Susanna Gregory is a Cambridge academic and the creator of the Matthew Bartholomew medieval series. She has previously been a police officer and now lives in Wales with her husband, also a writer.

Visit the author's website at www.susannagregory.co.uk

THE WESTMINSTER
POISONER

Susanna
Gregory

SPHERE

First published in Great Britain in 2008 by Sphere
This paperback edition published in 2009 by Sphere

A CIP catalogue record for this book
is available from the British Library.

ISBN 978-0-7515-3955-4

Typeset in Baskerville MT by Palimpsest Book Production Limited,
Grangemouth, Stirlingshire
Printed and bound in Great Britain by
Clays Ltd, St Ives plc

Papers used by Sphere are natural renewable and recyclable products sourced
from well-managed forests and certified in accordance with
the rules of the Forest Stewardship Council.

Mixed Sources
Product group from well-managed
forests and other controlled sources
www.fsc.org Cert no. SGS-COC-004081
© 1996 Forest Stewardship Council
FSC

Sphere
An imprint of
Little, Brown Book Group
100 Victoria Embankment
London EC4Y 0DY

An Hachette UK Company
www.hachette.co.uk

www.littlebrown.co.uk

For Carolyn and Craig

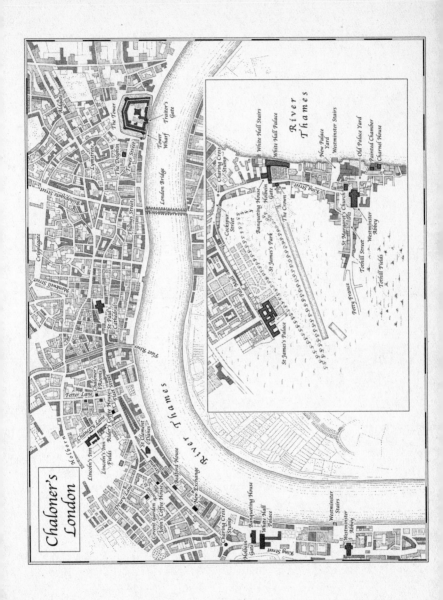

Chaloner's London

Prologue

Henry Scobel, Clerk of the House of Lords, was dying. His physician had confidently informed him that he was afflicted with a 'sharpness of the blood', a painful ailment from which few recovered. Scobel had always lived a clean, decent and sober life, and had no idea why his blood should so suddenly have become sharp, but he was unwilling to waste his last hours pondering on it. He was a religious man, and if God had decided it was time for him to die, then who was he to argue? And, if the truth be told, he no longer had much appetite for life, anyway – he had liked England under Cromwell, but detested it under the newly restored Charles II. The King and his Court had only been installed for a few months, but already they were showing themselves to be corrupt, debauched and treacherous. Scobel was appalled by them, and deplored the notion of such men ruling his country.

'You will be better soon, uncle,' said Will Symons, trying to control the tremor in his voice. He loved his kinsman dearly, and hated to see him suffering. 'And in

1

the spring, we shall ride out together to see the cherry trees at Rotherhithe, just like we do every year.'

Scobel was sorry to be the cause of his nephew's distress: Symons was a good man, who was hard-working, honest and reliable, and Scobel thought it disgraceful that he had recently been ousted from his government post, just because the Royalists wanted it for one of their cronies. Of course, Symons was not the only one to be shabbily treated – honourable men all over the country were facing hardship and ruin for no reason other than that they had worked for the Commonwealth. It made Scobel furious, especially as the newcomers were not only unqualified for the jobs they were being given, but many were brazenly corrupt, too.

'Do not worry,' said Symons kindly, when his uncle began to voice his concerns. 'Have you forgotten our last prayer meeting? Everyone promised – swore sacred oaths – to live righteous and godly lives, no matter how wicked the world becomes. Others will follow their example, and evil will *never* triumph.'

Scobel was not so sure about that, but he summoned a smile when he thought of his friends. 'They are decent souls, but these are difficult times. It would not be the first time an upright man fell by the wayside, and I fear for their—'

'They are successful and happy,' said Symons firmly, to quell the dying man's growing agitation. 'And they know it is God's reward to them for being good. They also know He might take it all away again if they let themselves be seduced by sin. Do not fret, uncle: they will not stray.'

Scobel's expression was pained. 'But I do not want them to uphold their principles because they are afraid

2

their luck will change if they transgress. I want them to do it because they love God and desire to do His will.'

'They will,' said Symons soothingly. 'I will see they do.'

Scobel closed his eyes wearily, and hoped the younger man was right. He could feel his life ebbing away faster now, and had no energy for debate. All he hoped was that his beloved country would survive the corruption that was taking hold in Westminster and White Hall, and that good people, like the men who attended his prayer meetings, would stand firm against sin and encourage others to do likewise. A tear rolled down his cheek when he thought about what might happen if they failed. Poor England! Would her suffering never end?

Westminster, Christmas Day 1663

The Palace of Westminster was an eerie place after dark. It was full of medieval carvings that gazed down from unexpected places, and when the lantern swayed in his hand, it made some of the statues look as though they were moving. The killer was sure he had just seen Edward the Confessor reach for his sword, while a few moments before he had been equally certain that a gargoyle had winked at him. He took a deep breath and tried to pull himself together, increasing his stride so he could complete his business and go home. It was no night to be out anyway, with a fierce storm blowing in from the east, carrying with it needles of rain that hurt when they hit bare skin.

He walked towards the building called the Painted Chamber, which was a long, draughty hall hung with tapestries so old they were grey with dust. Ancient kings

3

had once used it to receive important guests; nowadays it was where the two Houses of Parliament met when they needed to confer. However, as Commons and Lords rarely had much to say to each other, a few high-ranking government officials had taken it over. Desks were placed at irregular intervals along its length, while around its edges were chests full of documents, writs and books.

The Painted Chamber was empty now, of course, because it was eight o'clock on Christmas night, and the clerks had gone home early, eager to gorge themselves on rich seasonal foods, sing carols and enjoy visits from friends and family. Cromwell's Puritans had done their best to curb the revelries associated with the Twelve Days of Christmas, but December was a dark, cold, dreary month, and people needed something to cheer themselves up – the Puritans' efforts had never had gained much support, and the Restoration had seen the festival revived in all its pagan glory. Christmas was more popular now than it had ever been.

The killer nodded to himself when he opened the Painted Chamber's door and saw a lamp gleaming at the far end. *Most* clerks had gone home early: James Chetwynd was still at his desk, chin resting on his left hand while he wrote with his right. The killer did not blame the man – Chetwynd's kin were quite open about the fact that they cared nothing for him, and that they hoped he would die so they could inherit his money; he would have to be insane to want to spend Christmas with *them*. The killer took a deep breath, and supposed they were going to be rich sooner than they had anticipated, because tonight was going to be Chetwynd's last on Earth.

He advanced stealthily. Chetwynd was engrossed in

4

his papers, so certain he was safe inside the great hall that he did not once look up. The killer wondered if the clerk preferred the stillness of evening to the commotion of daylight hours – if he was able to think more clearly when there were no distractions. Regardless, the killer was glad he was there, because what better place for a murder than a deserted room in a palace that had been all but abandoned for the night? It afforded both privacy and space, allowing him to take his time and ensure he left no clues behind him. His smug musings meant he did not concentrate on where he was going, and he stumbled over a loose floorboard, a sound that made Chetwynd's head jerk up in surprise.

'Is anyone there?' the clerk called, peering into the darkness beyond the halo of light around his desk. 'Show yourself!'

There was no fear in his voice – he assumed anyone entering the Painted Chamber would be a friend, and did not for a moment imagine he might be in danger. The killer did not reply. He waited until Chetwynd's attention drifted back to his documents, and then he made his move.

Chapter 1

Westminster, 27 December 1663

There was a belief, common among many folk, that an unusually high wind was a sign that a great person would die. Thomas Chaloner was not superstitious, but even he could not deny that it was the second time in as many days that a gale had descended on the nation's capital with a terrifying savagery, and that an eminent man had died on each occasion. He would not have said James Chetwynd or Christopher Vine were 'great' exactly, but they were high-ranking officials, and that alone was enough to attract the Lord Chancellor's attention. And when the Lord Chancellor expressed an interest, it was Chaloner's responsibility, as his spy, to provide him with information.

He stared at the body that lay on the floor of the Painted Chamber, listening to the wind rattling the windows and howling down the chimney. The lamp he held cast eerie shadows, and when a draught snaked behind the tapestries on the walls, the ghostly grey figures swayed and danced in a way that was unsettling. Beside him, the Lord Chancellor, created Earl of Clarendon at the Restoration, regarded it nervously, then shivered in the night's deep chill.

'Why is it called the Painted Chamber, sir?' Chaloner asked, breaking the silence that had been hanging between them for the last few minutes, as they had pondered Chetwynd's mortal remains. 'There is no artwork here.'

The Earl almost leapt out of his skin at the sudden sound of his voice, although Chaloner had not spoken loudly. He rested a plump hand over his heart and scowled, to indicate he did not appreciate being startled. Chaloner bowed an apology. He was uneasy in the hall, too – and he knew how to defend himself, thanks to active service during the civil wars, followed by a decade of spying on hostile foreign governments.

'There were frescos,' replied the Earl shortly, flapping chubby fingers towards the ceiling. 'Up there, but they have been plastered over. How can you live in London and not know this?'

Chaloner did not answer. His overseas duties had made him a virtual stranger in his own country, and he was acutely aware that he needed to remedy the situation – a spy could not be effective in a place he did not under-stand. Unfortunately, he kept being dispatched on missions abroad, so never had the opportunity to familiar-ise himself with England's biggest city.

'You are supposed to be telling me what happened to Vine, not quizzing me about architecture,' the Earl continued waspishly, when there was no reply. 'I need to know whether his death was natural, or whether you have a *second* murder to investigate – this one, as well as Chetwynd's.'

Chaloner dragged his attention away from the ceiling, and knelt next to the corpse. Vine had not been dead long, because he was still warm to the touch. The spy glanced around, feeling his unease intensify. The Painted Chamber was so huge and dark that it was impossible to see far, and a killer – or killers – might still be there. The dagger he always carried in his sleeve dropped into the palm of his hand as he stood.

'What is wrong?' The Earl sensed his disquiet, and scanned the shadows with anxious eyes. 'Is someone else in here? Turner told me the place was deserted.'

'Turner?' Chaloner began to prowl, taking the lamp with him. Loath to be left alone in the dark, the Earl followed. He wore fashionably tight shoes with smart red heels, which made his feet look disproportionately small under his portly frame. Their hard leather soles pattered on the floor as he scurried after his spy, short, fat legs pumping furiously.

'Colonel James Turner,' he panted, tugging on Chaloner's sleeve to make him slow down. 'You must know him – he declared himself for the King during the wars, and championed our cause all through the Commonwealth.' There was a hint of censure in his voice: Chaloner's family had been Parliamentarians, while the spy himself had fought for Cromwell in several major battles. In other words, Turner had chosen the right side, Chaloner had not. 'It was Turner who found Vine's body.'

The spy frowned. The Painted Chamber was not a place that would attract most people on such a wild night, so what had Turner been doing there? Besides being vast, dark and full of disquieting noises, it was bitterly cold. But the colonel had been right about one thing: it *was* deserted, and it was not long before Chaloner had satisfied himself to that effect. He returned to the body.

9

'He said he saw a light as he was walking home from church,' the Earl elaborated, resting his hands on his knees to catch his breath. 'So he came to investigate. He found Vine, and, knowing my interest in Chetwynd's murder, he came to tell me that a second prominent official lies dead.'

'How did he know about your interest in Chetwynd?' asked Chaloner suspiciously. Sudden deaths among government employees were for the Spymaster General to investigate, and the Earl had no business commissioning his own enquiry. So, when he had ordered his spy to look into the affair, he had promised to keep it a secret, to avoid unnecessary trouble – the Spymaster hated meddlers.

The Earl looked sheepish. 'I may have mentioned to one or two people that I dislike the notion of our officials being murdered in Westminster, and that I have a man asking questions about the matter. Turner probably heard it from them.'

Chaloner stifled a sigh, and wished his master knew how to keep a still tongue in his head – he was always sharing information he should have kept to himself. But what was done was done, and there was no point in remonstrating, not that the Earl would take notice anyway. 'Where is Turner now?'

'I sent him to fetch Surgeon Wiseman.' The Earl held up a hand when Chaloner opened his mouth to object. 'I know you dislike Wiseman – and his gleeful penchant for gore *is* disconcerting – but he is good at distilling information from corpses. Turner must be having trouble finding him – I expected them to arrive before you, given that you have had to travel all the way from Wapping.'

'I was there shadowing Greene,' said Chaloner, keeping

his voice carefully neutral. 'The man you suspect of killing Chetwynd.'

'But Greene *did* murder Chetwynd,' declared the Earl uncompromisingly. 'I know a scoundrel when I see one, and I was right to order you to watch his every move.'

Chaloner made no reply. He had been tailing Greene for two days now – ever since Chetwynd's body had been found – but felt it was a complete waste of his time. Moreover, it was unreasonable to expect one man to follow another for twenty-four hours a day without help. He was exhausted, and had been relieved when the Earl's steward had arrived to tell him he was needed urgently at Westminster.

'Where is Haddon?' demanded the Earl, seeming to realise for the first time that the steward was not with them. 'Did he go home after delivering you my message?'

'You said you wanted Greene under constant surveillance,' explained Chaloner. 'So Haddon offered to monitor him while I came here.'

The Earl smiled smugly. 'He is a dedicated soul, and I am glad I hired him. He will do anything for me – even lurk around outside on foul-weathered nights.'

Chaloner nodded, not mentioning that Greene's house was mostly visible from a nearby tavern, and Haddon was comfortably installed there with a jug of ale and a piece of plum pudding. Just then an especially violent gust of wind hurled something against one of the windows, hard enough to shatter the glass. Chaloner whipped around fast, sword in his hand, and the Earl released a sharp yelp of fright.

'Where is Wiseman?' he demanded unsteadily, peering out from behind the spy: being in a deserted hall with a corpse was taking a heavy toll on his nerves. 'What is

11

keeping him? Perhaps *you* should examine the body. I know you are no surgeon, trained to recognise foul play in the dead, but you spotted the signs readily enough on Chetwynd two days ago. So do the same for Vine now.'

Chaloner obliged, performing a perfunctory examination that entailed inspecting the inside of Vine's mouth to look for tell-tale burns. They were there, as he had known they would be the moment he had set eyes on the man's peculiarly contorted posture – it had been this that had alerted him to the fact that Chetwynd's death was not natural some two days before.

'Poison,' he said, looking up at his master. 'Just like Chetwynd.'

The gale showed no signs of abating, and when the Earl opened the door to leave the Painted Chamber, he was almost bowled over by the force of the wind. It hurled a sheet of rain into his face, too, and deprived him of his wig. Without it, he looked older, smaller and more vulnerable. Chaloner retrieved it for him, then shoved him backwards quickly when several tiles tore from the roof and smashed to the ground where he had been standing.

'I should have stayed home, let you report to me in the morning,' said the Earl shakily, tugging the wig into position on his shaven pate. 'But I was worried. The government has many enemies, and we cannot have folk running around killing our clerks. I needed to see for myself what we are up against.'

'At least we know Greene is not responsible,' said Chaloner, careful to keep any hint of triumph from his voice. 'I have been watching him all day, and he is currently at home in bed. He cannot have killed Vine.'

'Nonsense!' cried the Earl. 'You are letting his meek manners and plausible tongue cloud your judgement – clearly, he found a way to slip past you. You argued against arresting him on Thursday, and I bowed – reluctantly – to your judgement. But it has cost Vine his life.'

Chaloner was not sure how to refute such rigidly held convictions, but was saved from having to try, because a bobbing lantern heralded the arrival of the surgeon.

Wiseman was enormous, both tall and broad, and it was said at Court that he had recently acquired a peculiar habit: he liked to tone his muscular frame by performing a series of vigorous exercises every morning. His eccentricity was also reflected in his choice of clothes: he always wore flowing scarlet robes, which he claimed were the uniform of his profession, although no other surgeon seemed to own any. His hair was red, too, and fell in luxurious curls around his shoulders. His whimsical unconformity might have been charming, had he not been one of the most opinionated, arrogant, obnoxious men in London. As far as Chaloner was concerned, Wiseman had only one redeeming character: his steadfast, unquestioning loyalty to the Earl.

'Where is the cadaver?' demanded the surgeon, never a man to waste time on idle chatter when there was work to be done. 'At the far end of the hall, like the last one you summoned me to inspect?'

'Good evening to you, too,' muttered Chaloner, as Wiseman shoved past him, hard enough to make him stagger. The surgeon was accompanied by another man, one whom the spy had seen at Court.

'Thank you for bringing Wiseman to me, Turner,' said the Earl, smiling pleasantly at the fellow. 'You have been of great service tonight, and I shall not forget it.'

13

Turner was tall, dark haired and devilishly handsome. He had a narrow moustache like the King's, and he wore an ear-string – an outmoded fashion that entailed threading strands of silk through a piercing in the earlobe, and leaving them to trail stylishly across one shoulder. Because the rest of his clothes were the height of fashion, the ear-string looked oddly out of place, and drew attention to the fact that the lobe had an unnatural hole in it. Chaloner had been told that it had been made by a Roundhead musket-ball, but was sceptical – the injury was too small and neat to have been caused by any firearm he knew. But no one else seemed to share his suspicions, and the colonel was always surrounded by doting admirers.

'It is a pleasure, sir,' gushed Turner with a courtly bow. 'And if I can be of further assistance, you only need ask. I have long held you in my humble esteem, and I am at your command *any* time.'

'What a charming gentleman,' said the Earl, watching him strut away. Chaloner said nothing, but thought Turner would go far in White Hall, if he was able to produce such nauseating sycophancy at the drop of a hat. 'But come back inside, Thomas. We had better hear Wiseman's verdict.'

The surgeon was humming when they reached him, suggesting he had not minded too much being dragged out to inspect corpses. His abrasive character meant he did not have many friends, so murder scenes were important social occasions for him. Chaloner's occupation meant he did not have many friends, either, and Wiseman's solitary lifestyle was a constant reminder as to why he needed to make some. It was not easy, though: his uncle had been one of the men who had signed the old king's death warrant, and people were still wary about fraternising with the family of a regicide. Indeed, it was only in the last few weeks that he had felt able to tell people his real name, instead of using an alias. He knew he was lucky the Earl was willing to overlook his connections – along with the fact that he had spent a decade spying for Cromwell – because employment was not easy to come by for old Parliamentarians, especially in espionage. And Chaloner was qualified to do very little else.

'Like Chetwynd, Vine has swallowed something caustic,' Wiseman announced, not looking up. 'It burned the skin of his throat and caused convulsions, which accounts for his contorted posture.'

'Poison,' said the Earl, nodding. 'Thomas was right.'

Wiseman regarded him haughtily. 'Since when did he become a surgeon, pray? However, in this case, his opinion happens to be correct, because it coincides with my own. Of course *I* can go one step further: I suspect both these men died from ingesting the *same substance*.'

'What substance?' asked Chaloner, hoping it would be something unusual that would allow him to trace it – and its purchaser – by making enquiries among the apothecaries.

Wiseman shrugged. 'There is no way to tell from a visual inspection alone. Vine's kin will have to let me anatomise him.' His eyes gleamed at the prospect.

'Thomas will try to get their permission,' said the Earl. Chaloner's heart sank; it was bad enough telling a family that a loved one was dead, without being obliged to put that sort of request, too. 'But do not hold your breath – Chetwynd's kin cared nothing for him, but even so, they were loath to let you loose on his corpse. So, I cannot imagine Vine's wife and son leaping to accept your offer.

15

Now, is there anything else we should know? Any clues that prove Greene is the killer?'

'You asked me that when you found Chetwynd,' said Wiseman, climbing to his feet. 'And the answer now is the same as it was then: no. There is nothing that will help you trace the culprit. Dissection is the only way forward.'

'I suppose we should be thankful he did not carve Vine up right here in front of us,' whispered the Earl, watching him stride away. 'Escort me home, Thomas. I have had enough of corpses and their vile secrets for one night. The wind seems to be dropping, so I should be safe from falling tiles now.'

Chaloner was acutely uneasy as he accompanied the Earl to his waiting coach. The gale had abated, but it was still blowing hard, and the racket it made as it whipped through trees and around buildings meant it was difficult to hear anything else. Unfortunately, darkness and driving rain meant he could not see very well, either. He disliked the notion that he might not have adequate warning of an attack, and although he was not afraid for himself, the Earl had accumulated a lot of enemies since the Restoration, and this was the perfect opportunity for an ambush.

'You should not have come, sir,' he said, as he helped his master into the carriage and climbed in after him. He banged on the ceiling with his fist, to tell the driver to move off. 'It is not safe for you to wander about so late at night.'

'So you have said before, but I refuse to let anyone dictate where I can and cannot go.' The Earl looked anxious, though, despite his defiant words. 'I have no idea why I am so unpopular – I seem to attract new enemies with every passing day.'

'Do you?' Chaloner immediately wished he had not asked, because he knew exactly why his master had more opponents than friends. The Court libertines despised him because he was prim, dour and something of a killjoy, while he had made political enemies by adopting uncompromising stances on religion and the looming war with Holland.

'It is because no one else knows what they are talking about,' stated the Earl. 'At least, not as far as politics, food, religion, art, horses, ethics, fashion or sport are concerned. I have been arguing all week, and I am tired of it. Why does no one ever agree with me about anything?'

'Who have you been arguing with, sir?' asked Chaloner politely. A list of sparring partners promised to be far less objectionable than being treated to a diatribe of the Earl's controversial – and sometimes odious – opinions.

'Well, the Lady, naturally.' So intense was the Earl's dislike for the King's mistress that he refused to say her name: Lady Castlemaine was always just 'the Lady'. 'And the Duke of Buckingham, who encourages the King to play cards instead of listening to me, his wise old advisor.'

'Who else?'

The Earl began to count them off on chubby fingers. 'Sir Nicholas Gold told me I was a fool for advising caution when declaring war on the Dutch. His young wife Bess, who has fewer wits than a sheep, told me my wig was unfashionable. Then that disgustingly fat Edward Jones accused me of cheating him out of the food allowance that goes with his post as Yeoman of the Household Kitchen.'

'You would never do that,' said Chaloner, indignant on his behalf. The Earl had many faults, but brazen dishonesty was not one of them.

'He is entitled to dine at White Hall, but his monstrous girth means he is eating more than his due. So I told him to tighten his belt, and take the same amount as everyone else. He objected vehemently.'

'Oh,' said Chaloner, supposing he would. 'That is hardly the same as accusing you of cheat—'

'Then Barbara Chiffinch took issue with my reaction to that practical joke – the one that saw White Hall decorated with *nether garments*.' The Earl lowered his voice at the mention of such a lewd subject. 'I ordered the offending items burned, and she called me an ass.'

'Because the prankster stole them from servants,' explained Chaloner. He liked Barbara, who was a rock of common sense in a sea of silly people. 'You should penalise the Lord of Misrule, not the poor scullions who cannot afford to lose their—'

'I *hate* that custom,' spat the Earl, grabbing Chaloner's arm as the carriage lurched violently to one side; Westminster's roads were notorious for potholes. 'Electing a "king of mischief" to hold sway over White Hall for the entire Twelve Days of Christmas is stupid. And I am always the butt of at least one malicious prank. Who is the Lord of Misrule this year, do you know?'

'No,' lied Chaloner, not about to tell him that the dissipated Sir Alan Brodrick had been responsible for the undergarment incident. Brodrick was the Earl's cousin, and for some unaccountable reason, the Earl was fond of him. He steadfastly refused to believe anything bad about him, despite Brodrick's growing reputation as one of the greatest debauchees in London.

'Then there was that horrible youth Neale,' the Earl went on, going back to the list of people who had annoyed him. 'He said I have poor taste in music.'

'Did he?' The spy started to think about his investigation, tuning out the Earl's tirade. He knew few of the people who were being mentioned, so the monologue was not particularly interesting to him.

'And finally, Francis Tryan charged me too much interest on a loan. How dare he! Does he think my arithmetic lacking? That I am a halfwit, who cannot do his sums?'

'I interviewed Chetwynd's heirs yesterday,' said Chaloner, when he thought the Earl had finished. 'Thomas and Matthias Lea. They work in the same building as Greene, so I was able to question them and watch him at the same time. Unfortunately, they have no idea why their kinsman—'

'And there was another idiot,' interrupted the Earl. 'Chetwynd attacked my stance on religion.'

The spy was not a devout man, but he disliked his master's attempts to impose Anglicanism on the entire country, and thought Catholics and nonconformists were justified when they said they wanted to pray as they, not the state, thought fit. 'Many people would agree with him,' he said carefully.

'Then many people are wrong,' snapped the Earl in a tone that said further debate was futile. He was silent for a moment, then resumed his list yet again. 'Did you know Vine criticised me for wanting to build myself a nice house in Piccadilly? Why should I not have a palace? I am Lord Chancellor of England, and should live somewhere grand.'

Chaloner found himself agreeing with Vine, too, although he said nothing. He knew, with all his heart, that the Earl's projected mansion was a bad idea – it was too ostentatious, and was sure to cause resentment. He had urged him to commission something more modest, but the Earl refused to listen.

'But enough of my troubles,' said the Earl, seeming to sense that his complaints were falling on unsympathetic ears. 'We should discuss these murders while we are alone.'

'So you knew Vine as well, sir?' asked Chaloner. 'You told me on Thursday that you knew Chetwynd.'

The Earl nodded. 'They were both high-ranking clerks – Vine in the Treasury, and Chetwynd in Chancery. Each had a reputation for being decent and honest, and it is a shame that two good men lie dead, when so many scoundrels remain living.'

By 'scoundrels', Chaloner supposed he referred to his various enemies at Court. 'Yes, sir.'

But the Earl knew a noncommittal answer when he heard one. He narrowed his eyes and went on the offensive. 'I have just one question for you: how did Greene kill Vine when you were supposed to be watching him? Or were you deliberately careless with your surveillance, because you refuse to see the obvious and accept that he is the culprit?'

Chaloner bit back an acid retort at the slur on his professionalism, knowing he would be doing himself no favours by offending the man who paid his wages. 'It is difficult to follow a suspect full-time, sir. Not only is he more likely to spot you if you are always there, but you cannot watch back doors and front ones at the same time.'

'Are you blaming *me* for the fact that Greene eluded you and went a-killing?'

'No.' Chaloner struggled for patience. 'I did not see Greene leave after he returned home this evening, but I suppose it is possible – his house has three exits, and I could not guard them all. However, I think it unlikely. He had no reason to kill Chetwynd, and I imagine we will find he has none to kill Vine, either.'

'So you say,' snapped the Earl. 'But let us review the tale he spun when he discovered Chetwynd's corpse. He *claims* he was working late, although it was Christmas Day and he should have been at home. Then he says he ran out of ink, so he went to the Painted Chamber to borrow some. But it was almost ten o'clock at night, which is an odd time to go rooting about for office supplies. And when he arrived, he maintains he found Chetwynd, dead on the floor.'

'He raised the alarm—'

'But only because you and I happened to be walking past, and we saw him dashing out,' interrupted the Earl.

For the past week, Chaloner had been hunting for a statue that had been stolen from the King, and the Earl had heard a rumour that it was hidden in a nearby stable. The pair had been on their way to see whether the tale was true. Fortunately for the Earl, Chaloner had suspected a trick the moment he had been told the 'news' and he had been right to be sceptical – his wariness in entering the stable had prevented his master from being doused with a bucket of paint. It was a jape typical of the Season of Misrule.

'Greene told us Chetwynd was dead,' the Earl went on. 'So we went to investigate. You took one look at the corpse's peculiar contortions, and declared a case of foul play. Poison.'

Chaloner nodded. 'A liquid toxin, which would have

been delivered in a cup or a bottle. We searched, but found no vessel of any kind – not in the hall and not on Greene's person. There is only one logical conclusion: the real killer took it away with him when he left.'

But the Earl was not about to let an inconvenient fact get in the way of his theory. He ignored it, and continued with his summary. 'After Spymaster Williamson's men had finished taking Greene's statement, they let him go home, and I ordered you not to let him out of your sight.'

Chaloner had taken the opportunity to interrogate the clerk on the journey to Wapping. Greene had been shocked and deeply frightened, both from stumbling over a corpse in the dark and by the fact that a powerful noble thought him guilty of murder. He had been shaking almost uncontrollably, and Chaloner knew he was not the brazen slaughterer of the Earl's imagination.

'I watched his house for the rest of the night,' he said. 'The next day, he went to church, then took a boat to his office in Westminster. He went home at dusk, then followed exactly the same routine today – only he stopped to dine at the Dolphin on his way home. He is probably in bed as we speak.'

'But you cannot say for certain,' stated the Earl. 'You said yourself that it is impossible to watch three doors at once. He must have slipped past you.'

'It is possible, but unlikely, because—'

'You need a colleague,' said the Earl, somewhat out of the blue. 'And I know just the fellow. Colonel Turner is said to be looking for something useful to do. I shall hire him.'

'Turner?' Chaloner thought, but did not say, that if Greene was to be branded a killer because he had found Chetwynd, then why was Turner rewarded with employment when he had found Vine? It made no sense. Not that he expected sense from the Earl in matters of intelligence: the man might be a fine politician and a skilled diplomat, but he was a menace when it came to investigations.

'He is a likeable fellow, and I am sure you will get along famously.' The Earl beamed, pleased with himself. 'Engaging Turner is an excellent notion, and I should have thought of it sooner. My enemies multiply daily, and you are unequal to the task of monitoring them all – not to mention catching killers and hunting down stolen statues.'

Chaloner was not sure what he was suggesting. 'You want us to work together?'

The Earl shook his head as the carriage pulled up outside Worcester House on The Strand, where he lived. 'Separately – but on the same cases. A little healthy competition never did anyone any harm, and we shall see which of you is the most efficient.'

'Christ!' muttered Chaloner, appalled. 'We will be falling over each other, asking the same people identical questions. It will almost certainly impede—'

'Nonsense! You are just afraid Turner will transpire to be better than you. I want this case solved, and Greene brought to justice. You have until Twelfth Night – ten days – to prove him guilty.'

'And if he is innocent?'

'He is not,' said the Earl firmly, allowing Chaloner to help him down the carriage steps. Without another word, he stalked inside his house and nodded to the footman to close the door behind him.

The bell in Westminster's medieval clock tower was chiming midnight by the time Chaloner had escorted

Christopher Vine's body to the nearest church, and was free to break the news to the man's family. He had been the bearer of bad tidings many times before, and knew how to do it gently, but it was not a task he relished even so. He walked slowly to New Palace Yard, where Vine had lived, and spent a few moments bracing himself before knocking on the door. Then he did not know whether to be relieved or shocked when Vine's wife informed him that it was the best news she had had in weeks.

'Since word came that Queen Katherine was ailing,' she elaborated, when the spy found himself at a loss for words. 'The woman is barren, and I prayed she would die, so the King can marry a fertile Protestant instead. He should never have wed a Catholic.'

Aware that people were seldom themselves after being told their spouses were dead, Chaloner did not take her to task for maligning a lady he liked. 'The King's marriage alliance with Portugal was—'

'Portugal!' sneered Mrs Vine. 'Who cares about Portugal? All they do is fight Spaniards and eat olives. But I did not drag myself out of bed at such an hour to discuss royal matches with the likes of you. What happened to Christopher? Did he die of shock, because he heard someone swearing? Or did he spend so long at prayer that God grew tired of listening and struck him down?'

Vine's only son, George, snickered. He was in his mid-twenties, and looked like his father in that he was tall and thin, but there the resemblance ended. George's eyes were bloodshot from high living, and he reeked of brothel perfume. He was a far cry from his respectable sire, and Chaloner did not believe the rumour that said he had once tried to assassinate Cromwell – George simply did not have the mettle.

'Perhaps he died of shame, because he found an inconsistency in his accounting,' the young man said with a smirk. 'And he was afraid folk would find out that he had wantonly mislaid a whole groat.'

Mrs Vine cackled with laughter, then went to pour two cups of wine. She gave one to her son, and raised it in salute. 'To a future without old Dreary Bones!'

'You did not like him, then,' said Chaloner drily.

Mrs Vine snorted. 'The man was a bore, with his prayers and his sickly goodness – always helping the poor and the sick, weeping every time he saw an injured dog . . .'

'And then there was the Lord of Misrule,' added George resentfully. 'We all know the tradition is great fun, but father said it was cruel, and forbade me to have anything to do with it. Well, he cannot stop me now, and I shall offer my services as soon as I wake up tomorrow afternoon.'

'Your father was poisoned,' said Chaloner, wondering whether they had heard what had happened to Chetwynd, and had conspired to duplicate the crime in order to be rid of a hated kinsman. But then would they be so openly gleeful at the news of his death? He decided they would, on the grounds that people would know relations within the family were strained, and to feign grief would certainly arouse suspicion. Or was that attributing them with too much intelligence?

Mother and son were exchanging a glance he found impossible to interpret. 'Then we demand an investigation,' said Mrs Vine slyly, 'with a view to claiming compensation for our loss. If Christopher died in the service of his country, I shall demand a pension.'

25

George emitted a sharp squeal of delight, and clapped his hands together. 'Yes, yes! He earned a princely living, and his family cannot be expected to endure poverty just because he has been murdered. Oh, this is tremendous news!'

'Do you have any idea who might want to harm him?' asked Chaloner. 'Other than you two?'

'Us?' asked George, the glee fading quickly from his eyes. He shot his mother an uneasy look. 'We had nothing to do with his death. You heard us – we thought it was natural until you said he was murdered. You cannot blame us for what has happened.'

'The villain will be someone at White Hall,' added Mrs Vine hastily. 'Perhaps a colleague who wanted his government post – it is a lucrative one, and lots of folk are jealous of his success.'

'Or maybe someone did not like the fact that he was so revoltingly honest,' mused George. 'The Court understands that corruption is a necessary part of modern life, but Father never did. I will be more tolerant, when *I* take over his duties.'

Chaloner was bemused – Vine's post was not hereditary. 'You intend to step into his shoes?'

George shrugged. 'Why not? I will be better at it than he was, because I shall not offend people by rejecting their bribes.'

'I see,' said Chaloner. 'But I was thinking more in terms of your safety. Your mother has just said Vine might have been killed by someone who wants his job. If you are appointed, you will be at risk from poison, too – unless you are the culprit, of course.'

George opened his mouth, but then seemed unable to think of a suitable response, so snapped it shut again. It was left to his mother to protest his innocence. Chaloner listened to her list of alternative suspects, but it soon became clear she was naming everyone and anyone in an effort to divert attention from her son.

'The Court surgeon wants to examine your husband's remains more carefully,' he said, interrupting her tirade, and supposing there was no harm in putting Wiseman's request. After all, they were hardly prostrate with grief. 'May he have your permission to—'

'No,' interrupted George. He shot his mother another unreadable glance. 'I have seen Wiseman in action, and it is disgusting. Dreary Bones might have been a trial, but I will not see him hacked to pieces by that ghoul. He will go in the ground whole, with all his entrails where they are meant to be.'

'Why was your father working so late tonight?' Chaloner asked, not sure what to make of the refusal. 'Everyone else had gone home.'

Mrs Vine shrugged. 'Christopher and I live separate lives, which suits us both. To be frank, I thought he was upstairs asleep, and had no idea he was out.'

'Did he know a clerk called Chetwynd?'

'Of course,' said Mrs Vine. 'Why do you ask? Is it because Chetwynd was poisoned, too?'

'The news is all over London,' said George, before Chaloner could ask how she knew. 'Everyone is talking about it, because it is not every day that government officials are unlawfully slain.'

'No, it is every *other* day,' quipped his mother. 'Chetwynd on Thursday, and Christopher tonight. We shall dine on this for months, because *everyone* will want to befriend the kin of a murdered man.'

'I imagine that depends on who is revealed as the

27

killer,' said Chaloner, aiming for the door. He had had enough of the Vines for one night. 'And the authorities *will* catch him. You can be sure of that.'

'Why bother?' asked George, going to refill his goblet. 'Dreary Bones will not be missed.'

Although the wind was not as fierce as it had been earlier, it was still strong enough to make the trees in nearby Tothill Fields roar. The air was full of flying debris – mostly twigs, dead leaves and dust, but also human rubbish, including discarded rags, sodden bits of paper and even scraps of food. Chaloner was disgusted when a rotting cabbage leaf slapped into his face, and was relieved when he finally managed to flag down a carriage to take him back to Wapping.

It was a long way to Greene's house, which, at sixpence a mile, delighted the hackneyman. The coach was determinedly basic, with a wooden seat bristling with splinters and a mass of squelching straw on the floor. It stank of horse and vomit, and there were no covers on the windows to protect passengers from inclement weather – the owner was apparently of the belief that if he was obliged to sit outside, then so should his fares. The vehicle lurched along the empty streets at a furious lick, forcing Chaloner to cling on tight or risk being tossed out. By the time he reached the tavern where Haddon was waiting, he was cold, tired and wet.

'It is still raining, then,' said Haddon, when the spy slipped into the seat next to him. The steward was a slight man of about sixty, whose baggy skin made him look as though he had once been much larger, and he wore a wig to conceal his hairless pate. He had a pleasant face, with laughter lines around his mouth and eyes, and he owned a passion for dogs that verged on the obsessive. He had been appointed the previous year, when the Earl had complained that his current staff could no longer cope with the volume of work, and so had been granted funds to expand his retinue.

'It is always raining in this godforsaken country,' grumbled Chaloner, weariness making him irritable. 'It makes me wish I was back in Spain – and the last time I was there, I was almost killed.'

Haddon raised his eyebrows. 'Do you realise that is the first information about yourself you have ever volunteered to me? The Earl must have driven you to distraction with his demands to prove Greene is the killer, because you are usually far more guarded.'

Chaloner supposed he was right. He had been trained never to yield personal details, which was a considerable stumbling block in making new friends. It was a problem for his latest relationship, too, because Hannah Cotton was eager to learn all about her new lover, but he found himself reluctant to tell her what she wanted to know. Secrecy was not so important now he was no longer a foreign spy in a hostile country, but it was a difficult habit to break after so many years regardless.

'You should go home,' he said to Haddon. 'I heard a rumour that the Lord of Misrule plans some sort of attack on the Earl soon, and you cannot defend him if you are half asleep.'

'What about you?' asked Haddon. 'How will you find Chetwynd's real killer after a third night spent out here? You will be too tired to catch a cold, let alone a murderer.'

'You do not think Greene is the culprit, then?' Chaloner asked, intrigued by Haddon's use of 'real'.

'Of course not,' said Haddon scornfully. 'I have known

29

him for years, and he would not harm a fly. You have talked to him – you must see the Earl is wrong about the poor fellow.'

Chaloner nodded. 'I thought Vine's death would give the Earl pause for thought, but it has only convinced him that Greene managed to outwit me – slipped past when my attention wavered.'

Haddon grimaced. 'Vine was a decent soul – kind to stray dogs. Was he poisoned, too?'

'Wiseman thinks so.'

'Then it must be true.' Haddon was silent for a moment. 'After you left, I walked around Greene's house, and learned that there are three different ways he can leave it, only two of which are visible by one pair of eyes. So, perhaps he *did* go to the Painted Chamber tonight without you noticing.'

Chaloner stared at him. 'I thought you just said he is no killer.'

'I genuinely believe Greene is innocent of these heinous crimes, but I am not such a fool as to ignore facts that do not support my theory. Of course, there is a way to determine once and for all whether he is involved in this nasty business.'

'There is?'

'If Greene has indeed been out a-killing, then his coat and shoes will be wet. Agreed? It is a filthy night, and no one can move about without a drenching, not even if he hires a hackney. The Earl's secretary tells me you own some skill at breaking into houses, so break into Greene's. If his clothes are dry, then it means he has been nowhere, and we can abandon this ridiculous vigil.'

Chaloner raised his eyebrows in surprise. It was an eminently sensible idea, and one he should have thought of himself. He might have done, had he not been so unutterably tired.

Haddon smiled when he saw the spy's reaction. 'Stewards can be relied upon to provide intelligent notions occasionally, so do not look so startled. Come, we shall do it together.'

'I had better go alone.' Chaloner disliked company when he was committing burglary, especially that of amateurs. 'Although it is good of you to offer.'

Aware of Haddon watching through the window, he trotted across the road and made his way to the most secluded of Greene's three doors. He picked the lock with the easy confidence of a man who had invaded other people's property many times before, and found himself in a tiny kitchen. Beyond it was a hall, with doors leading to more rooms and a flight of stairs. Chaloner headed for the latter, knowing from his surveillance that Greene slept in an upper chamber that overlooked the street.

Through a crack in the bedroom door, he saw his quarry reading by candlelight, although the troubled expression on Greene's face suggested his thoughts were a long way from his book. Chaloner supposed it was not surprising: he would not have been slumbering peacefully if the Lord Chancellor of England had deemed *him* guilty of murder, either. He crept back to the kitchen, closed the door and lit a lamp. Then he inspected the pegs on which Greene kept his outdoor clothes.

The clerk had worn a rather shabby cloak that day, and it was hanging on the hook nearest the door. It was damp, as would be expected given that it had been wrapped around him while he had travelled home from Westminster at dusk, but it was certainly not

31

sodden: clearly, it had been drying for several hours. Chaloner knelt to look at the footwear. Greene owned two pairs of shoes and one set of boots. The boots were stuffed with paper, to prevent the leather from shrinking, but again, they were damp rather than wet. Meanwhile, the shoes had not been worn that day, because they were bone dry.

'Well?' asked Haddon, when Chaloner rejoined him in the tavern. 'What did you find? Is the Earl right about Greene, or am I?'

'You are. He has not been out since returning home this evening, so he cannot have given Vine the poison. Of course, he might have hired someone to do it for him.'

Haddon nodded slowly. 'I cannot imagine there are many poisoners among his acquaintances, but I suppose it is something you should explore.'

'What do you know about James Turner?' asked Chaloner, thinking again that if the Earl regarded Greene as a suspect for discovering Chetwynd, then the flamboyant colonel should be treated likewise.

Haddon was surprised by the change of subject, but answered anyway. 'He likes the company of ladies, and I predict hearts will be broken, because he cannot possibly please them all. He is egalitarian in his tastes – he enjoys a romp with Meg the laundress just as much as one with Lady Castlemaine.'

'Anything else?'

'He seems personable enough to me, although I doubt the hole in his ear was made by a musket-ball, which implies a tendency to moderate the truth. And I would not trust him with my daughters.'

'You have daughters?'

32

'It is a figure of speech. My wife died many years ago, and I have no other family – unless you count my dogs, which are like children to me. And you? Sir George Downing, with whom you worked in The Hague, told me last week that you married a Dutch lass when you first went to Holland.'

'It was a long time ago.' Chaloner liked Haddon, but did not feel equal to an exchange of confidences that night – although a nagging voice at the back of his mind warned him that he was never in the mood for personal conversations, not even with Hannah. How was he going to develop friendships, if he could not bring himself to confide in the people who were trying to get to know him? 'Even if Greene is a killer, there is no point in watching him now, because I doubt he will strike twice in one night. We should both go home.'

'It is late for travelling, so I suggest we hire rooms here,' said Haddon, adding with an impish smile, 'then you can tell the Earl truthfully that you remained within spitting distance of Greene all night.'

It was another good idea, and Chaloner was asleep the moment his head touched the pillow.

A lifetime of travel meant Chaloner had developed the ability to rest tolerably well in most strange beds, and the one in the Wapping tavern was surprisingly comfortable. The following morning Haddon complained that he had been kept awake by howling winds and the thunder of rain on the roof, but Chaloner had noticed none of it. There had not been much of the night left by the time they had retired, but even so, he felt reasonably well-rested when he joined the steward for a breakfast of bread and ale.

They hired a skiff to take them to White Hall, leaving as soon as it was light enough for the boatman to see. It was a bumpy ride, because the wind had churned the Thames into a confusion of waves, most of which were going against the tide. The boatman moaned about the conditions all the way, oblivious to the fact that spray from his oars drenched his passengers at almost every stroke. Haddon was shivering miserably by the time they alighted at the Westminster Stairs.

It was not a pleasant day, even once they were off the river. The sun began to flash from behind the clouds occasionally, although never for long enough do any useful warming. It was bitterly cold, and there was a wavy fringe of ice all along the beach. Because it was Sunday, bells were ringing all across the city. The wind played with the sound, making a deafening jangle one moment, and a distant tinkle the next.

Chaloner and Haddon walked up Cannon Row, a well-maintained street with gates giving access to a number of elegant mansions, as well as to the King's private orchard in the Palace of White Hall. Haddon stopped outside a pretty cottage that had a dog-shaped weather-vane on the roof.

'This is my humble abode. Since we are passing, I shall change my clothes before I take a chill. Come in and wait for me, and when I am warm and dry again, I would like to ask your opinion about something – a matter that is worrying me deeply.'

He had opened the door and stepped inside before the spy could demur, and immediately, two lapdogs scampered at him with frenzied yaps of delight. They were brown and white with long, silky ears. Their fur was glossy, their noses shiny, and their necks adorned with bows of silk. Haddon knelt and greeted them with professions of such love that Chaloner wondered whether he should wait outside. The spy could not have made himself speak such words to a woman, let alone an animal.

'Do you own a dog?' asked the steward conversationally, when the pooches were bored with affection and began to clamour for food. He fed them prime cuts of meat on solid silver platters.

'Cat,' Chaloner replied, grateful it was not in the habit of overwhelming *him* with gushing adoration every time he arrived home.

'You should get a dog,' advised Haddon, shooting his charges a doting glance as they ate. 'I would not be without my little darlings for the world, and cats have too many unpleasant habits.'

Chaloner was not sure what he meant, but time was passing, and he did not want to waste the few hours of winter daylight on a debate about pets. He gestured that Haddon should hurry, and while the steward went to remove his sodden clothes, he prowled around the parlour, reading the titles of the books on the shelves – mostly religious tracts and tomes about dogs – and then picking out tunes on a virginals that stood by the window.

'What did you want to ask me about?' he called, frowning when he made a mistake in the music. He was an adequate virginalist, but his real love was the bass viol, which he played extremely well.

Still fastening the 'falling band' that went around his neck like a bib, Haddon went to a desk, and removed a piece of paper. 'I found this lying on the floor after Brodrick visited the Earl last night.'

The spy was puzzled. 'It is a plan of our master's White Hall offices. But Brodrick is his cousin, and does not need a map to find his way around – he knows the place inside out.'

'I think he drew it yesterday, but dropped it by mistake on his way out. You mentioned rumours that the Lord of Misrule intends to play a prank on the Earl . . .'

'And Brodrick is the Lord of Misrule,' finished Chaloner in understanding. 'So he sketched the layout of the Earl's domain to help him with whatever piece of mischief he intends to perpetrate.'

'*Brodrick* is the Lord of Misrule?' echoed Haddon in astonishment. 'I have been trying to find that out since Thursday, but everyone keeps telling me they have been sworn to secrecy.'

They had told Chaloner the same thing, but it had not stopped him acquiring the information anyway. He handed back the paper. 'It is a stroke of luck for the Earl, because Brodrick will never harm the one person who keeps trying to get him a high-paying post in government. Whatever Brodrick plans, I doubt it will be too terrible.'

Haddon's expression was troubled. 'I disagree. Libertines like Buckingham and Chiffinch have been jibing him about his affection for the Earl recently, so he might devise something especially horrid, just to prove himself to them. After all, the Lord of Misrule's identity is a secret, so how will the Earl ever know who is to blame for whatever outrage is inflicted on him?'

'Then you must stop it.'

'I can only act if I know what Brodrick intends. That means I need you to make some enquiries for me.'

'I cannot. The Earl intends to pit me against Turner, to see who can solve these murders fastest. I will not have time to—'

'It will not matter which of you is best if our Earl's feeble grip on power is loosened by some prank of the Lord of Misrule. You *must* oblige me in this, Thomas – there is no one else.'

'There is Secretary Bulteel. He will not stand by and see our master harmed.'

'Yes, but he hates me, because he thinks I am trying to steal his job. Meanwhile, I dislike him, because he is uncommunicative and sly. I need *your* help.'

Supposing he was going to be in for a busy time, Chaloner nodded reluctant agreement.

The Palace of White Hall was a sprawling affair, said to contain more than two thousand rooms in edifices that ranged from tiny medieval masterpieces to rambling Tudor monstrosities. Most had never been designed to connect with each other, but connected they were, resulting in a chaotic tangle of winding corridors, dead-ended alleys, oddly shaped yards, mysteriously truncated halls and irregularly angled houses. It was rendered even more confusing by the fact that most of its buildings were more than one storey, but the layout of their upper floors seldom corresponded to the layout at ground level. It had taken Chaloner weeks to learn his way around, and even now, there were still pockets that confounded him.

He and Haddon entered the palace via the Privy Garden, a large area of manicured splendour that was used by courtiers for gentle exercise. As they walked, Haddon happily informed the spy that he took his dogs there most evenings, and that the King found them captivating. Chaloner could not imagine His Majesty being charmed by a pair of yapping rats, but kept his thoughts to himself. He glanced up at the sky as Haddon chattered;

grey clouds scudded across it at a furious rate, while trees whipped back and forth in a way that was going to damage them. Several were already at unnatural angles, and would have to be replanted.

They parted company in the main courtyard, Haddon to check on some arrangements for a state dinner, and Chaloner to see whether the Earl was in his office. The spy was just jogging up the marble staircase – the Earl's suite was on the upper floor – when he met someone coming down. It was Turner. The colonel looked particularly dashing that morning, in a black long-coat with yellow lace frothing at the throat and wrists, colours that were reflected in his trademark ear-string. His hat was pure Cavalier, with a huge amber feather, and when he smiled, his teeth were impossibly white.

'We were not properly introduced last night,' he said, effecting one of his fancy bows. 'I am James Turner. Perhaps you have heard of me?'

'Should I have done?' asked Chaloner.

Turner nodded cheerfully, unabashed by the spy's less-than-friendly manner. 'Yes – either for my valour during the wars, or my exploits during the Commonwealth. I am sure you remember how Cromwell had a clever Spymaster called Thurloe? Well, I was the bane of Thurloe's life. In fact, I annoyed him so much that he put up a reward for anyone who could bring him my head.'

'Does the offer still stand?' Chaloner doubted the claim was true, because he knew Thurloe well, and he was not the type of man to provide money in exchange for body parts.

Turner laughed. 'Why? Do you wish to claim it? If so, you will have to behead me the *next* time we meet, because His Portliness is keen to see you, and you should not keep him waiting. He is in a snappish mood, probably because his shoes are too tight, and they hurt his gouty ankles.'

'You mean the Earl?' Chaloner was a little taken aback. *He* would never discuss his master in such uncomplimentary terms with someone he barely knew. For a start, the Earl was sensitive about his weight, and any hint of mockery would see the joker dismissed in a heartbeat.

The merry grin was still plastered on Turner's face. 'He wanted us to meet each other this morning, and discuss tactics over these Westminster poisonings, but he grew tired of waiting for you, and dispatched me on a solo mission instead.'

'What mission?' asked Chaloner. Turner clearly liked to give the impression that he was a Court cockerel, all frills and no substance, yet there was something about him that suggested he was rather more. Chaloner supposed his affable buffoon act was an attempt to lull rivals into a state of false security, but the spy had met such men before, and knew better than to be deceived.

'I am to go to the Shield Gallery, and inspect it for clues regarding the statue that was stolen last week – the one you have been hunting. His Portliness says the place is closed because of a leaking roof, so I shall have it to myself. Is it worth my time, do you think? Will I learn anything useful?'

'You never know. However, I examined it very carefully the morning after the theft, but the culprit left no clues that I could find.'

Turner chuckled. 'That is what I suspected, so I shall not waste too much time on it. However, the morning will not be a total loss, because the Shield Gallery has a passageway that leads to the Queen's private apartments

– and where there is a queen, there are ladies-in-waiting. I warrant they will be delighted to have a bit of unscheduled manly company.' He waggled his eyebrows.

Chaloner could only admire his audacity. 'That is probably true, but the Queen has armed guards as well as ladies-in-waiting, and I imagine they will be rather less delighted by your arrival.'

Turner treated him to a conspiratorial wink. 'Thanks for the warning – I shall do the same for you some day. I see we will work well together, you and me.'

'I understand you found Vine's body,' said Chaloner, deciding it might be a good time to pump the man for information. 'That must have been unpleasant for you.'

'I am a soldier,' said Turner with a world-weary shrug. 'So I am used to corpses. Of course, most of my experience is on the battlefield, where you tend not to encounter ones that have been poisoned. Then I come to London, and within three days, I lay eyes on two: Chetwynd and Vine.'

'I thought Greene found Chetwynd's body.'

'He did,' said Turner, rather hastily. 'I saw it later, along with a host of other courtiers who were curious to see the mortal remains of a murdered man. I never knew Chetwynd – when I looked at his corpse, his face was unfamiliar – but I did have the misfortune to meet Vine. He was a sanctimonious old fool who called me a libertine, just because I have twenty-eight children. I assured him they are all legally begotten, but he did not believe me.'

Chaloner laughed. 'I wonder why! Are you a bigamist, then?'

'I married young,' replied Turner, with another wink. 'My *illegitimate* offspring are another tally altogether, but

I had better keep that number to myself. How about you? How many do you have?'

'Vine,' prompted Chaloner, wondering whether Haddon had been gossiping about the family Chaloner had had, and lost to plague, in Holland more than a decade before. Regardless, he was not about to discuss them with a man he did not know. 'You were telling me how you came to find his body in a part of Westminster that is usually deserted at night.'

'Was I indeed?' asked Turner, with one of his rakish grins. 'Well, as we are colleagues, I suppose I can trust you with a confidence. I went to the Painted Chamber for a midnight tryst with a lady who works in the laundry. We arranged to meet there because it is usually empty at that hour. But when I arrived, I found not the lovely Meg, but Vine. Stone dead.'

'Is the lovely Meg the kind of woman to poison someone?'

Turner shook his head vehemently. 'She is a gentle child, and would never harm a soul.'

Chaloner would make up his own mind about that when he interviewed her. After all, it was not inconceivable that Vine had happened across her while she was waiting for her lover to arrive, and had made disparaging remarks about her morality. Some women in White Hall were sensitive about that kind of accusation, and men had been killed for far less.

'But you found Vine a long time before midnight,' Chaloner pointed out. 'Why did you arrive so early for this assignation?'

'Because I hoped she would come a bit ahead of schedule, and I was at a loose end, with nothing else to do. Now I wish I had visited Lady Castlemaine instead,

41

although you had better not tell her so – I doubt she will appreciate knowing I view her as somewhere to kill time between *amours*.'

Chaloner was sure she would not. 'Where is Meg now?'

Turner frowned. 'I have not seen her since we made the arrangement, and I can only assume she has decided to keep a low profile, lest someone start pointing accusing fingers. You see, it was not the first time she and I used the Painted Chamber for a nocturnal romp.'

'When you found Vine, what were your immediate thoughts? Death by poison is rare, so I doubt it was the first thing that entered your mind.'

'Actually, it was – because of Chetwynd. I noticed spilled wine on Vine's chin, indicating he had been drinking when he died, but there was no sign of a goblet, which struck me as odd. It told me someone else had been there – someone who had taken the cup with him. The killer, no less.'

Chaloner studied him thoughtfully, aware that here was a man whose powers of observation equalled his own, and it reinforced his initial impression – that there was more to Turner than met the eye. 'Do you think Greene did it?'

'I do not. It takes courage to commit murder, and Greene is a mouse. Besides, he believes everything in life is preordained, so he never bothers to do much of anything, on the grounds that it will make no difference to the general scheme of things anyway. You have met him – you know this is true. His Portliness refuses to be convinced, though. What about you? What do you think?'

'That Greene did not leave his house last night, so he cannot have killed Vine.'

Turner looked pleased. 'We think alike, you and I.

42

I imagine we share the same taste in women, too. As far as I am concerned, they only need one qualification to secure my favour: they must have teeth. I cannot abide making love to bare gums. I am sure you will agree.'

He sauntered away, whistling to himself, before Chaloner could frame a suitable answer.

Chapter 2

The Earl's White Hall offices comprised a suite of rooms overlooking the Privy Garden. They were sumptuously furnished and snug, with the exception of one: Secretary John Bulteel occupied a bleak, windowless cupboard that was so cold during winter he was obliged to wear gloves with the fingers cut out. He glanced up as Chaloner walked past and gave him a friendly wave, baring his rotten teeth in a smile as he did so. He was a slight, timid man, who was not popular among his colleagues, although Chaloner liked him well enough. His wife baked excellent cakes, and he often shared them with the spy – a diffident, shy gesture of friendship that no one else at White Hall ever bothered to extend.

Bulteel took a moment to blow on his frozen hands, then turned back to his ledgers, looking like a scarecrow in badly fitting, albeit decent quality, clothes. Chaloner often wondered why the Earl treated him so shabbily, when he was scrupulously honest, hard-working and loyal, and could only conclude it was because Bulteel was so singularly unprepossessing – that the Earl could not bring himself to show consideration for someone who was not only physically unattractive, but socially inept, too.

In contrast to his secretary's chilly domain, the Earl's chambers were sweltering, heated not only by massive braziers, but by open fires, too. They had recently been redecorated, although Chaloner thought the man responsible should be shot. A massive chandelier now hung from the main ceiling, and while the Earl was short enough to pass underneath it without mishap, anyone taller could expect to be brained. Meanwhile, the walls were crammed with paintings from the newly retrieved collections of the King's late father – Cromwell had sold these after the execution of the first Charles, and the Royalists were currently in the process of getting them all back again. Chaloner found the sheer number of masterpieces in such a small space vulgar, although no one else seemed bothered by it.

He walked through the open door, ducked to avoid the chandelier, and approached the desk. The Earl leapt violently when he became aware that his spy was standing behind him.

'How many more times must I tell you not to sneak up on me like that?' he snapped angrily, hand to his chest. 'I cannot cope with you frightening the life out of me at every turn.'

'I am sorry, sir. It is these thick rugs – they muffle footsteps.'

'They are for my gout. Wiseman says soft floor coverings are kinder on the ankles than marble. He also said I would be more comfortable if I was thinner. I confess I was hurt. Do you think me fat?'

'I have seen fatter,' replied Chaloner carefully. He did not want to lie, but suspected the Earl would not appreciate the truth. He changed the subject before the

45

discussion could become awkward. 'I interviewed Vine's family last night. They do not seem overly distressed by his death.'

'That does not surprise me. Young George is a nasty creature, and I do not believe he tried to assassinate Cromwell, as he claims. I suspect he made up the tale, to curry favour with us Royalists.'

'There was no love lost between father and son. They—'

'George did *not* dispatch his father,' interrupted the Earl, seeing where the conversation was going. 'Vine was killed in an identical manner to Chetwynd – with poison. Since there cannot be two murderers favouring the same method of execution, we must assume a single culprit: Greene. Besides, while George may be delighted to lose his sire, he has no reason to want Chetwynd dead.'

'Perhaps that is what he hopes you will think. Chetwynd might be a decoy victim.'

'Why must you always look for overly complex solutions?' demanded the Earl. '*Greene* killed Chetwynd, as I have told you dozens of times. And now he has attacked Vine.'

'But I was watching his house when Vine was killed. He cannot be—'

'He hired an accomplice. He can afford it, because his job pays him a handsome salary. But I fail to understand why you cannot see his guilt. He "discovered" Chetwynd's body, and you once told me yourself that the discoverer of a murdered corpse should always be considered a suspect until he can prove his innocence. Moreover, Greene and Chetwynd worked in adjoining buildings and were acquaintances, if not friends. I know Chetwynd ranked higher than Greene, but that is irrelevant.'

'Irrelevant?' Chaloner was unable to stop himself from

pointing out an inconsistency. 'But when we caught Greene running away from Chetwynd's body, you said it *was* relevant, because it was Greene's motive for murder: jealousy.'

The Earl glared at him. 'You really are an insolent dog! But you should watch your tongue from now on, because if Turner transpires to be better than you, I shall appoint him in your place and dispense with your services. There are those who think I am rash to employ a man who was a member of Cromwell's secret service, and I am beginning to think they may have a point.'

'You mean Williamson?' The government's most recent spymaster held Chaloner responsible for the death of a friend earlier that year, and hated him intensely. It was unfortunate, because Chaloner had hoped to continue spying in Holland after the Restoration – the King needed experienced men to watch the Dutch just as much as Cromwell had, and his record was impeccable. Moreover, he had only ever provided reports on alien nations, never on the exiled King. But he would never be sent to the Netherlands as long as Williamson was in charge of intelligence.

The Earl nodded. 'He says that hiring ex-Parliamentarian agents may make folk question my loyalty to the King. And he is right – I have many enemies at Court, and one might well use my employing of you to harm me.'

'But none of them know about my past,' objected Chaloner. 'Unless you have told them?'

'I have not,' said the Earl firmly. 'Do you think me a fool, to provide them with ammunition? And Williamson knows better than to tell them, too, because he is afraid of your mentor. Cromwell's old spymaster may have lost his government posts and a good slice of his wealth when the Royalists returned, but he still wields enough power to make him dangerous.'

Unfortunately, though, the fear in which men had once held Thurloe was beginning to wane as time passed. Chaloner was not worried about what that meant for himself, although the prospect of an unleashed Williamson was not something he relished, but about the repercussions for his friend. There were those who thought Cromwell's chief advisor had no right to be living in peaceful retirement, and should suffer a traitor's death.

'Greene, sir,' Chaloner prompted, supposing he would have to prove his loyalty yet again to the Earl and the new government – and keep proving it until he was fully trusted. It was a miserable situation, because there was little about the Earl *or* the work that he liked, but he needed to earn a crust, and no one else was lining up to hire him.

The Earl pursed his lips. 'When Greene came slithering out of the Painted Chamber, just as you and I happened to be walking past, he behaved very suspiciously.'

'He was frightened,' said Chaloner reasonably. 'He had just found a dead senior official, and then the Lord Chancellor accused him of murder. I would have been frightened, too.'

'But you would not have tried to run away. You would have stayed and explained yourself.'

'He panicked – it could happen to anyone under such circumstances.'

'Rubbish,' declared the Earl, with a note of finality that told Chaloner any further debate would be a waste of time. 'But I told Colonel Turner that I want this killer – whether it is Greene or someone else – behind bars by Twelfth Night. He assures me that it will be done. What will you promise?'

'To do my best. I will not lie to you, or make pledges I may not be able to fulfil.'

The Earl stared at him for a moment. 'Very well. Go and do your best then, and let us see where it leads. However, I see no point in continuing to watch Greene – he slipped past you to murder Vine, after all – so give up the surveillance and concentrate on other leads instead. And incidentally, these deaths do not mean you can forget about the previous task I set you.'

Chaloner regarded him blankly. 'What previous task? Finding out what the Lord of Misrule plans to do over the next ten days?'

The Earl grimaced in distaste. 'You had better *not* waste your time on that nonsense! No, I mean the King's missing statue. He remains grieved by its loss, and I would like to be the one to hand it back to him. You will be busy, because I give both these enquiries equal status.'

The Earl of Clarendon was not normally a stupid man, and Chaloner could not help but wonder whether there was more to his dislike of Greene than he was willing to share. It would not be the first time he had been less than honest with his spy before sending him off on an investigation, and Chaloner knew from bitter experience that this could prove dangerous. But such subterfuge was the Earl's way, and Chaloner had come to expect lies and half-truths, so he resigned himself to fathoming out the mystery without his master's cooperation. It was a wicked waste of his time, especially given that he had two other enquiries to conduct, but it could not be helped, and there was no point in wasting energy by railing against it.

'He is in a bad mood this morning,' said Bulteel, following the spy down the stairs with some letters to post. 'His gout must be aggravating him.'

'He is always in a bad mood,' Chaloner replied tartly. 'So goutiness must be his permanent state.'

'Do not be too hard on him,' said Bulteel quietly. 'He is under a lot of pressure, what with the bishops demanding new laws to suppress nonconformists, the Court popinjays clamouring for war with the Dutch, and people muttering that the Queen – the wife *he* chose for His Majesty – is barren.'

'How is your family?' Chaloner was loath to discuss the Earl's concerns, because he and Bulteel held diametrically opposite views on most of them. Bulteel tended to accept whatever the Earl told him, whereas Chaloner had seen enough of the world to make up his own mind.

Bulteel blinked at the abrupt enquiry. 'Well, we would like to provide our little son with a sibling, but I fear for my future employment. Haddon has only been here a few months, but the Earl already prefers him to me – he is taking over duties that should be mine.'

'But that is why he was hired,' Chaloner pointed out. 'You were overwhelmed, struggling to keep up, and Haddon is meant to be taking some of your work. The Earl expects you to be grateful, not nervous.'

'Well, I *am* nervous,' snapped Bulteel, uncharacteristically sharp. 'This job is important to me. And I do not like Haddon, anyway. He smells of dog and is always smiling at people. It is not natural.'

'Right,' said Chaloner, not sure what else to say. Haddon did smile at people, but no more than was necessary for normal social intercourse, and the spy had not noticed any particular odour of pooch. He changed the subject before the discussion went any further – he did not want to take sides when he had to work with both secretary and steward. 'I do not suppose you have heard any rumours about these murders, have you? About potential culprits?'

'I am afraid not,' replied Bulteel. 'All I know is that neither victim will be mourned by his kin, although London will be a poorer place without them. They were good men.'

'You knew them well?'

'No, but I wish I had – they were gentle and kind. And Vine funded a hospice for stray dogs. Perhaps *that* is why they were killed – the Court is so full of vice that decency is considered a fault.'

'Is Greene the kind of man to despise goodness?'

'I do not know him well, either, but I would not have thought so. He is very devout, by all accounts – attends church most mornings, and does charitable work in Southwark.'

'Then what about the missing statue? There must be *some* gossip regarding its whereabouts?'

'Not that I have heard. Colonel Turner has been told to make enquiries, too, but I would rather you were the one to find it.'

Chaloner shrugged. 'It does not matter which of us succeeds, only that the King has it back. He is said to be very distressed about its disappearance.'

Bulteel was silent for a moment, then began to speak. 'Turner is a danger to your future. And Haddon is a danger to mine. You and I have worked together before to our mutual advantage, so what do you say to renewing our alliance? You tell me if Haddon confides any plot that might prove detrimental to me; I tell you anything I hear about the statue or the murders. Agreed?'

'Very well,' said Chaloner, confident that the steward would confide nothing of the kind, so betraying one colleague to another would not be a quandary he would ever be obliged to face.

Bulteel smiled. 'Good. And to seal our agreement, I shall go with you to the Shield Gallery. Turner should be gone by now, because we both know there is nothing to find – you have already looked.'

'So why should I go there with you now?' asked Chaloner warily.

'Because I have been thinking about the theft, and I have a theory. It involves keys.'

The ease with which the thief had entered the Shield Gallery on the night the statue had gone missing was something that had troubled Chaloner from the start, and he was more than willing to listen to Bulteel's ideas on the subject. The secretary had a sharp mind, and might well have an insight into how the crime had been committed – and Chaloner needed all the help he could get now he was in competition with another investigator. He nodded assent, and they began to walk in that direction.

The Shield Gallery was a long hall, so named because trophies won during tournaments in the nearby Tilt Yard had once hung there. No such chivalrous pursuits took place now, though – Chaloner thought there was more likely to be a tally of sexual conquests pinned to the walls.

The gallery was on the upper floor of an Elizabethan section of the palace, and at one end was a large, mullioned window that overlooked the river. On the ground floor, directly beneath the window, were the so-called Privy Stairs, which were basically a private wharf for the King and Queen. It was convenient for them to jump into a boat there, because the Queen's quarters were through a door in the gallery's northern end, while the King's lay to the south. The gallery was handsomely appointed – its floor was tiled in black and white granite, and paintings by great masters hung along its length, interspersed with sculptures on plinths.

As it was so close to the royal apartments, the chamber was usually kept locked. Bulteel opened it with a key, and Chaloner saw Turner had not been exaggerating when he had mentioned a leaking roof: there were puddles on the floor and water-stains on the walls. There was no sign of the colonel, although there was a lot of noise coming from Her Majesty's rooms – squeals, giggles and bantering conversation. The spy was impressed: it was not easy for a man to inveigle his way into that Holy of Holies. But there was work to be done, and Chaloner had more important concerns than Turner's silver tongue. He turned his attention to the matter in hand.

'The statue was there,' he said, pointing to the one plinth that was bereft of its masterpiece.

Bulteel ran wistful fingers across the empty marble. 'Bernini captured the old king's likeness to perfection when he carved that bust. Did you know it was one of the pieces Cromwell hawked, because he needed money to pay off his army? You, in other words.'

Chaloner was taken aback by what sounded like an accusation. 'Hardly! I fought in the wars, but was never in the peacetime militia – I was overseas by the time the old king's goods were sold.' He frowned. 'I did not know you were a connoisseur of art.'

Bulteel shrugged. 'You have never asked. But I do like sculpture. When the King decided to reassemble his late father's collection, I was one of those employed to make a list of what had gone, so the commissioners would know what to hunt for. I hope you find the Bernini, because it would be a crying shame if that disappeared into some private vault.'

'Yes, it would, so we had better get to work. The Shield Gallery has four doors: one leads to the Queen's apartments; one leads to the King's; the tiny one in the corner leads to a spiral staircase that exits into a lane – we just used it to come here; and the last one leads to the Privy Stairs and the river. All are locked at night. What is your theory about keys?'

'There was no sign of forced entry, which means the culprit had one. The King rarely uses his door – you can see from here that it is currently blocked by a chest. By contrast, the Queen uses hers a lot, because she likes to walk in here if the weather is damp.'

'You think the thief is one of her ladies-in-waiting?' Chaloner was amused. 'She must be a very hefty one, then, because those busts are heavy.'

'You are mocking me,' said Bulteel reproachfully. 'I was going to say that the ladies can be eliminated as suspects, because they would have stolen something more easily portable.'

Chaloner inclined his head to accept his point. 'I know the thief did not use the Privy Stairs door, because that was barred from the inside. So, we are left with the one that gives access to the lane. Who has a key to that? You do, for a start.'

Bulteel held it up. 'It is the Earl's, and one of my responsibilities is to keep it for him. It was a duty he wanted me to pass to Haddon, but I prevaricated for so long that he has forgotten about it.'

'Who else?' asked Chaloner, not very interested in Bulteel's machinations to foil his rival.

'And *there* is your problem. I made enquiries, and was

told they were issued to at least forty nobles – women and men – at the Restoration. Brodrick has one, for example. Perhaps *he* stole the statue, and intends to make it look as though his cousin is the thief, as one of his pranks as Lord of Misrule.'

Chaloner was troubled, because it was exactly the kind of jape Brodrick might dream up. Unfortunately, what sounded like harmless fun might have devastating consequences, because the Earl's detractors would use it to question his probity – and England would not want a Lord Chancellor with accusations of dishonesty hanging over his head.

'Is that why you brought me here?' he asked. 'To tell me Brodrick is the guilty party?'

'Actually, no. I brought you here because I wanted you to understand that the thief is either a courtier or a high-ranking, well-trusted servant. It will not be a common burglar or some lowly scullion. It means you need to be careful, because the culprit may be powerful enough to do you real harm as you close in on him.'

Chaloner was thoughtful as he left the Shield Gallery. He had known from the start that the theft was the work of someone familiar with the palace, but he had been working on the premise that it was some greedy nobody. Bulteel's theory made sense, though, and he supposed he would have to tread warily from now on.

'What will you do now?' asked Bulteel, breaking into his thoughts.

'Go to discuss the problem with an old friend.'

London had not fared well in the recent gales. Trees had blown over, and several had fallen on buildings and smashed through their roofs. Bits of twig and broken tile littered the ground, and people were struggling to repair the damage with hammers and nails. The rhythmic clatter could barely be heard over the noise of the street – iron-shod cartwheels rattling across cobbles, the insistent hollers of tradesmen, and the jangling peals of church bells. The dying wind could barely be heard, either, although it made the hanging signs above doorways swing violently enough to be unsafe, and played a dangerous game with the creaking branches of some elderly oaks.

Many folk had marked the Twelve Days of Christmas by tying wreaths of holly, bay and yew to their doors. Most had been torn away, and sat in sodden heaps in corners, or blocked the drains that ran down the sides of the main streets. With indefatigable spirit, children were collecting them together, shaking out the water and filth, and pinning them back up again. Their noisy antics brought back happy memories of Chaloner's own boyhood in Buckinghamshire, making him smile.

He walked along The Strand, then up Chancery Lane until he reached the building known as the Rolls Gate, next to which stood Rider's Coffee House. Rider's was not the most comfortable of establishments, because it was poky, dimly lit and badly ventilated. It did, however, roast its beans without burning them, so the resulting potion was better than that served in most other venues.

Chaloner was not overly fond of the beverage that was so popular in the capital; he found it muddy, bitter and it made his heart pound when he drank too much of it. It was, however, better than tea, which he thought tasted of rotting vegetation. And tea was infinitely prefer-able to chocolate, which was just plain nasty, with its rank, oily consistency and acrid flavour. That day, though, it was not coffee he wanted in Rider's, but the companionship of the only man in London he considered a true friend.

He smiled when he opened the door and saw John Thurloe sitting at a table near the back. The place was busy with black-garbed lawyers from the nearby courts, all perched on benches and puffing on pipes as they discussed religion, current affairs and whatever had been reported in the most recent newsbooks. The spy was greeted with the traditional coffee-house cry of 'what news' as he aimed for Thurloe, but shook his head apologetically to say he had none.

Thurloe, who had run Cromwell's spy network with such cool efficiency, was a slight, brown-haired man with large blue eyes that had led more than one would-be traitor to underestimate him. He was softly spoken, slow to anger and deeply religious. He could also be ruthless and determined, and his sharp mind was the reason why men like Spymaster Williamson continued to fear him, even after he had been stripped of his government posts. There were those who said the Commonwealth would not have lasted as long as it had without Thurloe, and Chaloner was inclined to agree, despite the man's quiet and almost diffident manner.

As usual, Thurloe sat alone. At first, Chaloner had assumed no one wanted to hobnob with a man who had been a powerful member of a deposed regime, but it had not taken him long to learn that the choice was Thurloe's. Would-be table-companions were repelled with a glacial glare, and now the regulars left him to enjoy his coffee in peace. But he beamed in genuine pleasure when Chaloner slid on to the bench next to him.

'Tom! Where have you been these last few weeks? You told me your Earl was sending you to Oxford, to investigate a theft in his old College, but I did not imagine you would be gone so long. When did you come home?'

'Last week,' replied Chaloner, knowing he should have visited sooner. One reason he had not was Hannah, who had claimed a disproportionate amount of his time – and he found himself willing to let her. 'I have been looking for a missing statue ever since.'

Thurloe raised his eyebrows. 'The Bernini bust? That is unfortunate. Everyone is talking about how it was a perfect crime, because the thief left nothing in the way of clues. I suspect there may be some truth to these claims, because you do not look exactly flushed with victory.'

'No,' agreed Chaloner ruefully.

'I do not suppose you visited our friend Will Leybourn on your way home from Oxford, did you?' asked Thurloe, when the spy said no more. 'To see how life in the country is suiting him?'

'He seemed all right,' replied Chaloner vaguely. The ex-Spymaster did not need to hear that the mathematician–surveyor had taken up two new pastimes since leaving the city: one was watching his neighbour's wife through a binocular-telescope in the attic; the other was visiting her when her husband was out. Chaloner sincerely hoped he would come to his senses before there was trouble.

'Are you well?' asked Thurloe, when he saw that was all the news he could expect of their erstwhile companion. 'You are very pale.'

As a man obsessed with the state of his own health, Thurloe tended to assume there was something wrong with most people, even when they were blooming. He claimed he had a fragile constitution, although Chaloner suspected that he had nothing of the kind, and was as robust as the next man.

The spy smiled. 'It is dark in here. You cannot tell what shade I am.'

'I can see well enough,' said Thurloe tartly. 'Perhaps you should take one of my tonics.'

Chaloner was saved from having to devise an excuse – Thurloe's tonics had a reputation for turning even strong men into invalids – by the arrival of the coffee-boy, who slapped a bowl of dark-brown liquid down in front of him, then demanded to know whether he wanted green-pea tart or sausages. Coffee houses did not usually sell food, but Rider disliked the way his patrons disappeared for dinner at noon, so he provided victuals between twelve and one o'clock in an attempt to keep them there. Chaloner opted for the pie. A second servant flung it on the table as he passed, so carelessly that the spy was obliged to grab the flying platter before it upended in his lap. It transpired to be a pastry case filled with dried peas, sugar, spices and enough butter to render the whole thing hard and greasy.

'Christ!' muttered Chaloner in distaste. 'No wonder the King prefers French food.'

'You should have had the sausages,' remarked Thurloe unhelpfully. 'Only a lunatic orders something called green-pea tart.'

Chaloner sipped the coffee and winced – even when the beans were not burned, the beverage did not make for pleasant drinking. He swallowed the rest quickly, like medicine, then set the bowl down, repelled by the thick, sandy residue that remained at the bottom. He glanced up and was disconcerted to see Thurloe eating his sludge with a spoon.

'Are you sure that is good for you?' he asked uneasily, certain it was not.

'Coffee grit is a digestive aid – it helps grind up food in the stomach, allowing it to pass more easily through the gut. At least, that is what my old friend Chetwynd told me, when he was still alive.'

Chaloner laughed. 'You are losing your touch, because that was *not* a subtle way of learning whether the Earl has charged me to investigate Chetwynd's murder. Three years ago, you would have been aghast at such transparency.'

Thurloe set his dish back on the table with a moue of distaste. 'I am not sure Chetwynd knew what he was talking about, and my delicate constitution may take harm from following the advice of the ignorant. What do you think?'

'About what? The possibility of you being harmed by coffee grounds, Chetwynd's competence in medical matters, or the manner of his death?'

Thurloe opened a small box, the label of which proudly claimed the contents to be *Stinking Pills, guaranteed to purge phlegm, clear the veins, and cure gout and leprosy.* Chaloner hoped his friend knew what he was doing when he took a handful and began to chew them.

'The answer to any question would be acceptable, Thomas. You have volunteered virtually nothing since you arrived, avoiding even my innocuous enquiries about your health. If this is what happens to a man when I train him to spy, then I am sorry for it.'

'So am I,' said Chaloner, supposing that working at Court, moving among people who were subjects for investigation rather than friendship, was beginning to take an unpleasant toll on his manners. If he could not hold a normal conversation with his closest friend, then it was not surprising that he often felt lonely in London.

He tried to explain. 'I am forced to be constantly on my guard at White Hall – against being told lies, against physical attack, and against harm to my master.'

Thurloe regarded him thoughtfully. 'But that has always been the case. When you were working for me in Holland, France and Portugal, the strain must have been even greater, given that a careless slip would have cost you your life. White Hall cannot be as bad as that.'

Chaloner was not so sure. 'Williamson is proving to be an unforgiving enemy.'

Thurloe's expression was one of disgust. 'Williamson is a fool! If he had hired you as his spy in The Hague, as I recommended, we would not be nearing the brink of war with Holland now. You would have provided him with information that would have averted the crisis.'

Chaloner was astonished by the claim. 'I sincerely doubt it! The government thinks we can win an encounter with the Dutch, and no spy will convince them otherwise. I cannot imagine where their bravado comes from, given that they have dismissed the standing army, and the navy is full of unpaid criminals who will desert at the first cannonball.'

'The Royalists are like children, playing games of war. But they will learn, although not before English blood is needlessly spilled. I only hope none of it is yours. The situation is now so dangerous that I would urge you to refuse, should the Earl order you to gather intelligence in Holland. Look what happened when you went to Spain and Portugal earlier this year. You barely escaped with your life.'

'He is more concerned with the missing statue than with the Dutch,' said Chaloner, changing the subject, because he did not want to think about his harrowing experiences in Iberia.

Thurloe raised his eyebrows. 'So, you are *not* investigating what happened to Chetwynd?'

'I am expected to do both.' Chaloner hesitated uncertainly. 'I would not mind telling you all I have learned about the murders, to see if you can think of any way forward. The Earl is determined to see Greene hanged for killing Chetwynd and Vine, but I am sure he is innocent.'

Thurloe listened without interruption as the spy outlined all he had discovered. 'I met Greene once,' he said when Chaloner had finished. 'He is a nonentity – an unassuming fellow without the vigour to kill two men. Why does the Earl dislike him so intensely?'

'I do not know – and I suspect I never will. He has never really trusted me, and I think he intends to replace me soon, with a man called Colonel Turner. Have you heard of him?'

'Yes. He was a minor nuisance during the Commonwealth – he liked breaking into the Post Office and stealing letters. He never laid hold of anything important, but it was an annoyance, regardless.'

'He says you put a price on his head.'

'Then he is lying – he would not have been worth the expense.'

'What else can you tell me about him?'

'Only that he has twenty-eight children, and he trained as a solicitor. And that he could never match your expertise as an intelligencer, and the Earl is an ass if he thinks otherwise.'

But the Earl *was* an ass in matters of espionage, thought Chaloner dejectedly, and might well dismiss him in favour of a flamboyant Cavalier. And then what? The spy could not foist himself on his family, because, as fervent supporters of Cromwell, they were being taxed into

62

poverty by vengeful Royalists. He wondered, not for the first time, whether he should abandon England, and go to live in the New World. The only problem was that he had been there once, and had not liked it.

'What do you know about the victims?' he asked, changing the subject. 'Vine and Chetwynd?'

'Just that they were pillars of decency in a government that seethes with corruption. It was not like that when Cromwell was in charge – as absolute ruler, he had the power to dismiss or arrest anyone he deemed less than honest. As I have said before, a military dictatorship is the best form of govern—'

'What about their families?' asked Chaloner, interrupting before they could argue. He did not share Thurloe's views on the joys of repressive regimes. 'George Vine told me he tried to assassinate Cromwell. Is it true?'

Thurloe grimaced. 'I did have wind of a plot, but it transpired to be so outlandish that I did not bother with a prosecution. He planned to give the Lord Protector an exploding leek, but failed to take into account that most men are not in the habit of devouring raw vegetables presented to them by strangers. And we all know you cannot pack enough gunpowder inside a leek to kill anyone.'

'No,' agreed Chaloner. 'You would need a cabbage, at the very least.'

Religion was a contentious issue in England, and as far as the bishops were concerned, a person was either a devout Anglican who attended his weekly devotions, or a fanatic who should be treated with suspicion. Some churches kept registers of which parishioners stayed away, and because Chaloner had been trained never to attract unnecessary attention, he always tried to make an appearance at St Dunstan-in-the-West on those Sundays when he was home. He did not usually mind, because the old building was a haven of peace amid the clamour of the city, and the rector's rambling sermons gave him a chance to sit quietly and think of other matters.

But he resented the wasted time that day. There was too much to do, and Rector Thompson was holding a sheaf of notes that suggested his congregation might be trapped for hours while he ploughed through them all. Chaloner exchanged amiable greetings with him in the nave, ensured his name was recorded on the attendance list, then escaped through the vestry door when no one was looking. Once in the street, he headed for Westminster, walking with one hand on his hat to prevent the wind from tearing it from his head. It had been a gift from a lady in Spain, and its crown was cunningly reinforced with a metal bowl. It had saved his life on several occasions, and he did not want to lose it.

Westminster was different from White Hall, despite the fact that both were medieval palaces. White Hall was brazenly secular, alive with the colours of Court – the reds, golds, oranges and purples of balls and banquets. Its larger buildings were built of brick, although most were in desperate need of painting, and fountains and statues adorned its open spaces. By contrast, Westminster was dominated by its abbey and Norman hall, and had a monastic feel. Its buildings were characterised by lancet windows, stained glass and pinnacles, and there was an atmosphere of sobriety and business. Policy might be decided in White Hall, but the documents and writs to make it legal came from Westminster.

At the heart of Westminster, in the open area known

as New Palace Yard, was the medieval Great Hall. As Chaloner walked past it, he paused to stare up at the severed heads that had been placed on poles outside. Cromwell's was there, although the spy had no idea which of the blackened, almost inhuman objects belonged to the man who had ruled the Commonwealth. Some had long hair that waved in the wind, but most were bald, picked clean by crows. They had a tendency to blow down in rough weather, and he could see at least two on the ground. People were giving them a wide berth, because Spymaster Williamson's men were in the habit of lurking nearby, ready to arrest anyone who attempted to rescue the pathetic objects and give them a decent burial.

Chaloner cut through a series of alleys until he reached the narrow lane that gave access to the Painted Chamber, intending to inspect it more thoroughly than he had been able to the previous night. He was unimpressed to find it very busy, not only with the clerks who had turned it into their personal office space, but with spectators who wanted to see the spot where two men had been murdered. A search was out of the question, so he lingered unobtrusively near the tapestries, eavesdropping on the discussions of the ghouls. It did not take him long to realise that he was wasting his time, and that the chances of overhearing anything relevant were negligible, so he left.

Unfortunately, he had no clear idea of how else to proceed, so he spent the rest of the day lurking in the kitchens, cook-houses and public areas of both palaces. But although there was a lot of talk about the murders – the statue was not mentioned, because it was old news and no longer of interest – it was all gossip and speculation, and nothing was based in fact. And the Lord of Misrule was being unusually close-lipped about his plans, so the spy made no headway there, either. He did learn that an event was planned for that evening in the Great Hall, though – it was something to do with Babylon, and necessitated the preparation of vast platters of a glutinous, rose-flavoured jelly.

The daylight faded and darkness fell. People began to dissipate, either to go home, or – if they were important enough to be invited – head for the Great Hall to enjoy whatever Near Eastern extravaganza Brodrick had devised. Among the latter was George Vine, who wore a bizarre combination of clothes meant to make him look like a sultan. The wind caught his turban and sent it cart-wheeling across the courtyard; Chaloner stopped it with his foot, and handed it back to him.

'What do you think?' asked George, twirling around then grabbing Chaloner's arm when a combination of wine and a sudden gust of wind made him stagger. 'I am a Babylonian prince.'

'Very pretty. Have you made arrangements for your father's funeral yet?'

'Do not think to berate me for merrymaking while he lies above ground, because old Dreary Bones was buried this morning.' George smirked at Chaloner's surprise. 'I wanted to make sure Surgeon Wiseman did not get him, so time was of the essence.'

'I see,' said Chaloner, wondering why George was so determined to prevent an examination that might yield clues. It was clearly nothing to do with filial love. 'Can you tell me anything about his last day? What time did he leave home?'

'At dawn. I remember, because we met at the door,

and argued over the fact that he was going to work, while I had not yet been to bed. He was like that, always criticising me for having fun.'

'And what did his work at the Treasury entail, exactly?'

'He dealt with large quantities of money. I suppose I shall have to find out more, given that I intend to take over his duties. But I refuse to work as hard as he did – *I* am no bore.'

'I am sure the King will be impressed by your dedication.'

George curled his lip, jammed his turban on his head and began to totter away. He called back over his shoulder as he went. 'The wind is picking up again, and we all know what that means.'

Chaloner had no idea what he was talking about. 'What?'

'That a great person will die. People said it blew for my father, but it persists, so obviously it gusts for someone else – old Dreary Bones was not a "great person" after all. You had better make sure the Lord Chancellor is tucked up safe in his bed.'

Chaloner darted after him, gripping his shoulder hard enough to make him squeal as he jerked him to a standstill. 'Are you threatening my Earl?'

George was frightened – by the spy's speed, strength and the expression on his face. 'No! I was just blathering. I did not mean anything by it, I swear!' His bloodshot eyes lit on a nearby lane, and he jabbed a desperate finger at it. 'Look, there are Thomas and Matthias Lea. Go and interrogate them – they also benefited from the murder of a kinsman, and I am not the only one who is suddenly rich.'

Chaloner peered into the gloom, and saw Chetwynd's

heirs climbing into a hackney. They were looking in his direction, but when he released George and took a few steps towards them, one said something to the driver and they rattled away. He could have caught them, had he run, but it was not worth the effort. They had left abruptly because they did not want to deal with him, and chasing them was not going to change that fact. He would simply have to wait for a more opportune moment.

He lingered a while longer, standing in the shadows of White Hall's largest courtyard, and watching gaggles of courtiers set off towards Westminster together. Most wore costumes that showed they had not the faintest idea of what Babylon had been like. Eventually, only the stragglers remained. One trio comprised a girl with woolly hair who wore nothing around her midriff and bells on her ankles, a youth dressed as a genie, and an old man whose sole concession to the occasion was a fez. He appeared to be deaf, and kept turning questioningly to his companions, who made no effort to speak at a volume that would help him. Chaloner knew they were rich when a coach came to collect them, although it was too dark to make out the insignia on its side. He could tell from their gestures that the youngsters were annoyed about being late, while the ancient gave the impression that he would rather be at home with a good book and a cup of warm milk.

But then even they had gone. There was no point in remaining, so Chaloner set off for Westminster himself, not to spy on the ball, but to see whether the Painted Chamber was empty at last.

When he reached New Palace Yard, the twang of foreign-sounding music and a cacophony of voices emanated from the Great Hall. A few revellers spilled into the street, one or two to vomit up the unpalatable mixture of wine and rose-flavoured jellies, and others to snatch kisses and fondles in the darkness outside. Several enterprising businesses had stayed open in the hope of attracting late trade, although Chaloner could not imagine many courtiers being interested in legal books or porpoise tongues, which seemed to be the two main commodities on offer.

The area around the Painted Chamber was deserted, though. It was illuminated by the odd lantern, but not many, because fuel was expensive and the government saw no point in spending money on a part of the complex that was usually abandoned at night. The occasional clerk risked life and limb to work late – the Palace of Westminster was surrounded by tenements and hovels, so violent crime was rife – but they were not many. One shadow sidled up to Chaloner with the clear intention of relieving him of his purse, but it melted away when he started to draw his sword.

The Painted Chamber was unlocked, and he supposed the guards had yet to make their rounds and secure the building for the night. He opened the door to its lobby, then ascended the wide stone steps to the main hall. He paused by the entrance, listening intently for any sound from within, more from habit than any expectation of detecting anything amiss. But George had been right when he said the wind was picking up again – it screamed down the chimney and roared across the roof, and Chaloner could barely hear his own footsteps, let alone anyone else's. He scanned the shadows for any flicker of movement that might tell him someone was there, but the place appeared to be empty. It was lit by a lamp at its far end, near the spot where Vine and Chetwynd had died, but was otherwise in darkness.

It was a large building, perhaps eighty feet long by twenty-five wide, and showed signs of serious long-term neglect. The great tapestries depicting the Trojan Wars were grey with filth, and the ceiling was black from years of smoking candles. The stone tracery in the windows was crumbling, and the floorboards needed replacing – there were gaps between some that could swallow a small foot.

He walked to the far end, and gazed at the place where the bodies had been found. The first victim, Chetwynd, had been working at his desk. So what had happened? Had the killer arrived, amiably offering to share a cup of wine with him? If so, then Chetwynd must have known his murderer, because government officials did not accept refreshments from just anyone in the depths of night. The fact that no cup was anywhere to be found when the chamber was later searched told Chaloner that the culprit had been careful to leave nothing in the way of clues.

And Vine? The building where he worked adjoined the Painted Chamber, so perhaps he, like Greene, had run out of ink, and hoped to borrow some from Chetwynd's well-supplied table. Or perhaps the killer had invited him there, offering to share his deadly brew on the pretence that it was a toast to a dead colleague. And that meant the killer knew *both* his victims – knew them well enough that Vine was not suspicious, despite almost certainly being aware of what had happened to Chetwynd.

The spy took the lamp and began to examine the floor, although not with much hope of finding anything useful – the hall had been graced by too many visitors that day.

He was on the verge of giving up and going home, when he spotted something gleaming faintly between two floor-boards. It was a ring, but when he tried to pick it up, he found it was solidly wedged. There was a smear of mud on it, which told him someone – possibly its owner – had trodden on it, probably by accident, crushing it even more firmly into the slit. New scratches on the floor around it indicated someone had tried to prise it out, but had given up. Chaloner saw why when his dagger proved too unwieldy for the task, and he was obliged to use one of his lock-picking probes. It was not easy, but he succeeded eventually.

The ring was small – too tiny to fit even his little finger – and beautiful in its simplicity. It comprised a plain gold band with a clasp that held a deep-red ruby. The size of the gem and the quality of the workmanship told him it was valuable. Did it belong to one of the ghouls who had visited the Painted Chamber that day? He did not think so, because they would not have abandoned their efforts to retrieve it – they would have fetched a more suitable implement with which to lever it out.

Had it belonged to Vine, then, and his attempts to rescue it had been interrupted when the killer had arrived? It would have been too small to fit his fingers, but there was a current fashion for wearing rings suspended from cuff-strings, so its size meant nothing. Or was Chaloner holding something that belonged to the murderer, ripped away as Vine thrashed around in his death throes? He was sure of one thing, though: it was not Greene's. The clerk was something of a Puritan, and favoured clothes devoid of extravagant accessories, jewellery included.

There was no more to be learned from the Painted

Chamber, so he decided to go home. He was halfway down the hall when he heard a creak over the racket being made by the storm. It sounded like the main door being opened. Instinctively, he slipped into the shadows and watched it intently – so intently that he made a basic mistake. The room had other entrances, one of which was directly behind him. He spun around the moment he detected the rustle of clothing, but it was too late – a cudgel was descending towards his head. He managed to deflect it by throwing up his arm, but it was a violent blow, and sent him staggering backwards.

There were six of them – three had entered through the main door, and three from the entrance behind Chetwynd's desk – and they meant business. Chaloner whipped out his sword to parry a thrust that was obviously intended to disembowel him, then was obliged to retreat fast when the rest came at him in a tight phalanx of flashing blades. His left arm was numb, and the ring slid from his nerveless fingers. He barely noticed it go: all his attention was focussed on staying alive.

He fought furiously, using every trick and feint he knew in an effort to gain an advantage. But it was an unequal battle, and although he injured two who were reckless enough to come within his range, they were simply too many for him. Moreover, they wielded their weapons with an easy confidence that said they were professional soldiers, and he could tell, from the way they anticipated each other's moves, that they had been fighting together for years – they operated like a well-oiled machine, one stepping forward the moment another fell back. A detached part of his mind knew it was only a matter of time before he was skewered, because he could not fend them off indefinitely – he was already tiring.

'I've found it,' said one, bending to retrieve something from the floor. 'We can go.'

Immediately, a warrior tried to manoeuvre his way behind Chaloner, who was forced to back up against the wall. Then three attacked at once, and he was hard-pressed to repel them. He was aware of movement on either side of him, but did not realise what was happening until someone gave a yell and started to haul on something. He glanced up in time to see the tapestry tear free from its moorings. The soldiers leapt away, but Chaloner was knocked from his feet as the heavy material enveloped him. He was encased in darkness, and completely help-less. He was aware of blades stabbing into the floor around him, then something struck his head, hard enough to knock him out of his senses. The last thing he heard was retreating footsteps.

When Chaloner opened his eyes, his nose and mouth were full of dust, his head hurt, and he could not see. It was several minutes before he remembered what had happened, and several more before he was able to struggle free of the suffocating tapestry. The soldiers had gone, and a quick search revealed that the ring had gone, too. He removed his hat and ran his fingers across the crown, to discover a vicious jab from a blade had caused a substantial dent in the metal lining. Once again, it had saved his life, and he gave silent thanks to Isabella, his brief but passionate Spanish *amore*, who had given it to him. He was sure the soldiers had not expected him to survive.

He had no idea how much time had passed since the attack, but he peered carefully around the main door anyway, just in case the men were still there. They were not, for which he was grateful, because he was in no state to tackle them again, and they were unlikely to let him live a second time. So, who were they? The killers of Vine and Chetwynd? He doubted it – why waste time with toxins when they had swords to hand? He recalled one soldier bending to pick something up from the floor, telling his colleagues that he had 'found it'. Clearly, he referred to the ring, but why? Had the killer charged them to retrieve it, because it was evidence that would trap him? Chaloner rubbed his aching head as he thought about it. The Painted Chamber had been busy all day, right up until the ghouls had gone to Brodrick's ball. So, like Chaloner, it would have been the soldiers' first opportunity to enter unseen.

So what did that tell him? That the killer controlled an elite gang of warriors, as well as having access to deadly potions? They had reminded him of the 'train-bands' of the civil wars – a group of friends or neighbours who had learned their martial skills together, and who could be mobilised at a moment's notice. Did it mean their leader – or their master – was rich and powerful? Or did it mean the killer was a woman, because while she might be capable of handing goblets of poison to her victims, tackling armed investigators was a different proposition entirely?

He became aware that he was standing directly underneath the lamp that lit the Painted Chamber's entrance, providing a perfect target for anyone who meant him harm. Disgusted, he tried to pull himself together, taking a deep breath in the hope that it would clear his wits. It did not, and he reeled dizzily, forcing him to wait for the weakness to pass. Then he started walking, but had not taken many steps before he was obliged to stop and steady himself against a wall.

'Too much Babylonian punch?' came a familiar voice.

'I warned people to treat it with caution, but did anyone listen? No! I only hope it does not put the King in a deadly stupor, because he has an important meeting with the Swedish ambassador tomorrow. Perhaps I should remain on hand tonight, lest my services are needed.'

Chaloner whipped around in alarm. The combination of noisy gale and befuddled senses had let Wiseman approach to almost within touching distance, and he had not heard a thing. He knew he needed to be a lot more careful, or the train-band would easily finish what they had started.

The surgeon, clad in his trademark red, was with a courtier, a plump man whom Chaloner had seen before – it was the fellow Greene had met in the Dolphin tavern the previous evening. The two men had shared a meal, talked amiably for a while, then parted ways. And they had done something else, too, but the memory was just out of Chaloner's reach, no matter how hard he struggled to recall it.

'Babylonian punch?' he asked dully, aware that Wiseman was waiting for a response.

'Brodrick's unique concoction of ale, limejuice, brandywine and spices,' elaborated Wiseman. 'I recommended he omit the brandywine, but he said Babylonians downed barrels of the stuff with no ill-effects. They did nothing of the kind, of course – it was only invented recently.'

'Actually, brandywine is what made them so famously garrulous,' countered his companion authoritatively. He was a bland-looking fellow, and his only outstanding feature was a very long nose. 'Babylonians babbled a lot – and they babbled because they were drunk on brandywine. It is a well-known fact. Brandywine made them wildly licentious, too – another well-known fact.'

Wiseman shot him an arch look. 'Not that well known, because *I* was unaware of it. But I am forgetting my manners. Langston, meet the Lord Chancellor's man. Chaloner, this is Francis Langston, one of the officials who works in the Royal Household.'

Chaloner started to bow, but changed his mind when the movement made the ground tip and he thought he might be sick. He wanted to ask what they were doing in a dark alley so late at night, but his tongue felt too big for his mouth, and Langston began to speak before he could form the words.

'I am a great admirer of your master – I wrote a play about him once, but it turned out badly. He is a fine, upright fellow, but literary heroes need more than morality to make them great – he came over as a pompous, overbearing bigot, so I thought it best not to present him with a copy.'

'Never mind that,' said Wiseman curtly. He looked enormous in the darkness, all barrel chest and powerful arms. '*I* have something important to say. As I watched folk swigging Brodrick's brew with gay abandon earlier this evening, it occurred to me that brandywine might have been used in the potion that killed Chetwynd and Vine.'

'So we went to visit Kersey, to find out,' said Langston, taking up the story. 'Wiseman sniffed Chetwynd's corpse – his kin refused the offer of dissection, but they said nothing about sniffing – and brandywine was indeed one of the ingredients.'

'No doubt it was added to disguise the taste of the toxin,' added Wiseman. 'Plain wine would have been unequal to the task. Unfortunately, Brodrick bought vats of it for his punch – all that was in London, apparently

– and the cellar staff say it is impossible to tell whether any is missing.'

'Who is Kersey?' asked Chaloner, struggling to understand what they were trying to tell him.

'The Corpse Keeper.' Wiseman frowned when he saw Chaloner's blank look. 'Do you know nothing? Everyone has heard of Kersey.'

'Well, I have not,' snapped Chaloner, his aching head making him irritable.

Wiseman sighed, and began to speak in a way that could only be described as patronising. 'When people die in Westminster – and thousands live and work here, so there is always someone breathing his last – their bodies go to Kersey until they are either buried or claimed by kin.'

'His charnel house is near here,' added Langston. 'It is not a place I like to visit, but needs must. Chetwynd and Vine were colleagues, and I do not like the notion of them being murdered.'

'Greene is your colleague, too,' said Chaloner, recalling what he had seen the previous night.

Langston shook his head. 'Greene is a *friend*, not a colleague. I am very fond of him, which is why I agreed to visit a charnel house with Wiseman – to see if we could prove his innocence.'

'And how does brandywine do that?' asked Chaloner, becoming confused. He wished he was home, lying in bed, not trying to talk to two men whose conversation was making no sense.

Wiseman peered at him. 'You are slow on the uptake tonight. Are you unwell? Perhaps you should go home, and I will explain my clever theory tomorrow. I do not want to have to repeat myself.'

'Have you seen any soldiers?' asked Chaloner tiredly. He raised a hand to his head, which felt as if it might explode. 'Not the palace guards, but a train-band, like the ones from the wars. They—'

Langston looked alarmed. 'You were attacked! Is that why you are swaying like a drunk? They knocked you out of your wits? I heard a gang of villains has taken to infesting these parts, so we had better leave while we can. Come. We shall walk to the Great Hall together.'

He took Chaloner's arm, and it was not many moments before they reached the light and noise of the ball. The music that wafted through the open door was curious and not entirely pleasant, as if someone had decided that the best way to emulate the tunes of the Ancient Near East was to take familiar melodies and play them sharp. Langston immediately disappeared inside, muttering something about it being safer than streets crawling with train-bands.

'Go home and rest,' ordered Wiseman, when he had gone. 'I shall stay here and eavesdrop. And if I hear anything useful about these killings, I shall tell you tomorrow.'

Chaloner stared at him. 'You want to help me?'

'I want to help the Earl,' corrected Wiseman. 'I refuse to stand by and watch him make a fool of himself by persisting with his irrational belief that Greene is the killer. Do not worry about me. *I* am a surgeon, and my lofty intelligence is more than a match for any mere poisoner.'

Chaloner could not think of anything to say in the light of such hubris.

Chapter 3

The wind blew hard all night, whistling through the loose windowpanes in Chaloner's room, bellowing down the chimney, and ripping across the roof. Exhausted though he was, it was not conducive to restful sleep, and he woke every time there was an unfamiliar bump, scrape or rattle. And each time he did, he found himself reaching for the dagger under his pillow, which reminded him unpleasantly of his recent mission to Spain, where constant and unrelenting danger had forced him into a similar state of high vigilance. He sincerely hoped London was not about to become the same.

It was not just the sounds of the storm that made him uneasy. An explosion in the neighbouring house the previous year had rendered his own building unstable. His landlord claimed there was nothing wrong, but cracks in the walls, window frames that suddenly did not fit, and a distinct list to the floor indicated otherwise. Chaloner was acutely aware that a high wind might tear the destabilised roof from its moorings, and as he lived in the attic, this would be a problem. He considered going to visit Hannah, but their courtship was very new

– they had graduated to the bedchamber only the previous week, upon his return from Oxford – and he did not think she would appreciate being woken in the small hours by a lover whose sole intention was to secure a good night's sleep.

It was four o'clock before the gale blew itself out. Chaloner dozed for another hour, then reluctantly prised himself out of bed. He lit a lamp, and saw water had seeped under cracked and missing tiles to dribble through the ceiling and down the walls; green stains indicated it was not the first time this had happened. Most men would have abandoned the place and found better accommodation, but the garret in Fetter Lane suited Chaloner for a number of reasons. Firstly, the structural hiccups meant it was leased at an attractively low rate, an important consideration for a man whose master did not always pay him on time. Secondly, Fetter Lane was a reasonably affluent street, and its residents kept it lit at night – a spy always liked to see who was going past his home in the dark. And finally, it was convenient for White Hall.

After positioning bowls to catch the worst of the drips, he sat on his bed and stared into space, feeling drowsy and sluggish. His head ached, his arm was bruised, and at some point during the skirmish, he had jarred his leg – an exploding cannon during the Battle of Naseby had left him slightly lame. In all, he felt decidedly shabby. He closed his eyes, and was almost asleep again when his cat jumped into his lap, jolting him awake. He had not known it was home, but was pleased to see it. He fed it some salted herring, which it devoured greedily. Then it left without so much as a backwards glance, its cool independence a far cry from Haddon's fawning lapdogs.

Despite his weariness, Chaloner knew he could not

afford to waste the day. He shaved quickly – it was cold in the room, and the water was icy – then donned a clean linen shirt, black breeches and stockings, and a blue 'vest' – a knee-length, collarless coat with loose-fitting sleeves. Unwilling to risk another blow to the head, he wore Isabella's metal-lined hat again. Thoughts of her made him smile, and he wished there was a way they could have been together. Unfortunately, their blossoming romance had come to an abrupt end when he had been exposed as a spy, leading to his arrest, imprisonment and an escape so narrow that it still haunted his dreams.

And now there was Hannah. Her father had been a favourite of the old king, and the new one had drafted her into the Queen's service after the death of her husband. Chaloner was not sure why he had been attracted to her – or her to him – because they had little in common, and he wondered whether it was an affection born of mutual loneliness. Yet he hoped the relationship would develop into something meaningful even so, assuming he did not ruin it by being reticent about his personal life – he had learned through bitter experience that most women did not like uncommunicative men.

'A great person has died,' announced Landlord Ellis, when he saw his tenant descend the rickety stairs and aim for the front door. Chaloner was surprised to see him, because dawn was still some way off, and Ellis was not an early riser. 'One always does when there is a strong wind. Did you hear about Chetwynd, who perished during that terrible blow we had on Christmas Day?'

Chaloner nodded, but declined to say he was one of those charged to find the man's killer.

'Chetwynd was not what I would have called great, though,' Ellis went on, standing in front of the tin mirror in the hallway and attempting to straighten his wig. 'You cannot be great if you are corrupt, in my humble opinion.'

Chaloner blinked in surprise. 'Chetwynd was corrupt? I thought he was one of the few honest men at Westminster – devout, hard-working and upright.'

'He was a lawyer,' countered Ellis tartly. 'And a Chancery clerk into the bargain. Of course he was corrupt. And if you do not believe me, ask Thomas Doling. And that young rascal Neale, who was rendered penniless by Chetwynd's duplicitous manoeuvrings.'

'Who are Doling and Neale?'

'Doling was a Commonwealth clerk, and Neale is a penniless courtier. They both haunt the Angel Inn on King Street, although not together obviously – Roundhead henchmen and Cavalier fops do not befriend each other, even if they *are* both victims of the same crooked lawyer. The man who died during the latest gale was great, though. No one can argue with that.'

'Was he?' asked Chaloner. A number of people had remarked on Vine's innate decency, so he supposed the fellow really had been a paragon of virtue.

Ellis nodded. 'I heard all about it this morning, when I went to my coffee house.'

'You must have gone very early,' said Chaloner, immediately suspicious. 'It is not yet light.'

Ellis looked sheepish. 'I could not sleep with all that rattling and howling, so I went out at midnight. I dislike storms, and there is nothing like coffee-house discourse to take one's mind off one's worries.'

As he spoke, he moved furtively to one side, and Chaloner saw he was trying to stand in front of a strongbox, to hide it from sight. It had a substantial lock, and was clearly for transporting valuables.

'You mean you were afraid the house would tumble about your ears, so you took your gold and spent the night somewhere safe. Why did you not warn your tenants to do likewise?'

Ellis became indignant. 'My house is safe – I was just not in the mood for taking chances. But we were talking about gales. The wind blew for Chetwynd on Thursday, and then it blew until a second great man died – a fat one, this time. "Great" can mean fat, you know.'

Chaloner frowned: Vine had not been fat. 'Who are you talking about?'

'Francis Langston,' replied Ellis. 'He was murdered last night.'

'Langston?' asked Chaloner, thinking of the plump fellow with the long nose he had met with Wiseman outside the Painted Chamber. Could it be the same man? 'Are you sure?'

'Yes – the storm died out at four o'clock, precisely when he was said to have breathed his last.'

'How do you know all this?' Chaloner estimated it was not quite six, so the news must have travelled very fast, even for London.

'One of the palace guards is a regular in my coffee house, and he told us the tale. The story is that Langston's corpse was found by the Lord Chancellor, who is said to be in a state of high agitation about it. And who can blame him? Apparently, he was going to hire Langston to be his personal spy.'

The news of Langston's death – and the unsettling notion that the Earl was expanding his intelligence network without telling him – was enough to drive Chaloner to White Hall immediately. He walked as fast as his sore leg would let him. As he limped across the Palace Court, he saw the day was not quite advanced enough for the King and his Court to have retired to bed, and the rumpus emanating from Lady Castlemaine's apartments suggested an extension of the Babylonian escapade was still in full swing. He heard the King's distinctive laugh, followed by the bleat of a goat, and then something that sounded like a musical instrument being smashed. He did not like to imagine what they were doing, but suspected that whatever it was would transpire to be expensive for the taxpayer.

He was just walking up the stairs to the Lord Chancellor's offices, when he heard a scream. It was his master, and he sounded terrified. Chaloner broke into a run, ignoring the protesting twinge in his leg as he took the steps three at a time. When he reached the Earl's door, he threw it open with a resounding crack, sword in his hand. The Earl knelt precariously on top of his desk, while his steward stood on a chair next to him. They were clutching each other, white-faced and frightened, and Chaloner was immediately struck by how old and vulnerable they both looked.

'Help me!' cried the Earl, when the spy edged into the room, every sense alert for danger. It appeared to be deserted, and there was no sign of assassins or anything else that might have driven the Lord Chancellor and his steward to take refuge atop the furniture. Chaloner took a step towards the window, but was brought up short when he cracked his head on the inconveniently placed chandelier.

'Help you with what?' he asked, hand to his scalp. Once again, he was grateful for Isabella's hat, because he suspected he would have knocked himself insensible without it – the fixture seemed to be made of especially unyielding metal.

'Look, man, look!' screeched the Earl, pointing unsteadily at a chest in the corner, where he kept a few changes of clothes and a spare hairpiece or two. 'It is the Devil's work!'

Assuming some sort of explosive device was hidden there, Chaloner gestured that his master was to walk towards him, intent on getting him out before anything detonated. 'Come,' he said, a little impatiently, when the Earl merely shook his head and refused to move. 'You must leave now.'

'I am not jumping down while that ... that *thing* is there!' declared the Earl vehemently.

Bemused, Chaloner studied the chest more closely, and saw a wig on the floor next to it. It was one of the larger ones, a magnificent creation of golden curls that hung well past the Earl's shoulders. They were rumoured to have come from a Southwark whore, who was currently in the process of growing a new set for the Duke of York. As he looked, Chaloner became aware that it was twitching. Then it began to slide along the floor of its own volition, slowly at first, but then with increasing speed as it approached the desk. The Earl howled again, and so did Haddon. Chaloner started to laugh.

'Do something!' shrieked the Earl. 'Before it races up the table and attaches itself to my person.'

'Or mine,' added Haddon fearfully. 'There is witchery in that periwig, and I am not sure such spells are very discerning. The evil may be meant for him, but it might harm me instead.'

Struggling to control his amusement, Chaloner jabbed the tip of his sword into the wig as it slithered past him. It stopped dead, although he could feel it tugging as it tried to continue its journey.

'Do not damage the hair!' squawked the Earl, watching

85

him in horror. 'Do you know how much those things cost? More than *you* earn in a year!'

'Perhaps I should ask for a pay-rise, then,' muttered Chaloner, keeping the sword where it was until he had reached down to grab the wig. It squeaked as he picked it up. Then it bit him. With a yelp of his own, he dropped it, and it was off again, skittering towards the window.

'It has teeth,' wailed Haddon, clutching the Earl so hard that he threatened to have them both on the floor. 'It is truly a demon sent by the Devil!'

The Earl closed his eyes and intoned a prayer of deliverance. 'Stab it again, Thomas,' he ordered. 'But without spoiling the wig, if you please. Then you can stay here and guard it, while Haddon and I fetch a priest. We shall have to exorcise this vile fiend, since it seems determined to do violence.'

Flexing his smarting hand, Chaloner went after the wig, which sensed him coming and began to move faster still. It shot under a chest, and emerged at high speed through the other side. Then it whipped across the floor, aiming for the door and the freedom beyond. Chaloner slammed the door shut before it could effect its escape, ignoring the Earl's furious reprimands for not letting it become someone else's problem. Eventually, he managed to pin it down on one of the Turkish carpets. When he picked it up a second time, he was rather more careful.

'A ferret,' he said, examining the wriggling creature within. 'I thought it would be a rat.'

The Earl peered at it, still holding on to Haddon. His expression was already turning from fearful to indignant. 'A ferret? You mean an animal dares to make its nest inside my favourite headpiece?'

'It is tied there,' explained Chaloner, using his dagger to cut through the knots. The little creature was incensed by its rough treatment, and squirmed vigorously, making his task more difficult. 'I imagine this comes courtesy of the Lord of Misrule.'

'A trick?' demanded the Earl, anger growing. 'I have been driven on top of my desk by a *trick*?'

Haddon climbed off his chair, his lips tight with fury. 'I fail to see the humour in torturing an animal. It is a despicable thing to do, and they should be ashamed of themselves. Have they hurt it?'

Chaloner shook his head. 'It is just frightened – but not nearly as much as you two were.'

The Earl glared at him. 'This situation is *not* amusing. And if you tell another living soul about this, I shall . . . I do not know what I shall do, but suffice to say I shall not be pleased.'

Chaloner held the ferret by the scruff of the neck, so it could neither bite him nor escape. Haddon took it from him, and began to soothe it by rubbing the soft fur on its head. Beady eyes regarded him crossly at first, but then it snuggled into the crook of his arm.

'It is tame,' the steward said, touched. 'It will be someone's companion. Poor thing!'

'I will take it to St James's Park and release it,' offered Chaloner. 'It will—'

'No!' cried Haddon, cradling the animal protectively. 'You will not! A dog or a fox will have it. It probably belongs to one of the kitchen boys, who will be heart-broken to find it missing.'

'Go and find him, then,' said the Earl tiredly. 'There is no need for a child to suffer, just because the Lord of Misrule – whom I suspect is that vile Chiffinch – sees fit

87

to mock his Lord Chancellor. We shall put it about that his trick was discovered *before* my periwig started racing about the floor. I do not want him to know it worked, because he might try it again with something larger.'

Haddon covered the ferret with his hat, to protect it from the cold, and went to do as he was told. Uncomfortable with the notion that someone had entered the offices illicitly, Chaloner searched them, to ensure no other pranks were waiting to unfold. The Earl watched uneasily, and only relaxed when his spy assured him that all was in order.

'I have had a terrible day,' he said mournfully, flopping into a chair and mopping his brow with a piece of lace. 'And it is not even light yet. Did you know I found Langston dead earlier?'

Chaloner raised his eyebrows. 'It is true? I hoped it was just coffee-house gossip.'

'You heard it in a coffee house?' The Earl was aghast. 'Is nothing sacred? I suppose the guards must have blathered. It gave me a terrible fright, you see, and my cries of alarm brought them running.'

'What were you doing at Westminster so early, sir?' asked Chaloner, trying to keep the reproach from his voice. 'You know it is not safe.'

'I had important business there – urgent missives for France, which were scribed overnight and required my seal before being dispatched to Dover today.'

'Could these documents not have been brought to your home?'

'I grew anxious waiting for them, and Haddon and Turner were to hand, so I told them to accompany me. Turner is good with a sword, so I felt quite safe. We were cutting through the Painted Chamber, when we discovered Langston. Dead.'

'Poisoned?'

'Turner thinks so. It was just like the first two: a corpse lying on the floor, with no sign of a cup or a jug. He has gone to find out where Greene was at the salient time, even though he was exhausted – he spent all last night at that ridiculous Babylonian ball, listening for gossip about the murders. He is a diligent fellow, working on my behalf. Where were you last night? Asleep in bed?'

Chaloner was tempted to say he had been resting after an attack intended to kill him, but managed to hold his tongue. The Earl could not be trusted to keep the tale to himself, and Chaloner did not want the train-band learning they had left a survivor just yet. He addressed another issue instead.

'I also heard you had asked Langston to be your spy. Did you?'

The Earl glowered at him. 'You spend too much time in coffee-houses, and too little on your duties. Turner would never waste *his* energies listening to gossip.'

'You just said he spent all last night doing exactly that, at the Babylonian ball,' Chaloner pointed out before he could stop himself. He rubbed his head and closed his eyes, wishing he had not spoken. Aggravating the Earl was not a wise thing to do.

'You presume too much on my patience,' said the Earl coldly. 'Either find evidence that shows Greene is the killer, or find yourself another employer. Do you understand me?'

Chaloner frowned. 'I am not sure. Are you ordering me to look *only* for evidence that proves Greene is guilty, and ignore anything that might point to another culprit?'

The Earl flung up his hands in exasperation. 'What is wrong with you today? Can you not string two words

89

together without abusing me? Of course Greene is guilty, and I cannot imagine why you refuse to believe it – the *Lady* is going around declaring his innocence, for a start. Did you know that? That is as good as screaming his culpability from the rooftops as far as I am concerned. The King's mistress does not demean herself by taking the side of insignificant clerks without good reason.'

Chaloner gazed uneasily at him. 'Lady Castlemaine has taken Greene's side? I did not know.'

'Well, you do now,' snapped the Earl.

Chaloner left the Earl with his thoughts in a whirl of confusion. He looked in Bulteel's little office, hoping to obtain some confirmation of their master's claims, but it was too early for the secretary, and his desk was empty. Why would Lady Castlemaine take Greene's side? Was it because she hated the Lord Chancellor with a passion, and tended to support anyone he disliked, as a matter of principle? Or was she involved in the murders somehow? Chaloner could not imagine why she should stoop to such dark and dangerous business, but she was an incorrigible meddler, so perhaps she could not help herself. The Lady was not someone he wanted to confront, though – at least, not until he had more information.

It was still dark when he reached the bottom of stairs and stepped outside, and there was not the slightest glimmer in the eastern sky to herald the arrival of dawn. The lights in Lady Castlemaine's rooms were being doused, indicating her soirée was at an end. Her guests spilled into the Privy Garden, laughing and shouting as they went, careless of the fact that most White Hall residents would still be sleeping. Chaloner thought he saw a face peer out of the Queen's window, then withdraw quickly. When he looked back to the garden, he saw the King weaving across it, arm around someone dressed as a concubine. The slender perfection of the near-naked limbs led him to suppose it was the Lady, but she wore a mask, and he could not be sure. He loitered until he spotted Brodrick.

'I am sure no harm will befall the Earl in the coming week,' he said, approaching soundlessly, and speaking just as his master's cousin was about to relieve himself against a statue of Prince Rupert.

'God's blood!' cried Brodrick, spinning around so fast he almost lost his balance. He scrabbled with his clothing, mortified. 'Must you sneak up behind a man when he is engaged in personal business? As Lord of Misrule, I could fine you for— *Damn* my loose tongue! I did not want anyone in my kinsman's retinue to know it is me who is elected this year.'

'I am sure you do not. But I repeat: no harm will come to the Earl.'

Brodrick looked pained. 'I shall have to make him the subject of one or two japes, because people expect it, and it is more than my life is worth to disappoint. But I will not do anything that will hurt him physically, or anything that will allow his enemies to score points against him politically. Beyond that, my hands are tied. You will just have to trust my judgement.'

Chaloner eyed him. Brodrick looked debauched when he was sober and properly dressed, but that morning he was neither. He had lost his pantaloons during the night, leaving him in his undergarments, and his turban had unravelled at the back. His eyes were bloodshot, and he reeked of strong drink.

'Your judgement,' Chaloner repeated, not bothering to hide his disdain.

Brodrick's expression turned spiteful. 'Why do you care about him, anyway? He is hiring new staff as though there is no tomorrow, and it is only a matter of time before you are displaced. He already prefers Turner to you, and I learned last night that he wants Langston to be his spy, too. But Langston refused outright – he told me so himself.'

Chaloner recalled Langston heading for the ball after visiting the charnel house with Wiseman, so supposed it was not inconceivable that he had chatted to Brodrick there. 'Why did he refuse?'

'Because spying is sordid,' replied Brodrick, taking the opportunity to fling out an insult of his own. 'Langston is honourable and, like any decent man, wants nothing to do with a profession that is so indescribably disreputable. Although, to be frank, I suspect my cousin's real aim is to populate his household with upright souls, and he did not think that offering to hire Langston as an intelligencer might be deemed offensive.'

'Langston is dead,' said Chaloner, watching him closely for a reaction.

Brodrick gaped. 'Dead? No, you are mistaken! I was talking to him not long ago. You did not swallow any of that Babylonian punch, did you? Surgeon Wiseman told me it might be dangerous, and my head tells me I should have listened to him. I have rarely felt so fragile after a drinking bout.'

'Did you notice whether anyone took an unusual or sinister interest in Langston last night?' Chaloner asked, although not with much hope of a sensible answer.

Brodrick shook his head apologetically. 'I was more concerned with my own pleasures than in observing what others were doing. I recall him regaling me with his indignation about the Earl, but that is about all.'

Chaloner tried another line of questioning. 'Does Lady Castlemaine ever employ Greene?'

'You want to know why she is going around telling everyone he is innocent, when my cousin is so adamant he is guilty.' Brodrick shrugged, grabbing Chaloner's arm when the gesture threatened to tip him over. 'I suspect she is just taking the opportunity to oppose an enemy. I doubt it is significant.'

The discussion ended abruptly when Brodrick slumped to the ground and closed his eyes. Supposing he should not leave him there to freeze, although it was tempting, Chaloner summoned the palace guards and ordered them to carry him indoors. Then, craving the company of someone who would not fall into a drunken stupor in the middle of a conversation, or accuse him of negligence, disloyalty and choosing an unsavoury career, the spy set off for Lincoln's Inn.

When he arrived, Lincoln's Inn was still mostly in darkness, although lamps gleamed in the occasional room, showing its lawyer-occupant was already hard at work. White Hall had put Chaloner in a sullen mood, and he did not feel like exchanging pleasantries with the porter at the gate, so he walked to the back of the building and scrambled over a wall. His temper was not improved when he misjudged the drop and jarred his bad leg. He hobbled to the courtyard called Dial Court, then climbed the stairs to Chamber XIII, aware of the familiar, comforting scent of wood-smoke and beeswax polish.

Thurloe was sitting at a table in the room he used as an office, poring over documents and sipping one of his infamous tonics. The spy shook his head when he was offered a draught, but accepted a slice of mince pie. It

93

had been made by the Inn's cook, and contained chopped tongue, as well as apples, dried fruit and spices. The taste transported Chaloner back to his Buckinghamshire childhood, when he had been safe and happy. He recalled singing Christmas carols with his brothers and sisters, and watching his parents hold hands in the ridiculously affectionate way they had with each other. He experienced a sharp pang of sadness for an age and a contentment that were lost to him forever.

'Well?' prompted Thurloe after several minutes, during which the spy's only words were a greeting so terse it was barely civil. 'Did you come just to stare into space and devour the best part of my pie?'

Chaloner saw the plate was indeed a good deal emptier than it had been when he had arrived. 'It is a very good pie.'

'But not as fine as my wife's. Come home with me and try some – you look in need of a rest. I plan to leave for Oxfordshire at the end of the week, and will probably be gone for several months.'

Chaloner struggled to conceal his dismay. London would be a bleak place without Thurloe. 'I see.'

The ex-Spymaster gave one of his rare smiles. 'Ann and the children like me home on Twelfth Night, to give them presents and join the festivities. Come, too – they would love to see you.'

Chaloner was sorely tempted, but shook his head. 'Greene might hang if I do not find the real culprit. And my Earl will not escape unscathed if he sends an innocent man to the gallows, either. His enemies will use it to destroy him.'

'Your devotion does you credit, but is it worth it? The Earl will not thank you for proving him wrong, especially now I hear Lady Castlemaine has joined the affray, and is championing Greene's cause. You are effectively taking her side, and he will not appreciate that.'

'No, but what sort of retainer would I be, if I let him make a fool of himself? Besides, I cannot leave now – he is hiring more spies, and if I go to Oxfordshire, he may use the opportunity to replace me permanently. Then I shall have to take a ship to the New World, and try to earn a living there, although it is a terrible place – full of frozen rivers, tangled woods and dangerous animals. I would rather go to Spain, and that . . .' He faltered, not wanting to talk about Spain.

Thurloe gazed at him. 'You are in a dark mood this morning! But do not worry – I shall help you with your investigation before I leave. Do you have any questions I might be able to answer? Or would you like me to help you interview suspects?' He misunderstood Chaloner's rising alarm and grimaced. 'I was a Spymaster General, Thomas. I do know what I am doing.'

'But I do not want you involved!' Chaloner stood abruptly. 'I should not have come. It was selfish.'

'It was nothing of the kind,' said Thurloe sharply. 'And I shall be hurt and offended if you decline to confide in me because of some misguided notion that I need to be protected. So sit down and ask me your questions, before I become annoyed with you. What do you need to know?'

'Chetwynd,' said Chaloner, relenting when he saw the determined set of Thurloe's chin. 'You said he was your friend, but my landlord told me he was corrupt.'

'There *were* claims that he was crooked. But he was a Chancery clerk – his chief duty was to dispense rulings in those cases where a plaintiff felt common law was not up to the task – and the folk he ruled against were invariably bitter. *Ergo*, accusations of misconduct were an occupational hazard.'

'So he was not corrupt?'

'I do not believe so. And you must remember that the two men who were most vocal in their allegations bore him a grudge.'

'Doling and Neale?' asked Chaloner, thinking about the names Landlord Ellis had mentioned.

'Yes. They were furious when he ruled against them. But I read those particular cases myself, and I would have come to the same conclusion: they *should* have lost.'

Chaloner frowned. 'Why did you read them?'

'Because of the rumours that Chetwynd had been less than even-handed – I was curious. Moreover, both cases were heard in the summer, when you were in Iberia, and I was bored and lonely without you to cheer me. I did it to pass the time.'

As always when Thurloe made references to the depth of their friendship, Chaloner was surprised, not sure what he had done to earn the affection. He was grateful, though, to have secured the amity of a man he respected, admired and trusted. He found himself telling Thurloe all he had learned and surmised since they had last spoken.

'And Langston is the third man to be poisoned,' said Thurloe, turning the new information over in his mind. 'Langston knew Chetwynd and Vine – he told you so when you met him last night.'

'He said he was a friend of Greene's, too.'

'More than a friend – I happen to know that he rented rooms in Greene's house. He fancied himself a playwright, and wanted a peaceful place to pen his masterpieces. He told me himself that Wapping fitted the bill perfectly.'

'But I did not see Langston when I was watching Greene's house,' said Chaloner doubtfully.

'Langston was a busy man with lots of friends at Court,' explained Thurloe. 'You not spotting him means nothing. And I imagine he spent more time there during the day, when Greene was out at work and the place was quiet.'

Suddenly, a connection snapped into place in Chaloner's mind, and he remembered what he had been struggling to recall the previous night, when the blow to his head had scrambled his wits. Greene had visited the Dolphin tavern on his way home from work on Saturday, and he had met Langston there. But what the spy had failed to recollect was a detail of their meeting – namely that Greene had given Langston a purse, a heavy one that looked as if it contained a substantial amount of money.

'So Greene paid Langston for something, and now Langston is poisoned,' mused Thurloe, when Chaloner told him. 'Of course, there are dozens of perfectly innocent explanations for what you saw. Perhaps Greene was making a charitable donation – Langston was on the board of St Catherine's Hospital, so it is not impossible. Or maybe he was repaying a debt. You say they made no attempt to hide what they were doing, so I doubt the transaction involved anything untoward.'

'Perhaps they made no attempt to hide because they did not know a spy was watching.' Chaloner was angry with himself. 'I should have questioned Langston about it last night, but I was too befuddled. Now he is dead, and the opportunity is gone. I suppose I shall have to talk to Greene instead.'

'However,' said Thurloe, ignoring the interruption, 'the incident should not be discounted, either. You think

Greene is being victimised by the Earl, but do not let sympathy cloud your judgement.'

'It is not sympathy – it is caution. There is something odd about this case, and I am unwilling to jump to conclusions before having all the facts.'

Thurloe stood. 'Then we had better find you some. I knew all three victims, albeit not intimately, but I may be able to wheedle something useful from their heirs on your behalf.' He sighed as he donned his cloak. 'Why can people not see that a military dictatorship has so much to offer? We never had all these horrible murders under Cromwell's iron fist.'

It was not far from Chancery Lane to Westminster, where Chetwynd and Vine had lived, but Thurloe insisted on taking a hackney, claiming there was so much debris on the roads from the storm that there was a danger of stepping in something nasty. Chaloner climbed in the vehicle after him wondering whether he had been so oddly fastidious when he had had weighty affairs of state to occupy his mind.

It was light at last, and bells were ringing to announce it was eight o'clock. London was wide awake now – with the notable exception of White Hall's debauchees – and the city was alive with noise and colour. Daylight showed that some of the houses along The Strand had been washed clean of soot for the Christmas season, and their reds, yellows and blues were bright in the sunshine. A group of players was performing a mime in the open area around Charing Cross, and the audience that had gathered to watch was obstructing the flow of traffic. Carters and hackneymen objected vociferously, and in one or two places, fights had broken out.

Thurloe's lips compressed into a disapproving line, and Chaloner supposed he was thinking that Cromwell's repressive regime would not have countenanced such unseemly public behaviour.

As the coach drew closer to Westminster, the spy's misgivings about involving Thurloe intensified. Talking to his friend had helped him see connections he would otherwise have missed, but the price was too high – and the previous night's attack weighed heavily on his mind. Thurloe might be full of good ideas and logical conclusions, but he was no fighter, and the spy did not like the notion of putting him in danger. It would only be a matter of time before word spread that Cromwell's chief minister was visiting the kin of murdered clerks, and the spy did not like to imagine what Thurloe's enemies would make of that – if Thurloe was less feared now than he was at the beginning of the Restoration, then he should be keeping a low profile, not jaunting around with one of his former intelligencers. It was not long before Thurloe grew tired of the litany of objections.

'How many more times do I need to remind you of who I was?' he snapped. 'You, of all people, should know I have been enmeshed in far more serious – and deadly – matters in the past. Besides, I am not visiting these folk as an investigator, but as an acquaintance concerned for their welfare. But if it makes you feel better, we can call on them separately, and pretend not to know each other.'

It was an improvement on arriving together. 'You go ahead, then. I need to stop at the Angel tavern first, to see if Doling and Neale are there.'

'They might be having breakfast, I suppose,' acknowledged Thurloe. 'But they will not be doing it together. Neale is a fey youth, in London to make his fortune;

Doling is a dour old Roundhead who hates everything about the new regime. He clerked for Cromwell's government, and resents the fact that he was ousted so a Royalist could have his job.'

'Resentful enough to kill Royalists in revenge?'

'Possibly, although I imagine he is more of a knifeman than a poisoner. I doubt Neale killed Chetwynd, though. He would never be sober enough. I shall come with you, to point them out.'

The Angel was a small, cramped place. It comprised a single chamber with benches near the hearth, and a table in the window. It was not very busy – thanks to the smelly rushes on the floor and the over-friendly pig that charged forward to greet newcomers – but it had its share of patrons. The air was dense with smoke, mostly from a badly swept chimney, but also from pipes.

'Doling is near the fire,' said Thurloe, wiping his streaming eyes. 'He is the one glaring at his ale as though he would like to strangle it. And Neale seems to have persuaded Sir Nicholas Gold's wife to join him; they are together in the window seat. What in God's name are they wearing? Is it legal?'

Chaloner regarded the young couple with interest. He had seen them in White Hall the previous evening, waiting for a coach to take them to the ball. Lady Gold still wore nothing around her middle and bells on her ankles, while Neale was the genie. Both costumes were ripped and soiled, and he wondered what they had been doing; he could only surmise that it had involved time spent on the floor.

Neale possessed a mop of golden curls that would not have looked out of place on a cherub, and his youthful face was more pretty than handsome, like an overgrown choirboy. Meanwhile, Lady Gold was a plain girl, with pale, tightly curled hair and vacant eyes that put Chaloner in mind of a sheep.

Leaving Thurloe in the shadows, Chaloner identified himself to Neale as the man investigating the clerk murders on behalf of the government. He declined to mention the Earl, on the grounds that the case was Spymaster Williamson's to explore, and his master should have had nothing to do with it.

'Call me Bess,' simpered Lady Gold, when Neale introduced her. 'Everyone else does, and "Lady Gold" makes me sound boring. Besides, you might confuse me with Nicky's previous wives and I would not like that. They were *old*, whereas I am only nineteen.'

'I see,' said Chaloner. 'Are you recently wed, then?'

'Oh, no! Nicky and I have been married for three months now, which is absolutely *ages*.'

'Where is your husband now?' Chaloner was perfectly aware that courtiers did not let a small thing like marriage interfere with their fun, but he was astonished that Gold was willing to let his wife sit half-naked with a youth who was quite so obviously intent on bedding her.

'He went home at ten o'clock last night,' replied Bess, fluttering her eyelashes coquettishly. 'That is his bedtime, and he said he was not going to change it on account of Babylon. He missed a treat, though, because the ball was lovely – except the bit when Brodrick made us all jump in a vat of mud to wrestle with each other. Lady Castlemaine did not mind, though – she was in like a shot.'

'That was because Colonel Turner was already there,' remarked Neale snidely. 'She wanted to make a grab for him under the surface, where no one could see what she was doing.'

'I would have taken the plunge for Colonel Turner,'

said Bess with an adoring sigh. 'He is *very* handsome. He gave me this.' She brandished a crucifix, which, given the current unpopularity of Catholicism, was not the wisest of objects to be toting around. 'Is it not pretty?'

Neale regarded it disparagingly before turning to Chaloner. Clearly, he both disliked and disapproved of the competition. 'You said you wanted to talk about Chetwynd. What do you want to know? About his corrupt verdict on my legal case?' His tone was petulant.

'Chetwynd was *dull*,' declared Bess. 'He used to visit my husband, and they sat in our parlour for hours, praying together. When I told Nicky I would rather go to the theatre, he sent me to my room.'

'I am not sorry Chetwynd was poisoned,' said Neale defiantly. 'Personally, I think it serves him right. You see, I was hoping to inherit my grandfather's fortune, but he decided it should go to my older brother instead. It was a stupid decree – I would have put the money to good use, whereas John will squander it all on drink and gambling.'

Chaloner was bemused by Neale's resentment, because primogeniture was law, and the moral character of an heir was irrelevant – Chetwynd would have had no choice but to find in favour of the older brother. Thurloe was right: Neale disliked Chetwynd purely because he had lost his claim, and his accusations had no basis in fact. He stood to leave, feeling he was wasting his time.

Thurloe accompanied him when he went to talk to Doling, because the two had been colleagues during the Commonwealth, and he felt his presence might work to the spy's advantage. Doling was a squat, dark-haired, powerful man with an unsmiling face. He reminded Chaloner of the tough, cynical soldiers he had served with during the wars, and nodded when the spy asked if he had seen active service.

'Naseby,' he replied. 'You are too young to remember, but it was a glorious victory.'

Chaloner remembered it all too well, as did his leg. And he should have been too young, but his regicide uncle had taken him away from his studies at Cambridge, because he said Parliament needed every able body it could get. By the time the two opposing armies had assembled at Naseby, Chaloner had been a seasoned warrior, despite being only fifteen.

'General Fairfax noticed me at Naseby,' Doling went on, eyes gleaming at the distant memories. 'And later, he got me a post in government. But I was rudely dismissed when the Cavaliers strutted back to take over the country, and for a while I was destitute.'

'And now?' asked Thurloe encouragingly. 'I recall writing a testimonial for you a few months ago.'

Doling nodded. 'For which I am grateful. It earned me a job guarding Backwell's Bank – they were robbed last summer, and decided to upgrade their security. It is not a very interesting occupation, but I am well paid and no one tells me what to do. I am happy enough.'

He turned to his ale, glaring at it in a way that made Chaloner wonder whether he was telling the truth about his contentment. Or was he just one of those men who looked angry even when he was in high spirits? Chaloner decided Backwell's Bank had made a good choice, though, because Doling's saturnine visage alone would be enough to deter most would-be thieves from trying their luck.

'My case was a complex one,' Doling replied, when Thurloe asked him about Chetwynd. 'It concerned fishing rights in the river that forms the boundary between my garden and estates owned by a man called Hargrave. But Chetwynd took a mere ten minutes to decide in Hargrave's favour.'

Thurloe frowned. 'I examined your case, too – it *was* complex, and took me the best part of a week to unravel. However, Chetwynd's decision was the right one: you should not have fishing rights.'

'I know that now. However, my grievance lies not in the fact that he ruled against me, but in the speed he took to reach his decision. And then later, I learned that he and Hargrave were friends – and that Chetwynd rented his London house from Hargrave.'

'Really?' asked Thurloe, troubled. 'That is the kind of behaviour that gives lawyers a bad name. Your case should have been adjudicated by someone who was a stranger to you both.'

'And do you know the final indignity?' Doling went on bitterly. 'A few weeks later, Hargrave gave Chetwynd a gift – a cottage on his estate with access to the river. Chetwynd visited it every Sunday, and never failed to catch a trout.'

'I knew none of this,' said Thurloe unhappily. 'And I am shocked, because Chetwynd had a reputation for being honest.'

'And that is why no one will listen to my complaints,' said Doling morosely, 'although the facts are easy enough to check. Look into the matter, Mr Thurloe. You will find I am telling the truth.'

Thurloe was keen to investigate Doling's claims for himself, but insisted on accompanying the spy to see Chetwynd's heirs first. When Chaloner had broken the news of their kinsman's death on Christmas Day, the Lea brothers had been so delighted to hear they were going to inherit sooner than they had anticipated, that they had literally danced for joy. He had given up trying to elicit sensible answers while they were pirouetting around the room, and had elected to leave the interview until they were more calm. He had managed a brief word with them while he had been shadowing Greene, but that was all, and a serious discussion was now long overdue.

'Who is investigating these poisonings for Williamson?' asked Thurloe, as their coach rattled up King Street towards St Martin's Lane. 'As Spymaster General, it is his responsibility to produce a culprit.'

'I have no idea,' replied Chaloner. 'But if he has appointed someone, then the fellow is keeping a very low profile, because I have not come across him.'

Thurloe frowned. 'How odd! Most spymasters would consider poisoned government officials a priority case, and would insist on a highly visible investigation. I know I would. But I suppose Williamson knows what he is doing.'

Chaloner was not so sure, having scant respect for the man. 'Here we are,' he said, as the carriage came to a standstill.

'The Lea brothers live here?' asked Thurloe, regarding the grand house in puzzlement. 'They were not so well paid when they worked for me – they were just minor bookkeepers then.'

'It is Chetwynd's home,' explained Chaloner. 'He had paid the rent until August, so they abandoned their own cottage in Holborn, and moved here instead. They did it the day after he died.'

Thurloe made a moue of distaste. 'I wonder why the Royalists kept them on when they dismissed virtually every other Parliamentarian. The Lea brothers were not particularly good at their work, and I doubt they were retained for their affable personalities – they are horrible fellows. All I can think is that they must have said or done something to persuade the new government to look favourably on them.'

Chaloner had an uncomfortable feeling he might be delving in some very murky waters if he tried to find out. But find out he must, because it might have a bearing on their kinsman's death.

'Give me a few moments to condole them on their loss, then come in,' ordered Thurloe, alighting from the carriage. 'We shall pretend to be strangers, to ease your worries about my involvement.'

While he waited for a suitable amount of time to pass, Chaloner studied the house. As befitting his lofty status as a Chancery clerk, Chetwynd had opted for a residence that was imposing. It had ornate brickwork, smart window shutters and a new front door. When Chaloner eventually knocked on it, a servant conducted him to a spacious parlour, where the Leas were entertaining the ex-Spymaster with spiced wine. A fire blazed in the hearth, and woodwork gleamed under a coating of new wax. Even so, there was an underlying scent of mould, and patches of damp on the walls – Chetwynd's mansion was not as well-maintained as its immaculate exterior suggested.

On their first meeting, Chaloner had been unable to determine which brother was Matthias and which was Thomas, because they wore identical clothes and had a disconcerting habit of finishing each other's sentences. They were both tall, lean and leered in a way that made them look predatory. He had not taken to them at all.

'It is the Lord Chancellor's creature,' said one, as Chaloner was shown in. He turned to Thurloe. 'He came on Saturday, demanding to know who might want to kill Chetwynd. We told him to—'

'—question someone else,' finished the other. 'We loved Chetwynd dearly, but this man acted as though *we* had killed him. We find that deeply offensive. He can close the door on his way out.'

Chaloner sat down. 'Why did you run away from me last night? What were you afraid I might ask?'

'We did not run,' objected the first indignantly. 'We drove off in a carriage. We had been invited to the Babylonian ball, and did not want you to delay us with—'

'—impertinent questions. It is the first such invitation we have ever received – our new wealth is already working its magic – and we did not want to offend anyone by arriving late.'

It was an oddly plausible explanation, and Chaloner was inclined to believe it.

'Are you the sole beneficiaries of your kinsman's will?' asked Thurloe. Both brothers nodded gleefully. 'How marvellous for you.'

One tried to look mournful. 'His death was a terrible blow to us both, of course.'

'But inheriting all his money will help to soften the loss,' added the other. He sniggered suddenly. 'We intend to sell the cottage Hargrave gave him. Perhaps Doling will buy it from us.'

'How did you keep your government posts after the Restoration, when everyone else lost theirs?' Chaloner's dislike for the Lea brothers was intensifying, and the blunt question was intended to unsettle them, hopefully enough to provide him with some truthful answers.

The first Lea glared at him. 'Because we are good at

107

what we do. Not everyone can count money and never make a mistake, but we can. We are indispensable.'

'No one is indispensable, Matthias,' said Thurloe quietly. 'And these are dangerous times.'

His sombre words caused a flash of unease to pass between the pair, but it was quickly suppressed. 'You know nothing of Royalist politics,' said Matthias contemptuously. 'Times have changed since—'

'—you wielded power. You are compelled to live quietly now, but our fortunes are on the rise at last. Chetwynd's death is just one more step up the ladder of success.'

'Did you know Vine and Langston?' asked Chaloner. The brothers were exchanging grins of pure pleasure, and he was keen to keep them talking lest they started dancing again.

'Yes, of course,' replied Matthias. 'We all work for the government, so we were colleagues. We used to meet socially, too – or rather religiously: we prayed together.' He raised his eyes heavenwards, and his brother sniggered at his display of false piety.

'What about Greene?' asked Chaloner. 'Did you pray with him, too?'

'There is a rumour that Greene killed Chetwynd,' said Matthias to his kinsman. 'So this question is designed to discover whether we hired him. But the Lord Chancellor's creature is wasting his time, because there is nothing that can connect us to our kinsman's murder.'

His brother's expression was cold and hard. 'Yes, but he will almost certainly learn that Greene *was* one of those with whom we once fraternised, and may draw his own – erroneous – conclusions. Personally, I never liked Greene. He is too gloomy, always saying that everything is preordained, and that nothing we say or do can change the outcome. Well, he is—'

'—wrong. We took control of our destinies – decided to make our way with the Royalists – and look at us now. We have everything we ever wanted.'

'Chetwynd does not,' said Thurloe softly. Chaloner saw he was repelled by their self-congratulatory gloating. 'Can you think of a reason why anyone would want to kill him? He was a decent soul, and it is hard to imagine him acquiring enemies.'

Matthias looked smug. 'Between you and us, Mr Thurloe, he was not as scrupulous as you might think. You must have heard the rumours that say he took bribes in exchange for favourable decisions? Well, they are all true—'

'—although we are not in a position to give any of them back,' added his brother hastily. 'But a more corrupt man never walked the streets of London, although he was careful to present an honest face to the world. And if you do not believe us, then look at the verdicts he gave on the cases he was asked to resolve. It will not take you long to see that he was a villain.'

Thurloe looked stricken, and Chaloner changed the subject, to spare him more of the Lea brothers' revelations. They were only confirming what Doling and Landlord Ellis had said, but Thurloe did not need to hear *them* vilify a man who had been a friend. 'Did he own a ruby ring? Or do either of you?'

Both brothers leaned forward acquisitively. 'He might—'

'He *did*,' corrected Matthias. 'I remember it quite clearly. I imagine it has been found, and the authorities are keen to return it to its rightful owners. You can tell them we will be happy to accept it.'

Chaloner was sure they would. 'What did it look like?' he asked.

'Silver,' said Matthias, watching the spy for a reaction that might help with the description. He was out of luck, because Chaloner was used to concealing his thoughts, and his expression was unreadable. 'Or maybe gold. I am not very good at identifying precious metals. And it had a large ruby.'

'But not overly large,' said his brother. 'Respectable. Show it to us, and we will identify it.'

Chaloner took his leave, even more revolted by them than he had been the first time he had visited. They could not describe the ring, so did that mean they were innocent of murder? Or were they more clever than they seemed?

'So, it is true,' said Thurloe sadly, following him out of the house. 'Chetwynd was not the paragon of virtue he led us all to believe. This is a bitter blow – enough to shake a man's faith in humanity.'

But Chaloner's faith had been shaken – well and truly shattered, in fact – a long time before.

Thurloe wanted to accompany Chaloner to see the Vine family, but the spy refused to let him. George was a courtier, and would almost certainly gossip about the fact that he had received a call from the Commonwealth's old spymaster, and the spy did not want *that* reaching Williamson's ears. He was relieved when Thurloe agreed, albeit reluctantly, to wait in the carriage.

'Do not ask about the ring,' warned Thurloe, catching his sleeve as he started to climb out. 'If it does belong to the poisoner, you are effectively telling him that you have a clue regarding his identity. And those soldiers wanted you dead, so you would not be a witness to them *or* what they were sent to retrieve. So you should not advertise the fact that they failed, because they may try again.'

'But the ring is my only clue. If I do not ask, how will I find out who owned it?'

Thurloe looked unhappy. 'I do not like this enquiry, Thomas. I wish you would abandon it and come to Oxfordshire with me. I will find something for you to do – clerking, perhaps.'

But Thurloe's estates were already full of displaced friends and kin who had lost all at the Restoration, and there was no room for yet another penniless petitioner. Chaloner promised to be careful, and walked to Vine's house.

George had only just returned from his night out, and was having a bedtime snack in the parlour – his 'meal' appeared to be a glass of wine with a raw egg beaten into it. His mother was with him, and Chaloner was astonished to see her wearing an outfit that would not have looked out of place on a Southwark harlot. When she said Brodrick had asked her to attend the ball as a Babylonian concubine, he thought it explained why she was dressed in such a bizarre fashion, but not why she should have accepted the invitation in the first place.

'Why should I not go?' she demanded, reading his thoughts. 'Old Dreary Bones never let me do anything fun, and I am owed something for twenty-five years of boredom. Do you think I should don black and sit behind closed curtains, instead? That would make me a hypocrite!'

'God forbid,' said Chaloner, thinking it was not surprising Vine had kept her indoors, if her idea of entertainment was to go into high society dressed like a whore. He changed the subject when he saw her lips press together in anger – he did not want to waste time debating with her. 'I have been told that your husband owned a ruby ring, and—'

'He owned no rings of any description,' interrupted Mrs Vine firmly. 'He said they got in the way of his writing, and preferred other forms of jewellery, like lockets and brooches.'

'Then how about you?' asked Chaloner, noting her fingers were well adorned in that respect.

'No,' she said sullenly, putting her hands out of sight under the table. 'And neither does George.'

Chaloner knew she was holding out on him, because she had not asked why he wanted to know, as most people would have done. He could not decide whether she, Vine or George *had* owned a ruby ring, and she was denying it because she knew it was connected to her husband's murder, or whether she was just unwilling to commit herself until she understood the implications of his questions. He glanced at George, wondering whether she suspected him of the crime, and was trying to protect him. And was he guilty? Chaloner had no idea. However, one thing he did know was that his enquiries about the ring were going no further, so he changed the subject.

'How well did your husband know Langston and Greene?'

'Quite well,' replied George. He spoke cagily, as if he was afraid that even the most innocent reply might see him in trouble. 'He did not invite them here to dine, but then he never brought friends home. It was almost as if he was ashamed of us.'

'I wonder why,' muttered Chaloner.

'You had better be frank with him, George,' said Mrs Vine, leaning back in her chair. 'Someone is sure to gossip about us, and I want him to hear our side of the story. Tell him what a drab bird we have lived with all these years.'

George shrugged, but his expression was uneasy. 'My father was a vile man. He carped incessantly against wickedness and sin, but he made our lives a misery – which is a sin, is it not? To make another person unhappy? And he was furious when my mother took a lover.'

'Well, why should I not have one?' demanded Mrs Vine, seeing Chaloner's startled look. 'He never came to my bed after George was born. And George is twenty-four!'

'His piety was disgusting,' George went on, angry now. 'He gave money to the poor, but refused to buy me new clothes. What kind of father deprives his son of decent clothes? He was a hypocrite, with his stupid principles and out-dated morality, and I am surprised he lasted three years at Court.'

'We thought one of those gay libertines would have dispensed with him long before now,' agreed Mrs Vine. She grinned suddenly. 'The Lord of Misrule has some wonderful japes planned for the Christmas season, and this year I shall be able to enjoy them all. Did you know it was Brodrick?'

George gaped at her, grievances against his stern father forgotten. 'Really? Everyone else is saying it is Chiffinch.'

'Then everyone else is wrong,' gloated Mrs Vine. 'He is trying to keep it secret, but he talks in his sleep, and Lady Muskerry overheard. She knows about some of his plans, too. One is to decorate the Lord Chancellor's offices in the style of a Turkish brothel – complete with concu-bines. Another is to send love-letters in Bess Gold's writing to the Bishop of London.'

George giggled. 'Gold will be furious.'

'But unable to do anything about it,' said Mrs Vine maliciously. 'Feeble old fool!'

'He did not look feeble when he threatened to run me through last week,' said George, turning sullen again. 'It was Bess's fault – she should not have squealed so when we frolicked in her parlour. Do you think Neale has managed to bed her yet? I shall be vexed if *he* wins her affections, because I am a far better proposition – not that I need Gold's fortune now old Dreary Bones is—'

'Greene,' interrupted Mrs Vine abruptly. Chaloner was under the impression that she was afraid her son might say something he would later regret, and was blurting the first thing that came into her head. 'There is a rumour that he killed my husband – and Chetwynd, too. It is almost certainly true.'

'Is it?' asked Chaloner. 'Why?'

Mrs Vine grinned slyly. 'For two reasons. First, because the three of them were in the habit of meeting mutual friends every week at John's Coffee House in Covent Garden – perhaps they had some kind of falling out there. And second, because I understand Langston has also been poisoned.'

Chaloner frowned. 'I am not sure I follow—'

'Then think about it. Where did Langston live? With Greene in Wapping. Obviously, Greene killed Chetwynd and my husband, then Langston discovered something incriminating. So Greene was obliged to murder him, too.'

114

Chapter 4

'We had better travel to Wapping and interview Greene immediately,' said Thurloe, when Chaloner returned to the carriage and told him what he had learned. 'The Earl will certainly be suspicious when he finds out that Greene's tenant is the poisoner's latest victim, and might order his arrest. So, if Greene has an alibi, you should check it as soon as possible, to prevent your master from making a fool of himself.'

'He tried to hire Langston as a spy,' said Chaloner, banging on the roof of the hackney with his fist to tell the driver to go. 'Although it seems his offer was rejected in no uncertain terms. Why would he recruit the house-mate of the man he is so intent on destroying?'

Thurloe shrugged. 'I imagine he was unaware of the connection. He does tend to be ignorant about such matters – unless someone like you chooses to enlighten him. Unfortunately for him, you are not very good value as a scandal-monger. You listen and analyse, but you fail to pass on.'

'Did your mother never teach you that gossiping is wrong?'

'You had no problem passing me information when I sent you to spy overseas, so why do you baulk at keeping your Earl abreast of happenings in the place where he lives and works? If you obliged him with Court chatter from time to time, he might be more inclined to continue employing you. After all, no one wants an intelligencer who keeps all the interesting tittle-tattle to himself.'

If keeping his post at White Hall meant turning into a rumour-monger, then Chaloner supposed he had better start planning his voyage to the New World, because there were some depths to which he would not sink. He said nothing, and stared out of the window, watching the familiar landmarks whip past – the Royal Mews and the New Exchange, the latter of which had a large and angry crowd outside it. He wondered what was happening there, but there was no time to stop and indulge his curiosity.

It was a long way to Wapping, so Thurloe used the time to effect a disguise, in an effort to alleviate Chaloner's concerns about him meddling in government business. From supplies he kept in his pockets, he donned a cap and wig that hid his hair, slathered his face in a paste that made him look sickly, and attached a remarkably authentic false beard. Chaloner was impressed at the speed with which he changed his appearance, and although it would not fool someone who knew him well, no casual observer would recognise him.

Wapping was separated from the city by the grounds of St Catherine's Hospital – Langston's favourite charitable concern – and had the scent of the sea about it. Greene's house was on the edge of the village, looking across farmland to the north and the river to the south. The spy was about to knock on the door when it was opened and the clerk himself stepped out, apparently ready to go to work. He sighed when he saw Chaloner and his 'servant', and wearily gestured that they were to enter.

Greene did not look like a killer. He was stooped, thin and always seemed ready to burst into tears, although, in his defence, Chaloner had only ever met him when he had had good cause to be distressed. His plain, Puritan clothes were of decent quality, because his government post was a well-paid one, and he wore a wig that would not have been cheap. After watching him for the best part of two days and nights, Chaloner suspected there was little about him that would raise any eyebrows. Greene was a dull, uninteresting man, who lived a predictable, unexciting life, and the spy could not imagine why the Earl had taken against him so violently.

The clerk's front parlour was large, but cold without a fire, and there was not much furniture in it, so their voices echoed when they spoke. There was a table in the window, which was covered in papers; an open ink-bottle suggested that someone had recently been working there.

'Langston,' said Greene, as Chaloner picked up one of the sheets. It was a page from a play. 'He liked to see the river when he was writing. Are you here because he is dead? I heard the news at dawn this morning. However, I assure you I had nothing to do with it.'

'Where were you last night?' asked Chaloner.

Greene blinked back tears. 'So, the Earl *does* think I am responsible. But I am not! I went to the Dolphin for some ale and a pie after I finished work, and then I came home. I went to church at four o'clock this morning, and was praying there when Swaddell arrived to tell me what had happened.'

'Who is Swaddell?'

117

'A fellow clerk. It was good of him to come, because Wapping is hardly on his way. However, this time I *can* prove my innocence, beyond the shadow of a doubt.'

'You can?' Chaloner hoped so, for his sake.

'Swaddell told me Langston was still alive at four o'clock this morning – he was seen by Lady Castlemaine – but I was with my vicar at that time. Go and talk to him, if you do not believe me.'

Chaloner nodded to Thurloe, who immediately left to do so. 'Why were you with a priest at such an odd hour?' he asked, when the ex-Spymaster had gone.

'I always pray before work – I am a religious man. Four o'clock is not an odd hour for me.'

Chaloner knew that was true, because he had watched him at his devotions. 'You did not mention Langston sharing your house when I questioned you before.'

'It did not occur to me to do so. Why would it, when neither of us could have predicted that he would become this fiend's next victim?' Tears began to fall, great salty drops that rolled unheeded down his face. 'Why is this happening? What have I done to incur the Earl's hatred?'

'I wish I knew. Tell me again what happened when you found Chetwynd.'

Greene closed his eyes in despair, but he did as he was told. 'I was working late, and went to the Painted Chamber to borrow ink. When I arrived, Chetwynd was dead on the floor. I was frightened – it was dark and that gale was raging. I ran away, but you caught me at the door. I should not have panicked, but it is easy to be wise with hindsight.'

'You met Langston in the Dolphin on Saturday, and you gave him money. Why?'

Greene's eyes snapped open to gaze at the spy in

astonishment. 'Have you been spying on me?' He sighed miserably. 'But of course you have – the Earl would have demanded it. The answer to your question is that I lent Langston ten pounds. He did not say why he wanted it, and I did not ask. We were friends, and friends do not quiz each other.'

'Ten pounds?' It was a good deal of money, and men had been killed for far less.

'It was not unusual – he often borrowed from me, but he always paid me back. But surely, this is a reason for me *not* harming him? Now he is dead, I am ten pounds poorer.'

Chaloner looked hard at Greene, trying to understand what it was that had turned the Earl against him so zealously, but could see nothing, as he had seen nothing the other times he had done it. 'Is there anything else I should know?' he asked eventually. 'I cannot help you unless you are honest with me.'

'I cannot think of anything,' replied Greene wearily. 'But I *am* innocent. As you pointed out when Chetwynd died, there was no poisoned cup in the Painted Chamber or on my person. That should have been enough to exonerate me straight away. Meanwhile, I have an alibi for Langston's death – and perhaps I have one for Vine's murder, too, if you have been watching me. But I shall put my trust in God. If He wants me to hang, then I shall face my death with courage and fortitude.'

'Right.' Chaloner had forgotten Greene's peculiar belief that everything happened according to some great and immutable divine plan. 'Did you know Chetwynd took bribes?'

Greene gaped at him. 'He did not! He was a good man, and if you think to help me by tarnishing his reputation, then I would rather hang. I have my principles.'

He would find out the truth soon enough, thought Chaloner. 'Mrs Vine told me you met her husband regularly at a coffee house in Covent Garden. Is it true?'

Greene nodded. 'Yes, I mentioned it when you first interrogated me. A group of like-minded men often gather to discuss religion and scripture. Besides Chetwynd, Vine, Langston and me, there are Nicholas Gold, Hargrave and Tryan the merchants, Edward Jones, Neale and a number of others.'

Chaloner had met Neale, and he knew Gold was the elderly husband of Bess. Meanwhile, Jones was a Yeoman of the Household Kitchen – he was the enormously fat fellow who ate so much that the Earl had ordered him to tighten his belt. But Chaloner had never heard of Hargrave or Tryan. Or had he? He frowned when he recalled the dour Doling mentioning someone called Hargrave – he had given Chetwynd a cottage after the lawyer had taken ten minutes to decide a complex legal case. He frowned at the connections that were forming, unable to make sense of them.

'What was Langston like?' he asked, changing the subject when answers continued to elude him.

Greene shrugged. 'Kind, generous, but a little secretive. Yet who does not have things he would never tell another? Do not tell me *you* share everything with friends!'

Chaloner ignored the challenge in the clerk's voice. 'Do you own a ruby ring?'

Greene blinked at the question, then held up his hands, to show they were bereft of baubles. 'Jewellery is for courtesans and Court fops, not Puritan clerks.'

'What about Langston?'

'If he did, then I never saw it. Search his rooms if you like.'

It was too good an invitation to decline, regardless of the fact that the soldiers had taken the ring and it was not going to be in Wapping. While Greene watched listlessly, Chaloner went carefully through all Langston's belongings. Unfortunately, his efforts were wasted, because he found nothing of interest, except a letter from Backwell's Bank. It said robbers had been in their vault, but they fully intended to honour the three hundred pounds he had deposited with them – just not for a few months. It was dated in the summer of the previous year.

'I know,' said Greene, when Chaloner showed it to him. 'A lot of people were inconvenienced by that crime, and the bank was so shaken that it hired a man to overhaul its security – Doling.'

There was no more to be learned, so Chaloner took his leave. Thurloe was still talking to the priest, who insisted on repeating to Chaloner what he had told the ex-Spymaster – that Greene had come to the chapel at roughly four o'clock that morning. Greene had prayed for help with his predicament, while the vicar had prayed for the roof, which he had been certain was going to blow away.

'Greene is a melancholy fellow,' said Thurloe, as they left Wapping. 'I believe God looks after His own, too, but that does not mean we should sit back and do nothing to help ourselves. His belief in predestination will see him hang, unless he pulls himself together and stops feeling sorry for himself.'

'If I asked *you* for money, as Langston did Greene, would you hand it over?' asked Chaloner. 'Or would you want to know what it was for?'

'Both. But Greene's gloomy nature means he does not have many friends. Perhaps he did not want to lose one by asking awkward questions. You may never know why Langston needed ten pounds.'

It was late afternoon by the time Chaloner left Thurloe at Lincoln's Inn and headed towards White Hall. It was warmer than it had been earlier, and a greyish-yellow sun gleamed in the smoke above the city. As he walked past the New Exchange on The Strand, he could not help but notice how shabby it looked that day. Its gothic façade was dark with soot, and the Christmas garlands that had been hung along its eaves were torn and limp.

Outside it, Chaloner was surprised to see that the fracas he had observed earlier was still in full swing. It had attracted a mass of spectators, some of whom had simply ordered their carriages to stop in the middle of the road so they could watch, causing a serious impediment to traffic. He listened to the yells of the protagonists as he threaded his way through the mêlée, aiming to be past it as soon as possible and about his own business.

'The King ordered it closed – and I have been charged to ensure it remains that way,' one man was shouting. Chaloner smiled wryly when he recognised the voice of Edward Jones, thinking it odd that he should encounter the Yeoman of the Household Kitchen so soon after he had been mentioned by Greene as someone who met him and the three murdered men in Convent Garden.

Jones was a contender for the title of Fattest Man in London – he verged on the grotesque, and there was a rumour that Surgeon Wiseman had arranged for him to be measured, only to discover that he weighed precisely three times as much as the King.

'But half the city does business here,' objected an elderly merchant. He had impressively bandy legs, and his handsome clothes said he was very rich. 'His Majesty *cannot* close the New Exchange!'

'He can do what he likes, Alderman Tryan,' replied Jones soberly. 'He is the King.'

'But he no longer wields that sort of power,' argued Tryan. 'And rightly so, if he is the kind of man to shut down important places of commerce on a whim. We went to war for this, and if he has not learned his place, then we shall have to fight him all over again. Is that not so, Hargrave?'

Hargrave, thought Chaloner, stopping dead in his tracks to look at the man who had given Chetwynd a cottage in exchange for a speedy verdict on his dispute with Doling – and who had rented Chetwynd his house. Hargrave and Tryan, like Jones, were also among those Greene had met at the Covent Garden coffee house. The spy decided to loiter instead of returning immediately to White Hall, to watch the three men and see what he might learn.

'He and his Court are all rakes,' declared Hargrave. He was not an attractive specimen. Savage red marks on his shaven pate suggested he had recently enjoined a major battle with fleas or ringworm, and wigs were not recommended until the skin had had time to heal; it was not only the poor who had trouble with parasites. 'They do nothing but drink, frolic with whores and play cards. Why should we be taxed to support them?'

There was a rumble of agreement from his fellow merchants, and Chaloner was appalled to see how far from favour the King had fallen. It was only three years since he had been welcomed into the capital with cheering crowds and showers of roses. Now his people deplored the way he lived, and resented the cost of maintaining him and his Court.

'The bishops get all,' chanted Tryan, beginning a popular ditty that could be heard in London's streets with increasing frequency. It was not just merchants who sang it, but apprentices, children and even clerics, too. 'The courtiers spend all, the citizens pay for all, the King neglects all, and the Devil takes all.'

Jones blew out his chubby cheeks in a sigh. 'I understand your frustration, Alderman Tryan, but one of His Majesty's coachmen lost an eye in the fight here this morning, and traders from the New Exchange cheered for his opponent. Now the King believes it is full of traitors.'

'Traitors?' demanded Tryan angrily. 'We love our country, but what does he do for it? Or does sleeping until noon, and waking only to cavort with his mistress count as patriotic service?'

'*We* are not debauchees, who care only for our own comforts,' added Hargrave. 'We are hard-working men, and it is on our labour that this fine country is built. So open the damned Exchange!'

'I cannot,' said Jones, clearly uncomfortable with the position he had been forced to take. 'His Majesty wants it to remain closed until further notice, and I am duty-bound to obey. Soldiers from White Hall will be here soon, and it would be better for everyone if you all just went home.'

There was a menacing growl from the people. Free Londoners had never appreciated being ordered about by the military, and Chaloner could see the apprentices readying themselves for battle.

124

'You can try to keep it shut,' challenged Hargrave, aware that he had the crowd's support. 'But we will have it open – no matter whose blood is spilled.'

While Hargrave and Tryan basked in their colleagues' approbation for their brave stance, Chaloner approached Jones, who was wringing his fat hands in dismay.

'I hate to be the bearer of bad news,' he said in a low voice, 'but the road is blocked by carriages, and the guards will be unable to get through. So do not expect reinforcements any time soon.'

'Chaloner,' breathed Jones, recognising him. 'Thank God for a friendly face! You must be right about the soldiers, because they should have been here ages ago. I was a fool to have tackled these rebels alone.'

'They are not rebels,' said Chaloner, not liking to think what might happen if that description of the crowd reached the nervous ears at White Hall. 'Just angry citizens.'

But Jones was not interested in splitting hairs. 'What am I to do? I cannot disobey a direct order from the King, but I do not love him so much that I am willing to be torn limb from limb. And if you ever repeat that, I shall deny saying it.'

'Then turn the situation to His Majesty's advantage,' suggested Chaloner, thinking the solution should have been obvious. 'Tell these merchants that you have just received word from the King, who has decided to reopen the Exchange as a mark of affection for his loyal subjects.'

Jones gazed at him. 'But that would be untrue! He hates these upstarts.'

Chaloner was surprised Jones had managed to secure a Court post, if he baulked at telling lies. 'The alternative is to keep the place closed and increase the King's unpopularity – and risk losing your life. There must be upwards of five hundred people here, with more flocking to join them by the moment.'

Jones hesitated until someone threw a clod of mud that narrowly missed his tent-sized coat. 'I have just received word from the King,' he shouted, raising a plump hand to gain attention. 'He orders that the Exchange be opened for business immediately. And he sends warm greetings to all his people, whom he loves like his own children.'

'Steady!' murmured Chaloner in alarm. Londoners were not stupid.

'He does not have any children,' said Hargrave, bemused. 'The Queen is barren.'

'She is not,' declared Chaloner, stepping forward before he could stop himself. He liked the Queen, and objected to anyone abusing her. His quiet words, the expression on his face, and the confident stance of a man who knew how to handle himself made Hargrave scuttle back in alarm.

'Actually, the King has plenty of children,' countered Jones. 'The only problem being that none of them are legitimate. But time is passing, and I have much to do. Good afternoon, gentlemen. God save the King, and so forth.'

'God save the King,' echoed Tryan mechanically. A few others joined in, but not many and none were very enthusiastic.

'God might prefer saving the Devil to that scoundrel on the throne,' muttered Hargrave. He cleared his throat and raised his voice. 'And now let us to business. Too much time has been wasted today.'

'Thank God that is over,' breathed Jones, watching the

mob disperse. Many went reluctantly, giving the impression that they would rather have had a skirmish; it underlined what a volatile place the city could be. 'But what shall I tell the King? He will ask why the Exchange is open.'

'Say his people appreciated his magnanimity in permitting the resumption of trade,' suggested Chaloner. 'And that money made today can be taxed tomorrow. That should mollify him.'

Jones invited Chaloner to ride with him to White Hall. The carriage listed heavily to one side, leaving Chaloner gripping the window in order to prevent himself from sliding into the large courtier's lap.

'I understand you have competition in the form of one Colonel Turner,' said Jones conversationally as they jolted along. 'The Earl has appointed him as his new spy, and he is doing rather well with his investigation into these murders.'

'Is he?' asked Chaloner uneasily.

'He told me he is coming close to a solution. Little Bulteel follows him around in the hope of finding out what he has learned, because he is determined that you should win the contest. You should let Bulteel befriend you, Chaloner, because his wife makes excellent cakes.'

'Always a good reason for developing relationships,' said Chaloner facetiously, before realising that for an obese man like Jones, it probably was.

'Do not develop one with Turner, though,' advised Jones, leaning towards him confidentially. 'He is a liar – he told me he has twenty-eight legitimate children, and that he intends to increase his brood the moment he finds himself another wife. And would you believe that women are eager to be considered for the honour – even those who are already married?'

'I heard he attracted the attentions of Lady Castlemaine last night. In a mud bath.'

Jones shuddered as he nodded. 'It was rather horrible, if you want the truth. He will cavort with anyone. That poor young Meg from the laundry is under the impression that he is going to wed *her*, but of course he will do no such thing. Perhaps that is why she has not been seen since Saturday – she has learned his intentions are less than honourable towards her.'

Chaloner frowned, recalling that Turner had been due to meet Meg for a midnight tryst, but the colonel had been unable to fulfil his obligations, on account of him finding Vine's body. 'She is missing?'

'Yes. It is a pity, because she is a pretty little piece.'

Chaloner's frown deepened. Had the laundress arrived early for the assignation, and seen the killer at work? And had she then fled, to ensure she was not his next victim? Or had she screamed or announced her presence in some other way, and so was lying dead somewhere? The Painted Chamber was not far from the river, which was an excellent repository for corpses. He supposed he would have to ask the charnel-house keeper whether any bodies had been washed ashore. Of course, all this assumed Turner was telling the truth. What if *he* was the killer, and he had been obliged to 'find' Vine because Meg had caught him in the act of dispatching his victim? Either way, Chaloner did not hold much hope that the laundress was still alive.

When they reached White Hall, they paid the driver and were just walking through the gates, when two people hurtled towards them, intent on a game that involved a

128

ball and two curved sticks. One stick caught Jones a painful blow on the shin, causing him to howl and jump about in agony. Lady Castlemaine put her hand over her mouth when she saw what she had done, but her remorse did not last long: she took one look at the fat man's undulating jig, and immediately burst into laughter. Her partner in crime, the Duke of Buckingham, ignored Jones altogether as he took aim and hit the ball as hard as he could, sending it whizzing towards a fountain. Whooping and shrieking, he and the Lady hared after it. They appeared a little too intimate together, indicating their relationship was probably sexual, as well as one of co-conspirators against the Lord Chancellor.

Chaloner watched them disapprovingly. The Lady reminded him of a cat – smug, sensual and vain, with claws ever at the ready. She was still young, but lines of spite and bad-temper were beginning to etch their way around her mouth and eyes, and the spy had never understood why so many men found her irresistible. Meanwhile, Buckingham was a tall, athletic fellow in his mid-thirties, who should have known better than to play rough games in a place where people might be hurt. Chaloner turned to Jones, offering an arm for balance as the fat man bent to inspect the damage to his leg.

'I have been looking for you, Jones,' came a voice from behind them. 'I have a message: the King wants you to re-open the Exchange as soon as possible. Apparently, keeping it shut entails too much paperwork.'

The speaker was a clerk, and Jones straightened up to stare at him. 'What?'

'He realised it was more trouble than it was worth shortly after he dispatched you to The Strand. He apologises for not sending word sooner, but says he has been engrossed in a game of blind man's buff, and forgot about you. Indeed, it was only by chance that he happened to mention the matter to Williamson, who then ordered me to look for you and tell you of the decision.'

'I see,' said Jones. He looked deflated, hurt by the revelation that the unpleasant episode outside the New Exchange had all been for nothing.

'You work for Williamson?' asked Chaloner of the clerk. He had not seen the man before, and was curious about his relationship to the Spymaster. The fellow was clad in black from head to toe, with the exception of his spotlessly white neck-band. The effect might have been smart on another person, but on the clerk it was sinister, although Chaloner could not have said why. Perhaps it was something to do with the dark, close-set eyes, which never seemed to settle on anything.

Jones remembered his manners. 'This is John Swaddell, Williamson's new secretary, whom he says is indispensable.' He gestured to Chaloner. 'And this is—'

'I know,' interrupted Swaddell. 'The Lord Chancellor's intelligencer, and the current beau of Hannah Cotton. My master has mentioned him on several occasions.'

Chaloner was uncomfortable with the notion that he – and his friendship with Hannah – had been the subject of discussions involving Williamson. 'What did he say?'

Swaddell shrugged. 'Only that he dislikes you, and that I am to ensure you do not harm him.'

'Harm him?' echoed Chaloner in disbelief. 'He is Spymaster General, with an army of highly trained men at his command. I would not dare go anywhere near him!'

This was not entirely true, because Court security was so lax that Chaloner knew he could 'harm' anyone he pleased. However, he did not want Williamson thinking him dangerous, and was keen for Swaddell to report there was nothing to worry about. Enemies of Williamson were apt to disappear, and Chaloner did not want to be stabbed in a dark alley just because the Spymaster was uneasy.

Swaddell was about to add more, but was distracted by a sudden screech of rage. It came from the Lady, who was given to abrupt displays of temper. This time her ire was focussed on a couple who had just alighted from a splendid carriage. It was Bess Gold and her elderly husband. A number of male courtiers were beginning to converge, eager to offer Bess an arm across the cobbles – a young woman with an ageing and very rich husband was an attractive target for the fortune-hunters who haunted White Hall. However, the moment they realised she was engaged in an altercation with Lady Castlemaine, they melted away like frost in the sun.

'I said I *like* it,' the Lady was yelling, eyes flashing as she fixed Bess with a glare that held poison. 'That means I *want* it, and you should give it to me. Do I have to spell it out, you stupid child?'

Buckingham was trying to calm her, although his impatient manner was doing little to ease the situation. 'It is just a bauble,' he snapped irritably. 'I will buy you another. But you cannot have this one, because its owner is unwilling to part with it.'

'You are right, kind sir,' simpered Bess, batting her eyelashes at him. 'I am.'

Chaloner watched with interest as the scene unfolded. Gold was cocking his head in a way that suggested he could not hear a word that was being said, while Buckingham was itching to get back to his game. Bess beamed at the Duke, and seemed wholly unaware that she was playing with fire by refusing a 'request' by the Lady – and by flirting with her handsome playmate.

'I am a Catholic,' the Lady announced in a ringing voice. 'A secret one, it is true, but I am a faithful daughter of the Church, and I do not yet have a crucifix. Yours has rubies in it, which would look nice with the gown I intend to wear to confession. I want it, and you will give it to me.'

'Eh?' said Gold. 'Speak up.'

'It is not a crucifix,' objected Bess. The object in question hung around her neck, and she fingered it possessively. 'It is a cross with a figure of Jesus on it. And it was a special gift from Colonel Turner, so you cannot have it.'

'You should not wear rubies to confession, anyway,' said Buckingham, grabbing the Lady's arm and attempting to haul her away. She flashed her teeth at him, apparently threatening to bite, and he released her hastily. 'The priest would demand them for the poor, and, as a "faithful daughter of the Church", you will be obliged to hand them over for the Pope's coffers.'

'Bess is not my daughter,' declared Gold loudly. 'She is my wife. And I would rather you did not mention coffins in my presence, not when I am fast approaching the day when I shall be in one.'

'I shall buy you a nice casket when the time comes,' offered Bess brightly. 'Although it should not be too expensive, given that you will only be using it the once.'

All four turned when one of the hovering courtiers, braver than his fellows, strode towards them. It was the cherub-faced Neale. 'What seems to be the trouble, Bess?' he asked. 'May I help?'

'You may not,' snapped Lady Castlemaine, giving him

a shove that was hard enough to make him stagger. 'Go away and mind your own business, boy. You are not wanted here.'

'You may not want him, but I do,' said Bess, with something of a leer. Fortunately for Neale, Gold's ancient legs were tiring, and his attention was fixed on holding himself upright by hanging on to Buckingham, so he did not see her expression. The Duke grimaced and tried to extricate himself, but Gold's gnarled fingers were stronger than they looked.

'I shall accompany you home, Bess,' declared Neale gallantly. 'Away from this place.'

'It is a disgrace,' agreed Gold loudly, shifting so the hapless Duke bore almost his entire weight. 'Uneven cobbles should be banned by royal decree – a man could break his neck in this yard.'

Lady Castlemaine ignored him and put her hands on her hips. 'Excuse me,' she snarled at Neale. 'But I just told you to mind your own business. You had better oblige or Buckingham will run you through. He can do it, you know. He has a rapier.'

'Not with me, though,' said Buckingham with a grimace, struggling to stay upright under Gold's dead weight. 'So it will have to be later. Tomorrow at dawn, in Lincoln's Inn Fields? That is where such matters are usually settled.'

'That is very kind, Buckingham,' bellowed Gold. 'I would be honoured to be your guest at Field's tomorrow. I understand it is one of the more exclusive coffee houses, patronised by members of Court and parliament. Dawn is too early, though, and a man of my mature years needs his sleep. Midday would be much more convenient, so I shall see you then.'

He grabbed the arm Neale was proffering to Bess, and leaned on it so heavily that the young man was hard-pressed to keep his balance. As Bess and Neale escorted him away, Gold began a litany of compliments about Buckingham's gracious manners. Chaloner laughed when he saw the stunned expressions on the faces of the Duke and the Lady, although not loudly enough for them to hear him.

'It was a paltry crucifix anyway,' said Buckingham, when he had regained his composure. 'And those were not rubies, but coloured glass. I shall buy you a much nicer one.'

'For my priest to steal?' asked the Lady icily. 'No, thank you! Perhaps I will return to Anglicanism, if papists are going to prove miserly. I am bored of the religion, anyway, and only converted to annoy the Queen. She wallows in her Catholic devotions, and I wanted to show her that I can wallow just as prettily. I can produce royal children prettily, too. Unlike her.'

'You can produce royal bastards,' corrected Buckingham tartly. 'Only a queen can produce royal children, but our dear Lord Chancellor has ensured that we shall never see any. He did England a grave disservice by foisting a barren wife on our King.'

Chaloner was spared from having to report his progress – or lack thereof – to the Earl, because his master was at a meeting of the Privy Council, and so unavailable. He ate some seedcake made by Bulteel's wife, listened to Haddon wax lyrical about the delights of owning a dog, and spent the first part of the evening in the Banqueting House, where the Court had gathered for a performance of the King's Musick. He made a few desultory enquiries,

134

but Locke was one of his favourite composers, and it was not long before he became lost in the exquisite harmonies. Afterwards, guilty that he had squandered so much time – especially as Turner was busily darting from woman to woman, looking as though he was gathering intelligence aplenty – he went to the kitchens, hoping the servants would be in the mood to gossip. They were, but he learned nothing useful anyway.

He was on the verge of giving up when he saw Hannah, who had come to fetch warm milk for the Queen. Hannah was small, fair and her face was more interesting than pretty. Unlike the Lady, she could be witty without resorting to cruelty, and one of the things Chaloner liked best about her was her ability to make him laugh. He loitered, waiting for her to finish her duties, then escorted her to the pleasant cottage in Tothill Street where she lived. The road was bounded by the rural Tothill Fields to the south, and the landscaped splendour of St James's Park to the north, and was a quiet, peaceful place. It smelled of damp earth and dew, and owls could be heard hooting in the woods nearby.

Hannah was livid, because one of Buckingham's footmen had made some impolitic remark about the Queen's failure to produce children. She had left the fellow in no doubt as to what would happen if she heard him utter such treasonous statements again, but his stammering apology had done nothing to appease her: she remained incandescent.

'How can people be so heartless?' she raged as they walked. Her voice was loud enough to cause a few residents to peer through their curtains, and Chaloner supposed it was no surprise that word had spread about their blossoming friendship. 'The Queen is doing her best to achieve what is expected of her, but these . . . these *pigs* are implacable.'

'It is unfair,' agreed Chaloner.

'It is more than unfair – it is a scandal! They exclude her from their revelries – she was not even invited to the King's Musick tonight – they shun her when she speaks to them, and they laugh at her attempts to learn English. She is the Queen, but they treat her with rank disrespect.'

She continued to rail while Chaloner lit a fire and warmed some wine, so he listened patiently and without interruption until her temper burned out. Then he spent the night, and was tired enough after several nights of poor sleep that he did not wake until an hour after dawn the following day. Alarmed by the loss of time, he slipped out of bed, dressed and walked briskly to White Hall. The weather had continued to improve, and patches of blue let shafts of sunlight dance across the winter-bare ground.

He climbed the stairs to the Earl's office slowly, wondering what he could say about his progress. To postpone the inevitable reprimand for his lack of success – when the unctuous Turner was probably on the brink of a solution – he went to speak to Bulteel first. The secretary was good at gathering information, and now they had a formal pact to help each other, Chaloner was hopeful that he might have learned something useful. Unfortunately, he had nothing with which to reciprocate.

He met Haddon first, in the hallway outside Bulteel's little domain. His dogs were with him, straining against their leashes and making breathless, gagging sounds.

'I thought I would bring my darlings to work today,' the steward said beaming merrily, 'The Earl is having a

136

soirée tonight, which means a lot of running about to arrange food, guests and music, and my beauties like a bit of exercise.'

'Music?' asked Chaloner keenly. 'What manner of music?'

'Viols, I believe, although stringed instruments sound like a lot of screeching cats to me. Give me a trumpet any day. A trumpet is like a dog – loud, clear and commanding of respect.'

Chaloner looked at the glossy, pampered creatures that panted and gasped at his feet. 'Is that so?'

'Come along, my lovers,' trilled Haddon. 'The Earl wants us to hire Greeting's consort because Brodrick's is unavailable. Shall we look for Greeting in the chapel first, or his coffee house?'

'His coffee house,' replied Chaloner. 'He will not be in the chapel at this time of day.'

'I was talking to the dogs, actually,' said Haddon jovially. 'But your advice is welcome, and we shall do as you suggest, although my sweethearts dislike coffee houses. They tell me the smell of burned beans irritates their little noses.'

'They talk to you?' asked Chaloner, regarding him warily. Men had been taken to the lunatic house at Bedlam for less.

'Of course they do! Surely you converse with your cat?' Haddon smiled at the spy's bewildered expression, then patted him on the shoulder. 'Perhaps you should try it. It keeps the loneliness at bay, and animals are a great comfort to those who live a solitary life.'

He bounced away whistling, openly delighted at the prospect of a day with his canine companions. Chaloner watched him go, and supposed he had better spend more time with Hannah or Thurloe, lest his isolated lifestyle drove him to imagine his cat might have something worthwhile to say. He would not be able to do his job if he was mad, and then he would starve.

Bulteel leapt in alarm when Chaloner tapped him on the shoulder, not having heard him approach. He clutched his chest and regarded the spy balefully, then gave a reluctant grin and offered him a piece of his wife's Christmas gingerbread. Chaloner sat on the desk while he ate it. It was excellent, as usual, and he wondered how the secretary had managed to capture himself such a talented cook. He found himself thinking about Hannah, but their relationship was at such an early stage that he did not know if she could bake. He decided he had better find out.

'Did you hear about the third poisoning?' asked Bulteel in a low voice, so the Earl would not hear and come to find out why he was chatting when he should be at his ledgers. 'Langston – the plump fellow with the long nose – is dead.'

Chaloner brushed crumbs from his coat. 'What was Langston like? I met him with Surgeon Wiseman the other night, but only briefly. And I was not really in any condition to take his measure.'

Bulteel shrugged. 'Honest, kind and considerate. I cannot imagine why anyone would want to kill him. Kersey has him in the charnel house, so you should inspect him before you see the Earl – he is sure to ask whether this death is the same as the others. And you should examine the Painted Chamber, where Langston died, too. Perhaps the killer left a clue this time. Williamson told me . . .'

He faltered, and Chaloner frowned. 'You have been talking to the Spymaster? Why?'

Bulteel grimaced, angry with himself. 'Damn! That slipped out because I am frightened.'

Chaloner regarded him askance. 'Frightened by what? These murders? But why? Chetwynd, Vine and Langston were all government-appointed officials, but you are an earl's private secretary. I doubt the killer will regard you as a suitable victim.'

But Bulteel disagreed. 'It is well known that I refuse bribes, and the three dead men had one thing in common: their integrity.'

Chaloner hastened to reassure him. 'Chetwynd was not as honest as he liked people to think, so I doubt probity is the motive for their murders. Is that why you were talking to Williamson? You are afraid, and think he might be able to protect you?'

Bulteel looked miserable. 'Williamson has had his claws in me for a lot longer than that. A few months ago, he came to me and said that unless I provide him with the occasional report on the Earl, he would start rumours that would see me dismissed.'

'Rumours about what? I doubt you have ever done anything unsavoury.'

Bulteel shot him a wan smile. 'Your confidence is generous, but unfounded. You see, during the Commonwealth I worked for a bookseller who believed Cromwell was a hero. I told Williamson I did not think the same way, but he said it was irrelevant. He left me with no choice but to do as he asked.'

Chaloner thought Bulteel was a fool for letting Williamson use such a paltry excuse to intimidate him. He shrugged. 'A spymaster *should* have eyes all over White Hall, to keep him appraised of what is happening. But I am sure you never impart information that shows the Earl in a bad light.'

Bulteel was indignant. 'Of course not! I like this job, and a steady income is important for a man with a new

139

baby. But it is not easy. Williamson is always after me for snippets, and now Haddon is here, it is only a matter of time before I am ousted. I do not suppose you have learned anything that may give me an advantage over him?'

Chaloner shot him an apologetic look. 'But he will never displace you – he is a steward, not a secretary, and he could never manage the Earl's accounts like you do.'

Bulteel did not look comforted, although he produced another of his sickly smiles. To anyone who did not know him, it was a sinister expression, and one that would have most men reaching to secure their purses. 'You *must* catch this killer, Tom – I shall not feel safe until you have tracked him down. Did you know the Earl invited Langston to work as his spy, but he refused?'

Chaloner nodded. 'That would have made three of us, with Turner. What does he want, an army?'

'Yes, actually. He is worried that his enemies will start accusing him of ordering these deaths, because all three victims were men with whom he has had arguments over the last few weeks.'

Chaloner recalled the Earl ranting about his detractors after they had inspected Vine's body, when the spy had escorted him home in his carriage. He had put the incident from his mind, because it had seemed more of a diatribe than a flow of information, but now he understood. Without admitting that he had done anything wrong, the Earl had been telling his spy about his own uncomfortable association with the victims – and with others who had crossed him.

'He said Chetwynd disapproved of his unbending stance on religion,' he mused, thinking about what had been confided. 'And Vine objected to his gaudy house.'

140

'And Langston was deeply offended by his offer of employment – a lot of people heard him call the Earl a villain. I imagine it will not be long before our master's opponents notice that men who disagree with him end up being poisoned in the Painted Chamber. And then they will start braying about it.'

'He is not a murderer,' said Chaloner firmly. 'He may not be a saint, but he has his principles.'

And yet, he thought, the Earl was inexplicably determined to see an innocent man hang. Perhaps he had decided principles were putting him at a disadvantage in a place where no one else had any. It would not be the first time a good man had attempted to combat wickedness on its own terms.

Chaloner decided to take Bulteel's advice and inspect Langston's body before it was either moved to a church or shoved in the ground, depending on how well he had been loved by his next of kin. The Earl was ensconced with Brodrick anyway, and said he was not to be disturbed, not even to be briefed about murder or lost busts.

He walked to Westminster, and was halfway across New Palace Yard when he was sidetracked by a spectacle. Colonel Turner had dressed for the ladies that day, eschewing the current taste for lace, and opting instead for a plain blue suit with a silver sash and matching earstring. The attire made him look martial and manly, and he was surrounded by women, all clamouring for his attention. He stood among them like a god.

Bess Gold was at the edge of the gathering. She fingered her crucifix, and simpered in a way that was brazenly provocative. Her husband clung to her arm, but his attention was on his feet, to ensure he did not stumble on the uneven ground. The cherub-faced Neale was hovering nearby, full of envious resentment that Turner should be the object of Bess's admiration. He tried to slip around Gold to speak to her, but the old man grabbed him as he passed, ostensibly to hold himself up. Chaloner frowned. Was it a deliberate ploy to keep Neale away from his wife, or simple bad timing on Neale's part? But there was nothing in Gold's demeanour to suggest he objected to the young man's presence. On the contrary, he seemed grateful for another source of physical support.

The remaining women were members of the Queen's bedchamber, although Chaloner recognised only two. There was Lady Muskerry, reputed to be a willing partner for any man, but not overly endowed with wits; like Bess, she fingered a trinket that hung around her neck. And there was Hannah.

'Did I dream you were with me last night?' Hannah asked in a low voice, detaching herself from the throng to talk to him. Her face was serious, but her eyes danced with mischief. 'I must have done, because I am sure you would not have sneaked off before dawn without a parting kiss.'

'It was not before dawn. The sun was up and half the morning was gone.'

'Why the rush? Was it because I did not stop chattering last night – did not draw breath to ask after your day – making you eager to escape? Or is it just that you are trying to solve these recent murders?'

Chaloner's immediate inclination was to evade her question with a comment about Lady Muskerry's necklace. But it had been his reluctance to talk about himself that had driven wedges between him and several previous lovers, and he was determined not to repeat the mistake.

Unfortunately, it was difficult to break the practice that had kept him alive for so many years, and he much preferred the times when Hannah did all the talking.

'The Earl has hired Turner and me to look into them,' he forced himself to say.

Her expressive face crumpled into a grimace. 'Then be sure you do not do all the work, while he steps in to take the credit. He thrives on adulation, and will be keen to secure your Earl's good graces.'

Chaloner raised his eyebrows, surprised – and gratified – that she could see through the colonel's flamboyant charm. 'Every other lady at Court seems to think him a gift from God.'

'Oh, he is a gift, all right. I am told – by several impressed friends – that there is no one like him for making a girl feel special in the bedchamber. However, a pretty face and a perfect body are not high on my list of requirements in a man.'

'That is a relief.'

She nudged him playfully. 'You will suffice.' Then her impish smile faded, to be replaced by an expression of concern as her attention was caught by something else. 'Look – there is Margaret Symons! I am sure she is ill – do you see the taut way she holds herself, as if every step hurts?'

Chaloner glanced to where she pointed. A woman was walking slowly from the direction of the abbey, leaning heavily on the arm of a man. She was thin and pale, and did appear to be unwell; her companion was conspicuous for his mane of spiky ginger hair. Both wore respectable clothes, but ones that had seen better days, indicating they had once been much wealthier. London was full of people just like them – folk who had

143

prospered during the Commonwealth, but who were now suspect to the new regime. No one would do business with them, and some were finding themselves reduced to desperate poverty.

'Her husband – the man with her – is Will Symons,' Hannah went on. 'He was a government clerk until the Restoration, at which point he was ousted to make room for Royalists. He is a pleasant man. Margaret is a sculptress – my husband liked statues and commissioned one from her.'

'From a woman?' asked Chaloner, startled. He shrugged at Hannah's indignant expression. 'You do not hear of many female artists. I am not saying Mrs Symons is not good, just that it is unusual.'

Hannah sniffed, not entirely mollified. 'My husband almost cancelled the work when he learned "M. Symons" was a lady, but I informed him that he had better think again. And I was right to force him to reconsider, because the piece she made for us is exquisite.'

'But you think she is ill?' Chaloner knew he was drawing out the discussion, so Hannah would have less time to ask him questions about his work, but he could not help himself.

'Yes – you can see from here that Will is being very solicitous of her. They are a devoted couple, and it grieves me to see him look so worried. I should go to talk to them.' She started to move away, but then turned back. 'Will you visit me again soon? I enjoyed your company last night.'

He said he would try, and had not taken many steps towards the charnel house when he heard his name being called. It was Turner, who had managed to extricate himself from his adoring throng. He was adjusting his clothing, as though leaving had involved the prising off of fingers.

'There is scant information about murder to be had from those lasses,' he declared, smoothing down his moustache, 'but their company is a delight – I shall be doubling my tally of children, at this rate! But while we are speaking of ladies, have you heard anything of Meg the laundress? I have not seen her since we failed to meet for our midnight tryst – the night I found Vine murdered.'

'Has it occurred to you that she might have stumbled across the killer, and he has ensured she will not be around to provide a description of him?'

Turner shook his head. 'It is more likely that she has found out about my growing affection for Barbara – that is Lady Castlemaine to you – and is jealous. Damn! I was growing fond of Meg, too.'

'You should find her,' advised Chaloner, feeling the man should not need to be told. 'If she is alive, she might be in danger, or frightened and in need of your protection.'

Turner brightened. 'Oh, I can do protection. I am good at gallantry. Where shall I start looking?'

Chaloner regarded him askance. 'How should I know? Try her home, or the place where she works. Does she have family in the city?'

'I have no idea. I want to bed her, not marry her, for God's sake – I am not interested in her kin. But perhaps I will have a bit of a hunt for her tonight, when I am done with His Portliness's affairs.'

'You think you will have solved the case by then?' Chaloner wondered whether Turner intended to present Greene as a culprit, simply because it was the easiest option and would please the Earl.

But Turner shook his head again. 'Unfortunately, it is proving more complex than I imagined. Incidentally, His Portliness says I can have a permanent post with him if I beat you to the answer, and he and Haddon have taken bets on which one of us will win.'

Chaloner was disgusted. 'Murder is hardly a subject for wagers.' And neither was his future.

'That is what I thought – I was under the impression they had more decorum. But Haddon believes you will succeed, while His Portliness is backing me. However, both agree that neither of us has a hope in Hell of locating this missing figurine – the one by Barocci.'

'Bernini. And it is a bust, not a figurine.'

Turner flapped a hand, to indicate details were irrelevant. 'Suffice to say it cost the old king's wife a diamond ring, which was valued at a thousand pounds.'

'You do not know the sculptor's name, but you know what he was paid?' Chaloner was amused.

Turner grinned back. 'I know what is important. Where are you going? To see Langston's corpse? I have already done that, but it yielded nothing in the way of clues. And it cost me threepence, too.'

'What did?' asked Chaloner, puzzled.

'Viewing the corpse,' explained Turner. 'Because there has been such a demand to see it, Kersey has opened his mortuary to spectators, and is making a fortune in entry fees. But I had better talk to Bess Gold, before her husband takes her away. She was one of the last people to see Langston alive, and might have something useful to impart.'

But Chaloner had interviewed Bess at the King's Musick the previous evening, and had discovered that her powers of observation were negligible – she barely

146

recalled what she had been wearing, let alone anything to solve a murder. He watched Turner strut away, but did not tell him he would be wasting his time. The tale about the Earl's wager had annoyed him, and he found himself determined to prove his master wrong. And if that meant not sharing information with his rival, then so be it.

The charnel house was located near the river, sandwiched between a granary and a coalhouse. As Turner had warned, it was full of spectators – it was not often three clerks were murdered in the same week, and people were eager to view the victims. They handed over their coins and disappeared into the mortuary's dark interior, pomanders pressed to noses. None lingered long, so although there was a queue, it moved quickly. Chaloner loitered, waiting for the horde to dissipate, because there was no point going inside if he could not see Langston for sightseers.

The first person he recognised among the ghoulish throng was the grim-faced Doling, who stamped out looking as black as thunder. Chaloner might have assumed the fellow had seen something to enrage him, but then recalled the way he had scowled at his ale in the Angel the previous day: Doling was just one of those men who frowned at everything. His expression blackened further still when the wind caught the lace at his throat and whisked it off to reveal skin that was old, red and wrinkled, like that of a turkey. The lace was retrieved by Hargrave, whose flea-ravaged head was wrapped in a scarf that made him look like a fishwife, and who was in company with the elderly Tryan. The three exchanged a few words, then walked away together, Tryan's bandy legs pumping nineteen to the dozen as he struggled to keep up with his younger companions.

Moments later, George Vine reeled out, a Lea brother on either side. He lurched to a doorway and was promptly sick, although Chaloner could not tell whether it was at the sight of a man who had suffered the same fate as his father, or his stomach rebelling at the amount of wine that had been poured into it the previous night. The Leas were spitefully amused by his misery, and were still sniggering when they helped him into a hackney carriage some time later.

They were watched in rank disapproval by a number of courtiers, among whom was the obese Jones, still limping from his encounter with Lady Castlemaine's gaming stick. He grimaced, and pointedly leaned down to rub the afflicted limb when she and Buckingham arrived a few moments later. It was then that Chaloner saw he was not the only one observing the proceedings: so was Williamson's clerk, who skulked in the shadows of a nearby doorway, almost invisible in his black clothes.

Eventually, the queue dwindled to nothing. Chaloner prised a stone from the road, and lobbed it at the glass window of a nearby warehouse. Immediately, the owner tore out, and began to accuse a departing courtier of the crime. While Swaddell's attention was fixed on the resulting fracas, Chaloner left his hiding place and slipped inside the charnel house unseen.

Kersey's domain was larger than it looked from the outside, and the main section comprised a long, windowless hall with lamps hanging at irregular intervals from the ceiling. There were a dozen wooden tables, each graced with either a cadaver, or a neatly folded sheet. Kersey – a dapper, well-dressed little man – was holding forth to the last of his visitors, informing them that on a good week, he might have as many as twenty corpses to mind. His audience, however, was more interested in clucking over his charges than listening to him. Chaloner waited until they were all gaping at the remains of a drowned apprentice, then turned to inspect the poisoner's most recent victim.

Langston lay next to Chetwynd, identifiable by his large nose and plump body – Chaloner recalled that Vine had already been buried, and so was spared the humiliation of being turned into an exhibition. He was devoid of all clothing except a strategically placed handkerchief, and the spy shuddered, not liking the notion that anyone who happened to die in Westminster could expect to be laid out and exposed to all and sundry. It was undignified, and for a moment, he had a disturbing vision of his own violent demise, and the Earl coming to gawp at his naked corpse. He took a deep breath, to clear his mind of such dark thoughts, and turned his attention to Langston.

A quick glance at the mouth and lips revealed blisters that were reminiscent of the poison used on Chetwynd and Vine, which came as no surprise. Surreptitiously he looked for signs of other injuries, but there was nothing he could see. He was on his way out when a familiar figure strode through the door. Kersey opened his mouth to demand an admission fee, but closed it again when he recognised the newcomer.

'Good God!' boomed Wiseman, red robes billowing around him as he regarded the spectators in distaste. 'Can you find nothing better to do than drool over the corpses of your colleagues?'

'You are a fine one to talk,' flashed a courtier named Peters. His expression was malicious: Wiseman's blunt

149

tongue had made him unpopular at Court. 'I hear that you have recently taken to hefting heavy objects about with a view to acquiring larger muscles. If that is not a damned peculiar way of carrying on, then I do not know what is.'

'I do it for the benefit of my health,' replied Wiseman imperiously. 'And I feel ten years younger, so it is certainly working. I firmly believe that exercise is the best way to prolong life and promote wellbeing, and anyone who does not agree with me is a fool.'

'*You* will not live a long life, no matter how fit you think these odd habits are making you,' sneered Peters contemptuously. 'And why? Because someone will dispatch you, on the grounds that you are conceited, arrogant and rude, and no one likes you.'

Wiseman regarded him in silence for a moment, and when he spoke, his voice was soft. 'I can see from here that you are afflicted with the French pox, so I shall not take your words to heart – I am a surgeon, and know how these diseases can rob a man of his wits. However, you may like to know that I have identified the source of the current outbreak: it is Lady Muskerry.'

Chaloner was not the only one to be taken aback by this announcement. There was a collective gasp of astonishment and shock, and then people began to edge away from the woman in question. They edged away from Peters, too, who was gaping in disbelief, staggered that the surgeon should stoop to such low tactics just in order to win a petty spat.

'I have devised a cure, though,' Wiseman continued, relishing his opponent's mortification. 'It works like a charm, and will save sufferers from the embarrassment of unwelcome sores – and from the embarrassment of making unwarranted verbal assaults on fellow members of Court, too. I recommend you try it, Peters – French pox can be fatal, if left untreated.'

He was going to add more, but Peters shouldered past him and headed for the door, determined to leave before any more of his intimate secrets could be brayed to the world at large. The other courtiers followed, all careful not to meet the surgeon's eye, lest they be singled out for a tongue-lashing, too. When they had gone, Wiseman turned to the spy. Chaloner took a step away from him, not sure he wanted his company when he was in such a bellicose frame of mind.

'Colonel Turner told me you were here, so I came to see if I could help you. Bulteel says the Earl will dismiss you if you do not find this killer, and I do not want you gone from White Hall. You are one of the few people there who are acceptable to me.'

'Thank you,' said Chaloner warily, wondering whether the surgeon's temper was spent or whether he had yet more vitriol to expel. He braced himself, ready to follow Peters's example and leave if he did – he had better things to do than exchange insults with the razor-tongued Wiseman.

But the surgeon's expression had gone from haughty to troubled. 'Is it true?'

Chaloner frowned. 'Is what true?'

'What Peters said – that no one likes me.'

Chaloner was inclined to tell him the truth, in the hope that it might imbue him with a little humility, but when he saw the genuine anguish in the man's eyes, he found he could not do it. He flailed around for a noncommittal answer. 'The Earl likes you,' he managed eventually.

'And you?' asked Wiseman, regarding him intently. 'What do you think of me?'

Chaloner was not sure how to reply. He did not want to make an enemy of Wiseman by answering honestly, but he did not want to lie, either. 'I think you are an innovative surgeon,' he hedged. But a glance at Wiseman's agonised expression told him this was not enough. He cleared his throat, uncomfortable with the discussion. 'And you are one of the few people who are acceptable to me.'

It seemed to satisfy the surgeon, because he smiled briefly, and then waved a hand towards the two corpses. 'Langston, like Vine and Chetwynd, died when a virulent toxin seared the membranes of his mouth and throat. It caused immediate swelling that restricted the flow of air to his lungs. In essence, he suffocated. I imagine I would see bleeding in his stomach, too, were I to slice him open.'

Chaloner winced. He was not unduly squeamish, but there was something about Wiseman's grisly enthusiasm he had always found unsettling. 'Do you know the nature of this poison yet? You said you would find out.'

'That was assuming I had a corpse to dissect, but the kin of Vine, Chetwynd *and* Langston have refused me permission. However, there are many such substances in the modern pharmacopoeia, and I doubt knowing a name will help you catch your killer. Most have perfectly innocent applications, such as scouring drains, making glue or cleaning glass.'

'So I will be wasting my time if I try to track it down?'

Wiseman nodded. 'Although I intimated to Turner that it was worth doing. However, I can tell you that all three men were killed by the same potion – there is no

152

question about that – and they probably died quickly. And, as I said the other night, the poison's odour was disguised by brandywine.'

'Do you still think Greene is innocent? You have not discovered anything to suggest otherwise?'

'Greene does not have the strength of mind for killing, and the Earl is a fool for thinking he does. But we shall ensure he does not embarrass himself.'

'Shall we now?' murmured Chaloner.

'We shall,' declared Wiseman, 'because I am *not* working with that popinjay Turner – not on this case, and not in the future, either. So, I have a clue to share with you, something I discovered when I examined the bodies: namely that the purses of all three victims were missing, along with any jewellery they might have owned. I am surprised Mrs Vine did not comment on it.'

'Perhaps she did not notice.'

Wiseman snorted his derision. 'She would have noticed. And so would her snivelling son.'

Chaloner nodded his thanks, but thought it did not help much to know he was dealing with a killer who stripped his victims of valuables – the Court was full of avaricious people. He tried to set the 'clue' in context. Did it mean the ruby ring had belonged to Vine, dropped as the killer had looted the corpse? It was obviously worth a lot of money, so why had Vine's wife denied him owning it? Or had she sent a train-band to retrieve it when she realised it was missing? With a sigh, Chaloner realised Wiseman's information posed more questions than answers.

Chapter 5

As Chaloner left the charnel house it was more desperation than any real expectation of finding answers that drove him to the Painted Chamber. He was surprised to find it deserted – it was usually busy during the day – but then he realised it was the time when folk went for their midday meals. His footsteps echoed hollowly as he walked, and he noticed that the tapestry used to incapacitate him had already been rehung.

A dark, sticky stain on the floor indicated where something had been spilled. He knelt to inspect it, and saw the edges were slightly frothy, while the bulk smelled of brandywine. It was almost certainly the remains of whatever had killed Langston, although Bulteel had told him that – like the first two murders – there had been no sign of a cup. He could only surmise that the killer had taken it with him when he had left. Of course, it did not explain why Langston should have accepted a drink in a place where two of his colleagues had died doing the same thing. The only answer was that all three had known the killer, and trusted him.

'Taste it,' urged a soft voice from behind him. 'Swallow some, to see if it contains poison.'

Chaloner was not so engrossed in the stain that he had dropped his defences, and knew perfectly well that someone had been slinking towards him. The knife he carried in his sleeve was in his hand, and he could have had it in the fellow's heart in an instant, had he wanted. He stood and turned, feigning surprise to see someone behind him – it was Spymaster Williamson, and he was loath to antagonise the man by informing him that elephants could have effected a more stealthy approach.

Williamson was tall, impeccably dressed and an expression of lofty disdain was permanently etched into his face. He had been an Oxford academic before embarking on a career on politics, and there was no question that he possessed a formidable intellect. Unfortunately, his unattractive personality – he was vengeful, condescending and greedy – meant he was unlikely to be awarded the promotions he doubtless thought he deserved. Chaloner was not the only man to have earned his dislike, although he was the only one still living in London – the others had either run for their lives or had disappeared under mysterious circumstances. In other words, people crossed the Spymaster at their peril.

'According to our records, your family were late paying their taxes again this year,' Williamson said. His voice was low and full of pent up malevolence. 'They supported Cromwell during the wars, so I imagine depriving the government of its revenues is their way of continuing to fight against us.'

'Then you imagine wrong,' said Chaloner coolly. 'The taxes imposed on old Parliamentarians are colossal, and my kin are not the only ones struggling to pay what is being demanded from them.'

'If they default, then they are traitors, as far as I am concerned,' said Williamson silkily.

'Them and half of England,' retorted Chaloner. He was appalled by the discussion – shocked to learn that the Spymaster was the kind of man to strike at an enemy through his relations. Chaloner's siblings were peaceful, gentle folk, who lived quietly on their Buckinghamshire estates; they should not have to suffer more hardship, just because their youngest brother had antagonised someone in London.

'I could prosecute them,' Williamson went on, casually examining his fingernails. 'Or do you think I should leave them alone? Of course, if I do, you will have to make it worth my while.'

Chaloner was ready to do virtually anything to protect his brothers and sisters, but was careful to keep his expression neutral, aware that the Spymaster would exploit any sign of weakness. 'I doubt the Earl pays me enough to satisfy a man of your standing.'

Williamson gave what Chaloner supposed was a smile, although it did not touch his eyes. 'I am not thinking about money – I am more interested in you doing me a service. You see, I am aware that the Earl has ordered you to explore these clerk-killings, despite the fact that they come under my remit.'

'You want me to stop?' It would mean his dismissal for certain, but Chaloner was willing to do it.

'I want you to continue,' came the unexpected reply. 'The city is full of treasonous talk at the moment, and my spies are hard-pressed to monitor it all. Moreover, *I* want to be the one to find the King's missing statue and earn his undying gratitude, so I must expend manpower on that, too. I do not have the resources to catch a killer, as well.'

'But the victims were government officials,' said Chaloner, puzzled by the Spymaster's priorities. 'And their deaths may be an attempt to destabilise the Royalist administration. Surely, finding the killer is more important than locating a piece of art?'

'Not necessarily,' replied Williamson smoothly. 'Stealing from the King is a very serious matter.'

But Chaloner did not believe it, and was sure there was another reason for the Spymaster's curious position. 'I do not suppose the King ordered you to find the statue, to prove yourself, did he?' He could tell from Williamson's pained expression that he was on the right track. 'What did he say? That if you cannot do that, then how can you be trusted with the nation's security?'

Williamson glowered. 'He did not put it in quite those terms, but, as it happens, I *have* been asked to demonstrate my agency's efficacy by tracing the bust. So, I am loath to waste my time on murder.'

'And you want me to do it instead?'

'Yes, because you are right – finding the killer *is* important. However, it is not as important as me keeping my job. So, do we have an agreement? I will overlook your family's persistent late-payment of taxes, and you will hunt down the villain who is murdering officials?'

'Very well,' said Chaloner stiffly. He disliked the notion of entering a pact with such a man.

'Good, although I should warn you that I *will* prosecute them if you fail to solve the case – and I mean solve it properly, not just present me with Greene because your Earl believes him to be guilty.'

'You think Greene is innocent?'

'Let us say I am sceptical, although my opinion is

157

based solely on the fact that I have met Greene, and he does not seem the murdering type. But before I ordered my spies to concentrate on the statue, I heard their reports on the crimes. They uncovered three facts that may help you. First, Chetwynd, Vine and Langston had public arguments with your Earl in the last few weeks.'

'I know,' said Chaloner, struggling to mask his unease. Had Williamson joined the Earl's enemies, and intended to use the case to help topple him from power? The Spymaster had so far declined to pick a side, although his neutrality had nothing to do with professionalism or fair play: he was just waiting to see who would win before committing himself. 'He told me.'

Williamson ignored him. 'Second, all three frequented John's Coffee House in Covent Garden, as does Sir Nicholas Gold. You might want to speak to him in the course of your enquiries.'

'I know this, too. They also met Greene, Neale, Hargrave, Tryan, Jones, and several others.'

Williamson ignored him again. 'And third, the three dead men used to be regular and enthusiastic members of prayer meetings held at the home of a man named Henry Scobel.'

'Scobel?' echoed Chaloner, not sure whether to believe him. 'He was a Commonwealth clerk, who died a few months after the Restoration. Why would he entertain Royalists in his home?'

'I have no idea, but entertain them he did, right up until his death. I heard the testimony of reliable witnesses – men with no reason to lie – with my own ears.'

Chaloner would make up his own mind about whether these 'reliable witnesses' had no reason to lie – being interrogated by Williamson alone might have been enough to send them into a frenzy of fabrication. 'Why do you think this is important? Scobel died more than three years ago.'

Williamson shrugged. 'Perhaps it isn't important. I am merely reporting facts – interpreting them is your business, and you may pursue or dismiss them as you see fit.'

'It was just four of them at Scobel's meetings?' asked Chaloner, trusting neither the Spymaster nor his information. It was not inconceivable that he was trying to sabotage the Earl's investigation by muddying the waters with untruths. 'Scobel himself, Vine, Chetwynd and Langston?'

'No, there were many others, including the men you listed as enjoying each other's company at John's Coffee House – Greene, Jones, Neale, Gold, Hargrave and Tryan. In addition, Will Symons went, and so did an old Roundhead soldier called Doling. And the Lea brothers.'

Chaloner kept his expression blank, but his thoughts were racing. What did it mean? That this eclectic collection of men had prayed together in Scobel's home during Cromwell's reign, and had moved their devotions to a coffee house after his death? And that one of them had decided to kill some of the others? But why?

'Will Symons is Scobel's nephew,' Williamson was saying. 'He was a Commonwealth clerk, too, but lost his post at the Restoration. So did Doling, and both are bitter. Like you, I imagine. You must be disappointed that I decline to employ you in Holland, after all your efforts to integrate yourself so seamlessly into that country – speaking their language, adopting their customs, learning their politics.'

Chaloner shrugged, unwilling to give him the satisfaction of knowing he was right. 'I am happy here.'

'Are you?' asked Williamson softly. 'Then I must see what I can do about that.'

Chaloner was resentful as he left the Painted Chamber. He disliked his family being used as pawns to secure his cooperation, and he distrusted Williamson with every fibre of his being. However, if the Earl *was* connected to the murders, as Williamson obviously suspected, then Chaloner did not blame him for keeping his distance from the investigation – the King would not thank him for revealing that his Lord Chancellor was involved in something sinister. And the statue? Chaloner had no intention of giving up his enquiries on that, just so Williamson could prove the efficacy of his intelligence service. He would have to be careful, but he took orders from no man except the one who paid his wages. And that was the Earl – for the time being, at least.

He thought about the new information. Three years before, Thurloe had written him a letter, expressing his deep grief at Scobel's death – Scobel was gentle and kind, and Thurloe had liked him. Had there been something suspicious about his demise, too? Thurloe had not mentioned anything amiss, but perhaps it had not occurred to him to look. Chaloner rubbed his head as he walked across New Palace Yard. What had the Earl let him in for this time, if the enquiry necessitated peering back into the mists of time?

Confused and a little bewildered, he reviewed all he had learned. He knew the three victims had been killed by the same poison and thus probably by the same person. They had been robbed of purses and jewellery. All had died in the Painted Chamber. They had prayed in the home of a Parliamentarian official, and after Scobel's death had continued to meet at a coffee house in Covent Garden. Chetwynd had pretended to be upright, but had been corrupt, although Vine and Langston were said to be decent men. And that was all he knew – the rest was speculation and theory.

Frustrated, he turned his thoughts to the missing statue. No one had admitted to seeing anything suspicious the night it disappeared, and there had been no sightings of it since. But who would steal a bust of the old king? It was valuable, but hardly something that could be hawked on the black market – too many people knew it was stolen, so buyers were unlikely to be lining up. Had it been acquired for someone's private collection then, because to own a work of art by Bernini was its own reward? Should he start investigating wealthy men, to ascertain whether any had a penchant for sculpture? Merchants, perhaps? Or some of the more affluent courtiers? But that represented a lot of people, and with disgust, Chaloner acknowledged that he was no further along with that enquiry than he was with the murders.

He arrived at the Earl's offices, treading lightly as was his wont, and was rather surprised to catch Haddon in the act of rummaging through Bulteel's desk – the secretary was out delivering letters. Haddon stopped what he was doing, and gave the spy a sickly, unconvincing smile. His dogs were with him, and Chaloner supposed they had not been trained to bark a warning as someone approached.

'I was looking for a pen,' explained the steward, straightening up furtively.

Chaloner pointed to the box of quills that stood in plain view. 'What is wrong with those?'

161

Haddon grimaced. 'I know what you are thinking – that I am searching Bulteel's drawers because I intend to see him ousted and me appointed in his place. He accuses me of it every time we meet.'

'Perhaps he has a point.'

Haddon winced. 'But I do not *want* his post. I would hate being cooped up in this dismal hole all day, writing letters and making dull little entries in ledgers. The reason I am invading his domain is because I do not trust him. I think he may have drawn that map of the Earl's rooms I showed you. Unfortunately, he is too clever to have left any clues that will allow me to prove it.'

'Bulteel did not make that sketch,' said Chaloner firmly. 'Brodrick did, as you first assumed – you said you found the drawing after he had been to visit. I imagine it has something to do with his plan, as Lord of Misrule, to decorate the Earl's offices in the manner of a Turkish brothel.'

Haddon gazed at him, then sighed in relief. 'Is that what he intends to do? Then it is not as bad as I feared! It will be inconvenient, but we can cope with that. I shall have to take the Earl away for a few hours, to ensure they have enough time to accomplish their mischief, but that should be no problem.'

Chaloner was puzzled. 'You will let them proceed?'

Haddon regarded him as though he was insane. 'Of course! If I thwart him, Brodrick might devise something much worse – and better the devil you know. Not a word to the Earl, though. He will refuse to play along, and that would be unfortunate, because I *know* it will be better for him if he just lets matters run their course.'

Chaloner left thinking the steward was wiser than he looked, and that the Earl was fortunate in his servants.

It was a pity Bulteel and Haddon disliked each other, because together they would make a formidable team, and would increase the Earl's chances of besting his enemies permanently.

He tapped at the door to the Earl's offices, expecting to be reprimanded for taking so long to report his findings. The Earl opened it furtively, and when he recognised Chaloner, he slipped out and led his spy a short distance down the corridor, evidently intending to have the discussion there. Chaloner was bemused, because the hallway was draughty, which the Earl always said was bad for his gout. His mystification intensified when he glanced behind him, through the door that had been left ajar, and glimpsed a visitor. It was Sir Nicholas Gold.

'I am sorry to take you away from your company, sir,' he said, apologetically.

'I am alone,' said the Earl rather too quickly. 'But I have confidential papers out on my desk – ones I cannot let anyone else see.'

'I see,' said Chaloner, taken aback. He had never known the Earl to lie quite so brazenly before. Uncharitably, he wondered whether he was asking Gold about the murders, and planned to pass any clues to Turner. Then Turner would solve the case, and the Earl would win his bet with Haddon.

'Well?' demanded the Earl, when the spy said no more. 'Have you proved Greene's guilt yet?'

'No, I came to report that—'

The Earl raised a plump hand to stop him. 'I want a culprit, not a résumé of your discoveries. And while you waste time here, Turner is in the charnel house, watching those who gawk at Langston's corpse – he tells me killers

163

often gloat over their handiwork. He knows a lot about such matters.'

'Does he?' asked Chaloner curiously. 'How? I thought he was a soldier.'

'Like you, he has enjoyed a colourful career, although *he* was never a Parliamentarian spy or an officer in Cromwell's New Model Army.'

There was no answer to a statement like that, and Chaloner did not try to think of one. 'How violently did Chetwynd oppose your stance on religion, sir?' he asked instead. It was a blunt question, but he was beginning to think the Earl would hire Turner in preference to him no matter what he did, and felt he had nothing to lose by impertinence.

The Earl regarded him through narrowed eyes. 'I hope you are not intimating that I might have wanted Chetwynd dead because he attacked me in public! Or that I had designs on Vine's life, because he condemned my new house.'

Not to mention your ire when Langston declined to become your spy, thought Chaloner. He shook his head. 'Of course not, sir. I ask because I need to be ready to answer any accusations from your enemies. That will be difficult, if I do not have all the facts.'

The Earl mulled this over. 'My disputes with Vine and Chetwynd did turn nasty,' he conceded reluctantly. 'I was furious when they presumed to question my judgement. And I was angry with Langston for refusing to work for me, so yes, I had reason to dislike all three. But anyone who thinks I had anything to do with their deaths is a fool. Damn Vine! Why did *he* have to be a victim?'

Chaloner frowned. 'Why do you single out him in particular?'

164

The Earl jutted out a defiant chin. 'I do not want to talk about it.'

Chaloner would find out anyway, although it would save time if he did not have to. 'I would rather hear it from you, than from one of your detractors, sir,' he said reasonably.

The Earl eyed him balefully. 'You really are a disrespectful rogue! No wonder Thurloe kept you overseas all those years – he would have been compelled to slit your throat, had you worked here.'

Chaloner was growing tired of the Earl's reluctance to trust him. Why could he not be more like Thurloe? Not for the first time, the Spy wished Cromwell had not died, the Commonwealth had not fallen, and Thurloe was still in charge of the intelligence services. 'Then I will ask Vine's family—'

'No,' snapped the Earl. He sighed irritably, and went to close the door to his office. He lowered his voice when he returned. 'If you must know, Vine was blackmailing me.'

Chaloner regarded him askance. 'I doubt *you* have ever done anything worthy of extortion.'

For the first time in weeks, the Earl smiled at him. 'A compliment! There is a rare event – I was under the impression you consider me something of a villain. But your good opinion is misplaced, I am afraid. Vine knew a terrible secret about me, which he threatened to make public. He said he would hold his tongue only if I agreed not to build my home in Piccadilly.'

'Did he think it too grand?'

'Yes, but that was not his main complaint. Raising Clarendon House will necessitate the destruction of some woods. Nightingales sing in these woods, apparently, and he did not want their song silenced.'

Chaloner struggled to understand. He liked birds himself, and the haunting sound of nightingales was a source of great delight to him, but there were other trees nearby, and the ones that would be felled to make way for the mansion were something of a jungle. Then he considered the geography.

'Did his objections arise from the fact that he could hear these birds from his house?'

The Earl nodded. 'It took me rather longer to grasp the selfish rationale behind his demands, but you are right. He said it was a crime against God to render nightingales homeless, but the reality was that *he* liked them. His family hated him, and listening to these birds was the only thing that made being at home with them tolerable. And now I had better tell you what Vine knew about me – my awful secret.'

Chaloner doubted he was about to hear anything overtly shocking. 'It might help, sir.'

'It involves something that happened a few months ago, when the Lady was moving from her old rooms in the Holbein Gate to fabulous new quarters overlooking the Privy Gardens. To furnish them, she looted works of art from the King, from public rooms, and from any White Hall resident too intimidated to oppose her plunder.'

'I remember. She put White Hall in a frenzy of chaos for about a week.'

'One night, just before she moved in, I found myself with an opportunity to inspect her new domain alone. When I saw the beautiful things she had appropriated for herself, I was overcome with a deep and uncontrollable anger. I did something of which I am deeply ashamed.'

166

'And Vine saw you?'

'Yes. He was also taking the opportunity to admire what the Lady had accumulated, and was standing quietly in the shadows, so I did not see him until it was too late. Needless to say, he was shocked when I . . . did what I did. He said he understood the reasons for my uncharacteristically loutish behaviour, and promised to overlook the matter like any decent man – until the matter of the nightingales arose, and he threatened to tell everyone.'

Chaloner was silent, wondering whether the Earl was the kind of man to hire an assassin to prevent the revelation of an embarrassing secret. He would have said no a few months before, but now he found he was not so sure.

'What did you do?' he asked eventually.

The Earl lowered his voice to a whisper, and his eyes were huge with mortification. 'I drew on the Lady's portrait – the one painted by Lely. I gave her a beard and a moustache.'

Chaloner gazed at him for a moment, then started to laugh. 'Really?'

The Earl glared at him. 'It is not funny! We are talking about the King's favourite mistress here, and that portrait cost a lot of money. I defaced it so vigorously that it is far beyond repair.'

'You should have given her a pair of horns, too, and sketched in a pitchfork.'

That coaxed a reluctant smile. 'I wish I had thought of it. But this unedifying tale tells you something new about Vine, this noble, upright man, does it not? That he was willing to resort to underhand means to get his own way?'

Chaloner nodded. 'So Vine was a blackmailer and

167

Chetwynd was corrupt, although they both presented godly faces to the world. I wonder what we will learn about Langston.'

'Nothing,' said the Earl firmly. 'He really was a decent fellow.'

The short winter day was almost over, and dusk was falling fast. Chaloner was hungry, having eaten nothing that day except Bulteel's cakes. Fortunately, the Earl was in one of his conscientious phases, and had been paying his staff on time, so the spy was currently solvent. It was not always so, which was another reason he missed working for the Commonwealth – Thurloe had paid regularly and well, allowing Chaloner to live respectably and even invest funds for the future. It had all disappeared at the Restoration when, for the first time in his life, he had experienced genuine poverty.

But he had money to spend that evening, so he went to New Palace Yard, on which were located three establishments called Heaven, Hell and Purgatory. It depended on their owners' whim whether they were taverns, coffee houses or cookshops on any particular week, but it was usually possible to purchase victuals of some description, and he liked their dark rooms, worn benches and convivial atmospheres. He was heading towards them when he spotted some familiar faces.

Turner was sitting on a bench near the central fountain, stretching his long legs in front of him as though he was relaxing in the sun, rather than perching on a stone monument in the middle of winter. His trademark ear-string fluttered in the breeze. With him were the bandy-legged Tryan, and Hargrave with his scarred and shaven head. Neither merchant looked as comfortable as

168

Turner, and huddled inside their coats. The bench was protected by an awning, and at that time of night, the trio were virtually invisible under its shadow. Intrigued as to why they felt compelled to meet in such a place, Chaloner eased his way behind them, aiming for a position where he could eavesdrop.

'Of course I can read the contracts for you,' Turner was saying amiably. 'If they are anything like the ones I did last week, they will be easy.'

'You are most kind,' said Hargrave, scratching his scalp. 'But are you sure it is no bother? I thought you were employed by the Lord Chancellor these days, to catch him a killer.'

'I am,' said Turner. 'But I am perfectly capable of helping you at the same time.'

'We would have lost a fortune in the past, without solicitors to safeguard our interests,' said Tryan soberly. 'It is a sad state of affairs when a man cannot trust a fellow merchant not to cheat him. We are indebted to you, sir.'

'Lord, it is cold!' exclaimed Hargrave, pulling his coat more tightly around him. 'I rarely noticed bad weather when I had hair, and I should never have listened to Chetwynd – it was he who suggested I cut it all off, and have it made into a wig. But the damned thing has been nothing but trouble.'

'You cannot blame Chetwynd for the lice, though,' said Tryan. 'You got them from that brothel.' He pursed his lips disapprovingly.

'It was not a brothel,' objected Hargrave, stung. 'It was a gentleman's club. Besides, I suspect I actually picked them up from the New Exchange – the Lea brothers have never been very scrupulous about hygiene.'

'Do either of you know who murdered Chetwynd?' asked Turner conversationally. 'I hate to admit it, but my enquiries have reached something of an impasse.'

'Greene did it,' replied Tryan, sounding surprised that he should need to ask. 'The Earl told me so, when I met him in the cathedral the other day. I confess I was astounded: Greene does not seem the type.'

Turner's expression was pained. 'He only *thinks* Greene is guilty – he has no evidence to prove it.'

Tryan's face was a mask of horror. 'No evidence? But he informed me of Greene's culpability as though it were beyond the shadow of a doubt. Are you saying poor Greene might be innocent?'

'I always thought the Earl was decent,' said Hargrave, when Turner nodded. 'But this makes me realise he is no different from the rest of Court – a liar and a scoundrel. We should never have invited the King back, because it is His Majesty's fault that there are so many villains in White Hall.'

'Stop,' said Turner sharply. 'I lost part of my ear serving the old king, and I am loyal to the new one. So keep your treasonous thoughts to yourself, if you do not mind.'

Hargrave regarded him disparagingly. 'You were wounded for the Royalist cause, but what has the King done for you in return? Made you his Master of Horse? A Groom of the Bedchamber? No! You are palmed off on an earl who goes around making false accusations against hapless clerks.'

'Gentlemen, please!' said Tryan hastily, raising his hand to prevent the colonel from responding. 'How many more times must you argue about politics before you realise you will never agree?'

Hargrave shot Turner a conciliatory smile. 'My apologies, friend. I mean no offence.'

Turner inclined his head graciously. 'And no offence is taken. However, we *do* agree on one thing: it is too cold to meet out here again. Next time, we shall discuss our business in a tavern. I know tobacco smoke makes you sneeze, Tryan, but the chill cannot be healthy, either.'

'There will be smoke galore when you join the dean of St Paul's for those Twelfth Night ceremonies in the cathedral,' Hargrave said to Tryan, as he helped his colleague to his feet and they prepared to take their leave. 'I told you not to accept the invitation.'

'I could never refuse a clergyman,' said Tryan reproachfully. 'He might think me irreligious.'

When Turner sauntered off in the opposite direction, Chaloner caught up with him, making him jump by grabbing his shoulder. He was disappointed that his eavesdropping had revealed nothing useful, but it was as good a time as any to exchange meaningless pleasantries with the colonel – Turner was not the only one who wanted to lull his rival into a false sense of security.

'God's blood, man!' exclaimed Turner. 'Watch who you sneak up on! I might have run you through before I realised who you were.'

Chaloner showed him the dagger in his hand. 'You would not have succeeded.'

Turner smiled. 'I am glad. I have no desire to harm a fellow veteran of the wars, although His Portliness tells me we fought on opposite sides. Have you found the missing statue yet?'

'Not yet,' replied Chaloner, wondering what else the Earl had said about him.

Turner grimaced. 'Between you and me, I have reached

a dead end with it. I got Lady Muskerry to escort me to the Shield Gallery again – she took me once before, when the damned thing was still there – and I stared at the empty plinth for ages, but no solutions occurred to me. I am fed up with espionage, and plan to take tonight off, to renew my energies by visiting a few ladies. Bess Gold will appreciate my company, if I can get rid of that tiresome Neale.'

'He does pay her close attention,' agreed Chaloner.

Turner looked disgusted. 'Damned fortune-hunter! She will be a widow soon, and Neale intends to marry her. Gold must be worried, to see his successor champ so hard at the bit. Still, if Gold is murdered, we shall know where to look for a suspect. Even I will be able to solve that one.'

'Will you visit Meg the laundress tonight, too?'

'There is nothing I would like more, but I hunted high and low for her today, and could not find the merest trace of her. She seems to have disappeared off the face of the Earth. I hope you are wrong, and the clerk-killer has *not* drowned her. She has the best thighs in London.'

Chaloner watched him swagger away, doffing his hat to various ladies, all of whom he seemed to know by name. Where was Meg? The spy rubbed his chin thoughtfully when it occurred to him that it was odd that Turner should think she had been drowned, rather than poisoned, stabbed or strangled. Did he know something he was unwilling to share with his rival investigator?

It was Hell's turn to sell food, and delicious smells wafted from it when Chaloner opened the door. His intention was to find a corner where he could keep his own company, but Bulteel was at a table near the fire and waved him over. The secretary was with a dozen other White Hall officials, although he was not really one of them: they formed a tight, comradely cluster, and he was slightly outside it. Williamson's clerk Swaddell was part of the throng, though. He was holding forth in an affable manner, although his dark, restless eyes were everywhere, missing nothing.

'It is noisy this evening,' Chaloner remarked to Bulteel, surprised to find the place so busy.

Bulteel nodded. 'Because it is Tuesday – Sausage Night. People travel for miles to be here.'

Looking around, Chaloner realised it was true, and was amazed to see so many familiar faces. Greene was at a crowded table near the back. He was talking to Gold – or rather he was bawling in Gold's ear, and Gold was frowning to say he could not hear. So hard was Gold concentrating that he was oblivious to the flirtatious activities of his wife and Neale at the other end of the bench. Chaloner watched Greene, and wondered why the Earl should think him a killer. There was something pitiful and limp about him, and the spy was sure he did not have the resolve to hand men cups of poison, watch them die, then calmly hide the evidence. Besides, he had alibis for two of the crimes.

He turned his attention to Neale, who had hated Chetwynd for passing an unfavourable verdict. Did the young man's cherubic looks hide the dark visage of a killer? But then why kill Vine and Langston? As decoy victims, to ensure investigators looked elsewhere for the culprit? Neale was not stupid, so it was certainly possible that he had devised such a plan. Of course, it was equally possible that George Vine had murdered his father – and that he had killed Chetwynd and Langston to cover *his* tracks.

Also at Greene's table were the couple Hannah had pointed out that morning – Scobel's nephew, the orange-haired Will Symons, and his sickly, artistic wife Margaret. Had Williamson been telling the truth when he claimed Symons had joined the three murdered men at prayers in his uncle's house? Did he resent all he had lost at the Restoration, and was avenging himself on those who had done rather better? Symons looked tired and drawn, and he and Margaret appeared shabby and down-at-heel compared to the bright company around them.

The door opened, and the spy glanced up to see the unsavoury Lea brothers enter. They exchanged boisterous greetings with the clerks at Chaloner's table, then squeezed themselves in at the opposite end, amid laughter and general bonhomie. Then the door opened again, this time to admit the dour-faced Doling. Doling headed for a place near the window, but was so morose and unfriendly that the men already sitting there soon made excuses to leave. Bulteel muttered something about Sausage Night enticing all manner of vermin from their nests.

'You do not like Doling?' said Chaloner.

'I do not like any bitter old Roundhead who holds us responsible for his misfortunes – and Doling has gone from government official to security minion for Backwell's Bank. Incidentally, the Earl is losing patience with you over your refusal to see Greene as the killer. Turner is not so foolish as to oppose him – he tells the Earl he is right, and keeps any reservations he might have to himself.'

'How do you know he has reservations? Has he mentioned them to you?'

Bulteel looked pained. 'No – I cannot get him to tell

me anything, although I have tried my best to worm my way into his confidence. However, do not be too ready to dismiss Greene from your inventory of possible villains. He knew all three victims, and he was caught trying to sneak away from the scene of Chetwynd's murder. Of course, there are other suspects, too.'

'Who?' Chaloner was interested to know whether Bulteel's list matched his own.

'Well, the Lea brothers have expensive tastes, and wasted no time claiming Chetwynd's fortune. Meanwhile, Neale hated Chetwynd, George Vine hated his father, and Doling hates everyone. Then there are the victims' so-called friends. I saw them at John's Coffee House about a month ago, and they were all arguing furiously – Gold, Jones, Tryan and Hargrave, to name but a few.'

It was a depressingly long list, and reminded Chaloner of the enormity of the challenge he was facing. He fell silent, listening to Swaddell talk about the Spymaster's new-found passion for cockfighting. Sourly, he thought it unsurprising that a man of Williamson's brutal tempera-ment should take pleasure from such a barbaric activity.

'Fine company you keep,' he remarked acidly to Bulteel. 'Men like the Spymaster's toady.'

'Hush!' whispered Bulteel in alarm. 'Swaddell has uncannily sharp hearing. Besides, we are all just clerks in here – it is a place where we forget our differences, and enjoy easy company and good ale.'

Chaloner doubted Swaddell felt the same way, and was sure he would use such occasions to gather intelli-gence for his master. 'If you say so.'

'I do say so,' said Bulteel firmly. 'But I am glad you came tonight, because there is something I want to ask you. Will you stand as godfather to my son?'

Chaloner stared at him, certain he had misheard. 'What?'

'My boy means more to me than life itself, and I want him to have the best godfather I can procure. Will you oblige? It would make me very happy.'

Chaloner was at a loss for words, astonished to learn that Bulteel liked him well enough to extend such an offer. No one had asked him to be godfather to their children before, not even his siblings.

'But I have no money and no influence at Court,' he said, aware that Bulteel was waiting for an answer. 'I will not be able to help him in the way he will need.'

'You will be able to teach him decency, though,' said Bulteel quietly. 'And there are not many who can do that in this place. I would rather have him virtuous and poor, than rich and rakish.'

'You may not think so when he comes of age and needs a patron. I am not a good choice, Bulteel. My life is dangerous – there are not many elderly spies in London, in case you have not noticed.'

'But you are more careful than others, more experienced,' persisted Bulteel stubbornly. He laid a thin hand on Chaloner's arm. 'And do not refuse me without giving my request proper consideration. Come to share our Twelfth Night dinner, and see the baby. Then decide.'

Chaloner smiled back. 'Thank you. It is an honour. My hesitation only stems from my own shortcomings – the fear of letting you down.'

'You will not,' stated Bulteel firmly. 'Not ever.'

The sausages arrived on huge platters, one for each table. They comprised tubes of seasoned meat stuffed into the intestines of a sheep, and the combination of gristle and rubbery guts provided a serious challenge for even the sharpest of teeth. Once scullions had slapped down the plates, the noise level dropped dramatically as people struggled to chew. The sausages were criminally hot, and more than one man was obliged to cool a burned mouth with gulps of ale. Chaloner was just wondering how Bulteel had managed to finish his before anyone else, when his teeth were by far the worst in the tavern, when the door opened and a vast figure materialised. It was Jones, the obese Yeoman of the Household Kitchen who had closed the New Exchange.

'Am I too late?' he cried, dismayed. 'Buckingham delayed me on a matter concerning the Lord of Misrule, and was unsympathetic when I told him I did not want to miss Sausage Night in Hell.'

Voices assured him that there was plenty left, although no one seemed keen on him joining their particular group. Men spread out along to benches to repel him, reluctant to share with someone who was likely to eat too much. Eventually, he arrived at Greene's table. Because most people were now chewing rather than talking, Chaloner found he was able to hear what was said.

'Make room for a little one,' ordered Jones, sliding his vast posterior along the wood with grim determination. Protesting men were crushed into each other, and Greene dropped off the far end.

'I will sit elsewhere, then,' said the clerk in his gloomy, resigned voice as he picked himself up. 'It was draughty there, in any case, and breezes around the ankles predispose a man to gout.'

'I never gloat,' declared Gold, looking up from his repast in surprise. 'It is bad manners.'

'That does not stop people from doing it, though,' said

Symons, shooting Jones a look that could only be described as resentful. 'Folk gloat over me all the time.'

'My Nicky has good cause to gloat,' said Bess, running her fingers down her husband's sleeve. She looked particularly ovine that evening, because her dress was the colour of undyed wool, and she had dressed her white-blonde hair into tight little ringlets. 'He has earned lots of lovely money, and tells me I will be a wealthy widow one day.'

'Do not wish it too soon,' said Margaret softly. She looked at her husband, and her thin, wan face softened into a smile. 'If you have a good man, I recommend you keep him alive for as long as possible.'

'There are plenty of fish on the beach,' countered Bess carelessly. 'I shall find another one I like.'

'Fish in the *sea*,' corrected Neale, to remind her that he was at her side. She had been flirting with Peters – French pox notwithstanding – and Neale did not like it.

'I adore tea,' said Gold, flinging a couple of sausages at his rivals, ostensibly to ensure they did not miss out now the gluttonous Jones had arrived, but one fell in Neale's lap, leaving a greasy stain that necessitated the use of a damp cloth. Chaloner thought he saw the old man smirk. 'The Queen quaffs it every day, and what is good enough for Her Majesty is good enough for me.'

'I have never had any,' said Greene miserably. 'No one has ever offered it to me. Although there was once a man from Barrington who—'

'The Earl of Clarendon?' demanded Gold aggressively. 'I did not take tea with him today, and anyone who claims otherwise is a damned liar!'

Chaloner regarded him in surprise. Was it the ritual of tea-drinking that had elicited such a vehement denial, or was it his conference with the Earl? The spy was just trying to imagine why Gold should object to people knowing about either, when he became aware that Swaddell was also listening to the exchange – he was nodding at Bulteel's monologue about a batch of bad ink, but Chaloner was too experienced an eavesdropper himself to be deceived.

But Swaddell was wasting his time, and so was Chaloner. The rest of the discussion around Greene's table could not have been more innocuous, and the most contentious subject raised was whether the sausage casings came from a sheep or a pig.

Eventually, Gold stood to leave, hauling Bess away from Peters and Neale, who were vying for her attention in a way that was beginning to be uncouth. It was the cue for a general exodus as, food eaten, people began to make their farewells. Outside, patrons waited for each other – crime was rife in Westminster, and only a fool walked there alone after dark. They began to wander away in groups of three or four, while a gaggle of about two dozen headed along St Margaret's Lane. Chaloner followed when he saw Greene, Jones and the Symons couple were among the throng, with Gold, Bess, Peters and Neale trailing along behind them.

When the company reached Old Palace Yard, most began to climb into the hackney carriages that were for hire there, but Greene and his companions lingered, talking in low voices. Chaloner eased closer, but stopped short of the alley he had been aiming for when he saw someone was already in it. It was Swaddell, listening intently to what was being said.

'. . . not meet for a while,' Jones was suggesting. 'It is the most sensible thing to do.'

'I disagree,' said Symons. He sounded almost tearful.

'Now is the time we need it most, and I refuse to countenance what you are proposing. It is wrong!'

'My husband has a point,' said Margaret quietly. 'You should not allow—'

'It is only for a while,' interrupted Jones. 'Just until this blows over. Then we can resume, if you feel we must, although I believe it is unnecessary. What do you say, Gold?'

But Gold's eyes were on Bess. 'Did Peters just put his hand on my wife's rump?'

'On her hips,' corrected Greene. He stiffened suddenly when Swaddell's foot clinked against something metal that had been left in the alley. 'What was that? Is someone spying on us?'

Jones drew his sword, and so did Gold. Swaddell promptly beat a hasty retreat down the lane. His footsteps rang out, and Jones immediately waddled off in pursuit. Meanwhile, Gold gave a howl of outrage, and dived after Peters with his naked blade. Suddenly, he was not a feeble old man, and Symons, Neale and Greene were hard-pressed to restrain him. Peters ran for his life, Bess pouted, and Gold's friends bundled him into a coach before he could do any harm.

'Impertinent dog!' Gold roared. 'Get in the coach, friends. We shall hunt him down like vermin!'

'What about Jones?' asked Greene uneasily. 'He heard someone in that lane, so we should wait for him to come back and tell us—'

'It was probably a rat,' said Bess, shooting her husband a sulky look. 'There are a lot of them about at this time of night. Great big ones that spoil a person's fun.'

'Symons! Greene! Neale! Get in the carriage,' yelled Gold, still incensed. 'You, too, Margaret. I am sure *you*

180

know how to deal with Court cockerels. When we catch him, you shall chop off his—'

'I am taking Margaret home,' interrupted Symons. 'It is too cold for her to be out. But Jones knows how to look after himself, and if he did hear someone, it will only be a beggar. He can deal with one of those without our help. He was once a soldier, after all, and distinguished himself during the wars.'

'You are probably right,' said Greene, although he did not look happy. 'He should be able to manage a beggar.'

Chaloner watched them leave, then turned towards the alley, which he knew led to a wharf – a gloomy, ramshackle dock that was used by the fuel barges that came from Newcastle. He moved cautiously, ready to hide in the shadows when Jones and Swaddell came back – which he knew they would, because it was a dead end, and there was nowhere else for them to go.

But they did not return, and eventually he arrived at the pier. It was lit by a lantern on a pole, which swung gently in the breeze. He wondered why anyone would bother to illuminate the place, when fuel was expensive and the lamp itself was likely to be stolen by anyone who knew it was there. He looked around, and saw the wharf was bounded on three sides by high walls, while the fourth was open to the river. There were no doorways, alcoves or sheds, and the only way out was the way he had come. Thus he was astonished to find no sign of Swaddell or Jones.

Puzzled, he walked to the wharf's edge, and looked into the water. The only place for them to have gone was the river, but it was bitterly cold and he did not see either eager to take a dip. Yet he could see something bobbing there, and was about to kneel for a closer look, when he heard a sound. He spun around, and saw half a dozen figures converging on him from the alley. All carried swords.

'Never meddle in matters that do not concern you,' said one softly. Like his companions, he wore a wide-brimmed hat that concealed his face, and he moved with an easy confidence. Chaloner knew, beyond the shadow of a doubt, that they were members of the train-band from the Painted Chamber.

'What matters?' he demanded, drawing his own weapon as they advanced on him.

'Murders and rings,' replied the leader in the same low whisper. 'It will be the end of you.'

His sudden attack forced Chaloner to jerk away, and his colleagues lunged forward before the spy had regained his balance. Chaloner fought hard, using every trick he had ever learned, but they were experienced warriors, and although he managed to score hits on two, he was no match for so many. He was going to be killed unless he did something fast. He drove them all back with a wild, undisciplined swipe that took them off guard, then turned and leapt into the river.

Water roared in Chaloner's ears, and seaweed brushed his face as he sank. The tide was in, and the river ran deep and agonisingly cold. His downward progress ended when his feet sank into a layer of silt. It clung to his legs, and he could not kick himself free. He struggled violently, but the mud was reluctant to relinquish its prize. It was not long before his lungs began to burn from the lack of air, but just when he thought he might drown, one foot came free, followed by the other. He propelled himself upwards, emerging next to one of the wharf's thick wooden struts. A light above his head told him that his attackers had removed the lamp from its post, and were using it to search. He paddled under the pier and tried to control his ragged breathing, aware that he was a sitting duck if they had guns. Suddenly, a great, whale-like form surfaced next to him in a violent explosion of spray.

'Help!' Jones gurgled in a voice that was full of water. 'Help me!'

Instinctively, Chaloner moved towards him, intending to direct one of the flailing arms towards the weed-encrusted pillar, so Jones could keep himself afloat. But the fat man grabbed him, and they both went under. Chaloner tried to punch his way free, but Jones's grip was made powerful by terror. The spy's feet touched the river's sticky bottom a second time, and he was aware of mud sucking at his ankles.

He fought harder, and felt his knuckles graze against something hard: it was one of the pier's legs. He grasped it, and used it as an anchor to tear free of Jones's panicked clutch. The move seemed to weaken Jones, enabling Chaloner to spin him around, to prevent him from grabbing his rescuer a second time, then kick upwards, keeping a firm grip on the man's collar as he did so. It was like dragging lead, and there was a moment when he thought Jones was just going to be too heavy for him – that he would have to let him go. But then he glimpsed light shimmering down through the black water, and seeing it so close gave him the strength he needed to swim the last few feet.

'There!' snapped the train-band leader, as spy and Yeoman of the Household Kitchen surfaced at last and took great gasps of sweet air. 'Shoot him!'

183

Immediately, something zipped past Chaloner's face. They were using a crossbow, presumably because the discharge of firearms on government property would attract unwanted attention.

'Save me!' screamed Jones, oblivious to the danger. 'I cannot swim!'

'Quickly,' hissed the leader. 'Make an end of this before someone hears.'

Jones was thrashing furiously, creating great spumes of foam that made it difficult for Chaloner to see. He lunged for the spy again, but missed. Was this what had happened to Swaddell? He had been ensnared by a drowning man, and had been unable to escape? Suddenly, there was a crack as the crossbow was fired again, audible even over Jones's noisy splashes. Then the fat man was gone. Silence reigned, broken only by the sound of lapping water and the distant barking of dogs.

'It is done,' said the leader eventually. 'You two stay here, on the chance that he escaped and is waiting to climb out. The rest can go home.'

While he talked, Chaloner forced himself underwater, groping in the darkness for Jones, but he soon gave up. The tide had just turned, and the current had almost certainly swept the hapless Yeoman downstream. It tugged at Chaloner as he clung to the pillar, and made the seaweed undulate. He saw a ladder leading up to the quay, but he had lost his sword, and he could not fight the two remaining guards without it. He realised he was going to be trapped in the water until either they left or the tide went out, allowing him to walk to safety along the beach.

He knew he should concentrate on devising a solution to his predicament before the icy river sucked away his life, but his mind kept wandering. He thought about the fact that the pier was provided with a lantern, even though coal was unlikely to be landed at night. *Ergo*, it was used to light some other activity. Then he considered the trainband. They had appeared very suddenly, and were determined that he would not escape. Of course, the leader had mentioned the ring, which meant they knew it was him they had met in the Painted Chamber. And after he had jumped, they had referred to him in the singular. He could only assume that they thought he and Jones were one and the same – that the feeble lamplight had not allowed them to see two men in the water. Three, counting Swaddell.

His grip on the pillar was starting to loosen, and he was aware of a warm lethargy taking hold of him. It would be easy to close his eyes and sleep, but something deep within him stirred, and he felt his resolve begin to strengthen. He could not climb this ladder, but there were other public stairs. All he had to do was let the current take him. He would have to ensure it did not sweep him to the middle of the river, because then he would never escape its frigid embrace, but he could stay near the edge. Without giving himself too much time to think, he took a deep breath, let himself slide under the water, and gave himself to the pull of the tide.

He stayed submerged until his lungs felt as though they would burst, then surfaced with a gasp that sounded deafening to his ears. He glanced behind him and saw the lamp, but he had been carried beyond the point where the soldiers would be able to see him. He was safe – or as safe as he could be in a fast-flowing river in the dark. He could see the Westminster Stairs a short distance ahead, so he struck out towards them. But the current was too strong, and carried him past.

He swallowed water, and began to cough. Then he saw lights ahead, and knew they were his last chance, because the cold was now seriously weakening him. Mustering every last ounce of his strength, he swam towards them. Were they closer, or was he imagining it? He closed his eyes, summoning reserves of energy he did not know he had. Then he felt something solid beneath his feet, and could hear the lap of waves on stone. Struggling to make his limbs obey, he clambered out of the water, and collapsed in an exhausted heap at the top of a flight of steps. He was not sure how long he lay there, but it was enough to bring back the warm lethargy. He forced himself to stand.

He knew, from the number of lights, that he was at White Hall, but he was not on the main pier. His heart sank when he realised he had fetched up on the Privy Stairs, which led to the rooms used by the King and his Queen. Now what? he thought. He was not inclined to jump back in the river and aim for a more suitable landing spot, so he supposed he would just have creep through the royal apartments without being seen. It would not be easy, but his cold-numbed mind was failing to come up with any other options. With water squelching in his boots and weighing down his clothes, he picked the lock at the top of the stairs, and let himself inside.

It was a relief to be out of the wind, although the little chamber in which he found himself could hardly be described as cosy. He climbed more steps, then picked a second lock, to find himself in the Shield Gallery with its long line of statues, ghostly sentinels faintly illuminated by the light of the lamps in the alley outside. Happier now he was in familiar territory, he stumbled along it, aiming for the door that led down to the lane. From there, he could reach the Earl's offices, where there would be a fire – the Earl liked his rooms permanently heated on account of his gout, and kept blankets to hand for the same reason. Chaloner would thaw himself out, then go home. Or better still, visit Hannah, who would know how to banish the aching chill from his bones.

He had almost reached the end of what felt like an inordinately long chamber, when a door opened. Instinctively, he dodged towards a statue, aiming to hide behind it, but his legs would not do what his brain suggested, and he did not move nearly quickly enough. Light from a powerful lantern flooded the chamber, and there was nothing he could do to prevent himself from being caught.

Chaloner waited for the yell of outrage that would see soldiers racing to arrest him. Then he would be bundled into some dismal cell until the Earl rescued him, which was likely to be hours, given that they would be loath to disturb the great man until morning. Chaloner hated gaols with a passion, and did not relish being locked up when he was soaking wet. Briefly, he considered fighting his way free, but he was in no condition to do battle with anyone – especially without his sword.

'Thomas?' came a voice full of astonishment. 'Is that you?'

Chaloner blinked against the light. It had sounded like Hannah. Footsteps clattered towards him.

'It is your lover?' The question was asked in heavily accented English, and Chaloner was horrified to recognise Queen Katherine. He tried to bow, but was too cold to move properly, and Her Majesty was lucky he did not topple into her arms.

Soldiers immediately seized him, and he resigned himself to a night in prison. He hoped the Earl would not arrive too late for work the following day – or worse, decline to take responsibility for him, because it would be an easy way to dispense with his services. Being caught near the Queen's bedroom was not something that could easily be explained away, and he saw he was in very grave trouble.

'My *friend*,' corrected Hannah primly. 'The Earl charged him to investigate the King's missing statue, which I imagine is what he is doing here.'

'Let him go,' ordered the Queen, addressing the guards. She was not long recovered from a serious illness, and her small, delicate face was far too pale.

'That would be unwise, ma'am,' said the captain, stepping forward to prevent his men from doing as they were bid. He pointed at the water that had gathered in a pool around Chaloner's feet. 'I do not believe he is investigating the theft, because he would have used the door from the lane, like any normal person. But he came via the river, suggesting he plans to steal something himself.'

'Steal what?' demanded Hannah archly, gesturing at the large paintings and heavy sculptures that surrounded them. 'Some of these? How? By swimming off with them? He is not a fish!'

'My husband's statue was stole at night,' said the Queen slowly. 'It is recreating the crime.'

'Of course!' cried Hannah in delight. 'How exciting! We shall help you, Tom – Her Majesty cannot sleep, and this will be much more fun than walking up and down until she wears herself out.'

'She should not be here anyway,' muttered the captain. 'The roof was damaged in the last storm, and it has not been mended yet. It may not be safe.'

188

'I play this game,' said the Queen, smiling. 'But not here. Too cold. My chambers has fire.'

With open unease, the soldiers escorted her, Hannah and Chaloner to the room in question. Once there, they did not close the door all the way, but stayed to peer through the crack, ready to dash in the moment there was any hint of a threat. Chaloner was pleased they took their duties seriously, because the Queen was the one person at Court whom he thought was worth protecting.

Hannah handed him a blanket, and the Queen gestured he was to sit opposite her, by the fire. As he warmed up, he began to shiver, almost uncontrollably, and it was difficult to keep his teeth from chattering. Hannah knelt between them, poking the flames with a stick, while the Queen studied him with dark, sad eyes. Politely, he waited for one of them to speak first.

'We shall use my language,' the Queen said in Portuguese. 'I do not have the opportunity very often, now the King has sent my tiring women home. Incidentally, I never thanked you for travelling to Spain on my behalf this summer, or for sending me all those intelligence reports. My brother the king was able to make good use of them, and the result is a cessation of hostilities.'

'But an uneasy one, ma'am,' replied Chaloner in the same tongue. He saw Hannah regarding him in astonishment, and supposed he had never mentioned his skill with languages. 'It will not last.'

'I pray that it will,' said the Queen, crossing herself. 'Now, what were you really doing in the Shield Gallery? It was nothing to do with locating my husband's bust, because there are no clues to be gained from studying an empty room, especially so long after the original theft.

189

And your explanation does not account for the fact that you are soaking wet.'

Chaloner was not sure how much to tell her. 'The investigation led to a skirmish that saw me fall in the river,' he replied, not about to admit that the 'investigation' he had been following had nothing to do with statues.

'Well, I am glad you are safe, because there is something I want you to do for me.'

Chaloner experienced a lurch of alarm. The Earl had almost dismissed him the last time he had accepted a commission from the Queen, and had made it clear that he would not countenance it happening again. Of course, that was before the Earl had appointed a rival investigator. Perhaps this time he would not care.

The Queen interpreted his silence as acquiescence. 'My marriage contract stipulated that I was to have forty thousand pounds a year for my household expenses. The money was deposited in the Treasury, and I was to apply for funds as and when I needed them. I am not extravagant, like . . . like other women. My expenditure for this year amounts to less than four thousand pounds.'

It was common knowledge that 'other women' – namely Lady Castlemaine – could go through that in a single night. Chaloner waited for her to continue, wishing he could stop shivering. Meanwhile, Hannah frowned; the rapidly spoken Portuguese was excluding her from the discussion.

'I should have thirty-six thousand pounds left, but when I requested funds to travel to Bath – to partake of the healing waters – I was told it had all gone.'

'What happened to it, ma'am?' Thirty-six thousand pounds was a staggering sum to go adrift.

'That is what you must find out. All I know is that the money has disappeared, and I am prevented from accessing the waters that may help me conceive.'

She looked away, and Chaloner's heart went out to her. He recalled the rumour that she was barren, and could not do the one thing the King demanded of her: provide him with an heir.

'This is important to me,' she continued softly. 'I want you to find out what happened to my money, and then I want enough of it back to let me go to Bath.'

'I am not qualified for this task, ma'am,' said Chaloner gently. 'You need someone to go through records and other expenditures. If your lost money was in silver pieces, then I might be able to hunt it down for you, but this is a crime of embezzlement, and will only be solved by someone skilled at interpreting complex accounts.'

The Queen's eyes brimmed with tears. 'No one wants to help me. I have appealed to the King and the bishops, but they all hate me, because they think I am infertile. But when I offer to immerse myself in stinking water – a desperate remedy, but I will do anything to fulfil my duty – the government refuses to advance me the money. What am I to do?'

Chaloner felt wretched. 'I would help if I could, but it would be like asking Hannah to translate the Bible into Portuguese. She does not have the necessary skills, despite her devotion to you. It would be beyond her – and identifying accounting errors is beyond me.'

The Queen wiped her eyes, and attempted a smile. 'And I imagine you are busy with the missing statue anyway, and have no time to devote to a trifling matter like mine. You served me well once, and I suppose it is unreasonable to expect more. But I can do something for you.'

'You can?' Chaloner hoped it was not arresting him for declining to do as he was told.

'Your master would like to find the bust, but Williamson is determined to reach it first. However, the Earl has always been kind to me, whereas Williamson is cold and aloof. I want the Earl to win this race, so I shall tell you something that might bring about a result that will please me.'

'No,' said Chaloner firmly. 'Williamson is vindictive and ruthless, and you should not risk his wrath for any reason. Keep your secret – do not become involved in his affairs.'

'No one else would decline free information on the grounds that it puts me in danger,' said the Queen bitterly. 'But I am going to tell you anyway. I trust you not to tell Williamson the source.'

Chaloner wished he was more alert, because he could not think of a way to stop her. He opened his mouth, but she raised her hand to prevent him from speaking.

'My servants gossip in front of me, in the mistaken belief that I cannot understand a word they say. I overheard one mention that my husband's statue has been offered for sale to a clerk called Greene.'

Chaloner gaped at her, forgetting himself as his thoughts whirled. 'Who offered to sell it to him?'

'They did not seem to know. Then they went on to say that he declined in horror, and so the same proposal was made to a woman named Margaret Symons. Will this information help you?'

'It might,' said Chaloner gratefully. 'Thank you.'

Chapter 6

When the Queen declared she was tired at last, and was ready to try sleeping again, Hannah was released from her duties. Chaloner escorted her home, and she invited him to stay. He accepted partly because her house was always warm, but mostly because he felt a need for human companionship. The Queen's painful loneliness had upset him, and he wished there was something he could do to help her.

'What was she telling you?' asked Hannah, when they lay in bed a little later. He was still chilled to the bone, and was holding her more tightly than was comfortable for either of them. 'I had no idea you could speak Portuguese.'

Her profile was etched against the light from the fire, and Chaloner gazed at it. 'I had no idea you could not. How can you serve her, if you do not know her native tongue?'

'She is Queen of *England*, Tom. She must forget her old language and customs, and embrace the new ones – unless she wants people accusing her of spurning things English. And she has enough hatred directed at her already, for not getting pregnant. She cannot afford more.'

'Poor Katherine,' said Chaloner softly, his heart going out to her.

'Did you hear her household allowance has gone missing?' asked Hannah, full of indignation. 'She tried to impress everyone with her frugality, using a mere fraction of what she is entitled to take, only to find someone has stolen the rest. I suspect Lady Castlemaine, personally. She probably ran up some gambling debts, and the Queen's thirty-six thousand pounds was used to pay them off.'

'You may be right.'

'Did she ask you to find it? She has been petitioning everyone she knows, although she has had scant success so far. You see, until she produces an heir she has no influence, so no one is willing to waste his time by doing her favours.'

Chaloner knew that was the way things worked at Court, but was disgusted nonetheless.

'Did you refuse her, too?' asked Hannah. She saw his apologetic expression and grimaced. 'That is a pity, because I have been extolling your virtues to her, although she tells me you have already been to Spain on her account. Speaking of which, why have you never mentioned it to me? It means we served the same mistress, which I would have been interested to hear.'

'It was—' He was about to dismiss the escapade as of no consequence, loath as always to discuss his work, but then remembered his new resolution not to drive her away with half-answers and lies, as he had previous lovers. He did not want Hannah to despair of him at quite such an early stage in their relationship. But he found he could not summon the words to explain what had happened to him. It had been one of the worst experiences of his life, and he did not know how to begin telling another person about it.

'It was what?' asked Hannah, peering at him in the firelight. 'Hot? Full of flies? Beautiful? Dull?'

'Not dull.'

Hannah sighed. 'Well, that is a start, I suppose. Spain is not dull. The Duke of Buckingham told me the opposite, and said he would not return there for a kingdom.'

'You discussed Spain with Buckingham?' Chaloner sat up, not liking the notion of such a reprobate engaging any decent woman in conversation.

'I like him,' said Hannah with a shrug. 'He is kind, amusing and generous.'

'*Buckingham?*' asked Chaloner, wondering whether there was more than one of them.

'I know he has a reputation for being a libertine, but he has his virtues, too.'

Chaloner lay back down and hauled up the bedclothes. He was still freezing, and was beginning to think he would never be warm again. 'Next you will be telling me that Lady Castlemaine is chaste.'

She gave him a jab with her elbow that was rather too hard to be playful. 'You have friends whom *I* consider dubious. Barbara Chiffinch for example. She is a sharp-tongued shrew and I have never liked her, yet you and she rub along famously together. She is old enough to be your mother.'

'She gives me information that . . . helps my work. And she does remind me of my mother, now you mention it. She would have liked you. My mother, I mean. She played the viol.'

Hannah laughed. 'You are trying your best to overcome your natural reluctance to discuss private matters, and the result is a jumble of statements that are supposed to be revealing, but that make no sense whatsoever. Your mother would have liked me because she played the viol? Really, Tom!'

Chaloner was not sure what to say. 'I cannot talk about Spain. It was too . . . I did not think I would be coming back.'

She regarded him silently for a moment, then patted his chest. 'Then we shall talk about other things instead. Do you know Sir Nicholas Gold? I like him *very* much, although his wife is a dolt. And I deplore that vulture Neale, waiting to step in and claim her the moment she becomes a widow.'

'Is Gold ill, then? Set to die?'

'He is just old, although I suspect he is not as frail as he looks. But Bess is not yet twenty, and will certainly outlive him. She will be one of the richest widows in London when he dies, and Neale wants to ensure he will be the one to snare her. Of course, he has his work cut out for him, because she is inclined to be flighty, and Colonel Turner is just one of many who compete for her affections.'

'Is that so?' Chaloner was more than happy to let her talk.

'He gave her a crucifix, and regards her as more special than the others. Except for Meg, perhaps.'

'Meg the laundress?' asked Chaloner. She nodded, and he continued. 'He was supposed to meet her for a tryst on Saturday night, but she never arrived. Have you seen her since then?'

'No, why? Do you think something untoward has

happened to her? She is a dreadful harlot – I have seen her smuggling lovers in and out of White Hall myself, on her laundry cart.'

Chaloner stared at her. 'Do you think Turner found out she was unfaithful, and dispatched her?'

'That would make him a hypocrite, would it not? Killing her for infidelity when he is in the process of sampling every woman at Court? But men are mysterious creatures, and who can fathom the illogical mush that passes as their minds? If he did kill her, I would be appalled, but not surprised.'

Chaloner continued to stare. 'Has Turner . . . Did he . . . Have *you* . . .'

'Has he made a pass at me? And did I succumb? Is that what you cannot bring yourself to say aloud? You should credit me with more taste, Tom – Turner is a rake.'

'But a likeable one.' He listened to the fire settling in the hearth, then said, 'You pointed Margaret Symons out to me earlier. You said your husband commissioned a sculpture from her.'

Hannah pointed to a delicate figurine that stood near the window. 'She made us that statue of Venus, which is as fine a piece as any in the royal collections. Why do you ask?'

'I heard she liked art.' Chaloner was aware that he was being less than honest, but he hesitated to confide in her for reasons he did not quite understand. It had been obvious the Queen had not told Hannah that Margaret had been invited to buy the stolen bust. Why was that? Did she not trust her with the information? Or had she just not considered the rumour worth the effort of translating into English? He closed his eyes tiredly. What was wrong with him? Why could he not give straightforward answers to the woman with whom he was trying to develop a meaningful bond?

'You are holding back on me again,' said Hannah, almost as if she had read his thoughts. She was smiling, but the mischievous gleam was gone from her eyes: he had hurt her feelings. 'But no matter. You can answer some questions to make up for it. Why *were* you swimming in the Thames in the depths of winter?'

'I became involved in a skirmish and fell in.'

'You are no raconteur, are you?' she said drily. 'It was probably an exciting adventure, but you make it sound boring. However, it was my quick thinking with the excuse about the statue that saved you from being arrested, so you owe me some explanation.'

Briefly, Chaloner wondered why she should want to know, but he was exhausted, his defences were down and he was weary of being suspicious of everyone he met. So he struggled to supply an explanation she would accept, but that would not reveal too much about his business.

'I was following two men down an alley. Then a pack of soldiers appeared, and jumping in the river was the only way to escape. Next time, I will settle for being skewered, because I am still freezing.' Hannah wrapped her arms around him, although it did nothing to dispel the chill that had settled deep in his bones. He hunted for something to say that would let him change the subject without sounding as though that was what he was doing. 'Bulteel asked to me to be godfather to his son. Should I do it?'

Hannah was silent for so long that he thought she was angry with him for not elaborating on the Thames incident. By the time she replied, he had dozed off, and her voice roused him from a dream in which he was swimming across the Painted Chamber while the Queen informed everyone that the waters would make him pregnant.

'You should decline. There is something about Bulteel that is not entirely nice, although I have heard he is the most honest clerk in White Hall. I know it is an expression of friendship on his part, but I do not think you should accept it.'

'Why not? You have just said he is honest.'

'Is that all you require in a friend? Honesty? What about sharing interests? Music, for example.'

'He does not like music,' acknowledged Chaloner. He recalled his surprise when Bulteel had informed him of the fact. He had thought everyone liked music.

'Think carefully before you give him your answer. Do not dwell on what you might be able to do for the child, but on what such an association means for *you*. You are a good man, Tom. It would be unfortunate if Bulteel dragged you down.'

It was late morning when Chaloner woke the next day, and Hannah was gone. He supposed it was her revenge on him for doing it to her, and was concerned that he had not heard anything. He was normally a light sleeper, and anyone moving about in a room where he was resting usually had him snapping into immediate wakefulness. But he did not feel well that day, and it took considerable effort to dress and walk to Westminster. His lame leg hurt from being so cold the night before, and his head ached miserably.

So, what *had* happened the previous night? He had been so intent on surviving the encounter, that he had given little thought to what it meant. Jones and Swaddell were dead – at least he assumed they were – but what had caused them to go into the river in the first place? Had Jones caught Swaddell and killed him for eavesdropping? Or had they fought and fallen in together?

And why had the soldiers so suddenly appeared? Had they been tracking him, aware that he had escaped alive from the Painted Chamber? He did not think so, because he was sure he would have noticed. So, that meant their appearance was coincidence – he had just happened to blunder into an area they considered their own. Did they think he was dead now, because they assumed Jones, shot and drowned, was him? It did not seem likely that they would believe a man would leap in the river to escape them one moment, then call for their help the next. But in his experience, professional warriors were an unimaginative lot, and it was entirely possible they had not stopped to question what they thought they had seen. So did that mean he was safe for a while? He did not feel safe, and decided the first thing he needed to do that day was to visit the wharf, to see what might be learned from the place where he was attacked.

The alley was a dark, sinister slit, as uninviting in daylight as it had been during the night. He was less than a quarter of the way down it when the hairs on the back of his neck stood up – something was moving in the shadows ahead. He gaped in astonishment when he saw it was the guards who had been detailed to watch the pier the previous evening – they were still at their posts, and he realised he had underestimated their determination to be thorough. Suspecting there would be nothing to see anyway – and he had no sword to let him fight his way past them to look – he left.

Wiseman was in Old Palace Yard, resplendent in a tall red hat and a new scarlet cloak that swirled about him as he walked. Both made him more imposing than ever, which Chaloner supposed was the point – the surgeon liked to be noticed. His self-imposed exercise regime obviously suited him, too, because he radiated vitality and fitness. His skin was clear, his eyes bright and although he had been walking at a rapid clip, he was not even slightly breathless. Uneasily, Chaloner saw he would be a formidable opponent in a fight, and sincerely hoped he would never decide to change sides.

'You look as though you need my services,' Wiseman began imperiously. 'You are limping and—'

'No,' said Chaloner firmly. He would have to be at death's door before he let a surgeon loose on him. 'I do not suppose you have heard rumours about a train-band lurking around here, have you?'

'I have, as a matter of fact. A gang of soldiers has taken up residence – and their presence has virtually eradicated petty crime. Why? Was it they who attacked you the other night?'

'Who controls them? Pays their wages, buys their equipment?'

'No one knows. The obvious candidate is Williamson, although he has never cared about policing the area in the past. However, I can tell you that they are secretive and deadly, and that you should be wary of tackling them. Personally, I do not believe they are kindly Robin Hoods, ousting felons to protect the innocent – I think they crushed rival villains because it suited them to do so.'

'Do you know anything else about them?'

'Nothing – except that the charnel house currently

houses the corpses of two men and a woman who were rather vocal in demanding to know who these men are. *Ergo*, I recommend you keep your questions to yourself, because I do not want to anatomise your cadaver just yet.'

Chaloner was grateful for the warning, because investigating the train-band was exactly how he had planned to spend the morning. So, because he did not feel equal to tackling dangerous men again that day, he concentrated instead on trying to learn more about Chetwynd, Vine and Langston from the men who had worked with them. He also made discreet enquiries about ruby rings, but was disheartened to learn that they were rather common, and that at least a dozen people had a penchant for them. Wearily, he followed as many leads as he could, eliminating suspects where possible, but his efforts led nowhere. Occasionally, an opening occurred when he could ask obliquely about the train-band, but he found that either people had no idea what he was talking about or, like Wiseman, they had heard that discussing the mysterious soldiers was bad for the health and declined to do it.

He met Turner, who was surrounded by women as usual. The colonel broke away from them to inform the spy that he had just conducted a search of Greene's Westminster office, and had discovered a large supply of brandywine hidden beneath a window.

'Perhaps he was drunk when he murdered his colleagues, and does not remember anything,' he suggested. 'He denied the stuff was his, but who knows whether he is telling the truth? Meg is still missing, by the way, and I spent ages hunting for her this morning. But, look! There is Lady Muskerry. I must pay my respects.'

And he was gone before Chaloner could tell him that Surgeon Wiseman thought brandywine had disguised the taste of the poison fed to the three dead clerks.

The spy had wanted to talk to Greene anyway, to question him about Scobel's prayer meetings and being offered the stolen statue. He went in search of him, and found him still in his office. The clerk was pale and drawn, and had lost weight over the past few days. He sat at his desk sorting documents into piles. Chaloner watched, bemused. If he had been in Greene's position, he would have been out looking for evidence that would exonerate him. Or, if he was guilty, then he would be halfway to France. But here was Greene doing paperwork.

'I put my trust in God,' replied the clerk, when Chaloner questioned him about it. 'Besides, I have alibis for the murders of Vine and Langston, and that should be enough to deliver me from the Earl.'

'It should,' agreed Chaloner. 'But he does not believe Lady Castlemaine saw Langston alive when you were with your vicar in Wapping, and nor does he trust me when I say you were home when Vine died. We shall have to find something else to prove your innocence.'

'Then God will provide it,' said Greene quietly. 'Or not. What will be will be, and there is nothing you or I can do to change the outcome.'

His passivity was incomprehensible to Chaloner. He shook his head, and began to ask his questions. 'I understand you once attended prayer meetings with the three dead men in the house of a man called Scobel, and that you later met them in John's Coffee House in Covent Garden. Is it true?'

Greene sighed. 'Yes. I have already told you about the coffee-house gatherings. However, the prayer meetings were years ago, and it did not occur to me that they might be relevant. I went to a morality play with them all once, before the old king was beheaded, and we sometimes attended the same church during the wars. Do you want to know all that, too?'

Chaloner had no idea what he needed to solve the case, and addressed another matter. 'I am told you were invited to buy a certain piece of art recently.'

Greene looked pained. 'Yes, but I refused to have anything to do with it. Will the Earl hold that against me now? It was hardly my fault someone approached me with a suspicious offer.'

'Who was this someone?'

'A go-between, who declined to tell me the identity of his master. I followed him, to see where he went, but I am no spy and I lost him within moments. And do you know why I was singled out for this honour? Because it is common knowledge that your Earl hates me, and this villain said I could use the statue to buy back his favour.'

'I do not understand.'

'In return for virtually everything I own, I would get the bust. Then I could take it to the Earl, and offer it up in exchange for a pardon for these murders. But I am innocent – I should not need a pardon. And I would not buy a stolen masterpiece anyway, especially one that belongs to the King.'

Chaloner felt sorry for him. Greene was right: it was not his fault the thief had picked him. 'Did you notice anything that may allow me to trace this go-between?'

Greene thought hard. 'He kept his face hidden with one of those plague masks, but his dirty clothes told me he was a labourer. He was taller than the average man, and a bit more broad.'

Chaloner grimaced: the description was worse than useless. He was disappointed, because it was another dead end. He turned to the last of the subjects he wanted to air.

'Turner said you keep a supply of brandywine hidden here. Why?'

'It is not mine – I dislike the stuff. I have no idea who hid it here, but I assure you it was not me.'

'Brandywine was used to disguise the poison that killed Chetwynd, Vine and Langston,' said Chaloner to see what sort of reaction that particular snippet of information would provoke.

Greene's jaw dropped in horror. 'No! Will you tell the Earl? He will have me hanged for certain!'

Chaloner inspected the place where the drink had been found, but a number of people had already told him the office was never locked, so Greene was right in his insistent claims that anyone could have put it there.

'Who dislikes you enough to want you accused of murder?' Chaloner asked, sitting back on his heels. He was disgusted with himself – he should have discovered the cache when he first explored the room. Was it a sign that Turner was a better investigator?

'No one,' replied Greene, white-faced. 'I am not popular, but I am not hated, either. I imagine most people barely know I exist.'

Chaloner suspected he was right, and left him reciting prayers for deliverance from his troubles, although his dull, resigned expression suggested he did not think there was much chance of his petitions being granted.

By the evening, Chaloner had asked so many questions but received so few useful answers in return, that he was tired and dispirited, and knew he would be sullen company for Hannah. He decided to go home instead, but she met him as he was leaving White Hall. Buckingham was with her, intent on escorting her home – he claimed he was concerned for her safety, but Chaloner saw the lustful gleam in the man's eye. The Duke was loath to relinquish her at first, but then Lady Castlemaine appeared, and he excused himself with unseemly haste. Hannah did not see the reason for his abrupt departure, and extolled his virtues all the way home.

'He is a wonderful man,' she said dreamily, unlocking her front door. 'His wife is a lucky lady.'

Chaloner did not think so. 'Can you cook?' he asked, mostly to change the subject before they argued, but also because he was hungry and experienced a sudden hankering for cakes.

She regarded him in surprise. 'I can manage a pickled ling pie, but not much else. Why?'

Chaloner shuddered at the notion of pickled fish in pastry, and supposed he would have either to maintain his friendship with Bulteel or forgo cakes in future – unless he learned how to bake them himself.

Chaloner awoke the next morning feeling rested and much more optimistic about his investigations. While Hannah freshened his shirt and lace collar with a hot iron, he went to buy bread for their breakfast. He also purchased the latest newsbook, although *The Newes* contained no reports from foreign correspondents, nothing of domestic affairs, and its editorial was a rant on the poor workmanship to be found in viols made anywhere other than England.

'That is untrue,' he said to Hannah, pacing back and

forth as he read. 'There are excellent viol makers in Florence.'

'We shall have some nice music on Twelfth Night eve,' said Hannah. 'I forgot to tell you last night, but Sir Nicholas Gold has invited me to dine at his home, and said I might bring a guest. Bess sings and he plays the trumpet. With your viol and my flageolet, we shall have a lovely time.'

The combination of instruments was worthy of a wince as far as Chaloner was concerned, but he was not often asked out, so any opportunity to play his viol was to be seized with alacrity. Of course, Gold was deaf, which did not bode well for the quality of the music, but the spy was willing to take the chance. When Hannah had finished primping his clothes, he walked to Lincoln's Inn, to ask what Thurloe recalled of Scobel's death – and whether the ex-Spymaster knew anything about prayer meetings with men who had later become Royalist clerks.

When he arrived, Thurloe was at a meeting of the 'benchers' – the Inn's ruling body. They were a verbose crowd, who felt cheated unless they had repeated them-selves at least three times before any decision was reached. Used to the trim efficiency of the Commonwealth, Thurloe found the occasions a chore, and was more than happy to use a visitor as an excuse to escape.

'I checked Doling's claims about Chetwynd with several informants,' the ex-Spymaster said, walking with Chaloner in the Inn's garden. Winter should have rendered it bleak and unwelcoming, but the benchers had hired professional landscapers to design an arbour that was a delight in any season. Gravel paths prevented expensive footwear from getting wet, while evergreen shrubs supplied year-long colour.

'What did they say?' asked Chaloner, hoping Thurloe knew what he was doing when he removed three bright blue pills from a tin and ate them.

'That Hargrave *did* bribe Chetwynd by gifting him a cottage. I am disappointed, because I respected Chetwynd. He hid his corruption well.'

'And Neale's accusations?'

Thurloe's expression was pained. 'There is irrefutable evidence that Neale gave Chetwynd a substantial sum to secure himself a favourable verdict. Unfortunately for Neale, his brother paid more. Chetwynd accepted both bribes, then refused Neale a refund. And what could Neale do? Nothing! Bribing government officials is a criminal offence, so he could hardly make a formal complaint. No wonder he is bitter.'

'Meanwhile, Vine was in the habit of blackmailing people. He was not a virtuous man, either.'

Thurloe shook his head sadly. 'I had no idea. However, I heard there was some great falling out between him and Gold not long ago. I shall endeavour to find out what it was about.'

'Please do not,' begged Chaloner. 'It is unwise for prominent Parliamentarians to explore the embarrassing failings of Royalists.'

Thurloe shot him a reproachful glance. 'I am quite capable of asking my questions anonymously. You need not fear for me.'

'But I *do* fear for you. You are an excellent master of intelligence, able to see patterns in half-formed facts, but that is not the same as going out to gather the data yourself.'

'You underestimate my skills,' said Thurloe coolly. 'Why do you think I am still alive, when, as Cromwell's chief advisor, my head should be on a pole outside Westminster Hall, next to his? I do not suppose you have noticed whether it is still there, have you? I cannot bring myself to look.'

'It is impossible to tell. But please do not meddle in—'

'I shall do as I think fit,' interrupted Thurloe, uncharacteristically sharp. 'And I shall be gone from London soon, anyway, so if I make a mistake, it will be forgotten by the time I return. These affairs never last long in people's memories.'

'I disagree. Royalists seem to have extremely long memories, and they are bitter and vengeful. Ask Doling and Symons. They lost everything when—'

'That is different,' snapped Thurloe impatiently. He changed the subject, to prevent a quarrel. 'Why did you come to see me? Just for confirmation of Chetwynd's corruption?'

Chaloner was tempted to say yes, because he did not want his friend involved any further, but Thurloe fixed him with steely blue eyes, and the spy knew better than to lie to him.

'Scobel,' he said reluctantly. 'He hosted meetings – for prayers, apparently – which all three murder victims attended. So did a number of other people, including Greene, Jones, Doling, Symons, Gold, the Lea brothers, Hargrave and another merchant called Tryan.'

'But Scobel died three years ago,' said Thurloe doubtfully. 'How can these gatherings be important now? Moreover, there are probably other connections between these men, too – such as a shared interest in poetry, or a liking for pigeons. Are you sure these meetings are relevant?'

'No, but it is a lead I feel compelled to follow. According

to Williamson, they convened in John's Coffee House after Scobel died, so it looks as though the men involved thought the assemblies were important. What can you tell me about him?'

Thurloe shrugged. 'Not much. He was clerk to both Houses of Parliament during Cromwell's reign, and did well for himself. He died of a sharpness of the blood. Very nasty.'

Chaloner had never heard of this particular affliction, but was not surprised Thurloe had, obsessed as he was by matters of health. 'What is a sharpness of the blood?'

'It entails aching pains, shortness of breath and violent shuddering. As I said, very nasty.'

'Poison can produce those symptoms,' said Chaloner, wondering what was going on. 'It will not be the same toxin that killed Chetwynd, Vine and Langston, because that was caustic, but there are plenty of others. I will confirm it with Wiseman, but I am sure I am right.'

'Why would anyone kill Scobel?' asked Thurloe. 'He spoke out against the Court when it first arrived in London – saw it as a nest of corruption and vice – but no one took issue with him, because everyone knew he was right. His was not a lone voice – many people felt the same. Most still do.'

'What else can you tell me about him?'

'That his nephew, Will Symons, inherited all his worldly goods. Symons lost his job at the Restoration, and if it had not been for Scobel's bequest, he and his sculptress wife would have starved. Scobel was also friends with Doling and the Lea brothers, but dropped his association with the latter when they turned Royalist – you may recall they were the only clerks to retain their positions.'

'So, there are four suspects for Scobel's murder: Symons and Margaret may have wanted to inherit his money sooner rather than later, and the Leas might have objected to him rejecting their friendship.'

Thurloe wagged a finger. 'You are jumping ahead of yourself. First, Scobel may not have been murdered – people do die of natural causes, you know, even in London. And second, even if he was unlawfully killed, there is no evidence with which to accuse anyone.'

'Those four are the ones with the motives.'

'The ones with the motives that you know about,' corrected Thurloe. 'The Leas are sly and self-serving, but I cannot see them having the courage to kill, while Symons was very fond of his uncle. Scobel was a lovely man.'

'Another saint,' said Chaloner with a weary sigh.

Thurloe glanced sharply at him. 'He *was* a saint, and I consider it an honour to have known him. He had a dog, which sat by his grave and howled for two weeks solid. It would probably be howling still, if someone had not shot it. Did you never meet him?'

Chaloner shook his head. 'But you mentioned him in your letters. Often.'

Thurloe had been an avid correspondent, and the friendship between him and his spy had developed almost entirely through letters for the first decade of their acquaintance. He had written at length about all aspects of his life, his work, his friends and his family.

'Yes, I would have done,' he said sadly. 'I liked him enormously. And he *did* hold prayer meetings in his home, although I cannot tell you who joined him. He invited me, but I prefer to meditate in private, so I never went. He gave thanks, mostly.'

'Gave thanks for what?'

'For everything – his success at work, his nephew, his friends, the food on his table. He sincerely believed thanking God was a vital duty, and encouraged others to do the same. You look sceptical, Tom, but you must remember that he was rather more pious than you. He went to church because he loved God, not because he did not want to be seen as a nonconformist.'

'What did he look like?' asked Chaloner, ignoring the dig. Religion was something about which they would never agree – Thurloe was a committed Puritan, while Chaloner was not sure what he believed.

'A short, fat fellow, bald as an egg, who sported a huge black beard. He refused to conceal his pate with wigs, because he said God had made him hairless and he would never try to improve on His handiwork. Unfortunately, it made him look as though his head was on upside down.'

'Was he tedious about religion, then? Overly zealous?'

'No. People attended his meetings because they wanted to be there, not because he forced them to go – he was devout, not a fanatic. Incidentally, he foretold the exact time of his death. Did I write to you about that? It was eerie, and folk talked about it for weeks afterwards.'

'Not that I remember.'

'He had a premonition that he would breathe his last on a specific date, and although we all told him that sort of thing was for God to decide, he transpired to be right. He *did* die on the day he predicted.'

'Do you think he knew someone was going to poison him?'

'It did not occur to me at the time,' replied Thurloe soberly, 'but now I find myself wondering.'

*

It was mid-morning by the time Chaloner left Lincoln's Inn. He stopped to collect his spare sword on the way to White Hall, feeling naked and vulnerable without one. Most men wore them as fashion accessories, and rarely, if ever, drew them in earnest, but Chaloner's were working weapons, and he kept both oiled and well honed.

His cat padded to greet him when he opened the door, and he spent a few moments petting it. He was unimpressed when he found dead mice secreted in several different places, but the cat purred when he glared at it, and the show of affection made it impossible to stay angry. With a sigh of resignation, he went to the window and lobbed the bodies into the street below. He aimed for, and was pleased when he hit, the sign of the Golden Lion opposite. He ducked back inside when one of the furry corpses bounced off the board and ricocheted into a passing carriage. The coach bore the Muskerry coat of arms, and Chaloner was almost certain it was Colonel Turner who reached across the female occupant and chivalrously removed the dead rodent from her lap.

'The man is insatiable,' he remarked to the cat, then stopped abruptly. Haddon talked to his dogs as though they were people, and the spy considered it a peculiar habit. He was appalled by the notion that he might be in the process of acquiring it himself – that people might think *he* was short of a few wits.

He left his garret and began to walk towards White Hall, mentally reviewing the connections that linked his three victims. All were government officials, their corpses had been stripped of valuables, they had argued with the Earl, they had attended Scobel's prayer meetings *before* the Restoration, and they had met in John's Coffee House *after*. Common acquaintances included Gold, Bess, Neale,

Greene, Hargrave, Tryan, Scobel, Symons, Margaret, the Lea brothers, Doling and Jones. There would be others, too, but these were the names that kept cropping up, and which seemed worth exploring.

He turned his thoughts to the missing statue. Thanks to the Queen, he now had one lead to follow – two people had been invited to buy it, which suggested the thief was getting desperate. Chaloner rubbed his chin. He knew the culprit's reason for approaching Greene, but why Margaret? She was a sculptress, but not nearly wealthy enough to buy stolen art and keep it hidden for the rest of her life.

So, there were several things he needed to do: ask Margaret about the statue, question her husband about his uncle's prayer meetings, and visit John's Coffee House to learn more about the nature of the gatherings that took place there. There was also the ruby ring, but he had asked virtually everyone in White Hall about that, and had met with no success. He decided he had taken that as far as he could, and although he would bear it in mind, he would not waste any more time on it.

He walked through White Hall's main gate un-challenged, because the guards were busy watching Lady Castlemaine wave a handgun at someone in the middle of the Palace Court. They were not the only ones taking the opportunity to gawk: the yard was fringed with spectators. Careful to keep a wall between him and the weapon, Chaloner went to where Haddon was standing with his dogs.

'She says she will blow out Turner's brains unless he gives her what she wants,' explained Haddon, seeing the spy's questioning look. 'I dare not move from here, lest she discharges her dag, and hits one of my darlings by mistake.'

Chaloner saw that the object of the Lady's hostility was indeed the colonel, who looked particularly dashing that morning in a dark green suit, red ear-string and a hat with a vast white feather that trailed down his back. When Chaloner glanced across the yard, he saw the Muskerry coach, and wondered whether the sight of Turner in company with Muskerry's wife was the cause of the Lady's wrath.

'What does she want?' he asked. 'His romantic services? She does not need to threaten him with death for those – I suspect they are available to anyone who asks. As long as she has teeth.'

'The Lady has plenty of those, believe me. But she is after his hat. The feather belonged to an ostrich, apparently, and is the only one of its kind in London.'

'How does he come to have it, then?' asked Chaloner curiously. A man who took work as a spy was unlikely to have money to squander on fripperies, especially if he had twenty-eight children to support.

'Bess Gold won it from Buckingham at cards, and I imagine it went from her to Turner in the usual manner,' replied Haddon, a little primly. 'The Lady is extremely jealous, and so is making a fuss.'

'It was a gift, madam,' Turner was saying softly. He smiled at her, a sweet, gentle expression that saw the gun wobble in her hands. 'And thus an object to be cherished. You would not respect me, were I to hand tokens of affection away to anyone who asks for them.'

He touched a brooch on his coat and treated her to a knowing wink, indicating Bess was not the only one who paid him the compliment of extravagant presents.

Chaloner looked at the many baubles that adorned the colonel's neck, wrists and fingers, and wondered how he managed to remember what came from whom. He shook his head in grudging admiration: the gifts Turner received were far more costly than the tawdry trinkets – like the coloured-glass crucifix – he dispensed to his swooning ladies.

'But this is *me*,' declared the Lady. Her face was bright with righteous indignation, and there was real malice in her eyes. Chaloner would not have wanted to be Turner at that moment. 'I shall have whatever I like. And I like that hat, so if you do not give it to me, I shall shoot you and take it from your corpse. I shall need it if I am to go riding this afternoon. The hat I mean.'

'For God's sake, woman!' bawled Buckingham, who was watching the proceedings from the safety of the gate. 'Use another headpiece. You have enough of the damned things.'

'One never has enough,' snapped Lady Castlemaine, rounding on him. He dived behind the door in alarm when the gun came around with her. 'Of anything.'

Chaloner laughed softly, and Haddon turned to him in surprise. 'You think this is funny? We may be about to see murder committed in front of our very eyes!'

'The gun is not primed. She could not kill anyone, even if she wanted to, and Turner knows it. That is why he is not unduly concerned.'

'Be reasonable,' came Buckingham's voice from behind the gate. 'Let the captain keep his hat.'

'Colonel,' corrected Turner, rather grandly.

'Really?' asked Buckingham. He did not sound convinced. 'Under whom did you serve?'

'Dear Lady,' said Turner, ignoring him and focussing

his attention on the King's fuming mistress. 'Perhaps you will allow me to accompany you to your chambers, where we can discuss this matter in private. I have something I warrant you will like a *lot* more than a hat.'

It was an offer no woman with teeth could decline, and the Lady permitted Turner to take the weapon and push it into his belt. Then she strutted across the court-yard on his arm, head in the air and exuding a sense of wounded dignity. Seeing the crisis had been averted, people began to go about their business again. One was Greene, who slouched towards the Banqueting Hall with all the cheer of a man going to his execution. As their paths crossed, Lady Castlemaine nodded a greeting to him. Chaloner frowned. The Lady had a reputation for slighting people she did not like, while she considered servants so far beneath her that she never acknowledged their presence. And yet she had favoured the unprepos-sessing clerk from Westminster with a salutation. Why? Was it because the Earl had taken against him, and any victim of the Earl's was a friend of hers?

'Turner will be trapped with her for hours now,' Haddon was saying. 'She has a voracious appetite for pretty men. And that works to our advantage, because as long as he frolics, he cannot investigate.'

'*Our* advantage?'

'I have five pounds wagered that you will catch the killer before he does,' explained Haddon, bending to pet his dogs. 'The Earl believes Turner will win. However, his preference for the colonel has nothing to do with who is the better investigator – it is based on the fact that Turner is beginning to accept Greene as the killer.'

'And the Earl wants a solution that proves *him* right,' said Chaloner gloomily.

'No – he wants a solution that is fast,' corrected Haddon. 'But I would rather the enquiry took longer and the real culprit is exposed, so I am backing you.'

'Then let us hope it does not cost you five pounds.'

'It had better not, because I cannot afford it. Incidentally, you will find the Earl in a sour mood this morning, because Brodrick played his Turkish-harem trick last night – our master arrived to find his chambers bedecked in billowing silk and forty harlots. So, let us hope the Lord of Misrule moves to other targets now. Come along, precious ones. We do not want your little paws chilled on these nasty cold stones.'

Chaloner had only taken a few steps towards the Earl's offices when he spotted Barbara Chiffinch. He went to speak to her, wondering what it was about her that Hannah so disliked. Barbara was married to Will Chiffinch, a courtier of infamous depravity who was said to procure women for the King when his mistresses were unavailable. Barbara was not depraved, though, and led a perfectly respectable life. It was said that she and her husband had not shared the same bed in forty years.

'I have been looking for you, Tom,' she said as he approached. She was a comfortable, matronly woman with grey hair, an ample bosom and hazel eyes that glowed with intelligence. 'Turner tells me your Earl has employed him as a spy. Have you been dismissed, then?'

'Not yet – but I will be, if I cannot catch this clerk-killer and locate the King's stolen statue.'

Barbara was thoughtful. 'There is all manner of gossip about both, but no one has any idea who the culprits might be. However, I can tell you one place to go for clues: to Temperance North.'

Chaloner was puzzled. Temperance – a friend of his – ran a stylish 'gentlemen's club' in Hercules' Pillars Alley, near The Strand. 'What does she have to do with dead clerks and missing art?'

'My husband patronises her establishment, and he was waxing lyrical about an evening he enjoyed there a couple of weeks ago, when he said something odd. Apparently, Temperance had quizzed him about Bernini – the sculptor who carved the bust. She had never expressed an interest in art before, and he was delighted with himself for feeding her a lot of bogus information.'

'I do not understand.'

'He told her Bernini is a Swedish hermaphrodite, whose hobbies include rope-dancing and keeping hedgehogs. But that is beside the point – which is, what prompted her questions in the first place?'

'Perhaps she heard a Bernini masterpiece was stolen from the King,' suggested Chaloner, still not sure what she was trying to tell him.

'But this discussion occurred *before* the statue went missing. Of course, it may mean nothing, but that is for you to decide. Have you heard the news this morning? Poor Edward Jones is drowned.'

'What about Williamson's clerk, Swaddell?' asked Chaloner. 'Is he drowned, too?'

Barbara raised her eyebrows in surprise. 'No, but he is missing. I shall not ask whether you had anything to do with it, but I hope not, for your sake. Williamson is livid.'

'Why? What does Swaddell do that his other spies cannot?'

Barbara's eyebrows went up a second time. 'You do not know? Swaddell is his assassin, the man who wields

219

knives in dark alleys. Williamson is by the gate, look, interrogating people about the fellow's whereabouts as they pass. He is speaking to Lady Muskerry at the moment, although he should not expect sensible answers from her, poor lamb. She is far too silly.'

Chaloner watched the Spymaster grab the woman by the arm and shake her. She looked frightened, and when she started to cry, he was tempted to intervene. Barbara stopped him.

'Your gallantry is commendable but misguided. Do not worry about Muskerry – she will have forgotten Williamson exists by the time she reaches the other side of the courtyard, while he will not appreciate being berated for ungentlemanly behaviour. Damn it! Now he is coming towards us.'

'I hoped I might run into you, Chaloner,' said Williamson unpleasantly. 'Swaddell is missing, and I am told you and he dined together in Hell on Tuesday – the night he disappeared. Where is he?'

Chaloner shrugged. 'I really have no idea,' he answered truthfully. 'And we did not dine together – we sat at opposite ends of a table, separated by a dozen clerks.'

'I have been told that, too,' said Williamson. 'By Neale and Matthias Lea, who were also there.'

It was not a good idea to make free with the names of informants, and once again, Chaloner was unimpressed by the man's approach to intelligencing; his loose tongue was likely to see people killed. But he said nothing, and it was Barbara who broke the uncomfortable silence that followed.

'Swaddell is a loathsome fellow, and he will not be missed by decent folk.'

'He will be missed by me,' declared Williamson.

'Point proven,' said Barbara coldly. 'But Thomas has an alibi for Tuesday, so leave him alone.'

Williamson sneered at her. 'What alibi? You have not entertained a man in your bed for decades, so do not expect me to believe you made an exception for *him*.'

Chaloner regarded him with dislike. 'Such vile remarks are hardly appropriate for a government minister to—'

But Barbara put a hand on his shoulder, to stop him. 'His alibi is the Queen, if you must know,' she said, addressing the angry Spymaster. 'She told me she met him on a matter of business. Ask her, if you do not believe me.'

Williamson regarded her icily. 'Oh, I shall. But he cannot have been with her all night, and it takes but a moment to slip a dagger in a man's gizzard and toss his body in the river – and I should know.'

'Then perhaps your time would be better spent questioning your own people,' said Barbara tartly. 'You hire some very disreputable villains, so ask *them* what has happened to your assassin.'

Williamson ignored her, and fixed Chaloner with glittering eyes. 'Bring me Swaddell, or I shall assume the obvious – that you killed him.'

'But I barely knew him,' objected Chaloner indignantly. 'Why would I mean him harm?'

'So you say,' snarled Williamson. 'Find him, or suffer the consequences.'

'Take no notice,' said Barbara, as the Spymaster stalked away to interrogate someone else. 'He is so agitated by Swaddell's disappearance that he is threatening anyone and everyone. Of course, he is not so much afraid that Swaddell is dead, as that he might still be alive.'

'What do you mean?'

'I mean that Swaddell is said to have undertaken some very dark tasks for our Spymaster, tasks that Williamson will not want revealed to anyone else. He will relax when Swaddell's corpse appears.'

'And if it does not?'

'Then I suspect the uncertainty will render him unpredictable and dangerous.'

Edward Jones, courtier and gourmand, was in the charnel house, awaiting collection by his next of kin. Unfortunately, his next of kin took one look at the mammoth cadaver and decided it could not be safely toted around the city, and asked Kersey to care for it until the funeral. Surgeon Wiseman offered to reduce the scale of the problem, but his services were rejected in no uncertain terms – Jones had sons, and although they had not been close to their father, they still took their filial duties seriously.

The mortuary boasted two reception rooms, as well as the long, low hall in which bodies were stored. One was Kersey's office, and the other was a surprisingly tastefully decorated chamber used for explaining formalities to grieving relatives. Kersey introduced Jones's sons to Chaloner in the latter, when the spy said he had come to convey the Lord Chancellor's sympathy to them. They had just arrived from the country, and it did not take many minutes for Chaloner to ascertain that they knew virtually nothing about their father or his life in London.

'I would not accept the post of Yeoman of the Household Kitchen for a kingdom,' said one with a shudder. 'I hope to God it is not hereditary, because I could never live in White Hall.'

'It is full of rogues,' agreed the other, blithely oblivious to the fact that such an opinion might be construed as treason. 'All they do is eat and enjoy orgies. Father was never so fat when he lived at home.'

'I see,' said Chaloner, although he suspected that such a monstrous girth was a lot more than three years in the making, so the Royalist government could not be held solely responsible for its development. 'I do not suppose you know if he owned any rings, do you?'

'Oh, lots,' replied the eldest carelessly. 'Most are in a box at home, but Mr Kersey has just given us the ones he was wearing when he died. He had a particular penchant for green ones.'

'They were all green,' added his brother. 'Except for the ones that were red.'

'His sons cannot be suspects for pushing him in the river,' said Kersey to Chaloner, after he had shown them out. He started to gnaw on something that looked like a stick of dried meat, although the spy could not bring himself to study it too closely. 'They told me earlier that they have recently inherited a fortune from an uncle, which means they have no need to pick off a father.'

'You think Jones was unlawfully killed?' asked Chaloner uncomfortably. He hoped no one had seen him follow Jones – and Swaddell – into the alley, because fending off accusations of murder would not be easy. He did not think anyone had been watching him, but could not be certain.

Kersey jerked a thumb towards the dark recesses of his odoriferous hall, where Surgeon Wiseman could be seen hovering over a corpse like a massive red bird of prey. 'That is the kind of question you should be asking him. Were you telling the truth when you said the Earl sent you to offer Jones's kin his condolences? Because if you are actually here to admire the corpse, it will cost you threepence.'

Chaloner handed over the coins, which Kersey added to a bulging purse. Then the spy walked with soft-footed tread to stand behind Wiseman.

'Damn it, Chaloner!' cried Wiseman, whipping around in alarm at the cough so close to his shoulder. 'That is not a wise thing to do when a fellow is holding a scalpel.'

Chaloner looked in distaste at what the surgeon was doing. 'I thought permission to make off with parts of Jones had been denied.'

'This is too good an opportunity to miss.' Wiseman's voice dropped to a conspiratorial whisper. 'Look at the size of him! I would be negligent to let him go to his grave without furthering medical research, and I am doing no harm.'

'I am not sure Jones would agree,' said Chaloner uneasily. He thought, but did not say that Wiseman represented no mean specimen himself, with his height and muscular bulk. 'You will be hanged if you are caught chopping up courtiers without the permission of their relatives. There are those who think anatomy is a dark art, and you take too much pleasure in it.'

'There is nothing wrong with enjoying the pursuit of knowledge,' declared Wiseman, lending a grandeur to his actions Chaloner felt was undeserved. 'Would you like to see something interesting?'

'Not if it has anything to do with his innards.'

'He drowned.' The surgeon leaned on Jones's chest and pushed down, pointing to the foam that began to ooze from the corpse's mouth. 'You only ever get that when the lungs are waterlogged. And they are only waterlogged if a man is trying to breathe underwater.'

'He was found in the river. Of course he drowned.'

'But he did not go easily.' Wiseman picked up a hand. 'Look at these broken nails – he fought violently to save himself. And there is a hole in his shoulder that may have been made by a crossbow bolt.'

Chaloner already knew all this. 'I imagine most men who fall in the Thames struggle.'

Wiseman gave his superior smile. 'But here is the interesting part: he could have struggled all he liked and still never clawed his way to safety. He sank like a stone. And do you want to know why?'

He unbuttoned Jones's coat and pulled aside the left-hand flap to reveal a number of pockets in the lining. Each pocket held a purse, and each purse contained ten gold pieces. Then the surgeon opened the right-hand flap, and repeated the process until a mound of bright discs lay on the table.

'Is this interesting enough for you?' he smirked.

Chaloner picked up a coin and weighed it in his hand. It was heavy, and he imagined it was worth a significant amount of money. 'It is unexpected,' he said, in something of an understatement.

The surgeon chuckled. 'Then what about this?'

Jones was wearing a vest under his coat, and Chaloner gaped when Wiseman revealed a second lair of hidden pockets. He went to lock the door, not liking the notion that someone might come in and find them with such vast riches, then joined the search for more. There were secret pouches in Jones's breeches, boots, the sash that held his sword, and even in the lace at his throat and wrists.

'I am surprised he could move,' Chaloner said when they had finished. 'No wonder he was so heavy when I . . . No wonder he sank.'

'No wonder indeed. How much do you think it is worth?'

Chaloner shrugged. 'Thousands of pounds. What are you going to do with it?'

'Me?' Wiseman was alarmed. 'I want no part of it! I wager anything you like that he did not come by this legally, or he would not have felt compelled to carry it about on his person. It is lucky you happened by, because I was in a quandary regarding what to do.'

'You would not confide in Kersey? You must have some kind of understanding with him, because I doubt anyone else would let you stay in here unattended, knowing what you are likely to do.'

'He gives me access to interesting corpses, and I invite him to dine at Chyrurgeons' Hall on occasion – as you know, the Company of Barber-Surgeons puts on some very sumptuous feasts. That is the nature of our arrangement. However, he is not a man I would approach for advice about large sums of money.'

'Well, this belongs to Jones's sons, just like the jewellery that was removed from his corpse.'

'Only if he acquired it honestly, which I seriously doubt. Besides, it would be unkind to foist this kind of fortune on those hapless bumpkins – it is likely to see them killed.'

'Then I will give it to Bulteel to look after until we can identify its rightful owner. He has safe places for treasure, and can be trusted not to steal it – which cannot be said for many clerks at White Hall. Of course, I will have to ask him not to mention it to Williamson.'

'Yes, we do not want *him* near it,' agreed Wiseman. 'He is an avaricious devil, and fearfully dishonest. It is hard to see him as a fellow intellectual.'

Chaloner looked around, and his eye lit on a pile of sacks – roughly made bags used for storing a corpse's personal effects. He took one and began loading the gold into it. 'Have you heard of anyone else being washed up by the river today? Swaddell is missing, and Williamson wants me to find him.'

'I usually look at what the river spits out – I am always alert for decent specimens – but there was no Swaddell. Of course, Father Thames does not always relinquish his catches immediately. It might be weeks before Swaddell appears – if ever. What makes you think he drowned?'

'He and Jones ate in the same cookhouse on Tuesday,' replied Chaloner vaguely.

'Perhaps Swaddell knew how Jones padded out his already-rotund figure,' suggested Wiseman. 'I would not put it past the little weasel. Now *there* is a corpse I would not touch with a bargepole. Who knows what might come slithering out once you had it open.'

It was an unsettling image, and told Chaloner that he had had enough of the surgeon's company for one day. He left him to his illicit anatomising, and lugged the sack to the Earl's offices, praying that the material would hold and that a fortune in gold would not suddenly burst all over the street.

Bulteel was aghast when he saw what the spy wanted him to hide. 'Are you insane?' he hissed angrily. 'God alone knows how Jones laid hold of all this, but it cannot have been legitimate.'

'No one knows we have it except Wiseman. He can be trusted to say nothing.'

Bulteel nodded reluctantly. 'Yes, he can, but my office is no longer the safe haven it was, not with Haddon prowling around. He often has his dogs with him, and one might sniff out this hoard.'

'I think they prefer the scent of food to precious metals, and will be more likely to lead him to one of your wife's cakes.' Chaloner looked around hopefully. It had been a while since breakfast.

But Bulteel's attention was on the money. 'I wonder if Jones was drowned deliberately – someone knew he had a fortune and wanted him dead, so he could get it for himself.'

'If that were the case, the killer would have removed the purses before abandoning the body,' said Chaloner, choosing his words with care.

Bulteel gave a crafty smile and wagged a finger at him. 'But that assumes the culprit knew where Jones kept them, and you must admit that carrying such a vast sum in hidden pockets is an odd thing to do – you cannot blame a killer for not thinking to search the corpse. Or perhaps the weight of the gold meant Jones sank so fast that the killer had no chance to grab him.'

Chaloner did not want to discuss it. 'Do not tell Williamson about this,' he warned, watching the secretary load the money into the plinth of a statue.

Bulteel regarded him askance. 'Do you think me a lunatic? He would have it away from us before you could say "corrupt spymaster", and it would never be seen again. He has a weakness for yellow metal. And silver metal. And glittering stones of all colours. He would kill to lay his hands on this.'

Chapter 7

The Lord Chancellor was standing at the window when Chaloner entered his office, and the spy saw immediately why he was loath to be at his desk. His chamber still bore evidence of Brodrick's practical joke, with scraps of bright silk dangling from the ceiling, and lewd murals daubed on the walls. An attempt had been made to wipe them off, but the pranksters had used waterproof pigments, so some serious scrubbing would be required to remove them. The place reeked of cheap perfume, and there was a brazenly feminine undergarment entangled in the chandelier. Chaloner used his sword to hook it down.

'Thank you,' said the Earl, not looking around. 'Toss it on the fire, if you please. I cannot do it myself, because I decline to soil my hands by touching such a filthy article.'

Chaloner did as he was told, then joined him at the window. He was watching the Queen with her ladies-in-waiting in the Privy Garden, and Chaloner smiled when he saw Hannah among the throng. The Earl grimaced when Lady Castlemaine glided to join them, but not nearly as much as the Queen. Katherine had objected furiously when the King had appointed his mistress to Her Majesty's Bedchamber, but she had been no match for the combined might of husband and paramour. They had won the battle handily, and the Lady attended the Queen when she felt like it and ignored her when she had more interesting things to do.

'I heard the Lady has converted to Catholicism,' said the Earl, making it sound as though she had made a pact with the Devil. Of course, Chaloner thought grimly, he doubtless thought she had, given his narrow-minded views on religion. 'It is supposed to be a secret, but everyone knows.'

'Probably because she is going around demanding crucifixes from people. She almost had Bess Gold's the other day.'

The Earl shook his head in disgust. 'The woman has no shame.'

The ladies were skipping and cavorting happily, while the Queen moved more slowly, as if exercise was still an effort after her illness. She did not join in the laughter when Lady Castlemaine made some quip that had the other women doubled over, and Chaloner was pleased to note that Hannah did not, either. She went and slipped her arm through the Queen's, whispering something that brought a reluctant smile to the thin, wan face.

'The Lady is telling everyone that the Queen is barren,' said the Earl unhappily. 'And I fear she may be right, because the King has no trouble siring brats with other lasses. The consequences for me are dire, given that it was I who arranged the match.'

'I suppose they are, sir,' said Chaloner, thinking they were a lot more dire for the Queen.

'There is no need to agree quite so readily,' snapped the

Earl, turning to face him with a scowl. 'If you were any kind of diplomat, you would rush to offer words of comfort.'

'That would be disingenuous.'

The Earl sighed miserably. 'Yes, it would, and deceit is something of which I could never accuse you. You are later than I expected. Is it because you have been busy arresting Greene?'

Chaloner smothered his exasperation. 'I was watching his house when Vine died, sir. He cannot be the killer. Meanwhile, he was with his parish priest when Langston was dispatched. He is—'

'You do not need to be with someone when they drink the poison *you* provide,' the Earl shot back. 'You told me that yourself.'

'The victims were not fools, sir – they would not have accepted wine from some hireling in a dark hall after everyone had gone home. The killer is someone who knew them, someone Vine and Langston trusted enough to drink with, despite knowing what had happened to Chetwynd. Greene does not have the strength of character to persuade such a man to kill on his behalf.'

'But the Lady is going around telling people that he is innocent. What greater proof of his guilt can you want than that?'

Chaloner tried to make him see sense. 'I could arrest Greene, but what happens when the killer claims his next victim? Everyone will know we have made a mistake. And Greene may sue you for making damaging allegations,' he added, resorting to a financial argument to make his point.

The tactic worked, because the Earl rubbed his chin thoughtfully. 'Very well. We shall leave Greene for now, although I want you to keep an eye on him. He is one

231

of those sanctimonious Puritan types, for a start, and I dislike them. What is wrong with the Church of England, for God's sake? Why must people insist on following these bizarre sects?'

'They do as their consciences dictate – just as you remained an Anglican, even though you were in Catholic countries when you shared the King's exile.'

The Earl gaped at him. 'You overstep the mark, man! A fellow's religion is his own affair, not to be remarked upon by others.'

The Catholics, Baptists and Quakers would agree, thought Chaloner – that was their point exactly. He changed the subject before it saw him in trouble. 'I spoke to Greene about Langston, and—'

'Yes – tell me how he reacted to the news that his housemate was poisoned,' ordered the Earl.

'He seemed distressed, although I did not tell him about it. Williamson's clerk did.'

'Swaddell? Then Greene is lucky not to have had a blade shoved between his ribs. Swaddell is a deadly assassin, although he tells everyone he is a clerk. Did you hear he is missing? There is a rumour that he tried to steal Jones's purse, and they both fell in the Thames during the ensuing skirmish. It is nonsense, of course: Swaddell is an experienced killer, and would not have bungled a simple robbery.'

'Was Jones rich enough to warrant Swaddell attacking him, then?' asked Chaloner innocently.

The Earl nodded. 'Yes he was, but men do not carry their worldly goods about on their person – they invest it in banks, or they hide it in their houses. *Ergo*, Jones must have been killed by some low villain, who thinks a few pennies is worth a man's life.'

232

'Yes, sir,' said Chaloner, declining to comment.

The Earl became animated – he liked talking about money. 'Do you know a bandy-legged merchant called Tryan? He is said to have a fortune in coins and jewels, all locked up in his front parlour.'

'Swaddell may still be alive,' said Chaloner, to steer the discussion back to the missing assassin.

'Williamson certainly hopes so,' said the Earl, clearly disappointed that a chat about fiscal matters was to be cut short for something rather less interesting. 'He has come to rely on him, and they are one of a kind – ruthless, ambitious, greedy and cruel. But it will take more than a river to be rid of Swaddell, just as it will take more than a river to be rid of you.'

Chaloner looked at him sharply, wondering what was meant by the remark. Did he know about his spy's last encounter with the train-band, and was surprised to see him alive? Or was he just complimenting him on his survival skills? Chaloner had no idea, but did not appreciate being likened to a man who was 'ruthless, ambitious, greedy and cruel', regardless.

'The rumours that you argued with the three victims are spreading,' he said, after a short and slightly uncomfortable pause. 'It is—'

'Yes,' interrupted the Earl. 'I know what people are saying, because Turner came today – rather earlier than you deigned to appear – and gave me a full report. I am well aware that my disagreements with Chetwynd, Vine and Langston are common knowledge, and that the Lady is using them to make me a villain. Turner understands the urgency of the situation, and has promised me a speedy solution.'

Chaloner said nothing, but thought Lady Muskerry's

233

carriage and Lady Castlemaine's boudoir were not places *he* would have gone to investigate the murders. Perhaps Turner did intend to take the easy way out, and have Greene blamed for the crimes.

'I understand Bulteel has asked you to be his son's godfather,' said the Earl, breaking the silence that followed his remarks. 'I confess I am astonished, because I assumed *I* would be his first choice.'

'Perhaps he thought you would consider it beneath you,' suggested Chaloner.

The Earl nodded. 'Well, it would be, of course. But you should accept. You are unlikely to be in a position where you can help the brat with influence or money, but you are good with a sword.'

'You mean I should teach him how to fight?' asked Chaloner, startled. 'I doubt that is what his father has in mind. I imagine he expects him to become a clerk or a secretary.'

'Actually, I was thinking that you could use your skills to keep him alive. We shall be doing battle with the Dutch soon, while rebels and fanatics itch to overthrow the monarchy and plunge us into another civil war. You will be able to protect the boy in a way that I never could.'

Chaloner was unsettled, because he had never heard the Earl issue such a bleak forecast for their country's future before. 'You think Bulteel wants a bodyguard?'

The Earl shrugged. 'I would, if I were a new father. But time is passing, and it is already noon. Come with me to the Tennis Court.'

'The Tennis Court?' echoed Chaloner. He had not imagined the Earl fit or lithe enough to engage in that sort of activity. Tennis was strenuous.

'Not to play,' explained the Earl testily, seeing what he

was thinking. 'The King has challenged Buckingham, and I should be there to cheer him on. Everyone else will be, and I cannot have him thinking I do not care.'

'But I need to visit Symons,' objected Chaloner, loath to waste time. 'And your household guard—'

'My household guard is away practising for the King's Twelfth Night military parade,' interrupted the Earl. 'But Jones's death makes the fourth in a week, and that is a lot, even for White Hall. I do not feel safe, so you will escort me.'

'Now *you* want me for a bodyguard?' asked Chaloner, wondering whether his White Hall acquaintances thought he was good for nothing else.

The Earl nodded, unabashed. 'If you would be so kind.'

Chaloner understood exactly why the Earl was keen to have a guardian when they entered the newly refurbished Tennis Court. Word had spread that His Majesty had challenged Buckingham, and all the Court sycophants were in attendance. They included a large number of people who disliked the Earl, and when he stepped into the spectators' gallery, everyone stopped what they were doing to glare. The response was so unanimous that Chaloner half-expected the ball to freeze in mid-flight, too. His hand went to the hilt of his sword, and he glanced around apprehensively, alert for trouble.

'Do not fret, Thomas,' whispered the Earl, patting his arm. 'I am used to icy atmospheres. It is when these stares turn to more naked hostility that I shall be worried.'

Chaloner thought the hostility was more than naked enough for him, and wondered why the Earl put himself through it, especially as it did not look as though the

King cared whether he was there or not. Indeed, he had been distracted by the abrupt silence, and was scowling.

Buckingham, sulky and petulant because he was losing, mimicked the Earl's waddling gait, and the tense hush among the spectators was shattered by a burst of spiteful laughter. The King's frown deepened, but he made no attempt to defend his Lord Chancellor. He retrieved the ball and hit it, catching the Duke off-guard and forcing him to scramble.

The Earl sat on a bench, but the people nearby immediately moved away, leaving him isolated. Chaloner was acutely uncomfortable: so many enemies had crowded into the place that there would be little he could do, should they decide to attack *en masse*. He reminded himself that this was London, and that courtiers did not rush in shrieking mobs to murder their ministers. But then he remembered what had happened to the old king, and the bloody executions that had followed the new one's coronation, and was not so sure.

'I do not understand this game at all,' declared the Earl, when Chaloner came to stand behind him; at least the spy could make sure that no one stabbed him in the back. 'Do you?'

'Yes.'

The Earl swivelled around to give him a look. 'And do you care to explain it to me, or shall we just leave it that you know the rules and I do not?'

'Brodrick, Chiffinch and Jermyn are plotting something. They keep looking at you.'

'And you do not wish to be distracted by chatting to me about sport. Very well. However, bear in mind that my cousin will not harm me, although I cannot say I approve of the company he keeps. Do you think Jermyn

236

is the Lord of Misrule? Filling my office with women of ill repute is exactly the kind of low trick I would expect from that foul-minded villain.'

Chaloner did not reply. He watched the trio leave the gallery, and appear a few minutes later on the court itself. Brodrick had donned a suit designed to make him look like a chicken, and he strutted on to the playing field amid a chorus of laughter. The King pursed his lips, disliking his concentration broken by foolery, but Buckingham guffawed heartily. Chaloner, however, was more interested in Brodrick's companions, who were doing something to the box of spare balls. Whatever it was did not take long, and, as soon as they had finished, Brodrick bowed and retired from the court to a standing ovation. Then the King and Buckingham resumed their game, and for a while nothing happened.

As Chaloner scanned the spectators, alert for any hint of mischief, he saw a number of familiar faces, some of which he would have expected to see at such an occasion, and some he would not. Gold was asleep on a bench at the back, while Neale sat closer than was decorous to Bess. Bess, however, was more interested in Turner, who was surrounded by so many ladies that all that could be seen of him was the top of his hat. They were all laughing merrily, paying no attention at all to the tennis.

Not far away, Symons's ginger head could be seen with Hargrave's bald one; they sat with Tryan, Greene and several merchants. When Chaloner asked the Earl why tradesmen should be present, he was told the King had invited them – his Majesty had heard what had happened when Jones had closed the New Exchange, and had been unsettled by the fact that so many Londoners had taken against him. So, he had decided

237

to win back their affection by issuing the kind of invitation reserved for his intimates, to beguile them into thinking he considered them friends. Chaloner almost laughed: showing off the Court in all its unbridled, dissolute glory was unlikely to make anyone think restoring the monarchy was a good idea, or to make them eager to pay the taxes that funded it.

He narrowed his eyes when Greene slunk up to Symons and whispered in his ear. Symons nodded, but did not take his eyes off the game. His orange hair stood in unkempt spikes across his head, and his face was unnaturally pale; Chaloner wondered whether he was ill. Then Greene glanced up and saw the spy was watching them. The clerk immediately darted through the nearest door. Chaloner would have chased him, had he not been afraid to leave the Earl unattended. Therefore, he was surprised when Greene materialised breathlessly in the entrance behind him, and indicated that he wanted to speak.

'I have just heard about Jones,' Greene whispered, speaking softly so the Earl would not turn around and see him. 'And I wanted to tell you that I was with Gold, Bess and Neale the night he went missing. *I* did not kill him.'

'I know.'

'Does your Earl know, too? Or am I still the arch-villain in his eyes?'

'There must be some reason why he has taken against you,' said Chaloner, most of his attention still on the spectators. 'Have you argued with him? Defied him? Done something to make him think you are corrupt or debauched?'

'No! I cannot imagine why *anyone* should hate me. Or do you think your Earl is the killer, and I am just a convenient scapegoat? Perhaps Turner put the brandy-wine in my office, on his orders.'

'No,' said Chaloner firmly. 'He is not that kind of man.'

Or was he? The Earl had changed since his political rivals had tried to impeach him that summer, and had become harder and more bitter. Chaloner was no longer sure to what lengths he might go to fight the people who were so determined to see him fall from grace.

Greene forced a smile, which served to make his gloomy face more morose than ever. 'If you say so. But the afternoon is wearing on, and I have a lot to do – I take pride in my work, and want everything in order, so that if I am arrested, my successor will . . .' He trailed off miserably.

'You seem very certain this affair will end unhappily,' observed Chaloner, regarding him curiously.

Greene's expression was glum. 'Of course it will end unhappily – for me, at least. I have never been blessed with good luck, but it is God's will, so I shall not complain.' He hesitated, then grabbed Chaloner's hand, eyes glistening with tears. 'But if by some remote chance you *do* prove my innocence, it would be rather nice. Please do not give up on me yet.'

Chaloner was moved by the clerk's piteous entreaty, but there was no time to think about it, because something was happening on the court. Buckingham had taken a new ball from the box, and the spy could tell from the way he handled it that something was amiss. The Duke weighed it in his palm for a moment, then turned and lobbed it directly at the Earl, who shrieked in alarm. But Chaloner was ready. His sword was drawn and he used it like a racquet, to hit the missile as hard as he could.

There was a dull clang as the two connected, and the ball shot back the way it had come.

It did not go far. It exploded mid-air with a sharp report, releasing a cloud of pink dust. It was coloured flour. Buckingham took another ball and hurled it, rather more playfully this time, at Bess. Her jaw was hanging open so far that Chaloner wondered whether she might catch it with her teeth. It dropped into her lap, where a second crack saw her enveloped in blue powder. Gold woke with a start, and people howled with laughter when they saw the old man's shock at Bess's azure appearance. More balls followed, and although Chaloner was ready to field any that came in the Earl's direction, none did. Buckingham knew it would be a waste of a missile, and there were plenty more targets available.

'Enough, friends, enough,' said the King good-naturedly, when he felt the joke had run its course. 'The Lord of Misrule has played a clever trick, but let us return to more serious matters. What will our guests think? We promised them tennis, not japes.'

Tryan and Hargrave were smiling, but their expressions were strained, while the other merchants were openly disapproving. The King sighed, but did not seem overly concerned that there would be more damaging rumours about his Court circulating by morning. He turned his attention to the game.

'Good play, Your Majesty,' called the Earl after the first serve. It was unfortunate timing, because the King had just made a mistake, and the remark made him sound facetious. His smile was fixed as he muttered to Chaloner, 'I hate this game. It is all rushing about in sweaty shirts, like peasants.'

After a while, the Queen arrived, and her reception

was almost as chilly as the one that had been afforded the Earl. She maintained her composure, though, nodding greetings to people, even when they barely acknowledged her. No one offered her a seat, and it was left to Barbara Chiffinch to scowl at her husband until he obliged; he did so with ill grace, and ignored the Queen's shy murmur of thanks.

'Why does the King permit such low manners, sir?' asked Chaloner, itching to box a few ears.

'I imagine because the Lady will make trouble for him if he complains,' replied the Earl. 'It is easier to pretend nothing is wrong, and he always was a man for choosing the least demanding option.'

'She is the Queen,' said Chaloner angrily. 'They should pay her proper respect.'

'Yes, they should,' said the Earl, struggling to his gouty feet. 'So *I* shall go and bid her good afternoon. I know what it is like to be shunned.'

He engaged the Queen in meaningless conversation, and Chaloner was sorry that even the prim, overly formal attentions of the Lord Chancellor brought a rush of gratitude to her wan face.

'I want Bath,' she said in her low, deep voice. 'You help?'

The Earl blushed furiously. 'I think your ladies-in-waiting are better equipped to assist you with your private ablutions, ma'am. And I am a married man.'

'She wants to take the healing waters, sir,' explained Chaloner. 'In Bath. And she needs funds.'

'Oh, I see,' breathed the Earl, relieved. He smiled at her, then started speaking loudly, as if he thought her English might improve if the words were bellowed. 'Unfortunately, there is no money left in your household

241

account, ma'am. I have inspected the books, but cannot tell what happened to it – I can only assume it was diverted to some other account when you failed to use it. In other words, there is no money available for travelling.'

'He speaks too fast!' cried the Queen in Portuguese. Her eyes were full of anguished tears as she turned to Chaloner. 'But tell him I *must* go. It is my only hope. People may not hate me so much when I have a son.'

The Earl waited until she had finished speaking, then immediately started to talk about the weather, unwilling to pursue a subject that might see him asked to pay for the venture himself. He did not let Chaloner translate what she had said, although the spy was sure he had understood the desperation in her voice well enough. The Queen listened intently to his monologue, but it was clear she understood little of it. There was hope in her eyes, though, suggesting she thought the Earl's chatty, friendly tone meant he approved of her intention to visit a spa, and that he might help to facilitate the matter. Chaloner looked away, unable to watch.

Lady Castlemaine had arrived with the Queen's party, but did not stay with them for long. She began to strut about, tossing glances at past, present and future lovers that told of all manner of shared secrets. Her presence was a distraction to both the King and Buckingham. They started to play poorly, and their game degenerated into chaos when she descended to the court and tried to catch the ball. Eager to be on her good side, others rushed to assist her. Lady Muskerry fell, and landed with her legs in the air. There was a cheer of manly appreciation, so Lady Castlemaine contrived to do the same. And then there was a forest of naked calves being waved this way and that.

'I am not staying here to witness such an unedifying spectacle,' announced the Earl, surveying the scene in open disgust. 'Haddon's dogs are better mannered than this rabble!'

It did seem unsuitable behaviour from people who were supposed to be running the country, and the merchants were aghast. Chaloner was relieved to leave the place, and escort his master home.

Haddon was waiting in Worcester House when the Earl and Chaloner arrived there, his dogs curled around his feet. There was to be a dinner for a few of the Earl's closest friends that night, mostly pompous clergymen and high-ranking lawyers, and the steward wanted to check one or two last-minute details.

'All is ready, sir,' he said, almost falling into the Earl's arms when one of his pooches tripped him. He made sure it was unharmed before he resumed his report. 'I cancelled the viols, as you asked, and arranged for violins instead.'

'Good,' said the Earl. 'Viols sound so crude when one is used to the lighter tones of the violin. Do you not agree, Thomas?'

'No,' said Chaloner shortly. To his mind, nothing could compare to a consort of viols, and he thought the Earl did not deserve to hear one if he was incapable of appreciating its haunting beauty.

The Earl shot him an unpleasant look. 'Then it is just as well you are not invited.'

He bustled away to change his clothes before his guests arrived, and Haddon took the opportunity to pull the spy to one side.

'You asked me to listen for rumours pertaining to the

243

murders, but I am afraid there is little point in repeating what I have heard, because it is all nonsense. However, there is one snippet that you may find interesting. Do you recall Turner saying he had arranged a midnight tryst with a lover when he stumbled upon Vine's body?'

'With Meg the laundress. She has not been seen since.'

Haddon smiled. 'Ah, but she has! You see, I complimented Alderman Tryan on his beautifully clean lace today, and we got talking. Boastfully, he told me that his laundry is done by the same lass who does the King's. Then he said Meg had delivered him a batch of clean shirts only last night.'

Chaloner was pleased, because he had been certain she was dead. 'Are you sure?'

Haddon nodded. 'She has been away, visiting kin in Islington. But now she is back, so you can interview her about what she saw on the night of Vine's death. Perhaps she spotted the killer slinking out of the Painted Chamber, and can describe him for you. If so, then it is good news for Greene.'

'Did she tell Tryan anything about the murder?' asked Chaloner, hoping the Westminster poisoner would not hear about her return and move to ensure she did not provide investigators with clues.

'Not that he shared with me. I have a friend – a fellow dog-lover – who works in the laundries, and he is going to find out where she lives. The moment I hear from him, I shall let you know.'

Chaloner thanked him and left Worcester House, intending to track Meg down himself, but he had not taken many steps before he collided heavily with someone. Symons reeled from the impact, which had been entirely his fault – the spy had done his best to move out of the

244

way, but Symons had been so preoccupied that he had ploughed ahead like a runaway cart. He mumbled an apology, bowed his orange head as if the weight of the world was on his shoulders, and continued on up The Strand.

Chaloner's first instinct was to call him back, to ask about his uncle's prayer meetings and the curious combination of men they had attracted. But Symons was moving very purposefully, so he started to follow him instead. Once past the New Exchange, Symons turned left, threading through a maze of lanes until he reached Covent Garden. By then, Chaloner knew exactly where he was going: to John's Coffee House, perhaps for one of the assemblies Greene had mentioned. It seemed as good a time as any to find out whether the gatherings had any bearing on his investigation, so Chaloner decided to eavesdrop.

John's had once been a tavern, and still looked like one. It was a great sprawling place, with upper storeys that overjetted the street like a looming drunk. It was run by John Ravernet, a thin, sallow-faced man who liked to tell everyone he had been a Royalist hero during the wars. Unfortunately for his credibility, Chaloner recalled visiting the place a decade before, and hearing Ravernet talk about his bravery when he was serving in Cromwell's army. It was hard to blame anyone for embroidering their past in the current climate of unease, although it occurred to the spy that there might be less mistrust if everyone just told the truth.

He followed Symons inside, and took a seat near the back of the room, where thick shadows and a lack of natural light rendered him virtually invisible. Symons went to a table where several men already sat. They greeted him with friendly calls of 'what news?' so he told them about the King's tennis, although his voice was flat and dull, as if the Court's antics were of no interest to him. They were of interest to his companions, though: they shook their heads in salacious disgust. After a while, some left, making room for new arrivals. Chaloner frowned thoughtfully when he saw his suspects turn up one by one, as and when they managed to escape from the Tennis Court.

Within an hour, they were all there – Symons, Greene, Gold, Neale, Hargrave and Tryan. Chaloner wondered whether Doling and the Lea brothers might appear, too, but then recalled that although they had attended Scobel's prayers, they did not seem to belong to the coffee-house set. Four seats were ominously empty, and the spy noticed several of the gathering glance sadly at the places that had presumably been occupied by Chetwynd, Vine, Langston and Jones.

Others arrived to join the assembly, too, and Chaloner was disconcerted to see Turner among them. The colonel wore a disguise, but his confident swagger and the hole in his earlobe gave him away. He was not the only one who had tried to conceal his identity. So did two more men: hats shielded their faces, and they did not remove them, even when Ravernet arrived with a tray of coffee and they all took a dish. Chaloner studied them hard. Did he know them? Unfortunately, their shape and size told him nothing, and he suspected he could stare at them all day and still have no answers.

Eventually, Symons said something that resulted in them all huddling together with their heads bowed and their hands clasped together. Their voices dropped, and Chaloner found he could not hear a word. He edged

246

closer, but it made no difference. He watched with a puzzled frown: it looked as though they were praying. It did not seem very likely, especially in a coffee house, but he could not imagine what else they could be doing.

After a while, Greene went to order more drinks. As he did so, the man next to him glanced up, and Chaloner finally caught a glimpse of the fellow's face. It was heavily bearded and dominated by a large nose; the nose looked artificial and Chaloner knew he had never seen it before. Yet there was something vaguely familiar about the rest of the face. It took Chaloner a moment, but then recognition came. Swaddell's disguise was excellent, and the spy might have been deceived had he not been trained to notice such details – Swaddell's restless black eyes were distinctive.

So what was the Spymaster's assassin doing in such company? Clearly, Williamson did not know what Swaddell was up to, or he would not have asked Chaloner to look into the man's disappearance. Or was the Spymaster playing a complex game that entailed convincing everyone that his agent was missing? Chaloner frowned, feeling his investigation had just taken a distinctly sinister turn, if Williamson and his favourite henchman were involved.

It was not much longer before Symons stood to leave, which brought the meeting to an end. Chaloner followed the participants outside, and found himself faced with three choices. He could trail Symons home, and interview him and his wife. He could attempt to find out what Swaddell was doing. Or he could concentrate on the last man of the group, the one whose face he had been unable to see, and try to learn his identity. Unfortunately, the last man had used a different door from the others, and had already disappeared, so Chaloner waited just long enough to satisfy himself that Symons was heading in the right direction for his house, then set off after Swaddell.

The Spymaster's man did not go far before ducking into a doorway. Chaloner crept forward cautiously, aware that if Swaddell was half as dangerous as everyone claimed, then he would know he was being followed and would react with his knife. He waited until the assassin's attention was fixed on removing his nose, then stepped up behind him and wrapped an arm around his neck.

'Your master is worried about you,' he said softly. 'He thinks you are drowned.'

Swaddell's instinctive struggles ceased abruptly when he felt the spy's dagger against his throat. 'Chaloner? Yes, it is you – I recognise your voice. What do you think you are doing, assaulting me like this? Let me go at once!'

'I will consider it, when you have answered some questions.'

'And what if I refuse?'

'Do you really want to find out?'

Swaddell was silent, weighing his options. He strained briefly against Chaloner's arm, testing its strength, then gave a sigh of resignation. 'Very well. What do you want to know?'

'Why were you with those people?'

'That is none of your business.'

It was not an auspicious start, and Chaloner moved the dagger slightly, to remind him it was still there. 'They are suspects for killing Chetwynd, Vine and Langston, so it *is* my business.'

Swaddell sighed again, impatiently this time. 'Then

why do you *think* I was there? I am also trying to find the villain who is killing government officials.'

'Why? Williamson said he has ordered all his people to concentrate on finding the King's statue.'

Swaddell grimaced. 'Yes, he has, but where does that leave me? Vulnerable to accusations, that's where – I am an assassin, and here are three men poisoned. How long do you think will it be before folk put these two "facts" together? To my mind, solving this case is a matter of self-preservation.'

'You are afraid you will be blamed for committing these crimes?' Chaloner was bemused.

'It would not be the first time. And while Williamson is generous with his pay, I am not sure he can be relied upon to stand by me should certain matters come to light. You are a spy, so you understand what I mean. Thurloe would have denied knowing you, if you had been caught . . . breaking the rules.'

Chaloner was not sure whether to believe him. 'And does "breaking the rules" entail dispatching the killer when you catch him? Is that why you attended this meeting?'

'No!' objected Swaddell. He sounded indignant. 'I may be an assassin, but I do not spend *all* my time stabbing people – I have other duties, too. And if you must know, I infiltrated this group some weeks ago, because Williamson was suspicious of its combination of government officials, ex-Commonwealth clerks and wealthy merchants. He thought they might be plotting something dangerous.'

'And are they?'

Swaddell made a disgusted sound at the back of his throat. 'I have rarely met a band of men less interested

249

in politics. All they do is pray, plan their next prayers, or debate whether the past ones were sufficiently devout. And occasionally, they talk about what is reported in the newsbooks.'

Chaloner frowned. 'It is a religious assembly, then?'

'It is – and tedious in the extreme. When Chetwynd was killed, I wondered whether one of these pious fellows might have done it, because Chetwynd was secretly corrupt, while they are all nauseatingly honest. So I have continued to attend their meetings, to see what I could find out.'

'And what have you learned?'

'Nothing!' spat the assassin, clearly exasperated. 'I have probed, hedged, blithered, done everything in my power to encourage the culprit to say something incriminating, but my efforts have gone nowhere. I am beginning to think these men might be innocent.'

'What is the name of the person who did not remove his hat? Not Turner – the other one.'

'He calls himself John Reeve, but it is probably an alias. I have bumped against him, spilled his coffee, sneezed at him, dropped my pipe in his lap, but even when I do glimpse his face, it is so plastered with pastes and paints that it is impossible to identify. He is not the only one to disguise himself, though. Chetwynd used to do it, and so does Hargrave, on occasion.'

'Why, if all they do is pray?'

'You tell me – I am damned if I understand. Now let me go. Standing like this is hurting my back.'

'What happened to you on Tuesday?' asked Chaloner, not relinquishing his hold. 'Jones chased you with a sword, but then you disappeared.'

Swaddell had been trying to ease himself into a more

comfortable position, but he stopped moving abruptly. 'Were you following me?'

'Why would I do that?'

It was no kind of answer, and Swaddell knew it, but he did not demean himself by asking for a better one. He winced when the dagger nicked his throat. 'All right! I was trying to listen to what Jones and the others were saying, but I tripped over some rubbish. Jones heard, and came after me like a rampaging bull. The alley I ran down leads nowhere but the river, and I found myself trapped.'

'Did you push him in the water?'

'No! Basically, he was such a fat man that he could not stop once he was on the move, and he managed to knock us both in, although I seriously doubt it was deliberate. He sank like a stone, and I managed to climb out. I was sorry for it, but it was hardly my fault.'

'I see,' said Chaloner, not about to contradict him and reveal his own role in the incident.

'The place is deserted at night,' Swaddell went on. 'So there was no one about to help me save him. However, it is a rough part of the city, so I do not recommend going there to confirm my tale. No, on second thoughts, *do* go. There are no ruffians to beat you to a pulp for poking around their domain. None at all.'

Chaloner processed the information. Perhaps Jones *had* careened on to the wharf too fast to be able to stop, but had Swaddell really been carried in with him? If he had, then it meant he must have been in the water when Chaloner had arrived, because not enough time had passed for him to have climbed out. Moreover, the train-band had been watching the pier hours later, which meant Swaddell must either have swum away, like Chaloner had done, or had waited for the tide to drop. The latter was unlikely, because the cold would have killed him. Or did Swaddell know the soldiers, and they had turned a blind eye when he had scrambled to safety?

The other alternative was that Swaddell had not fallen in the river at all. But then where *had* he gone? There were no other ways to leave the alley, and he had not been on the pier, because Chaloner would have seen him. The spy was about to demand a more honest explanation when it occurred to him that either scenario meant Swaddell would have seen or heard the train-band fighting with him. Did the fact that he had neglected to mention the incident mean he did not know it was Chaloner who had been doing the battling? Of course, he would know if Chaloner revealed his role by asking questions about it, and as the spy was keen for the train-band to assume he was dead, he decided that learning how Swaddell had extricated himself from his predicament was not as important as staying alive. He went back to the murders.

'What have you learned about the three victims?'

Swaddell seemed relieved to be talking about something else. 'Vine had a nasty habit of blackmailing people and Chetwynd seldom gave honest verdicts in the cases he heard, so neither were the saints they would have had you believe. And Langston was just as bad.'

'In what way?'

Swaddell shrugged. 'I am not sure, but there was something amiss. I suspect it has something to do with Hargrave and the Lea brothers, because I have seen them glancing at each other when Langston is mentioned. Everyone else leaps to say he was a virtuous man, but they do not.'

252

Chaloner was not sure what to believe. Some of Swaddell's answers were plausible, while others were clearly lies or half-truths. 'Perhaps you *are* the poisoner,' he said. 'And you have gone into hiding so you can continue to murder at will.'

He felt Swaddell wince. 'There! You see? You cannot find the real killer, so who do you blame? The poor assassin! I knew it would only be a matter of time before fingers started to be pointed. Of course, I happen to have an alibi for all three murders, but has anyone bothered to ask about it? No!'

'Your indignation is hardly warranted,' said Chaloner, amused. 'You are a self-professed killer who has disguised himself to spy on three men who have been murdered – four, if we count Jones. But what is your alibi?'

'I was with Williamson when Chetwynd, Vine *and* Langston died. Ask him, if you do not believe me. But I have answered enough of your questions. Let me go.'

'No,' said Chaloner, feeling an alibi from the Spymaster was less than worthless, as far as he was concerned. 'You are coming to White Hall with me. Your master thinks I killed you and dropped you in the river, and I would rather he did not hold me responsible for the death of one of his creatures.'

'I am afraid that is out of the question. You see, I had the misfortune to witness Lady Castlemaine commit an indiscretion with a certain gentleman, and she offered to cut out my tongue if I show my face there again. She will forget me eventually, but I intend to keep a low profile until she does. The rumours about my death suit me very nicely.'

'They will not be rumours if you refuse to come with me.'

'You cannot march all the way to White Hall holding me like this, and I will not go willingly. You will have to find another way to convince Williamson that you have not murdered his best man.'

'Then tell me your password – all intelligencers have a code that only they and their Spymaster know.'

'That is a clever idea! Unfortunately, we do not. Take my brooch instead – he will recognise it as mine.'

Chaloner laughed softly. 'And then he will arrest me for stealing it from your corpse! Keep it. It will be more trouble than it is worth – and so are you.'

He released his captive suddenly, shoving him so hard that Swaddell stumbled into a pile of rubbish. The moment he regained his balance, the assassin whipped out his dagger, an expression of deadly purpose on his face. But Chaloner had already melted into the shadows, and was nowhere to be seen.

Symons had not travelled far while Chaloner had been interrogating Swaddell. He had wasted time trying to flag down a hackney, but it was raining, and other people had the same idea, so carriage after carriage had rolled past with shakes of the head from the driver. After a lot of futile waving, Symons accepted it would be quicker to walk, and began to plod along with his head down and his shoulders slumped. Eventually, he reached Axe Yard, a small cul-de-sac off King Street, which boasted twenty-eight houses of varying levels of grandeur. He headed towards one of the smaller homes, which was neat and clean, but in obvious need of fresh paint and new window shutters. It was exactly what Chaloner would have expected from a respectable clerk who had lost all at the Restoration.

A lamp hung above the door, and its unsteady light showed Symons's clothes were greasy and unwashed, while his carrot-coloured hair had not seen a brush in days. Moreover, he had been crying – his eyes were red-rimmed and his cheeks were puffy. Chaloner frowned as he approached. What was wrong with him?

'I have no money,' blurted Symons, assuming the sudden appearance of a stranger in the dark meant only one thing. 'Take my purse, if you will, but it is empty.'

'I am not here for your money.'

Symons peered at him. 'I know you! Greene spoke to you at the Tennis Court today. Surely he has not sent you to call me to yet another prayer meeting? We have only just finished the last one.'

Chaloner was not sure what to make of this assumption, but was prepared to take advantage of it. 'Does he often send you summonses, then?'

A flicker of suspicion crossed Symons's face, but quickly faded, leaving Chaloner with the impression that he did not really care why anyone should be asking him such questions. He wondered again what ailed the man.

'Yes, he does,' replied Symons. 'The others, being employed by the Royalist government, have the luxury of telling each other when to meet. I, being ousted, must wait for messengers.'

'You go to these meetings to pray?'

'*I* go to pray. The others are obsessed by these murders at the moment, although I suppose that is understand-able – the victims were our friends.'

'I find it strange that you – a dismissed clerk from the Commonwealth – should count Royalist officials among your acquaintances.'

Symons shrugged. 'I do not begrudge them their

success. They are all good men, unlike the Lea brothers whose prosperity derives from corruption. Well, I assume they are all good men. Before he died, my uncle Scobel said he suspected Chetwynd was a rogue, but I did not believe him. However, Greene told me today that he was right.'

'I met your uncle once,' lied Chaloner. He tried to recall what Thurloe had written in his letters. He did not think remarking that the man's bald pate and beard made him look as if his head was on upside down would endear him to his nephew, so he thrashed around for something else. 'At a firework display he funded, in the grounds of St Catherine's Hospital.'

Symons leaned against the door, oblivious to the rain that dripped from the eaves, and smiled for the first time. 'He often did things like that, to cheer folks' lives. He was a wonderful man.'

'How did he die?'

'A sharpness of the blood. People say I benefited from his death, because I was his heir. But first, I did not inherit much of his estate – the bulk went to pay debts. And second, I miss him horribly and wish he was still alive.'

'I am sorry,' said Chaloner, hearing the genuine grief in his voice. 'It is never easy to lose kin.'

Symons regarded him curiously. 'You speak from personal experience?'

Chaloner did not reply. There were some depths to which he would never plunge, and using dead loved ones to elicit information was one of them.

'Everything went wrong three years ago, and it has stayed that way,' Symons said bitterly when there was no response. 'After the Restoration, I lost my job, my uncle died, my wife became ill, and now the prayer meetings – once such a source of strength for me – have turned into occasions for trite social chatter. Some of our number even go as far as to say the gatherings have become a chore, and they want to withdraw. Of course, they never will.'

Chaloner raised his eyebrows. 'Why not? Is attendance obligatory, then?'

'No, but most of them are afraid that their luck will change if they resign. After all, look what happened to Langston when he left us last summer. Do you know Langston? He is the plump man with the long nose – the third of the poisoner's victims. He pretended to be virtuous, but he was not. He wrote plays.'

Chaloner was bemused by the disjointed chain of confidences. 'Do you object to the stage, then?'

Symons shook his head. 'But I object to the kind of filth Langston penned. His dramas were obscene, all about unnatural forms of love and . . . things I cannot bring myself to mention. They could never be performed in public, but he wrote them for the Court, which has an appetite for lewdness – especially Lady Castlemaine, who is said to have paid him a fortune for them.'

'How do you know what he wrote?'

'Because he accidentally left a manuscript behind once, after one of my uncle's meetings. We were deeply shocked. Langston came to retrieve it, but not before we had seen what sort of mind he had.'

'Did he know you read it?'

'No! I put on an innocent face, and my uncle pretended to be asleep, so he would not have to speak to him. And they never met again anyway, because my uncle died a few days later.' Symons saw Chaloner was

257

sceptical. 'If you do not believe me, then ask the Lea brothers – they made copies for Langston's actors. And ask Hargrave, too, because his apprentices built the sets at White Hall.'

Chaloner thought about what Swaddell had said – that the Leas and Hargrave had exchanged meaningful glances whenever Langston was mentioned, and that they, unlike everyone else, declined to proclaim his virtue. So, the assassin had been telling the truth about that, at least. 'You said something happened to Langston last summer,' he prompted.

Symons nodded. 'I am coming to that. He withdrew from our gatherings, because he said our beliefs were obsolete and silly. But within days, disaster struck – his bank was robbed, and all the money he had earned from his plays was stolen.'

'You think the robbery occurred because he left your meetings?' asked Chaloner, unconvinced.

Symons shrugged. 'Why not? He stopped praying for success, and immediately he lost his fortune. Backwell's have pledged to repay their customers eventually, but in the interim, Langston was penniless. He came back to us with his tail between his legs, and he is lucky our friends are open-hearted, because they welcomed him like a prodigal son. They also lend him money, to tide him over until Backwell's make good.'

'Why should he need to borrow?' asked Chaloner, supposing it explained why Langston had taken ten pounds from Greene. 'Was his White Hall pay insufficient?'

'I believe he spent a lot of money visiting brothels, to gain inspiration for his writing – and I am told the higher sorts of establishment are expensive.'

'Did Greene know what kind of plays he wrote?'

Symons hesitated. 'He invited Langston to live in his house after the robbery. I visited them there once, and Langston was using the parlour in which to write. Perhaps Greene never looked at the papers scattered about his table, but I find that hard to believe.'

'He seems to keep some very dubious company,' Chaloner remarked. There was an uncomfortable feeling at the pit of his stomach, which told him he might have made a mistake – that perhaps he had been wrong to champion Greene's cause.

Symons looked hurt. 'Actually, he keeps very *good* company. Chetwynd, Vine and Langston may have strayed from the straight and narrow, but most of the men who meet in John's Coffee House are above reproach – Francis Tryan, John Reeve, Nicholas Gold. Do not tar us all with the same brush.'

'I do not know Reeve.'

'He is a corn-chandler, who insists on wearing a disguise to our meetings. So does Swaddell, the Spymaster's man, although we guessed his identity the first time he joined us. Langston and Jones wanted him expelled, but the rest of us felt sorry for him. It cannot be easy for assassins to make friends, and we hope that praying with us might encourage him to adopt a gentler profession.'

Chaloner frowned. 'You keep saying that you meet to pray. Is it the sole function of these gatherings?'

'It used to be, to thank God for our good fortunes. My uncle believed that too many folk ask Him for favours, and too few are grateful for what they already have. But these days we spend most of the time chatting to each other. And since Chetwynd died, we have done little but talk about murder.'

'You clearly disapprove, so why do you continue to go?'

'Because I told my uncle I would. He thought I would be able to keep the others from sin, but I have failed miserably – just as I have failed in everything else. But a promise is a promise, and I have some honour left, so I head for John's Coffee House each time I am summoned. I imagine that is why Greene sent you now – one of them has learned something new about these horrible deaths, and we are all beckoned forth to hear about it.'

'Greene did not send me. I am investigating the murders for the Lord Chancellor.'

Symons closed his eyes. 'Then you should not have let me waste your time with my blather. My wife is dying, and if I appear unhinged, it is because I do not know how to cope with the calamity.'

He spoke so softly that Chaloner thought he might have misheard. 'She seemed all right yesterday.'

'She has the same sharpness of the blood that took my uncle. She told me she would die tonight.'

Chaloner was not sure whether to believe him. 'Then why are you not with her?'

'Because I needed the others to pray for her recovery. My own petitions have gone unanswered, and I thought theirs might do better. They did pray, but now I find myself too frightened to go inside and see whether . . . I do not suppose you would come with me, would you?'

Symons opened the door, and indicated the spy was to follow him inside. He started to cry the moment his eye lit on an unfinished piece of embroidery, so Chaloner fetched a cloth from the kitchen and indicated he was to wipe his face. When he had regained control of himself, he led the spy up a narrow staircase to a bedchamber.

Margaret was lying in a fever, while a servant held her hand.

'It is the same sickness that took Mr Scobel,' the maid whispered to Symons. 'I am sure of it. She has been talking nonsense, just like he did.'

'Have you summoned a physician?' asked Chaloner. It occurred to him that if Scobel had indeed been poisoned, as he suspected, then perhaps someone was attacking Margaret, too.

'They will not come, because they know we cannot pay,' said Symons miserably.

Chaloner told the maid to fetch Wiseman, whom he knew would be at White Hall. The surgeon was usually there of an evening, because he did not like being alone at home – and he had no friends to invite him out. When she had gone, Margaret opened her eyes and looked at the spy.

'Visitors?' she asked in a weak voice. 'I must scrub the floor, or he will think us slovenly.'

'It is perfectly clean,' said Chaloner gently, not sure he was ruthless enough to ask about the statue. He wanted answers, but there were limits to what he was prepared to do to get them.

Margaret drowsed a while, then spoke again. 'Do you like our fine mansion? My husband is a government clerk, and works very hard, while our uncle Scobel often buys us beautiful paintings.'

'She thinks we are in my uncle's house, before the Restoration,' explained Symons in a whisper. 'He used to purchase art for her.'

'I do not suppose he owned a bust by Bernini, did he?'

Symons shook his head. 'There were no sculptures, just pictures. They were in the room where he held his

261

prayer meetings, so people could see them and reflect on the glory of God. As I said, he was a devout man, who believed prayer can bring happiness, wealth and success.'

'Actually, you told me the opposite – that he thought there was not enough thanking going on, and that too many people were demanding favours.'

Symons made a dismissive gesture. 'You are splitting hairs. He believed that prayer lay at the heart of his achievements, and felt that God had been exceptionally good to him. He had a position of power, a family who loved him, and he was forever smiling. People asked for his secret, and he always told them it was his communications with God.'

Chaloner raised his eyebrows. 'Is that why people flocked to his gatherings? They saw his accomplishments, and thought that if they prayed with him, they would share his luck?'

Symons nodded reluctantly. 'Although my uncle did not realise it. Of course, most of the men who came to these meetings *have* found a measure of personal triumph – Langston, Vine, Jones and Chetwynd flourished while they were alive. Tryan, Hargrave and Gold are all fabulously rich, while even young Neale is on the brink of securing himself a wealthy widow.'

'But not Greene. He told me himself that he is unlucky.'

Symons grimaced. 'He has done well enough, despite his melancholy nature. He was a penniless nobody at the Restoration, but now he owns a pleasant house and has a decent post in government.'

There was a thunder of footsteps on the stairs, and Wiseman's bulk loomed in the doorway. Chaloner braced himself for strident declarations about superior medical skills, but the surgeon simply perched on the edge of the bed and began a silent examination. Margaret stirred as he touched her, and he whispered something that soothed her back to sleep. Eventually, he stood and indicated the maid was to go to the kitchen with him, where they would concoct a potion together.

'You can cure her?' asked Symons, eyes burning with sudden hope.

'I am sorry,' said Wiseman quietly. 'Sharpness of the blood is usually fatal, and there is nothing I can do. My medicine will ease her passing, no more.'

Chaloner pulled the surgeon to one side, so Symons and the maid would not hear. 'Are you sure it is a disease that is killing her? Not poison?'

'It is impossible to say. Many toxins mimic the symptoms of natural illnesses, and this may well be one of them. However, I shall explore the kitchen while I brew this medicine, and perhaps remove one or two items for analysis.'

'Will you send me word if you reach any conclusions?'

'I will send it with my bill, although I doubt you earn enough to pay the princely sums I charge. However, I am prepared to accept an evening of your company in lieu of silver.'

Chaloner thought that price was rather too high, and wondered how he could lay his hands on some money to settle the debt. Wiseman disappeared, and a while later the maid came with the potion they had prepared. It was green, smelled of drains, and Chaloner would not have swallowed it to save his life. Margaret gulped it thirstily, and claimed it to be excellent wine.

'Uncle Scobel was here earlier,' she said. The servant shook her head, but Margaret was insistent. 'He was!

He stood at the end of the bed and told me he liked roses. Then he sang a hymn.'

'Was he well, love?' asked Symons, forcing a bright smile. It emerged as a grimace.

'You know I will die tonight, Will? You say I will not, but I am quite certain. I am not afraid, so you should not be, either.'

Chaloner edged towards the door. He had no place in the sickroom, and it reminded him too acutely of the family he had lost in Holland. The maid followed him down the stairs, to see him out.

'Scobel has been in his grave these last three years,' she said, more to herself than Chaloner. 'It frightens me to hear her talking like that.'

'You say he died of the same ailment?'

'The medical men call it a sharpness of the blood, but I think it is a melancholy. It happens when good people see the wickedness of the world. They despair, then they sicken and die.'

'Margaret is good?'

'A saint, sir. She is honest, kind and sweet. Did you know she was offered a statue for next to nothing the other day? But she said it was sure to be stolen, and refused to buy it, even though she has a great love for such things. She is a talented carver herself.'

Chaloner's hopes rose. 'Were you with her when this happened?'

The maid nodded. 'A man came with a letter, but he wore one of those plague masks, to keep us from seeing his face. He waylaid us in Westminster Abbey, as we were passing through it. He waited until she read it, then asked for a reply to take to his master. He did not say who his master was.'

'Do you know why was she chosen?' asked Chaloner.

'Because she is a sculptress. The letter said she could either keep the bust as a work of art, or refashion it into something of her own. He only wanted five pounds, which is cheap for marble.'

And there was the problem, thought Chaloner: the thief had committed a brilliantly successful crime, but was unable to turn it to his advantage. He suspected it would not be long before Bernini's masterpiece was furtively disposed of in the Thames.

Chapter 8

The notion that the thief was growing desperate, and the statue might soon be destroyed, drove Chaloner to spend a good part of the night in White Hall, listening to conversations not meant for his ears. But the only thing he learned was that Lady Castlemaine was taking a rather sinister interest in the King's oldest illegitimate son, which led him to surmise that it had been young James Croft with whom Swaddell had caught her cavorting. He was not surprised she wanted it kept quiet: the King was protective of his offspring, and would be outraged if he learned what the Lady was doing.

The Lord of Misrule had decreed that anyone in the palace grounds after dark that night should be wearing nothing but red, and courtiers disobeying his edict could expect to have the offending garments removed. Chaloner took care not to be caught, but he witnessed what happened to others who were less wary. He was obliged to rescue Haddon with his fists when a gaggle of drunken youths laid hold of him. Prudently, they slunk away when they saw their high spirits were likely to end in a trouncing.

'Thank you,' said the steward unsteadily. The encounter

had frightened him, and he was on the verge of tears. 'I am glad my dogs are not here – they would have raced to save me, and those vile ruffians might have hurt them.'

'Shall I escort you home?'

Reluctantly, Haddon shook his head. 'I had better warn the Earl, or he might suffer the same fate.' He looked across the vast open space of the courtyard in front of him. 'Although it is a long way to his offices. I do not suppose you would mind . . .'

Chaloner took him on a circuitous route that avoided the roistering mobs. While they went, Haddon said that he had managed to find out where Meg lived: with a friend on a street called Petty France.

'She has quit her post in the White Hall laundry,' the steward elaborated. 'Apparently, she thinks there are too many difficult stains involved in washing for the Court. But everyone says she will have no difficulty in recruiting private customers, because she is so good at ironing.'

'I will visit her first thing tomorrow morning,' said Chaloner.

'Good,' said Haddon. 'Let us hope it brings you one step closer to catching the killer – and me one step closer to keeping the five pounds I wagered on your success.'

When they arrived at the Earl's offices, Turner was there, drinking wine in social bonhomie with his master. He was clad in crimson from head to toe, even down to his ear-string. The Earl was remarking on his attire with uncharacteristically good-humour, indicating he had no idea the colonel was obeying the dictates of the Lord of Misrule.

'You should follow his example, Thomas,' the Earl said jovially. 'Wear pink perhaps. Or yellow.'

267

Chaloner regarded him quizzically. 'Are you unwell, sir?'

'I have never felt better,' declared the Earl, standing to stretch his plump arms. The movement caused him to totter. 'And now you will all escort me home. There is a lot of shrieking and cackling outside, and I do not want to be made the subject of some practical joke by drunken youths.'

The empty jug on his desk suggested it was not just youths who were drunk that evening.

'Very wise, sir,' said Turner smoothly. 'You will be safe with us.'

Chaloner was not so sure, because the Lord Chancellor was a tempting target, and they might be overwhelmed by the sheer number of people who wanted to pick on him. He and Turner were armed, but so were many courtiers, and although most were poor swordsmen, others were highly adept. Besides, Chaloner did not want to stab influential noblemen if he could help it.

'I will fetch your carriage, sir,' he said, heading for the door. 'This is not a good night to wander—'

'No, I shall walk,' countered the Earl. 'I feel like some fresh air, and I refuse to let this misrule nonsense dictate my movements. Take my arm, colonel. That wine seems to have gone to my head, and I do not want to take a tumble, because I know what my enemies would make of *that*.'

'Have no fear, My Lord,' said Turner grandly, stepping forward to offer his hand. The Earl lurched, but managed to right himself. 'I will give my life before letting harm come to a single hair on your head.'

'That is not saying much,' quipped the Earl merrily. 'I am virtually bald! Incidentally, did I tell you I am invited to a play in the Banqueting House on Saturday? It is called *The Prick of Love*.'

'Christ,' muttered Chaloner, eyeing him uneasily. 'I hope you do not intend to go.'

'Of course I shall go! I like a good drama as much as the next man.'

With grave misgivings about the nature of the Earl's future entertainment – and his determination to stroll around White Hall on this particular night – Chaloner followed him down the stairs. When his master started to take a route that would lead him directly across the middle of the Palace Court, he jumped forward to stop him, but the Earl pushed him away furiously.

'How dare you presume to tell me where I can and cannot walk! I shall go where I please.'

'Do not waste your breath, Thomas,' whispered Haddon, watching the Earl weave off into the open with Turner at his side. 'He is drunk, which means he will not listen to you or me. Unfortunately, he *is* listening to the colonel, who is almost as inebriated as he is, so cannot be relied upon to dispense sensible advice. I have a very bad feeling about this.'

'He does not normally drink to excess,' said Chaloner, setting off after them. 'What happened?'

'The Bishop of London sent him some wine,' explained Haddon, trotting to keep up. He had grabbed a poker from the hearth before he had left the Earl's offices, and was clutching it fearfully. 'And he has been quaffing it all night. He gave me some, but I found it rather strong.'

Chaloner shook his head in disgust. 'The Lord of Misrule will be behind this, providing a powerful brew in the hope that the Earl will commit an indiscretion – or be befuddled enough to walk out dressed in something other than red. He will lose his clothes, not to mention his dignity.'

'Lord!' exclaimed Haddon in alarm, glancing behind him. 'You are right. Here they come!'

Upwards of thirty people had materialised from the shadows, and they began to converge on the Earl with hoots and jeers. They wore masks that concealed the top halves of their faces, although Chaloner recognised Brodrick, Buckingham and Chiffinch by their voices; the Lady he identified by her malicious grin. He pulled his sword from its sheath, wondering what he could do against so many.

'Oh, dear,' gulped the Earl, suddenly sober enough to appreciate the danger he was in. 'They look as though they mean business. What shall we do?'

'Draw,' said Chaloner urgently to Turner. 'They may think twice if they see they will not have him without a tussle.' He glanced to where the colonel was standing with his mouth hanging open. 'Tonight would be good.'

Turner fumbled with his scabbard. 'Damn! I cannot get it out – the hilt seems to be jammed.'

Chaloner regarded him askance. 'I thought you were a soldier! How can you have a broken sword?'

Turner edged behind him, and began to explain in a voice that was too low for the Earl or Haddon to hear. 'I was not a soldier of the fighting variety. I was more of a strategist, performing behind the lines. Baking, for example. An army is nothing without its food.'

'God help us!' muttered Chaloner, thinking it was not a good time to find this out. 'I thought you were wounded in the King's service.'

'I *was* wounded. Cooking is dangerous, especially if

your assistant is in the habit of brandishing skewers when he is in his cups. Besides, everyone exaggerates what he did in the wars – do not tell me you were really at Naseby. You would have been too young.'

'I need your help,' said Chaloner, alarmed to see more courtiers flocking to join the mob by the moment. 'I cannot protect the Earl on my own.'

'I could try to reason with them,' offered Turner, although not with much enthusiasm. 'I am a solicitor, which means I am good at sly persuasion. When I first arrived in London, my intention was to practice law, but loitering around the Court was a lot more fun. Then His Portliness invited me to—'

'Turner!' snapped Chaloner. It was not the time to hear the man's life story. 'If you cannot draw, then be ready to pull the Earl to safety while I create a diversion. One the count of three. One, two—'

'Wait!' ordered Turner unsteadily. 'We should think this through first. Give me a moment to . . .'

But it was too late. His hesitation had lost them the advantage, and the crowd surged around them.

'You dare point weapons at the Lord of Misrule?' demanded Brodrick. The Earl gulped audibly, and Haddon brandished his poker. Several courtiers laughed when they saw how much it shook. 'And flout his edict that all should wear red tonight?'

'We did not know about your decree, noble sir,' lied Turner, taking several steps to distance himself from Chaloner. 'But we shall fetch some crimson finery immediately. So, if you will excuse us—'

'Your clothing is acceptable, colonel,' declared Brodrick. 'So *you* may join us. But your three companions must pay the price for their disobedience.'

'And the Earl will pay for accusing innocent men of murder, too,' hissed the Lady. 'Poor Greene!'

Turner said nothing, and Chaloner saw he was seriously tempted to abandon his responsibilities and accept Brodrick's invitation. While he dithered, Chaloner stepped protectively in front of their master. Unfortunately, the Earl chose that moment to lurch forward, and the resulting collision made him stagger. He flailed with his arms for a moment, desperately fighting for balance, but he had swallowed far too much wine, and his equilibrium was gone. He sat down hard, legs splayed in front of him. There was an astonished silence, and then Buckingham started to laugh. He had an infectious guffaw, and it was not many moments before the whole mob had joined in.

'Come, friends,' said Brodrick, putting his arm around the Duke's shoulders and leading him away. 'We have had our fun here, and I am bored. Let us find some other entertainment.'

In moments, the crowd was gone, skipping and cavorting around their Lord of Misrule, and singing a popular Christmas song. Lady Castlemaine looked disappointed that her enemy was not to suffer further abuse, but seemed to sense there was only so far Brodrick would go as far as his cousin was concerned. She was the last to leave, but leave she did.

'I shall never forgive you for this, Chaloner,' snarled the Earl, as Turner helped him to his feet. 'You pushed me deliberately, to make me a laughing stock. Consider yourself dismissed – and fortunate that I do not send you to the Tower for . . . for treason!'

'He was trying to save you,' said Haddon quietly. 'He could not have fought all those courtiers single-handed, and would almost certainly have been killed. But he was ready to do it anyway.'

Something in the rational tone of his voice penetrated the Earl's drink-sodden mind, and most of the rage drained out of him. He sighed wearily.

'Take me home. I shall reconsider my position in the morning.'

As soon as the Earl was safely inside Worcester House, Turner headed back towards White Hall, obviously intending to rejoin the revelries. Chaloner walked Haddon to Cannon Row.

'Brodrick would have *tried* to stop the horde from attacking us,' the steward said. 'But Buckingham and Chiffinch are not the kind of men to take orders from him, Lord of Misrule or no. There would have been blood spilled tonight if the Earl had not fallen when he did – and, as far as I am concerned, his dignity is a small price to pay for our lives.'

'The Earl does not think so,' said Chaloner, wondering whether he was going to be unemployed sooner than he had anticipated.

'He will in the morning, when he is sober and has had a chance to reflect on what happened. I was singularly unimpressed by Turner's performance, though. For two pennies, he would have stepped over to Brodrick, and abandoned us. But I am glad we survived the encounter. What would my dogs do without me? Who would sing them to sleep at night?'

'You sing them to sleep?' Chaloner shot him an uneasy glance.

'The darlings would not have it any other way.'

The incident in the Palace Court had unsettled

Chaloner, and even an energetic session in Hannah's bed did not calm him. He dressed while she slept, and slipped out into the night. He prowled restlessly, a silent shadow that no one noticed. Just before dawn broke, he went to the address Haddon had given him on Petty France, but was informed that Meg had not returned home the previous evening. Her housemate did not seem unduly concerned, and said Meg often stayed out all night when she had a man.

The Earl was in a foul mood when the spy went to his office. His eyes were bloodshot and he smelled of vomit. He mentioned neither his undignified tumble nor dismissing Chaloner, and the spy wondered whether he remembered them. Or perhaps he just did not want to think about an episode that was so painfully embarrassing. He barely looked up from his work when Chaloner made his report, and when the spy asked whether he had any specific instructions, he made an impatient gesture with his hand and grunted something inaudible.

Haddon smiled warmly when they met on the stairs, though, evidently feeling the danger shared as they faced the mob together had created a special bond between them. Bulteel regarded Chaloner with reproachful eyes when he saw the exchange, clearly thinking this represented a betrayal of their own friendship. To mollify him, Chaloner took him to a coffee house.

They had not been there many moments when Williamson arrived. He selected a table at which to sit, then raised his eyebrows in astonishment when the men already there promptly made their excuses and left. At the remaining tables, conversations began to revolve around the weather and the state of St Paul's Cathedral

– no one was foolish enough to talk about politics or religion when the Spymaster was listening. He saw Chaloner and Bulteel and waved, inviting them to join him. But the secretary was listening to a sail-maker hold forth about the recent gales and did not see the gesture, while the spy pretended not to notice it.

For a while, the status quo continued, but the Spymaster soon grew tired of being ignored. He stood, and began to stroll from table to table, greeting men who responded with suspicious nods or insincere smiles. While his attention was taken by two surly bakers, Chaloner took the opportunity to slip through the back door. He hid in the darkness of the hall beyond, just out of sight, listening.

'Where is your friend?' Williamson asked, when his perambulation brought him to Bulteel.

'He is—' The secretary stopped speaking in surprise when he realised Chaloner had disappeared. 'He was here a moment ago. Where could he have gone?'

'You tell me,' said Williamson drily. 'I wanted to talk to him. Tell him to come and see me at his earliest convenience. I am sure he knows what happened to Swaddell.'

'I sincerely doubt it,' said Bulteel, swallowing nervously. 'He is not acquainted with Swaddell.'

'He is acquainted well enough to appreciate that Swaddell is important to me,' said Williamson. His voice was cold. 'And I *will* have answers about my spy's disappearance. Will you pass Chaloner my message? To come to my offices?'

'I will tell him,' replied Bulteel uncomfortably. 'But that does not mean he will do it.'

Williamson gave a smile that made him look like a crocodile. 'Then he will wish he was more sociable and so will his treacherous family. You can tell him that, too.'

He had stalked out before Bulteel could respond. The secretary finished his coffee, then left himself. Chaloner joined him in the street, making him jump by falling into step at his side.

'Did you overhear my exchange with the Spymaster?' Bulteel asked. 'You really should do as he says. It is better to visit of your own accord, rather than to have him drag you there.'

Chaloner supposed he would just have to stay out of Williamson's way, because he had no intention of entering the man's lair – voluntarily or otherwise. 'I met Swaddell last night, as it happens, but he refuses to return to White Hall. Perhaps he is afraid of Williamson, too.'

'Too?' echoed Bulteel. 'You mean as well as you? Good. You *should* be frightened of him.'

'I mean as well as *you*. He does not worry me.' But that was untrue: the Spymaster worried Chaloner a great deal when he started threatening his family.

The rest of the morning was spent in a fruitless search for Greene, because the spy wanted to ask him about Langston's skill in penning saucy plays. He gave up at noon when one of Greene's colleagues was able to tell him that the clerk had gone to Southwark.

'He does charitable work there,' the fellow elaborated. 'But I do not know the details.'

The afternoon was devoted to Jones, in an effort to discover more about his personal finances. It was not easy, because Chaloner did not want anyone to know he had found the gold, but his carefully phrased questions yielded nothing of value anyway. And although he learned that Jones had indeed owned a fine ruby ring, he was unable to determine whether it was the same as the one retrieved by the train-band in the Painted Chamber.

At dusk he returned to Meg's lodgings, but the laundress was still out. He went to see Thurloe instead, only to be told the ex-Spymaster had retired to bed with a headache. Loath to disturb him, Chaloner left Lincoln's Inn feeling as though he had wasted an entire day. He only hoped the evening would be more profitable, because it was time he visited his friend Temperance North.

Temperance's gentleman's club was a stylishly tasteful establishment in Hercules' Pillars Alley. It was just beginning its operations, and several coaches were outside, disgorging customers. The club catered primarily for men, but a few liberal-minded women sometimes came to enjoy its witty conversation, professional musicians and French cuisine. Lady Castlemaine was often one of them.

It was unusually busy that evening, because the Twelve Days of Christmas meant people were in the mood for fun. At its door, ready to refuse entry to anyone who looked as if he could not pay, was a man named Preacher Hill. Hill was a nonconformist fanatic, who saw nothing incongruous in the fact that he earned his living in a brothel at night, then went out to condemn such places during the day. Chaloner had warned Temperance against employing someone whose poisonous tongue might cause trouble for her, but she remained doggedly loyal to the man who had been friends with her dead parents. When the spy approached the door, Hill grabbed him by the arm.

'This is a respectable place,' he declared, although 'respectable' was not a word Chaloner would have used to describe a brothel, even a fashionable one like Temperance's. 'So *you* cannot come in.'

'Is that so?' asked Chaloner dangerously, shrugging him off. It had been a frustrating day, and he was not in the mood for Hill. 'And who is going to stop me?'

Despite his bluster, Hill was frightened of Chaloner. He pretended to reconsider, determined not to lose face by backing down too readily. 'All right – I will let you in this time, but you had better behave yourself. I have a lot of brawny friends, and if you make trouble, I will see you are sorry.'

Chaloner treated the threat with the contempt it deserved by ignoring it. He stepped across the threshold and looked around in awe. More money had been spent on the club since he was last there, and the entrance hall was now opulent, with mural-covered walls and curtains screening the stairs. Maude, the formidable matron who was Temperance's helpmeet, sat at a desk at the bottom of the steps, ensuring no one gained access to the ladies on the upper levels without her say-so. Everything was managed with the utmost decorum, so there were never unsightly queues as patrons waited their turn – if a man wanted a woman, he passed word to Maude, and was escorted to a bedroom only when the previous client had gone and the occupant was properly ready for him.

The main room, or parlour, was another glorious affair, with tapestries on the walls, works of art set on marble plinths around the edges, and Turkish carpets on the floor. A separate antechamber held a consort of musicians, usually professionals good enough to hold Court appointments, who played medleys of popular tunes. It was background music, designed to complement the genteel conversation in the parlour, although they were often drowned out in the early hours when the atmosphere became rather less refined. But it was early by club standards, and only novices or youths were drunk so far.

Temperance sat at a large gaming table, holding a hand of cards. At first Chaloner thought she was someone else, because he barely recognised her. She had always been plump, but her tight purple gown made her look fat, and the neckline was low enough to be indecent. A formal wig masked her beautiful chestnut curls, and her fresh, pink skin was smothered in a paste intended to give her a fashionable pallor. With a stab of sorrow, Chaloner realised the demure teenager he had befriended barely eighteen months before no longer existed.

She spotted Chaloner, and gestured to say she would speak to him when her game was over – gone were the days when she would have exclaimed her delight and dropped everything to greet him. While he waited, he wandered through the parlour. Several more card games were in progress, while other men preferred flirting to gambling, and were enjoying the company of the girls who had draped themselves at strategic intervals about the place. He was not surprised to see Turner there, but he *was* surprised to see him in company with Neale, whose cherubic face was flushed with wine and whose golden curls were in wild disarray. When he saw the spy, Turner came to talk.

'I am sorry about last night,' he said with an apologetic grin. 'It was that wine His Portliness fed me. He said it came from the Bishop of London, although the Bishop denies making any such gift. However, it was unusually powerful stuff, and I think it might have been tampered with.'

'You mean it was poisoned?' asked Chaloner in alarm.

No wonder the Earl had looked shabby that morning, and he sincerely hoped it was not a toxin that had long-term effects.

'No, I mean it was dosed with something to make it stronger. All I can say is that he is lucky he shared it, because if he had swallowed the whole jug himself, he would still be insensible tonight. I know it is no excuse for not being able to draw my sword, but I feel I owe you some explanation.'

Chaloner nodded acceptance of the tale, although Turner had not seemed that drunk to him. He looked to where Neale was pawing a woman named Belle. She was unimpressed by the lad's clumsy gropes, and was having trouble fending him off. Turner followed Chaloner's glance and grimaced.

'We had better rescue her – I shall escort her some-where to recover, while you deal with Neale.' He shot Chaloner a conspiratorial grin. 'Last time I was here, she waived her fee for the romp we enjoyed, and I have hopes for a repeat performance tonight. You are a man of the world – you understand.'

'Understand what?' asked Chaloner, but Turner was already in motion. With one smooth, suave movement, he had plucked the prostitute from Neale's gauche embraces and had whisked her away. The young man tried to follow, tripped, and was only saved from falling face-first across one of the gaming tables because Chaloner caught him. The spy half-carried him to a chair near the window, and gave him a cup of water. Petulantly, Neale flung it away and grabbed a jug of wine instead. He took a gulp, and Chaloner stepped back smartly when Neale's hand shot to his mouth in a way that presaged vomiting. When he had fought off the nausea, Neale inspected his rescuer through bleary eyes.

'The Lord Chancellor's man,' he slurred. 'Investigating Chetwynd's poisoning. You asked me about it in the Angel tavern, when I was trying to charm Bess Gold.'

'She will not be very charmed if she learns you frequent this sort of place,' remarked Chaloner.

'But she is the one who drove me here,' said Neale, full of sullen self pity. 'You see, she refuses to lie with me while that deaf old turkey still breathes – and I am a red-blooded man with needs. Still, the old bird cannot last much longer, and then I shall have her body *and* her widow's fortune.'

Chaloner was taken aback by the bluntness of the confession. 'How much have you had to drink?'

'Enough to know I shall have a sore head tomorrow. But where has Colonel Turner gone? He has been plying me with wine in exchange for information all night, but the moment *I* want him – I need some silver if I am to win Belle – he is nowhere to be found.'

'What sort of things did he want to know?'

Neale peered at him through glazed eyes. 'He was asking about Greene, so I told him how I often meet the fellow at John's Coffee House in Covent Garden. Have you been there? It is very nice.'

'Is Greene a friend of yours, then?'

'Not really. He is too religious for my taste, although he does share my taste for whores.'

'Whores?' Chaloner was not sure whether to believe him, because Greene had not seemed that kind of man, and he had certainly visited no bawdy-houses when the spy had been following him.

Neale nodded vigorously. 'He likes the ones that do

not cost much, such as can be got in Southwark. He entertains several at a time. I saw him myself once, when I was out with Brodrick and Chiffinch, and he was obviously a regular, because they all knew him by name. They were laughing and joking together, like old friends.'

His eyes started to close, so Chaloner kicked his foot, knowing he did not have much time before wine won the battle for what remained of the young man's wits. 'What do you discuss at John's?'

Neale jerked awake. 'Mostly we pray for good fortune – for money, happiness and success. I am not averse to having those, so I do not mind spending the odd evening on my knees. And we exchange news about people we know, the weather, the King's skill at tennis. But we never debate politics. The others always override me if I try to bring up anything contentious, the boring old . . .' He waved an expressive hand, his vocabulary apparently having deserted him.

'You misled me the last time we spoke,' said Chaloner softly. 'You neglected to mention that you had bribed Chetwynd.'

Neale slid a little lower in the chair, and his voice became bitter. 'You think I should have told a stranger how I corrupted a royal official? I may be young, but I am not a fool! But it was a rotten business, if you must know – Chetwynd took the last of my money, then found in my brother's favour. Bastard! So, here I am, forced to make eyes at a sheep, so I can marry her when Gold dies.'

Chaloner regarded him with distaste. 'What else did you tell Turner?' He kicked Neale's foot a second time when the young man's eyelids drooped.

'What? Nothing. No, wait. I told him about the river.'

'What about the river?' Chaloner hated interviewing drunks; it was like drawing blood from a stone.

'I saw Greene throw something in it on Thursday morning. Something leathery. Purses, I think.'

'Purses?'

'Three purses. But they were empty. I could tell by the way they hit the water. No splash, see.'

Three purses, three robbed corpses, thought Chaloner uneasily, as Neale finally descended into a snoring stupor. For the second night in a row, he wondered whether he had been right to champion Greene's innocence. But how could the clerk be guilty, when he had alibis for two of the crimes? Engrossed in his thoughts, Chaloner lifted Neale into a position where he would not choke, and placed an empty bowl at his elbow. Neale would need it when he woke, and Chaloner did not see why Temperance should have to clean up the mess.

The music was louder than it had been, to make itself heard above the rising clamour of people having a good time. Women shrieked, men laughed, and there was a constant chink of coins changing hands and goblets being refilled. Belle excused herself to confer with Maude, which left Turner at a loose end for a while. The colonel rolled his eyes when he saw the state of Neale, but did not seem unduly concerned that his informant would not be doing any more talking that night.

'Working for His Portliness is fun, is it not?' he remarked jovially to Chaloner. 'I mean, what other employer leaves a man to his own devices day and night, and reimburses his expenses in the morning?'

'Not yours,' said Chaloner. 'He will be horrified if he thinks you frequent brothels – whether you do it on his

283

behalf or not – and if you present him with a bill for women, he will dismiss you.'

Turner regarded him uncertainly. 'You jest. He is not *that* prudish.'

'Try him, and see.'

Turner grimaced. 'Then I had better curtail my spending. Neale can pay for his own whore.'

Chaloner doubted the lad would be needing one that night. 'Has he been worth the expense?'

'He provided me with a snippet or two. What about you? What have you learned so far?'

'Not nearly enough,' replied Chaloner gloomily.

Turner looked pleased with himself. 'I, on the other hand, have done rather well – with the murders, at least. I have had no luck at all with the statue. The thief is clever. He removed it with no one seeing – no mean feat, considering its weight – and has contrived to make it disappear completely.'

Chaloner disagreed. 'He is not clever, or he would have stolen a piece that is less famous. Everyone knows the old king's bust is stolen, and he will never sell it for what it is really worth.'

Turner raised his eyebrows. '*Is* it famous? I thought it was just one in a whole room of similar tripe – worthy and full of artistic merit, to be sure, but not something you would want in your own house.'

Chaloner was surprised he should be so dismissive. 'Bernini is the greatest living sculptor in the world.'

Turner grimaced. 'Well, perhaps he was having a bad day when he made that one.'

Chaloner did not want to discuss art with someone who knew even less about it than he did. 'What have you learned about the murders?' he asked instead.

Turner preened. 'I have uncovered evidence that points to Greene's guilt. I know you do not share His Portliness's suspicions, but it seems the old goat *was* right. In fact, it was because he seemed so certain that I decided to concentrate all my efforts on Greene, to see what I could learn about him.'

It was not a bad strategy, and Chaloner wondered whether he should have done the same. It would have pleased the Earl, and might even have secured his future employment. 'What did you find out?'

Turner's expression was amused. 'Is this to be a one-way exchange of intelligence, or do you intend to reciprocate? I do not want you to claim all the credit for solving the case, because I enjoy spying for His Portliness and would like to carry on working for him.'

'I doubt he has the resources to hire us both long-term. I know he was recently awarded additional funds to expand his staff, but that was for administration, not the kind of work that we do.'

'Shall we be rivals, then?' asked Turner, fingering his ear-string.

Chaloner shook his head tiredly. 'That might mean more murders. If the best way to catch this villain is by pooling our resources, then that is what we must do. So, you can tell me what you have learned about Greene, and I will tell you what I have learned about the victims.'

'You first, then,' said Turner slyly.

'I devised a list of common acquaintances – not casual ones, such as might be made by working in the same place, but more meaningful ones. They include Neale, Gold and his wife Bess, Doling, the Lea brothers, Hargrave, Tryan and of course Greene. And Jones, who is dead, too.'

He omitted Swaddell because of the assassin's connections to the Spymaster – Chaloner did not understand what Swaddell was doing, but it seemed wise to keep his suspicions to himself – and Symons because he did not want Margaret disturbed during her final hours. Of course, Turner already knew the names of the men Chaloner had listed, because he had inveigled himself into their society when they had met at John's Coffee House.

The colonel waved a dismissive hand, unimpressed. 'If Greene is the killer, then these other "suspects" are irrelevant. Tell me something useful, or I shall keep my own information to myself.'

'Is Greene the killer? He was in Wapping with his priest when Langston was killed, and I was watching his house when Vine died.'

'And we know what time Langston breathed his last, because of Lady Castlemaine's testimony,' mused Turner. 'She saw him alive just before four o'clock in the morning – and the Earl found the body not long after that. However, what if the Lady is mistaken? And what if Greene managed to slip past you the other night? Neither alibi is perfect.'

'But *why* would Greene kill these men? All had dark pasts that may have earned them enemies: Chetwynd was corrupt, Vine blackmailed people, and Langston wrote bawdy plays. However, these are not reasons for *Greene* to kill them.'

Turner frowned. 'I do not follow you.'

'The culprit will be someone who was a victim of Chetwynd's corruption or Vine's penchant for blackmail. And he will be someone who was shocked by Langston's bawdy plays – Greene may well have enjoyed them, given what Neale says about his liking for brothels.'

He ignored the clamouring voice in his head that demanded to know why Greene should have been throwing three leather purses in the Thames.

Turner's expression was doubtful. 'You have made this very complicated. But let me tell you what I have found out. On Thursday and Saturday evenings – the nights when Chetwynd and Vine were murdered – Greene went to the cellars and begged for brandywine. He told the man in charge, a fellow called Munt, that he was working late and needed refreshment. But Munt passed Greene's office later, and said it was in darkness *both times.*'

Chaloner had been watching Greene on Saturday, but had not seen him visit the cellars. However, the building in which Greene worked had far too many doors for a lone man to monitor, so he supposed it was possible the clerk had eluded him.

'Are you sure Munt is telling the truth?'

'Yes, because he was indignant about being played for a fool – Greene preyed on his sympathy as a man obliged to slave long hours, then sloped off. And he did it not once, but twice. But I know what really happened: Greene added poison to this brandywine and fed it to his victims.'

Chaloner frowned. 'Is Munt certain about the days – Thursday and Saturday?'

'Ask him yourself. And let us not forget the brandy-wine I found hidden in Greene's office, either. It all adds up to something suspicious.'

'If you are so certain Greene is the killer, then why have you not arrested him? That is what the Earl wants, and he will certainly continue to hire you if you prove him right.'

For the first time, Turner's cheery confidence wavered. He frowned uneasily. 'Because arresting Greene will lead to a speedy conviction and death at the end of a rope. If I am to be instrumental in sending a man to the gallows, then I must be certain of his guilt.'

Chaloner regarded him quizzically. The colonel did not seem like the kind of man who would allow scruples to interfere with his plans for a comfortable future.

'You do not believe me,' said Turner, seeing what he was thinking. 'But it is quite true. I was obliged to break the law during the Commonwealth, when self-declared Royalists like me struggled to earn a living, and I might have been executed myself. So, I shall tell His Portliness my findings only when I am *sure* Greene is guilty, and not a moment before. That is where you come in.'

Chaloner smothered a smile. 'It is, is it?'

'I want you to confirm what I have learned. Then we can share responsibility for Greene's death.'

'It will also mean we shall share credit for a case you have solved.'

'Yes, but at least I shall be able to sleep at night – and the importance of guilt-free slumber should never be underestimated. However, I do not plan on doing much dozing this evening. I shall have Belle first, but then who else? Which of these lovely lasses will best appreciate my company, do you think?'

'Whoever you pay the most, I imagine.'

Turner gazed at him in astonishment. 'Pay? I have never paid for a woman in my life.'

'Perhaps so, but this is a brothel. These women are not here for their health.'

Turner waved a dismissive hand. 'You underestimate my charms. Oh, I shall hand a few coins to that fierce matron in the hall, but the ladies I choose to accompany me upstairs will give me keepsakes that will be worth ten times that amount. Did you notice that locket around Belle's throat? Ten shillings says that will be mine tomorrow.'

'How will I know you have not stolen it?'

Turner was shocked. 'I am no thief! Besides, you will be able to ask her whether she parted with it willingly. Well, what do you say? Will you accept my wager?'

Chaloner nodded. He had known Belle for some time, and she was not the kind of woman to hand hard-earned wealth to a customer, no matter how pretty he thought himself. Turner, he thought, was not a good judge of character.

Temperance was still engrossed in her game of cards, and the stakes were now more than Chaloner earned in a year. He was staggered by the amount of silver and jewellery that was being tossed on the table as bets were made, and was reminded that she now inhabited a very different world from his own. Eventually, she stood, offering her seat to Chiffinch. Brodrick objected to losing her company, but she ruffled his hair and planted a kiss on the top of his head to appease him.

'Chaloner!' he shouted, as she went to join the spy. 'Have you come to play the viol? I wish you would. Greeting is drunk and keeps bowing sharp. It hurts the ears, and you have such a lovely touch.'

'I have heard the same,' drawled Chiffinch. 'My wife says he has exquisite fingerwork.'

There was a gust of manly laugher, accompanied by nudges and winks, so those of slower wits would appreciate that a lewd joke had been made.

'She would say no such thing,' said Chaloner coolly, disliking the notion that Barbara should be the subject of conversation among such depraved company. 'She has too much decency.'

Chiffinch's eyebrows shot up, and he leaned back in his chair. 'You accuse me of being indecent? I should call you out, and teach you a lesson with my sword.'

Chaloner wished he would, so he might rid Barbara of the man who had brought her nothing but trouble and unhappiness for the last forty years, but Temperance stepped in before he could reply.

'You are *very* indecent, Mr Chiffinch,' she said with a smirk. 'Which is just how we like you.'

There was another manly cheer, and Chaloner allowed her to bundle him out of the room while the laughter lasted. She ushered him down the corridor and into the kitchen. This had always been a warm, quiet place, but since his last visit it had become the domain of a shrieking Frenchman, who screamed orders at his bewildered assistants in an anarchic mixture of Latin and Spanish. There was a lot of confusion, and Chaloner was not surprised his soufflés had collapsed.

'He is telling you to use butter,' he said to the cooks as he passed. 'You used lard, apparently. He wants you to start again.'

There was an immediate sigh of understanding and work resumed, although the Frenchman's squawks remained just as frenzied. Temperance led Chaloner to the little office where she and Maude counted their nightly takings. As usual, there was coffee simmering in a pan over the hearth, while a pair of cushion-loaded chairs provided somewhere the two ladies could rest, should the carousing in the parlour become too much for them. The room stank of pipe smoke and expensive perfume.

'You once said you would teach me French,' said

Temperance, flopping into one of the seats and indicating he was to perch opposite. 'The language of love.'

'There is not much love in what your cook is screeching.'

Temperance smiled dreamily. 'I was not thinking of using it on him.'

As Temperance rarely went out, Chaloner could only assume she had fallen for one of her patrons. 'You have a . . .' He was not quite sure how to phrase the question, given that 'liking for a client' was unlikely to be very well received. '. . . a friend?' he finished lamely.

'A certain person *has* become rather special during the last few weeks. I did not think I would ever be smitten by a man, but this one is different – worthy of my affection. I think I shall marry him.'

'Really?' Chaloner was amazed: Temperance had always been of the firm opinion that matrimony was a condition to be avoided at all costs. 'Who is he?'

'Someone you will like. He is not here tonight, though, or I would introduce you. But you should meet him. Come to dine with us on Twelfth Night, although you must promise to behave – no turning taciturn if he asks you questions, and no caustic remarks about the morality of the Court, either. He is a gay sort, and will think you a prude.'

'I cannot,' replied Chaloner, a little dismayed that she did not trust him to be amiable. 'Bulteel has asked me to go to his house on Twelfth Night – he wants me to be godfather to his son.'

'Bulteel? Ugh! It will be like dining with a Puritan, and you are sure to come away hungry. And you should not agree to be the godfather, either. The poor brat deserves better.'

'You think I am not good enough?' It was one thing to believe himself unequal to the task, but quite another to hear it so baldly stated from someone who was supposed to be his friend.

'I mean better in terms of *fun*,' elaborated Temperance. 'You seldom have any, and he will need someone to show him the ways of the world. And I do not mean how to kill people in dark alleys, speak peculiar languages, or pick locks, either. I refer to dancing and cards.'

'The important things in life.'

Temperance shot him an unpleasant glance. 'Quite. However, these two invitations will not conflict – Bulteel's soirée will be during the day, while mine will be the night before – so you can attend both. Come at midnight. I will make sure you are with your dull little colleague by the following noon.'

Chaloner should have known she was unlikely to do anything in daylight. She was seldom up before three, by which time the winter sun was already setting. 'That is a singular time for dinner.'

She shrugged. 'You let yourself be too constrained by tradition, Tom, and it is turning you into a bore. You should adopt my motto: *carpe notarium*.'

'Seize the secretary?' translated Chaloner, bemused.

'Seize the *night*. I thought you knew Latin. Brodrick taught me that phrase, and I rather like it.'

Chaloner found he did not want to join her tradition-flaunting party, and tried to think of an excuse that would allow him to miss it. 'Actually, I have also been asked to Sir Nicholas Gold's—'

Temperance arched her eyebrows. 'You are a social creature these days! But Gold's invitation will not clash with mine, either. His soirée will start at dusk and be

292

over by ten, when he will retire to bed with a cup of warm milk. Do not look so dubious – you will enjoy being with me and James. We shall dine on mince-pies, venison sausages and a Double Codlin Tart. And I have ordered a pelican.'

Chaloner blinked. 'Have you? Whatever for?'

Temperance's expression was defiant, which told him she had probably never seen one. 'Brodrick said it is what the King is having, so I told my butcher to get us one, too. What is good enough for His Majesty is good enough for me, and I am not having another turkey. Did you know the beast we were going to eat last year has taken up residence on Hampstead Heath, and no one dares go near it?'

Chaloner was pleased. He liked birds, and had not relished the notion of such a fine specimen having its neck wrung. 'What is your friend's name?' he asked, suspecting she would not feel the same way, so changing the subject before they could argue about it.

'James Grey.' Her hand went to her bodice, where a square of red silk had been tucked down the front of it, clearly a love token. 'He plays the viol, which should commend him to you. You can bring yours, and we shall have music.'

Then perhaps the occasion would not be so bad after all, thought Chaloner, watching as Temperance reached up to the mantelpiece and took down a pipe. She had only recently acquired the habit when he had last seen her, but a few weeks had turned her into a seasoned smoker – her movements were deft and confident as she tamped the bowl with tobacco. When it was lit, and she was encased in a billowing haze, she regarded him reproachfully.

'You know you are always welcome here, Tom, but only if you agree not to insult my guests. They are volatile at the best of times, and I cannot afford to have you challenging them to duels.'

'Chiffinch challenged me,' Chaloner pointed out. 'All I did was defend his wife.'

'They insult their wives all the time, but it means nothing. They come here to forget them, and on the whole, I do not blame them. Barbara Chiffinch is a sharp-tongued shrew with no sense of humour.'

'She has an excellent sense of humour, despite being married to that worthless dog for forty years.'

'You and I always disagree these days,' said Temperance sadly. 'You never used to be like this. You have changed, and I am glad I did not marry you.'

Gallantly, Chaloner resisted the urge to say he had never considered asking her – and now he had seen what she had become, he was heartily glad of it. 'It is you who have changed. A year ago, you were spending half your life in chapel, and the other half helping the poor.'

'And I was deeply unhappy,' she shot back. 'Whereas now I run my own business, I am rich beyond my wildest dreams, James loves me, *and* I have a glut of wealthy and influential companions.'

'Chiffinch and Brodrick are fair-weather friends,' warned Chaloner, not liking the notion that she might think them dependable. When all was said and done, Temperance was barely twenty, and her strict Puritan upbringing meant she had little experience of the world. 'If there is a popular uprising against debauchery and vice – and it could happen, because Londoners deplore the Court's profligacy – they will not help you when your house is attacked.'

Temperance puffed smoke through rouged lips. 'That will not happen – the King will not let it, and I have James to protect me, anyway. You are beginning to sound like Thurloe – a tedious old misery.'

'I should go,' said Chaloner, standing abruptly. Thurloe had been good to Temperance after her parents had died, and he was sorry she had forgotten his kindness so soon. 'I only came to ask after your health.'

'I am well – it is you who is testy. Let me provide you with a lady, to put you in better spirits, so we can have a civilised conversation. You can have Snowflake. She knows how to make a man smile.'

'I am sure she does,' replied Chaloner coolly, 'but I did not come to inveigle a . . .' He waved his hand, not sure what was the correct term for an offer of a free whore. 'I came to see you.'

Temperance smiled at last. 'Then we should set aside our differences and talk. Sit down and have some coffee. Maude made it.'

Chaloner took a sip of the black brew, then fought the urge to spit it out. It was the most powerful thing he had ever tasted, so thick it was more syrup than beverage. Maude had a reputation for potent infusions, but this one was hearty, even by her standards. There was a rumour that her first husband had died from drinking her coffee, and Chaloner was perfectly willing to believe it.

'Christ, Temperance!' he managed eventually. 'Who taught her to make this? The Devil?'

Temperance laughed. 'Have some more. You will soon acquire a taste for it.'

But Chaloner did not want to acquire a taste for it. He pushed the dish aside, then shook his head when she offered him a pipe.

She raised her eyebrows. 'Shall I warm you some milk, then?'

'You have made some improvements to your parlour since I was last here,' he said, deciding he had better bring the conversation around to statues before they fell out in earnest.

She grinned. 'James suggested we commission Brodrick to purchase us a few masterpieces. We must have the best, because our patrons will notice if we opt for rubbish. And Brodrick may be an old reprobate, but he does know his way around an art gallery.'

'He does,' agreed Chaloner. 'But he also throws food about when he has had too much to drink. I hope he and his cronies do not damage anything irreplaceable.'

'That is why we decided to go for statues – Apollo was hit by a pineapple last night, but he suffered no ill effects whatsoever. I do not like sculpture, personally. Most of it seems to revolve around smug Roman emperors and fat Greek goddesses toting unlikely weapons.'

Chaloner made no comment, although he found himself thinking, rather uncharitably, that she had recently grown a lot more portly than any Greek goddess.

'But I got Brodrick to buy extras, so I can rotate them,' she went on. 'I do not want to be looking at the same stony visages every night for the next fifty years. The spares are in the cellar, and I gave myself *such* a fright the other day. You would have laughed! I went down there for wine, and glanced up to find Nero staring at me. I screamed so loud that Preacher Hill came racing to my rescue.'

'Who is the artist?'

Temperance frowned. 'Do you mean who crafted my Nero? Some Italian, I think. Why?'

'I wondered whether it was Bernini.'

'I do not approve of *him*. Did you know he is a Swedish hermaphrodite, who likes rope-dancing and hedgehogs?' There was a slight pause. 'What is a hermaphrodite, Tom? I do not like to ask James, lest he think me ignorant.'

'He will not think you ignorant. Are those the only reasons you do not like Bernini?'

Temperance shot him a sideways glance. 'Are these questions anything to do with the King's missing statue?'

'I heard you made enquiries about Bernini before his masterpiece was stolen.'

She gaped at him. 'You heard it from whom?'

'It does not matter. But your discussion was overheard, and your courtly friends cannot keep secrets. So take warning and be careful what you say in future. But why *did* you ask about the sculpture?'

'People were talking about it, and as I had been buying statues of my own, I had an interest. I asked Chiffinch what was so special about Bernini.'

Chaloner regarded her sadly. 'You would lie to me?'

'Why not, when you lie to me?' Temperance flashed back. 'You pump me for information, but seldom give anything in return. And you did not really come to see me tonight – you came because of an investigation. Admit it! Well, I am *not* telling you what prompted my interest in Bernini. You will have to find out another way.'

'Temperance, I—'

'Go home, Thomas. You presume too much on our friendship.'

Chapter 9

The spat with Temperance had upset Chaloner, and he did not feel like sleeping alone in his chilly garret, so he went to visit Hannah. She had only just returned home, and was so angry that she could barely form the words to tell him why. Apparently, the Queen had been invited to a ball that evening, and had been delighted to think she was included in a Court occasion at last. She had spent all day preparing, taking care not only with her dress, but also to learn new English phrases that she hoped would impress her hosts. But when she arrived at the Banqueting House, where the dance was to take place, she found it closed. Moreover, there was not a courtier to be found in the entire palace.

'My first thought was that it was the Lord of Misrule,' spat Hannah furiously. 'And a few enquiries revealed that Brodrick *has* declared White Hall off-limits to anyone who does not want to be doused in green paint tonight. But it was heartless to raise the Queen's hopes with a gesture of friendship, only to dash them so pitilessly, and I do not think Brodrick is that low.'

Chaloner was inclined to agree. The Earl's cousin was

dissolute and hedonistic, but he was not cruel. 'I do not suppose you noticed what Lady Castlemaine was doing all day, did you?'

Hannah nodded, eyes flashing. 'Encouraging the Queen in her excitement, telling her what a wonderful night it would be. But when it was time to go to the Banqueting House, she disappeared.'

'Then there is your culprit.'

'Damn her!' cried Hannah. 'No doubt she will be delighted when she hears how deep a wound she has inflicted. But I do not want to discuss it any more; I am too incensed. Tell me what you have been doing instead. Where did you spend your evening?'

'In a brothel,' replied Chaloner, loath to lie when there was a chance that someone like Brodrick or Chiffinch might report seeing him there.

But Hannah glowered at him. 'If you cannot tell me the truth for reasons relating to your investigation, then that is fair enough, but do not insult me by inventing wild tales. I am not in the mood. Tell about your *morning*, then, if your evening is off limits. Where did you go, and whom did you meet?'

'Why?' asked Chaloner warily.

'It is called making conversation, Thomas,' snapped Hannah, eyeing him balefully. 'What is wrong with you? Surely, your work cannot be so secret that you are unable to tell me that you exchanged greetings with Lady Muskerry, or that you prefer the coffee in John's to that served in the Rainbow?'

Chaloner raised his hands in a shrug, although he wondered whether it had been chance or design that led her to mention the establishment where his suspects met. 'I am sorry. It has been a long day.'

'So has mine,' she snarled, unappeased.

He tried to make amends, recalling his vow not to alienate her by being uncommunicative, but it was too late: nothing he said or did could placate her. Eventually, he left, although he was not impressed to find his landlord had been in his rooms to mend the roof, and had succeeded in exacerbating the problem. Irregular drips had been transformed into steady trickles, and Ellis had contrived to move the bed so it was directly under the worst of the holes. Chaloner woke in the night to find himself sodden as rain hammered down outside, and he was obliged not only to fetch bowls for the new leaks, but to hunt out dry spots for his bass viol and music chest, too. He went back to bed, and dozed fitfully until a curious combination of sounds woke him the following day.

He listened with his eyes closed for a moment, then shot to his feet, grabbing his sword as he did so, sure someone else was in the room. But it was only his cat. It regarded him through lazy amber eyes, then released the pigeon it had caught. The bird immediately flapped towards the window, which it hit with a thump before flopping to the floor, stunned.

'Oh, no!' cried Chaloner in dismay. 'I thought we had an understanding: rats and mice are fair game, but birds are forbidden.'

The cat meowed at him, and he sat heavily on the bed, resting his head in his hands. He was talking to the animal, and it had answered him! Was the insidious loneliness that had been a part of his life ever since he had become a spy finally taking its toll? Would it be only a matter of time before he ended up like Haddon, substituting animals for people? He decided to visit Temperance that evening and apologise, because he did not have so

300

many friends that he could afford to squander them in petty squabbles. And the quarrel had been entirely his fault – he should have told her why he needed to know about Bernini, not ambushed her with questions. She was right to be angry with him.

And he would see Hannah, too, and try to worm his way back into her good graces. Since arriving in London, he had met no one who had interested him for more than a casual encounter, but he was beginning to feel Hannah was different. She was intelligent, amusing and had shown a remarkable tolerance for his various flaws of character. He discovered with a pang that he did not want to lose her.

When the cat meowed at him again, he ignored it and went to let the pigeon – recovered and keen to be on its way – out of the window. When it had gone, he ran his hands over the smooth, silky wood of his viol. It had been some days since he had had time for music, and he felt the tension begin to drain out of him as he took his bow and began to play. It was not long before he became totally immersed, and only came to his senses when the bells chimed noon. At first, he thought he had misheard, and then was disgusted with himself for frittering away so many hours of daylight.

He donned clean clothes, and set off to Petty France, hoping Meg would be in, but there was no reply when he knocked at her door. He walked to the back of the house, and gained access to her room via a window. But his efforts were wasted, because his search told him nothing, other than that she kept an ear-string in a box next to her bed. He supposed it belonged to Turner, and the colonel had either given it to her, or she had snagged it without his knowing.

He went to Lincoln's Inn, feeling a need for Thurloe's companionship, but the ex-Spymaster was out, and his manservant did not know where he had gone. Chamber XIII was full of folded clothes, ready to be packed for the journey to Oxfordshire, which was a sharp reminder that Chaloner would soon be without his mentor. His sense of isolation intensified.

He emerged from Lincoln's Inn to see Haddon trotting along Chancery Lane, conversing merrily with his dogs and drawing wary looks from the people he passed. Not in the mood to be informed that a pooch could replace Thurloe, Chaloner ducked into the Rolls Chapel, a pretty building designed by Inigo Jones as part church and part repository for legal records. He was disconcerted when Haddon joined him there a few moments later.

'I have never been in here before,' said the steward, looking around appreciatively. 'It is beautiful.'

Haddon had always been friendly to Chaloner, and the spy was already regretting the attempt to avoid him. It had been rude. He knelt at the altar rail and pretended to pray, in the hope that Haddon would not guess he had darted into the chapel to effect an escape. When the steward walked towards him, he smiled and indicated Haddon was to kneel at his side. He was taken aback when the dogs followed their master's example, resting their front paws on the rail, and their back ones on a hassock.

'God's creatures,' said Haddon, beaming fondly at them. 'Is that not so, my beauties? They know how to behave in a church . . . Oh, Lord! They have never done *that* before.'

'I think we should leave,' said Chaloner, eyeing the mess uncomfortably.

302

'But you have only just arrived, and you should not let a mishap stand between you and God. I had not taken you for a religious man, Thomas – I am favourably impressed.'

'I am glad someone is,' muttered Chaloner, acutely aware that the verger was pottering nearby. If the man saw what the dogs had done, there would be a scene, so he stood and began to walk briskly towards the door, relieved when Haddon followed. 'Did you have something to tell me?'

'Yes, I have sad news to impart. Margaret Symons is dead. She foretold the exact hour of her passing, and she slipped away precisely when she said she would.'

'I am sorry to hear it.' Scobel had predicted the time of his death, too, and Chaloner wondered again whether it meant someone had helped them into their graves.

A tear sparkled in Haddon's eye. 'She was kind to me once, when I was ill. And she liked dogs.'

'So did Vine,' said Chaloner, remembering being told that the Treasury clerk had made donations to a charitable foundation that cared for strays. It was clearly a bad week for London's mutts.

Haddon sighed sorrowfully. 'Yes, he did, but I doubt George will continue his father's good work. Do you think the Earl might spare a few shillings each month to make a puppy happy?'

Chaloner resisted the urge to laugh at the notion of the Earl parting with money for something that would not benefit himself. 'You never know.'

'I have something else to tell you, too,' said Haddon. 'Turner visited our master this morning, and I eavesdropped on their conversation. He was in some sort of club with Brodrick last night, and they got talking.

Brodrick was drunk, and let slip a secret about fat old Jones who drowned the other day. Apparently, Jones liked robbing banks.'

Chaloner was not sure whether to believe Haddon's claim – Brodrick liked to spin Temperance wild yarns, so perhaps he had done the same to Turner, too. The colonel was not as gullible as Temperance, but the Earl's cousin had a clever tongue and a plausible manner, and it was not impossible that he had executed one of his practical jokes. Chaloner decided to speak to Brodrick directly, and set off for White Hall, leaving Haddon buying expensive pastries for his pampered dogs.

The first person he saw in the palace was Williamson, who waved to indicate he wanted to talk. Chaloner pretended not to notice, and stepped into a laundry to avoid him. The Spymaster followed, so Chaloner zigzagged through the steaming cauldrons and slipped out through a back door, hiding behind a stack of crates until Williamson threw up his hands in exasperation and gave up the chase. The second person he met was Barbara Chiffinch, who railed about the unkind trick that had been played on the Queen the night before. The King was said to be livid, and the Lord of Misrule had been ordered to leave her alone.

'Brodrick denies being the guilty party,' said Barbara angrily. 'But no one believes him. And quite right, too! Why else would he decree that anyone found out after dark would be doused in green paint? There is a rumour that the whole thing was Lady Castlemaine's idea, but no one likes to ask her and the King's fury means she is unlikely to confess, either.'

'I need to speak to Brodrick,' said Chaloner. 'About Jones.'

'I suppose you have heard that Jones robbed banks.' Barbara waved away Chaloner's surprise. 'The tale is all over White Hall this morning – Brodrick has a slack tongue. However, it is quite true. My husband has just confessed to me that he has known about Jones's illegal activities for years.'

Chaloner raised his eyebrows. 'And you believe him? I mean no disrespect, but your husband is not a reliable source of information.'

'I believe him,' said Barbara grimly. 'I can tell when he is lying – and he was not lying today. Besides, he also admitted to being Jones's accomplice once, helping to relieve Backwell's Bank of a thousand pounds. He knew details he could not have done, unless he had been directly involved.'

Chaloner rubbed his chin, thinking the story certainly explained why Jones had elected to carry his wealth about on his person – he would know from first-hand experience just how vulnerable banks could be. So, here was yet another government official who presented a respectable face to the world, but who was really something else.

'Why would he do such a thing?' he asked, more of himself than Barbara. 'He earned a good salary as Yeoman of the Household Kitchen, and his family is not poor.'

'It is not just a love of money that inspires men to steal.' Barbara's voice held a note of regret, and Chaloner supposed she was thinking about her husband. 'It is the thrill of playing with danger. Jones once told me he was bored with his job, so he obviously went out and found other ways to amuse himself. The Backwell's theft was meticulously planned – the thieves left no clues whatsoever.'

'Have you seen Brodrick this morning?' asked Chaloner, supposing he had better hear the tale from the source of the gossip.

Barbara grimaced. 'Try looking in the wine vaults. He usually visits about this time.'

Brodrick had been and gone by the time Chaloner had arrived, but the spy wanted to speak to the cellarer anyway, because of what the fellow had told Turner about Greene begging for brandywine. Daniel Munt repeated his story, indignation in every word.

'The first time, Thursday, I felt sorry for him, and let him have a jug, but then I saw his offices in darkness and knew he had played me for a fool. The second time he came, I sent him packing.'

'So he left empty-handed on Saturday?'

'I thought so, but after he had gone, I noticed some brandywine was missing. Now, I cannot be certain *he* took it, because a lot of men come here in the hope of a drink, and young Neale was particularly insistent that night. But it was there at the beginning of the evening, and gone when I locked up at midnight.'

Chaloner resumed his hunt for Brodrick, eventually tracking him down in the Banqueting Hall. In his capacity as Lord of Misrule, the Earl's cousin had hired the King's Players to perform a theatrical production, and was busy ensuring the set was built, the props were in place and the costumes were ready. While Chaloner waited for him to finish a frantic consultation with the stage-manager, he watched the actors rehearse, and the bawdy speeches told him *The Prick of Love* was probably one of Langston's masterpieces. One thespian cheerfully informed the spy that invitations had been issued to only a very select few, because the play was deemed too ribald for the average ear. After enduring two scenes of silly, predictable vulgarity, Chaloner was glad he was not on the guest list, because it was tedious stuff, and he had better things to do with his time.

'I am not sure picking this particular play was a terribly good idea,' confided Brodrick worriedly, as the spy approached. 'Lady Castlemaine chose it, but I did not realise it was quite so . . . The King will think me desperately lewd.'

'I am sure he has seen worse. It was unkind to invite your cousin, though.'

'The Earl?' Brodrick regarded him in horror. '*He* cannot come! He would have a seizure! My guests include His Majesty and a dozen close friends. But the Earl . . .' He shuddered at the notion.

'You had better warn him to stay away, then. I doubt he will listen to me, not after what happened the other night. You frightened him, Brodrick.'

Brodrick rubbed his eyes. 'It will not happen again – I think I have satisfied my cronies that the Lord of Misrule applies his mischief even-handedly. What did you want to ask me about?'

He confirmed what the spy already knew about Jones, adding only that Chiffinch had kept quiet about the fat man's penchant for theft while Jones had lived, but broke silence the moment he was dead. He had not gossiped about his own participation, though: he had disclosed that only to Barbara.

Chaloner left Brodrick to his preparations, and was about to walk outside when he saw a familiar figure lurking behind a stack of benches. The spy supposed he should not be surprised that Greene had wormed his way into a building where an obscene play was being rehearsed, bearing in mind his friendship with the author and his weakness for cheap whores. He regarded the clerk thoughtfully. Greene did not seem to be deriving any great enjoyment from the spectacle, though, and the expression on his face could best be described as haunted.

'I understand you have a liking for this sort of thing,' Chaloner said softly, watching the clerk leap in alarm at the voice so close to his ear. 'It was an interest you and Langston shared.'

'You are wrong,' replied Greene hoarsely. His face was very pale. 'I was aware that he wrote . . . a certain kind of verse, but I had never heard any of them until today. I find myself appalled.'

'I do not believe you. Witnesses say you frequent the lowest kind of brothels, and that you are well-known and popular in them.'

Greene closed his eyes. 'Then your witnesses have drawn conclusions from half-understood facts. Yes, I visit the Dog and Duck in Southwark, but not to avail myself of the women. I go to give alms, in the hope that some will take the money and make more respectable lives for themselves.'

Chaloner laughed, genuinely amused. 'Of course you do.'

'I have had two successes.' There was something in Greene's earnest, pleading voice that gave the spy pause for thought. 'One is now a cook-maid, and the other is a laundress. You may scoff, but I hope to save more young ladies in time. Of course, I cannot do it if I am hanged . . .'

Chaloner regarded him sceptically. 'And why should you want to rescue harlots?'

Greene swallowed hard, and looked away. 'Because my sister . . . during the Commonwealth, when it was hard for Royalists to earn a crust . . . It was the only way to feed her baby, her husband being killed at Naseby. I was unemployed myself then, and had no funds to share with her.'

'Your sister was a prostitute?' asked Chaloner in disbelief. His own family had endured struggles as hard as any, but his kinswomen had never resorted to those sorts of measures.

'Hush!' hissed Greene, distressed. 'There is no need to tell everyone. And she was *not* a prostitute – she just made herself available to one man in return for regular payment. After she died, I vowed to help other unfortunates. I do not know any gentlewomen in my sister's position, so I elected to save the poorest whores instead – the ones in the Dog and Duck, whom nobody else cares about.'

Chaloner was unconvinced. 'You have been seen laughing with them.'

'They are cheery company, and always greet me kindly. I have grown to like them, so yes, we laugh together. It makes for a pleasant change, because I seldom have cause to laugh with anyone else.'

'Then what about the three purses you tossed in the river on Thursday morning? Explain those.'

Greene looked unutterably weary. 'Again, your witnesses have misconstrued an innocent act. I did not throw *three* purses in the river – I threw *ten*. They belonged to Jones, and he left them at my house after Langston and I entertained him for dinner once. We always meant to return them to him, but we kept forgetting. They were a painful reminder of an evening with good friends, so I disposed of them.'

'Why hurl them in the Thames? Why not in a gutter? Or why not give them to your cheerful harlots? I am sure they would never refuse a free gift.'

'Because for me, dropping them in the river was a symbolic act,' whispered Greene miserably. 'Jones drowned, so it seemed fitting to . . . But I was not thinking clearly. I see now it was a stupid thing to have done, but that did not occur to me when I did it.'

There was a pitiful plausibility about the explanations, and Chaloner found he was not sure what to think. 'Then what about the brandywine?' he demanded. 'You told me you do not touch strong drink, yet you begged some from Munt on two occasions; and Turner found a secret supply in your office.'

Greene was close to tears. 'Damn! I was hoping no one would find out about Munt, because I knew how it would look. I asked him not to mention it, but I should have known he could not be trusted.'

'So, you lied to me,' said Chaloner flatly. 'The hidden brandywine *was* yours.'

'No! I do not drink brandywine, and I have no idea how those flasks came to be in my office. But I did ask Munt for some – on Thursday and then on Saturday. I told him I needed its stimulation, because I planned to work late. However, the real reason is because my vicar has a liking for it.'

Chaloner raised his eyebrows. 'Do you really expect me to believe that?'

'Ask him. He will tell you how I give him some most weeks. But Brodrick bought every last drop in London for his Babylonian punch, and I did not want to disappoint, so I inveigled some from Munt instead. So much for trying to be nice! But can you not see what is happening? Someone wants me accused, and is twisting innocent facts to trap me. I have explanations, but no one is listening.'

Chaloner regarded him thoughtfully. Perhaps the vicar of Wapping really did rely on Greene to provide him with a weekly dose of brandywine – and Chaloner knew from Wiseman that Brodrick *had* bought all the available supplies for his punch. It sounded ludicrous, but sometimes the truth was absurd.

'Who would do such a thing to you?' he asked eventually.

'You have asked me that before, and the answer is the same now as it was then: I do not know. I wish I did, because it must be a misunderstanding. I have lived a simple and godly life, and I cannot imagine why anyone should hate me so. All I can do is put my trust in God – and in you.'

Confused and uncertain, Chaloner decided to visit the Dog and Duck. He took a boat to the London Bridge, then made his way through the cramped, sunless alleys that formed the area known as the Bankside Stews. Mean houses, dirty taverns and filthy streets characterised that part of Southwark, and it teemed with life. The noise was deafening, with tradesmen declaring the virtues of their wares, carts clattering along cobbled streets, and a cacophony arising from an escaped and furious bull.

The Dog and Duck was famous for its willing ladies, and Chaloner supposed it was an obvious target for anyone wanting to save fallen women. He entered its vast, smelly interior, and found a seat in a corner at the back, intending to sit quietly and watch the prostitutes in action before selecting one he thought might answer his questions. But the lasses were used to men lurking in the shadows, and he was approached almost immediately by a sallow-faced girl who told him her name was Alice.

'Are you from Court?' she asked with a coquettish smile. 'You are very well dressed.'

Chaloner placed a coin on the table. 'Will you answer some questions?'

'For a silver shilling, I will do anything you like. Shall we go upstairs?'

Chaloner watched a rat strut boldly across the festering rushes on the floor, and did not like to imagine the state of the beds. He was not particularly fastidious, but nothing would be gained from rolling around among fleas. 'I would prefer to stay here.'

'Very well, as long as you promise not to do anything embarrassing. I got my reputation, see.'

'I shall do my best. Do you know a Westminster clerk called Greene?'

'Mr Greene? Of course! He visits us almost every week. Are you his friend? I am glad he got one, because he is a lovely man. He took us to St Paul's Cathedral on Christmas Day.'

'Did he? What for?'

'He said we deserved to see something beautiful. We got dressed in our best clothes, and he paid for a carriage *and* a nice dinner afterwards. Bless him.'

'Does he avail himself of your services?' asked Chaloner bluntly.

Alice's lips tightened in disapproval. 'That's none of your business, and—'

Chaloner removed the coin from the table. 'Then I shall ask someone else.'

312

She reached out to grab his hand, revealing black teeth in an ingratiating smile. 'No need to be hasty, sir. You cannot blame a girl for being wary of someone what comes in asking questions about her friends. Why do you want to know anyway? Is it about the trouble he is in? He told us about that – some Court bastard is after his blood. But he is a good man, so they should leave him alone.'

'I am trying to help him. And you can help him, too, by answering my questions honestly. So, I repeat: does Greene frolic with you?'

Alice prised the money from his fingers and shook her head. 'No. He comes to ask after our health, and he tries to persuade us to do other jobs. He paid for Meg to train as a washerwoman.'

'He told me,' lied Chaloner. He had actually failed to make this connection, but supposed it made sense. Of course, Meg had not moved too far from her old trade, if she was enjoying late-night trysts with the likes of Colonel Turner in the Painted Chamber.

'She is over there,' said Alice, pointing. 'She came back, because White Hall is too debauched.'

Chaloner looked to where she gestured, and saw a small, pretty woman with bright blue eyes. She was laughing with some of her colleagues, and he was not surprised that Turner had taken a fancy to her. She had all her own teeth, her skin was smooth and white, and she had more yellow curls than the Lord Chancellor's best wig. Alice beckoned her over.

'Dear Mr Greene,' said Meg sadly, after Chaloner had been introduced as the clerk's friend. 'The villains at White Hall are accusing him of murder, but he would never hurt a fly. He is gentle and kind, and that is the

313

reason they hate him – his goodness makes them ashamed of themselves.'

Extraordinary though it might seem, Chaloner saw Greene had been telling the truth about his clandestine visits to Southwark. More probing told him the clerk had never taken advantage of any woman in the brothel, although all had offered him their services free of charge. He also gave them money when they were ill, tired or distressed. They looked on him as a father, and it was not long before Chaloner was surrounded by prostitutes, all eager to convince him that Greene was next in line for sainthood. Moreover, Meg confirmed the tale about Greene's fallen sister, and said that he and Langston had indeed hosted a dinner for Jones, at which the fat man had accidentally left behind ten leather purses. She had been employed to wash the dishes afterwards, and had seen them.

Chaloner tuned out the chattering voices and thought about what he had learned. If Greene had been honest about Southwark, then there was no reason to doubt his other claims, either. And that suggested he was right: someone *was* trying to have him wrongfully accused of murder. But who? Someone who disliked his integrity? Or someone who thought the Southwark harlots did not deserve a friend?

By the time he left the Dog and Duck, dusk was fast approaching, bringing with it a bitter, sleety drizzle that turned Southwark's streets more dismal than ever. Meg begged a ride in the hackney he took back to the city, saying she had laundry to deliver to Tryan the merchant in Lymestrete. Chaloner was going to Hercules' Pillars Alley, because he wanted to apologise to Temperance, so Lymestrete was not far out of his way.

'People have been worried about you,' he said, as they thundered across the Bridge. The driver's recklessly selfish speed reminded him of why he did not like walking across it.

'About me?' asked Meg, startled. 'That is nice. Who?'

Chaloner looked at her in the fading daylight, and found he could not answer. Her housemate had not been overly concerned when she had failed to return home, assuming – doubtless on account of her previous occupation – that she was with a man. Turner had been anxious, but only because he thought he might have lost out on a romp. Or was he doing the colonel an injustice?

'Turner,' he replied, for want of anyone better.

Her pretty face split into a hopeful grin. 'Really? I thought he did not care about me when he failed to turn up for our tryst. I waited until nightfall on Saturday, but there was no sign of him.'

Chaloner frowned. 'Nightfall? I was under the impression that he expected you much later.'

'He told me to meet him at the witching hour.'

'That is midnight.'

'No, it is dusk. Everyone knows witches come out when daylight fades, so the witching hour is between sunset and total darkness. Why? Are you saying he thinks it was another time?'

'It *is* another time, Meg. He expected you at twelve o'clock.'

Meg's eyes were huge. 'Lord! He will think *I* abandoned *him*! The dear man! I should have known better than to question his love for me. He said he adores me, and he does. And I was so angry with him! I kept thinking he had deserted me, after all I had done for him – all

315

that smuggling him in and out of the palace on my laundry cart every time he had a meeting with Lady Castlemaine.'

'Why would you do that?' asked Chaloner, wondering how on earth Turner had managed to persuade one lover to facilitate his visits to another.

'Because she needs him to protect her from that awful Earl of Clarendon,' explained Meg, earnestly ingenuous. 'The Earl keeps foisting his attentions on her, see. But that was before he hired my colonel as his spy – now my dearest has an official post, he can come and go as he pleases.'

'I see,' said Chaloner, not sure whether to be more impressed by her absolute credulity or Turner's colourful lies.

'You have made me *so* happy with this news! I should have known he thought I was special, or he would not have met me so often. Did I tell you that we have enjoyed secret assignations in the Painted Chamber every Monday and Thursday for the past two months?'

'Even last week?' asked Chaloner, wondering whether it was significant: Chetwynd had died on a Thursday, and Langston on a Monday. And both bodies had been found in the Painted Chamber.

She nodded, smiling gleefully. 'That was when he gave me one of his ear-strings.'

'How long do these sessions last?'

Meg's grin broadened. 'From dusk until dawn. We meet in the Painted Chamber, and then he takes me to an inn in Chelsey. But our last tryst was arranged for a Saturday, at a different time than usual, which explains my silly confusion. So, now you have cleared that up, all I have to worry about is Mr Greene. I *must* do something to get

316

him out of trouble. I owe it to him, after all he has done for me.'

Chaloner did not think the interference of a harlot would do Greene much good. 'May I come with you to Lymestrete? Tryan is a friend of Greene's, and might know something that will help him.'

'I will do anything for Mr Greene,' said Meg gamely. 'Even be seen in company with a rogue from White Hall. You will have to carry the washing, though. I feel an aching back coming on.'

Lymestrete was an ancient road full of buildings that did not really go together. Precarious hovels rubbed shoulders with wealthy merchants' homes, while shops that sold expensive jewellery sat next to ones that hawked cheap candles. Tryan's house was near St Dionis Backchurch, a handsome fifteenth-century chapel with a lofty spire.

Meg and Chaloner – the latter toting a sack of clothes – were shown into Tryan's parlour. It was a pleasant room, with a roaring fire, chestnuts roasting in a tray, and books everywhere. There was a chest under the window, armed with three heavy locks that suggested valuables were within. The spy wondered why Tryan did not conceal it with a cloth – as it stood, most would-be thieves would view it more of a challenge than a deterrent.

'Meg!' cried Tryan in pleasure. 'I was beginning to think you had made off with my shirts. You are not usually late with your deliveries.'

The bandy-legged merchant was sitting at a large, polished table, surrounded by papers. A brief glance at one of the ledgers revealed some staggering sums of money, indicating business was booming. He was not

317

alone, because Hargrave was with him, dividing his attention between finance and relieving his itching scalp with the sharp end of a quill.

Meg began to dance around with Tryan's shirts, explaining what she had done to render them so pristine. He was captivated by her youthful exuberance, and Chaloner was sure she was earning herself a handsome bonus by taking the time to charm him. Meanwhile, Hargrave frowned at the spy.

'You have a curious way of spending your time,' he said suspiciously. 'I would have thought the Lord Chancellor's intelligencers have better things to do than carry laundry for harlots.'

'And how many Lord Chancellor's intelligencers do you know?' asked Chaloner, amused.

'Two: you and Turner. I might have known three, had Langston chosen to accept the commission. He was outraged when the Earl first approached him, but I told him he should have taken it.'

'Why?' asked Chaloner curiously.

'Because your Earl *was* a good man, but White Hall is beginning to turn him wicked. However, he is probably redeemable, and I felt Langston was the fellow to save him.'

'You are in no position to criticise another man's virtue,' said Chaloner coolly. 'I understand you provide materials for Langston's dramas, but, judging from the rehearsal I saw today, they are hardly morality plays.'

Hargrave's face flushed red. He shot an uneasy glance at Tryan, but Tryan's attention was fixed on the cavorting Meg, and he would not have noticed an earthquake. 'Langston did ask me to help him,' he muttered uncomfortably. 'As a favour to a friend. But I had no idea of the lewd content of his—'

'You must have done,' interrupted Chaloner, tired of lies, 'because of the manner of props required. I saw some this morning, and you cannot possibly have been ignorant of what they are required to do.'

Hargrave shot a second uneasy glance in his colleague's direction. 'Can we discuss this later?' he whispered. 'Perhaps in a tavern? Tryan has a high opinion of me, and I do not want that to change. And I am sure we can come to some arrangement – you will keep a silent tongue, and I will provide you with a little something in return. What do you say to five pounds?'

Chaloner hated it when people tried to bribe him; it told him they held no regard for his integrity. 'I do not want your money.'

Hargrave winced when the spy made no effort to lower his voice. 'What then?' he asked, a little desperately. 'Information? Such as that the Lea brothers knew about Langston's obscene dramatics – they wrote out the different parts for the actors to learn.'

'What about Greene?' asked Chaloner, to see whether Hargrave would confirm what the hapless clerk had claimed. 'Did *he* know what these plays entailed?'

'I sincerely doubt it. He is a prudish fellow and would have been deeply shocked.'

'Then tell me about the prayer meetings you attended with Scobel.'

Hargrave blinked at him. 'Scobel? But he died years ago. What can possibly interest you about—' He saw Chaloner's expression, and hurried on quickly. 'They took place in his home, and comprised a group of men who joined together to thank God for His goodness.'

'I do not believe you. I think there was more.'

'I could lie, and so end this embarrassing interview,'

said Hargrave quietly, 'but we really *did* meet for prayers. Scobel felt not enough people were thanking God for their good fortune, and set out to rectify the matter. And, for a while, it did seem that we – the grateful men – enjoyed better success than those who just kept asking for things. Obviously, once we realised it, we were keen to continue.'

'So, it went from being a religious occasion to one of superstition?'

Hargrave winced. 'You put it bluntly, but yes. Personally, I feel it is time to move on – to end these gatherings and stand on our own two feet. But the others are afraid their luck will change if we stop. They point out that when Langston left, his bank was robbed. Then there is Doling, who renounced us because he objected to what he called our pagan slavishness to Lady Fortune – he lost all at the Restoration, and has continued to lose since.'

'He certainly lost the court case that came before Chetwynd,' said Chaloner. 'Although I imagine your bribe of a cottage had something to do with that.'

Hargrave's eyes bulged in horror, and he shot another uncomfortable glance at Tryan. 'I admit I gave Chetwynd a small property, but it had nothing to do with Doling's claim for fishing rights. The two incidents are entirely unrelated. Perhaps my colleagues are right, and that if Doling had not abandoned our prayer meetings . . .' He let the suggestion hang in the air.

Chaloner regarded him in silence for a moment. 'I do not believe that everyone who attends these gatherings enjoys good fortune.'

'And you would be right – Symons has not, despite his regular appearances. However, most of us have done

320

extremely well, although I still feel it is time to end them. Unfortunately, Scobel made us promise to remain friends and pray together. We were stupid to have sworn sacred vows to do as he asked – it was a different world then, and we were different men.'

'I am not sure I understand.'

Hargrave clawed at the scabs on his head. 'Scobel predicted the Restoration would bring a change in morality, and he wanted to ensure a spark of virtue remained. However, while he was right in that standards *have* changed since the King returned, I think it is a mistake to follow outdated principles.'

'So you approve of what you saw at the Tennis Court? You prefer those values to Scobel's?'

'I would not go that far,' said Hargrave stiffly. 'But I am not comfortable with rabid sanctimony, either. I wish I had the courage to break away from the others, but their superstition has started to infect me – I do not want to end up like Doling, so I keep waiting for someone else to leave first.'

'What are you two talking about?' asked Tryan, smiling as Meg flounced merrily through the door, clutching a full purse. She winked before she left, making him blush with pleasure.

'Our prayer meetings,' replied Hargrave quickly. 'And how I think we should end them.'

'That would be madness,' said Tryan, turning to give him his full attention. 'You are wealthy, blessed with a good wife and obedient children. Why would you risk all that? Besides, Scobel made you swear an oath, and you do not want God angry with you for vow-breaking.'

The two merchants began a debate on the matter, and when he saw he would learn nothing more from listening

321

to them, Chaloner bowed a farewell and left, thinking of how little he had achieved that day. He had reinforced his conviction that Greene was innocent, but was no further forward with identifying the real culprit. However, he was determined to put the evening to good use, so he headed for Hercules' Pillars Alley.

It was early by club standards, and the atmosphere in the parlour was still quietly genteel. Pipe smoke hung blue and hazy in the air, overlain by the scent of 'burnt' claret and orange-rind comfits. Temperance was playing cards with Chiffinch. She smiled when she saw Chaloner, and he sighed his relief – it told him she was sorry about their row, too, and was willing to make amends.

'The Earl's man,' said Chiffinch, regarding the spy in icy disdain. There was a network of broken veins across his nose and cheeks, and the whites of his eyes were yellow, both the result of a life spent in pursuit of hedonistic pleasures. 'I am surprised he pays you enough to let you come here.'

'Tom is my personal guest,' said Temperance, intervening before there was trouble. She need not have worried, because Chaloner was not going to let himself be needled by the likes of Chiffinch. Unless he insulted Barbara, in which case the man could expect to be punched.

'I thought you would be watching the play in the Banqueting House tonight,' Chaloner said to him amiably. 'The one Langston wrote.'

'I have seen *The Prick of Love* before,' said Chiffinch sourly. 'It is far too rude for my taste. The occasion might have been amusing, had your Earl been there, but he sent word that he is ill. He is in perfect health, of course, and I suspect Brodrick lost courage and warned him off. The man is a base coward.'

Chaloner did not like to imagine what the Earl would have made of the performance, if the likes of Chiffinch considered it excessive.

'I shall fetch you some syllabub, Mr Chiffinch,' said Temperance, standing and indicating that Snowflake was to take her place at the table. 'My cook tells me it is the best he has ever made. At least, I think that is what he was saying – he is not always easy to understand.'

Chaloner followed her into the hall. 'I am sorry about last night,' he began, the moment they were alone. 'I was wrong to question you about Bernini—'

'And I am sorry, too,' interrupted Temperance. 'You should have told me I am a suspect for stealing the King's statue, but I should have explained myself when you asked. We were both at fault.'

'You are not a suspect. At least, not to me. Spymaster Williamson might reach other conclusions, though, which is why I warned you to be wary about confiding in your patrons.'

'You still trust me, then?'

'Of course. I do not believe you have changed so much that you would steal.'

'And you would be right. Reputation is everything in a place like this, and I cannot afford rumours of deceit or dishonesty. So, are you still coming to meet James on Twelfth Night eve?'

Chaloner smiled. 'If I am still invited.'

She kissed his cheek with the sisterly affection he had missed since they had started to grow apart. 'He is eager to meet you, and I have a feeling you will be good friends.

323

However, there is one thing I should tell you in advance: we will not be eating pelican.'

Good, thought Chaloner. 'Why not?'

'Because it was delivered this morning, and it was such a sweet thing that I could not bring myself to wring its neck. Maude took it to St James's Park instead, and released it into the company of its fellows.'

Chaloner smiled again. 'I should go,' he said, watching her select a bowl of syllabub for Chiffinch. He was hungry, but the thick, plum-flavoured beverage did not tempt him at all. 'You are busy.'

'Never too busy for you, and I owe you an explanation about Bernini, anyway. I asked questions about him, because Brodrick and Chiffinch kept talking about his fine carving of the King's head. They chatted about it for weeks – so long that my interest was piqued.'

Chaloner frowned. 'Do you think *they* stole it, perhaps because Brodrick plans to use it in one of his japes as Lord of Misrule?'

'Yes, I do, and so does James. I told him everything last night, and he said there is no other explanation. He also told me I should confide all this to you as soon as possible.'

'Why would he do that?' asked Chaloner, puzzled.

'Because he is an art-lover himself, and thinks the bust might get broken if it is used in some wild caper. He says that would be a tragedy.' Temperance was silent for a moment, then touched his arm. 'Chiffinch told me you asked him and Brodrick whether they owned a ruby ring. Presumably, you have reason to believe that either the clerk-killer or the statue-thief might own one. Am I right?'

'Yes,' agreed Chaloner cautiously, but did not elaborate.

'If it was small, then perhaps it belonged to a lady,'

suggested Temperance tentatively. 'There is a tendency for men to forget that we can steal and commit murder, too, so do not fall into that trap. And there are a lot of ruthless women at Court.'

Chaloner nodded, and did not tell her that the notion had already occurred to him. He did not want to risk another quarrel by being ungracious. 'I will not forget,' he promised.

When Chaloner returned to his rooms, the bowls he had set to catch the drips that morning were so full they had overflowed, and the floor was awash. There was a note pinned to the door from the instrument-maker who rented the room below, complaining of water streaming down his walls. Landlord Ellis had been to inspect the trouble – his muddy footprints were everywhere – but in a rare moment of self-doubt, he had apparently decided repairs were beyond him, and had not attempted any. Normally, he was only too pleased to ply his dubious skills to effect even more dubious remedies, and the fact that he was daunted by the scale of the problem did not bode well for the future.

As it stood, the place was not at all inviting, and it was raining again – Chaloner did not want to spend a second night dodging deluges, so he decided to leave. Before he went, he fed his cat with some salted meat from the pantry, although it ate only two mouthfuls before going to wash itself by the fireplace, and he supposed it had found itself something more appetising during the day. He hoped it had not been a bird. He spent a few moments teasing it with a piece of ribbon, just to prove he could be in its company without resorting to meaningless chatter – or, worse yet, a serious conversation – then left for the greater comfort of Hannah's house. She was asleep when he arrived, but moved over so he could climb into the bed beside her.

'Where have you been?' she murmured drowsily, nestling against him. 'You smell of smoke.'

Remembering her response the last time he had admitted to visiting Temperance's club, he was uncertain how to reply. He flailed around for something that was true, but that she would believe.

'Not again,' she said with a groan, when he took too long. 'Surely, you cannot have been engaged in secret business *all* day? Or is the Earl getting every last penny's worth out of you?'

'Yes, he is,' said Chaloner, feeling this at least was something that could not be disputed. 'I think I have finally eliminated Greene as a suspect for the murders, but I have made no progress in identifying the real killer. Or in locating the King's statue.'

She climbed out of the bed, and went to prod the fire. He supposed his answer had not been to her liking, but did not know what else to say. It was not a good idea to lie every time the truth was unacceptable, because there was a danger that he might forget what he had told her, and contradict himself later. Thurloe had taught him that liars needed very good memories, and he had always preferred avoiding questions to fabricating replies. But he did not want to do either with Hannah.

'I talked to my cat this morning,' he gabbled, rather desperately. 'It had caught a pigeon.'

She turned to look at him, but her face was backlit by the fire and he could not see her expression. 'Did it answer back?'

'It made a noise,' replied Chaloner cagily. 'Is that what you mean?'

'That poor animal,' said Hannah. He could hear laughter in her voice. 'Attached to a man who is so unforthcoming that it takes a captured pigeon to elicit a reaction from him.'

Chaloner struggled to make her understand why the incident had unsettled him. 'It is because of Haddon. He converses with his dogs out of loneliness. He is quite peculiar over them.'

She stared at him. 'And you think that by passing the occasional fond remark to your cat you may become as odd as him? That is foolish, Thomas! You are not lonely – you have lots of friends.'

'In London, I have two: Temperance and Thurloe.'

'And not me?' She sounded hurt. 'Or Barbara Chiffinch, who, for all her faults, is fond of you. Or Bulteel, who has asked you to stand as godfather to his only son? Or even Haddon, who will not let the Earl say anything bad about you? We are nothing, are we? And here I was about to suggest that you come to sit next to me at the fire, and allow me to help you solve your mysteries.'

'Now?' asked Chaloner uneasily.

'Yes, now,' she said impatiently. 'Why do you think I have been stoking it up? You sound tired and dispirited, and I thought you might appreciate some help. It is what *friends* do for each other.'

'I see. But how—'

'You will tell me everything you have learned, and I shall see if I can spot connections you may have missed. You look suspicious. Why? Do you imagine *I* am the killer, and I am trying to ascertain how much you have found out about me?'

327

It was not easy for Chaloner to put aside his natural reticence and confide his discoveries – he could do it with Thurloe, but Thurloe had been his spymaster, and was different – and discussing his work with Hannah felt very wrong. But images of Haddon's eccentricity kept flooding into his mind, so he ignored the clamouring instincts that urged him to silence, and began.

'Greene is not the killer,' he said, speaking slowly to give himself time to assemble his thoughts in a sensible manner. 'Which means someone else is the culprit.'

'Impeccable logic,' said Hannah, beckoning him to sit next to her. 'Is there anything else, or is that the sole conclusion you have reached?'

He knelt by the fire and prodded it absently. 'The obvious suspects are the men who attend these prayer meetings. For example, Hargrave – he wants the occasions to end, so perhaps he killed the three clerks because they did not.'

But, he thought, Tryan did not want them to end, either, and *he* was not dead. Did that mean Hargrave was innocent? Or was Tryan spared because he was Hargrave's friend, and murdering mere acquaintances was not the same as dispatching a man he obviously liked and respected?

'Who else is on your list?' asked Hannah, when he faltered into silence.

'Gold.'

'Sir Nicholas? No! He has asked us to his soirée on Monday – in two days time – and a killer would not do that. Besides, he is too old to go a-murdering.'

Chaloner smiled at the notion that issuing invitations to parties should be considered an exonerating factor.

328

'He is not as frail as he looks. I saw him attack a man who assaulted Bess the other night.'

'Neale!' pounced Hannah. 'Now there *is* a man who would not hesitate to kill by poison.'

Chaloner inclined his head to acknowledge it was possible. 'Meanwhile, Doling left the prayer group after the Restoration. Perhaps envy drove him to kill three men who have been very successful. The same is true of Symons. Or perhaps I am over-complicating matters, and the Lea brothers or one of the Vines are the culprits – killing an unloved kinsman in order to secure an inheritance.'

'And dispatching two more in an attempt to lead you astray,' mused Hannah, nodding. 'Do not forget George Vine devised a plot to assassinate Cromwell, either – that shows him to be murderous. Are there any other suspects?'

'A corn-chandler called Reeve, who wears a disguise when he goes to John's Coffee House.'

There were also Turner and Swaddell, both of whom had infiltrated the meetings to spy. Could one of them be the killer? There was certainly more to Turner than the amiable buffoon he liked to project, while Swaddell was a spymaster's assassin. And, of course, there was Williamson himself. But Hannah did not need to be told about any of them – the knowledge might prove dangerous to her.

'Was there any other link between the victims?' she asked. 'Besides these religious assemblies?'

'They all argued publicly with my Earl. And they all appeared to be virtuous, but transpired to have the usual human flaws – dishonesty, corruption, licentiousness.'

'So your killer dispatched not good men, but sinners? Are there any vicars among your suspects?'

Chaloner shook his head. 'I should visit John's Coffee House tomorrow, and talk to the owner. So far, only the people who actually take part in the meetings have told me what transpires in them.'

'So, I *have* helped,' announced Hannah with satisfaction. 'I have given you a new direction to follow. Now, let me see what else I can accomplish. Tell me what you know of the culprit himself.'

'He used poison to kill his victims. And he may have dropped a ruby ring – a small one, like a woman's – then sent members of an elite train-band to retrieve it for him.'

'A woman's? Then it will be irrelevant,' declared Hannah immediately. 'The killer is not a lady, and you had better ignore this bauble, or it will mislead you.'

'Very well,' said Chaloner, although he had no intention of doing so. He wondered why she was so vehement, and recalled Temperance's words about the same clue: that he should bear in mind that a lady *could* be responsible. It was odd to hear two such different views within a short space of time.

'What about the statue?' asked Hannah, changing the subject rather abruptly. 'Any progress there?'

'None,' replied Chaloner gloomily.

Hannah was silent for a moment, then started to speak. 'When Bernini finished the bust, a courtier was charged to escort it from Rome. It took him three months of dangerous travel to bring it to London. His name was Thomas Chambers, and he was my father.'

Chaloner stared at her, asking himself why she had not mentioned it sooner. Was this why the Queen had elected not to share with her the tale about it being offered to Greene and Margaret Symons? Because

Hannah had a curious and unique connection to the thing? 'I see.'

'I was a child at the time, but I remember him coming home, and telling my mother and me about his adventures. The other thing I recall is that the bust was very heavy.'

'Large pieces of marble usually are.'

Hannah pulled a face at the coolness of his voice. 'I am trying to help, Tom, so do not be acerbic with me. If the Bernini bust was weighty, then a thief cannot have shoved it under his arm and walked off with it. He would have needed transport. Or a large and very strong sack. *Ergo*, there will be a witness to the crime. You just need to find him.'

'I have asked virtually everyone in the palace, and if there is a witness, then he is not talking. And the area around the Shield Gallery is deserted at night, anyway, and security is minimal. I could steal anything I like, and no one would be any the wiser.'

'That is not a good thing to claim – it could see you in trouble. But you should sleep.' Hannah ended the discussion by jumping back into bed. 'You will need your wits about you tomorrow, if you are to fathom any sense into these mysteries.'

It was raining hard when Chaloner woke the next morning, and windy, too. He wondered what state his Fetter Lane rooms were in, and was glad to be in Hannah's cosy home. She toasted bread over the fire for breakfast, smearing it thickly with a marmalade of quinces. She chattered happily as she worked, asking about his plans for the day, and demanding to know how he intended to prove he was a better investigator than

331

Turner. He gave monosyllabic answers, most of his attention on the statue of Venus that Margaret Symons had carved. It really was exquisite, and he thought it a pity she had died before achieving the recognition she had so clearly deserved.

'You will have to find time for church, too,' Hannah babbled on, handing him a cup of warmed ale. 'It is Sunday, and you do not want to be on a list that says you are a Catholic. Like me.'

'You are on a list?'

'No, I am Catholic. I converted when I was appointed to serve the Queen. Does that shock you?'

'Oh, deeply.' He saw her wince, and hastened to be serious. 'Of course not. Besides, the crucifix by your bed is something of a giveaway, and so are the specific times you tend the Queen.'

She regarded him curiously. 'You are not going to suggest I change back again?'

'Why would I do that? Your devotions are your own business.'

'That is an unusually enlightened attitude, especially from a man who serves the Earl. I suppose it comes from spending so much time overseas.'

Or from seeing the trouble religious dissent could cause, thought Chaloner, as he and Hannah set out for White Hall together. He abandoned her when he saw their path was going to intersect that of Williamson, and went to lurk in an alley near the Tennis Court until the Spymaster had gone. As he peered out from his hiding place, he saw Williamson and Hannah stop to talk to each other. The exchange appeared to be cordial, and Chaloner frowned, wondering why she should deign to associate with such a fellow.

Knowing the Spymaster was loose in White Hall made Chaloner decide to go to Westminster instead. He went a second time to look at the lane where Jones had died, but it was jammed tight with carts, all waiting to be loaded with coal from a barge that was docked at the pier, and there were too many people around to permit useful skulking. He decided to come back when it was less busy. He met Symons in Old Palace Yard, and offered his condolences for Margaret's death, but the man barely acknowledged him before shuffling away with his spiky orange head bowed.

'Poor Margaret,' said Doling, appearing suddenly at Chaloner's elbow. The spy jumped, astonished that anyone should be able to come so close without him hearing. All his senses were on full alert, because he was determined to avoid Williamson, which meant the surly ex-Commonwealth official possessed a very stealthy tread. 'And poor Symons, too. They were a devoted couple.'

'She seemed a decent woman.' Chaloner did not like the way Doling was standing so close to him, and the knife in his sleeve dropped into the palm of his hand.

'She was the best,' replied Doling with one of his scowls. 'And it is a pity she is gone. She will not be properly mourned, though, except by Symons and me.'

It was a curious thing to say. 'What do you mean?'

'I mean the acquisitive vultures who gather in Covent Garden do not appreciate her goodness, even though she was a shining light at the meetings in Scobel's house. Of course, that was before he died. Once he was gone, they effectively banished her from the gatherings by electing to hold them in a coffee house, where women are not permitted to tread. It broke her heart, poor soul.'

'She wanted to be there?'

'Yes.' Doling clenched his fists, as if he was considering thumping someone. 'She told me that if she had been allowed to pray with them, her husband might have enjoyed greater success. Of course, it is all superstitious nonsense. Scobel was wrong to make us take that vow.'

'You swore it, too?' asked Chaloner. 'And then broke it?'

Doling grimaced. 'The others say that is why I have been unlucky, but I disagree – God does not reward people for praying in a specific place or with specific people.'

'I suppose not.'

Doling's expression was distant, almost as if he was talking to someone else. 'Scobel thought he could keep his friends godly by making them promise to pray with each other, but he reckoned without White Hall. All of them – Chetwynd, Vine, Langston, Jones, Gold and others – used to be decent, upright souls, but White Hall has sucked the goodness out of them. Now they are just like everyone else.'

'Except you? You have retained your lofty principles?'

Doling glowered at him, and for a moment, Chaloner thought the man was going to swing a punch. He braced himself to duck, but Doling took a deep breath and it seemed to calm him.

'I am not perfect, but I have done my best. I wish Scobel was still alive – if ever his sober, gentle guidance was needed, it is now. Did you ever meet him?'

Chaloner tried to recall what Thurloe had said about the man, but found he could only remember one thing. 'He looked as though his head was on upside down.'

Doling's eyes opened wide with astonishment, and Chaloner wondered whether the remark might induce him to react with violence, but then, unexpectedly, the dour Parliamentarian cracked a smile. 'I suppose he did, with his thick beard and bald head. That has never occurred to me before. Dear Scobel!'

Still smiling, Doling stamped away.

Great sheets of rain were gusting across the courtyard when Chaloner arrived in White Hall, and no one ventured across the middle of it, preferring instead to take advantage of the scanty protection around the edges. Gold, Neale and Bess were among the cowering throng, and, as they walked, Bess's hat was ripped from her head and went skittering through the mud. She bleated her dismay, so Gold elbowed Neale and indicated he was to retrieve it. Obligingly, Neale hurried into the rain, golden curls whipping about his face, but each time he came close to the headpiece, the wind tugged it away again. Chaloner saw Gold snigger, confirming his suspicions about the man: he was *not* the feeble ancient he wanted people to see.

Eventually, Neale snagged the hat by jumping on it, and hurried back to present Bess with a soggy, dented mess of wet material and broken feathers. She simpered her appreciation before jamming it on her head, apparently oblivious of the fact that it was well past salvation. Then she gaped blankly when Lady Castlemaine asked if it was worn by decree of the Lord of Misrule.

'Stupid woman,' muttered Munt, who had stopped next to Chaloner to watch the incident unfold. 'I cannot imagine what possessed a sane fellow like Gold to marry her – she looks like a sheep. But he made his fortune in wool, so perhaps she reminds him of the beasts that set him on the road to riches.'

'I have been told his success is the result of prayers with his friends,' said Chaloner.

335

'Well, there is that, I suppose,' acknowledged Munt. 'I went to a few meetings myself, when Scobel was alive, but then he asked me to sign an oath, promising to be virtuous, so I left. We live in an uncertain world, and no man should swear vows that might hinder him later.'

'I suppose not,' said Chaloner, thinking it was uncertain indeed, if people were unwilling to commit to a future where they might be asked to uphold their principles.

'Did you hear Greene did it again last night?' asked Munt. His expression was indignant. 'At about eight o'clock, he came to my cellar and asked for brandywine, spinning some wild tale about it being for his vicar. I told him where to take his lies, but, like last time, when I did an inventory, I found a flask of the stuff was missing. I wager you anything it was him.'

'His vicar does like brandywine,' said Chaloner, thinking Greene was a fool to indulge his priest's penchant for strong liquor at such a time. Theft from the King's cellars was a serious charge, and he was doing himself no favours. Or had someone else stolen the flask, knowing what Greene had asked of Munt, with the express purpose of seeing him in even deeper water? Still pondering the question, he made his way to the Earl's office, nodding to Bulteel and Haddon as he passed. Haddon was looking thoroughly dejected, while Bulteel wore a smile that was uncharacteristically vengeful: clearly, one had scored a victory over the other. Chaloner stifled a sigh. Their squabble was ridiculous, and beginning to be annoying.

He stepped into the Earl's office, and was making his way towards the desk when he tripped over one of Haddon's dogs. He stumbled forward, and his head connected sharply with the chandelier. He staggered, seeing stars – he was not wearing his metal-lined hat this time. The Earl grinned when he turned to see the spy gripping his head with both hands.

'That will teach you to try to sneak up on me,' he said spitefully. 'Incidentally, Turner has been to see me twice this morning already. He came to say he has almost enough evidence to arrest Greene. I said Greene was the killer, and should never have listened when you said he was not. And Haddon was wrong to take your side against me, too, although he will pay for his folly with five pounds.'

'It is unfortunate,' said Chaloner, fighting the urge to voice a few pithy objections to the Earl's dangerously placed ceiling fixture.

'What do you mean by that?' demanded the Earl suspiciously. 'What is unfortunate?'

Chaloner had meant it was unfortunate that the Earl might be about to look foolish, given that the 'evidence' was not as solid as Turner had probably led him to believe. However, he had blurted it out because he was in pain, and wished he had been in sufficient control of his wits to say nothing. 'What is that noise?' he asked.

The Earl raised his eyebrows. 'I hear nothing. And you owe me an apology – you were stupid to champion Greene, and your unwillingness to accept the truth has cost the lives of two men. Vine and Langston were not particularly *good* men, it would seem, but they did not deserve to be poisoned.'

'There is a snuffling sound.' Chaloner glanced around the Earl's sumptuous chamber, but could see nothing amiss.

'Haddon's dogs. Why do you keep trying to change the subject? Are you knocked out of your senses? Turner

337

would never walk into a chandelier. He is a fine fellow: tall, strong, and *obedient*.'

Chaloner supposed his unwarranted assault on the light fitting was the final straw, and the Earl had decided he was inferior to the colonel in every way: he was about to be dismissed. Absently, he wondered whether he had enough money to buy a berth on a ship to the New World, or whether he would have to acquire some illicitly. There was always Jones's hoard, which no one had stepped forward to claim. He brought himself up sharply when he realised what he was contemplating – he had stolen in the past, but only in the course of his duties, and never for his own benefit. Were Hargrave and Doling right, and there *was* a poison at White Hall that sapped the goodness out of people?

'There *is* an odd sound, sir,' he said, snapping out of his reverie when he heard it again. 'It is coming from your other office.'

'Dogs,' repeated the Earl. 'I asked Haddon to leave them at home, but he looked at me as though his world would end, and I did not have the heart to press the matter. Besides, I like dogs.'

Chaloner drew his sword when a low, guttural grunt emanated from the chamber in question. 'Have you been in there today?'

'You know I seldom use it in winter – it is too cold.' The Earl narrowed his eyes. 'Is this a ploy to prove your value as a bodyguard, in the hope that I will not oust you in favour of Turner?'

'Leave,' ordered Chaloner urgently, now certain something was wrong. He took a firmer grip on his sword and started to walk towards the door that linked the two rooms. 'Take Haddon and Bulteel with you.'

'How *dare* you tell me what to do! It is—'

Suddenly, the door swung open, and a bear shambled through it. It wore a muzzle over its grizzled nose, suggesting it was one of the performing beasts that provided Christmas entertainment. It had small, glittering eyes, and when it spotted Chaloner and the Earl, it immediately went up on its hind legs. It was enormous, and made a curious huffing sound, which the spy took to be some sort of warning. He stepped in front of the Earl, shielding him from it.

'Walk slowly towards the door,' he said quietly. There was no reply, and he glanced behind him to see the Earl's mouth hanging open in mute horror. 'Do not run, or it will—'

But the Earl was not listening. He issued a sharp shriek that made both bear and spy jump in alarm, then turned to flee. The sudden movement secured the animal's undivided attention, and it dropped to all fours to lumber after him. Chaloner hurled himself at it, so the weight of his body knocked it away from its intended target, but it had moved faster than its shambling gait suggested, and its slashing paw missed the Lord Chancellor by less than the width of a finger. The Earl reached the door and hauled on the handle for all he was worth, but panic made him clumsy and he could not get it open. He wailed in terror as the bear stalked towards him, long claws clicking on the marble floor.

'Hey!' shouted Chaloner, scrambling to his feet and prodding it with his sword. The creature whipped around and snarled at him. He regarded it dispassionately, assessing the best spot for a fatal stab. He did not enjoy killing animals, but he was not about to stand by and let one maul his master.

'Wait!' A figure tore from the spare office and flung itself between bear and spy. 'Do not hurt her! I should never have agreed to this – it was a ridiculous idea. Come, Barbara. We are going home.'

'Barbara?' echoed Chaloner, watching the man soothe the agitated beast by rubbing its ears. It whined, then strained in the direction of the windows. It wanted to be outside.

'Named for Lady Castlemaine: strong, beautiful and proud.' The man slipped a leash through a loop on the muzzle, and led Barbara out of the office, adding under his breath, 'And a bit bad tempered.'

Chaloner was about to sheath his sword when a flicker of movement caught his eye. He braced himself for more trouble, but the door was thrown open and people began to pour out, all masked against recognition. At their head was a man wearing a golden cloak and a paper crown. The courtiers scampered through the Earl's domain, shrieking with laughter and congratulating the Lord of Misrule on the success of his prank. The Earl's fright gave way to rage, and he began to chase them, giving even more cause for amusement, because he was far too fat and slow to catch anyone.

'You said you had finished tormenting the Earl,' said Chaloner fiercely, grabbing Brodrick's arm and swinging him roughly around. 'And this prank may have seen him harmed.'

'He was in no danger,' objected Brodrick, trying to free himself. 'That is why we brought its owner with us – to control it.'

'It lashed out with its claws,' argued Chaloner, furious with him. 'It has been trained to dance about outside, and being penned up with all those sniggering wastrels

340

frightened it into aggressive behaviour. It was a dangerous trick, one that came close to going badly wrong.'

'You saved him,' said Brodrick dismissively. 'As I knew you would, should matters not go according to plan. Why do you think I waited until you arrived? It was not easy persuading that lot to be patient, and you came much later than I anticipated. Let go of me, man! He is looking this way, and I do not want him unmasking me.'

'I will unmask you, if you pick on him again,' vowed Chaloner. 'You will leave him alone from now on. Do you understand?'

Brodrick's eyes glittered behind the mask, although the spy could make out nothing more of his expression. Then the Earl's cousin gave a terse nod, before spinning on his heel and heading for the door. Haddon and Bulteel were in his way, and they stood their ground as he strode towards them. He was obliged to ask them to move, and they did so in their own time, regarding him so coldly that Chaloner suspected the man would not be paying any social calls to his kinsman's offices for a while.

'Damn you!' the Earl cried after him. 'I am going to complain to the King about this. If Thomas had not been here, I might have been killed.'

'You had better not dismiss him in favour of Turner, then, sir,' said Bulteel with a grin that revealed his brown teeth. 'It would not be right, not after he risked his life to rescue you. Again.'

'Much as it pains me to agree with the likes of Bulteel, your secretary is right,' said Haddon. 'You cannot reward his courage by dispensing with his services.'

'I shall dismiss whoever I feel like,' shouted the Earl, incensed that minions should dare tell him what to do. 'And I stand by my original deadline. It is Sunday today, and Twelfth Night is Tuesday, so Thomas has two days to prove his worth. After that . . . well, suffice to say I cannot maintain *two* spies.'

Chaloner began to wish he had let the bear have him.

Chapter 10

Time was running out for Greene, and for Chaloner, too, and had reached the point where it was necessary to stop chipping at the edges of the investigation and go for the heart. And the spy could think of no better way forward than to corner Greene and demand a list of anyone with whom he had had even the slightest disagreement over the years. He walked to the clerk's Westminster office, but was told Greene was not expected in that day – he had sent a note informing his colleagues that he planned to work at home.

The spy headed for the river, where he hired a boat to take him to Wapping. It was a miserable trek, with a spiteful wind blowing needles of rain into his face the whole way. They 'shot' London Bridge, something that was perilous when the tide was in full flow, but that was uneventful that morning because it was on the turn, and continued east. Chaloner huddled inside his cloak, his mood growing blacker and bleaker when he realised he was as far from solutions now as he had been ten days earlier.

He strode to Greene's house as fast as he could, partly

because he needed answers as a matter of urgency, but also because he was cold and a brisk walk was a good way to warm himself up. He hammered on Greene's door, but there was no answer, and the building had a peculiarly abandoned feel to it. He wondered if the clerk had had enough of waiting to be arrested, and had finally run away. If he had, then Chaloner did not blame him, although the Earl was going to see it as a sign of guilt.

Glancing around to ensure he was not being watched, he picked the lock and let himself in. Then he began a systematic search, not sure what he was looking for, but determined to be thorough. And if Greene returned and caught him, then so much the better – it might make the clerk understand that he would hang unless he put his mind to identifying the person who was so determined to see him in trouble. The spy finished exploring the ground floor without learning anything useful, and turned to the upper one. He had already searched Langston's room, so this time he concentrated on Greene's.

The chamber was almost Spartan in its neatness. It contained a bed, two chests, and a shelf of books. The tomes were almost entirely devotional tracts – with the curious exception of Michel Millot's *L'Ecole des Filles*, widely condemned as pornographic, although it was tame by Langston's standards. Chaloner opened it, and was surprised to see an inscription in the front, written in a flowing hand he recognised as Lady Castlemaine's. It directed the reader to the particularly juicy sections, although there was no indication that the recommendations were aimed at Greene. Chaloner frowned. Had Greene stolen it? Or was it actually Langston's, and Greene had borrowed it out of salacious curiosity? There was one explanation he refused to entertain, though: that the Lady had given it to Greene herself. She would simply not waste her time on a lowly official, especially one who was unlikely to please her in the bedchamber. He put it back and resumed his search.

He was about to give up, when he realised that although the curtains were drawn, they did not quite meet in the middle. He stood on a stool and ran his hand along the top of the rail. His groping fingers encountered a small box, no bigger than the length of his hand. He took it down, and opened it to find it full of papers.

The first document he inspected was an oath, and its brownish colour led him to wonder whether it had been written in blood. The language was Latin, and promised the reader that God's commandments would be followed and a righteous life led. It was signed with Greene's name, and was so well worn that Chaloner suspected it had been taken out and read a lot. So, he thought, the vow sworn by members of Scobel's prayer group had included a written declaration, as well as a verbal one. The man had obviously done his utmost to prevent his flock from straying, although, as Doling and Hargrave had said, he had reckoned without the corruptive influence of White Hall.

The remaining papers were lists of various expenditures. Chaloner sat on the bed and studied them carefully, but they seemed to be exactly what they appeared: household accounts for the previous year. He read that purchases of ale, wine, coal, cloth, utensils and barley had been made, and the cost was carefully recorded each week. They were dull and uninteresting, and he could not imagine why Greene should have considered them important enough to hide. He slipped them in his pocket anyway, and was about to leave when he became aware that the bottom of the doorframe was glittering slightly. He crouched down, and saw a tiny hole made by a knot in the wood. Something had been pressed inside it, and it was not many moments before he had prised it out.

It was a ruby ring.

He gazed at it in confusion. Was the Earl right after all, and Greene *was* the killer? His first reaction was disgust at himself: he was a professional spy, and should not have been deceived like some inexperienced novice. But then questions flooded into his mind, and he forced himself to stop leaping to conclusions and analyse the evidence logically, as Thurloe had trained him to do.

He had inspected the ring only briefly before the train-band had reclaimed it, but he had a good memory, and was fairly sure that the bauble he held now was not the one from the Painted Chamber – it felt lighter and cheaper, and lacked the quality of the other. So, had someone left it to incriminate Greene, because that person knew Chaloner was aware of the ring's existence and the implications of owning it? Uncomfortably, he wondered whether the Earl had contrived to plant it there, because he was tired of his spy's unwillingness to accept his point of view.

He swore softly when it occurred to him that he had asked virtually everyone he had met about the ring – not just his suspects, but anyone he thought might recognise it. *Ergo*, his questions had ensured that a huge number of people knew it was central to his investigation. He had even told Hannah about it. The upshot was that anyone wanting to incriminate Greene would know that hiding a red-stoned ring among the man's possessions would do the trick.

He continued to stare at it, wishing there was some way it could tell him its story. But gawking was not going to provide him with answers – he needed to find Greene, and fast. He stuffed it in his breast pocket, next to the documents, and headed for Wapping church, recalling its vicar saying that Greene was a regular and punctilious visitor.

'Greene,' he said without preamble, when the cleric gave him a wary smile, recognising him from the last time he was there. 'Where is he?'

'I wish I knew. He failed to return home last night, and this morning he missed dawn prayers for the first time since the Restoration. I am worried, because there have been some very nasty characters asking after him of late.' The priest swallowed uneasily when he realised what he had said. 'Not you, of course—'

'Turner?' interrupted Chaloner. 'A handsome man with an ear-string?'

'Yes, he was here, but he was all smiles and good manners. I refer to the group of men who look like soldiers. Their commander treated me like dirt, and I do not mind admitting that he terrified me.'

'Describe him.'

The vicar shuddered. 'Rough, brutish and bullying. He and his louts asked me question after question, but it was more of an interrogation than a conversation.'

'What did they want to know?'

'Details of Greene's activities, where he kept his valuables, whether he had secret hiding places.'

'And does he?' asked Chaloner, to see whether Greene had trusted him enough to mention the little box above the curtains. Or the hole in the doorframe.

'Not that I know of. We only ever talk about God.

Poor Greene! They terrified me into telling them about his daily visits to church, and now he is missing. How could I have blathered about him, when he has been nothing but kind to me? He knows my weakness for brandywine – it is difficult to buy, but he never fails to provide me with a weekly flask. And what do I do? Repay him with betrayal!'

Chaloner was not sure what to think about the brandy-wine. 'Was there anything about these soldiers that will allow me to identify them?'

'They wore masks to conceal their faces, but the commander has a scar on his neck. It will not be obvious unless you stand close to him, but it is there.' The priest regarded Chaloner thoughtfully. 'Greene tells me you are the only one who believes his innocence, so I shall confide something I managed to keep from those ruffians: he has an understanding with Lady Castlemaine.'

Chaloner regarded him askance. 'You mean he is one of her lovers?' It did not sound very likely, given that Greene was an unattractive specimen, but with the Lady, anything was possible.

The vicar was horrified. 'Lord, no! I mean that Langston and Greene worked for her. Secretly. They ran errands, although I have no idea what kind. Greene never said, and I never asked. I would rather not know anything that involves *her.*'

Chaloner was beginning to see the glimmer of a solution at last: Lady Castlemaine knew Langston from his ribald writing, and he must have introduced Greene to her as a dependable sort. Perhaps she *had* made Greene a gift of *L'Ecole des Filles*, or one of his 'errands' was to deliver it to someone else. It certainly explained why she had challenged the Earl's belief that Greene was the killer – it was not just to oppose an enemy, as everyone assumed, but because she did not want to lose a servant. Chaloner recalled the way she had nodded to Greene when their paths had crossed at White Hall, and how he had been puzzled by it, given that she never acknowledged minions. But trustworthy staff were not easy to find, and she must have been keen to retain Greene's goodwill. And Greene was clearly among the best, because Chaloner had detected no hint of his association with her, despite more than a week of interviewing his closest friends and associates.

The priest had nothing else to add, so Chaloner boarded a skiff and headed back to the city. The boatman was the garrulous sort, who insisted on regaling his fare with a list of men who had drowned in the Thames. The depressing monologue, along with the fact that the wind rocked the little craft in a way that made him seasick, meant Chaloner was relieved to arrive back in the city.

'There was a corpse washed up just this morning,' the boatman continued, as the spy rummaged in his purse for coins to pay him. 'Kersey will keep it in his charnel house, and if no one claims it within a week, it will be buried in St Margaret's. There are hundreds of drowned men in that churchyard, and they wail whenever there is an especially high tide. I have heard them myself.'

'Is that so?' asked Chaloner, his mind more on where to find Greene than the dismal stories.

The fellow saw he was not believed, and became indignant. 'Ask Kersey. He hears them, too. You can see him today, and view the new corpse at the same time. After all, threepence is not much for a bit of light entertain-ment – less than the price of a night at the theatre, and a lot more memorable.'

'Who drowned last night?' asked Chaloner, loath to offend him. He might have to use the fellow's boat again in the future, and did not want to be 'accidentally' tipped in the water.

'Kersey said it was a clerk,' replied the boatman, gratified by the interest.

Chaloner regarded him sharply. 'What was his name?'

'He did not say – he just mentioned that it was the fifth government official to die since Christmas Day. Dangerous place, Westminster.'

Chaloner could not agree more. He walked briskly along Canning Street, although even the smart pace he set himself did not dispel the cold, unsettled feeling that had seeped deep inside him. He felt a sudden, almost desperate need for the company of a friend, and although he knew he should visit Kersey as a matter of urgency, he stopped at Lincoln's Inn first.

His search of Greene's house had taken much longer than he had anticipated, and the daylight was fading as he walked across the yard, heading for Chamber XIII. The journey to Wapping had yielded some clues, but the ring had only served to deepen the mystery, while learning about Greene's association with Lady Castlemaine was interesting, but would probably not help in identifying the killer. Chaloner felt he had wasted the best part of yet another day, and by the time he reached the top of the stairs he was in a melancholy frame of mind. His spirits plunged further still when Thurloe opened the door to reveal packed chests and sheet-draped furniture.

'Ah, Tom.' Thurloe was dressed for travel in heavy

cloak, woollen hat and sturdy boots. 'I am glad you came. I am leaving in a few moments, and did not like to disappear without bidding you farewell.'

Chaloner struggled to mask his dismay. 'You are going now? But surely, no carriage will venture out onto the King's highways at night. It would be madness!'

'Robbers were never a problem in the Commonwealth,' agreed Thurloe grimly. 'A military dictatorship knows how to secure safe roads.'

'Actually, I was thinking about the more immediate danger of floods, broken wheels and getting lost. No self-respecting driver travels a road he cannot see.'

'I shall sleep at an inn in Aldersgate this evening, and be ready take the coach at first light tomorrow. You are very wet. What have you been doing?'

'Squandering time on the river,' replied Chaloner despondently.

Unfortunately, repeating what he had learned did not help him this time. The ex-Spymaster asked several intelligent questions, but was also unable to make any sense of the confusion of facts.

'And I am afraid I have gleaned nothing of any great use, either,' he said apologetically. 'At least, nothing you have not already discovered for yourself. Greene and Langston *did* work for Lady Castlemaine, although only as agents for organising her various trysts – they were not entrusted with anything politically significant. And I have found no one who admits to owning a ruby ring.'

'Does this look valuable to you?' Chaloner passed him the one he had found in Greene's house.

Thurloe did not take long to assess it. 'No. In fact, there is a shop that sells dozens just like it in the New Exchange. Your killer would not have hired a train-band to retrieve this bauble, so I can only assume you are right: someone left it in Greene's house to incriminate him. And the culprit has done a good job – if I were your Earl, I would have issued a warrant for Greene's arrest days ago.'

'Then why does he hold back?'

'I imagine because of you. You have been proven right on a number of occasions, and it is enough to make him stay his hand. Clearly, he trusts your judgement, even if he is unwilling to admit it. However, he is beginning to lose patience with the ponderous pace of your investigation, so you had better find him some answers fast.'

'It is too late. I am almost certain the drowned clerk in the charnel house will transpire to be Greene, and I cannot see answers appearing by Tuesday.'

He knelt next to the fire, trying to thaw his frozen hands. Was it his fault Greene was dead? Would the clerk still be alive if he had worked harder to find the killer? He sighed, thinking of how much he would miss Thurloe's calm logic – he knew from previous Oxfordshire expeditions that his friend was unlikely to be back before spring, and was glad he had made his peace with Temperance. At least he would have one friend in the city. Thinking of her reminded him of the man she claimed to love.

'James Grey,' he said, looking up at Thurloe. 'Have you met him?'

'No. I asked Temperance to bring him to me, but he declined to come – said he could not risk his reputation by drinking ale with ex-Commonwealth spymasters. I suppose I cannot blame him.'

'She intends to wed him, which surprises me. I thought she was against marriage.'

'I may be responsible for her change of heart,' said Thurloe sheepishly. 'I told her marriage was a blissful state – that I would not be without Ann for the world. If ever I am sad, I just think of her sweet face, and all unhappiness vanishes, like mist in the sun.'

'Really?' asked Chaloner. He vaguely remembered feeling that way about his own wife, but they had only been married a year, so he had no way of knowing whether the affection would have lasted.

Thurloe nodded, rather dreamily. 'However, I am uncommonly blessed, and I hope I have not led Temperance to imagine that all matches are perfect.'

'Have you investigated him?' asked Chaloner. 'Ascertained whether he is suitable?'

Thurloe smiled. 'And what kind of man do you think is "suitable" for a brothel-keeper?'

Chaloner grimaced. 'You know what I mean.'

Thurloe patted his shoulder. 'I do. But she guessed what I might do, and came to tell me not to – she does not want him thinking she has overly protective friends. I agreed to comply, although not happily. Perhaps you will learn something when you meet him on Twelfth Night eve.'

'Perhaps.'

'Did you know Margaret Symons is dead? She breathed her last at the exact hour she predicted. Apparently, as soon as she had her premonition, she wrote out a list of tasks for her husband, to keep him occupied during the first few weeks of his bereavement. She was wise, because he is the kind of man to mourn over-deeply.'

'I am not convinced her death was natural. Surgeon Wiseman said it was impossible to tell whether she had a sharpness of the blood or whether she had been poisoned, although he offered to run some experiments. Regardless, her demise sounds uncannily similar to Scobel's.'

Thurloe regarded him sombrely. 'I am not happy about leaving you here alone. There is plenty of room in the carriage, and I cannot see how this affair will end happily. You say the Earl was on the verge of dismissing you today. Leave him of your own accord, and come with me.'

The prospect of spending time with a happy family, away from the scandals and intrigues of White Hall, was an appealing one. And what did London hold for him, other than a leaking garret, a master who did not like him, and a cat that had started to hunt birds? He supposed there was Hannah – and there was his self-respect. He had never abandoned a case because he was uneasy before, and he did not want to start now. Reluctantly, he shook his head.

He escorted the ex-Spymaster to where a coach was waiting to take him to Aldersgate. But although he was sorry to see Thurloe go, there was also an element of relief. He had not liked the notion of his friend involving himself in the investigation, and now he would be safely away from the city and its myriad dangers. He watched the carriage rattle away, then turned towards Westminster. It was cold, dark, pouring with rain and not a time when most men would pay a visit to a charnel house, but if Kersey had gone home, then Chaloner would just have to break in to see Greene's body.

The foul weather meant the roads were essentially deserted – even the festivities for the Twelve Days of Christmas could not induce people to leave their warm homes and brave these elements. Chaloner trudged wearily along The Strand, thinking the tattered, wind-torn greenery that bedecked its buildings was more depressing than decorative. A group of beggars had been hired to sing carols outside the New Exchange, but there was no one to hear them, and their voices formed a mournful duet with the desolate sigh of the wind.

He reached Westminster, and left the relatively well-lit Old Palace Yard to head for the darker streets near the river, where the mortuary was located. He thought about Greene. Had the clerk been drowned by the same person who had put the ring in his house? Did the killer hope Greene's death would mark the end of the matter – that it would be assumed he had committed suicide, sick with remorse for his crimes? The more Chaloner thought about the callous campaign waged against the hapless clerk, the more he became determined that the killer would not get away with it.

He was so engrossed in his ruminations that he almost missed the shadow that flitted towards the wharf where Jones had died. Snapping into a state of high alert, he followed.

He reached the alley's entrance and peered down it. The blackness was impenetrable, and totally silent. However, it was not silent behind him, and he whipped around when he heard the unmistakeable sound of a shoe scraping on cobbles, drawing his sword as he did so. He was only just in time. Two men were bearing down on him, blades at the ready. He parried their attack, but then became aware of footsteps coming from the alley, too. Two more soldiers were emerging from the darkness, aiming to trap him in a pincer-like movement. Their confident manoeuvres told him they were members of the train-band. Again.

'What do you want?' he demanded, backing against a wall so they could not outflank him.

'You should have gone to Oxfordshire.' Chaloner recognised the voice of the leader from the last time they had met. 'It is a pity you stayed.'

The spy's stomach lurched at the notion that they knew Thurloe. 'Who are you?'

'You think Greene killed those officials,' the leader went on. 'You have been listening to the Lord Chancellor and that idiot Turner, and you let them convince you. You are a fool!'

Chaloner's thoughts reeled in confusion. 'How did you—'

'Our orders were to kill him, not engage him in conversation,' muttered a soldier who was bigger than the others. 'You are too fond of your own tongue, Payne.'

Payne was clearly irked by the reprimand, but was too professional to start an argument when there was work to be done. He nodded to his comrades, who began to advance. Chaloner was heavily outnumbered, but was not about to go down without a fight. He launched himself at Payne, taking the man off-guard with the ferocity of his attack. Even so, Payne managed a thrust that punched a hole through his coat, although the wad of documents he had taken from Greene saved him from injury.

Then the big man was on him. Chaloner fended him off, then attacked Payne again. Backing away fast, Payne missed his footing, and stumbled into his larger colleague, so they both fell. And suddenly, there was no one between Chaloner and the road leading to Old Palace Yard. If he reached it, he might yet escape, because he did not think the train-band would kill him in front of witnesses – and there was always someone about in Westminster's busiest square, even on a dark, filthy night like this one.

He began to sprint towards it. Payne released an angry yell and started to follow, his comrades streaming at his heels. Chaloner did not look around, but powered on, dropping his sword because holding it was losing him speed. Ahead, he could see that some kind of function had just ended in Parliament House, and carriages were converging there to take the participants home. Chaloner tore towards them. He gained the edge of Old Palace Yard, and heard several of the soldiers skid to a hasty standstill, clearly loath to enter such a well-lit area.

Unfortunately, no such reservations hampered Payne. He ran harder, single-mindedly determined that his quarry should not escape a third time. By contrast, Chaloner's leg was starting to hurt, and it was slowing him down. Payne was gaining on him, and he knew it would only be a matter of moments before he was caught – and he had thrown away his sword, so would be unable to defend himself. Payne would strike him down the moment he was in range, then disappear into the night.

He was vaguely aware of a coach bearing down on him, travelling far too fast. The driver gave a warning yell when he saw Chaloner, and the spy only just managed to jig to one side, narrowly avoiding the thundering hoofs. Lightning quick, he reached up to grab the door-handle as the carriage hurtled past. The manoeuvre almost ripped his arm from its socket, and for one agonising moment, he thought he was going to be dragged under the wheels. But he managed to gain a toehold on one of the coach's steps, and then he was being carried along as the vehicle charged towards St Margaret's Street.

The driver did not see what had happened, but the

coach's occupant had heard the thump of someone landing on his private conveyance. Outraged, he stuck his head through the window to see what was going on. It was Brodrick. His eyes widened in astonishment when he saw Chaloner, and they widened even more when Payne leapt up beside the spy and tried to stab him.

It was not easy clinging to a speeding carriage with one hand while trying to defend himself against a flailing dagger with the other, and Chaloner was struggling to hold his own. But with unexpected aplomb, the Earl's cousin produced a sword and poked Payne in the shoulder. More startled than hurt, Payne dropped away, hitting the ground and rolling several times. Amazingly, he staggered to his feet and tried to give chase, but managed only a few faltering steps before collapsing. Chaloner saw his comrades surround him quickly, and bundle him down a quiet lane, away from curious eyes. Relief slackened the spy's grip on the door, but Brodrick grabbed him before he fell, and supported him until they had cleared Westminster and were cantering along King Street. Only then did he shout to the driver to stop.

'You lead an exciting life,' he said drily, watching the spy climb to the ground. 'Fighting bears, tackling mobs, indulging in reckless chases. What next? Seducing Lady Castlemaine?'

'I am not that brave,' said Chaloner, brushing himself down and feigning nonchalance. The truth was that his heart was pounding and his legs were wobbly.

'May I offer you a ride somewhere? To Hercules' Pillars Alley, perhaps? Or would you prefer the more tender ministrations of Hannah Cotton?'

'Thank you for your help,' said Chaloner sincerely. 'I am in your debt.'

358

'Really?' Brodrick looked sly. 'Then how about saying nothing to my cousin about my involvement in the bear incident? You were right this morning – it was a stupid thing to have done.'

'So why did you do it?'

Brodrick looked pained. 'The bear was supposed to wander into his office and eat some nuts we had left it. The damned thing was not supposed to start swiping about with its claws. I knew I should not have accepted the Lady's advice for a jape. Well? Will you be discreet about my role in the affair? You owe me something for saving your life.'

Chaloner gave his promise, then watched the carriage rattle away. When he turned, he saw two members of the train-band running towards him. He melted into the shadows, and when the soldiers arrived moments later, he was nowhere to be found.

The next day was so foggy that when Chaloner opened the door of Hannah's house, he could not see the opposite side of the street. It made London dangerous, because hackneys still raced along at a furious lick, hoping the clatter of their wheels and the occasional yell would be enough to warn pedestrians of their approach. Those on horseback were almost as bad, and Chaloner only just managed to haul Hannah out of the path of one pack of snorting stallions. It was Buckingham, Chiffinch and their cronies, riding home after a night of debauchery at Temperance's club.

'Buckingham is such a scamp,' said Hannah indulgently, as the cavalcade galloped on. 'London would be so dull without him. Speaking of fun, you have not forgotten that we are to dine with Sir Nicholas Gold this evening, have you?'

'No,' lied Chaloner. He brightened at the prospect. 'You said there would be music.'

'And food,' added Hannah wryly. 'And perhaps even conversation. What will you do today?'

'Why do you ask?' he said, before he could stop himself.

She gave a long-suffering sigh. 'Because you listened to me for hours last night – virtually my entire life story – and it is only right that I reciprocate by enquiring after you in return.'

'Visit the charnel house, to view Greene's body.' Chaloner had not felt up to breaking into Kersey's domain and inspecting corpses after his encounter with the train-band the previous evening. He had not really felt up to listening to Hannah, either, but had forced himself to pay attention. When she had finally gone to sleep, he had been restless and uneasy. Questions whirled about in his mind, and he had spent most of the night sitting by the window, staring into the street as he tried to reason some sense into all he had learned. Dawn had found him tired, haggard and frustrated by the lack of answers.

Hannah heard the unhappiness in his voice. 'It is not your fault he is dead, Tom. You tried to prove him innocent. But people – including Greene himself – were not honest with you, so how could you be expected to solve the mystery under those circumstances?'

'Would you mind telling my Earl that? Of course, it does not explain why I have neglected to locate the stolen statue, as he is sure to point out.'

'Then he is a fool,' she declared. 'You have done your best, and he has no right to expect more. What will you do after you have stared at Greene, and blamed yourself for the fact that he is dead?'

'Speak to his colleagues and show them a ring I found.

Visit John's Coffee House, to ask its owner about the prayer meetings that take place there. Return to the wharf where the train-band seems to lurk – I need to learn more about them if I am to survive our next encounter.'

Hannah regarded him uneasily. 'What next encounter? Surely, it is better to stay away from them?'

'That may not be possible – I did not exactly seek them out yesterday. And I cannot avoid them if they are involved in the clerk murders – at least, not today. It will not matter tomorrow, because the Earl's deadline will have passed, and I will either be victorious or dismissed.'

'Then why not go to the Queen, and tell her you will look into her missing money? It would be a lot safer than risking your life for a man who keeps threatening you with unemployment.'

'I wish I could – she is worth ten of him – but her loss is one of embezzlement, and the only way to find out who cheated her is to comb through dozens of palace accounts.'

'Then comb.'

'I cannot, I am not qualified. Only someone with accounting experience will catch the culprit.'

Hannah looked as if she did not believe him, but he did not know what more he could say to convince her. They parted at the Court Gate, where he decided to visit John's Coffee House first, hoping to catch the proprietor before his establishment became busy. Greene could wait – he was not going anywhere, and Chaloner was not sure what he could accomplish by looking at a corpse anyway.

'What news?' the coffee-house owner called, as the spy walked in. John Ravernet did not look up from his perusal of *The Intelligencer*, and the greeting was automatic rather than a genuine request for information. As Chaloner had hoped, the place was virtually empty, and the only customer was a morose-looking fellow with a wart between his eyes.

'A body was washed up near Westminster yesterday,' replied Chaloner.

'That is not news,' said the customer disdainfully. 'That is an everyday occurrence.'

'Not in this case,' argued Ravernet, folding the news-book and going to give his roasting coffee beans a stir. 'Because word is that the corpse was yet another of the King's clerks. It seems to be a bad time for them, because not only were three hapless souls poisoned, but poor Jones drowned last week, too. Unfortunately, no one is quite sure how it happened.'

'And no one is asking, either,' said the customer, fixing him with a meaningful look. 'Jones was a high-ranking official, and he ended up in the Thames, but no one is curious to learn why. And after three of his colleagues were murdered, you would think *someone* would be looking into the matter. But no one is, not even Spymaster Williamson.'

'You see conspiracy everywhere, Hawley,' said Ravernet. 'However, in this instance, you are right. No one is investigating, which means someone is glad he is dead. Someone important.'

With a start, Chaloner realised it was true, and wondered why it had not occurred to him before. Other than the ghoulish curiosity common to all violent deaths, no one had asked why Jones had drowned, not even his colleagues from the prayer meetings. Of course, it had worked to Chaloner's advantage, because an investiga-tion might have uncovered the fact that *he* had followed Swaddell and Jones down the alley, and he could imagine what Williamson would make of that small fact. Had Jones's death gone unremarked because the Spymaster's men were too busy hunting the statue? Or was there a more sinister reason – which seemed eminently likely, given that Jones had been loaded down with stolen gold when he had died?

'Mr Greene recommended your coffee house to me,' he said, intending to lead the discussion around to the gatherings. He could not afford to waste time on Jones when he had only one day left to solve the murders of Chetwynd, Vine and Langston. 'And so did Sir Nicholas Gold.'

Ravernet looked pleased. 'They have been loyal customers for years. They used to meet at Scobel's home, but when he died, they elected to come here instead. They are an amiable crowd.'

'But sadly depleted by death,' said Hawley. 'Jones was the fourth of their number to perish. Now there is only a handful left: Greene, Tryan, Hargrave, that angel-faced Neale. Swaddell comes in disguise, but we all know he is the Spymaster's assassin. Colonel Turner attends the odd meeting these days, too.'

'And do not forget Reeve,' added Ravernet. 'He never misses.'

'I do not know him,' said Chaloner.

'Neither do we,' said Hawley ruefully, 'although I have done my best to penetrate his cover – I like a challenge. Personally, I think he is a woman, because of the slight mince he has when he walks. And his beard is patently false.'

Chaloner stared at him. Could 'Reeve' be Bess Gold? Was she sufficiently clever to carry off a convincing disguise? Or was it Margaret Symons, whom Doling said was heartbroken to be excluded from the meetings by virtue of her sex? But that was not possible: Margaret had been at home dying when Chaloner had seen Reeve with his companions. Or was it Lady Castlemaine, determined to secure herself a prosperous future by spending the occasional hour with devout men? Mrs Vine could not be forgotten, either. She had, after all, been suspiciously vehement in her denials that her husband had owned a ruby ring, and the spy did not trust her or her testimony.

'They used to pray a lot,' Ravernet was saying. 'But they are just like any other group of friends these days. They talk about the news and the weather, and Symons is the only one who tries to impose religion on them. They oblige, but with increasing reluctance.'

'Then perhaps they should have listened to him,' suggested Hawley soberly. 'Because if they had, God might have watched over them, and four of their number might not be dead.'

Unwilling to spend the day without a sword, Chaloner borrowed one from his landlord, who had a large collection. None were very good, because Ellis was in the habit of using them as tools to effect repairs around the home, but they were better than nothing. Chaloner picked one, then set off towards Westminster, knowing he could postpone inspecting Greene's body no longer. He was just crossing New Palace Yard, alert for any sign of the trainband, when he met Haddon. The steward looked out of sorts, and his usually kindly face was angry and flustered.

'Bulteel fed pepper cake to my dogs,' he explained bitterly, as their paths converged. 'The poor darlings do not know what to do with themselves for the pain. How could he do such a cruel thing?'

'Are you sure?' asked Chaloner doubtfully. 'His wife's cakes are usually—'

'Brodrick commissioned it, to feed to Lady Muskerry as a joke,' interrupted Haddon. 'And some was left over. A man who harms a dog is a low creature, as I told Bulteel to his face. Perhaps I *should* work to see him ousted, since he believes I am doing it anyway. Hateful fellow!'

'I am sure he did not mean to hurt them,' said Chaloner, although he was not sure at all. Bulteel, like Chaloner himself, was not very keen on the yappy little lapdogs. Nonetheless, he hoped they would recover from their ordeal, because Haddon would be devastated if one died.

Haddon shot him a look that said he knew better. 'They are resting by the Earl's fire at the moment. *He* has been very kind.' Tears sparkled in his eyes briefly, and he brushed them away, embarrassed.

'Where are you going now?' asked Chaloner curiously. They were walking towards the charnel house, which seemed an odd destination for the steward.

'The Earl wants me to view the corpse that was found yesterday, given that you have not been in to tell him about it. He tried to send Bulteel, but the villain fabricated some sly excuse to get himself exempted.'

'Turner could not oblige?'

'He has been ordered to concentrate on the stolen statue now he has solved the murders to the Earl's satisfaction. So, which clerk do you think lies in Kersey's horrible mortuary? It would be good to be able to brace myself. I am not very good with corpses – they make me feel queasy.'

'Greene has been missing since Saturday night.'

Haddon raised his eyebrows. 'Are you sure? Only I

saw him on Saturday night myself, here in Westminster. He was working – or so he told me when I asked him what he was doing out so late.'

'When we last spoke about him, you said you thought he was innocent. Do you still believe that?'

Haddon took a moment to reply. 'Turner has amassed a lot of evidence that says he is guilty, but Greene has always seemed a decent sort to me. It is hard to see him as a ruthless slaughterer.'

But Chaloner knew the most unlikely of people were capable of doing terrible things, and being a 'decent sort' meant nothing, as far as he was concerned. He followed the steward inside the mortuary, where Kersey bustled forward to greet them, holding out his hand for the requisite fee. The charnel-house keeper was clad in a set of brand new clothes, and was smoking a pipe.

'People are very interested in these clerk-killings,' he said gleefully, counting the coins carefully before adding them to his bulging purse. 'Will there be many more, do you think?'

'Perhaps *he* is the killer,' murmured Haddon to Chaloner in distaste. 'He is the one who is benefitting from the deaths – they are making him a fortune!'

Kersey's domain was crowded. The only poison victim to have been buried was Vine, hastily shoved in the ground before Wiseman could ignore his family's wishes and dissect him anyway. The others remained in Kersey's tender care. Chetwynd lay between Jones and Langston, and the charnel-house keeper said there had been three stabbings that week, too. Before Chaloner or Haddon could stop him – neither wanted to view more corpses than necessary – he had whisked away some sheets, to reveal two men and a woman. The shapes of the wounds were more indicative of swords than daggers, and Chaloner recalled Wiseman's claim that the trio had asked questions about the train-band.

Then Kersey whipped the cover off his most recent acquisition. But it was not the gloomy clerk who lay naked on the table.

Haddon turned accusingly to Chaloner. 'You led me to believe it would be Greene!'

'I thought it *was*,' said Chaloner, equally astonished. 'I do not understand!'

Kersey puffed contentedly on his pipe. 'You are obviously looking for intrigue, because so many government clerks have died of late. But the simple fact is that people sometimes just fall in the river and drown. Perhaps this is one of those occasions.'

'So, who is this man?' asked Haddon tiredly.

'Matthias Lea,' replied Chaloner, staring down at the body. 'One of Chetwynd's heirs.'

'His brother was missing a kinsman,' elaborated Kersey. 'And he came to look when he heard I had charge of an unidentified cadaver. He was very upset when he discovered it was indeed Matthias.'

While Kersey described in ghastly detail how most drowned men were bloated beyond recognition if the Thames did not give them up immediately, Chaloner stared at Jones's massive bulk, thinking about Ravernet and Hawley's contention that no one had bothered to investigate his death.

'How many people have been to see him?' he asked, cutting across the grisly exposition and nodding towards Jones. Haddon, who had been listening with increasing horror, breathed his relief.

'Lots,' replied the charnel-house keeper smugly. 'He has

367

been popular because of his mighty girth. We do not get such vast specimens in very often, and he is impressive.'

'Has anyone asked any questions about him?' pressed Chaloner. 'Other than about his size.'

Kersey shook his head, then grinned. 'His kin said I could keep his clothes, and I am thinking of creating a display out of some of the more unusual items I have collected through the years. His massive drawers will provide the centrepiece. People will pay handsomely to see *them*.'

Haddon put his hand over his mouth, and his face was so pale, that Chaloner took his arm and led him outside, afraid he might faint. When he had recovered, they began to walk towards White Hall together, and were almost there when they met Wiseman. In a rather piercing whisper, the surgeon confided that Lady Castlemaine had strained a groin muscle during the night. Neither Chaloner nor Haddon cared to ask how, but Wiseman was ready with the information anyway.

'She was following a special exercise regime devised by me. If she pursues it diligently, she will develop limbs a man will die for.'

'She already has those,' said Haddon, rather wistfully. 'Of course, they are nothing compared to those of my dogs, whose legs are an example of God's perfection.'

'Did you hear about Matthias Lea?' asked Wiseman, regarding the steward dubiously before changing the subject. 'Yet another government official gone. Perhaps we should defect to another employer while we are still alive.'

'Defection is a young man's game, and I am past sixty,' said Haddon, taking him seriously, although Chaloner suspected Wiseman was just being flippant. 'However, I take sensible precautions – I try to stay in at night, I have not touched wine since Chetwynd was killed, and my sweethearts bark at any uninvited visitors to my home. Of course, if they are sick from pepper cake, they may not be as vigilant as usual.'

He went to report to the Earl, walking rather more slowly than was his wont; Chaloner was not sure whether the mistreatment of his pets or the sights in the charnel house had distressed him more.

'Did Kersey tell you Matthias had drowned?' asked Wiseman, when the steward had gone.

Chaloner nodded grimly, recalling the beginnings of the vivid lecture.

'Then he has made an erroneous assumption,' asserted Wiseman pompously. 'Just because a corpse is found in the river, does not mean it perished there.'

Chaloner frowned. 'What are you saying? That Matthias was thrown in the water *after* he died?'

'Yes, because the cause of his death was poison, not drowning,' announced Wiseman, relishing Chaloner's surprise. 'The blisters in his mouth indicate he swallowed a corrosive substance.'

'The same corrosive substance that killed the other three?'

'I cannot say with certainty, but my informed guess would be yes.'

'Do you have any idea *when* he might have died?'

'He was last seen alive on Saturday, at about nine o'clock in the evening, and his body was found yesterday morning – Sunday – just before dawn. Obviously, he died between those two times.'

'Christ!' muttered Chaloner. He saw Wiseman regarding him quizzically and hastened to explain. 'The cellarer

369

said Greene asked for brandywine on Saturday night. It was refused, but a flask was later found missing.'

'And now we have Matthias dead of poison, which we know has been delivered in brandywine in the past,' mused Wiseman. 'As a scientific man, I find the evidence against Greene compelling.'

Chaloner was not sure what to think, but the nagging worry that he might have made a terrible mistake had returned. He had known from the start that Greene could have slipped out of the back door of his house to go and kill Vine, while Lady Castlemaine had good reason to lie about the timing of her last sighting of Langston.

So, where *was* Greene? Chaloner had been so certain he was dead, that he had given no consideration to where the clerk might have gone. Or was this the line of reasoning the real killer hoped people would take – to wrap the noose even more tightly around an innocent man's neck?

'Has anyone asked you about Jones's death?' Chaloner asked the surgeon, wanting to think about something else. 'Or about the gold we found?'

'No. I have been listening out for rumours relating to his hoard, but there has not been so much as a whisper. It is all very mysterious.'

'His gold must have come from the thefts he committed, which explains why he chose to carry it on his person. After all, he could hardly invest it with Backwell's Bank – they are its rightful owners!'

'I do not believe the tale that has Jones responsible for what happened at Backwell's,' began Wiseman dismissively. 'It is—' But then he stopped speaking abruptly. His jaw dropped, and he looked staggered. 'Jones and I discussed that particular incident. He . . . Oh, Lord! Now it makes sense!'

'What makes sense?'

'He said Backwell's had only themselves to blame, because they had not locked up their wares properly before closing shop for the night. I asked him how he knew, and he winked at me.'

It was not far from the charnel house to the building the Leas had inherited from their murdered kinsman Chetwynd. When Chaloner arrived, he found the surviving brother being visited by Gold and Bess. Gold was doing his best to comfort the bereaved man, but Bess was standing in the window, happily waving at people who passed by outside. She wore a new hat – a red creation, with even more feathers in it than the one that had been damaged the previous day. She waved to Neale, who immediately decided that *he* should come in and console Lea, too.

'I will kill him!' Lea wept, while Gold patted his hand. 'Whoever pushed Matthias in the river is a dead man. I will hunt him down and strangle him with my bare hands. How could he?'

'*Pushed* him in the river?' echoed Neale. He did not look so cherubic that morning, with bloodshot eyes, a pale complexion and a trail of dried vomit down the front of his coat.

'Yes, pushed,' howled Lea. 'Matthias would never have gone near the Thames on his own, so some vile beast led him there and murdered him. It is someone here!'

'You mean one of us?' asked Neale, gazing around the room in confusion. Gold cocked his head, straining to hear. 'Bess, Gold, the Lord Chancellor's man or me?'

'I mean someone at White Hall or Westminster.' Tears gushed down Lea's face. 'There is slaughter everywhere

371

these days. It is like a disease.' The last part was delivered in a shriek that hurt the ears.

'White Hall is full of disease,' agreed Gold, entering the conversation with some relief. He had not liked being excluded. 'It is being spread by Lady Muskerry, apparently. Wiseman says she has an advanced case of the pox, so I stopped sleeping with her immediately.'

Chaloner blinked, but his astonishment was not nearly as great as that of Bess. She gaped at her husband, and her eyes were suddenly full of flashing emotion. It was the first expression approaching intelligence the spy had ever seen in her, and the transformation was chilling. It was quickly masked, though, and the ovine blankness came down like a steel trap. He recalled Hawley's theory – that Reeve the corn-chandler might be a woman. *Could* Bess be a contender?

'Well,' drawled Neale, smirking at her. 'This puts a different complexion on matters, does it not?'

'Do you know anyone who wanted to harm Matthias?' asked Chaloner of Lea, interrupting before the conversation could range too far along that road.

'Doling and Symons were always jealous that we kept our jobs while they lost theirs,' wailed Lea. 'Doling went around telling people that we were corrupt, although we never left any evidence of . . .' He stopped when he realised what he was saying.

'Matthias was not abrupt,' said Gold kindly. 'He was very patient, especially with old ladies.'

Lea began to sob at the compassion in his voice, and Chaloner saw he was going to have no sense from the man while he was distraught – or when Gold was there to lead the discussion astray. He took his leave when Bess asked her husband whether Lady Muskerry snored. Gold did not hear, but Neale's expression was predatory, and Chaloner suspected the young man would have her between the sheets before the day was out. He wondered whether it would be before or after the soirée Gold had planned for that evening.

His mind was full of questions as he headed towards White Hall. It was not so full that he failed to notice Williamson bearing down on him, however. This time, though, there was nowhere to hide, and he was not inclined to run. He braced himself as the Spymaster came closer, not liking the dangerous expression on his face. Williamson raised his hands to show he was unarmed.

'Do not confuse me with the rough villains with whom you usually consort,' he said coldly, while Chaloner thought he would never insult a rough villain by mistaking him for Williamson. 'Have you done as I ordered, and located Swaddell?'

'He was at John's Coffee House last week, in disguise and infiltrating one of the meetings you told me about. I suggested he make contact with you, although it looks as though he has not bothered.'

Williamson stepped back, startled. 'He is alive? I was certain you had murdered him.'

'Why would I do that? I barely know him.'

Williamson sneered. 'Because you think it will damage me, and we are not exactly friends. Incidentally, I hear Turner has proved Greene is the clerk-killer. What will you do now? Your Earl will not keep you on his payroll when Turner is your superior in every way.'

'Not every way,' said Chaloner, recalling the colonel's pitiful performance when threatened with the Lord of Misrule and his mob. 'Have you found the King's statue yet?'

'No, but I will provide him with what he wants, even if it means sending to Bernini for a replacement. How much do you think it will cost?'

'The last one was exchanged for a diamond ring worth a thousand pounds. But I understand Bernini prefers rubies. Do you happen to have one?'

Williamson regarded him oddly. 'I shall rummage in my jewellery box, and see what I can find.'

Chaloner was still pondering what he might have meant by the enigmatic reply – if anything – when he met Turner, swaggering along King Street as if he owned it. Women called greetings to him as they passed, and he acknowledged every one of them by name. The lowest street-trader was treated to the same merry charm as the highest duchess, and Chaloner realised that Turner was just a man who adored women. Age, shape and economic status was immaterial to him, and only the toothless could expect to be shunned.

Turner grinned as he approached the spy, brandishing something provocatively. It was a locket. 'You owe me ten shillings! You said I could not persuade Belle to part with it, yet here it is.'

'You also said I was free to ask her whether she had handed it to you willingly.'

Turner looked hurt. 'You think I would try to cheat you?'

Chaloner smiled. 'I am sure of it.'

Turner laughed. 'Belle will tell you the truth. Give me the ten shillings – unless you think me such a liar that you do not trust my word?'

Chaloner supposed Turner was unlikely to fabricate tales knowing they were likely to be verified. He handed over the coins. 'I hear you have gathered enough evidence to arrest Greene.'

Turner's jovial expression faded, and he began to count facts on his fingers. 'He begged brandywine on the nights Chetwynd and Vine were murdered. He was actually found with one victim, and I am unconvinced by his tale of borrowing ink. He had a secret life in that he was an errand-boy for Lady Castlemaine – and God alone knows what she asked him to do. And if all that is not enough, I have learned that he argued with Matthias Lea, just hours before the fellow was found dead.'

'He was seen? By whom?'

'By His Portliness. Bulteel was with him, so it is not a figment of the old goat's imagination.'

'Do *you* think Greene killed Matthias?'

'Matthias was not poisoned, as far as I know, but perhaps the river was to hand, so Greene just pushed him in. However, I am still uncomfortable with the whole business – I do not like the notion that my evidence will send a man to the gallows, whether he is guilty or not. It sounds womanish, but there is something about hanging that turns my stomach. You probably do not understand.'

Chaloner understood only too well, because he felt the same way about prisons, and did not know what he would do if his spying ever saw him incarcerated again. 'I thought Greene was dead – that the drowned clerk was him, not Matthias. He has been missing for the right amount of time.'

'Of course he has,' said Turner bitterly. 'He killed Matthias, then decided he had better flee before the Earl decided he has stayed his hand long enough. Perhaps we should have put him behind bars when His Portliness first suggested it. Then Vine, Langston and Matthias would still be alive.'

Chaloner was finally beginning to accept that he might be right.

The atmosphere was strained when Chaloner arrived at the Earl's offices. Bulteel was working in his antechamber, and had pinned a notice on his door saying dogs were not welcome. Haddon was sitting in the hallway, writing out a list of guests for the Earl's next soirée. There was no sign of his pets, and although Chaloner did not ask, he was told they were at home, recovering. Haddon shot a reproachful glare in the secretary's direction as he spoke, which Bulteel pointedly ignored. Before he could be drawn into the spat, Chaloner knocked on the Earl's door and entered his domain.

'I saw Greene bickering viciously with Matthias just hours before his body was found in the river,' said the Earl when he saw his spy. 'And now Greene is nowhere to be found. Of course, you and Turner have discovered some very nasty truths about his victims – they were not the good men they would have us believe.'

Chaloner nodded. 'Chetwynd, Vine and Langston were not the only ones with dubious secrets, either – the Lea brothers probably acted as scribes, producing copies of Langston's indecent plays.'

'Really?' The Earl's voice dripped disapproval. 'I did not know that. My objection to Matthias lies in another direction. He said he was loyal to the new government when we reappointed him at the Restoration, and swore all manner of oaths to "prove" it. But he was a liar.'

'You mean he was a traitor, plotting rebellion?' It did

not seem very likely – treachery took hard work and sacrifice, and the Leas were far too selfish for either.

'Williamson has learned that they accepted large sums of money to write seditious pamphlets. I am sure they do not applaud the sentiments themselves – they are too worldly to hold with anything that might be construed as principle – but they accepted money for their literary talents. Such as they are. Still, at least Matthias did not pretend to be saintly, like the other three.'

'There is a witness who believes Greene stole brandy-wine on the night Matthias died,' said Chaloner tiredly. 'Just as he did on the nights Chetwynd, Vine and Langston were poisoned. You were right all along.'

'And yet I still detect a note of hesitation,' said the Earl curiously. 'Why? Is it because you cannot believe you might have made a mistake? I had not taken you for that sort of fellow. You are stubborn, but I did not think you were a sulker.'

The truth was that Chaloner could not rid himself of the nagging notion that someone was framing Greene. But trying to explain his concerns would be a waste of time, so he handed the Earl the ring he had found. His master had a good eye for jewellery, and might well have noticed Greene – or someone else – wearing it. 'Have you seen this before?'

'No, but it is a woman's ring – it would be too small for a man. Why? Is it something to do with the murders? Or a clue in the mystery of the missing statue?'

'I am not sure.' Chaloner passed him the documents. 'I also found these hidden in Greene's house. They mean nothing to me, but you may understand their significance.'

The Earl's eyebrows shot up when he saw the damage

377

they had suffered during the encounter with the train-band: Payne's sword had punched a hole almost all the way through them. 'I shall not ask what you did to acquire these – what I do not know cannot plague my conscience. I will review them later, after I have seen the King about this visit of the French ambassador. What will you do now?'

'Try to find Greene.'

'You will be wasting your time: he will be in Holland by now. So, you had better concentrate on locating the statue, because I meant what I said – you only have until tomorrow to prove yourself.'

Haddon had gone when Chaloner left the Earl, so the spy took the opportunity to speak to Bulteel alone. Hannah and Temperance had told him to refuse the invitation to be godfather, while the Earl had recommended that he accept. He wished he had asked Thurloe, the one person whose opinion he truly respected. But Thurloe was gone, so he would have to make up his own mind. Bulteel's face fell when Chaloner told him of his decision.

'So, I have no idea how to find the King's statue,' the spy concluded tiredly. 'The Earl will dismiss me, and your son deserves someone who at least has a job. I am sorry.'

'You are giving up?' demanded Bulteel. 'Why? You still have twenty-four hours left, and you are not a man to be deterred by insurmountable odds. And do not forget Jones's gold, either. Retrieving that for Backwell's Bank must count for something – they may give you a reward, and you can share it with the Earl. He likes money.'

'Bribery?' asked Chaloner mildly. 'I thought you were above that.'

'I am above it – I was thinking it was something you could do. I refuse to see Turner win this race when he has done nothing to deserve it. Besides, there are a lot of questions raised by saying Greene is the killer – such as the fact that he had alibis for Vine and Langston. And why would he run away now? It makes no sense.'

'Because he killed Matthias, and knew it was one victim too many.'

'Rubbish!' declared Bulteel with uncharacteristic force. He changed tack. 'What about Jones, then? No one seems to care that *he* should die in the same week as the other three, whereas I think it is extremely odd. Look into his death, Tom. I am sure you will find something amiss.'

Chaloner stared at him. 'You seem very determined that I should succeed.'

'I *am* determined,' said Bulteel vehemently. 'But even if you fail, I still want you to be godfather to my baby. You are my friend, and that is more important than anything else.'

Chaloner continued to stare. He liked Bulteel, and liked even more the notion of being part of a family again. And while he might not be able to help with money or influence, he could teach the boy Latin, Greek and French – and other languages, too, if he had an aptitude. He could also show him how to fight, ride and play musical instruments.

'All right, then,' he said. 'As long as you are sure.'

Bulteel's thin face broke into a broad grin. 'Really? And will you come to dine on Twelfth Night?'

Chaloner nodded.

Bulteel clasped his hand. 'Then go out and show that arrogant Turner what *real* investigations are all about. Solve the riddle of Jones's death. Meanwhile, I shall double my efforts to locate the bust. We make a formidable team, you and I – sly thieves and wicked murderers cannot pull the wool over *our* eyes.'

Chapter 11

The fog had almost completely dissipated by the time Chaloner headed for Westminster, with only the occasional wisp lingering near the river. A bitter wind sliced in from the north, though, and he wondered whether there would be snow. It felt cold enough, and the clouds that hung overhead were a dirty yellow-grey, which he was sure could not be entirely attributed to London's soot.

As he walked, he did what Bulteel had suggested, and turned his thoughts to Jones. The train-band had contributed to the fat man's death by failing to pull him from the water when he was drowning, and by shooting at him with crossbows. Chaloner decided they would face justice for what they had done, regardless of the fact that Jones was a criminal himself.

The soldiers seemed to have some association with the alley that led to the pier, so it was high time the area was subjected to a proper search. He would look for evidence that would prove they were killers – not just of Jones, but of the two men and the woman who had been stabbed, too – so it could be passed to the appropriate authorities. And then he would present Jones's gold to the Earl, and let him take the credit – and the reward – for returning it to the bank. Bulteel was right: it might be enough to earn him a reprieve.

The towering buildings on either side rendered the alley dark and gloomy, even in broad daylight. They formed a solid brick slit, with no windows or doors to break the monotony. Near the middle, the lane curved to the left, and a slight bulge there made him wonder whether a gate might be concealed among the shadows. It would make sense: the soldiers had to have come from somewhere. However, he suspected going to inspect it would be tantamount to suicide – the train-band clearly went to great lengths to ensure no one knew anything about them.

As he pondered what to do, a wagon trundled out, piled high with coal, and he heard someone shout that the barge was almost empty – one more load should see the job finished. Another cart stood nearby, and he guessed it was the one designated to transport the last of the cargo. He hopped into the back, burrowing beneath a tarpaulin; it stank of wet, mouldy canvas, and he was aware of an oily black grit staining his clothes.

It was not many moments before a driver arrived, clicking at his horse to indicate it was to trot down the alley. There was a long metal hook near Chaloner's foot, used for freeing the tarpaulin when it became snagged under cargo, and he grabbed it as a plan began to form in his mind. He watched the left side of the alley intently, until he saw what he had suspected: there *was* a door in the shadows. It was virtually invisible, because it was flush with the wall and had been painted to look like the surrounding bricks. It would certainly go unnoticed by anyone who was not looking for it.

He jammed the hook into the moving wheel. Immediately, there was a screech of tortured metal, which made the driver haul on the reins to bring the cart to a hasty standstill. Swearing under his breath, the man jumped down and came to inspect the damage.

'The hook is mangled in the wheel,' he called to the bargemen waiting on the pier. 'You will have to wait until I fetch a smith to cut it free.'

'But that will take ages,' one objected. 'We shall hire someone else.'

The carter sounded smug. 'The alley is too narrow for anyone to get past me. And I am not going anywhere until my wheel is fixed.'

The bargeman glared. 'Then hurry up. We will be in Heaven, having a pipe and a drop of ale.'

'Do not offer to help, boys,' muttered the carter to their retreating backs. 'I can manage alone. It will take longer, of course. A *lot* longer . . .'

Chaloner watched as the secret door opened and Payne stepped out. Behind him was a short hallway, with doors leading to a room on either side and a flight of stairs at the far end. Men emerged from both chambers, to listen to what was going on.

'Get this thing out of here,' Payne ordered curtly. 'It is blocking the way.'

The carter started to walk away. 'Too bad. You will have to wait until I have hired a—'

'Stop,' commanded Payne. Something in his voice made the carter turn to look at him. 'Shift it now. This lane is in constant use.'

The carter put his hands on his hips. 'How, when the wheel is jammed? By magic? Besides, I have never seen anyone else use this alley, so it is *not* in constant use.'

Payne addressed one of the men in the hall. 'Fetch the captain.'

The man snapped a salute that was reminiscent of Cromwell's New Model Army, although his moustache and hat were all Cavalier. He was back in moments with someone who wore plain, practical clothes and a dour expression on his heavy featured face.

'What is going on?' demanded Doling. 'Move this thing, or we will move it for you.'

So, thought Chaloner, here was the man in charge. However, he knew for a fact that Doling was not the 'commander' who had questioned the vicar of Wapping so ruthlessly, because he had no scar on his neck: Chaloner remembered seeing his turkey-skin throat outside the charnel house, when his lace had blown away. The soldiers had another leader, one who was vicious and determined. Was it someone Chaloner knew? Payne, for example? One of the prayer-group men, perhaps? Or someone at Court?

The situation with the wagon had reached an impasse. Even with the best will in the world, the carter could not do what he was told, and the vehicle would remain where it was until the wheel could be made to turn again. At least, that was what Chaloner thought. But Doling nodded to his men, who proceeded to position them-selves around it, while Doling himself climbed into the driver's seat. He clicked his tongue at the horse, and the men started to push.

'Hey!' shouted the carter angrily. 'What do you think you are doing? If you move it when the wheel is stuck, you will damage it even more. And who are you anyway, that you cannot wait?'

'Busy men,' replied Doling tersely, as the vehicle began

to creak forward. The broken wheel skidded through the mud. 'And that is all you need to know.'

His voice was low and dangerous, and the carter backed away in alarm. The wagon continued to inch ahead, but it was heavy work and progress was slow. After a while, during which scant headway was made, Doling told Payne to fetch 'all the others'. The men who had been pushing took the opportunity to catch their breath, going to stand in a menacing circle around the hapless carter.

Assuming Doling's order meant the soldiers' lair was going to be temporarily empty, Chaloner knew it was an opportunity he had to seize. He peered out from under the tarpaulin, mind working furiously as he tried to devise a plan. Then he smiled when he saw the door opened outwards into the lane – and that the cart and soldiers were well beyond it. As soon as he was sure they were not looking in his direction, he abandoned his hiding place and ran towards the door, ducking quickly behind it. As long as no one closed it, or walked to or from the main road, he would remain hidden.

A dozen more soldiers trooped into the lane and ranged themselves around the vehicle. Doling flicked the reins, the men began to heave, and the cart was on the move a second time, the immobile wheel digging a deep furrow as it was forced along. This was too much for the carter – no man likes watching while his means of making a living is manhandled. He threw a punch at Payne. Chaloner expected him to be run through, but then realised that would attract too much attention – the bargemen would wonder what had happened to him, and their curiosity would be a nuisance to men who clearly preferred the shadows. Payne shoved the carter away, and the resulting set-to kept anyone from noticing

384

Chaloner ease around the door and dart into their domain.

He inspected the room on the left first. It was a barracks, with bunks around the wall and a table in the middle for communal eating. A chamber at the back served as a storage place for ammunition, food and clothing. All was scrupulously clean, and the weaponry was new and of unusually high quality. In short, the place smacked of the professional warrior.

The room on the right was smaller and dominated by a desk. Chaloner leafed through a handful of documents. They were mostly rotas, listing which men had worked which shifts, with remarks in the margin about individual performances. Doling had signed each one. There were also requisition forms for specific pieces of equipment.

Chaloner was bemused. Doling said he had been hired by Backwell's to improve their security after a robbery – the one masterminded by Jones, presumably. Did that mean the train-band was the bank's personal army? But Chaloner did not think a modest commercial enterprise would run to such an expensive operation, and suspected Doling had other uses for his men. Was he a rebel, aiming to overthrow the Royalist government? If so, then surely it was chancy to base the operation in Westminster? The train-band obviously took precautions against discovery, probably using the wharf, rather than roads, to travel around the city – which explained why it was lit at night – but it was still a risk of enormous proportion.

So what did all this tell Chaloner about Jones? Had the fat Yeoman of the Household Kitchen stumbled across the train-band's lair, and been allowed to drown to ensure his silence? Or was the opposite true – that Jones knew exactly who operated from the alley, and he had followed

Swaddell to make sure *he* did not live to talk? But then surely the train-band would have rescued Jones?

Of course, there was yet another possibility, which was that Swaddell knew about the train-band, and had led Jones down there on purpose. And what did that suggest? That the soldiers were working for the Spymaster? That answer made sense on two counts: the train-band's location at the heart of government, and the fact that the soldiers were provided with decent clothes and good weapons. Chaloner supposed he would have to find out whether Swaddell or Williamson had a scarred neck.

Aware that time was passing, he began to root through more papers, looking for a clue that would tell him why the train-band had been established in the first place. It did not take him long to find a log-book. Like most military officers, Doling kept a record of what his unit had been ordered to do. There was an entry referring to 'information gathering' at Wapping, which corresponded to the day the vicar had been interrogated. There was also a note marking the fact that Payne had been detailed to collect a red hat from a fashionable milliner.

Was Gold involved, then, thought Chaloner, recalling Bess's new headpiece? He had never seen the man's neck, but he knew for a fact that Gold was not the harmless old ancient he wanted everyone to see. But it was not the time for analysis, and Chaloner felt he had pushed his luck far enough. He replaced everything as he had found it, and aimed for the front door. He was about to slip through it when he heard footsteps in the alley. He had taken too long, and the soldiers were coming back.

Fighting his way past a score of skilled warriors was not an option, so Chaloner's only hope was that the stairs went somewhere he could hide until it was safe to come out. He climbed them quickly, praying they did not lead to a dead end. He was not a moment too soon, because the soldiers moved fast, and he had only just reached the shadows when Doling stamped through the door. The captain was unsettled by the incident, and was telling Payne that nothing like it was ever to happen again.

'We depend on the alley being clear,' he snapped. 'Without it, we are fish in a barrel.'

Chaloner sincerely hoped that did not mean there was only one exit, because it might be days before they all went out again, and he did not want to miss the music at Gold's house that night – or the opportunity to see whether his host had a scar on his neck.

Suddenly, Doling went quiet. It was an unnatural silence, and Chaloner eased into a position where he could see what was happening. Doling was examining footprints. A lot had been tracked inside, but the train-band wore military-style boots, while Chaloner had donned shoes that day. Doling's head snapped up, and he looked directly at the stairs.

'After him!' he cried.

Chaloner turned and fled. There was a door after two flights, but it had been nailed closed – apparently, the soldiers did not want anyone from the adjacent building to stumble into their domain by accident. He headed upwards again, hoping they had not done the same on every floor.

But they had. The third level was similarly barricaded, and so was the fourth. He was nearing the roof, and could hear the thunder of footsteps close behind him – the warriors were gaining, because of the vital seconds Chaloner was losing to check doors. They were not shouting, as many might have done in the excitement of the chase, but continued at a steady pace. Their discipline was formidable, and suddenly the spy's chances of surviving another encounter seemed very slim.

What should he do? Continue upwards, and die when there was nowhere else to go? Turn and fight now? But Chaloner had never liked giving up, and something kept him running until the stairs ended in a tiny door that had daylight and a howling wind coming through cracks in its wood. Now he understood why Doling had been so keen to keep the alley open – there really *was* nowhere else to go.

The door was locked, but Chaloner's probe was at the ready, and he had it open in a trice. He jumped through it, and braced it shut with a piece of timber. The lead soldier slammed against it, and Chaloner heard him swear when he found it blocked. The man began to hit it, not wild, undisciplined blows, but methodical ones aimed at a spot where the wood was most rotten. It would only be a matter of time before he was through. Chaloner glanced around quickly, assessing his options.

He was at the edge of a sharply pitched roof. There was only a five-storey drop to his left, so he turned right, scrambling upwards towards the apex. Loose tiles rattled beneath him, slick with damp and moss. He missed his footing and began to slide back down, only arresting his downward progress by grabbing a hole provided by a missing slate. The soldiers were almost through the door. He began climbing again, faster this time, just as the door finally collapsed in an explosion of splintering wood. He reached the top of the roof, and clambered across it.

The pitch was not so steep on the other side, but it

still ended in a five-storey drop – this one down to the alley. He looked at the building opposite, the roof of which was lower. The soldiers were almost on him, and he could not fight them all – he would either be run through or pushed to his death. But the roof opposite offered a chance, so he took several steps back, then ran forward and propelled himself into space with every ounce of his strength. He heard wind whistling past his ears, but his flight lasted only a moment, and then he was across.

He landed hard, driving the breath from his body and cracking several tiles. He tasted blood in his mouth, and for a moment, he could not move. Just when he was beginning to think he might have done himself a serious injury, his legs finally obeyed the clamouring orders from his brain. He began to scramble away, aiming to put as much distance between him and the train-band as possible.

Then there was an almighty crash, and he glanced back to see he was not the only one capable of death-defying leaps: Payne had followed. He wondered what sort of man would risk his life just to catch an intruder. Meanwhile, the remaining soldiers were putting away their daggers, and turning to retrace their steps. They appeared unconcerned, as if there was no question that Payne would succeed.

Chaloner found himself amid a chaotic jungle of rooftops that formed some of Westminster's poorer houses, shops and taverns. Most were in a dismal state of repair, and the going was treacherous. Fortunately the same was true for Payne, who took a bad tumble that lost him vital seconds. It was just as well, because not only was Chaloner tiring, but he had jolted his lame leg, and was limping badly. He tried to increase his speed, but found he could not do it.

He was obliged to make a second leap when the roof along which he was crawling ended in a dizzying drop. It was not across as great a gap, but he almost did not make it regardless. For a moment, he hung in space, suspended by his hands. It was Payne's jeering laugh that gave him the impetus to swing up his legs, and begin running again, this time along the edge of a large hall. It ended in another sheer drop, so he made a right-angled turn, heading for the distinctive mass of the Painted Chamber. Payne was hard on his heels, swearing foully, and promising all manner of reprisals for the trouble the spy was causing. Chaloner glanced behind him, wondering whether to stand and fight now Payne was alone. But a rooftop was a precarious battlefield, and there was always the danger that his bad leg would turn traitor and tip him into oblivion.

The Painted Chamber had a turret on one of its corners, and Chaloner could tell from its narrow windows that there was a spiral staircase inside. He staggered towards it, and ripped open the door. There was no way to secure it behind him, so he began to descend, hurling himself downwards three steps at a time, trying to ignore the burning pain in his knee. He could hear Payne following, breathing hard and still full of curses and threats.

Eventually, he reached the door that led to the main hall, while the staircase wound on down towards the basement. He hauled it open, then turned back, grabbed a wooden grille – placed in a window-slit to keep out birds – and hurled it down the steps. Then he darted through the door and closed it behind him, listening with baited breath to see whether Payne would fall for the ploy. He breathed a sigh of relief when he heard the soldier continue down, following the clatter made by the tumbling grille in the belief that it was his quarry.

He braced a chair under the handle, then peered out from behind a pile of chests to see he was near the spot where Chetwynd, Vine and Langston had died. The hall was full of people – clerks labouring over documents, government officials issuing orders, and members of the House of Lords in their ermine-fringed robes. A row of pegs hammered into the wall next to him held a variety of garments, so he grabbed a coat and a peculiar three-cornered hat, and donned them quickly to conceal his filthy clothes. Then he strode boldly through the throng, trying to look as though he had every right to be there. No one stopped him, and it was not many moments before he reached the main exit.

Out in the street, he saw members of the train-band everywhere, scanning the faces of passers-by. He reached Old Palace Yard undetected, but Doling blocked the way to the comparative safety of White Hall – and while Chaloner's disguise might fool the captain from a distance, he was too dishevelled to risk passing too close. He needed somewhere to improve his disguise, so he aimed for the abbey.

Westminster Abbey was always a curious combination of busy and deserted. The makeshift booths, selling books, food and candles, that had once thronged the church-yard had gradually eased their way inside, so parts of the nave now resembled a marketplace. But there were also a number of chapels and alcoves that were away from the bustle, providing small havens of tranquillity.

Chaloner found a quiet corner, and sat for a few moments, feeling his heartbeat return to normal and the ache recede from his leg. He would have rested longer, but time was passing, and he could not afford to waste any. He stood, removed his own coat and bundled it under his arm, so the stolen one did not make him seem quite so bulky, then washed his face and hands in a puddle near a leaking window. By the time he had cleaned his shoes and donned the hat, he appeared reasonably respectable – or at least, did not look as though he had been leaping across rooftops.

He was about to leave, when he saw a familiar figure. It was the surviving Lea, sobbing as he knelt at an altar. There was no one else around, and although he knew he should respect the man's privacy Chaloner had questions to ask and time was of the essence.

'I really am sorry about your brother,' he said gently, kneeling next to him.

Lea spoke with difficulty. 'His funeral is supposed to be in St Margaret's Church, but he died serving his country, so I want it here. In this grand abbey.'

'How did he die serving his country?' Chaloner raised his hands defensively when Lea turned on him, eyes blazing with anger. 'Forgive me, but I thought he fell in the river.'

It was clearly not the time to mention that Matthias had been poisoned.

'He could swim,' said Lea fiercely. 'And he should not have been near the river anyway – when we got home that night and realised we had no bread, he went to the bakery in King Street, which is a long way from the Thames. It is obvious what happened: he was taken to a quiet place and pushed in. He was *murdered*.'

'Who do you suspect of the crime?' asked Chaloner.

Lea gazed at him. 'You believe me? No one else does. I wish we had never inherited Chetwynd's beastly fortune, because it has brought us nothing but trouble. Hargrave is a dishonest rogue.'

'You think Hargrave killed Matthias?'

'He might have done. He let us move into the fine house Chetwynd rented from him – and had already paid for – but it leaks like a sieve and stinks of mould. We were better off in our old place.'

'Is Hargrave your only suspect?'

'Oh, no!' said Lea bitterly. 'There are plenty who wish us ill. There are the hypocrites who meet at John's Coffee House to ask God to make them richer and more powerful – Gold, Neale, Tryan and Symons. They hated Matthias for writing a pamphlet about false piety, in which he named them.'

'But you and Matthias attended these meetings, too,' said Chaloner, not bothering to point out that the hapless Symons was neither rich nor powerful. 'I have witnesses who will swear to it.'

'Yes, but that was years ago, when Scobel was still alive. Then there was talk of a Restoration, and it seemed foolish to hobnob with men like Symons and Doling – faithful Commonwealth clerks. So we stopped going.'

'Your strategy worked, because you retained your posts, while they were dismissed.'

'No, we retained them because we took matters into our own hands. We told secrets about former colleagues, which persuaded the right people we were loyal.' Lea saw Chaloner's distaste. 'Well, what else were we to do? A man has to eat! Scobel died of a sharpness of the blood soon after, but Symons said it was a broken heart, because we had betrayed him. Of course, Symons had his revenge.'

'What do you mean?'

'He would not let us rejoin the prayer meetings when all the fuss had died down. Our fortunes have bubbled along at a constant rate, but they have not exploded, like those who continued to pray – Gold, Jones, Chetwynd, Vine, Langston, Tryan and Hargrave.'

'Do you suspect anyone else of killing your brother, other than the prayer-group men?' asked Chaloner, wondering why so many intelligent people should be prey to such rank superstition.

'I barely know where to begin.' Lea's expression was vengeful. 'There is Spymaster Williamson, who does not like the way we earn extra pennies – the government will not fall to rebellion now, so what is the harm in penning a few manifestos?'

'Quite a bit, if enough people agree with the sentiments expressed in them.'

Lea grimaced. 'I doubt it. However, Williamson concurs with you, because Swaddell said he would kill us if we did not desist. Well, we did not desist, so perhaps he carried out his threat. Then there is Doling, who . . . But no, we should not discuss him. He is too deadly for *me* to cross.'

Chaloner was thoughtful. 'You work in Westminster, near a certain alley—'

Lea's face was a mask of fear. 'What of it? We never saw anything that led us to . . .' He trailed off.

'You learned about the train-band,' surmised Chaloner. 'Dangerous men, who probably have a wealthy and powerful master.'

Lea put his face in his hands. 'I told Matthias we should pretend not to have noticed them, but he said our fortunes were on the rise at last, and we should seize every opportunity that presented itself. He left a letter, suggesting Doling might like to pay a small sum to keep his activities secret.'

It was a misjudgement on an appalling scale, and Chaloner wondered how Matthias could have been so recklessly stupid. He took his leave of Lea, and walked outside to find it was dusk, the short winter day over almost before it had begun. The soldiers were still prowling around Old Palace Yard, discreetly scanning the faces of the people who passed, but the gathering gloom helped Chaloner to elude them. He met Wiseman as he was approaching White Hall. The surgeon was trying to hail a hackney to take him home.

'You are limping again,' said Wiseman, abandoning his increasingly bellicose attempts to attract a driver's attention, and turning to assess Chaloner with a professional eye. 'Would you like my—'

'No,' said Chaloner shortly. 'Have you heard whether Greene has been found?'

'A warrant has been issued for his arrest, but the palace guards have had no luck in tracing him. His friends say he has no reason to disappear, and fear he is poisoned or adrift in the river. His detractors say he has gone into hiding, so he can continue to murder as he pleases.'

'Then have you seen Turner?'

'He has spent the day hunting the lost statue.' Wiseman grabbed the spy's shoulder suddenly, startling him with the strength of the grip – the muscle-honing was clearly paying off, because it was like being held by a vice, and Chaloner could not have broken free to save his life. 'Have you been invited to Gold's home for dinner and music tonight?'

'Yes,' replied Chaloner warily, wincing as the surgeon's fingers tightened further still. 'Why?'

Wiseman released him abruptly, and when he spoke, his voice was uncharacteristically bitter. 'I knew it! Gold has invited everyone except me. I am never included in these affairs, although I cannot imagine why. I come from a respectable family, *and* I hold high office in the King's Court.'

'Perhaps it is because you describe surgical techniques while people are eating,' suggested Chaloner, knowing from personal experience that Wiseman's dinner-table conversation could spoil even the most resilient of appetites.

'What is wrong with that? Anatomy is a fascinating subject, worthy of discussion at any social gathering.'

'Actually, I have been asked to two dinners tonight.' Chaloner had only a few hours left before the Earl dismissed him, and while he had hopes that Gold's soirée might lead him to answers, the same was not true of Temperance's. He was sure she would understand why he could not go when he explained the situation. He smiled rather wickedly at the notion of sending the haughty surgeon to a brothel. 'The other is due to begin at midnight, but I have work to do. I do not suppose you would—'

'Where is it?' demanded Wiseman eagerly. 'I shall take your place.'

'Hercules' Pillars Alley.' Chaloner regarded him quizzically. 'You do not mind accepting second-hand invitations?'

'Not when they are the only ones I ever get,' replied Wiseman ruefully. He grinned suddenly, clearly delighted by the prospect of a night out. 'Now, what shall I wear? Will red be suitable, do you think?'

'Oh, yes,' said Chaloner innocently.

*

There was no time to go home before setting out for Gold's mansion in Aldgate, so Chaloner went straight to Hannah's house. She still had some clothes that belonged to her husband, and was more than happy to see them worn. Most were in better condition than Chaloner's own, and far more suitable for attending elegant receptions in fashionable parts of the city. She was horrified when she saw the state he was in, and insisted that he washed, despite his objections that they would be late. Then she selected a handsome blue coat with ruffles down the front, a well-laced shirt, and a pair of 'petticoat' breeches. They were not *au courant* – her spouse had died three years before – but the spy still felt quite respectable as he stepped outside and flagged down a hackney.

Nightfall had heralded a change in the weather. Clouds had raced in from the north, and there was snow in the air. It was bitter, far colder than it had been during the day, and puddles were beginning to turn to ice. The wind cut through clothes, straight to the bone, and Chaloner was tempted to forget the whole business and spend the evening indoors. The roof-top chase had exhausted him, and although the soirée would provide a chance to learn whether Gold was involved in the curious events that had seen so many people die, he was not sure his wits were sharp enough to capitalise on it. But he would be dismissed for certain if he failed to provide the Earl with some sort of solution by the following day, so he forced himself to rally his flagging energies. He glanced at Hannah, who was using his bulk to shield herself from the draught that whistled in through the hackney's badly fitting windows.

'Would you consider leaving London, and going to live in the New World?'

He felt her shudder in the darkness. 'I would not! I have heard it is a desolate place, full of Puritans and big snakes. And I like London, especially now I have you to keep me company.'

It was a long way from Tothill Street to Gold's home near the Tower, and Chaloner might have dozed off, had he not been so cold. The wind buffeted the carriage, making it rock furiously. Outside, the streets were almost empty, and those who were obliged to be out huddled deep inside their cloaks.

Eventually, the hackney rolled to a standstill outside a large house with a gravelled courtyard. Light blazed from every window, and Hannah murmured that she could not imagine the number of lamps required to produce such a dazzling display. Once inside, she disappeared to greet people she knew, flitting from group to group, while Chaloner kept to the edge of the festivities, watching and listening. Gold and Bess were at the centre of an appreciative crowd, and when the spy looked for Neale, he saw him, as expected, not far away, with his eyes fixed unblinkingly on the object of his aspirations.

A number of Chaloner's other suspects were present, too. Symons and the surviving Lea stood together, looking miserable. Lea was impeccably dressed, but Symons was wearing the same clothes had had worn the night Margaret had died. They were soiled and crumpled, and his ginger hair was dull with dirt, as though he cared nothing about any of it.

By contrast, George and Mrs Vine were part of a lively, laughing throng that included Turner, Barbara Chiffinch and Brodrick. Meanwhile, Hargrave and Tryan sat with other prosperous merchants, and their serious faces suggested they were discussing business. Chaloner watched them all, noting who spoke to whom, or ignored whom, and trying to understand the intricate social ballet that was being played out in front of him. He wished he was more alert, because he was sure it would have yielded clues, had his mind been agile enough to interpret them.

'Someone said it is snowing,' said Hannah chattily to Gold, when she dragged the spy to pay their respects to their host. Bess wore a fluffy white garment that looked like a fleece, while her hair had been arranged into woolly ringlets. Chaloner wondered whether the Lord of Misrule had bribed her maids to dress her like a sheep. It was, after all, Brodrick's last night in power – the Twelve Days would be over by the following morning – and the spy was sure he intended to make the most of it.

'You are going?' bawled Gold. 'But you have only just arrived. Stay and have some brawn.'

'There are pastries, too, made in the shape of angels,' added Bess, clapping her hands in childish delight. 'And the cook made a special one for me in the shape of a lamb.'

'Brawn is better for you than chocolate,' asserted Gold loudly. All around him, sycophants nodded simpering agreement. 'While coffee makes you bald. Surgeon Wiseman said so.'

'It is a bit late for *you* to be worrying about hair loss,' muttered Neale, gazing pointedly at Gold's expensive wig. 'Vain old dog.'

'Here comes your friend Turner,' said Hannah to Chaloner, as they walked away. She sounded disapproving. 'He has probably come to gloat, because he solved the case and you did not.'

The colonel looked magnificent that evening, in a black suit with scarlet frills that complemented his dark good looks. He had an adoring lady on each arm; they hung on his every word, and he was in his element. There were pouts when he asked them to fetch him some wine so he could speak to Chaloner in private, but they did as they were told. The moment they were out of earshot, he started to turn his oily charm on Hannah, but she stopped him with a look that said he might suffer serious bodily harm if he persisted.

'Lord!' he breathed in admiration, as she stalked away. 'There is one fiery wench! Does she have all her teeth?'

'Yes, and she is not afraid to use them,' replied Chaloner coolly, seeing the colonel was fully intent on adding her to his list of potential conquests. 'What do you want, Turner? The Earl tells me you have amassed enough evidence to prove Greene is the killer, so you no longer need my help.'

'But unfortunately, the wretched man vanished before I could arrest him. Do you have any idea where he might be? I promised His Portliness I would produce him by tomorrow.'

'That was rash. If he is in the river, it might be weeks before he surfaces.'

'He is not dead,' said Turner confidently. 'He has absconded. Incidentally, you gave the Earl some of Greene's documents earlier, and he, Haddon and Bulteel spent the afternoon studying them. Apparently, they are very revealing.'

'They were household accounts,' said Chaloner tiredly. 'What can be "revealing" about the fact that His Majesty's cellarer spent forty pounds on decanters last year?'

'The fact that Munt kept his own records, which say he only spent ten. But here *is* Haddon. Ask him for yourself.'

Chaloner supposed it was not surprising that Haddon had been invited – *sans* dogs – to the soirée, but Bulteel had not: Haddon carried himself in a way that said he was a gentleman, whereas Bulteel was socially inept.

'It is true,' said the steward, when Turner ordered that he verify the tale. 'In essence, these records show that the sum of forty pounds was *granted* to pay for decanters, but only ten pounds was actually spent. Thus thirty is unaccounted for. And that is only one entry out of hundreds.'

Chaloner stared at him. 'You mean Greene was embezzling from the government?'

'It looks that way,' said Turner gleefully, speaking before the steward could reply. 'We shall be asking him about it when he is arrested.'

'There is another possibility,' said Haddon quietly. 'Which is that Greene was gathering evidence to expose the real thief – that his motives are honourable.'

'And I am the Pope,' sneered Turner derisively.

Chaloner was thinking about the Queen. 'Her Majesty lost thirty-six thousand pounds this year. The money was put in an account for her use, but when she went to claim it, it had all gone.'

'Greene's documents contain a number of references to her so-called expenditures,' acknowledged Haddon. 'So I imagine they *do* explain what happened to her missing fortune, although she will not be pleased by the news – basically, they tell us that her money is irretrievably lost.'

'Thieves are everywhere these days,' said Turner in distaste. Then he grinned, unable to resist the opportunity to revel in his recent success. 'I am delighted to have solved these clerk murders to the Earl's satisfaction, even if it does mean sending a man to the gallows. Now all I have to do is find the King's statue, and my future with him will be assured.'

'The King's statue?' asked Hargrave, coming to join them. Tryan was with him, bandy legs clad in fine silk breeches. 'Are you still looking for that? I would have thought you had given up by now.'

'Do not give up,' said Tryan, rather wistfully. 'It was by Bernini, so no effort is too great to find it, as far as I am concerned. He is a genius, and I would love to own one of his pieces.'

'They are too expensive,' stated Hargrave authoritatively. 'And bankers do not like their customers removing vast sums all at once for costly bits of art, because it upsets their books.'

'I would never put my money in a bank,' declared Tryan. 'Look what happened to the fools who invested with Backwell's. Poor Langston was still waiting to be repaid, and the robbery was months ago. No, my friends, a man's money is safer in his own home. I have a box specially made for the purpose, and it is impossible to break into.'

Chaloner seriously doubted it – he had not met a box yet that could keep him out. 'Are you not afraid of burglars?' he asked politely, seeing the merchant expected some sort of response to his statements. 'Especially when you are out at night?'

'I am rarely out at night,' replied Tryan. 'Today is an exception – and I have been invited to join the dean of St Paul's later, too. But I am usually at home, and I have a gun. I am fully prepared to use it, too, should any vagabond dare tread uninvited in my property.'

'We had better not rob him, then,' remarked Turner

to Chaloner, amusement tugging at the corners of his mouth. 'We do not want to be shot.'

The evening wore on. Symons came to confide to Hannah that he would rather be anywhere than at such a happy gathering, given his recent loss, but Margaret had written a list of tasks that she wanted him to fulfil, and attending Gold's soirée was one of them. Another was dining with his old friend Samuel Pepys the following week.

'You have my sympathy,' said Hannah. In a motherly way, she reached out to smooth down some of the wilder ends of his orange hair. The gesture brought tears to his eyes, and Chaloner wondered whether it was something his wife had done, too. 'Pepys is such a smug little fellow.'

Symons nodded miserably. 'He is sure to gloat over his fine house, his success at the Admiralty, his new uphol-stery and his pretty wife. It will be difficult not to punch the man.'

'Then perhaps you should indulge yourself,' suggested Hannah wickedly. 'It might do him good.'

Symons gave a wan smile, then handed Chaloner a sheet of paper. 'Our maid wanted me to give you this. She said you were asking about it, and thought it might answer your questions – and we owe you something for persuading the surgeon to waive his fee when he came to tend Margaret.'

It was the letter offering the Bernini bust for a very reasonable sum. The handwriting was neat and familiar, and Chaloner knew immediately who had penned it. He put it in his pocket. It was certainly a clue, but unfortun-ately, it pointed him in a direction he would rather not look. He decided to put it from his mind and deal with it in the morning.

403

When Symons left, Haddon took up station at Hannah's side. The steward chatted amiably, mostly about dogs and the Queen, which he seemed to hold in equal regard. Chaloner half-listened, most of his attention on George Vine, who was talking to Hargrave. The spy was reasonably adept at reading lips, and knew George was regaling the merchant with a drunken monologue about old Dreary Bones' reaction when he had discovered his son's plan to assassinate Cromwell with an exploding leek.

'Did you know Gold is dying?' Haddon was saying to Hannah. Chaloner turned around in surprise. 'He will be in his grave in a matter of weeks. It is a sharpness of the blood, apparently.'

'The poor man,' said Hannah with quiet compassion. 'He should be in bed, not giving parties. But I think I can guess the reason why he organised this one: he is hoping to find a good match for that silly Bess – someone who will not marry her for the money she will inherit.'

'You are right,' said Haddon. 'He told me as much himself. He will leave her a fortune, and every wolf in the country will circle around, hoping for a bite of the prize. But he loves her, despite her faults, and wants her properly cared for.'

'Do you know what I think?' asked Hannah. 'That Neale has poisoned him. See how he looks at Bess – all avarice and lust? And she is too stupid to know him for what he is.'

'I suspect she has more wits than you think,' said Chaloner. He shrugged when Hannah started to tell him he was wrong. 'I am not saying she should be elected to the Royal Society, but she owns a certain innate cunning that will ensure she is no one's victim.'

'The Earl thinks the same,' confided Haddon. 'And he said so when Gold visited him the other day. Gold has asked him to guard Bess when he dies, you see, but the Earl maintains she is more than capable of looking after herself.'

Chaloner recalled seeing the old man in the Earl's chamber a few days before – and the Earl lying about being alone. Gold must have requested secrecy, so the Earl's fib must have been to oblige him. 'His frailty is not an act after all, then?' he asked. 'He really is ailing?'

'Yes, but he is a long way from being harmless,' replied Haddon. 'I have seen him draw his sword and wield it in a way that would put many of these youngsters to shame.'

'Whom did he threaten?' asked Hannah curiously. 'Neale?'

'Vine,' replied Haddon. 'Not George, but his father. I happened to be in John's Coffee House, at the time and I witnessed the incident myself. Gold said their gatherings had gone from the honourable business of praising God, to the superstitious nonsense of praying for their own good fortunes. He wanted to end them, but Vine was afraid that if that happened, he would start to experience bad luck. Vine was being stubborn, so Gold hauled out his weapon to make his point.'

'You have not mentioned this before,' said Chaloner, rather accusingly.

'Because I knew it would lead you to assume Gold was Vine's killer,' replied Haddon evenly. 'And I am sure he is not. I had five pounds riding on you solving the case, so I did not want you wasting your time on false leads. Of course, my ploy was all for nothing, because Turner won anyway.'

'These prayer meetings caused a lot of trouble,' said Hannah, speaking before Chaloner could inform the steward that he was quite capable of making up his own mind about what constituted a false lead. 'Scobel instituted something that should have been worthy, but that transpired to be distasteful.'

'So it would seem,' said Haddon. He grinned with sudden mischief. 'I told Turner about Gold's fight with Vine, though. He spent two days learning that Gold has alibis for all three murders.'

'Do you know what they are?' asked Chaloner, not sure they could be trusted.

'He was with the Queen when Chetwynd and Langston died—' began Haddon.

'He was,' agreed Hannah. 'I was not there myself, because Her Majesty had sent me home for the night. But the other ladies mentioned it the following day.'

'And he was with the Earl when Vine was killed,' finished Haddon. 'At Worcester House.'

Chaloner supposed the alibis were as solid as any he had heard, although that still left the possibility that Gold had hired someone else to do the killing. He rubbed his head wearily, and it occurred to him that he was wasting time at the soirée – and there was not even any music, as Hannah had promised. Perhaps he should be out hunting Greene, or re-interviewing the guards who had been on duty when the statue had gone missing. He looked at Hannah's sweet, happy face, and realised he did not want to leave London because the Earl no longer had a post for him. He wanted to stay.

His gloomy thoughts were broken by a sudden commotion. People began to gather around Gold, who sat in a great fireside chair. Bess was on his lap and his face was oddly serene. But Bess was screaming, because her dress was caught on some item of his jewellery, and she could not escape. It took a moment for Chaloner to understand why she was so determined to be away from him.

Gold was dead.

The party broke up once its host was no longer in the world of the living. Outside, Brodrick bemoaned the fact that it was so early, then launched into a sulky diatribe against Temperance for electing to close her club on an evening when not much else was on offer. And how dare she organise a private get-together and not invite him, her most faithful customer? He turned towards his carriage with the defiant declaration that he would find something better to do. After a moment of indecision – to go with Brodrick or stay to see if any inroads could be made on Bess – Neale followed. Hannah watched him through narrowed eyes.

'If he really cared for her, he would not be thinking about his own pleasures tonight. Sir Nicholas was right to elicit the help of a powerful baron to keep the vultures away. Unfortunately, it will be like trying to stop this snow from falling – you may catch a few flakes, but hundreds will get past.'

'Come with us,' Brodrick called jovially over his shoulder, one foot on the bottom step of his coach. He saw Hannah gird herself up for an acidly worded refusal, and added hastily, 'No, not you, madam. The invitation was intended for Thomas and Colonel Turner only. The kind of fun I have in mind will be unsuitable for a lady.'

'You mean you plan to visit whores?' asked Hannah, very coldly.

'Actually, I was thinking of serious music,' replied

Brodrick, equally icy. 'Of the kind that is beyond the female mind to comprehend. Thomas is an excellent violist, while the colonel played for the king of Sweden during the celebrations surrounding the Treaty of Roskilde, so he should be up to my exacting standards, too. Your squawking flageolet would be anathema to us, madam.'

'Will you let him insult me, Tom?' demanded Hannah, but Chaloner's thoughts were elsewhere. He had been at Roskilde, spying for Thurloe, but did not remember Turner among the entertainers. Being a music lover, he had paid more attention to the performers than he should have done, and that part of the occasion was etched vividly in his mind. Yet again, the colonel had lied.

But Turner spoke before Chaloner could challenge him. 'Not tonight, Brodrick. I am tired after hunting the statue all day, and would make a poor addition to your consort. I am going home.'

A number of women were openly crestfallen at this announcement, and he hastened to console them. Hannah glared at Chaloner for failing to defend her, but then snow began to fall in larger, harder flakes, driven by a cruel, north-easterly wind, and she declared it was no time for lingering. Brodrick clattered away with Neale, while Turner bade fond farewells to his entourage and started to walk towards his lodgings. Chaloner hailed a hackney, intending to see Hannah home, then spend the night looking for Greene and the King's bust. He was exhausted, but he would only have to keep going until the following noon – at which point he would probably be able to rest for longer than he would like.

'Nicholas died happy,' said Hannah, once she was settled in the carriage. The snow was so thick that the driver could not tear along at the usual breakneck speed, and the ride was pleasantly sedate. 'Although I imagine Bess will think twice before sitting on anyone's knee again!'

'It preceded her inheriting a fortune,' Chaloner pointed out. 'Perhaps she will think it was worth it.'

'I am surprised Turner has not made more of a play for her,' said Hannah, making a moue of distaste. 'He is a fortune-seeker, and Bess is foolish enough to fall for his shallow charms. The man is a snake, and I would not trust him with a . . . a coffee bean!'

'He does have a habit of stretching the truth,' acknowledged Chaloner, recalling that Turner had presented Bess with a crucifix, which suggested some kind of play had already been made.

'Stretching?' echoed Hannah in disbelief. 'He elongates it to the point where it is no longer recognisable. And he is brazen. Tonight, right in front of me, he told Bess that he hailed from Ireland, then turned around and told some other simpering fool that he was from Yorkshire. He even uses different names. He is not Colonel Turner to all his hopeful conquests.'

'No?' Chaloner was not really listening, thinking instead about which of the palace guards he should tackle regarding the stolen statue.

'No. He called himself Julius Grey when he was introduced to Margaret Symons, but then had to admit to the lie when someone called him "Turner" in front of her.'

That made Chaloner look up sharply. '*Julius* Grey?'

'No, that is not right,' Hannah frowned in thought, then brightened. '*James* Grey. That was it!'

'Are you sure? Only Temperance is in love with a man called James Grey. But it cannot be Turner.'

Hannah shrugged deeper inside her cloak; it was bitterly cold in the carriage. 'Why not?'

'Because she could not introduce us the night she told me about him, owing to the fact that he was not there. Turner *was* there, though.'

Hannah patted his knee, rather patronisingly. 'You have said before that she dislikes the way you condemn her lifestyle, so she probably wanted to give you time to get used to the idea, lest shock lead you to storm up to Turner and call him out for a rake.'

'You think she lied to me?' Why not? he thought. She had done it before.

'I have never met her, so I cannot say. Did she tell you anything about this James Grey?'

'Only that he played the viol.'

'Well, there you are, then. Turner plays the viol – you just heard him and Brodrick talking about it.'

'But Turner does *not* play the viol. Violists have toughened skin on the tips of their left-hand fingers, from pressing on the strings, but his fingers are soft. And he was not at Roskilde, either.' Chaloner frowned, as something else occurred to him. 'Grey gave Temperance a token – a piece of red silk that she wears in her bodice.'

'Turner has red silk in the lining of his coat,' pounced Hannah. 'It is newly sewn, because a couple of pins have not yet been removed, and I recall thinking that some poor lady was likely to feel a prick before the night was out. So to speak. He must have had a kerchief made of the scraps, and gave it to her as a keepsake. He does hand out keepsakes, although he usually confines himself to lockets.'

'I know he gave lockets to several ladies at Court.'

410

Hannah nodded. 'At least five that I have seen swooning over the things. I suppose he must have a ready supply.'

A sense of deep unease began to wash over Chaloner. 'Temperance said they were going to be married, but . . .' He trailed off, not knowing how to finish without sounding disloyal.

'But Turner has been frolicking with Lady Castlemaine, Lady Muskerry, Bess and several other very wealthy women,' supplied Hannah. 'So why would he deign to wed a brothel-keeper? Is that what you mean to say?'

'Actually, Temperance is probably richer than any of them, because her money is her own, and she is not obliged to rely on others to dole it out. I was thinking more of her . . . her . . .'

'Her looks,' finished Hannah, when he faltered a second time. 'Brodrick told me she is plain and fat. Why would Turner settle for an drab wife, when he can have a Court beauty?'

Chaloner looked away, watching the snow falling outside. Where there were lights, he could see it slanting down thickly. It was settling, and by morning, London would be covered in a blanket of white.

'You should warn her,' said Hannah, when he made no reply. 'You cannot stand by and let her make a fool of herself. Or worse. It would not be the first time a lonely girl snatched too eagerly at the prospect of a handsome darling, and lost everything to him.'

Chaloner did not think Temperance was lonely, but she did not confide in him any more, so who knew what she was really feeling? 'She will resent my interference,' he said uncomfortably.

'Of course she will, but that is what friendship entails

on occasion. You say she invited you to dine this evening, but you sent word asking to be excused. Go – say you changed your mind. When she introduces you to "James Grey", Turner will at least be shamed into telling her his real name. Perhaps that alone will be enough to make her wary.'

'He said he was going home,' Chaloner began lamely. 'And—'

'Because he wanted to avoid being exposed as a fraud when Brodrick put a viol in his hands,' said Hannah impatiently. 'I wager anything you please that he is on his way to Temperance as we speak.'

'You seem very keen for me to leave,' said Chaloner, wondering why she should encourage him to meddle in the affairs of a woman she had never met.

'I do not want you to feel guilty for letting down a friend.' Hannah hammered on the hackney roof. 'Driver! There has been a change of plan. Take us to Hercules' Pillars Alley instead.'

'Actually, I am letting you out here,' called the driver, and the coach came to a sudden stop. 'The weather is getting worse by the minute, and I am not risking my horse any longer.'

Chaloner could see his point: the snow was almost halfway up the wheels. He peered out of the window, and saw they were near Bishopsgate Street, where there were several respectable inns. Hannah would be safe there while he went about his business – he did not want her with him when he confronted Turner, and he did not have time to walk her all the way home.

'Can you reach the Mitre?' he asked.

The driver gave a reluctant nod, and it was not long before Hannah was installed in the best room the tavern could offer, with a roaring fire, mulled wine and clean blankets.

'That hackneyman exaggerated the severity of the storm,' she declared dismissively. 'If you keep to the smaller roads, you will find the drifts are much more manageable. But you must go now, Tom – by tomorrow, Turner's claws might be too deeply embedded for us to extract.'

'Easy for you to say,' muttered Chaloner, casting one last, longing glance at the fire before heading on to the streets again. It seemed colder than ever, and contrary to Hannah's assurances, the snow was knee-deep even in the narrowest of lanes. It was impossible to walk normally, and his leg hurt. Only the thought of Temperance drove him on. She might be slipping away from him as a friend, but he still felt a modicum of responsibility towards her, no matter how much she had changed.

Snowflakes whirled around him so thickly that he could not see, and he had reached St Mary Axe before he realised he was walking in the wrong direction. With a muffled curse, he turned down Lymestrete, where the blizzard drove directly into his face. He put his head down, and ploughed on, so tired now that he did not notice someone coming towards him until it was too late. His hand dropped to his sword, but a shoulder sent him crashing into a wall before he could draw it.

Winded and dazed, he pulled himself into a sitting position. His assailant was already some distance away, and his eyes focussed just in time to see him dart down an alley. The fellow was carrying a sack that was heavy enough to make him stagger. And then he was gone.

*

Slowly, Chaloner climbed to his feet, resting his hand on the wall to steady himself. He realised he needed to pay closer attention to his surroundings, because he had just learned the hard way that the instincts that normally warned him of impending danger were not functioning properly. He took a deep breath of cold air to clear his wits, then resumed his journey.

He was almost at the end of Lymestrete, when he happened to glance to his right. Most of the larger houses were owned by people wealthy enough to keep a lamp burning in their downstairs windows all night, as dictated by the city fathers, but one mansion was notable for its darkness. It took a moment for Chaloner to recognise it as Tryan's home, and was surprised – Tryan was an alderman, and was supposed to set a good example. Then he noticed the front door was ajar.

His senses snapped into a different level of awareness. No sane person left his door open at night, so something was wrong. Temperance momentarily forgotten, he stumbled towards it. He stepped inside and listened intently. The house was eerily silent.

'Tryan?' he called softly.

But of course the merchant was not home – he had been asked out by the dean of St Paul's and would be at the cathedral, shivering his way through a lengthy ceremony during which far too many clerics would be given an opportunity to speak. Tryan had bragged about the invitation several times, so doubtless all manner of folk knew about it. And someone had taken advantage of the information to burgle him, because the wood around the door was damaged, indicating a forced entry. Chaloner supposed the culprit was the man who had bowled him over, fleeing the scene of his crime with a sack of loot. It was a pity

Tryan was going to return to find his home had been invaded, but there was nothing the spy could do about it. He was about to go on his way when he heard a sound.

'Help,' came the merest of whispers. 'Please!'

It came from the parlour at the front of the house, and Chaloner could just make out someone lying on the floor. It was Tryan. Chaloner knelt next to him, and eased him into a more comfortable position. Then he fetched blankets and set about lighting a fire, because the room was deathly cold. As he worked, he looked around him. The heavy, iron-bound chest he had seen on his previous visit was open, and papers were scattered around its feet.

'The rogue knew,' rasped Tryan, his eyes huge in his white face. 'He knew I kept the key in my desk, because he went straight to it. And I did not even have time to aim my gun before he hit me.'

'Who have you told about the key?' asked Chaloner, tucking a blanket more tightly around him.

'Just my manservant and maid – I gave them the night off, because they have been so good to me.' Tryan's face was anguished. 'The thief took everything! I had one thousand and fifty pounds in cash, and four thousand pounds in jewels, which I keep here because I distrust banks. But now I am ruined! What have I done to deserve this terrible thing?'

Chaloner tensed when he heard footsteps in the hall. He drew his sword and stepped behind the door, assuming the burglar had come back to see what else he could steal. The blade wobbled in the hilt, telling him he had better buy a replacement as soon as possible, because the one he had borrowed from Landlord Ellis promised to fall apart at the first riposte.

'Hill! Susan!' cried Tryan, when two people walked in. They wore his livery, so Chaloner assumed they were his servants, returning from their night out. 'I have been robbed!'

The pair suddenly became aware of Chaloner standing in the shadows. Bravely, Hill raised his fists, although they would be of little use against a sword, even a defective one. Meanwhile, Susan grabbed a poker from the hearth and stood next to him, ready to protect her fallen master.

'No!' gasped Tryan. 'This man saw the door open and came to help me – he is not the thief.'

'I knew we should not have left you,' declared Hill, lowering his hands. His voice was full of bitter self-reproach. 'I told you it was not safe to be here alone, not when you have been telling everyone that you planned to be out this evening.'

'Not to mention your habit of saying you distrust banks,' scolded Susan, kneeling at Tryan's side and inspecting his battered face. 'It is asking for villains to come and try their luck.'

Chaloner helped Hill carry the old man to his bed, then Susan ordered them out while she tended his wounds, clicking and soothing like a mother hen. Tryan was fortunate to have such devoted staff, thought Chaloner, as the manservant escorted him towards the front door.

'I saw the thief,' he said, more to himself than Hill as they walked along the corridor together. 'At least, I saw someone carrying a heavy bag. He knocked me over.'

Hill was quietly furious. 'If I catch him, I will kill him! It is one thing to steal the old fellow's money, but did he have to beat him, too? And how did he know about the key? My master may blather about his distrust of banks and his invitations out, but he does not tell just anyone where he keeps his key. The thief will be someone who knows him and his habits.'

'Hargrave?' asked Chaloner. He seemed the obvious candidate.

But Hill shook his head. 'He is at St Paul's – when my master decided the weather was too foul for a man of his age to be traipsing about, Hargrave offered to go in his place.'

Chaloner was about to leave, when he saw something lying on the floor, dark against the pale wood. He bent to retrieve it. It was an ear-string. Hill snatched it from him.

'I have seen this before,' he said, turning it over in his hands.

'So have I,' said Chaloner softly. 'Worn by a man who does the occasional bit of legal work for Tryan, and who knows his foibles – the money chest, his plans to be out, and even, probably, where he keeps his key.'

'Turner!' exclaimed Hill in sudden fury. 'I knew he was a villain the moment I laid eyes on him.'

'I wish I had,' said Chaloner ruefully, stepping out into the blizzard.

Chapter 12

The snow was now swirling so densely that it was difficult to walk. Chaloner forced himself on, wishing he could go faster. The streets were deserted, and there was not a horse or a carriage in sight. If there had been, he would have hijacked it, so desperate was he to reach Temperance. As he struggled along, he tried to take his mind off his fears for her while he analysed what he knew of Turner.

He had known the man was a liar, but he had not imagined him to be a thief, too. However, the attack on Tryan was such an audacious, meticulously executed crime that the spy was sure it could not be his first. So what other felonies had he committed since arriving in London? He was not responsible for the business at Backwell's Bank, because that had been Jones, and the only other significant incident was the theft of the old king's bust. Chaloner stopped dead in his tracks.

'No!' he whispered into the blizzard, forgetting the frantic race to Hercules' Pillars Alley as answers came crashing into his mind like bolts of lightning. 'It cannot be!'

But when he reviewed the evidence, he knew he had

his solution, and it was so obvious, he wondered why he had not seen it before. The clues were there, but he had not put them together.

First, Turner said Lady Muskerry had taken him to the Shield Gallery before the statue had gone astray; he must have seen the priceless works of art then, and decided one would not be missed. Second, conversations had revealed his total ignorance of sculpture, indicating he would not have made a wise choice about what to steal – and taking the Bernini had been foolish. Third, Meg had smuggled him in and out of White Hall on her laundry cart, claiming Lady Castlemaine needed protection from the Earl – a ludicrous tale that should have warned Chaloner to look into it: clearly, Turner had needed the cart to transport his ill-gotten gains. And finally, there was his odd reluctance to arrest Greene – he felt a kinship with a fellow criminal, and wanted to give him every chance to escape or be exonerated.

'Damn!' Chaloner breathed, aghast at himself. 'How could I have been so stupid?'

So, where was the statue now? Turner was unlikely to have taken it home, but it was valuable, so he would have put it somewhere safe. Chaloner closed his eyes in disgust when he realised he knew the answer to that, too. 'James Grey' had encouraged Temperance to redecorate her brothel, purchasing sculpture rather than paintings, because her patrons were apt to be wild and carvings were more durable. The bust was not in the public rooms – someone would have recognised it – but she had spare pieces in her cellar, ready to be rotated when she grew tired of the ones on display. She knew nothing about art, either, and would not recognise Bernini's work, so it was the perfect hiding place. And if someone should happen to stumble across it?

'Then he would disappear and let her hang.' Chaloner was barely aware that he spoke aloud as anger boiled up inside him. He started to move forward again, cursing when his exhausted muscles were slow to respond to the urgent clamouring of his brain.

Rage kept him ploughing towards Hercules' Pillars Alley, allowing him to ignore the burning pain in his lame leg and the agony of frozen fingers. All he wanted to do was charge into the club and force a confession from the sly colonel with his fists. And then Temperance would see what sort of man she professed to love. But when he reached his destination, his training took over: his wild fury drained away and was replaced by the cool professionalism that had allowed him to survive ten years in espionage. So, instead of storming into the house like a lunatic, he slid into the shadows outside, and thought about what he was going to do.

Once his judgement was unimpaired by anger, he saw it would be foolish to dash into a situation that might see him killed. First, he was too tired for fighting. Second, his sword was broken. And third, Temperance might rush to her lover's defence, and then what would he do? Exchange blows with her, too? And would Turner even be there? He had just committed a violent crime, and was now more than five thousand pounds richer; perhaps he would decide that Temperance and the bust were not worth the bother. But indentations in the snow from the road to the club's front door told the spy that this was wishful thinking: Turner had been unable to resist the lure of easy pickings, and he was there, inside the house, plying his evil charms on the woman Chaloner loved like a sister.

The spy approached the building and tapped softly on the door, but the servants had evidently been given the evening off, because there was no reply. The door was locked, but that was no obstacle to him. His metal probe was in his hand without conscious thought, and he had it open in moments. He padded silently across the hall to the parlour, where he peered through a gap between door and wall. The snow that had caked on his coat and shoes began to melt, forming puddles on the floor.

Temperance was sitting at one end of a guest-filled table, and Turner was at the other. They held goblets, filled to the brim with wine, and were toasting each other's health. Chaloner winced when he saw the shining adoration in her eyes, and hated himself for what he was about to do. The colonel's face was red from his journey through the snow, and his cloak had been flung carelessly across the back of a chair. He looked remarkably lively, though, and Chaloner supposed he was buoyed up by the success of his robbery.

Turner and Wiseman were the only men present, the other guests being the 'working girls' and Maude. Belle was among them, and Chaloner shook his head when he saw she still wore her locket: Turner had shown him a duplicate in order to claim the ten shillings. Wiseman was relating some tale about a Public Anatomy he had performed, and his audience – a jaded group that was not easily entertained – was transfixed. The surgeon was unused to receiving such a positive reaction to his grisly anecdotes, and was happier than Chaloner had ever seen him.

While they were occupied, the spy decided to see whether his suspicions were correct. He headed for the cellar, lighting a lamp in the kitchen to take with him.

As he descended the stairs, he marvelled at the size of Temperance's collection. A dozen crates contained the most valuable items, while the more robust specimens sat out draped in sheets – with the notable exception of Nero, who glowered, uncovered, from the top of a tall box.

Chaloner began his search. The Bernini was in the third chest he opened, and he paused for a moment to admire it. He had seen the old king once, across a battlefield, but he recalled the pinched, arrogant features quite clearly. The artist had captured the hauteur and pride in the face, and yet there was also a touching vulnerability about it. He could see why Bernini was regarded as a genius.

He took a deep breath, trying to summon the energy he needed to confront Turner, and was about to walk back up the stairs, when he saw a trail of water splashes on the floor. He followed them to a sack that was heavily encrusted with snow. When he opened it, he found it full of money and jewels. He was still staring, disgusted that Turner should have beaten an old man to get it, when he heard a creak. He doused the lantern, ducked into the shadows and waited.

Turner walked into the cellar holding a lamp of his own. His eyes immediately lit on the opened box that contained the stolen masterpiece. He set the lantern on a crate and drew his sword.

'Come out,' he called softly. 'I know you are here, because you have left wet marks on the floor.'

Chaloner supposed he had. The snow that covered his clothes was continuing to melt, and he, like Turner's sack, left drips wherever he went. He stepped out, and thought he saw alarm flash in the colonel's eyes when he was recognised, but it was quickly masked.

'What are you doing here?' Turner demanded uneasily. 'Temperance will be hurt when she learns you declined her invitation to dine, just so you could use the opportunity to sneak into her home and help yourself to her things.'

'I am not the thief here,' said Chaloner quietly. 'I do not break in to the houses of elderly merchants when I think they are at church, and batter them half to death when I discover they are not.'

'What is this?' demanded Turner, struggling to feign bemusement. 'What elderly merchant?'

Chaloner pointed to the sack. 'The one you almost killed to get that. Do not deny it, Turner. Your ear-string dropped off during the attack, and identifies you as the culprit.'

Turner's hand flew to his empty lobe in horror. Seeing he was trapped, he dropped the pretence of innocence, and tried another tactic. 'This is not how it looks. I was worried about him keeping such a large sum in his house, so I decided to put it in a bank, where it will be safe. But he came back unexpectedly, and went for his gun. I panicked. I am not proud of myself, but it is what happened. It is all a terrible misunderstanding.'

'If you say so,' said Chaloner, too tired to argue with him. 'But that is for a judge to decide.'

Turner shook his head in stunned disbelief. 'This cannot be happening, not now! I have a job I love, wealthy ladies shower me with gifts, and Temperance is on the verge of giving me half her club. Those meetings at John's Coffee House work! You ask for success with like-minded men, and lo and behold, success is yours.'

Chaloner was taken aback by the claim. 'You attribute your recent rise in fortune to prayers?'

Turner shrugged. 'Well, something caused my luck to change. I joined originally to gain Tryan's confidence – to find out whether he really did have a fortune in his parlour. But when I realised prayers might be the key to my various triumphs, I decided I had better keep going. Do you want to enrol? I can get you in – in exchange for your silence about tonight's little episode, naturally.'

Chaloner regarded him in disdain. 'You are a callous dog, Turner. Or is your real name Grey?'

He drew his sword when Turner did not reply, glancing down when the hilt made a peculiar grating sound and something small and metallic fell from it and skittered across the floor. The blade was held in place by a thread, and would not survive the first parry. He cursed himself for not borrowing a better one from Tryan, because he should have anticipated how an encounter with Turner would end. At some point during his frantic race – probably when he had been knocked off his feet as Turner had been fleeing from Lymestrete – he had also lost the daggers he kept secreted about his person. Fortunately, the colonel noticed neither his lack of handy weapons nor the state of his sword. He began to back away.

'Please!' he cried, alarmed. 'I am sure we can work this out without resorting to violence.'

'We can,' agreed Chaloner evenly. 'And it entails you putting up your weapon and turning around.'

'No!' Turner's face was as white as the snow that was falling outside. 'They will execute me, and you know how I feel about hanging.'

Chaloner was unmoved. 'Then you should have thought of that before you broke the law.'

Turner swallowed hard, clearly loath to engage in a skirmish he thought he was unlikely to win. Then he closed his eyes in weary resignation, and slowly reached out to place his sword on the nearest crate. Unfortunately, Chaloner's blade chose that moment to drop out of its hilt. The colonel's eyebrows shot up in astonishment, but his reactions were fast. He snatched up his weapon again, even as Chaloner darted towards it, and the spy was lucky to avoid the lunge that was aimed in his direction.

'And you berated *me* for poor weapon maintenance the other night,' Turner crowed, his confidence flooding back now he had the advantage. 'Hypocrite!'

'You are still not leaving this cellar a free man,' warned Chaloner.

Turner laughed derisively. 'And who will stop me? Not you, because you will be dead. You seem to know rather too much about me, and I do not want you telling tales to His Portliness.'

Chaloner grabbed an old broom that had been left lying on the floor. Turner might have the upper hand at that precise moment, but the spy had faced worse odds. All he needed to do was even them out a little. He looked around quickly, and a plan began to form in his mind.

'I appreciate that the King's statue posed an irresistible temptation for you,' he said, jigging away from the stabbing blade. 'But I will never forgive you for involving Temperance. Or Meg, although I cannot imagine she knew why you needed her cart.'

'Meg would have demanded a share,' said Turner, watching Chaloner with narrowed eyes as the spy weaved between the crates. 'So I kept her in the dark. But how do you know I involved Temperance?'

The question took Chaloner by surprise, given where

they were. 'Other than the stolen bust being hidden in her cellar? Well, there is the note offering to sell it to Margaret Symons, which is in her handwriting. You persuaded her to scribe it, lest someone recognised your own scrawl.'

Turner grinned slyly. 'It suits me to be cautious. She had no idea what she was scribbling about, though – I doubt her affection for me runs deep enough to defraud the King on my account.'

Chaloner was not so sure about that. He moved further behind the sculpture as Turner continued to speak. His ploy to distract the man by encouraging him to gloat was working – like many criminals, he could not resist bragging about his achievements.

'I assumed some wealthy Royalist would buy it, but the King made such a fuss about its loss that I dared not approach any. I had no idea he would miss it so much. God knows why – it is ugly.'

'It is of his father,' said Chaloner, astounded not only by the man's ignorance of art, but by his lack of understanding for his victim. 'Of course he will miss it.'

'I tried selling it to artists in the end,' Turner went on, waving his free hand to indicate Chaloner did not know what he was talking about. 'And I even offered it to Greene, thinking he might exchange it for a pardon. He was a fool to refuse, because I do not see how else he will evade the noose.'

'You think he is guilty?' Chaloner stumbled when Turner managed to land a sly jab with his sword. It did no harm, but the colonel had moved fast, and Chaloner knew he would have to be careful. His lame leg was slowing him down, and the trek through the snow had taken too great a toll on his strength – unlike Turner, he did not have the exhilaration of a successful burglary to fuel him.

The colonel nodded. 'I wanted to believe he was the victim of a monstrous conspiracy, as you suggested, but there are too many inexplicable coincidences. He must have killed those three clerks because they were more successful than him, and he was jealous.'

One more jig put Chaloner in the position he had been aiming for – with Turner trapped between two tall boxes where he would be unable to make full use of his sword. He took a firmer grip on the broom, readying himself for attack. Turner was still chattering.

'I thought it would be easy to make a tidy profit from the statue, because everyone here is so fabulously gullible. For example, selling those lockets to swooning women has been child's play.'

The confession made Chaloner falter. 'You *sold* those keepsakes?' he asked, astounded by the man's audacity. 'I thought you dispensed them to make each lady think she was special.'

Turner's smug grin was back. 'I did – I just wheedled a small donation from her at the same time. They are wealthy lasses, and do not mind lending me money for my poor sick mother.'

'And then you make bets with men like me, saying you can charm these lockets away from their owners. But, of course, you do no such thing. Belle is still wearing hers, and the one you showed me this morning is a duplicate.'

'I keep a supply in my hat,' confided Turner, winking. 'I almost lost them when Lady Castlemaine demanded I hand it over – I had to pretend I wanted to keep it because it was a gift from Bess.'

'You could have returned the statue to the Earl,' said

Chaloner, aiming to disconcert him by turning the discussion to the crime that had transpired to be something of a disaster. 'He would have been far too delighted to ask awkward questions, and you could have secured his good graces permanently.'

Turner sneered. 'And what would he have given me for it? Nothing! However, I am beginning to see there is no alternative, so I shall make him a gift of it after I kill you. I will tell him *you* stole it.'

Chaloner dived forward, startling the colonel with the speed of his attack. Turner tried to fight back, but found he had insufficient room to manoeuvre. The spy met each feeble thrust with the broom, then jabbed hard, catching Turner a painful blow on the ribs. But Turner recovered quickly, and reciprocated by slashing at Chaloner's legs. He missed, but the move caused the spy to stagger, and Turner took the opportunity to dart around a crate and tip Nero off his pedestal. Chaloner hurled himself backwards to avoid being crushed, and fell awkwardly. Turner grinned when he saw the spy sprawled on the floor *sans* broom, and prepared to make an end of him.

Chaloner looked around desperately for some kind of weapon – anything that would slow Turner's relentless advance – but there was nothing. He took a deep breath and braced himself for the stroke that would end his life. But suddenly, there was a thud and Turner gave a sharp yelp of pain – someone had lobbed a wine decanter that had hit him square in the back. Temperance was on the stairs.

Turner whipped around, then started to stride towards her. Chaloner struggled to his feet, sure Turner was going to kill her, but his legs were like rubber, and he could not move nearly fast enough. The colonel reached her first.

'Dearest,' he said with one of his most winning smiles. 'Chaloner stole the King's bust, and hid it in your cellar. But he has been unable to sell the thing, so hopes to secure his future with the Earl by blaming you for the crime.'

'He is lying,' said Chaloner, although with scant hope of being believed. Why would she take his word over that of an adored lover?

'We have been fighting,' continued Turner, ignoring him. 'But I won, and it will not take a moment to finish him off. Go upstairs, love. You do not want to see this.'

'I heard you,' said Temperance in a low, broken voice. 'I was hard on your heels when you came down here. I heard everything you said.'

Unabashed, Turner winked at her. 'You heard me confounding him with a false confession. It is a technique I have used to corner felons before, and you should not worry your pretty head with it.'

While Turner was talking, Chaloner summoned the strength for a final assault. He tore across the room, and crashed into the man, bowling him from his feet. The sword flew from Turner's hand, and by the time he had gathered his wits, the spy was sitting astride him and his own dagger was being held to his throat. Turner regarded it in astonishment, as if he could not imagine how he had lost the encounter.

'Stand up,' ordered Chaloner, grabbing the sword. He was aware of Temperance's bitter weeping behind him, and it tore at his heart. For two pins, he would have run Turner through there and then.

'Do not let him take me,' Turner begged, climbing to his feet and stretching a pleading hand towards Temperance. 'I will be hanged. And anyway, I stole the bust for us, so we could—'

'No more lies, James,' Temperance sobbed. 'Do not talk to me.'

Turner was shrewd enough to recognise a lost cause when he saw one. He turned to Chaloner instead. 'If you let me go, I will tell you where to find Greene – or rather where Greene will be at dawn. The whores in the Dog and Duck have been sheltering him, but I met Meg earlier, and she could not resist confiding in me.'

Chaloner indicated that Turner was to precede him up the stairs. Temperance followed.

'He plans to visit the Painted Chamber at first light,' continued Turner, rather desperately. 'According to Meg, he wants to collect a few things before fleeing to France. You can go there and arrest him. It will delight His Portliness, and save you your job.'

'And why should I believe you?'

'Because I do not want to hang,' said Turner. His voice was unsteady. 'So I am offering you valuable information in exchange for an hour to leave the city. Besides, I suspect you think I am the clerk-killer – you seem to be blaming me for everything else – and I want to prove my innocence by giving you the real villain. Greene.'

'There is no need,' said Chaloner. They reached the top of the stairs, and Temperance stepped around them to open the door. 'You have an alibi for Chetwynd's murder: Meg said you and she meet each Monday and Thursday and stay together from dusk until dawn. You were with her when he died.'

He heard Temperance catch her breath, but did not

430

take his eyes off Turner. She tugged open the door, then stood aside for the colonel to pass. As he went, Turner reached out to touch her cheek. She ducked away violently, unwittingly placing herself between him and Chaloner's sword. As quick as lightning, Turner shoved her hard, so she toppled towards the cellar stairs. Chaloner tried to catch her, but she was a large woman and represented a lot of weight. She fell, dragging the spy down the steps with her. Then the door slammed, and Chaloner heard the key turn in the lock.

'Tom?' asked Temperance softly in the silence that followed. 'Are you all right?'

Chaloner was unable to answer until she had removed herself from his chest. Then he lurched up the stairs and hauled furiously at the door, disgusted with himself for letting Turner escape. By the time he had picked the lock, the colonel was long gone. He did not feel equal to a chase, so he limped back to the kitchen instead. Temperance was sitting at the table, sobbing so hard he was not sure how to comfort her. He said nothing, and knelt by her side, waiting until she was ready to talk. He was aware of the minutes ticking away, but nothing seemed more important than his friend at that moment.

While she wept, he thought about Turner's claim. Was he telling the truth about Greene being in the Painted Chamber at dawn? Or was it yet another lie? And how far off was daybreak anyway? He had lost all sense of time. In the parlour, he could hear Wiseman's voice, and the sound of women laughing. At least someone was having a good time.

'No!' exclaimed Temperance suddenly, brushing away her tears. She sat bolt upright. 'Oh, no!'

'What?' asked Chaloner uneasily. It was not a reaction he had been anticipating.

She leapt to her feet and began to bundle him towards the door. 'James – I have just realised what he is going to do. He will see us as the only thing standing between him and the fulfilment of his nefarious plans. He will run straight to your Earl and spin a web of lies that will see *us* blamed for robbing Tryan and stealing the statue.'

Chaloner disengaged his arm. Turner had just had a very narrow escape, and would be halfway to the coast by now, thanking his lucky stars for his deliverance. 'Even he is not audacious enough to—'

She punched his shoulder, hard, to express her exasperation. 'He *is*, Tom! He is the most plausible liar in London – he must be, if he can deceive me. And who do you think your Earl will believe? A Royalist colonel who solves murders, or you, who keeps to the shadows and insults him at every turn?'

'But you heard him confess,' said Chaloner tiredly. 'You will bear witness that—'

'You think the Earl will listen to a brothel-keeper, do you?'

She had a point. 'But it is not—'

'You do not know James like I do,' she snapped. 'He loves money, and we have just deprived him of five thousand pounds. He will be livid – itching for revenge. And what better way, than to see us accused of the crimes *he* committed? I cannot believe I have been such a fool.'

Neither could Chaloner. 'It could happen to anyone,' he began lamely.

'He used me to mislead you,' she went on bitterly. 'He encouraged me to think *Brodrick* stole the bust, in his capacity as Lord of Misrule. And then he urged me to share my so-called theory with you – to throw you off his own scent. He is a villain to the core! But do not stand there looking bewildered, Tom! Go! Take my horse.'

'You have a horse?'

'I did,' said Temperance grimly, when she led the way across the yard and saw the stable door ajar. Footprints in the snow showed where someone had dashed in and a nag had galloped out. 'You will have to run. Your life – and mine – depends on you reaching the Earl in time to refute James's lies.'

Chaloner tried to do as she ordered, but he was exhausted, and every inch was a struggle. The blizzard had dwindled to the occasional flurry, but the temperature had plummeted, and there was a crust of ice on top of the snow. Every step involved crunching knee-deep into it, and hauling the other leg out behind him. It would have been gruelling exercise had he been fresh, but his energy reserves were almost entirely depleted, and his leg ached badly.

He laboured along The Strand with his breath coming in sharp bursts. He began to sweat from the effort, but did not dare stop to remove his coat, afraid he would never start again if he did. When he reached Charing Cross, he was tempted to give up, and hope the Earl would be prepared to listen to him regardless of what Turner had said in the interim. But there was Temperance to consider. The Earl was not going to champion a woman who ran a bordello, whether she was innocent or not.

The city was eerily quiet, sounds being muffled by the blanketing snow. He heard the clocks strike five, and was surprised it was so late; it felt earlier, because most of London still slept. He did not imagine the Earl would be at his offices at such an hour, so he stopped at Worcester House, hammering on the door with a ferocity that hurt his hands. But the servant who answered it told him the Earl was not there – he had already gone to White Hall. Chaloner had miscalculated, and had lost valuable moments doing so.

He reached the palace after what seemed liked an age, and stumbled through the gate. He was able to put on a spurt of speed once he was inside, but knew it was too little, too late – when he arrived and placed his ear against the office door, he could hear Turner speaking. The monologue was occasionally punctuated by the Earl, and once by Haddon. Chaloner rested his forehead against the wall in weary despair. The colonel had already spun his tale, and he was elegant, plausible and charming. Temperance was right: the Earl would never believe Chaloner over his new darling.

So what should he do now? Slip away before he was arrested? But then what would happen to Temperance? He took a deep breath, and tried to hear what was being said.

'. . . Greene in the Painted Chamber,' Turner was declaring.

'Is he?' asked the Earl. 'Then why have you not arrested him?'

'I would have done, sir,' said Turner patiently. 'But, as I just told you, I have only just escaped from Chaloner and his friend the brothel-keeper. They locked me in their cellar all night, and I am lucky to escape with my life. It was they who stopped me from apprehending Greene.'

'I do not believe you,' said Haddon indignantly. 'Thomas would never do such terrible things. You are just trying to have him dismissed, so you can be appointed in his place.'

'Dismissed?' echoed Turner. 'I want him thrown into your deepest dungeon! He stole from the King, not to mention battering poor Tryan to within an inch of his life. And he told me he felt sorry for Greene, because he is a fellow criminal. A man like that cannot be allowed his freedom.'

'Put up your weapon, colonel,' ordered the Earl. 'I do not feel safe with you waving it about.'

Chaloner reached for his own sword, not liking the notion of Turner being in the Earl's company with a naked blade, only to realise he did not have one. The only remotely sharp implement to hand was Bulteel's paper-knife. He grabbed it, and had just put his ear to the door again when there was a shriek.

'Stop!' cried the Earl. 'I *command* you to disarm!'

'You do not believe me,' hissed Turner. 'You think I am lying.'

'We can talk about this like civilised men,' came Haddon's unsteady voice. 'But putting your sword at the Lord Chancellor's throat is not the best way to make your case.'

Chaloner had heard enough. He threw open the door and burst in, paper-knife at the ready.

'Thomas!' shouted the Earl in relief. Turner jerked around when the spy entered, enabling the Earl to scamper away from him. 'Thank God! Turner has taken leave of his senses, and means to kill us.'

'Well, why not?' demanded Turner. His voice was cold and dangerous. 'I have spent all night locked in a filthy basement on your behalf, and now you say you do not believe me! How can you take his side over mine? He is

435

a killer, trained by Spymaster Thurloe, no less – *and* he refused to accept that you were right about Greene. He *defied* you.'

'All that is true,' said the Earl. 'But you also said he was a thief, and that I will never believe.'

'Why not?' demanded Turner. 'Go to Hercules' Pillars Alley and see for yourself. He is—'

'Because he has had plenty of chances to steal in the past, and he never has,' replied the Earl. 'His honesty is beyond question. You, on the other hand, know a suspicious amount about these crimes.'

'Because I solved them!' yelled Turner in exasperation. 'You stupid, ignorant old fool! Why could you not have listened to me? We might have enjoyed a profitable partnership.'

'Partnership?' echoed the Earl in disbelief. 'How dare you presume! Well, what are you waiting for, Thomas? I have had enough of this ridiculous situation. Take him into custody immediately.'

Chaloner glanced at his paper-knife, wondering how he was expected to arrest the sword-toting Turner when he was basically unarmed. But the Earl pulled the kind of face that indicated this was an irrelevancy, and that Chaloner should get on with it and stop making excuses.

'Catch!' shouted Haddon, tossing his ornamental dress-sword towards the spy.

Unfortunately, Chaloner could not move quickly enough, and Turner reached it first. He kicked it under a chest, then launched a fierce and determined attack, apparently knowing that to lose this time meant certain death. The spy scrambled behind the desk, and lobbed the paper-knife. Had it been a dagger, it would have killed Turner instantly, but it was too blunt to penetrate and only bounced uselessly to the floor. Outraged, Turner lunged across the table towards him, forcing him to retreat faster than his leg appreciated. Meanwhile, the Earl's expression went from vengeful confidence to alarm when he realised his champion was not as invincible as he had thought.

Chaloner knew he was going to be skewered unless he thought of something fast. He glanced around quickly, then pretended to catch his foot in one of the Turkish rugs. The Earl gave a cry of dismay when he went sprawling. Grinning malevolently, Turner moved in for the kill. Chaloner waited for him to close, then kicked out hard, driving him backwards. There was a resounding clang as the colonel's head connected with the precariously placed chandelier. He crashed to the floor and lay still. Climbing quickly to his feet, Chaloner ripped a sash from one of the curtains and tied Turner's hands before he could regain his senses and create any more mischief.

'I had a feeling he was not all he claimed,' said Haddon, bolder now the danger was over. 'I have a gift for sensing wickedness, and there is a lot to sense in him – he is a liar and a thief.'

But the Earl was no longer interested in Turner. 'There is work to be done, Thomas. Greene is in the Painted Chamber, and it is time he was in custody. Go and apprehend him.'

'I will come with you,' offered Haddon kindly, reaching out to steady the spy when he reeled from pure exhaustion. 'But we had better hurry, or Greene may decide to leave.'

Numbly, Chaloner followed him out, hoping he would have the strength to carry out his orders – he did not

437

think he had ever been so tired. He was not so weary that he forgot to take Turner's sword with him, however.

Dawn was breaking at last, a pale, distant glow in the night sky. It revealed a world that was unrecognisable, with roofs coated in a thick layer of white, and great clots of snow lodged in the branches of trees. The streets around White Hall and Westminster were used by monarchs and nobles, so labourers had been employed to shovel paths along them, which meant the journey to the Painted Chamber was much easier than the one from Hercules' Pillars Alley. Even so, Chaloner struggled.

'What is wrong?' asked Haddon, eyeing him in concern. 'Did Turner score a sly hit? I find that hard to believe. The Earl said he could never best you in a thousand years.'

'Did he? When? Until a few moments ago, he was all for Turner.'

'Yes and no,' replied Haddon. 'He is not a fool, and detected inconsistencies in the tales he was spun – in response to a few hints by me, naturally. Moreover, he was unimpressed by the fact that Turner's sword broke when the Lord of Misrule attacked him, and asked me to investigate his military claims. I learned he was never a colonel in the Royalist army.'

'He probably cannot cook, either,' muttered Chaloner. He did not want Haddon with him when he arrested Greene. The steward would be in the way, and might be injured if there was a scuffle. He tried to think of an excuse to be rid of him. 'I saw Bulteel buying more spices yesterday.'

Haddon stopped dead in his tracks and regarded him closely. 'Did you? Do you think he might be planning a repeat performance of the pepper-cake incident? My poor darlings have still not recovered.'

'Perhaps you should check them,' suggested Chaloner, hoping his lies would not exacerbate the feud between secretary and steward to the point where it could never be mended.

'Perhaps I should,' said Haddon worriedly. 'But what about you? You need my help.'

'I will manage,' said Chaloner. 'It is only Greene – and I have a sword.'

Haddon's face was a study in indecision, but eventually affection for his dogs won out. With a muttered apology, he slipped off in the direction of Cannon Row. Relieved to be rid of the responsibility of protecting him, Chaloner toiled on alone. He sincerely hoped Greene would not elect to fight, because he suspected that even a clerk with no experience with weapons would best him at that moment.

It felt like hours before he reached the Painted Chamber, and when he did, he was obliged to take a moment to recover – to catch his breath and wait for the burning weariness to ease from his legs. Then he pushed open the door and entered its cold, dim interior. It was empty on two counts – it was still too early for the clerks to begin their work, and Twelfth Night was a popular holiday, when men tended to stay at home with their families. His footsteps echoed hollowly as he walked. Daylight was just beginning to filter through the windows, ghostly and grey from the reflection of the snow outside. It did not take him many moments to see that no one was there, and he was not sure whether to be disappointed or relieved.

Now what? He sat heavily on a desk, uncertain what

to do next. Should he hire a horse and ride to the coast, which was where any sane fugitive from justice would be heading? Or should he go to the Dog and Duck, on the off-chance that Greene had decided to remain in hiding with his prostitute friends? Unfortunately, either option required more energy than he had left.

'What are you doing here?'

Greene's voice was so close behind him that Chaloner leapt to his feet and spun around in alarm. He started to reach for his sword, but the clerk was holding a gun, and even in the poor light, Chaloner could see it was loaded and ready to fire. Greene did not look comfortable with the weapon, and the hand that held it shook.

'You lied to me,' said Chaloner, beginning to back away. 'I believed you when you said you were innocent – and I believed your reasons for why the evidence against you should be disregarded, too.'

'Yes, you did,' agreed Greene quietly. 'I cannot imagine why – I certainly would not have done. And stand still, or I shall shoot you.'

'So the Earl was right,' said Chaloner, doing as he was told – it was always wise to obey orders issued by men wielding firearms. By the same token, he knew it was reckless to taunt Greene with a discussion of his crimes, but he could not help himself. 'You *were* running away when we caught you outside this hall. You had just murdered Chetwynd. But what did you do with the cup?'

Greene smiled, although it was a pained, unhappy expression. 'I was not alone. I was never alone.'

For a moment, Chaloner thought he was claiming some sort of divine guidance, but then realised that God was unlikely to make incriminating goblets disappear into thin air. The clerk was talking about a real accomplice, one of flesh and blood.

'Who helped you?' demanded Chaloner. His hand was on the hilt of his sword, and he was ready to whip it out the moment Greene lowered his guard.

The clerk made a dismissive motion: he was unwilling to say. 'I was expecting Turner this morning, not you. He has finally grasped that I am guilty, so it was decided to entice him here and kill him. But as you are here and he is not, I suppose I shall have to poison you instead. I am sorry, but it must be what is meant to happen.'

'He will be here soon,' lied Chaloner. 'What will you do then? If you kill either of us, my Earl will hunt you down.'

Greene shrugged. 'How? He could not trap me when he had you and Turner, so how will he manage alone? Besides, I am taking a ship to the New World tomorrow, and that will be an end to the matter. My master, who has guided my hand in everything, will have to use other faithful servants to carry on his work – thanks to your Earl's determination to unmask me, my usefulness to him is at an end.'

'Are you saying someone *told* you to commit these crimes?' asked Chaloner in disbelief. 'How in God's name could you let yourself be used so? I thought you were an ethical man.'

'I have tried to be.' Greene looked miserable, a far cry from the gloating Turner. 'I swore an oath to be honourable, and I have followed it faithfully. You no doubt think that murder is *dis*honourable, but these were wicked men, and my master said God wanted them gone – that it was my destiny to dispatch them for Him. And I have always believed everything that happens is predetermined, so . . .'

441

'I suppose your master used your association with Lady Castlemaine to persuade you to do his bidding,' said Chaloner, more strands of the mystery coming together in his mind. 'You ran errands for her that decent men would have declined, and he threatened to tell. She gave you a book . . .'

'*L'Ecole des Filles*.' Greene blushed. 'I should not have accepted it, but I was curious and Langston said it was good. She lied about him being alive at four o'clock, by the way – I killed him at two. But she did not lie because she knows I am the killer – her sole objective was to oppose your Earl.'

'And everything Turner and I discovered about you was true: you *did* beg or steal brandywine from White Hall to disguise the taste of poison.'

'I did, although it was not my idea.'

'Chetwynd would have been easy to kill – he would not have been suspicious of a friend offering him a warming drink on a cold night. But how did you persuade Vine and Langston? With a gun?'

'I told them it is more pleasant than being gut-shot,' said Greene, gesticulating with his dag in a way that might see it go off. 'And we have all seen enough of war to know that is true. I shall offer you the same choice, but I recommend the poison. It is quick and relatively painless.'

Chaloner had no intention of swallowing anything. His fingers tightened around his sword, although Greene did not notice – he was still talking, using the flat, resigned tone that indicated he thought the whole business had been inevitable.

'None of it was my idea: I was his puppet in everything. He told me what time I was to go out, which routes

442

to travel, when I should approach Munt for brandywine, even which clothes to wear. And he told me to toss Jones's purses in the river, although your witness was mistaken in what he saw, because I really did throw ten, not three.'

'You are a fool! Can you not see what is happening? Someone left a red-stoned ring in your home and hid brandywine in your office. I suspect it is your master, and that he intends to have you blamed for these murders – you said yourself that your usefulness to him is at an end.'

Greene nodded. 'I *will* be blamed, but I shall be in the New World, where it will not matter.'

'Who is he?' asked Chaloner. He gestured at the gun. 'If I am going to be killed anyway, what does it matter if you tell me his name?'

Greene smiled. 'He will be here soon, and you can see for yourself. He always comes when I kill, probably to make sure I do not weaken and show mercy.'

But the last pieces of the puzzle had snapped into place, and Chaloner knew exactly who Greene's master was. 'My belief in your innocence was based on the fact that I was watching your house when Vine was killed, but now I see what happened. Your master told you to leave by another door when you went to commit the crime. And he suggested you hide your wet coat and shoes, too.'

Greene inclined his head. 'He has a mind for details.'

'And he was on hand to advise me to look for damp clothing when I returned from Westmister. He chose his victims because they were men who pretended to be upright but were flawed – Chetwynd's corruption, Langston's venality, Vine's liking for blackmail. Earlier, in the Earl's office, Haddon said he had a gift for detecting wickedness.'

443

'He told me the same. He said hypocrisy is endemic at Westminster and White Hall, and that it was necessary to take a stand against it. But here he is now.'

The door opened and the Lord Chancellor's steward walked in. He was not alone, because the train-band were with him, led by Doling and Payne.

While Greene's attention was taken by the new arrivals, Chaloner darted towards him. Startled, Greene raised the gun and jerked the trigger, but the weapon flashed in the pan. Chaloner snatched it from him and hurled it through a window. Perhaps someone would hear the smashing glass and send for the palace guards. Regardless, he felt better once it was no longer in Greene's unsteady grip.

He whipped around when the soldiers started to stride towards him, weapons drawn. Their message was unmistakeable: there would be no escape this time. He glanced at Haddon. The walk through the snow had warmed the steward, and he had loosened his collar. There was a faint scar on his throat, like the one the Wapping vicar had described. Chaloner also noticed he was wearing a ruby ring on a string around his neck. Haddon saw him looking at it.

'Vine ripped it off me in his death throes,' he explained, tucking it back inside his coat. 'It belonged to my wife, and I did not want to lose it. Payne retrieved it for me, although I understand you got it first.'

Chaloner gazed at him. 'I thought you were a gentle man, but you are responsible for four murders: Chetwynd, Vine, Langston and Lea.'

'I did what was necessary. And I am sorry it must end like this – I had hoped to spare you. My plan was to kill

Turner, and have you continue to assert Greene's innocence, but that is no longer a viable option. Lay hold of him, Doling.'

Chaloner drew his sword as Doling approached, and they exchanged a series of vicious ripostes. But Payne circled behind them, sword jabbing at the spy's back. When Chaloner spun around to tackle him, Doling knocked the weapon from his hand, enabling the others to seize him. He struggled when he was searched for knives, but it was a token effort, and he knew he was well and truly their prisoner. He did manage to kick Payne on the shin, though, causing the man to leap away with a howl of pain.

'Do not harm him,' shouted Haddon urgently, when Payne prepared to exact revenge. 'We need him unmarked if my plan is to work – Wiseman will notice any suspicious wounds.'

'He will,' agreed Chaloner. 'And he will know I am not the kind of man to swallow poison—'

'You *will* drink it,' interrupted Payne with grim determination. 'We will make you.'

Chaloner bucked, aiming to free a hand and grab a dagger from one of his captors, but they were too professional to fall for such a trick, and all he did was encourage them to hold him more tightly.

'You cannot escape from us,' Payne jeered, clearly delighted to have the troublesome spy at his mercy at last. His grip was hard enough to hurt. 'Not this time.'

Chaloner was beginning to believe he might be right. But he was not going to go without some sort of fight, and he had two weapons left to him: his tongue and his wits. He would just have to keep Haddon and his cronies talking until he could devise a solution to his predicament.

Of course, his wits were like mud, and he could barely put together sensible sentences, let alone formulate a plan that might save his life. But he had to rise to the challenge, because he was determined not to give Payne the satisfaction of defeating him.

'You are Reeve the corn-chandler,' he said, trying to force his exhausted mind to function. 'You disguised yourself to attend the coffee-house meetings, because you wanted to monitor the activities of your victims—'

'He actually wanted one of us to go,' interrupted Payne. 'But Doling refused to be in company with such low villains, while I am not very good at subterfuge. He decided to watch them himself.'

Haddon said nothing, and for a moment there was silence. Chaloner flailed about for something else to say. 'Why did you use Greene to kill, when you have a trainband at your disposal?'

'Because it suited me,' replied Haddon shortly. He turned to Doling. 'I do not anticipate many clerks will arrive for work this morning, but we should hurry regardless. Besides, I do not want to leave my dogs alone for too long. I am sure I saw Bulteel lurking in Cannon Row when I went there just now.'

Doling did not answer, and his dour face was cold and hard as he watched the steward remove two bottles from a satchel and begin to mix them. The aroma of brandywine began to pervade the hall. It made Chaloner queasy. Payne noticed his reaction and grinned nastily.

'Matthias Lea declined our concoction at first,' Payne said. 'But he drank it in the end. He was a vile creature – he betrayed his old colleagues in order to get a post with the Royalist government. So did his brother, who

446

will shoot himself this evening, wracked by grief over the loss of his kinsman.'

'You told me Greene was innocent when we met near your lair,' said Chaloner, supposing he would have to keep Payne talking, given that Doling and Haddon were disinclined to be communicative. Of course, chatting would do him scant good if his wits failed to keep their side of the bargain. 'Why?'

Payne shrugged. 'On the off-chance that you might escape. Haddon was not quite finished with him and your belief in his innocence was staying the Earl's hand – keeping him free to continue our work. It does not matter now, though. We have more villains to dispatch, but we shall use other means.'

'What other means?' asked Chaloner. Haddon seemed to be having trouble with his potion, because he was frowning in a way that said he was dissatisfied with it. Greene stepped forward to help.

'Accidental drownings come next,' replied Payne gleefully. 'And after that, mishaps with speeding carriages. Eventually, evil will be eradicated.'

'Drownings,' pounced Chaloner. 'Like Jones. He happened across your domain, so you pushed him in the river.'

'Actually, he came hurtling down the alley so fast, he could not stop – he sank like a stone. Then you came along. You jumped in the water rather than fight us, then surfaced screeching for rescue.'

'Jones was a thief,' said Doling grimly. '*His* death I do not regret. He stole from the bank that now employs me – the news is all over London.'

'Do you know why Jones was in the alley?' asked Chaloner. He could see from the bemused expressions

447

on the soldiers' faces that they had not thought to ask. 'Because he was chasing one of Williamson's spies – a man who subsequently escaped.'

'Our boat!' exclaimed Payne. 'We thought it had been swept away by the tide, but Williamson's man must have climbed into it and rowed away.'

'He will have told the Spymaster about you,' said Chaloner, aiming to give them cause for anxiety.

Payne laughed derisively. 'Who do you think provides us with quarters and weapons? Williamson often calls on our services, mostly to quell minor rebellions, which we do quietly and decisively.'

Chaloner was confused. 'So, you are not Haddon's men?'

'That is none of your business,' snapped Doling. 'Enough talking.'

Chaloner turned to him. 'How can you condone what Haddon is doing?' he demanded, hoping to appeal to some deeply embedded sense of military honour. 'You are a soldier, not an assassin.'

'We are warriors, fighting vice,' declared Payne, before Doling could speak. 'It is no different from any other war. I used to pray with Chetwynd and the others in Scobel's house, but their duplicity sickened me. The Restoration has allowed evil men to prosper at the expense of good ones. Look at Symons and Doling. They are decent, but they were dismissed to make room for scoundrels.'

'Hargrave will be next,' said Haddon casually, as though he was issuing invitations to dinner. 'He rents out sub-standard buildings, and profits from supplying materials for Langston's disgusting plays. Then Brodrick is a cruel man, who uses ferrets and bears for practical jokes, while Bulteel feeds pepper-cake to dogs, and embezzles money from his Earl.'

'No!' objected Chaloner, appalled. 'Bulteel is the most honest man in White Hall – more honest than you, because *he* does not pretend to be virtuous while he breaks the law.'

Haddon abandoned his chemistry, and strode forward to strike the spy. 'How dare you judge me!'

'So much for no suspicious marks,' muttered Payne, a little resentfully.

'And you can hold your tongue, too,' snapped Haddon, rounding on him. 'You have no business gossiping when I told you we need to hurry. Do you want to be caught?'

'We will not be caught,' said Payne confidently. 'Not when we have you to guide us. The best thing I ever did was swear that oath to you. You have led us down this glorious path—'

'We all swore it,' interrupted one of the soldiers, although he did not look entirely happy. 'We pledged to live righteous lives, and signed a pact in our own blood. But—'

'You swore to *him*?' Chaloner's thoughts whirled as he stared at Haddon. 'Thurloe said Scobel was fat and bearded, but sickness can waste a man, while beards can be shaved. You did not die . . . Margaret Symons *saw* you! She said her uncle stood by her bed, but we thought she was delirious.'

'She and my nephew nursed me back to health three years ago,' replied Haddon. He did not seem disconcerted that Chaloner had guessed his real identity – and why should he? The spy was in no position to tell anyone. 'And then I watched my so-called friends slide from the promises they had made. It has taken me all this time to decide to put an end to their sinfulness, but I wanted to give them every chance to reform.'

'It was futile thinking they would,' put in Payne. 'As I have told you before.'

'Symons should have inherited a fortune from you,' said Chaloner, speaking more quickly when he saw Haddon – he could not think of him as Scobel – inspect the contents of the cup, and give a satisfied nod. 'But he did not, because you were alive and still needed it.'

'It has all gone now. I enjoy working for the Earl, though. He is impatient, condescending and opinionated, but good at heart. And he likes dogs.'

'So did Scobel,' Chaloner recalled. 'One howled over his grave, apparently.'

'The coffin was stuffed with my clothes, and the poor beast was deceived. Payne killed the man who shot her.' Haddon gave the cup one last stir, then picked it up.

'I am not comfortable with this,' said Doling uneasily. 'Killing wicked men is one thing, but—'

'We cannot let him jeopardise our work,' said Haddon. 'And I have a plan that will ensure no questions are asked. Greene will kill him, then swallow the rest of the poison in a fit of remorse. The case will be closed, and I shall advise the Earl that nothing will be gained by further investigation.'

'What?' asked Greene in horror, as two soldiers stepped forward to hold him.

'I told you they could not be trusted,' said Chaloner.

Greene struggled instinctively when he was grabbed, but it was not long before the gloomy, resigned expression was back in his eyes. He went limp in his captors' arms. Chaloner tried to capitalise on the diversion by breaking

450

free, but Payne subdued him with several vicious punches that made his head spin, ignoring Haddon's protestations about suspicious marks. The spy had been in many difficult situations during his eventful life, but this was by far one of the most serious – he could not see any way to help himself, no matter how hard he tried to force his sluggish mind to work.

'Drink the wine,' ordered Payne, taking the cup from Haddon and holding it out to Greene.

'Refuse,' countered Chaloner. His voice sounded thick and slurred to his own ears. 'Do not make it easy for them – they promised you passage to the New World, but they repay you with death.'

'Perhaps it is for the best,' said Greene flatly. 'I never was easy with the notion of killing, even for God. And working for Lady Castlemaine made me feel . . . tainted.'

'You are tainted,' said Haddon softly. 'But if you take your own life, God will forgive you. Drink. It will soon be over.'

Greene indicated the soldiers were to release one of his hands, then he took the cup and held it to his lips. He hesitated for a moment, then tipped it back and swallowed. Chaloner watched in disbelief – he had expected the man to put up at least a modicum of self-defence. After a moment, the clerk doubled over and started to retch. Chaloner began to struggle again when Payne walked towards him, and succeeded in knocking the cup with his chin, so some of its contents slopped to the floor.

'Hold him still,' Payne snarled.

Chaloner summoned the last of his strength and fought, writhing and twisting with all his might, knowing resistance was his only chance of life. More poison spilled, and in frustration, Payne pushed his dagger against the

451

spy's throat. There was a sharp pain, but Chaloner knew it was a victory, because it was yet another mark Wiseman would question. More men came to pin him down. He managed to bite one and butt another in the face with his forehead. Curses filled the air.

'It will taste of brandywine,' snapped Haddon, becoming angry when he saw the length of time it was taking. 'Do not make such a fuss.'

'I do not like this,' said Doling, backing away from the fracas suddenly. 'I swore to fight evil, not to dispatch honest men for doing their duty.'

'We have no choice,' said Haddon impatiently. 'Do you want to hang for murder? No? Then help Payne restrain him. The longer you let him keep us here, the greater are our chances of discovery.'

Liquid splashed on Chaloner's cheek as the cup was lowered towards him, and he imagined he could feel it corroding his skin. He resisted with every fibre of his being, but his strength was spent, and Payne now gripped him so hard that he could barely breathe. His vision began to darken.

'No,' ordered Doling. 'That is enough. Let him go.'

Chaloner was astonished when the soldiers promptly stepped away. Unfortunately, Payne did not follow their example: he responded by tightening his hold further still, and the spy found he was too weak to break loose. Worse, he could not breathe at all, and it occurred to him that suffocation was just as effective a way to kill as poison. Payne was about to do his master's bidding without the toxin coming anywhere near him.

Suddenly, there was a tremendous crash, and the door flew open. The Earl stood there, Bulteel at his heels. The secretary looked terrified, and the Earl was panting hard.

452

'Stop!' the Earl bellowed. 'I command you to stop!'

For a moment, no one moved. The train-band gaped at him, while even Haddon seemed taken aback. He recovered quickly, though.

'Bulteel,' he said, ignoring the Earl. 'Your timing is impeccable. I said I would make you pay for what you did to my dogs, and I happen to have some spare poison. Fetch him, Payne. Doling can finish Thomas – we have wasted enough time on him.'

'What about the Earl?' asked Payne, releasing Chaloner and hurrying to do as he was told. The spy collapsed on the floor, gasping for breath. 'Can we dispatch him, too? He is from White Hall, so he *will* be corrupt.'

'He is—' Whatever Haddon was about to say died in his throat, and an expression of astonishment filled his face. He opened his mouth to speak, but nothing emerged. Then he pitched forward. Payne rushed to catch him, gazing in horror at the knife that protruded from his master's back.

Chaloner managed to raise his head, and saw triumph gleam in Greene's eyes. He could not imagine how the dying clerk had mustered the strength to lob his knife, but he had done it, and Haddon was choking as blood filled his lungs.

'You—' Payne's face was as black as thunder, and he dropped Haddon to take a menacing step towards the clerk. Doling interposed himself between them.

'Enough,' said Doling quietly. 'It is over.'

'Are you insane?' snarled Payne, trying to thrust past him. 'We must finish this – if we let these men live, we will be signing our own death warrants.'

'So be it,' said Doling, pushing him away. His men stood behind him, silent and obedient.

Eyes flashing with rage, Payne turned on Doling, but his hot-tempered lunges were no match for the older man's cool, practised ripostes. His eyes bulged as Doling's sword bit into his chest. Then he crashed to the floor, and lay still. There was a brief silence, then Chaloner heard the tap of the Earl's tight little shoes as he moved forward tentatively.

'London is no place for us,' said Doling softly. 'We thought we could stop the seeping wickedness that pervades the city, but we became as soiled as the men we sought to eradicate.'

'I should say,' agreed the Earl, looking around in distaste. 'And associating with Spymaster Williamson is unlikely to lead you along the path of righteousness, either.'

'Payne was the killer,' said one of the soldiers. 'He stabbed two men and a woman just for asking about us. Doling tried to stop him, but Scobel had Payne under his thumb, and it turned him mad.'

'I would like to take my men away from the city,' said Doling, in the same low, level voice. 'Lead them somewhere safe. Will you try to stop me, sir?'

'No,' said the Earl hastily, reading a threat in the quietly spoken words. 'However, I suspect Williamson will ensure you never reach a court if you are captured, because he will not want his role in this affair made public. So I advise you to leave the country with all possible speed.'

Doling gave him a curt nod, and strode out, his warriors streaming at his heels.

Chaloner forced himself to sit up, aware that by bursting in with only Bulteel at his side, the Earl had just committed an act of remarkable courage. 'What are you doing here?' he asked weakly.

The Earl raised his eyebrows. 'That is *not* my idea of a heartfelt expression of gratitude, Thomas. What is wrong with you? I have just risked my life to save yours, and I am not a naturally brave man – at least, not where dangerous villains are concerned.'

'How did you know . . .' Chaloner was too tired to think of the question he wanted to ask.

'You have Bulteel to thank for that. He happened to be near Haddon's house in Cannon Row, when he spotted him conferring with Payne – a man who is wanted for murder in Westminster. He came to tell me, and we set off together. The palace guards should be here at any moment.'

'Thank you,' Chaloner managed to say.

The Earl shrugged carelessly, although he looked pleased with himself. 'You are welcome. After all, I do not want to lose *both* my spies in the same day.'

Epilogue

Two days later

Although the Earl was eager for explanations, he appreciated his spy was in no condition to provide him with any, and took him to Fetter Lane in his own carriage. Chaloner was not sure at what point Hannah arrived, but he was aware of her stoking up the fire and soothing him as he lay in a fever of dreams. When he finally woke, stiff but refreshed, the sun was shining and the snow had melted so completely that he wondered whether he had imagined the entire episode.

'Your Earl wants you to visit as soon as possible,' Hannah said, as they ate the pickled ling pie she had made to celebrate his recovery. It was not very pleasant, but she was quite open about the fact that it was the only dish she knew how to prepare, so he supposed he would have to do all the cooking if he wanted a future with her. 'He is eager to know where you have hidden the missing statue.'

Chaloner set down his spoon, appetite gone as he thought about all that had happened. 'I was wrong about

Greene, and my arrogance allowed Haddon – Scobel – to claim more victims.'

'The Earl said you would think that, but he heard some of what was said in the Painted Chamber, and is convinced that Haddon and Payne would have devised other ways to kill, if Greene had been unavailable. And you were not wrong, anyway.'

'How was I not wrong? Greene poisoned Chetwynd, Vine and Langston.'

'Because he was *forced* to. Haddon planned everything, down to the last detail, and Greene was just his instrument.'

The difference was academic, as far as Chaloner was concerned, and he knew it would be a long time – if ever – before he forgave himself.

'Greene confessed to the Earl before he died,' said Hannah, when he made no reply. 'He said Vine, Chetwynd and Langston would not have accepted wine from "Reeve", as they called Haddon, because they did not trust him. They all knew he wore a disguise, which meant they were always wary of him. But no one thought Greene was a killer, which allowed him to do as Haddon ordered. I wonder why Haddon picked on him – and why Greene let him do it.'

'Because of the oath he swore,' explained Chaloner. 'He promised to be virtuous – and he tried, by helping the Southwark prostitutes – but he compromised his principles by working for the Lady and accepting obscene books. I imagine Haddon had him marked for death, anyway, and using him to kill the others was just a convenient way of dispatching yet another man he felt had let him down.'

'*L'Ecole des Filles* is not that obscene,' said Hannah. 'Not like Langston's plays.'

457

'You have seen them?' asked Chaloner, startled.

'Buckingham took me to watch one or two.'

'I made a lot of discoveries that had nothing to do with the murders,' said Chaloner, not wanting to know more. 'George Vine's hatred for his father, his mother's reluctance to tell me whether her husband had owned a ruby ring—'

'George said yesterday that she thought *he* was the killer, and was reluctant to say to anything that might implicate him. What a family!'

'Then there was Jones and his gold, and the fact that no one was investigating his death.'

'It was assumed he just drowned,' explained Hannah, 'as people do with distressing frequency. No one thought there was any need to ask questions, not even when it became known he was a bank robber.'

'For a while, I even suspected Gold of being the killer,' said Chaloner tiredly. 'But he was innocent.'

'He is guilty of marrying a very silly girl, though. I heard at Court today that Neale has asked Bess to wed him, and she has accepted. People are calling him Golden Neale for his good fortune. But I doubt they will make each other happy.'

'I misread what happened to Scobel and Margaret, too,' Chaloner went on. 'I thought they had been poisoned, but they were not.'

'Wiseman came to report that he found nothing amiss in the samples he took from the Symonses' house. Margaret died of natural causes. He also said that Scobel might well have recovered from his sharpness of the blood, but that it would have resulted in a dramatic loss of weight – which explains why Scobel was fat, but "Haddon" was thin.'

'I should see the Earl before he accuses me of malingering,' said Chaloner, standing reluctantly. 'He saved my life, so I should give him the opportunity to gloat.'

Hannah grimaced. 'I did not realise working for him was so dangerous. Perhaps I should not ask questions about your investigations in the future – what I do not know cannot worry me.'

Chaloner tried not to look relieved. Sharing his secrets had been a strain, and he realised he was far happier keeping them to himself. And if Hannah could not live with his reticence, then he would just have to get a dog. But he had a feeling she was growing as fond of him as he was of her, and that their relationship would develop at a calm, unhurried pace that would give them both the time they needed to adjust to their changing circumstances.

He decided to collect the statue from Temperance before going to see the Earl, although when he arrived at Hercules' Pillars Alley, he was surprised to find Wiseman in the kitchen, enjoying some of Maude's poisonous coffee. The surgeon was wearing an unusually vivid shade of red that day, putting Chaloner in mind of a bird in mating plumage, aiming to impress a pair of dowdy hens – Maude was clad in brown, while Temperance had donned grey. There were dark rings under Temperance's eyes, and there was a sadness in them that had not been there before.

'Delicious,' Wiseman declared, setting the empty bowl on the table and beaming at his hosts. 'I have no truck with these insipid brews, and yours is the elixir of champions, madam.'

'Only champions with iron stomachs,' muttered Chaloner.

Wiseman toted the heavy bust to a waiting cart as if it weighed no more than paper, and it occurred to Chaloner that there was something to be said for a regime of muscle-honing – he was strong himself, but the kind of brawn that Wiseman now sported would be a very useful asset to a spy.

While Chaloner set a pony in its traces, Temperance came to stand next to him, speaking in a low voice so the others would not hear. She need not have worried: Wiseman and Maude were engrossed in packing Bernini's masterpiece with straw to protect it from damage, and were not paying any attention to her.

'I am glad the Twelve Days are over. Bad things always happen at Christmas, and I was a fool to think this one would be any different.'

Chaloner touched her shoulder gently as she brushed away tears. 'I am sorry I did not . . .'

'Did not what? Warn me sooner? I am all grown up now, Tom, and can take responsibility for my own mistakes. Besides, I should have known James was a pig when he flirted with Belle in front of me. Will he hang?'

Chaloner nodded, not sure what to say to comfort her. She sighed, and walked slowly back inside the house. Maude hurried after her, and he knew she was in kind and understanding hands. He finished securing the statue, and, uninvited, Wiseman climbed on the cart to ride to White Hall with him.

'I like Temperance,' the surgeon said, glancing back over his shoulder. There was an odd expression on his face that Chaloner had never seen before. 'She is a charming lady, and told me I can visit her any time I please.'

'Do not go too early,' advised Chaloner, sure Wiseman

would not pursue the friendship once he realised what she did with her evenings. 'She seldom rises before three.'

'That will not be a problem,' said Wiseman with a happy grin. 'We surgeons are used to odd hours.'

The Earl was delighted when he saw what his spy had brought him. He clapped his plump hands and chuckled as he walked around the bust, viewing it from every angle.

'Bernini really is a genius,' he declared. 'He captured the old king's countenance perfectly.'

'I am sorry, sir,' said Chaloner. 'About Greene, and not believing you.'

The Earl started to look triumphant, but the expression faded before it was fully born. 'We both made mistakes, Thomas. Mine was hiring Haddon – a man I liked and trusted. But let us discuss happier things. Bulteel returned Jones's gold to Backwell's Bank this morning, but less than a quarter of it was theirs. The rest is still in my office.'

'Give some to the Queen,' pleaded Chaloner. 'So she can take the waters in Bath.'

'That is an excellent idea, especially in the light of what Bulteel and I discovered as we examined the documents you found in Greene's house. They allowed us to pinpoint innumerable cases of embezzlement, including Her Majesty's thirty-six thousand pounds.'

'Who has it?' asked Chaloner, sincerely hoping it was not Lady Castlemaine – or that he would be charged with the task of getting it back.

'No one. At least, no single person has the missing money in its entirety. Bulteel and I have identified at least three dozen clerks who have been manipulating the books.'

461

'Christ!' exclaimed Chaloner, overwhelmed by the scale of the problem.

'Most operated on a fairly modest level, but others were rather more greedy, and money was moved between accounts at an astonishing rate. A small percentage was siphoned off for personal use, but the bulk went towards pleasing patrons – to pay the Lady's gambling debts, to refurbish the Tennis Court and even, I am ashamed to say, to provide me with extra staff.'

'No wonder Haddon thought White Hall was full of thieves,' said Chaloner. 'He was right – it is! But how did Greene find out about it?'

'Because he was a clerk, too. He grew suspicious when the Queen complained about her missing money, and began to investigate. He gathered evidence, and was on the verge of exposing the villains when Haddon came along and distracted him.'

'How ironic,' said Chaloner softly. 'By making his findings public, Greene would have done far more to eliminate corruption at White Hall than helping Haddon murder sinful men. Haddon did the country a grave disservice by forcing Greene to kill.'

The Earl was silent for a moment. 'But at least I made Haddon pay me five pounds,' he said, as if that made everything all right again. 'When he lost his wager over whether you or Turner would solve the case first.'

'Perhaps that was a factor in why he was so determined to kill me,' said Chaloner wryly. 'I was responsible for losing him money.'

'I doubt it. He liked you, despite the fact that you were determined to expose his activities. He often told me he admired your integrity, doubtless because it is a virtue he lacked himself.'

'And credulity and stubbornness?' asked Chaloner with a crooked smile. 'Did he admire those, too?'

'Probably,' agreed the Earl with a grin of his own. 'But enough of Haddon. He is dead, as are Greene and Payne, while Doling is an ethical man who might do some good wherever he and his train-band happen to fetch up. The case is closed, and I think it is best we forget about it.'

Chaloner nodded agreement. He did not want to dwell on it, either.

The Earl turned his attention to the statue again. 'I *knew* you would find it for me. Now I shall be able to present it to the King as a post-Christmas gift.'

'I would not recommend that, sir. You see, although Turner stole it, using Meg as his unwitting helpmeet, he had an accomplice. I am afraid his partner in crime was Lady Castlemaine.'

The Earl's jaw dropped. 'What? But . . . how do you know?'

'Because there was no sign of forced entry in the Shield Gallery, which means someone opened it with a key. Turner had a lot of lovers at Court, but only two were issued with keys: Lady Castlemaine and Lady Muskerry.'

'And Muskerry is too dim-witted to have kept quiet during the rumpus that followed,' mused the Earl. 'But the Lady is not. It is exactly the kind of thing she would do. What was she hoping to achieve? To present it to the King, and earn his undying gratitude?'

'I suspect she already has that.' Chaloner hurried on when he saw the Earl's prim expression. 'She did it for money. But she judged others by her own corrupt standards, and assumed private collectors would turn a blind eye to where it came from. She is probably amazed to learn that is not the case.'

'This tale will put the cat among the pigeons!' gloated the Earl. 'Revenge at last!'

'No! If you expose her, her hatred will know no limits – she is bad enough now, but this would make her far worse. I would have nothing to do with it, if I were you.'

The Earl was crestfallen, but he was not a fool, and knew his spy was right. 'Then what shall we do with it? It cannot stay here, because someone might think *I* stole it.'

'Deliver it to Williamson, so he can give it back,' suggested Chaloner. 'He said he wanted the credit for its recovery, so let him have it – along with the consequences of crossing the Lady.'

The Earl looked uncertain, but nodded assent. 'Very well. You can arrange it, although you should be careful. His assassin Swaddell returned to him this morning, blaming his abrupt disappearance on a sick mother. However, I think he fled in terror because of what he saw.'

'He witnessed Lady Castlemaine entertaining a lover. Is that what you mean?' Chaloner had assumed the recipient of her dubious favours was the King's young son, given the rumours about her attempts to seduce the boy.

The Earl nodded. 'Swaddell spotted her smuggling this beau out of White Hall on a laundry cart. She is said to have been livid, and threatened to cut out his tongue.'

'A laundry cart?' Chaloner started to laugh. 'Then he probably saw the King's statue being spirited away and did not realise it. What a miserable band of incompetents!'

*

Because he had spent most of Twelfth Night asleep, Chaloner had missed Bulteel's invitation to dinner. He decided to make amends by visiting the family that evening, taking with him a set of silver spoons as a gift for his godson. He donned his best clothes and set off for Westminster, where the secretary lived in a small, but pleasant cottage that boasted a fine view of the abbey. He knocked on the door, and smiled when Bulteel answered it.

The secretary paled, then glanced around furtively. 'You did not tell me you were coming.'

Chaloner was taken aback by the cool reception. 'I came to see my godson, and to pay my respects to your wife. But if it is inconvenient, I can—'

'No.' With a smile that looked pained, Bulteel led him along a short corridor to a kitchen. The room was rich with the scent of baking, and on the table was a cake and a loaf of new bread. Chaloner looked around for the lady of the house, but the kitchen was empty of anyone except Bulteel. He also noted there was nothing to indicate a child lived there – no sets of tiny clothes drying, no cradle, no toys. And lastly, Bulteel's hands were dusted with flour.

'I like cooking,' the secretary mumbled. 'I always have. But it suits me to say my wife bakes, because people would laugh at me if I admitted to enjoying such a peculiar activity myself.'

Chaloner indicated Bulteel was to sit opposite him at the table. 'How long has she been gone?' he asked compassionately.

Bulteel hung his head, and when he spoke, he was difficult to hear. 'She was never here.'

With a start, Chaloner realised that Bulteel had never

465

taken his new son to be admired by colleagues, like most proud parents, and spoke of him only rarely. He frowned in puzzlement. 'But why did you ask me to be godfather to a boy who does not exist?'

'Because I wanted *you* to know the truth,' blurted Bulteel. He began to cry. 'It is hard maintaining the pretence, and I wanted one person to . . . You seemed more likely to understand than anyone else.'

Chaloner did not understand at all. 'I am?'

'The Earl hates me,' Bulteel went on, tears flowing down his cheeks. 'He relies on me, and trusts me with his business, but he does not respect me or like me. I invented a wife because I wanted him to think someone appreciated me, and then it seemed natural to have a child. And the lie *did* result in me being given this house, although the deception makes me uneasy . . .'

'He will find out eventually,' warned Chaloner. 'A neighbour will say he never hears the child cry, or someone like me will call. It is only a matter of time before—'

'No one is suspicious yet, and it has been three years. The truth is, no one cares enough about me to be curious. I could probably scream the truth from the rooftops and no one would be interested.'

Chaloner still did not understand, but he had been entrusted with far more peculiar secrets in the past, and at least this one did not entail anything illegal or treasonous. Sensing Bulteel's need to talk, he stayed with him, eating the cake while the secretary told the story of his life, and confided his various fears, dreams and ambitions. When he eventually stood to leave, Bulteel gave a shy smile.

'Perhaps you will introduce me to the ladies at Temperance's club,' he suggested.

'I doubt they will make very good wives.'

'Oh, I do not want a wife,' said Bulteel earnestly. 'I like living alone, and a spouse might bully me out of the kitchen. All I want is the occasional night of pleasure. Well, perhaps more than *occasional*.'

Chaloner blinked. 'I will see what I can do.'

The secretary escorted his guest out, and returned to the kitchen to wash the plates and wipe crumbs from the table. Almost immediately, a man emerged from a cupboard, brushing the cobwebs and dust off his new red hat. Bulteel turned towards him.

'I know you said I should borrow a baby for when he visits, but I suspect he would have been one of those godfathers who drop in unannounced. He would have caught me out sooner or later, and I am rather pleased by the way I resolved the situation.'

'Very clever,' grumbled Williamson. 'But did you have to keep him here quite so long? It was hot in there, and I kept thinking I would sneeze. What would I have said if he had caught me? I would have had to send Swaddell after him, and I do not want him dead just yet – not after he encouraged the Earl to let me return the statue to the King. I am surprised. I did not think he would do it.'

'He will have his reasons,' said Bulteel flatly. 'And you can be sure they will have nothing to do with pleasing you. When do you plan to deliver it to His Majesty?'

'Tomorrow night, at a reception in which all the Court favourites will be present – Buckingham, Brodrick, Chiffinch, Lady Castlemaine. I shall be feted.'

'I am glad to hear it. But what did you think of my performance just now? Was it acceptable?'

Williamson smiled. 'Actually, it was perfect. There is

467

nothing like arousing a man's sympathy to keep him on your side. Chaloner already stands up for you when people make accusations, and tonight you have sealed your blossoming friendship. His growing trust can only work in our favour.'

'Good,' said Bulteel. 'Because I do not want him suspicious of me. He is protective of the Earl, and if he ever finds out that *I* am one of those clerks who moves money from place to place – invariably to the Earl's detriment – he will show me no mercy.'

'Do not worry. He has no idea you are the biggest rogue in White Hall.'

'Second biggest,' retorted Bulteel, eyeing the Spymaster pointedly. 'And speaking of rogues, I delivered Jones's gold to the Queen this afternoon.'

'All of it?' asked Williamson innocently.

Bulteel handed him a heavy purse and revealed his brown teeth in a conspiratorial grin. 'Minus a commission, naturally.'

'Naturally,' said Williamson, returning the smirk as he slipped the coins into his pocket.

Historical Note

In July 1637, a carefully packed crate arrived in England, destined for Charles I's burgeoning private art collection. It was delivered by a man named Thomas Chambers, following a nerve-wracking journey that involved not only repelling pirates and thieves, but over-zealous customs officials, too. The crate contained the newly completed bust of the king by Gianlorenzo Bernini, a splendid masterpiece based on Van Dyck's *Charles I, King of England, from Three Angles*. It was paid for by Queen Henrietta Maria, who sent a diamond ring worth £1000 to the sculptor. The bust, along with many other masterpieces, was sold to raise quick cash during the Commonwealth, but was retrieved after the Restoration and put on display in the royal Palace of Whitehall. Unfortunately, a devastating fire swept through the complex in 1685, and the bust was one of its casualties.

Most of the deaths in *The Westminster Poisoner* really did occur between 1660 and early 1664. The first to go was Henry Scobel. He held several important and lucrative posts during the Commonwealth, including Clerk of the Parliament (1649–58) and Clerk to the House of Lords

(1659–60). His nephew Will Symons (who married Margaret in 1656) was one of his heirs; Symons lost his post as underclerk to the Secretary of State at the Restoration, and his kinship to a high-ranking Commonwealth official seems to have worked against him finding other employment. Both Margaret and Scobel were said to have predicted the exact time of their own deaths, and Margaret claimed to have seen Scobel standing at the foot of her bed not long before she died in December 1663.

Christopher Vine, of New Palace Yard, was a Chamberlain of the Receipt; he died in 1663. His son George went on to do the same job, and owned the famous Westminster tavern called Hell. Francis Langston was appointed Sergeant at Arms to the Royal Household in 1660, but was dead by March 1664. Edward Jones was a Yeoman of the Household Kitchen, and also died in 1664. Thomas Greene worked in the Treasury department, and died in 1663. Alexander Haddon resigned his Court post in 1663, although records do not tell us why.

Sir Nicholas Gold was a merchant and politician, who died in late-December 1663. He was married to Elizabeth, to whom he left a huge estate. Within five months of Gold's death, she had married the courtier Thomas Neale, who earned himself the nickname of 'Golden Neale' for his success in wooing her. Neale became an MP, and speculated in all manner of overseas trade, making and losing at least two fortunes. Elizabeth's family objected to the match, and even resorted to swords to keep Neale away from her. Neale was wounded in the ensuing fracas, but Elizabeth whisked him upstairs to bed, sent for a priest to recite the marriage service, and presented her furious kin with a fait-accompli.

It is not surprising that the victorious Royalists should

want to wrest the best jobs from their Parliamentarian incumbents, and a number of competent, well-qualified officials were dismissed to make way for the new order. One was John Thurloe, Spymaster General and advisor to Cromwell; he was living quietly between Lincoln's Inn and his Oxfordshire estate in 1663. Another was Thomas Doling, who had been Messenger to the Council of State. However, two men managed to weather the changes and retain their positions: according to the diarist Samuel Pepys, Matthias and Thomas Lea were the only under-clerks to the Council of State to be reappointed after the Restoration. Thomas Lea was related by marriage to a Chancery clerk named James Chetwynd, who lodged with Richard Hargrave in St Martin's Lane and died in 1663. Thomas Lea, Will Symons and Hargrave were executors of Chetwynd's will.

Notable courtiers and officials of the time include the Earl of Clarendon's secretary, John Bulteel, and Joseph Williamson, who inherited the intelligence services from Thurloe and had a clerk called John Swaddell. The brilliant and innovative Richard Wiseman was appointed Surgeon to the Person in June 1660. Will Chiffinch was one of the more infamous of the Court debauchees, and his wife was named Barbara. Lady Muskerry, said to be large and not especially lovely, was the butt of several unkind jokes by wickedly spiteful courtiers, especially during the Twelve Days of Christmas – the Season of Misrule.

Poor Queen Katherine was in a sorry state in December 1663. She was still recovering from an illness that had almost killed her, and was desperate to provide the King with an heir. She applied for funds to take the healing waters at Bath or Tunbridge Wells, but was told she had already spent all her annual household allowance of £40,000. Katherine was astounded: she had lived frugally, and her own accounts showed she was still owed £36,000. She petitioned the Lord Treasurer, demanding to know what had happened to her money, but his main response seems to have been an apologetic shrug. The £36,000 was gone, and there was no more to be had. It was July 1664 before funds were available for Katherine to go to Tunbridge Wells, but the spa did not help her conceive. Lady Castlemaine, by contrast, had provided the King with two sons by the end of 1663.

On the morning of 21 January 1664, Colonel James Turner was taken to the end of Lymestrete (Lime Street), where a scaffold had been erected. A few days before, he had burgled the house of Francis Tryan, a wealthy merchant and money-lender, and made off with £1050 in coins and £4000 in jewels. Turner may have been a solicitor, and had been employed by Tryan on several occasions.

Turner was the kind of man who gave cavaliers a bad name – there is no evidence that he was a real colonel, but he swaggered around boasting of his military prowess, and his behaviour was outrageous. He claimed to have sired twenty-eight children (counting only the ones born in wedlock), and on the scaffold, he announced to the crowd that his worst sin was swearing. He gave an inordinately long speech as the executioner waited to do his duty, confident that the King would pardon him. He had been warned that no such pardon would be forthcoming, but arrogant to the last, he refused to believe the King would not rush to his rescue. His Majesty wisely remained aloof from the affair, and Turner was hanged in the afternoon before an enormous crowd.

PELICAN BOOKS

A501

PREHISTORIC CRETE

R. W. HUTCHINSON

Richard Wyatt Hutchinson was born in 1894 and
educated at Birkenhead School and St John's College,
Cambridge. After serving in France and Belgium at
the end of the First World War, he was elected
Foundation Scholar and Craven Student at Athens in
1921, and later F.S.A. and F.R.A.I., and corresponding member of the German Archaeological Institute.
He was Curator in Crete for the British School at
Athens from 1934 until 1947, but actually served in
British G.H.Q. at Cairo from 1941 to 1945 during
the German occupation of the island. He was
appointed lecturer in classical archaeology at Liverpool University in 1948 and at Cambridge in 1952.
Since 1921 he has taken part in excavations at
Mycenae, Traprain Law, in Poland and Macedonia,
in Mytilene, at Nineveh, and at Colchester, besides
the 'digs' he conducted in Crete. Richard Hutchinson
has contributed articles to many learned journals and
collaborated in *A Century of Exploration at Nineveh*.

Cover design by Ole Vedel

R. W. HUTCHINSON

PREHISTORIC
CRETE

Penguin Books

Penguin Books Ltd, Harmondsworth, Middlesex
u.s.a.: Penguin Books Inc., 3300 Clipper Mill Road, Baltimore 11, Md
australia: Penguin Books Pty Ltd, 762 Whitehorse Road,
Mitcham, Victoria

—

First published 1962
Reprinted 1963

—

Copyright © R. W. Hutchinson, 1962

—

Made and printed in Great Britain
by Cox and Wyman Ltd,
London, Reading, and Fakenham
Set in Monotype Bembo

CONTENTS

LIST OF PLATES

Grateful acknowledgement is made to Dr Audrey Furness for Plates 1, 2; to Mrs Hilda Pendlebury for Plates 3, 4, 5, 6, 11, 12, 14*a*, 19 by J. D. S. Pendlebury; to Miss Natalie Lubowidsky for Plates 7, 8, 15; to Dr O. G. S. Crawford for Plates 10, 18, 21; to Mr G. Maraghiannis for Plates 9, 13, 14*b*, 17; to Mr E. M. Androulakis for Plates 21, 22, 23, 24, 25, 26; to the Society for the Promotion of Hellenic Studies for Plate 27; to *The Times* for Plate 16; to Mr R. E. M. McCaughan for Plates 28, 29, 30, 31, 32.

NOTE. The publishers regret that Plate 14*b* has been printed the wrong way round. All the symbols, and the spirals themselves, should face the opposite way from that shown in the photograph.

LIST OF TEXT FIGURES

9

LIST OF TEXT FIGURES

Grateful acknowledgement is made to Mr R. E. M. McCaughan for Figures 1, 2, 7, 10, 11, 18, 19, 20, 23, 35, 37, 38, 39, 44, 45, 46, 50, 52, 54, 55, 61, 71, and 73, and also for Figures 4, 5, 24, 25, 31, 33, 37, 65, 66, and 67 previously drawn to illustrate my article 'Prehistoric Town Planning in Crete' published in the *Town Planning Review* Vol. XXI (1950); also to Miss Honor Frost for Figures 6, 12–17, 41, 43, 49, and 64; to Mrs Hilda Pendlebury for Figure 51, reproduced from *Handbook to the Palace of Minos* (Macmillan), and for Figures 3, 21, 22, 26, 27, 30, 32, 34, 36, 53, 56, 59, and 60 reproduced from *The Archaeology of Crete* (Methuen) by J. D. S. Pendlebury; to the Consejo Superior de Investigaciones Científicas, Madrid, for Figure 8, reproduced from *Lexicon Creticum*, and Figure 9, reproduced from *Minoika* by B. Gaya Nuño; to the Society for the Promotion of Hellenic Studies for Figure 10, reproduced from *Journal of Hellenic Studies* (1953 issue) and Figures 38, 40, 42, and 63 reproduced from 1901 issue; to Macmillan & Co. Ltd, for Figure 18 from *The Palace of Minos* by A. J. Evans and Figure 70 from *How the Greeks Built Their Cities* by R. E. Wycherley; to the British School at Athens for Figure 52, reproduced from the *Annual*, 1951; to La Renaissance du Livre for Figure 61, reproduced from *La Civilisation égéenne*; to Vincent Desborough for Figure 58; to the Society of Antiquaries for Figure 62, reproduced from *Archaeologia*, 1905; to *Kretica Chronica* for Figure 68, reproduced from the 1950 issue; to Piet de Jong for Figures 47, 48, and 69; and to Mrs Corbett for Figure 72.

EDITORIAL FOREWORD

JUST over thirty years ago I travelled extensively in Crete and was shown round the island by Mr R. W. Hutchinson who was then Curator of the Villa Ariadne which Sir Arthur Evans had built next to the site of Knosos. It was fascinating to be in the company of a man who had dug with Evans, was familiar with everything that he had done and that he had found, and understood to the smallest detail the structure of the great archaeological framework which Evans had set up. From that time onwards I had it in mind to persuade Mr Hutchinson to put down on paper as much as he could of what he knew about ancient Crete, and it is fortunate that he has at last done so, for he is one of the few direct links with the great Evans who resurrected for us the ancient Minoan world.

Since this book has taken several years to write, the text was complete before the beginning of the more violent controversies on certain Minoan problems, so that on one of them, the question of the date of the Linear B tablets, Mr Hutchinson has had to comment in a brief additional note on page 90. He himself is in many ways uniquely fitted to act as a surviving personal liaison between Evans and Ventris whose genius deciphered the script after Evans's death, and to pass judgement on these additions to knowledge. The discussion in Chapter 3 on the 'Cretan Peoples, Languages, and Scripts' provides us with an important objective survey of the criticisms affecting the decipherment. These and other problems Mr Hutchinson contrives to view with an admirable freedom from personal bias. He has indeed at times inevitably criticized some of Evans's conclusions, not generally on matters of fundamental importance, although he has a well-imagined and well-reasoned reconstruction of the events which led to the catastrophe that overwhelmed Knosos; but archaeology would be a poor thing if one generation did not add depth to the achievements of another.

Arthur Evans had the acuteness to realize that a tripartite classification of the Minoan period – Early, Middle, and Late, with subdivisions of each – was comprehensive enough to cover the entire development and yet at the same time sufficiently elastic to allow for the inevitable modifications which subsequent discovery, not only at Knosos, but in other parts of the island, was bound to bring. It is at the very end of this period in the Late Minoan that his conclusions have been seriously attacked by Professor L. R. Palmer who, like others, found it difficult to account for the fact that the writings on the tablets at Knosos are, apart from a few minor details, extraordinarily similar to those found by Blegen at Pylos, and that Evans's findings imply a difference of at least two centuries between the two. Professor Denys Page in his great book on *History and the Homeric Iliad* (1959), while admitting that this was astonishing, accepted the chronological gap without further question. The fact is that many of the Linear B tablets were burnt, apparently in the holocaust of the late palace that was contemporary with them; we have no evidence for a subsequent burning and no adequate grounds for rejecting Evans's and Mackenzie's conclusions that the intact stirrup vases are later than the great conflagration.

As Mr Hutchinson has pointed out, Professor Palmer, whilst drawing attention to the difficulties, has not provided evidence to prove his case and his elaborate re-organization of the archaeological sequences does not commend itself to others who are still in agreement with the orthodox views. At the earlier end of the scale it is admitted by nearly all scholars that Evans's chronology for the Early Minoan period must be reduced, but the three sub-divisions of that period as organized by him would seem to be fully justified. It is most probable that continued work in Crete and indeed elsewhere in Greece and in the Aegean area will eventually provide solutions to all these questions.

No less exciting and indicative of the live state of Cretan archaeology, which first took sharp definition with Evans's work at the very beginning of this century, is the fact that within the last year excavations by Professor John Evans (not to be confused with Sir Arthur) in the deep Neolithic levels at Early Knosos have yielded C.14 dates which take us back to the sixth and fifth millennia B.C. and thus have rocked the top end of Mr Hutchinson's chronological table while the ink on it was still wet. Here again Arthur Evans, with a strange prescience, had himself suggested the possibility of dates even higher than those of these new findings.

30 April 1962   M. E. L. MALLOWAN

PREFACE

THIS book is intended not so much as a revision of but rather as a supplement to Pendlebury's *The Archaeology of Crete*, which dealt in more detail and so admirably with Minoan and Hellenic art in Crete, but left almost untouched the subjects of my Chapters 1, 3, 4, and 9. I have also endeavoured to summarize the results of later researches on Cretan prehistory, especially those of Dr Michael Ventris and of Dr John Chadwick in the decipherment of Linear Script B.

I am indebted to the help of various friends who are not, however, responsible for any of my statements. First and foremost I must thank Professor M. E. L. Mallowan for his trouble in reading and criticizing my original typescript, Mr R. M. E. McCaughan for his great kindness in drawing so many plans and figures, Dr J. C. Trevor who checked and revised my pages on physical anthropology, my mother who listened to much of my manuscript, and Mrs Hilda Pendlebury for permitting me to reproduce without charge many figures from her late husband's book.

I have benefited by conversations or correspondence with the late Sir John Myres, Sir Frederick Bartlett, Dr R. W. Hey, and Mr T. C. Lethbridge. I should also like to thank my cousin, Miss May Clarke, for typing numerous corrections and additions.

CHRONOLOGICAL TABLE

	CRETE	MAINLAND OF GREECE	EGYPT
5000	Neolithic		
3000	Post-Neolithic	Neolithic	Dynasties I and II
2800			
2700			
			Dynasty III
2600			
2500	Early Minoan I	Early Helladic I	Dynasties IV and V
2400			
2350			Dynasty VI
2300	Early Minoan II	Early Helladic II	
2250			
2200			First Intermediate Period
2150			
2100		Early Helladic III	
2050	Early Minoan III		Dynasty XI
2000			
1950			Dynasty XII
1900	Middle Minoan I		
1850		Middle Helladic I	
1800	Middle Minoan II	Middle Helladic II	Second Intermediate Period and Hyksos Kings
1750			
1700	Middle Minoan III	Middle Helladic III	
1650			

17

	CRETE	MAINLAND OF GREECE	EGYPT
1600			
1550		Late Helladic I	
1500	Late Minoan I		
1450	Late Minoan II	Late Helladic II	Dynasty XVIII
			Hatshepshut
			Thutmose III
1400			
1350			
1300			Dynasty XIX
1250			
	Late Minoan III	Late Helladic III	
1200		Trojan War	
1150		Return of the Heraclidae?	Dynasty XX
1100			
		Sub-Mycenaean	
1050			
1020			Dynasty XXI
1000	Sub-Minoan	Protogeometric pottery	
970			
950	Early Proto-geometric		
920			
900	Middle Proto-geometric		
870			
	Late Proto-geometric		
850		Geometric pottery in Attica	
835	Protogeometric 'B'	Homeric poems written?	Dynasty XXII
820			
800	Early Geometric		
770	Mature Geometric		
750	Late Geometric	First Olympiad	

18

	CRETE	MAINLAND OF GREECE		EGYPT
735		Protocorinthian pottery		Dynasties XXIII and XXIV
700	Early Orientalizing			
680				Dynasty XXV Esarhaddon conquers Egypt
	Late Orientalizing pottery	Early Dedalic sculpture		
650		Middle Dedalic		Assyrians evicted Dynasty XXVI
640				
635				
630	Archaic	Late Dedalic		
620				
		Post-Dedalic		
600				

INTRODUCTION

In historical times Crete has often appeared as a wild and unruly place, a mountain nursery for rebellions, massacres, and piracy – we remember the civil wars of the classical period, the nest of pirates destroyed by Metellus Creticus and Pompey, the Saracen raiders who dug the moat from which Candia took its name, the stories of the Venetians who used the island as a bastion against the Turks, and of the countless rebellions, savagely repressed, of the freedom-loving mountaineers of Crete against Roman, Saracen, Venetian, and Turk successively, and more recently against the Germans.

In the Bronze Age, however, Crete was a very different place, the centre of the first naval power known to history, a land where the people lived in peace and plenty with unwalled cities, a people boasting a culture that we term Minoan and that may be not unfairly compared to those of its great contemporaries in Asia Minor, Syria, Mesopotamia, and Egypt, a people that must certainly have regarded as barbarians their contemporaries in Europe.

For a millennium and a half this culture which we associate with the name of the legendary King Minos continued without any real break, though local disasters such as fires and earthquakes affected individual sites, and Mycenaean Greeks began to settle in the islands about 1500 B.C.

About 1400 B.C. a great catastrophe befell the island, a catastrophe of which we have no clear record in history, but one which is marked by destroyed and abandoned cities and villages, and from which the civilization as a whole never recovered. Most of the old sites, indeed, were reoccupied, but the next four hundred years were marked by the steady decadence of the splendid Minoan civilization.

Later a new life and culture arose in Crete, but it was primarily the creation of Greek colonists who had settled there, not of the survivors of the old Minoan race. Even this revival of culture in Crete, however, did not survive the seventh century B.C., and a new decline set in which lasted all through the great days of Athens and Sparta and the period of the Macedonian Empire.

The island of Crete was prosperous certainly in a humdrum way under the Roman Empire, but its inhabitants lived in a backwater, playing no great part in the more stirring events of the time. In the classical and Hellenistic period, when Athens, Sparta, Corinth, and the other mainland states were at their height, Crete was a land of internal strife, a land which supplied its more fortunate neighbours with bowmen and slingers, the poorer-armed type of mercenaries (a sure sign that all was not well at home), and reached its final period of degradation just before the Roman occupation, when it became the headquarters of the pirates in the Mediterranean.

Greek folk-memory, however, had always preserved the recollections of a golden age, when King Minos had ruled over Crete of the hundred cities and many islands, and when his navy had swept pirates from the seas around. Folklore had told too of the great engineer, the Athenian Daedalus, who had worked for Minos and had fashioned a dancing place for the Princess Ariadne, and had even manufactured flying wings which had caused the death of his son Icarus who had flown too near the sun and had been drowned near the island which still bears his name. We hear too, of the Minotaur, the monstrous man-headed bull, the offspring of Minos's wife Pasiphae, the monster to whom were sacrificed seven youths and seven maidens of Athens every nine years until Theseus, prince of Athens, slew the beast and escaped from the labyrinth where it had lived by means of a clue given him by the Princess Ariadne.

Folk-memory and the Homeric poems had dated Theseus only one generation before the Trojan war. Why then does the *Iliad* read like a saga with a historical background, while the story of Minos reads like a fairy tale? Some allowances must doubtless be made for the personality of the story-teller and the character of his audience, but I think there are two other major reasons why the historical element in the Cretan legends is so slight. Firstly, the inhabitants of Crete during the greater part of the Bronze Age probably spoke what the Greeks term a 'barbarian', that is a non-Greek, language, whereas those of the mainland were already speaking Greek. Secondly, the destruction of the Bronze Age settlements in Crete was far more thorough and devastating than on the mainland.

Classical Greece had no archaeologists, no antiquarian princes like King Nabonidus at Babylon. If a man opened an ancient tomb it was in the hope of finding jewels or gold to melt down; if he dug an ancient palace it was as a quarry for stones which he might use in some building he was engaged in constructing or repairing. Little therefore remained visible to the classical Greeks of the more monumental objects of Minoan culture. Engraved seals and beads continued to be handed down as ornaments, amulets, or milk-charms for nursing mothers (even up to the present day, when they are called 'milk stones'), but their original history and significance had been lost.

The Minoan people who had inhabited Crete during the Bronze Age had not been exterminated, and some of them were still speaking a non-Greek language up to Hellenistic times or later. The most permanent feature of Minoan culture, however, was their religion, which deeply affected the classical religion of Crete and to a lesser degree that of Greece as a whole. The amalgamation of Minoan and Hellenic cults must have started in the middle of the second millennium B.C., but even in the time of the Roman empire there remained cults and practices which were peculiarly Cretan, and of which the non-Hellenic elements were presumably inherited from the Minoan civilization of the Bronze Age. Some deities such as Britomartis, Velchanos, and Eileithyia were actually Minoan, but even Olympic figures such as Zeus, Hera, Apollo, and Athena were apt to retain Minoan features in their ritual and in the folklore referring to them.

It has been suggested that Plato's account of Atlantis, that island with its wonderful culture, its cult of Poseidon, and the emphasis on roads and water supplies, might be a reference, derived from folklore, to the lost island culture of Crete, and even that the reference to Solon deriving his information from Egypt might refer to information about Minoan Crete preserved in Egyptian records.[1] It is clear, however, that Plato himself did not identify Atlantis with Crete, and if he used folklore referring to Minoan Crete he was quite unconscious of any connexion between them. He knew the tradition about the laws of Minos and the relationship between the Dorian customs of Sparta and Crete, and of course, like all his contemporaries, he knew how Epimenides had been summoned from Crete to purify Athens after the murder of Cylon's associates in 632 B.C.

This eclipse of Crete during the classical period has left us with

1. Seltman, C., 'Life in Ancient Crete: Atlantis', *History Today*, 1952, p. 332.

little information from the classical authors, who in general were not particularly interested in the island. A few scattered but valuable remarks are preserved in the poems of Homer and the Histories of Herodotus and Thucydides, and we have to employ these as tests of the reliability of statements by authors of Hellenistic and Roman date. The poems of Epimenides, and the works of the historians who wrote specially on Crete in the Hellenistic period, have vanished, and practically all that remains of them is preserved in the history of Diodorus Siculus, an honest but uncritical historian who compiled his work about 40 B.C. His contemporary, Strabo the geographer, far more critical and better able to make use of the sources available to him, has left us some interesting information on Cretan religion, but practically nothing on the political history. Polybius, of course, is reliable on the political history of his own time, but in his days the Cretan forces were only as pawns moved about in the great game of chess played by the Hellenistic monarchs of Egypt and Macedon.

Sound evidence on many matters is provided by inscriptions and coins, but neither kind gives much information before 500 B.C., though from that time onwards these sources become more abundant and important. The most valuable evidence we possess from them is a long though incomplete inscription preserved on the walls of a Roman theatre at Gortyn in the Mesara giving the laws of that city mainly on questions of property valid in the fifth century B.C. The inscription is beautifully cut, and is a fine example of the local and rather archaic variety of the Greek script current in Crete, and of the local Doric dialect. It is even more valuable, however, as our longest and most complete account of the laws of property in a Greek city of the classical period.

After Diodorus there is no attempt by classical historians to delve into Cretan history, although writers on religion, both pagan and Christian, occasionally quote some detail of interest. Byzantine writers are no more curious, though chroniclers like Eusebius and Malalas quote from the older authorities, and the church historians give us interesting material about the early Christian church founded by St Titus.

In A.D. 832 Crete was seized by a band of Saracen adventurers from Egypt (and ultimately from Cordova in Spain) under the leadership of Abu Ka'ab and was held for Islam till it was recaptured by Nicé-phorus Phócas in A.D. 960.

The Saracens had founded the city of Candia, named after the 'Kandaiki', a moat they dug round their original settlement, but they were tough adventurers merely intent on plunder, and no Islamic university like those of Spain ever developed in Crete.[1] There is therefore practically no history of Crete during the period of the Saracen occupation, though we must note the effort made by the emperor Alexis Comnenus to replace the Saracen governing class by importing twelve noble Byzantine families known as the Archontó-pouloi.

In 1204 Crete was captured by the Crusaders and assigned to Boniface, Marquis of Montferrat, who sold his rights to Venice, and by 1210 a Venetian governor was appointed. The Venetians colonized the island, taxed it, exploited it, and suppressed rebellions, but they also built cities and introduced their own culture and the Latin church. Gradually the island settled down and some of the Venetian colonists, like the English colonists in Ireland, fraternized and intermarried with the Cretans, so that in 1363 many Venetians united with Cretans to rebel against the city of Venice and even went as far as to join the Orthodox church.

This union of Crete and Venice created not only a Creto-Venetian culture but also an interest in the earlier history of Crete, though the first medieval writer to display an interest in Cretan archaeology was the Florentine monk Buondelmonte, who visited the island in 1422, and whose observations were used by Cornelius in his *Creta Sacra* published in 1755. In 1596 Honorio de Belli dedicated his history of Candia, recording from personal observation many monuments and inscriptions. Of later writers Meursius in his *Creta* of 1675 and Hoeck in his *Kreta* of 1823 were both concerned with the history of the classical period derived from texts rather than from monuments.

Descriptions of the island itself and of contemporary Cretan life were given by Tournefort, Pococke, and others, but the first to combine classical scholarship with accurate topographical and socio-logical details was Robert Pashley in his *Travels in Crete* (1837) fol-lowed by Captain (later Admiral) T. A. B. Spratt in his *Travels and Researches in Crete* published in 1865, but embodying the results of a

1. No site even of a mosque of Saracen date has yet been discovered in Crete.

survey interrupted by the Crimean War. Spratt and Downes compiled the Admiralty Charts for Crete that were the best maps until the production of the staff maps during the Second World War. Victor Rawlin published his *Description physique de l'île de Crète* in 1869, an excellent account of the parts he had visited, but less comprehensive than the title suggests. It was not, however, till the last two decades of the nineteenth century that any serious attempt was made to excavate ancient sites in Crete, and the credit for the foundations of Cretan archaeology must chiefly be given to three men: Dr Joseph Hazzidakis, the founder of the Syllogos (the local Cretan archaeological society), Professor Federigo Halbherr, who conducted the first excavations of the Italian Mission in Crete, and Sir Arthur Evans, whose untiring efforts uncovered the Palace of Minos and revealed anew the great Minoan civilization of the Cretan Bronze Age and its neolithic predecessor.

Evans first visited Crete in 1893, attracted there by his study of the engraved seals then known as 'island gems', and the following year published the *Cretan Pictographs, and Pre-Phoenician Script*. In 1897 he acquired a permit for excavating part of the site of the Palace of Minos, then virgin ground, except for two small trial excavation pits, one sunk by Heinrich Schliemann and the other by Minos Kalokairinos. The Cretan rebellion of 1897 induced the Candia Turks to massacre some of the local Christians and rather unwisely to include in the massacre the British Vice-Consul and seventeen British sailors. Admiral Noel turned his guns on the city and gave the Pasha ten minutes to surrender. That, at least, is the local version of the story, and the name of Admiral Noel is still remembered with honour in Crete. Arthur Evans, whose liberal spirit had sympathized with this and other rebellions, was backed up by the new Cretan authorities and his title to the land was secured according to the new archaeological law proposed by Hazzidakis and Xanthoudides.

Hogarth describes the scene when he rode out with Evans, who was to start excavating his new site. 'For us then and no others in the following year Minos was waiting when we rode out from Candia. Over the very site of his buried throne a desolate donkey drooped, the only living thing in view. He was driven off and the digging of Knosos began.' On 23 March 1899 Evans, assisted by Duncan Mackenzie and by Theodore Fyfe as his architect, began those excavations which were to be continued every year until 1914 and again from 1920 until 1932. In 1901 Evans published his division of the Cretan Bronze Age into Early, Middle, and Late Minoan, and his article, 'The Mycenaean Tree and Pillar Cult'. In 1906 he published his *Essai de classification des époques de la civilisation minoenne* (a revision of his report to the Congress at Athens in 1905), a short but important article on Minoan weights and mediums of currency, and his *Prehistoric Tombs of Knosos*.

These discoveries attracted world-wide attention. The first general book to deal with them (a remarkably good one considering its early date) was H. R. Hall's *Oldest Civilization of Greece* published in 1901, followed by Miss Edith Hall's *The Decorative Art of Crete in the Bronze Age* (1907), L. P. Lagrange's *La Crète ancienne* and R. M. Burrows's *The Discoveries in Crete* (both 1908), and by Diedrich Fimmen's *Zeit und Dauer der kretisch-mykenischen Kultur*, C. M. Hawes's *Crete, the Forerunner of Greece*, and P. Kavadhias's *Proistoriki Archaeologia*, all in 1909.

In 1906 Evans had built the Villa Ariadne to serve as a permanent headquarters for his work, and in 1907 and 1908 he not only continued to excavate the Palace of Minos but also uncovered the Little Palace. In 1909 Evans published the first volume of his *Scripta Minoa* and in 1911 he was knighted for his services to archaeology.

Excavations in Crete were interrupted by the First World War but resumed in 1920, and in 1921 Evans published the first volume of his *Palace of Minos*. His devoted assistant Mackenzie was present at all the excavations until 1928, when ill-health forced him to retire, and he was succeeded as Curator at Knosos by J. D. S. Pendlebury. In 1932 Evans opened the Temple Tomb at Knosos, and in 1935 he visited Crete for the last time and published the fourth volume of his great book.

The British School of Archaeology at Athens started to excavate in Crete in the nineteenth century, when Hogarth opened the Dictaean cave at Psychro and the following year excavated a Minoan settlement at Zakros in the eastern end. In 1901 Bosanquet, who had been excavating the most important Bronze Age site in the Cyclades at Phylakopi in Melos, transferred his activities to Crete and excavated the archaic and Hellenistic site of Praisos, where he found an Eteocretan inscription (the first having been found by Halbherr).

In 1902 Bosanquet also began to excavate the Minoan city and tombs at Palaikastro on the east coast, and his work was continued by R. M. Dawkins.

In 1928 Evans presented his property in Crete to the British School at Athens, and from this date excavations at Knosos were conducted by the successive Directors – Humfry Payne, Alan Blakeway, Gerard Young, and Sinclair Hood – and by successive Curators, Pendlebury, myself, and P. de Jong. A large number of tombs of the early Iron Age were opened by Payne, Blakeway, Young, J. K. Brock, and T. J. Dunbabin.

In 1935 Pendlebury began an exhaustive examination of sites on the plain of Lasithi, a work terminated by the Second World War. During that war he made his gallant sortie against the German parachutists and was wounded, and later killed, in April 1941. Before his death, however, he had completely excavated the post-Minoan village of Karphi – a feat only equalled in Crete previously by Miss Boyd at Gournia – and also excavated a Neolithic cave site at Trapeza and other sites nearby.

In January 1940 I opened three tombs of the orientalizing period at Khaniale Tekke near Knosos, one with a rich treasure of jewellery of the seventh century B.C.

In May 1941 the Germans occupied the area round Knosos and the Villa Ariadne became the headquarters of General Ringel, who not only looted the antiquities in the house, but committed a much worse archaeological crime in destroying the Royal Tomb at Isopata to use the stones as foundations for three army huts. It should be remarked, however, that the German officers who succeeded Ringel treated the antiquities with great respect.

Halbherr had started excavating in Crete some years before Evans, but his earlier researches were concerned with remains of the classical period, including the famous inscription of the laws of Gortyn. In 1900, however, he began to excavate the palace site at Phaistos on the east end of an isolated ridge in the Mesara plain. In 1901 Professor Luigi Pernier took over the direction of the excavations. Pernier was able to complete the first volume of the final publication *Il Palazzo di Festos*, but the second volume, which he had left incomplete at his death in 1937, was completed and edited by Professor Luisa Banti in 1950. Further excavations have been made since the Second World

War by Professors Banti and Levi. Savignoni and Paribeni published their excavations of the cemeteries of Phaistos and Hagia Triada in the eleventh volume of the *Monumenti Antichi*. Only summary accounts have been published of the recent excavations at Phaistos.

The excavations of Pernier and Banti at Hagia Triada have not yet been published in full, though there are excellent preliminary reports. For the archaic and classical periods, Pernier gave an account of his excavations at Prinias in 1914, and Doro Levi of his work at Arkades in 1924. Last but not least there is the splendid corpus of Cretan classical inscriptions which Signorina M. Guarducci has been producing since 1935. The Americans were also early on the field and concentrated on the Gulf of Merabello.

During all this period a great deal of fine, if often unspectacular, work had been carried out by the Greek archaeological service under its successive officers Drs Hazzidakis, Xanthoudides, Marinatos, Theophanides, Platon, Petrou (a casualty in the Albanian war), and Alexiou.

The French School at Athens were slower to turn their attention to Crete, but in 1899–1900 P. Demargne excavated the interesting city of Lato. The French continued to be interested in this district, but of recent years they have devoted more attention to Mallia, where a splendid Minoan palace was uncovered on a site discovered and first tested by Joseph Hazzidakis.

The Germans took no part in Cretan excavations until their military occupation of Crete in 1941, but after that date they carried out a few minor excavations.

All these excavations had produced a mass of material which needed to be set in order and correlated with contemporary finds from other parts of the Levant.

A great deal of the preliminary spadework for this correlation of cultures was done by Evans himself in his great work *The Palace of Minos*, but there were many debatable points, and a battle royal developed between Evans and Wace on the vexed question of how far Mycenae might be said to be under Minoan influence or even domination during the Late Minoan I–II periods.

It is not possible here to give a bibliography of these excavations outside Crete, but readers may consult the various excavation reports by the scholars concerned.

CHAPTER I

The Islands of Crete: Geology, Geography, Climate, and Flora and Fauna

THE long mountainous island of Crete (Figs. 1 and 2) forms a natural stepping stone between Europe and Africa, and between Europe and Asia, but whereas there are many stepping stones for the latter interval, Crete is the only convenient link between Europe and Egypt. It was no accident therefore that this island became the medium for the transmission of cultural influences from the older civilizations of the Near and Middle East to barbarian Europe, and that the first civilization that we can term European was that of Crete.

In Late Miocene and Pliocene times the island seems to have been connected with Asia Minor rather than with Europe. Certain forms of land snails and wingless beetles appear on Crete and on Anticythera in forms akin to those of Asia Minor, whereas those of Cythera resemble those of the mainland of Greece, suggesting that at one time the strait dividing Cythera from Anticythera was the division between Europe and Asia. What is now the northern part of the Aegean Sea was then probably a lakeland, and as long ago as 1856 T. A. B. Spratt had noted that the Miocene deposits near Khersonnesos in Crete contained fresh-water molluscs in an abundance implying that the deposit was lacustrine, since the hills at this point would not have allowed the formation of so large a riverine deposit.

In the Pleistocene period there were evident convulsions which submerged the area now called the Aegean Sea, heaved up mountain ranges, and severed Crete from Asia Minor. Henceforward Crete was more nearly related to the mainland of Greece, and its present fauna and flora are European though retaining faint traces of their old connexions with Asia Minor and Cyrenaica. One such relic is the *agrimi*, the Cretan ibex, also found in the small Cycladic island of Antimelos; this splendid animal, though related to the ibex of Sardinia and Corsica, is more nearly akin to that of Cyprus and Asia Minor.

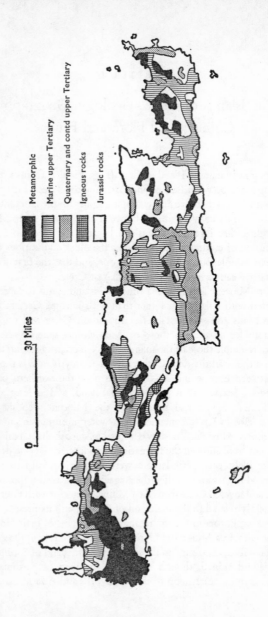

Fig. 1. Geological map of Crete

Metamorphic

Marine upper Tertiary

Quaternary and contd upper Tertiary

Igneous rocks

Jurassic rocks

30 Miles

0

The connexions with Europe were further strengthened by the fact that nearly all the harbours of Crete are on its north coast, and that after the first fifty miles there is a double string of islands joining Crete to the mainland of Greece. Another string of islands, Kasos, Karpathos, and Rhodes unites Crete to Asia Minor. On the south side, however, there is deep water and two hundred miles of open sea without any intervening islands between Crete and Africa.

The island has never yet been systematically examined by a geological survey though individual geologists have explored particular areas.[1]

The most recent geological map of Crete is the one based on the work of N. Liatsikos and published in the Rockefeller survey of Crete. Doubtless it corrects Captain Spratt's map in some parts, but for the general reader it is disappointing, because it is far more summary and leaves out a great deal of information contained in Spratt's work. According to Liatsikos the great limestone backbone of the island, including the promontories enclosing the bays of Kisamos, Khania, and Soudha in the west, the great ranges of the White Mountains, Ida, Lasithi, the Kophinos range in the south, and the moorlands beyond Seteia in the east are labelled as dark limestone and dolomite of the 'Tripolitza sub-zone'. Impure marly limestone, calcareous sandstone, and conglomerate mark the coastal plains of Khania and Rethymnon, all the valleys south of Herakleion between the Ida block on the west and the Pedhiadha valleys on the east, and also the quaternary alluvial plain of the Mesara on the south. In this rather mixed group Liatsikos evidently includes the white 'Kouskouras' marls, and though he marks gypsum outcrops on the Kisamos–Selinon boundary he does not mark either the historic hill of Gypsadhes, which provided the gypsum quarries for the Palace of Minos, or those in the Mesara, which furnished gypsum blocks for the palaces of Phaistos and Hagia Triada.[2]

The coastal district east of Kophinos and one or two other patches are classified by Liatsikos as limestone of the Adriatic–Ionian group.

1. e.g. west Crete by Ardaillon and Cayeux, *Annual of the American Geographical Society*, 1901, p. 445; and cave deposits in central Crete by Simonelli, *Rendiconti Accademia dei Lincei*, Rome, 1894, p. 236.

2. This observation is not intended as a criticism of Liatsikos, since these outcrops, though archaeologically important, are small in area.

Finally there is a solid block of country round Kandanos in the west, and smaller patches south of the Rethymnon plain and elsewhere labelled schist, phyllite, slate, quartzite, and marble.

Igneous rocks (serpentine, gabbro, syenite, and a little granite), mainly of the Jurassic and Cretaceous periods, but possibly including some of Eocene date, occur near the east end of the Asidheroto mountains and south of the Lasithi massif. Two small volcanic outcrops occur at Galatas and Xerokambos in the Khania district, and Spratt claims that the islands of Pondikonisi and Gaidharonisi are volcanic formations, though the latter is stated by a later authority to be Tertiary limestone.

In general, however, the base of the land of the island consists of metamorphic phyllites, slates, mica schists, and quartzites, and these crop out on the surface in the Kisamos and Selinon districts. Elsewhere the metamorphic rocks are usually covered by a vast mass of coarse-grained limestones of the Jurassic, Cretaceous, and Eocene periods often drained by swallow-holes rather than by streams. Caves are frequent and have so regularly provided refuges in troubled times that they added a word to the ancient lexicon, Kresphygeton, the Cretan refuge.

The lower areas were also largely covered by marine upper Tertiary rocks, especially conglomerates but including limestones, marls, chalks, and sandstones.

Quaternary and upper Tertiary deposits, though not extensive, form the most fertile areas such as the Mesara and the coastal plains of Herakleion and Rethymnon. Many details missing from the Rockefeller version of Liatsikos's map[1] may be filled in from the books and articles of earlier explorers such as that of Captain Spratt and M. Victor Raulin, summarized by Burchard.[2]

The province of Seteia was also discussed in detail in a book in German by L. Chalikiopoulos, and the same area was examined more recently by H. Lehmann, who in his brief summary of the districts he visited, states that east Crete is composed mainly of Mesozoic and old Tertiary limestone, crystalline schist and conglomerate overlaid

1. The original map, which I have not seen, may be much more informative.

2. Article 'Kreta' in the *Real-Enzyklopädie* of Paully-Wissowa-Kroll, pp. 174–9.

by late Tertiary limestone, conglomerate, and marls in the marginal troughs at Ierapetra and Seteia.

PIRACY AND THE DISTRIBUTION OF THE POPULATION

Lehmann's two plans illustrate how the Minoan settlements follow the alluvial deposits and the schist valleys and avoid the limestone. The schist not only breaks up more easily into cultivated terraces, but it also provokes intercommunication, forming natural roads along the hillside comfortable for a loaded mule, without any of the rough boulders that beset a limestone path. He also notes how the occupation zones swing away from the coastal plains to the uplands when there is increased danger from piracy. Thus Minoan sites are rarely more than a hundred metres above sea level, testifying to the power of the Minoan navy, and I think this is true of Minoan settlements elsewhere, though of course the rule only applies to villages, not to religious shrines such as peak and cave sanctuaries. In the Homeric and geometric period, however, when there was no Minoan navy and piracy was a fashionable profession, the villages spread into the higher dales and the lower slopes of the schist hills.

Piracy continued into classical times and reached a new peak of intensity in the late Hellenistic period, but after Metellus Creticus and Pompey had wiped out the Cretan pirates in the first century B.C. the island began again to enjoy peace and prosperity and the coastal plains filled up with a contented population of farmers, artisans, and traders. With the arrival of the Saracen raiders under Abu Ka'ab, however, in A.D. 825 the bad times began again, and the coastal plains hardly filled up again until the firm hand of imperial Venice had imposed peace (a peace less secure, however, than those of Minoan and Roman times).

A letter from R. C. Bosanquet to a friend alludes to more recent piracy on the coast by Palaikastro. 'Curiously enough until the Greek revolution the seas were so infested by pirates that no one dared to live on this exposed sea-board and the whole plain was uncultivated. ... A Venetian writer says it was uninhabitable on account of corsairs. ... We heard many stories of the last of the Christian corsairs, a certain Papa Boyatzes, "Father Dyer", a valiant priest who commanded a swift forty-oared galley and was the terror of the Turks.'

Admiral Spratt at an earlier date commented on the remarkable knowledge of the coastlines of Crete, Kasos, Karpathos, and Kastellorizo displayed by his ex-pirate pilot, 'the patient and gentle' Captain Manias. In the fourteenth book of the *Odyssey* the hero pretends to be a Cretan and boasts that 'nine times before the war at Troy I raided men of another race with my ships, and my house grew great and my reputation was established among the Cretans'.

EARTHQUAKES AND TIDAL WAVES

The only volcano at present active in Greece is that of the Cycladic island Thera, perhaps better known by its Italian name Santorini, but earthquakes affect many parts of Greece, and Crete averages about two severe earthquakes a century with minor tremors every year. Evidence of destruction by earthquakes was noted by Sir Arthur Evans when he excavated the Palace of Minos at Knosos, the clearest evidence being that of the House of the Fallen Blocks and the adjacent House of the Sacrificed Oxen. These two small houses had been destroyed by great blocks hurled southwards from the south-east part of the Palace, and it should be remarked that the earthquakes recurring now shake the island from north to south, the epicentre being presumably somewhere between Crete and Thera. The great fire which destroyed the Palace about 1400 B.C. was also supposed to have been the result of seismic activity, and Evans notes what he takes to be evidence of other earthquakes. This theory has been further developed by S. Marinatos and C. F. C. Schaeffer. (See page 301.)

SURFACE GEOLOGY AND TOPOGRAPHY

The surface topography of the island has been admirably treated by the late Captain J. D. S. Pendlebury in his *Archaeology of Crete* in which he summarized the previous evidence from the *Stadiasmus*[1] and from the earlier travellers, and supplemented them with his own

1. op. cit., pp. 13, 24; I think, however, that the temples cited in the *Stadiasmus* were quoted mainly as prominent landmarks for navigators rather than as 'facilities for devotion'.

unrivalled knowledge of the by-paths and mountains of Crete. Individual muleteers doubtless knew their own district better, but no man knew the whole island as well as Pendlebury, and he stresses the point, which may be forgotten by armchair archaeologists and historians, that distances on a map have little meaning in considering ancient trade routes, and that what really matters is the number of foot-hours occupied by a normal man walking between one site and another.

Pendlebury's first chapter, 'The Island', should be taken as a basis for surface topography, and it has since been supplemented by some further researches during and since the Second World War by the German archaeological expedition under Friedrich Matz in western Crete, by T. J. Dunabin in the Amari district, by N. Platon the Ephor of Antiquities, and by the survey of Crete executed for the Rockefeller Foundation under the direction of L. G. Allbaugh in 1948.

If the island is considered simply as an environment for human culture, we may divide Crete into the following types of country: (a) fertile coastal plains and valleys; (b) mountain-locked upland plains sometimes drained by a river but often drained only by natural swallow-holes (called *katavóthra* on the mainland but in Crete more often termed *chónoi*), often snow-bound in the winter and sometimes waterlogged if the swallow-holes get blocked; (c) low hills and table-land providing good pasture and even arable land; (d) forests; (e) the *madára* or bare lands on the higher mountains providing summer pasturage but snowbound in the winter; and (f) the high peaks, crags, and torrents that are unusable for pasture.

FAUNA

In the far west the schist valleys of the Kandanos and Ennea Khoria districts are better watered than the average and tolerably fertile, as are also the two coastal plains of Kisamos and Khania. In the White Mountains are the remains of the great cypress woods that still supplied material to the Venetian navy as late as the sixteenth century and which in the Keramia district still grow up to a level of 6500 feet. These parts have always been a refuge for the hunted, whether man or beast. In the time of Pliny, or at least in that of his authority, the province of Khania was the only part of Crete where deer still survived, and the wooded heights west of the Hagio Roumeli gorge are now the last refuge of the *agrimi*, the Cretan ibex which was still to be found in the Ida and Lasithi districts fifty years ago. Evans's statement, however, that they still existed on Dhia is not correct.

It will be remarked that among the recorded wild fauna of Crete not one is the ancestor of any domestic animal later found in the island; even the domestic cats of Minoan days would appear to be the offspring of Egyptian sires, not those of the native wild cat. The domestic animals of Crete must have been introduced in Neolithic times or later and are therefore more properly considered in the chapter on social organization. (See Chapter 8.)

There is no evidence on the varieties of fish available to the first settlers in Crete, but they must have included most of the Mediterranean varieties. Even now there are plenty of fish round the island, and before the Cretans began to fish with dynamite the fishing grounds must have been much more prolific; but fishing must always have been complicated by the fact that the main fishing grounds were off the south-east coast, where the off-shore water was very deep and there were no good harbours.

Game common on the island includes rock pigeons and red-legged partridges all the year round, and duck, snipe, woodcock, and quail at the migration times. Even storks have been seen in passage, but certainly the most exciting bird migration is that of the cranes, who fly in large flocks over Crete in a north-westerly direction in the spring, returning south-eastwards in October.

CLIMATE, RAINFALL, AND WATER SUPPLY

The Cretan climate varies greatly according to altitude. The plains have a pleasant, dry climate with practically all the rain falling between October and March, usually some heavy rain in October and again in February or March ('the former and the latter rains' referred to in the Bible). The temperature only occasionally falls below freezing point and snow is rare.

There is only one lake in Crete, Lake Kournas (160 acres in area), situated about eleven miles west of Rethymnon.

Allbaugh speaks of three permanent rivers, but this estimate

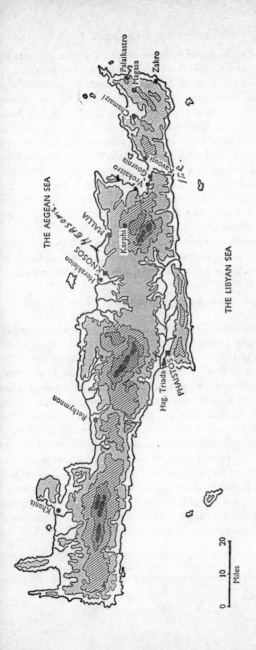

Fig. 2. General map of Crete

depends on where one draws the line between a river and a stream. Pendlebury quotes five that have never been known to dry up, namely the Platanias west of Khania (the ancient Iardanos), the Gazanos west of Herakleion ('formerly the Triton'),[1] the Metropolitanos or Yeropotamos (the ancient Lethaios) and the Anapodhiari (formerly the Katarrhactes) both in the Mesara, and the Mylopotamos (the ancient Oaxes) which flows out at the east end of the Rethymnos bay. Other places which have permanently flowing streams though they may not merit the title of rivers are Amnisos, Seteia, Zakros, and Kato Viannos. Water is thus relatively scarce (though usually quite good in quality); however, of the villages sampled by the Rockefeller Survey, only one had to carry its drinking water from a neighbouring settlement.

Springs are fairly common in the mountains and in the coastal plains water is drawn from wells (in the Mallia plain at a depth of only five metres, but at Knosos some twelve to fourteen metres).

MINERAL RESOURCES

The mineral resources of Crete are indicated by two reports presented to the Rockefeller Survey. One prepared in Herakleion indicated twenty appearances of iron ore, twelve of copper, ten of gypsum, and three to six each of manganese, talc, lignite, lead, and zinc. Another report alleged that in three unworked mines near Palaiokhora, Meskla, and Kastelli Kisamou there were precious stones, gold, silver, copper,[2] tungsten, platinum, magnetite, emery, graphite, and possibly tin apatite (most of them presumably in small quantities).

The forests, which still provided abundant cypress wood for the Venetian navy in medieval times, have now largely been destroyed. Half of the forest still remaining is in the province of Khania (half is scrub and half Aleppo pine mixed with scrub). There are also, however, some small chestnut forests in this province. Rethymnon has forests of carob and oaktrees. The southern and eastern slopes of the Ida range have oaks and conifers (constituting one fifth of the

1. I should have thought the Giophyros Potamos was more permanent and more likely to have been the Triton; in this I agree with Pashley.
2. Evidences of a Middle Minoan copper mine were found at Chrysokamino.

whole forest area of the island). Lasithi has almonds and carobs and there is a fine wood of *prinári* (evergreen oak) above Kritsa. The extreme east of the island is almost treeless except for plantations of olives or carobs, and the grove of wild palms at Eremopolis (traditionally supposed to have sprung from the date stones thrown away by the first Arab invaders).

EDIBLE PLANTS AND CULTIVATION

Very large areas of Crete are and always have been unproductive. No statistics are available for ancient times, but Allbaugh gives the following figures for 1948: eight per cent of the total land area was under cultivated crops such as wheat, barley, beans, etc., ten per cent was vine, olive, and other fruit orchards, five per cent was fallow land, seven per cent was grazing land and meadows of a permanent or semi-permanent type, two per cent was forests, no less than forty-eight per cent were lands used for nomadic grazing, and the remaining twenty per cent consisted of entirely unproductive land, such as mountain crags, torrent beds, and the like. It is impossible to form a fair estimate of what the proportions would have been in prehistoric times, but obviously much of the present *madára* – the bare lands used for nomadic grazing – would then have been virgin forest. At a very rough guess I should imagine that the cultivated land would not have been much less than the present and the unproductive twenty per cent of crags and torrents just the same, but that at least half of the present *madára* would then have been covered by cypress and other forest trees.

Before 1939 Cretan olive trees averaged a yield of five pounds of oil per tree, as compared with an average of 3·7 pounds for Greece as a whole and 3·1 pounds for Italy and Turkey, and the crop represented a large percentage – more than a third – of the Greek crop as a whole. Pre-war crops of wheat and barley in Crete averaged 12·8 and 15 bushels per acre respectively. Grapes, largely in the form of sultanas, form the largest Cretan export abroad now, though Pashley records that in his day oil paid 8,750,000 piastres duty against only 168,000 from raisins (which presumably includes sultanas). Today a considerable proportion of the olives exported from the island is simply sent to other parts of Greece. The annual output of olives is some 25,000 tons, and according to Elliadi[1] about 10,000 tons of grapes are exported annually.

Both olives and grapes were grown in Crete during the Bronze Age. How far they were exported is a matter for speculation, but it is of interest to note that Greek tradition attributed the introduction of the cultivated olive into the Peloponnese to the Cretan Herakles, who was said to have brought it from the land of the Hyperboreans, which Pausanias interprets as Crete; and very probably he is right in this instance, since the cultivation of the olive cannot have been introduced from a country in the far north. The actual development of the cultivated olive and the preparation of its fruit were attributed to the goddess Athena herself (who according to one tradition had been born in Crete).

Visitors to Crete are often surprised to find the valleys full of vineyards and wheat planted on the flatter tops and slopes of the lower hills – such wheat being said to produce whiter flour than that of the valleys – while the slopes of the lower hills are terraced for olives. In eastern Crete and in some western districts the carob bean tree vies with and even replaces the olive in popularity, while citrus fruits are grown in the valleys behind Khania; but the last-named are unlikely to have been known in Crete in prehistoric times. The present annual crop of carob beans amounts to about 20,000 tons.

The prehistoric Cretans were well supplied with leguminous plants, having peas, chickpeas and some form of beans, but for sweetening their food they must have relied mainly on honey.

NATURAL VEGETATION

The vegetation of Crete has probably not altered much since prehistoric times, with two great exceptions: the first, the diminution of forest timber, especially cypress, owing to excessive cutting, to fires, and to the failure to protect the young shoots from goats; and the second the introduction of numerous fruits, such as apples, peaches, apricots, plums, and citrus fruits in the west, and certain vegetables

1. In 1937, however, Crete produced 32,000 tons of olive oil and 2500 tons of table olives; Tournefort states that the crop of oil in 1699 was 300,000 measures, but cautions us that whereas the Rethymnon measure weighed 10 okes that of Canea weighed only 8½.

such as potatoes (now extensively grown on the Lasithi plain). If we bear in mind these exceptions we may take Rawlin's list, as modified by Trevor Battye, as a fair indication of what existed in ancient times.

From sea-level up to 500 feet we find common lentisk, large seeded juniper, tamarisk, a willow, *agnus castus*, and oleanders. The almond and quince, both probably native to Crete, are confined to this level. Elliadi, in 1933, quotes the crop of shelled almonds as averaging 600 tons and states it was increasing every year.

From 500 to 2000 feet up we find the terebinth (a softer lentisk), a deciduous oak, myrtle, arbutus, oleander, black mulberry, and styrax. From 2000 to 3000 feet, in the lower woods, we find dog rose, plane tree, and ivy (the latter two are also found lower). From 3000 to 4000 feet, in the higher wooded areas, there is the tree *salvia cretica* peculiar to the island, with oak, maple, and cypress, and spiny shrubs are common.

Between 4000 and 6000 feet, the limit of the true forest, we have the evergreen cypress, the Cretan maple, and the low prickly form of the *prinári*, or evergreen oak. Between 6000 and 8000 feet we find the bare subalpine slopes which the Cretans call *madára*. We still find there the common juniper, Cretan barberry (never more than bush size), and in the higher regions the woods flatten to creeping forms such as the creeping barberry, creeping plum, and buckthorn. The pine, chiefly *pinus haricio* or *pinus halepensis*, occurs at all levels up to 3000 feet, but the only considerable forests are in the Aradena district in the west and on the southern slopes of the Dhikte and Effendi Kavousi ranges.

Cypresses seem confined to the limestone country. Evergreen oak and myrtle are most common among, though not restricted to, the schist district.

Trees like the Cretan oak and myrtle tend to develop into prickly shrubs on the higher slopes. The centre of the island is now largely devoted to the culture of vines and olives, but in the Khania plain citrus fruits are grown. The wild pear may be found up to 3000 feet and the black mulberry up to 2000, but the latter was introduced probably for the silk trade, and there is a tendency for each village to have about one tree. White mulberries grow up to 3000 feet.

Cedar of Lebanon and Cefalonian pine have been identified in the remains of wood in the Palace, but whether these then grew in Crete or were imported is uncertain. We do know that Thothmes III used to import cedars from the Lebanon to Egypt 'in ships of Keftiu', but whether this means in Cretan ships is open to question (see page 108). There are a few natural salt marshes on the coast, but there is no evidence yet to show whether the Minoan people attempted to exploit these. Pepper, however, seems to be a pre-Hellenic word, and the Greek word for mustard also is of foreign derivation.

The wild vegetables include the wild forms of celery, carrot, cabbage, lettuce, and asparagus (of which only the young shoots are eaten, since the rest is spiny); but the Cretans also boil for the pot many *khorta* (grasses) which are despised by householders elsewhere, including the bulbs of asphodel and grape hyacinths.

The hills of Crete are particularly rich in aromatic herbs and bushes, of which the more fragrant are thyme, the various kinds of *cystus*, and sage, marjoram, and mint.

By July most flowers have vanished from the valleys, though even then the stony river beds grow pink with oleanders and the sandy river beds mauve with *agnus castus* (which is used for making baskets), and the vineyards are a rich green, only turning brown about the time of the autumn rains. But as the valleys grow brown, the snows melt from the high mountains, the upland plains of Nidha, Omalo, Lasithi, and others yield their best pasture, and many little flowers come out on the high mountains, such as chionodoxa, a rock-cress, forget-me-nots, and an alyssum (the last found by Trevor Battye right on the summit of Mount Ida).

CHAPTER 2

The Stone Age

PALAEONTOLOGICAL EVIDENCE

WE can say nothing definite about the existence of men in Crete during the Old Stone Age. A stone scraper resembling an Aurignacian type was discovered by Pendlebury in Lasithi, but not in a Palaeolithic context. It must be admitted, however, that the average archaeologist who works in Crete would not recognize the less obvious type of Palaeolithic tool, and is not a good enough geologist to look in the right places. One or two palaeontologists, however, have examined some early cave deposits, and so far have discovered no artefacts associated with the fossils contemporary with the Old Stone Age.

In 1893 Signor Simonelli excavated some caves in the Rethymnon district and identified bones of a large elephant and of a small deer which he named *Anoglochis cretensis*. In 1904 Miss Dorothea Bate spent some months in Crete examining Spratt's cave and some twelve others near Sphinari, two others at the north end of the Phalasarna plain, one each side of the promontory dividing Khania from Kisamos, four from within the limits of the Akrotiri peninsula, and a number of caves near Rethymnon. Later in the same year, she examined cave deposits in east Crete near Milatos, on Katharo plain, and at Kharoumes, recording the bones of pigmy elephants and hippopotami, as well as those found by Simonelli, and others existing on the island, such as the *agrimi*, or Cretan ibex (*Capra aegagrus cretensis*), but no *Bos primigenius*, nor any signs of man.

It would appear that the land bridge to Asia Minor had already sunk when the first Cretans came by boat from island to island by way of Karpathos and Kasos, and then sailed along the coast of Crete, which may perhaps help to explain the curious fact that no Early Neolithic pottery has yet been found except at Knosos. The first

Neolithic settlers in Crete cannot have arrived later than 3000 B.C. and probably arrived earlier.

Evans had early realized and stressed the Anatolian elements in Crete, such as the stone maces and the squatting figurines which seemed to imply the cult of a great mother goddess like that of Anatolia. This evidence has been reinforced by Dr Audrey Furness, who pointed out analogies between the decoration of the earliest Neolithic pottery in Crete and that of Chalcolithic pottery from the Alaca district of Asia Minor.

It may also be remarked that the colonization of Crete in such primitive boats as were likely to be available to the Neolithic inhabitants would hardly be practicable from anywhere except the Dodecanese or the Cyclades. (See p. 91 and Fig. 12.)

M. L. Franchet in 1912 examined a small habitation site on the coast three kilometres west of Herakleion, which he claimed to be earlier than that of Knosos and which produced some microlithic obsidian tools.

THE EARLY NEOLITHIC PERIOD

Apart from Franchet's site, of which the date is a little uncertain, we are dependent for our knowledge of the Early and Middle Neolithic culture of Crete entirely on the site of the Palace of Minos at Knosos. The permanent and abundant evidence from the deep test pits is preserved in the Stratigraphic Museum at Knosos. Recently this material has been studied in detail by Dr Furness. She retains Evans's division of the pottery into three main periods entitled Early, Middle, and Late Neolithic, but subdivides the first period into Early Neolithic I and Early Neolithic II. The pottery from these deposits was quite well made, well mixed, and tempered with powdered gypsum, and sometimes with larger grit, but rather irregularly fired, perhaps in an open fire, so that the colour of the surface varies from black through grey to buff and even red, though the fabric is tough and does not crumble. There is no slip, but the surface is usually very well burnished, although sometimes uneven burnishing left red scribblings on buff or black on grey. The commonest shape was a deep store jar, which might be anything up to half a metre in diameter, with large strap handles set vertically, occasionally on the rim, but usually some way below it. The profile seems to vary from cylindrical, through inverted conical, to round forms. Shallow bowls of various sizes, conical bowls with straight, thinning rims (a Neolithic trick common all over the Near East), round bowls with inverted rims, carinated bowls with similar rims: all these occur. Raking handles of wishbone type are not uncommon, and a broad, flat, double-horned type also occurs, though it is confined to Knosos and is not common even there.

Dr Furness divides the Early Neolithic I fabrics into (a) coarse burnished ware and (b) fine burnished ware, only differing from the former in that the pot walls are thinner, the clay better mixed, and the burnish more carefully executed. The surface colour is usually black, but examples also occur of red, buff, or yellow, sometimes brilliant red or orange, and sometimes highly variegated sherds.

Dr Furness justly observes that 'as the pottery of the late Neolithic phases seems to have developed at Knosos without a break, it is to the earliest that one must look for evidence of origin or foreign connexions', and she therefore stresses the importance of a small group with plastic decoration that seems mainly confined to the Early Neolithic I levels, consisting of rows of pellets immediately under the rim (paralleled on burnished pottery of Chalcolithic date from Gullucek in the Alaca district of Asia Minor), of large knobs singly, in threes, or in rows, mostly lower down on the vase, of curved mouldings running parallel with the scalloped rims that occur on certain bowls, of dentated rims, plastic imitations of a rope, unpierced lugs, and a few unclassified oddments. In all she noted that 137 sherds in the Stratigraphic Collection at Knosos, all probably Early Neolithic I in date, had plastic decoration of this kind. Incised ornaments were more rare and when they did occur were usually in the pointillé or punctuated ribbon style (Plate I), but also included filled triangles, chevrons, chequered stepped patterns, and fringed lines. Human and animal figurines in the same technique as the pottery also appear.

The Early Neolithic II period is marked by better mixed clay and better firing, which reduces the variations in colour, and by the disappearance of plastic ornaments, flanged handles, and certain forms of wishbone handle. Highly burnished black or red sherds are still normal, but they begin to be progressively replaced by less burnished buff or grey sherds. The shapes of the vases and handles are the same

chnique of the burnished ware, except that occasionally
rippled by the burnishing tool, a trick that appeared
e now but was to become more popular later.

ation was common (Plate 2 and Fig. 3) and was applied
to most of the fine pottery, except that, since it was only applied to
the exterior, the very wide bowls were usually left plain, while

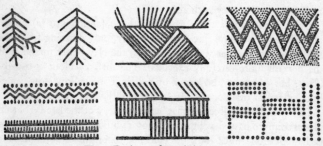

Fig. 3. Designs of Neolithic pottery

decoration was naturally more common on narrow-necked jars,
where it showed to better advantage. The designs included a plaited
ornament, zigzag and chevron bands, and fringed lines. It is also very
common arranged vertically on strap handles. Other ornaments
which occurred were hatched rectangles, chequers, and diamonds,
and sometimes the zigzag band or other ornament was reserved as a
pointillé background. Fragments have also been found of human and
animal figures with similar decoration.

THE MIDDLE NEOLITHIC PERIOD

In the Middle Neolithic period there appeared a growing tendency
to leave the coarser wares unpolished, possibly because they were now
better baked and therefore the polishing was less necessary to make
them impervious to water, and such polishing as did appear on the
coarse vases was of the scribbled type. The large coarse bowls and
jars continued to be common, though even in these there were some
changes, hard to define, in the profiles of the rims. True wishbone
handles were rare and the normal form was a large strap handle (not

flanged). Innovations of the Middle Neolithic period were the introduction of lugs, rectangular, round, or pointed, rising from the rim, and also loop handles set on the rim. There is one example on a coarse buff vase of a horizontal lug with two vertical perforations, a form characteristic of the earliest Bronze Age in Crete, the Cyclades, Mytilene, and Troy.

The shapes and fabrics of the Middle Neolithic fine pottery did not differ very much from those of the Early Neolithic period though the vase walls were rather thinner, nor did the incised designs differ much from the Early Neolithic II ones, but ornamentation by undulating ripples executed with a heavy polishing instrument became common, always as an alternative, never as an addition to the incised decoration. Middle Neolithic sherds in general might be jet black, brown, buff, bright red, or yellow in colour, but the rippled sherds were usually coloured a moderately uniform brownish black. Ribbon handles and tubular lugs were very common. The rippled bowls often had small token handles, obviously only a skeuomorphic ornament since they sometimes appear in vertical or diagonal rows.

At Knosos the people must have lived in mudbrick houses, but a large proportion of the population doubtless lived in caves. In the transition from Early Neolithic II to Middle Neolithic deposits, axes occur in greenstone, serpentine, dioprase, jadeite, haematite, and schist, usually either of a heavy type with roughened butt to facilitate hafting, or of a smaller trapezoid type for use rather as an adze or chisel. Obsidian blades and arrowheads are found, as are cores, which show that the material was imported, presumably from Melos, and worked on the spot. Bone pins and needles and clay spools and spindle whorls testify to the existence of spinning and weaving, probably as a household industry.

THE LATE NEOLITHIC PERIOD

It is not till the very end of the Neolithic period that we begin to form any idea of what a village of that period may have looked like, and by that time the basic principle, or lack of principle, that is so characteristic of the Minoan architecture of the Bronze Age is already manifesting itself. This is the characteristic which led one scholar to borrow a term from comparative philology and to refer to Minoan architecture as 'agglutinative', because the owner or architect, after constructing one rectangular room, would add others of varying sizes and shapes to it as the need arose. The resulting plan was rather haphazard in outline, giving the impression of an organic cellular growth rather than of an architectural design. Considerable ingenuity

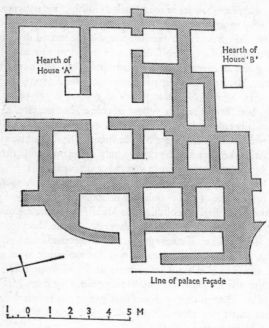

Hearth of House 'A'

Hearth of House 'B'

Line of palace Façade

|___|___|___|___|___|___|___|
    0   1   2   3   4   5 M

Fig. 4. Late Neolithic houses, Knosos

and architectural skill might be displayed in the design of individual parts of a building, but there was always an opportunist air about a Minoan building as a whole. The two late Neolithic houses uncovered in the central court of the Palace of Minos at Knosos (Fig. 4) already illustrate this cellular architecture. The individual rooms were rect-angular and well constructed but differ in size and shape, and two rooms of house A were only accessible from the street (conceivably shops, but perhaps only outhouses or stables for donkeys). House A had one rounded corner, doubtless because the village street took a turn at this point. Both houses had fixed hearths, an amenity which went out of fashion in the Bronze Age when palaces and houses alike seem to have relied mainly for their heating on small movable braziers, though two small houses of the Middle Bronze Age at Mallia had fixed hearths and Pierre Demargne has argued that the practice was not abandoned till that time, that is, till after 2000 B.C.

Fig. 5. Late Neolithic house, Magasa

At Magasa in the very east there was a small but well-built house of the type that the Scots term 'but-and-ben', with a fairly large square room opening out of a small outer room, and also a rock shelter roughly walled in front (Fig. 5). The latter was doubtless a shepherd's hut like many still used by the upland shepherds, but the former, to judge by the number of stone

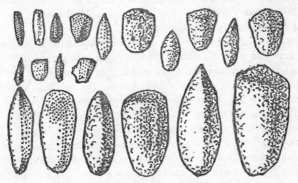

Fig. 6. Late Neolithic axes from Magasa

axes found there, may well have belonged to an artisan who made such tools and was living near his raw materials (Fig. 6).

Cave dwellings and rock shelters of the same period have been found, but are few in number and widely scattered, and were inhabited mainly, I suppose, by shepherds and hunters. One such cave at

Trapeza on the edge of the Lasithi plain was later in the Early Minoan period used as a burial pit. Another cave shelter of the Late Neolithic period was excavated at Miamou[1] in the long fertile valley connecting the Mesara plain with the bay of Lebena, and a third on the far west at Koumaro, where some of the bowls with scalloped or inverted rims recall Late Neolithic types on the mainland. Neolithic sherds have also been recorded from caves at Zakros, Sphoungaras, Skalais, and Hagia Photia in the east, at Mallia and Amnisos on the north coast, at Phaistos, Hagia Triada, and Gortyn in the Mesara, and at another cave on the island of Gavdhos. S. Alexiou excavated part of a Late Neolithic settlement at Katsaba just east of Herakleion.

In addition stone axes (mostly of local stones) have been picked up at various places, but some of these may have belonged to the Early Minoan period. The pottery of the Late Neolithic period has been discussed in detail by Dr Furness. The coarse ware consists chiefly of what she calls 'red wiped ware', and is no longer black grey in colour but usually fired an even brick-red right through, implying the use of a potter's oven. The pottery was less pervious now because of the better firing, so the burnishing of the surface was not necessary and the surface was simply rubbed with a cloth or brush leaving striations clearly visible.

The funnel-necked jars became more common, but the large bowls and stone jars were still normal, and (as in the earlier periods) there is still nothing we can identify as a cooking pot. Roasting and baking may have been done in the embers; but did the Neolithic Cretans never want to boil water or milk, or did they employ 'pot-boilers' for this purpose, as was done in more northerly parts? 'Wiped pottery' like that at Knosos has also been found in other parts of Crete, for example at Trapeza in Lasithi, where it persists as a sub-Neolithic fabric into the Early Minoan period, and constitutes the variety first identified and dubbed 'Trapeza ware' by Pendlebury. The shapes are chiefly large bowls and store jars; large strap handles are normal, but the wishbone type has vanished.

On the fine pottery of this period rippling almost died out. The fabric still resembles that of the fine pottery in the earlier periods, but the improved firing produced a chestnut brown, deep red, or wine colour beneath the surface burnish. Individual sherds may be buff

1. But S. Alexiou considers this to have been only a burial cave; see p. 138.

or light brown or have a red-flashed rim, but the genuine rainbow mottling of the early period was now rare, and the walls of the vases were usually thinner than those of the preceding periods. Spouts appear for the first time, including a bridged form which may be the ancestor of the bridged spouts so popular in the Middle Minoan period. Miniature vases continued to be common and so we find miniature token handles degenerating into incised dots and dashes with or without a small pinched knob.

At Phaistos some miniature vases of this type were discovered together with a clay figure of the squatting steatopygous type, a lump of magnetic iron, and a number of sea shells reminding us of shrines of Minoan date with figures and votive vases and shells; and we may therefore probably regard the deposit as the furniture of a small domestic shrine of the Late Neolithic period.

Incised decoration became less common on the fine ware and also less regular in form. Excised triangles appear occasionally, as on some of the earliest Bronze Age pottery of the Cyclades and the Greek mainland. There are various indications of foreign contacts, implying that the Bronze Age is near. Pierced stone maces like those of Mesopotamia appear for the first time in Crete, though they are still bored by hammering from both sides, not by the straight tubular drill employed during the Bronze Age. The most significant of the new foreign contacts is with Egypt. The late Neolithic levels at Knosos have provided an almost carinated macehead, a small limestone vase hollowed out with a tubular drill, and fragments of stone vases too small to identify but made of the variegated stones which tended to die out in Egypt at the end of the Pre-Dynastic period, all probably actual imports from Egypt.

Stone vases, however, remain in use sometimes for a long period, while the macehead and the small limestone vase are both definitely Proto-dynastic. The inference therefore is that the Late Neolithic period in Crete did not end until some time after the founding of the first dynasty in Egypt, which is now dated about 2900 B.C. by Stock and by most other Egyptologists at or about 3000 B.C., not 3400 B.C. as it was when Evans wrote the first volume of his *The Palace of Minos*.

PLASTIC ART

The people of Crete in prehistoric times never developed monumental sculpture, but they displayed great skill in modelling and carving on a miniature scale. Even in the Early Neolithic I period we find examples of clay statuettes in the form of squatting female figures or of animals. The fragments are too scanty to identify the animals, but if we may judge by later examples they would be the ordinary animals of the farm – cows, sheep, and dogs. The human figurines of the Middle Neolithic period are still all squatting females with the development of the lumbar region and the thighs so large that Evans, followed by Weinberg, called them steatopygous, a technical description of the abnormal development to be found in certain African tribes such as the Hottentots. This impression of steatopygy is given not only by Cretan Neolithic figurines, but also by others of Neolithic date from the mainland of Greece and from Early Bronze Age tombs in the Cyclades. The racial implications of this interpretation, however, are so serious and so strange that I am inclined to follow Hogarth in believing that most of these figurines were intended simply to represent very fat women.[1] Even today the Greeks are apt to equate plumpness with health and vigour, and their ordinary word for thin means powerless. Some of these figurines were relatively naturalistic. The body was modelled with some care, with the breasts, stomach, and rump carefully distinguished, though the heads were often treated much more summarily as a mere cruciform appendage of the body.

Other examples are more schematic in form, though this is perhaps due to clumsiness of execution rather than to deliberate stylization.

Of the naturalistic group of squatting figures the most magnificent specimen, which I would assign to the beginning of the Late Neolithic period, is the splendid figure from Kato Ierapetra now in the Giamalakis collection in Herakleion. It is much larger than any other complete statuette of this period, being 14·5 cm. in height and 9 cm. broad at the base. The figure squats with the left leg crossed over the right, providing the clue to what must have been the posture intended

1. D. G. Hogarth in *Essays in Aegean Archaeology*, 1927, p. 55; R. W. Hutchinson, 'Cretan Neolithic Figurines', *Ipek*, 1938, p. 50.

to be represented on so many figurines of a rougher and more schematic kind from various parts of the Levant in prehistoric times, especially that of a large group of figurines, known as the violin-shaped idols, common in Anatolia and the Cyclades but rare in Crete (though one example in clay, incised in the fashion of the contemporary vases, was found in a Middle Neolithic deposit at Knosos). The Giamalakis Figurine in a red fabric coated with a well-burnished grey slip was far more detailed in its execution. The short arms bent at the elbows, the breasts, the long neck, and the head with its flat triangular cap or coiffure are carefully modelled, and the face, with its aquiline nose, slightly modelled mouth, incised eyes, and back hair, is far superior to that of any other figurine preserved from this period. The fingers and toes are indicated by incisions, and the incised lines on the body seem to represent creases of fat.

Many of the Neolithic figurines and fragments from Knosos were not found in any particular stratigraphic context, but one interesting group consisting of two complete figurines and fragments of two others was found in a Late Neolithic house at Knosos. It is to be remarked that among the examples surviving there are no monsters like those of Mesopotamia and Egypt, no fabulous or even wild animals, but simply the familiar inhabitants of a Cretan farm, the cow, the goat, the dog, and the dove; whether these figurines were intended to be dedications or simply toys we know not, but they were as naturalistic as the potter was able to make them.

The purpose of the female figurines is also open to question. Evans saw in them evidence of the cult of the great mother goddess of Asia Minor; Hogarth saw the figures as similar to the Ushabtis of Egypt, intended to secure the comfort of the owner in the next world. Hogarth's explanation might serve for figurines of the Cycladic type found in tombs, but Cretan Neolithic figurines are found in houses and for these we must prefer Evans's explanation.

CHAPTER 3

The Cretan Peoples, Languages, and Scripts

SIR WILLIAM RIDGEWAY emphasized long ago the dangers of using the word Minoan as if it had a definite ethnic meaning like the word Greek, and I would like, therefore, to make it plain that if I use the terms Minoan people and language I simply mean the people who lived in Crete during the Bronze Age and the language or languages they spoke. We have evidence that at least one non-Hellenic language was spoken in Crete during the Bronze Age, but we have no right to assume that it was necessarily the only one.

Evans, in agreement with the chief linguistic scholars, stressed the number of apparently non-Hellenic places in Greece, including Crete, and in Asia Minor, ending in -ssos, -ndos, or -nda, and -nthos or -ntha, and remarked that such places had often been great cultural centres in the prehistoric period. From Asia Minor we can quote names such as Halicarnassus, Labraunda, Assos, and Perinthus, from the Cyclades Koressos and Prepesinthos, from the mainland of Greece Corinth, Tiryns (accusative case Tiryntha), Mykalessos, and from Crete itself Knosos, Tylisos, Karnassos, and Pyranthos. Platon has recently suggested that the tendency of modern Cretans to omit 'n' before 'th' may have existed in ancient times, and we may compare place names such as Marathon and Skiathos with plant names such as *marathos* and *aspalathos* or household names such as *kyathos* and *kalathos*.

Blegen and Haley discussed this group of names in an important little paper[1] and came to the conclusion that they had been brought to the mainland of Greece by the people who introduced the Early Helladic culture, the first metal users of the mainland. The natural inference is that the similar names we find in Crete were also intro-

1. J. B. Haley and C. W. Blegen, 'The Coming of the Greeks', *American Journal of Archaeology*, 1928, pp. 141–59 (the former discussing the pre-Greek place-names and the latter the prehistoric remains and other distribution).

56

duced early in the Bronze Age by a people with a similar language and a similar culture to that of the Early Helladic variety on the mainland and the Early Cycladic in the Cyclades. It is possible, however, that in Crete some of these names might even date back to Neolithic times, since we have reason for assuming an Anatolian element in the Cretan Neolithic civilization.

The ancient Greeks themselves were quite conscious of the fact that, from the earliest times preserved in folklore, Crete had been occupied by various nations of whom more than one had spoken a 'barbarian', that is a non-Greek, language. A celebrated passage in the ninth book of the *Odyssey* alludes to this mixture of nations: 'And one tongue is mixed with another; there are Achaeans therein, and great-hearted Eteo-Cretans, and Kydonians, and Dorians in their three tribes, and divine Pelasgians.'

The only non-Greek speaking people, the only barbarians in the Greek sense of the word, whom we can identify in Homer's passage are the Eteo-Cretans, who maintained their identity and to some extent their language up to Roman times. The Eteo-Cretan city of Praisos in the east of the island continued to be independent until about 140 B.C., when it was wiped out by a coalition of Hierapytna and Itanos.

There still survive a few fragmentary inscriptions from Praisos, and one from Dreros, written in Greek characters, but in an unfamiliar language which must be Eteo-Cretan. Most scholars regard this language as not belonging to the Indo-European group of languages; but the late Professor Conway argued strongly that it was an Indo-European language possibly related to Venetic, and Kretschmer calls it a mixed speech embodying early Anatolian elements related to Lydian in the east and to Tyrrhenian in the west. It seems likely that this Eteo-Cretan language was spoken during the Bronze Age, but was not necessarily the only language spoken in Crete in those times. The island of Karpathos, east of Crete, also possessed in classical times a survival of an earlier nation, people known as the Eteo-Karpathioi, but it would be very rash to assume that the Eteo-Cretans and Eteo-Karpathians spoke the same language.

Our doubts concerning the language spoken in the great cities of Knosos and Phaistos during the Early and Middle Bronze Age should be resolved when we can read their earlier inscriptions.

The passage in the *Odyssey* might be a later interpolation since Homer does not allude elsewhere in his poem to the Dorians, who appear to have been in western Macedonia at the time of the Trojan war. Was this an anachronism of Homer or his interpolator, or did a small band of Dorians settle in Crete even before the Trojan war? It is clear at least that the main Dorian settlement of Crete cannot have taken place before the latter part of the eleventh century B.C., and Greek traditions placed it one generation after the Dorian occupation of Sparta. What of Homer's other four nations? The Achaeans of whom Homer sings were certainly the Greek inhabitants of the Peloponnese before the coming of the Dorians. Pelasgian may be interpreted in many ways.[1] The Pelasgians of Herodotus's and Thucydides's histories were a small ethnic group in Lemnos and in two cities in Thrace speaking a 'barbarian' language. Many later writers, however, seem to use the word almost in the sense of pre-Hellenic, and even Herodotus almost uses it in this sense when he speaks of the Athenians having been formerly Pelasgians and of their becoming Hellenized later. We may therefore suppose that the Pelasgians of Crete, whoever they were, probably spoke a non-Hellenic language. The Eteo-Cretans, who claimed to be the original inhabitants, continued to speak a non-Hellenic language in eastern Crete up to Hellenistic times or later. They are usually supposed to be descendants of the Minoan people but they might possibly have been of Cretan Neolithic stock. The Kydonians were obviously the people who lived in and round the city of Kydonia and gave their name to it, but were they Greeks or barbarians? In favour of the latter theory is the fact that the people of Polyrrhenia to the south of them once spoke a barbarian tongue, and that Kydas, the legendary founder of Kydonia, was said to be the son of Minos's daughter Akakallis.

RACIAL CHARACTERISTICS OF THE CRETANS

The father of history, Herodotus of Halicarnassus, defined his conception of nationality as depending on common descent, a common

1. The word has been equated with 'Philistines' or with the 'peoples of the sea'; the most ingenious suggestion was that of Walter Leaf, who postulated that it might mean what Welsh meant to a Saxon, namely the neighbouring foreigners.

language, common religious beliefs, and common behaviour. His formula works well enough today, though we might add common economic interests and geographical position, and perhaps unified government. One of these factors alone will not make a nation, but no one is indispensable. England and the U.S.A. are different nations, but Switzerland is emphatically one, despite its three languages and its numerous religious sects.

Was Homer's idea of five nations in Crete true for the pre-historic period, or can we speak of a 'Minoan nation' occupying the whole or most of Crete during the Bronze Age?

Some of the factors required for qualification as a nation were present. Crete was a geographical unity, and though communications between its different valleys were difficult for wheeled traffic, they were easy enough for men and pack animals. The island could be self-supporting and function as an economic unity. We have reason also to believe that certain religious cults were common to various parts of Crete. The most important prerequisites in Herodotus's definition of 'nationality' however, are concerned with a common descent and a common language. Let us examine these in turn.

How far can we speak in Crete of common descent, the first essential according to Herodotus for the formation of a nation? The racial homogeneity of its Neolithic inhabitants must still be a matter of surmise, but it is clear that by the beginning of the Bronze Age the great bulk of the population belonged to what is usually known as the Mediterranean race.[1] The members of this are slender-boned people, of or below medium height, with dark hair and eyes and sallow complexions. Their small skulls are as a rule dolichocephalic or long-headed: that is to say the cranial index, or percentage ratio of the maximum breadth to the maximum length, falls below 75. Such a type is not uncommon round most of the Mediterranean, particularly in southern and central Italy, southern France, the Iberian peninsula, and North Africa. It also occurs in parts of Crete such as Lasithi. The majority of modern Cretans, however, are in the meso-cephalic or medium-headed category, which has cranial indices ranging from 75·0 to 79·9, while most mainland Greeks are today brachycephalic or broad-headed, with indices of or above 80. These

1. A. Sergi, *The Mediterranean Race*, 1901.

conventional limits for dolichocephaly, mesocephaly, and brachy-
cephaly are two units higher when measurements are taken on living
subjects as opposed to skulls.

Early in the Bronze Age a second racial element, the Tauric
('Armenoid'), began to enter Crete. This was taller than the Mediterranean and was brachycephalic. In Greece and the adjacent islands
broad-headed people are known from Neolithic times. Early Bronze
Age human remains from the Cyclades suggest varying degrees of
intermixture between the Tauric, broad-headed type and Mediterranean, long-headed. Thus, while skulls from Syros were on the
whole long-headed with a few broad-headed individuals, the opposite
situation was found in those from Paros, Oliaros (Antiparos), and
Siphnos, and mesocephaly characterized those from Naxos.

Anthropological research into the racial history of Crete has been
hampered by both the scarcity and also the bad state of preservation
of remains from most of the earlier periods. For example, the Neolithic burials at Magasa Skaphidia in the east, at Koumarospilio in the
west, and at Miamou off the Mesara, are too fragmentary to furnish
evidence of physical type, possibly having been disturbed by the
nature of the funeral sacrifices as suggested by Alexiou. Since women
are shorter in height and broader in the skull than men, large series
of well-dated skulls and other bones to which a probable sex can be
assigned are necessary for any sound conclusion. The only material
approaching such requirements so far available is that from British
excavations in eastern Crete in 1901, 1902, and 1903, first studied by
Sir Walter Boyd Dawkins, C. S. Myers, and W. L. H. Duckworth,
and later in part by A. Mosso, F. von Luschan, and J. C. Trevor,
and the skeletons which Hood excavated on the Aylias hill at Knosos
between 1950 and 1955, studied but not yet published by Trevor,
assisted by B. G. Campbell.[1]

According to Trevor, who has recently analysed Duckworth's
detailed measurements, Early Minoan I long bones from a rock-
shelter at Hagios Nikolaos and the Patema ossuary, sufficiently intact
for the statures of their owners to be determined, probably represented twenty-four persons, fifteen males and nine females. The
estimated height of the males is rather short – 162·7 cm. or 5 ft 4 ins.
The Hagios Nikolaos bones previously described as being of pygmy

1. Mr Hood has kindly allowed me to refer to this unpublished evidence.

dimensions seem all to have belonged to women. An Early Neolithic I series of sixteen skulls of adults from the same two sites, together with Boyd Dawkins's skull of a woman from the Epano Zakros cave, has cranial indices of 73·5 for ten supposed males and 74·9 for seven supposed females. No certain broad skulls were included in the figures on which these averages are based, but Duckworth noted that a six-year-old child at Hagios Nikolaos with a premature closure of the sagittal suture had a cranial index of just over 80, and he also omitted the indices of two apparently broad-headed females from his Patema total for that sex because of their unreliable measurements. Early Minoan skulls found elsewhere in Crete are rare. An Early Minoan I or II brain-case from a rock-shelter at Gournia measured by Hawes, was brachycephalic with a cranial index of 81·1. Its dimensions suggest a male sex. Hawes also recorded the index of an unsexed Early Minoan II skull from the large tholos tomb at Hagia Triada as approximately 77·6. Giuseppe Sergi gave indices of 74·4 and 76·2 for two of four more skulls from the same tomb, which are now in the Anthropological Institute of the University of Rome. The third he described as either long-headed or medium-headed, and the fourth as unmeasurable but broad-headed. Trevor, who examined the Hagia Triada skulls in Rome in 1955, considers that Sergi's Early Minoan II specimens are all male.

Hawes's index for an Early Minoan III skull excavated by Xanthoudides at Koumasa is 76·2. This would seem to be the same as the specimen which Max Kiessling has previously described as dolichocephalic and for which Mosso afterwards published an indicial value of 75·8. A photograph suggests that it is likely to have belonged to a male. The average cranial index of five skulls from Xanthoudides's other Mesara tombs, probably not earlier than Early Minoan III or later than Middle Minoan II, falls as low as 72·4, without distinction of sex. Though difficult to interpret for the period as a whole, the craniological data do indicate that, while the Early Minoan period was marked by a predominance of long skulls, a broad-headed minority was also present in Crete as far back as Early Minoan II if not Early Minoan I times. One Early Minoan I Patema man had an index of 79·7, which is on the verge of our broad-skulled proportions, and that of a Hagios Nikolaos woman reached 79·0.

After the exclusion of specimens distorted by earth-pressure, the

Middle Minoan I and II skulls from the two Roussolakkos ossuaries at Palaikastro yield cranial indices of 73·1 for thirty-eight males and 74·0 for fourteen females. Three males and one female are broad-headed. The few Roussolakkos limb-bones of which Duckworth was able to measure the lengths seem to have belonged to six men and three women, the estimated stature of the men being about 166·6 cm. or 5 ft 5½ ins. This apparent increase of height since Early Minoan times is confirmed by the average Trevor has found for eighteen Middle Minoan II and III males from the Aylias hill burials at Knosos, namely 167·9 cm. or 5 ft 6 ins., a value slightly below the figure of 168·5 cm. or almost 5 ft 6½ ins. obtained by D. F. Roberts from Hawes's measurements of nearly 2000 living Cretan men during the first decade of the present century. The cranial indices of the Aylias hill Middle Minoan II and III skulls studied in 1955 are 74·0 for twenty-nine males and 76·2 for eighteen females. Five of these Knosos males and three females are broad-skulled, as is another male skull excavated by Platon at Poros, near Herakleion, and accurately dated to Middle Minoan III B, a female specimen of the same date from this site being medium-headed.

Late Minoan skulls appear to number fewer than twenty, of which about a third can be sexed. Hawes gave an average cranial index for five unsexed specimens of Late Minoan I date from Gournia as 76·5. For two of four Late Minoan II or III crania from the chambered tombs at Hagia Triada, now in Rome, Giuseppe Sergi provided indices of 73·4 and 77·2. One other he stated to be long-headed and the last doubtfully broad-headed. Trevor regards them as those of males but believes that they are too fragmentary or distorted for anything but their general form to be determined. Hawes's statement that the average index of seven Late Minoan III skulls from various sites, none long-skulled but three medium and four broad-headed, is 79·1 does not agree with that calculated from his individual indices for specimens of this data in works published by him, namely a female from the rock-shelter at Aisa Langadha near Gournia, 80·2, and six unsexed skulls, four from Sphoungaras also near Gournia, 77·0, 79·0, 80·3, and 87·6, one from Sarandari, 75·9, and one from a hillside tomb near Knosos, 80·5. With the addition to these of Trevor's value of 72·4 for a male skull, part of an almost complete skeleton excavated by Platon and Huxley at Selopoulo in the Kairatos valley in August

1957 and dated to Late Minoan III B, the Late Minoan average for both sexes combined becomes as high as 79·6.

Tables purporting to show the percentages of various skull-forms for different periods may be misleading where the series are small and have not been sexed. Of the Middle Minoan I and II males from Palaikastro, 71 per cent are long-headed, 21 per cent medium, and 8 per cent broad-headed, while of the Aylias hill Middle Minoan II and III males from Knosos 49 per cent are long-headed, 34 per cent medium, and 17 per cent broad-skulled. If the scanty Late Minoan I evidence points to a mesocephalic trend, which perhaps continued through Late Minoan II, the all but brachycephalic average of the Late Minoan III skulls suggests more than a gradual secular change, in fact the arrival of a new element in the population. Whence did this come? Hawes believed that the modern broad-headed inhabitants of western Crete could be regarded as survivors of the Dorian invaders, and both he and von Luschan agreed that the later Saracens, Venetians, and Turks were unlikely to have had much influence on already established physical types. Since four of the eight late Middle Minoan III skulls belonged to people who were brachycephals, the cultural associations of a broad-headed strain entering Crete at this time would appear to have been Achaean rather than Dorian.

It seems, therefore, even on anthropological grounds that an Anatolian element may well have existed in Crete since Neolithic times. It is true that the squatting Neolithic ladies of Crete can be paralleled by the steatopygous squatting or lying figures of prehistoric Malta, but the parallel must not be pressed too far, since Malta occupied a marginal position in the Mediterranean, partly but never completely isolated, and with cultural connexions with both the western and the eastern Mediterranean. Weinberg is surely right in saying that if we are to seek outside the Aegean for an origin of the seated figurines with legs doubled under them, we must look towards Asia Minor and Syria, and perhaps farther east to northern Mesopotamia or even Iran, and he quotes the figurines from Adalia and Amuq to support this statement.

Did these immigrants from Anatolia come via Syria or did they come down one or other of the series of valleys opening into the Gulf of Iskanderun, a route which might be expected also to bring influences from Mesopotamia? Or if the immigrants came from the Afyon

Karahisar district, did they leave Asia Minor from the Gulf of Adalia or from the coast opposite Rhodes?

This south-western district of Asia Minor is marked by a considerable number of the place names ending in -ssos, -ndos, and -nda which we have noted in Greece and believed to indicate Anatolian influences. This brings us to the second factor demanded by Herodotus in the formation of a nation, the common language.

LANGUAGES AND SCRIPTS

What evidence have we from engraved seals and inscriptions of the languages spoken in Crete during the Bronze Age before the coming of the Mycenaean Greeks?

The rare seals with pictographic designs attributed to the Early Minoan I period are abnormal and not very accurately dated. It is not until the Early Minoan II period that we begin to find engraved seals in stratified deposits at Mochlos and Sphoungaras.

The designs of these seals have an Egyptian air and suggest that they were simply monomarks, signs of ownership, and had no particular hieroglyphic significance. It was, however, from seals of this kind that the Cretans began in the third Early Minoan period to develop a native hieroglyphic script which borrowed some symbols from Egypt but was in the main an independent growth. Many seals of this period, however, still have only one design, the monomark of the owner.

In the Middle Minoan I period, however, we find numerous seals with hieroglyphic inscriptions of several symbols, usually in the form of rather long triangular prisms, or, more rarely, four-sided seals cut in a soft stone, usually steatite. Thus, of a series of forty-nine such seals from the Giamalakis collection recently published by Mme Agni Xenaki-Sakellariou, forty-three were triangular prisms and only six four-sided.

Evans enumerated ninety-one signs in this script, which he termed Hieroglyphic Script A, and distinguished from a later development of it which he termed Hieroglyphic Script B. In both scripts together he identified a hundred and thirty-five signs, of which forty-four signs were peculiar to B, forty-two signs peculiar to A, and the remainder common to both scripts.

The hieroglyphs of class A were pictures easily recognized: a man walking, a man sitting, a ship, an eye, two crossed hands, a jug, a gate, a sistrum (an Egyptian form of rattle), the head of an ox or an ass, an arrow, or a plough. Sometimes we can even recognize animals no longer existing in Crete, such as the wolf and the horned sheep. The representations of ships, though summary, are interesting since they obviously depict sea-going vessels rigged like the Egyptian and Phoenician ships with a great square sail in the centre but, unlike the Egyptian, with an asymmetric hull with high prow at an angle of about 45° but with a low projecting stern. (See Chapter 4.)

Sundwall believed that most of the Cretan hieroglyphs had been derived from Egyptian prototypes and quoted parallels in Egypt for forty-four Cretan hieroglyphs and for nine symbols of the later Linear Script A. Evans, followed by Hall, while admitting that certain symbols were derived from Egypt, considered that the majority were Cretan inventions. The A hieroglyphs were usually executed as silhouettes, though sometimes internal details were carefully rendered; but those of Script B or 'the developed hieroglyphic script', as it is often called, were executed in a more summary fashion, in outlines, already suggesting that a conventionalized linear script would develop out of the old hieroglyphs.

At Knosos the seals with hieroglyphs of class B began in the second Middle Minoan period, and appeared in the following forms: (a) prism seals with three (or more rarely four) sides; (b) round seals with convoluted upper surface; (c) flattened cylinder seals; (d) signets, usually with loop handle for suspension, a form popular among the Hittites of Asia Minor; and (e) lentoid seals. These shapes continue with minor modifications into the third Middle Minoan period, the Middle Minoan II B and III seals being distinguished by increased naturalism of design and often by exquisite cutting, when the stone was hard enough to deserve it. Even many of the steatite seals are finely cut, but the best work usually appears on agates, rock crystals, jasper, and the like.

On the clay inscriptions, however, the designs were becoming less naturalistic and more schematic, a sure sign that they were in many instances ceasing to have ideographic value and were coming to represent sounds, so that the script was developing into a syllabary.

Many of the hieroglyphs shed a light on the culture of the time. The sacred double axe which gave its name to the labyrinth at

Knosos appears also as a hieroglyph and so does the Egyptian hieroglyph for palace.

Another hieroglyph shows a plough with stilt, pole, and share beam (the latter two probably in one piece, as recommended by Hesiod), exactly the same as the one depicted on some early Roman coins of Knosos, and not differing greatly from some ploughs still in use today (Fig. 44).

The clay inscriptions may occur in the following forms: (*a*) stamped on clay sealings of jars; (*b*) on clay labels shaped like a cockle shell with a suspension hole at the top; (*c*) on clay bars with a square section often with a suspension hole at one end; or (*d*) on clay tablets of oblong form. Occasionally the script appears on other objects such as a stone vase or a double axe. The most remarkable instance is a very well-cut line of hieroglyphs of class B on a rough boulder found just outside the Palace at Mallia, conceivably a boundary stone (Fig. 7).

Fig. 7. Hieroglyphic inscription, Mallia

The Phaistos Disk

This hieroglyphic script was succeeded at Knosos about 1700, and at an earlier date at Phaistos, by a Linear Script developed from it, which we know by the name assigned to it by Evans – Linear Script A. But before we discuss the Linear Script we must mention a hieroglyphic inscription of a different kind known as 'the Phaistos disk' (Plate 14*b*), a roughly circular disk of clay impressed on both sides before baking with a hieroglyphic text. It was discovered in a rectangular clay compartment in a room in the north east part of the Palace at Phaistos containing some Middle Minoan III B vases and also a tablet in Linear Script A. Professor Pernier, who published it, compared the fine clay to that of Kamares pottery, and thought that the hieroglyphics, though differing from the normal Cretan forms, might still represent a stage in their development. Mackenzie, however, thought the clay was foreign and Evans considered it might have been manufactured in south-west Asia Minor, stressing the parallels between the hieroglyph of the plumed head with the representations of Philistines on Egyptian monuments, and of the hieroglyph showing a wooden house with Lycian rock-cut tombs imitating wooden structures. The repetition of certain phrases he thought might indicate a metrical refrain, perhaps a hymn to the great goddess who was worshipped alike in Crete and in Asia Minor. He thought that the inscription started at the centre. It was clearly divided into words, but there were some slanting lines of which the significance was open to question (Plate 14b and Fig. 8).

The late Professor Macalister considered that the inscription started at the circumference. He also thought that the succession of words beginning with a plumed head were names of men, and that the large proportions of personal names indicated that the disk was not a hymn, but more probably a legal document with the names of the presiding magistrates, the witnesses, and the date. He proceeded in a less convincing manner to suggest that some of these symbols might have developed into the ordinary Phoenician letters of the tenth century B.C.

Two bold but unconvincing attempts were made in 1931 to translate the disk, by Miss F. M. Stawell, who rendered it as a hymn to Rhea in Greek, and by Mr F. G. Gordon, who translated it into Basque as a hymn to the 'rain lord', whom he identified with the constellation Aquarius.

There are 241 signs in all, arranged in a spiral on the two faces of the disk, and 61 sign groups, separated at irregular intervals by vertical lines which presumably represent the ends of words. The individual symbols are for the most part easily recognizable figures or objects. This fact, coupled with the rather large number of signs, suggests that the script is not yet fully developed syllabic script. Could it be another Cretan hieroglyphic script, either an earlier form or a variant from another part of the island?

Pernier, supported by Pugliese Carratelli, counted the disk as Cretan, and the latter scholar has remarked on the resemblance of certain signs to symbols on the Arkalochori axe and the stone block from Mallia.

Myres, Pendlebury, and Bossert all followed Evans in regarding

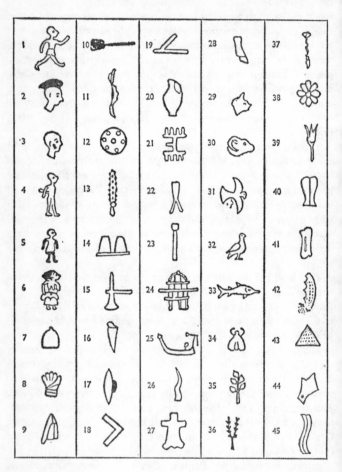

Fig. 8. Signs from the Phaistos Disk

the disk as an import from Anatolia. Dow's objection, that the disk was a fragile object to be exported so far, seems weak. Actually the disk is rather a solid object, much more so than the Kamares cups exported from Crete to Byblos and Ugarit, and it was probably an isolated gift or piece of plunder, not the Minoan equivalent of 'a present from Blackpool'. Different scripts of a pictographic character might have existed simultaneously in Crete. The solid argument, however, for assuming that the disk was of foreign manufacture lies in the presence of such exotic symbols as the Lycian house on piles, the lady with the very un-Minoan attire and figure, and the man with the feathered headdress.

At Phaistos an inscription in such an undeveloped syllabary was an anachronism in the seventeenth century B.C., since Levi's recent excavations have now revealed to us the surprising fact that the script we know as Linear Script A was already forming there, perhaps a couple of hundred years before the disk was placed there, and long before Script A was in use at Knosos.

The late Dr Paul Kretschmer discussed the punctuation of the Phaistos disk, and its relationship, if any, to the punctuation used in Etrusco-Venetic and late Greek inscriptions in diphthongs on the one hand, and the dots employed to modify consonants in Phoenician and other Semitic scripts on the other.

Marinatos has suggested that the late survival of hieroglyphs in Crete, such as those of the Arkalochori axe, the Mallia stone, and the Phaistos disk, might be explained by their use as a sacred script (as happened in Egypt) long after linear characters had been employed for secular purposes. This might be true of the axe and the stone in question, but the Anatolian features of the disk require more explanation. Who were the people with the feathered headdress whom Kretschmer connected with the Illyrians and with the Venetic name Fremaistina? (We may recall Conway's parallels between the Venetic and Eteo-Cretan languages.)[1] A feather headdress of this kind was worn by some of the peoples who joined the sea raid on Egypt in 1223 B.C., not only by the Philistines, but also by the Zakkarai and the Danuna. In classical times this headdress was regarded as so characteristic of the Carians of western Asia Minor that the Persians

1. P. Kretschmer, *Minos*, op. cit.; R. J. Conway, *Annual of the British School at Athens*, 1902, p. 125.

called them *Karka* (cocks), which is presumably the meaning of the word 'Carian'. Kretschmer also identified one of the signs on the Phaistos disk as the Carian round shield with the central handgrip which, according to Herodotus, was one of the military innovations of the Carians along with helmet crests and blazons on their shields. Herodotus also states in the same passage that the Carians, then termed Leleges, were subject to Minos, paying no tribute but providing feudal levies for his navy. Since the group of helmet and shield occurs thirteen times on the Phaistos disk, Kretschmer suggested that we have the names of thirteen soldiers, that Evans's suggestion that the disk was in a metrical form is therefore unlikely, but that it might be a Carian document. The later Carian script of the seventh and sixth centuries B.C. was partly syllabic, partly vocalized, and also had a slanting line dividing the words.

This mingling of Carian and Phoenician fashions of writing might have taken place in some Ionian colony such as Miletus, which claimed to have been founded by Cretans from Milatos before it received its Ionian settlers, and Kretschmer remarks that Priene once bore the name Kadme and claimed to have been founded by pre-Boeotian Cadmeans from Boeotia.

Linear Script A

By 1600 B.C., however, Linear Script A must have been employed by the priestly scribes at least over a large part of Crete, though older systems lingered in some parts and the mass of the population were probably illiterate. The list of sites where inscriptions in this script have been found as given by Pugliese Carratelli contained 219 inscriptions of which 186 texts and 86 scalings were found at Hagia Triada. To these must be added the Linear Script A inscriptions recently found at Phaistos. The inscription on the door jamb of the Tholos tomb I opened at Knosos in 1938 is intermediate between Scripts A and B. It should be remarked that tablets in Script A (Fig. 9) are very rare except at Hagia Triada, most of the other writing in Script A being in the form of short dedications on steatite lamps or libation tables.

The most westerly example was the inscription on a fragment of a steatite vase picked up by Pendlebury in the ruins of a Middle Minoan III house later excavated by Marinatos at Apodhoulou.

Evans noted resemblances between Linear Script A signs and some signs in the syllabary employed in Cyprus in archaic and classical times, and suggested the derivation of the latter from Linear Script A. Bennett admits this as a possibility but an unproven one. Of the classical Cypriot script, the signs for ka, ko, ku, lo, mo, mu, pa, pe, pi, po, pu, sa, se, si, su, te, ti, to, tu, ve, xe, and zo, and perhaps also la, li, na, and ra have possible prototypes in Linear Script B.[1]

The recent excavations of Levi at Phaistos, however, have completely upset the tidy evolution of Minoan scripts presented by Evans. In a general sense Evans's theory may still be defended as sound: probably hieroglyphic B did develop from A, and Linear A did develop from hieroglyphic B, but there was more overlapping of the systems than we dreamed of a few years ago. We can no longer say that the Cretans only employed hieroglyphic writing till the end of the Middle Minoan II period and that Linear Script A was invented in the Middle Minoan III A period.

At Phaistos Levi found clay tablets and labels with symbols in transitions to Linear Script A in the earliest deposits of rooms LI and XXVIII, suggesting that that script must have been in use there before 1850 B.C. at the latest.

The natural inference is that Linear Script A was an invention of the Palace scribes at Phaistos and was not in general use in northern Crete till a hundred, perhaps a hundred and fifty, years later. The objection to this very obvious theory, the scarcity of tablets in this script at Phaistos, is weaker than it appears to be. The presence of so many Linear Script B tablets at Knosos and Pylos is perhaps simply due to their being accidentally baked in a palace fire, and where no such conflagration

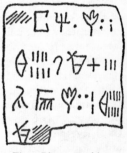

Fig. 9. Linear A tablet

took place the disintegration of such tablets was likely to be rapid.

If Knosos lagged behind Phaistos in the adoption of Linear Script A it appears that Mallia lagged further and was still employing the

1. But usually with syllabic values differing from those postulated by Ventris and Chadwick for the analogous signs in Script B.

later hieroglyphic system in Middle Minoan III A, but with numerals adopted from the Linear Script A then current at Knosos. The inhabitants of Mallia did finally adopt Linear Script A in the Middle Minoan III B period and continued to use it during the Late Minoan II period, but betrayed some influence from Linear Script B in that they used long thin tablets instead of the almost square tablets we associate with Linear Script A elsewhere. Indeed three of the Linear Script A tablets from Mallia were found in a deposit dated to the Late Minoan III period, so that the use of this script would appear to have continued on to the fourteenth century B.C. if not later.

The existing tablets seem to consist almost entirely of business documents or accounts. Many tablets begin with a single sign group, probably denoting the principal person concerned, followed by one termed 'the transaction sign', indicating the nature of the business, and by a series of signs followed by numbers, indicating either individual commodities in a single consignment or individual contributions (whether of persons or places) to a single transaction, referred to as the subsidiaries. The whole list may be followed by a total sign group followed by a numeral.

Myres quotes some Babylonian wage tablets as a parallel, though on these the name of 'the principal' and his errand come last. It is unfortunate that our only surviving documents seem to be accounts. Marinatos is probably right in saying that Linear Script A was invented for writing in ink or paint, not on clay,[1] for which the Mesopotamian cuneiform is far more suitable. It cannot be suggested that the Cretans had not thought of cuneiform since they were in regular communication at that time with Byblos and Ras Shamra, where cuneiform writing was normal. Marinatos notes that many of the clay sealings from Crete have traces of thin threads which appear to have been the letters of the papyrus documents to which the seal had been applied, and he remarks that the same signet had been used to seal letters at Sklavokambos in central Crete, at Hagia Triada in the Mesara, and at Gournia and Zakros in the east, implying widespread correspondence between different parts of Crete. The thin threads on the

1. Clay, of course, is a much cheaper and easier material to obtain, but the use of papyrus seems, as Marinatos suggests, to be implied by the type of the symbols and the thread marks of some of the sealings.

sealings implied that they were affixed to letters, not to heavy packages.[1]

The two surviving inscriptions written in ink on vases Marinatos would explain as incantations against evil spirits like those on Babylonian bowls.[2]

Fifty-four of the Linear A signs were used also in the Linear B Script, and it is a reasonable though not an inevitable assumption that most of these had the same phonetic values in both scripts. C. H. Gordon has recently used Ventris's transliterations for the Script B symbols (discussed on page 79) to provide a basis for transliterating and even translating Linear Script A. Hagia Triada tablet 31 has pictograms of various vessels with names in the Linear Script A, compared by Gordon to words in the cuneiform texts from Ugarit. Thus he compares Cretan SU-PU and KA-RO-PA to Ugaritic SP and Karpan and Cretan YA-MA-NA to Ugaritic Yaman in a passage referring to a Kaphtorian (Keftiuian) (see p. 108) God of craftsmanship.

Hagia Triada tablet 88 has A-PU followed by a pictogram for MAN + KA and may represent some sort of worker. Gordon cites Ugaritic APY = baker. Similarly A-DU-SI-SI on Hagia Triada 85 he interprets as perhaps = ADON-SISI = owners of horses. Other words he compares to Hebrew and Akkadian forms. Eleven of the nineteen identifications suggested by Gordon are Semitic, four Kaphtorian, three east Mediterranean, and one KU-ZU (compared to Ugaritic KZY = groom) of doubtful derivation.

Gordon concludes: 'While these notes tend to relate the language of Linear A to Semitic it is not my intention to oversimplify a highly complex situation. The east Mediterranean was already Levantinized by Linear A times, so that the interpenetration of cultures in the area had created a considerable east Mediterranean vocabulary that crossed linguistic boundaries. Often enough words in this vocabulary cannot yet be pinned down to any specific linguistic origin.' This solution is plausible but more speculative than that of Ventris. If the latter is wrong the former author is also; but Ventris could be right and Gordon still be wrong.

1. S. Marinatos, *Minos*, 1951, p. 39.
2. *British Museum Guide to the Babylonian and Assyrian Antiquities*, 1922, pp. 191–4; the examples in the British Museum are Mandäitic, but the practice seems to date back to late Babylonian times.

Linear Script B

At Knosos, but at no other site in Crete, Linear Script A was supplanted about 1450 B.C. by another, which Evans, who first discovered and identified it, christened Linear Script B.[1] This new script contained about seventy phonetic signs adopted from the Script A series and dropped another dozen of the A signs, but supplemented these by ten new phonetic signs, and by six or seven rebus signs for more syllables than one, expressed in sign groups, and by new pictorial signs for certain commodities (Fig. 10). Some fifty sign groups resemble Script A groups, but only ten are identical. The question arises: were the two scripts intended to transcribe the same language?

The signs are now always written from left to right, usually on long narrow clay tablets, sometimes termed palm-leaf tablets because of their shape. Occasionally a subsidiary group is written sign by sign between the stems of the principal signs, either to save space or perhaps to amplify or remedy an omission.

In the second volume of *Scripta Minoa* Myres suggested that 'the larger number of signs in Script B does not indicate a different language but rather a more refined distinction between sounds; it is the converse of the presumed development of the late Cypriot script from Minoan writing by elimination of similar signs for labials, gutturals, and so forth.' The total number of phonetic signs in Script B is not so large as is required for the syllabic equivalent of five vowels and the usual consonants b, p, f, v; k, g, ch; d, t, th, l, m, n, r; s, z, sh ($5 \times 17 = 85$), and this may account for the rare rebus signs already noted.

In *Scripta Minoa*, 1722 texts in Linear Script B were enumerated by Evans and Myres, and 1000 short ones were added by Bennett, but later joins will doubtless reduce this number. Similarly the tablets found at Pylos in 1939 were reported as 621 but later reduced by joins to 566. In 1952 another 352 tablets were reported from Pylos and thirty-eight tablets and one inscribed vase from Mycenae. Bennett reckoned that at least thirty scribes had been employed at Pylos and at least six on the Mycenaean tablets.

Up to 1950 most scholars had believed Linear Scripts A and B to have been written in the same language, a pre-Hellenic one, but after

1. See note on page 90.

74

Blegen's discovery (see page 85) it became obvious that there was at least a possibility that Linear Script B was a Greek script, since it had only been found in one part of Crete, whereas it had been found at several sites on the mainland. Knosos, however, was still the site with the greatest number of tablets, and appeared to have used the script over a hundred years before the mainland.

All scholars agreed that the number of signs in Linear Script B was too few for them to be purely ideographic and too numerous to be purely alphabetic, and that it was therefore probably a largely syllabic alphabet, without precluding the idea of certain signs having ideographic values.

Various attempts were made to translate Script B texts into Greek (Miss Stawell, Persson, and Mylonas) or Basque (F. G. Gordon) or to a purely imaginary Anatolian language by Hrozny, but none of these was convincing. A more recent attempt by B. G. Nuño to relate the Cretan texts to the Hurrian language is also unconvincing.

The general statement by Myres has, however, to be reviewed in relation to the recent finds from Pylos and Mycenae, of which the latter came too late even to be referred to in *Scripta Minoa* Vol. II, and the former, though mentioned, had not been adequately studied in relation to the researches of Ventris and other scholars.[1]

The Knosian tablets were examined and classified by their discoverer Evans who refrained from any attempt at translation, but whose monumental work in *Scripta Minoa* Vol. I laid a sure foundation for future research. The second volume dealing with Linear Script B was edited and produced after his death by Sir John Myres with such loving care and loyalty to his friend that his own very considerable share in the work is largely obscured. Much independent work on Linear Script B has also been carried out by other scholars such as Sundwall, Alice Kober, Emmett Bennett, Ventris, and Chadwick, and the whole outlook with regard to this script was changed by Blegen's discovery at Pylos in Messenia of a large hoard of Script B tablets followed later by Wace's discovery of other tablets at Mycenae, and by Ventris's work on the Linear B Script.

Bennett classified the Pylos tablets as follows:

Signs used in sign groups Probably chiefly phonetic and perhaps

1. See the bibliography compiled by M. Ventris and J. Chadwick, *Documents in Mycenaean Greek*, p. 428.

syllabic signs, though some might be determinatives of ideograms. The sign groups presumably represent names or other words.

Ideographic signs Always associated with numbers, and so representing the things numbered or measured.

Numerals, punctuations, and other marks The numerals had already been identified by Evans.

The repertory of the signs on the Pylos tablets is very nearly the same as that of the Script B tablets at Knosos, so that there can be no reasonable doubt that they were written in the same language.

Ventris's Solution of the Linear B Script

The first real step towards the decipherment of Linear Script B was provided by Dr Alice Kober who compared a series of triplets differing only in their final syllables and which she believed to be evidence of declension of nouns.

Ventris started his analysis of the tablets on the following assumptions: (*a*) most of the tablets were inventories, receipts, or accounts; (*b*) the commodities were listed by ideograms followed by names, words, and sentences written phonetically; (*c*) the commodities or persons could be recognized by their ideograms (men, women, chariots, wheels, etc.), or by their grouping (horses, cattle, etc.), or by the way they were measured; (*d*) there are eighty-eight linear signs in Script B at Knosos and many recur with little variation at Pylos and Mycenae, and also probably at Thebes and other mainland sites; (*e*) the signs were from a syllabary similar in principle to that used later in Cyprus; (*f*) signs can be classified as frequent, average, or infrequent and sometimes as predominantly initial or final; (*g*) the language is identical in all inscriptions of Linear Script B and shows inflexion for two genders, three cases, and two numbers of the noun and adjective; (*h*) many words exhibit a vowel variation in the last syllable.

A comparison of individual sign groups suggested that they might be grouped into: (*a*) place-names and names of buildings or departments; (*b*) personal names of men and women; (*c*) names of trades and professions; (*d*) general words describing commodities and their circumstances. One syllabic sign attached to the second word in a pair appeared to mean 'and' and to correspond to the Greek enclitic *-te* or the Latin *-que*, and was transliterated by Ventris first as *-pe* and later as *-qe*. This, preceded by another syllable, also appeared in pairs with different words and presumably meant 'either' and 'or' or alternatively 'neither' and 'nor'. Ventris transliterated the latter words as '*ouqe*' – '*ouqe*'.

The syllable for '*to*' had been suggested by Evans when he identified the word that meant 'total' and Cowley had suggested the symbol for '*qo*' when he identified the words for 'boy' and 'girl'. There were other couplets also which varied only in their last syllable and probably represented masculine and feminine forms of the same word. The syllabic symbol for '*a*' based on its relative frequency as an initial, had been suggested by Ktistopoulos and Dr Kober.

With the aid of these few symbols, Ventris proceeded to transliterate Dr Kober's series of triplets into the names of five well-known Cretan cities: Amnisos, Knosos, Tylisos, Phaistos, Lyktos.

A-mi-ni-so   Ko-no-so   Tu-ri-so   Pa-i-to   Ru-ki-to
A-mi-ni-si-yo   Ko-no-si-yo   Tu-ri-si-yo   Pa-i-ti-yo   Ru-ki-ti-yo
A-mi-ni-si-ya   Ko-no-si-ya   Tu-ri-si-ya   Pa-i-ti-ya   Ru-ki-ti-ya

Even the words quoted above illustrated the symbols for a, ki, ko, mi, ni, no, qe, ou, pa, ri, si, so, ti, to, tu, ya, and yo. The last two are written 'ja' and 'jo' by Ventris, but I have preferred to use 'y' as representing better the normal English pronunciation. On these foundations Ventris built up a grid which enabled him to translate most of the documents he tested into an archaic form of Greek which he calls Mycenaean and which resembles in many ways the dialect of the Homeric poems (Fig. 10). The early form of Ventris's grid, prior to the decipherment of the tablets, is given in Fig. 3 of *Documents in Mycenaean Greek* by Ventris and Chadwick.

The case endings of Homeric nouns afforded clues for the identification of certain vowels (provided that the language really was Greek). Thus personal and also professional names, such as *kerameús*, a potter, were apt to end in *-eus* in the nominative singular, *-ei* in the dative singular, *-eos* for an original *ewos* in the genitive singular, and *-eis* (for an original *ewes*) in the nominative plural. Nouns with a nominative in *-os* had a genitive ending in *-oio* (for an original *-owo*).

The final syllables of personal names or those that appeared likely to be descriptions of professions thus provided Ventris with the following syllables, e, we, wo, yo, etc., and it was possible to apply cross-checks: for example, to ascertain whether the symbol used for

WO in KE-RA-ME-WO was the same as that employed in KO-WO, where there were independent reasons for the assumption of the syllabic values. The evidence was cumulative so that even Ventris, most modest and scrupulously conscientious scholar that he was, was impelled to declare 'if the tablets are written in Greek they can hardly be explained otherwise than we have proposed; but if they are not, their language is probably, in the existing circumstances, unknowable.'

Ventris and Chadwick therefore compiled an experimental grid for the syllabic values of the signs, the horizontal lines consisting of the same consonants with different vowels while the vertical lines were comprised of different consonants followed by the same vowel (Fig. 10).

The results seemed most encouraging. The values assigned produced a list of intelligible Greek trade-names and place-names corresponding to famous ancient sites in Crete. To achieve this result, however, Ventris was obliged to formulate certain rules for the operation of his grid and to make the following assumptions:

(1) The syllabary differentiated five vowels A, E, I, O, U, but was indifferent as to their length.

(2) The second component of diphthongs in U was regularly indicated.

(3) The second letter of diphthongs in I was generally omitted except before another vowel and in the initial sign. (Where 'i' is added to endings in 'ai' or 'oi' we should probably count the syllables as 'ais' or 'ois'.)

(4) Vowels following I generally are indicated by the semi-vowel glide J,[1] those following U by W.[2]

(5) Apart from the semi-consonants J [my Y] and W the syllabary differentiates at least ten consonants D, K, M, N, P, Q, R (=L), S, T, and Z but does not indicate double consonants.

(6) There is no mark for the aspirate nor any differentiation of aspirated consonants.

(7) L, M, N, R, and S are omitted when final or when preceding another consonant.

(8) Initial S and W are apparently omitted before a consonant.

1. The German J which I have translated by Y.

2. Corresponding to the letter digamma (F), which appears in some archaic inscriptions but was gradually eliminated from the classical Greek alphabet.

Consonant	Vowel A	1	Vowel E	2	Vowel. I	3	Vowel O	4	Vowel U	5
(H-)	A, AI		E		I		O		U	
D-	DA		DE		DI		DO		DU	
J-	JA		JE				JO			
K- G- CH-	KA		KE, KWE		KI		KO		KU	
M-	MA		ME		MI		MO			
N-	NA, NWA?		NE, NEKO?		NI		NO		NU	
P- B- PH-	PA		PE, PTE		PI		PO		PU	
QU- GU-			QE		QI		QO			
R- L-	RA, RJA		RE		RI		RO, RJO		RU	
S-	SA		SE		SI		SO		SU	
T- TH-	TA, TJA?		TE		TI		TO		TU	
W-	WA		WE		WI		WO			
Z-			ZE				ZO		ZU	

Fig. 10. Ventris's grid for Linear B

(9) The consonant group NW is written NU-W; R before W is more often omitted.

(10) All stop consonants which directly precede another consonant are written with the vowel of the succeeding consonant. Thus KU-RU-SU for KHRYSOS.

Now several of these rules seem justified by the nature of a syllabary, and others, such as the dropping of initial W or the equation of L and R, by later Greek usages, but I must confess that I am troubled by rule 7, which allows so many variants and so greatly detracts from the apparent success of Ventris's method in producing so many intelligible Greek words. Thus under Ventris's system the same three letters can be used to transliterate Tokeus and Stoicheus and the same four letters to transliterate Polyphontes and Polybotes (in the genitive case).

Most classical scholars have accepted Ventris's system, though Bennett has been cautious, and even Ventris himself has been far more modest in his claims than some of his supporters. The arguments for and against Ventris's system have been summed up by Nicholas Platon in *Kretika Chronika*[1] as follows:

Arguments in Favour of Ventris

A. Recognition of characteristic categories of words.

(1) Place-names in appropriate contexts, including Knosos, Phaistos, Amnisos, Lyktos, and Tylisos on the Knosian tablets, and frequent mention of Pylos on the Pylian tablets.

(2) Recognition of Greek personal names such as Warnataios, Amaryntas, Antanor, Theseus, Eudamos, and names of Hellenic deities.

(3) Names of persons and professions with Greek endings.

(4) Names of materials and manufactured goods.

(5) Special and national epithets both male and female.

(6) Active, middle, and passive participles.

(7) Archaic forms of words.

B. Recognition of characteristic objects.

(1) A tablet from Pylos, published by Blegen, with the words for

1. In a joint review of recent articles by Ventris, Chadwick, and Blegen, in *Kretika Chronika*, April 1954, p. 143.

two tripods and one tripod accompanied by the ideograms, pictures of tripods followed by the figures for two and one, and the same for two-handled cups; also forms apparently meaning vases with four or three lugs or without lugs accompanied by the appropriate ideograms.

(2) A tablet from Pylos referring to rowers going to Pleuron.

(3) A tablet from Pylos enumerating *dorkeiai*, whatever they may be, and stating whether their fathers and mothers were slaves or not.

(4) A tablet from Pylos referring to coppersmiths in work or unemployed.

(5) A tablet referring to agricultural produce defining what belonged to the people, what to the temple, and what to the king.

(6) A Pylian text referring to a shepherd grazing sheep on the property of a certain person.

(7) A tablet enumerating payment by different classes for copper for the manufacture of weapons.

(8) A description of chariots and their parts.

(9) A string of names of Greek deities including Hera, Zeus, Hermes, and Poseidon and, best of all, a Knosian text apparently referring to a dedication of honey to Eileithyia in Amnisos.

C. Conclusions concerning the language. The language betrays the proper relationship to the Homeric dialect and to the Arcadian Cypriot dialect that one might expect of the Achaeans at this period, together with a considerable number of pre-Hellenic elements, and is still in an undeveloped state.

D. More general conclusions on the community and the state, its religious and historical inferences. The three chief estates of the realm are king, priests, and people. The professions are more developed and specialized than one might expect, certainly more so than in the Homeric poems.[1] The Achaeans have established a dynasty at Knosos from 1450 B.C. approximately, with Minoan subjects and with free intercourse with the mainland, though there is as yet no evidence for intercourse with foreign powers.

1. Ventris's picture of Mycenaean society recalls those of contemporary cultures in the Levant, but the simplification of this society as presented in the Homeric poems is far exceeded by the simplification of Roman life presented in the *Nibelungenlied*.

Arguments against Ventris

A. The relationship of Linear Script B to Linear Script A. Script B has fifty signs, and many combinations, in common with Script A, suggesting that the same names and words existed in both and that they had a common language. If so, and if B is in Greek, then the people in the older palaces of Phaistos and Mallia spoke Greek. (But we do not know for certain that they did not speak Greek in Middle Minoan cities.)

B. The relationships between Cretan and Cypriot scripts. The Cypro-Minoan script is usually derived from the Minoan, and from the former was derived the Cypriot syllabary of classical times. If so, however, it is strange that there should be no correspondence between the sounds of the Minoan script and those of the Cypriot syllabary.[1]

C. Cultural difficulties of accepting Greek as the language of the tablets of Script B. If Greeks were responsible for the Late Minoan II culture how can we explain: (a) the unbroken development of Late Minoan II art from that of Late Minoan I B; (b) the appearance in it of characteristically Cretan elements especially in architecture and religion; (c) the lack of evidence of destruction in 1450, when the Achaeans are supposed to have occupied Knosos, compared with the ample proof of total destruction in 1400 B.C.; (d) the fact that so many towns and flourishing districts in Crete were abandoned in 1500, and that although the other sites continued their Late Minoan I culture till 1400, there are no signs of conflict with the Achaeans at Knosos?

D. Imperfect system of the Script. The system is more ambiguous than any other known in the great centres of civilization. Owing to the omission of so many medial consonants and *iotas* in diphthongs, small words can sometimes be read in about fifteen different ways. If final s, n, and r were regularly omitted in Linear Script B how did they come to be represented in the Cypriot script? The exchange of l or r at such an early date is peculiar.[2]

1. The sounds of the Cypriot syllabary are established by inscriptions written both in the Greek alphabet and in the syllabary; J. F. Daniel (*American Journal of Archaeology*, 1941, p. 249) derived the Cypro-Minoan signs from Linear Script A.

2. Not so peculiar; they are sometimes confused in modern Greek, and Ancient Egyptian used one sign for both sounds.

E. The basis of the arrangement of signs on the grid is unreliable. The grid is based on the arrangement of syllables with the same vowels and different consonants, or with the same consonants but different vowels; but this depends on equations which are unreliable, some of the differences being due perhaps to different words rather than to changes in number or gender.

F. The first recognition of the phonetic values of the syllables pa, ma, re, po, and ro is unreliable. Thus on the tablet Py An 42 the object of the *dorkeion* is not clear, and so we cannot trust the *pater, mater* interpretation of it, nor can we trust the '*poro = polo* = horse' of the horse tablet Knosos 895, since only two of the horse ideograms have *poro* in front of them. The determined values for syllables are sixty-five and the undetermined twenty-three; moreover the latter include mu and su, syllables which occur very frequently in Greek.

G. The large number of unintelligible tablets. Platon attempted without success to read eighty tablets for which Ventris had found no satisfactory translation, and found difficulties and ambiguities in others which Ventris had translated. Sponsors of rival systems, such as Hrozny, had also failed to translate many documents.[1] Certain phrases with few syllables and no proper names fail to provide names of objects, though in these instances the possible variants are few.

H. Danger of *petitio principi*. We must not enthuse over the number of names ending in *-eus* since it was assumed at first that this ending would be common, nor at names like Knosos and Amnisos, and the same danger exists for 'the four-footed animal' in the 'shepherd' tables.

I. The purely hypothetical character of the list of subjects. The identification of the subjects depends on (a) that there is no mistake in the sound values accepted; (b) that the transcriptions of the words are those stated (since we have to allow for omissions and corrections); (c) whether the new words and strange forms are as suggested by the translator or are errors; (d) whether the suggested interpretation can be established by other texts.

1. The previous systems of Hrozny and others, as Platon would admit, are marred by many other defects absent from Ventris's system.

J. Anomalies of dialect. The dialect, according to Ventris's readings, has some rather strange features: unexpected Doricisms; words with an etymology obviously different from that recognized by scholars; late forms; some very improbable words and forms; the absence of the digamma where you might expect it and its unexpected appearance in other words; no difference between the dialect of Pylos and that of Knosos, though the inscriptions of the latter site were two centuries earlier and the site was presumably inhabited by a proletariat speaking a neo-Hellenic language.

Platon ends his review with the statement that, while he thinks these objections should be given due weight, he does not wish to belittle the very real achievement of Ventris's work and the hope it gives of a satisfactory translation of the Bronze Age tablets. In a tribute to Ventris written after his death Platon later expressed his conviction that Ventris's system was sound.[1]

In general, scholars agree on the validity of Ventris's system, though the variants permitted by it leave ample room for corrections and amplifications. The most compelling argument is the agreement with the grid values of the sounds implied by the pictograms on the vase tablet (Fig. 11).

It was emphasized by Evans that Minoan documents were likely to be only accounts and business records, and were not likely to give us any literature. This limited literacy devoted to one purpose only has been defined by Dow as 'special literacy'. 'Literacy arrived tightly associated with practical bread and butter. Created for these purposes it was all too adequate for them, writing remained specialized and ossified.' He suggests, however, that this designation may have been a blessing in disguise, that it may have fostered the oral tradition of the heroic lays that led up to the Homeric poems, and have saved the Greeks from the embarrassment of the persistence into classical times of an awkward and inadequate script, such as happened in Cyprus and even in Egypt.

A sober but favourable review of Ventris's work has been given by S. E. Mann,[2] who welcomes the rediscovery of the Mycenaean

1. N. Platon, 'Michael George Francis Ventris', *Kretika Chronika*, 1956, pp. 317-20.
2. S. E. Mann, 'Mycenaean and Indo-European', *Man*, February, 1956, No. 26.

Fig. 11. Tripod tablet from Pylos

TI RI PO DE / τι πο δε / tripod AI KE U / Αι γε υς / Aigeus KE RE SI JO / κ ρη σι ο / of Cretan WE KE / Fεργ ες / work TI RI PO / τι ρι πος / tripod 2 E ME / ? ? / PO DE / ποδε / foot OW O WE / ? ? TI RI O WE E / τ ρι ο Fε ε / threehandled TI RI PO / τι ριπος / tripod 1 KE RE SI JO / κ ρη σι ο / of Cretan WE KE A PU KA U ME / Fεργ ες α πυ κα υ με / work (burnt?)

KE RE A / στε λε α / (legs?)

QE TO / ? ? ME ZO E / μει ζο ε / large DI PA / δε πα / cup 2 TI RI O WE E / τ ρι ο Fε ε / threehandled DI PA / δι πα / cup 2 MEWIJO / μει Fι ο / small QE TO RO WE / ϙε το ρο Fες / fourhandled 2

QE TO / ? ? ME ZO E / μει ζο ε / large DI PA / δι πα / cup 3 WE KE / Fεργ ες / work KE RE SI JO / κ ρη σι ο / of Cretan QE TO RO WE / ϙε το ρο Fες / fourhandled ME ZO E / μει ζο ε / large DI PA / δι πα / cup 3

TI RI PO DE / τι πο δε / tripod AI KE U / Αι γε υς / Aigeus KE RE SI JO / κ ρη σι ο / of Cretan WE KE / Fεργ ες / work

QE TO / ? ? ME ZO E / μει ζο ε / large DI PA / δι πα / cup 3

DI PA / δε πα / cup MEWIJO / μει Fι ο / small TI RI JO WE / τ ρι ο Fες / threehandled

DI PA / δε πα / cup MEWIJO / μει Fι ο / small QE TO RO WE / ϙε το ρο Fες / fourhandled

DI PA / δε πα / cup MEWIJO / μει Fι ο / small A NO WE / ανοFες / handleless language in the following early characteristics: (a) the w phoneme; (b) Indo-European ā as in Doric and old Attic; (c) intervocalic yod (like the English 'y'), and (d) the labial triad (π, β, ψ) as distinct from the labio-velar group (represented by Q).[1] The unfortunate disappearance of so many medial consonants (if the transliterations are accepted) must, he says, be due to the phonetic poverty of the 'Eteo-Cretan' language. I should prefer to say 'pre-Hellenic' myself, since the few Eteo-Cretan inscriptions preserved seem to have almost a superfluity of internal consonants. 'As to the older language,' he continued, 'the values discovered in Linear B ("Mycenaean") have been applied to the older Linear A inscriptions ("Eteo-Cretan" dated tentatively about 1500 B.C.) but the resulting jumble of words cannot be interpreted, and its links, if any, with other Mediterranean languages cannot be established. The Ibero-Caucasian theorists will no doubt study it with interest.'[2] He concludes that, despite the numerous 'pitfalls and ambiguities', 'Mycenaean will in course of time supply the answer to many of our urgent queries'; and in a later review, though critizing the phonology, states that 'the work of Ventris and his able ally Chadwick rests on virtual certainty'.

A violent attack on the Ventris–Chadwick system has been delivered by A. J. Beattie. It is impossible to do justice here either to his arguments or the contrary arguments, but a brief summary must be given of his position.[3]

He thinks that the degree of conjecture demanded in the formation is higher than Ventris realized. The evidence for assuming the final values of the -eus -ewos declension is 'insufficient'. 'The intelligibility of the documents seems to decrease as their length increases.' ... 'There must be a limit to the number of phonemic differences that can be left. Otherwise the script will become too inexact to be of any use. So in Greek, if you do not show separately the five cardinal vowels and note the -i and -u series of diphthongs you run the gravest

1. For the suggested Mycenaean phonology see Ventris and Chadwick, *Documents in Mycenaean Greek*, p. 76 ff. (especially pp. 81, 82).

2. Compare P. K. Kretschmer, 'Die Vorgriechischen Sprach- und Volkschichten', *Glotta*, 1943, pp. 84–218, and O. J. L. Szemereny, *Classical Review*, March 1958, p. 57.

3. A. J. Beattie, 'Mr Ventris's Decipherment of the Minoan Linear B Script', *Journal of Hellenic Studies*, 1956, pp. 1–17; replied to by J. Chadwick, in 'Minoan Linear B, A Reply', *Journal of Hellenic Studies*, 1957, p. 202.

risk of being misunderstood. If you do not write u and s and i you destroy the syntax of your sentences. If you confuse r and l you obliterate the distinction between important suffixes and you obscure many roots. If in addition to all these things you omit a variety of medial consonants you create havoc. Mr Ventris's syllabic pattern is really far too simple, and we may say with confidence that it is insufficient for the writing and reading of Greek. It irons out the sound system of the language. On the other hand, just because it is so imprecise it enables Mr Ventris to discern Greek words in groups of syllables that look entirely un-Greek to classical scholars.'

Some of what Professor Beattie alleges against the decipherment would be admitted by Ventris and Chadwick and their followers, but is not particularly damning. The script postulated is admittedly very unsatisfactory for writing Greek, but this can be explained if we assume that Linear Script A, from which it was developed, had been devised for writing a very different language. The cuneiform script devised by the Sumerians was very unsatisfactory for writing Semitic languages (even though both had a distaste for closed syllables) until it had been amended and improved.

Beattie is, however, wrong in thinking he can refute Ventris's interpretation of TA-RA-NY as a footstool on the ground that the ideogram represents a flat pan with two handles. The gold ring from Tiryns proves clearly that such objects, whether pans or not, were certainly employed as footstools and this word represents one of the strongest individual arguments for Ventris's system.[1]

Beattie also raises objections to the reading of the tripod tablet. He notes 'the curious feature' of 'the writer's insistence on handles. ... We should in any case suspect the validity of a list that has no one-handled or two-handled pots but knows only those with three or four handles or none at all.' This is certainly curious but does not explain away the fact that such are the pots represented in the ideograms.

He also emphasizes the only weakness in the Ventris system which

[1]. The object bears a superficial resemblance to the hot water cans also used as footstools and employed to heat railway carriages before these were furnished with central heating, though I am not suggesting ta-ra-ny was such an article.

really troubles me – the number of possible variants. He asserts with reference to the tripod: 'If we apply these variations to the words in the text we find that TI-RI-O-WE might be interpreted in 5760 different ways and QE-TO-RO-WE in 92,160 ways. Even so short a word as DI-PA could mean about 300 different things.' I have not checked Beattie's figures but I think we may admit that the number of variants is uncomfortably large, and not quite so irrelevant perhaps as Professor Webster believes. The latter also complains, more justly, of Beattie's evasion of the evidence from 'the furniture tablets', his failure to recognize Ventris's symbols for sa, ke, ta, pa, yo, mu, za, and ro, and the weakness of his objections to the identifications of *Athena potnia*, *Paian*, and *Enyalios*.

Beattie's criticisms have been tested more carefully by A. P. Treweek, who, being a mathematician as well as a classical scholar, was able to assess the value of Beattie's computations of the possible ambiguities resulting from the rules of the Ventris grid. Beattie's individual statements of fact are usually correct except when based on an incorrect reading of the sign, but the inferences drawn are unjustifiable. 'Beattie's attack is in fact made from a bewildering variety of logically inconsistent positions. ... Had he warned us of the dangers of making wrong interpretations of the words written by the syllables in the language where we are still feeling our way, that would have been a salutary warning, but his attack was misdirected against the one part of the work where the results have been established with certainty.'

It is a great tragedy that the recent death of Mr Ventris has deprived Aegean studies of the man best qualified to answer these questions, a man whose modesty and conscientiousness never allowed his enthusiasm to lead him astray beyond reasonable assumptions.

Minoan Mathematics

The Minoan people evolved or borrowed from Egypt a mathematical notation (based on the ten fingers as are so many systems), but their mathematics does not seem to have reached a higher standard than was demanded for the keeping of accounts or the measurements made by masons and carpenters.

In the Cretan Hieroglyphic Script units were indicated by vertical or slightly curved lines, tens by dots, a hundred by a long slanting stroke, and a thousand by a lozenge. A v was used for some fraction, perhaps a quarter.

In Linear Script A the same decimal system persisted but the notation changed. Units were now always shown by straight vertical strokes. The dot for ten appears on some of the earlier tablets but was soon replaced by a horizontal line. A hundred was represented by a circle, and a thousand by a circle with four short lines projecting from the circumference. Quarters were indicated by an L.

The decimal system which we, like the Minoans, employ, is obviously inferior to the duodecimal. It is well enough for arithmetic, but breaks down badly for geometry because you cannot divide ten exactly by three or four. The ancient Sumerians realized this defect at an early date and combined both systems in a sexagesimal one. Sixty is an admirable number, being exactly divisible by 2, 3, 4, 5, 6, 10, 12, 15, 20, and 30. The Babylonians and Hittites followed suit and the Maya peoples of America were also not blind to the beauties of sixty. But the Greeks and Romans, as Dow remarks, 'copied the decimal system of the Egyptians and Minoans'; we are still paying the penalty.

The Greeks and Romans also followed the Minoans in having no symbol for zero, and the classical Greek phrase for nothing literally means 'not even one'. Bennett has shown that the Minoan symbol x was a check, not a symbol for zero. Addition and subtraction would have been easy for Minoan scribes but multiplication and division would have been as difficult for them as it was for the Romans.

Besides their ordinary decimal system of notation the Minoans had systems of weights and measures based on miscellaneous ratios: $1 \times 30 \times 4 \times 12$ for weights, $1 \times 3 \times 6 \times 4$ for liquids, and $1 \times 10 \times 6 \times 4$ for solids.

Bennett also remarked that while the Linear A scribes had a single set of fractional signs for all kinds of measurements wet or dry, Linear B scribes had a different set of fractional signs for each kind of measurement, each being an exact multiple of all smaller fractions; no sign for a numerical fraction had been discovered. The fundamental difference between the system of measuring quantities employed by the scribes of Linear Script A, as opposed to those of Script B, is well demonstrated by Bennett. The Script A store-keeper, after filling six unit measures of grain from a bin containing $6\frac{4}{5}$ units, would fill a half measure and then test the remainder by pouring it into smaller measures until he had several full, and the corn would finally be in the form $6 + \frac{1}{2} + \frac{1}{4} + \frac{1}{20} = 6\frac{4}{5}$. The Script B store-keeper, after filling his unit measures, would test the remainder by a tenth measure and the final tally would be $6 + \frac{8}{10} = 6\frac{4}{5}$. The second system is obviously quicker and more convenient, but it is of interest that the former system of counting corresponds rather to the Egyptian method, whereas the latter corresponds to the Babylonian.

A Mesopotamian system might have been introduced to the Peloponnese from Anatolia by Pelops himself, but the system could equally well have been introduced both to Crete and to the mainland by Phoenician merchants from Ugarit or Byblos, or by Mycenaeans trading with those ports.

NOTE: Professor L. R. Palmer in his recent book *Mycenaeans and Minoans* has attacked Evans's dating of the Linear B tablets, using material derived from the excavation notebooks of the late Duncan Mackenzie. He claims that these tablets were consistently found associated with pottery of Late Minoan III B, not Late Minoan II, date, and that the tablets should therefore be dated no earlier than the twelfth century B.C. This theory has been counter-attacked by Mr John Boardman who pointed out that Professor Palmer seemed to have supposed an other-wise unrecorded conflagration about 1150 B.C., since the Late Minoan III B pottery he quotes had not been damaged by the fire that burnt the tablets. Further, although in the 1900 excavation of the Stirrup Jar room Evans and Mackenzie had attributed tablets and vases to the same period, nevertheless after a subsequent excavation in 1901 Mac-kenzie reported: 'In no deposit which was recognized as belonging to this period of partial habitation at Knosos was a single inscribed tablet or sealing, broken or unbroken, ever found during the whole course of the excavation here.'

Mr Sinclair Hood has also defended Evans's dating of the tablets stressing that there is no evidence that Mackenzie ever disagreed with Evans on this point (both originally dated them Late Minoan III and both later dated them Late Minoan II). Recent excavations by Hood have confirmed Evan's account of the Late Minoan I B period also.

CHAPTER 4

The Minoan Marine, Trade, and Communications

THE EARLIEST CRETAN BOATS

THERE is no evidence of an indigenous Neolithic culture developing out of a Palaeolithic one in Crete, and the old land barrier between the island and Asia Minor had broken down long before the opening of the Neolithic period in Crete. The first Neolithic settlers must have come by sea. We have no evidence concerning the form of boats they employed, but we may exclude the idea of floats or canoes of reeds or rushes like those of Pre-Dynastic Egypt. Presumably the first settlers came in dug-out canoes of cypress wood of the type still used till recently on Lake Prespa in Macedonia. (I travelled on one there in 1927.[1] A pointed prow and stern had been added separately, giving the appearance of a rude gondola, but the otherwise primitive effect was somewhat marred by the fact that the dug-out had been liberally repaired with petrol tins.) Just such a dug-out canoe, except for the petrol tins, seems to be illustrated by a clay model found in an Early Minoan deposit at Mochlos (Fig. 13). Such a boat would serve well for offshore fishing,[2] but for inter-island traffic something larger would be required, even though it might still be a dug-out, since cypresses grow to a great height and have straight trunks capable of being turned into long boats. The first immigrants, like the first Viking explorers, probably relied on oars and not on sails,[3] and I

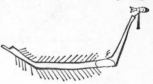

Fig. 12. Long boat from Cycladic vase

1. In A.D. 449 the general Maximinus and his suite, while on their way to meet Attila, were ferried across the Danube in dug-outs; compare L. Dindorf, *Historici Graeci Minores*, 1870–1, p. 292.

2. The two pairs of thole-pins are set as far apart as possible, presumably to leave the centre of the boat free for drawing in the net.

3. The Minoans, Mycenaeans, and Classical Greeks seem always to have used 'oars', not 'paddles', for which the Greek language appears to have no special term.

think they must have come via Rhodes, Karpathos, and Kasos, whatever may have been their original port of embarkation. Direct evidence for boats in the Early Minoan period is slight, but it would appear that besides the simple dug-out canoe of the Mochlos type, the Cretans also had a long boat with a high projecting bow and a low projection at the stern, interpreted by Evans as a fixed rudder. Such a boat is represented by a clay model of Early Minoan II date

Fig. 13. Mochlos dug-out

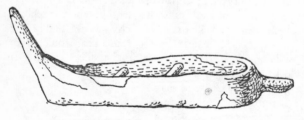

Fig. 14. Palaikastro model boat

from Palaikastro (Fig. 14). Some authorities would interpret the low projection as a ram on the prow and the high slanting projection as the stern, but Evans's interpretation is justified by the comparison with Minoan ships on Middle Minoan I seals and by Cycladic ships represented in the Early Cycladic vases known as frying-pans, where the fish at the prow shows clearly the direction in which the ship is travelling. Even in the Middle Bronze Age, when the Cretans were building ocean-going ships, this distinction between the high prow and low stern continued to distinguish them from the more symmetrical Egyptian and Phoenician ships.

The ships of the earliest dynastic period in Egypt were of the 'nuggar' type, of which Herodotus describes the construction, and which are still used on the upper Nile above the second cataract.[1] They were adequate for river work, but quite unsuitable for the open sea.

THE EARLIEST SEA-GOING SHIPS

By the time of the Third Dynasty, however, the Egyptians had already constructed a ship capable of sailing on the Mediterranean, though even as late as the Fifth Dynasty the ships of Sa-hu-re still preserve some characteristics of the old Nile 'nuggar', including the curious bifid mast, a relic of the reed-built boats which would not stand the strain of a mast stepped on the centre. Even as early as the Second Dynasty, however, we hear of a ship called the 'Byblos ship'. It is often assumed that this phrase simply means the ship employed on the Byblos run, as no doubt in fact it was. Nevertheless I think that if we consider the lack of timber suitable for ships in Egypt and its abundance on the Lebanon coast and the later shipbuilding traditions of the Phoenicians, we may perhaps go so far as to suggest that 'Byblos ship' meant the type of ship built at Byblos, without of course excluding the possibilities of Egyptians also building such ships either at Byblos or in Egypt.[2]

It is at least certain that by about 2000 B.C. we find on Minoan seals (Fig. 15) representations of large sea-going vessels which still preserve the high prow but low stern of the boats of Palaikastro and the Cyclades, but which have been transformed by the influence of ships of the Byblos type and now have a central mast with a square sail like the sea-going ships of Egypt.

Most representations of Minoan ships, however crude, display a triangle of lines each side of the mast illustrating a form of rigging

1. J. Hornell, 'The Sailing Ships in Ancient Egypt', *Antiquity*, 1943; 'nuggars' are characterized by their shallow depth, great width, and absence of ribs or any proper keel.

2. Probably the earliest ships of this type were built by Egyptians, but a local shipbuilding trade must have grown up at an early date on the coast of what was later termed Phoenicia, perhaps at the mouth of the Dog River.

which was normal during the Eighteenth Dynasty in Egypt and is described by Laird Clowes. The mast, which is a single pole, is stepped amidships, and the sail, of much greater width than that employed in the boats of the Twelfth Dynasty, has its foot extended by a heavy spreader yard. This lower yard, just as in these earlier boats, is supported by a number of lifts[1] which lead through a series of 'bees' lashed to the mast head very similar in form to the 'bees' of the eighteenth-century bowsprit. He remarks that 'each yard is formed of two spars fished together in the middle' and further that the

Fig. 15. Ships from Minoan seals

'vessel was sailed very much more by the manipulation of two braces or vangs, attached to the upper yard, than by means of the sheet which controlled the lower yard', and that the method of steering was essentially the same as that adopted by a whaleboat, where the very long oar used for steering is ordinarily rotated about the axis of its shaft by means of a short vertical handle, instead of its blade being bodily displaced from the side.

Minoan seals from the Early Minoan III periods onwards suggest that the rigging and method of sailing were the same as the Egyptian. It is true that most gem engravings only show the mast and the triangular rigging of the lifts but occasionally other details, such as the steering sweeps, the oars, the two-piece upper yard, and the lower spreader yard, are illustrated.

The Greeks later abandoned this system of the spreader yard and the triangular rigging of the 'lifts' required to sustain it. I do not know how early this improvement occurred, but the spreader yard

1. Diagonal ropes leading from the spreader yard to the mast head; the phrase 'eighteenth-century bowsprit' refers of course to the eighteenth century A.D.; there was possibly no bowsprit in the ordinary sense of that word in the eighteenth century B.C. despite the appearance of what looks like a bowsprit on some Minoan ships.

and its 'lifts' had both vanished before the middle of the sixth century B.C.

But the Minoan ships were not slavish imitations of the Egyptian, and from certain Cretan peculiarities we may infer the existence of a local shipbuilding trade, perhaps carried out at Nirou Khani, where the existence of two small dry docks suggests such a possibility.

Two idiosyncrasies which distinguish Middle Minoan ships from their contemporaries in Egypt are the very high prow rising at an angle of about sixty degrees, and the low stern with the keel projecting, a form persisting from the old long-boat type of the earliest Bronze Age both in Crete and in the Cyclades, and probably conditioned by the dug-out origin of the hull.[1]

The result of this lack of fore-and-aft sails, coupled with the fact that the regular Etesian winds, the summer winds of the eastern Mediterranean, now known as the *meltémi*, usually blow steadily from the north or north-west, probably implies that the ancient trading vessels (like the Lloyd Triestino vessels up to 1939) used to ply a circular route southwards from Crete to Egypt, up the coasts of Palestine and Syria, across to Cyprus, and back by way of the Dodecanese to whatever Cretan port they had sailed from.

We know now that fore-and-aft rigging was not unknown in the ancient world, since Professor Lionel Casson has recently published three illustrations of sprit-sails and one of a 'lateen sail' (better described as a short luff lug sail). I cannot quote any certain ancient example of a gaff sail or any reliable Minoan examples of sprit or lateen sails, but certain ancient illustrations suggest that the square sail could be pulled down at one corner and used (rather clumsily perhaps) as a lateen sail; oblong sails are employed in this way on the Malayan fishing vessels termed *perahu mayang*.[2]

Some Minoan seals depict ships with three masts joined by a lattice pattern with crescents on top giving an impression that it is a deck awning formed of matting slung on poles, as shown on Early Dynastic and Late Pre-dynastic drawings in Egypt. Marinatos, however, interpreted these as masts and sails, and Sir John Myres in a letter to me suggested that while the central line might represent a

1. Suggested to me by Mr T. C. Lethbridge.
2. H. M. Frese, 'Small Craft in the Rijks Museum van Volkerkunde, Leiden', *Mariners Mirror*, 1948, Fig. 2.

mast, the outer vertical lines might be halyards depending from the yard arm.[1] It might even be argued that these were sprit-sails. The sagging lines of the crescents seem also consistent with the suggestion of a tent-like deck cabin, but I must confess that such a cabin seems less appropriate for the Aegean Sea or the Libyan Sea than for the river of Egypt. Whatever be the true explanation, it is clear that this ship with the three masts or poles is a type quite distinct from the ordinary cargo ship with the great square sail. Small dinghies with transom sterns seem to be represented by the models from Christos (Early Minoan III–Middle Minoan I) and Hagia Triada (Late Minoan I).

SACRED BARGES

The gold ring from the Tiryns treasure (Fig. 16) illustrates yet another type of vessel, perhaps used as a sacred barge. The design appears to

Fig. 16. Ship from Tiryns ring

show the central mast with its normal rigging rising from the top of a square cabin, an impossible position since the mast would blow overboard with any wind. Either this is only a flagpole, which I think unlikely, or else we must imagine the mast as passing through the cabin down to the keel. The Tiryns boat may, of course, be a Mycenaean variant unknown in Crete, but there are other similar boats, except that they have no deck cabin as a rule, appearing on Minoan seals, usually in religious scenes. These boats resemble an old Mesopotamian type employed by the Marsh Arabs and illustrated by a silver model found in the royal graves at Ur.

DECKED MERCHANTMEN

The question how far Minoan merchant vessels were decked is open to dispute. The adoption of the watertight deck for warships was a

1. See the two right-hand seals in Fig. 15, one from an amygdaloid carnelian in the British Museum, the other from a similar seal in the Southesk Collection.

late innovation inasmuch as the Athenians had not yet adopted it for war-galleys at the time of the Persian invasions at the beginning of the fifth century B.C. Merchant ships, however, were sometimes decked during the Bronze Age, as is shown by the clay model of Late Minoan II date from Hagia Triada and by the painting on a Cypro-Mycenaean vase of a cargo ship decked from stem to stern.[1] We cannot prove that the Minoans had ships like the Cypriots, but I think it not unlikely. Pernice asserted that cargo ships of this kind relied entirely on their sails and had no oars, but the true distinction between the methods of propelling warships and merchant ships is more justly stated by Geoffrey Kirk (writing of ships in the Early Iron Age), 'Greek ships of all periods, both warships and merchant vessels, carried equipment for both forms of propulsion, although the primary motive power of the warship was undoubtedly oars and that of merchant ships sail. With favourable winds it would be foolish to row, but equally foolish not to have oars available for manoeuvring in harbour, or in case of calm, even for the most unwieldy vessel.' In other words, oars were employed like the engine of a *gasolina*, the modern fishing caique of the Greek islands fitted with a small subsidiary motor.

WARSHIPS

The earliest representation of a Greek warship is on a Protogeometric vase from Pylos, but it already foreshadows the archaic type, undecked save for small fighting platforms fore and aft – a form dictated by the necessity for manoeuvrability and the consequent need for more rowers and increased length of hull. 'The weight of a deck imposed severe strains, and it was only the lightly-built open-boat type which was found to support with safety the keel length of at least ninety feet [27 m.] necessitated by an increase to twenty-five rowers each side.'[2]

Apollodorus records a tradition that the first ship had been built by Danaus, and a scholiast more reasonably states that that king had constructed the first *pentekontor*, the first fifty-oared vessel designed

1. No. 262 from Tomb 3 at Enkomi; see E. Sjoqvist, *Swedish Cyprus Expedition* I, 1934, pl. XXXI, 3, 4.
2. Kirk.

purely as a warship. Danaus himself is a legendary character, but the nation of whom he was supposed to be the founder were the inhabitants of the plain of Adana who raided Ugarit in the fourteenth century and Egypt in the twelfth century B.C.[1] The chief port of this plain in the Late Bronze Age was Tarsus, so that even if the Biblical description for an ocean-going ship as a 'ship of Tarshish' refers to Tartessus in Spain or Tartous in Syria it is still not impossible that the story of Danaus's invention of the *pentekontor* may refer to an achievement of the shipwrights of Tarsus,[2] and most probably the Biblical Tarshish meant Tarsus.[3]

Greek traditions, however, also claimed Danaus for Argos, and our earliest representation of a Greek warship is on a twelfth-century B.C. vase from Pylos, so that we might also argue that warships of this kind were first laid down in the Peloponnese.

Both districts had ample supplies of suitable timber, and Barnett notes that the Biblical word for ship in the passages referring to Tarshish is not Semitic and might possibly be derived from the Hellenic *naus*.

Starr has vigorously attacked what he terms the 'Myth of the Minoan Thalassocracy' and makes some very good points. Even if we assign the greatest expansion of the Minoan marine to the Middle Minoan II period, we ought not to imagine that any prehistoric king of Crete (whether Minoan or Achaean) had a navy like that of fifth-century Athens, or regarded the Aegean Sea as *mare nostrum*. A Minoan warship would simply be a merchant vessel equipped with fighters. In England, writes Clowes, 'this interchangeability of the role of merchantman and man-of-war, as need arose, continued right up to the death of Queen Elizabeth'. Lionel Cohen's attempt to prove the existence of ships' rams in Minoan times was refuted by Marinatos.

The coasts of Crete were protected by the sea rather than by the fleet, and if any permanent naval force existed, which is doubtful,

1. Compare a note on Mopsos by R. D. Barnett in *Journal of Hellenic Studies*, 1953, pp. 140–3.
2. See T. C. Lethbridge, *Boats and Boatmen*, 1952, p. 117; R. Dussaud, *Topographie historique de la Syrie antique*, 1927, p. 121; and C. F. Schaeffer, *Ugaritica II*, 1949.
3. Barnett, 'Early Shipping in the Near East', *Antiquity*, 1958.

its function would have been rather the protection of its own merchant ships from piratical raids and the execution of piratical raids on enemy ships and ports, not coastal protection.

Starr, however, perhaps underestimates the size of Minoan ships. The fact that many representations of ships only show five or six oars may be due merely to the difficulty of representing them on a small seal stone (Fig. 15).[1] All the representations of Minoan ships are summarily executed and only illustrate the most salient features, yet one of them clearly indicates fifteen oars on one side apart from the steering sweeps, corresponding to the crew of thirty sent to Pleuron (Ventris and Chadwick, loc. cit., tablet 53). The same number of oars were used to propel Hatshepshut's ships on the expedition to Punt, and also the old ship preserved at Athens till Demosthenes's time and reputed to have been Theseus's ship.[2]

Marinatos has taken this ship as indicating the probable maximum for Minoan vessels and has estimated that it would have been about 21 metres long and about 4 to 4½ metres broad. He suggests that the large sail shown on Late Minoan ships may have implied the existence of vessels 30 metres in length but not much more. (The abnormally large barge constructed in Egypt for Hatshepshut's obelisk was 63 metres long, 21 metres broad, and had a displacement, according to Koster, of 1541·31 tons.)[3]

Some curious designs on Minoan seals of the amygdaloid form so popular in the Middle Minoan III period (but by no means confined to it) have been identified as sails with their buntline rings by Marinatos, who has suggested that these seals were the property of sailmakers.

Childe has commented on the relatively very large areas occupied by magazines and workshops in Minoan Palaces implying surplus products used for trade, and draws the conclusion: 'in other words the priest-king's economic power must to a quite high degree have depended on secondary industry and commerce as contrasted with agricultural production.'[4] Contrast Starr's remark that 'the splendour

1. Other seal stones depict seven a side, while the seal from Phaistos quoted above showed fifteen a side, apart from the two steering sweeps.

2. Plutarch, *Life of Theseus*, Chap. 23; Evans, *Palace of Minos*, Vol. II, Fig. 139.

3. Koster, A., *Studien zur Geschichte des Antikenseewegens*, 1934, pp. 1–10.

4. V. Gordon Childe, *What Happened in History* (Penguin Books, 1942), p. 173.

of its palaces rested mainly upon the work of farmers, and the Cretan artisans were fed from Cretan farms'. Cretan industries, however, must have depended very largely on imported materials. Gold, silver, tin, and lead all had to come by ship, and the island sources of copper must have been very inadequate for its needs. The luxury trades would also have imported ivory, lapis lazuli, musical instruments, and portable works of art from Egypt and Syria.

MINOAN HARBOURS

Platon has remarked how often Minoan ports were situated on small promontories affording a harbour on either side according to the direction of the wind;[1] to this category belonged not only Khersonnesos and Palaikastro, but also probably Amnisos and Mochlos before the sinking of the eastern coastline. The choice of such sites is reasonable and natural. It is less easy to conjecture why the ancient planners both in the Bronze Age and later should have displayed a preference for small islands lying a few miles off the coast; we may quote such celebrated ports as Tyre, Sidon, the Pharos, and Aradus in the Levant, and in Minoan Crete Pseira, Leuke, and perhaps Dia. (Mochlos, now an island, was perhaps a peninsula in Minoan times.)

Holland Rose offers two explanations, neither very convincing, but I have nothing better to suggest. 'Sometimes these islands or even ports on an open shore were placed under a kind of perpetual truce; or else exchange went on without the parties actually meeting. . . . It is probable,' he continues, 'that trade on these and many other islets long preceded trade on the mainland near by. . . . Note that early traffic avoided narrow inlets like the Piraeus for fear of being cut off'; and he points the moral by quoting how the Laestrygonian wreckers had trapped Odysseus's companions, whereas the hero himself, who had tied up at the entrance, escaped. Perhaps this explains why no important Minoan port developed in the splendid natural harbour of Suda Bay.[2]

1. I doubt whether the island at Amnisos was ever fully united to the mainland, but if a sandy bay had existed between it and the Kastro it would have provided some calmer water for boats beaching east of the Kastro.

2. Minoa, of which Theophanides discovered traces (Ephemeris *Archaiologiki*, 1950–1, Supp. 1–13), hardly appears to have been a port of any importance.

The numerous references to piracy in the Homeric poems[1] imply that it was a common practice in the Early Iron Age, and Thucydides's reference to the suppression by Minos of the Carian pirates obviously alludes to piracy in the Minoan period (whatever value we attach to the names 'Minos' and 'Carian').[2]

Signal flares were often lit on prominent headlands, both by coast-guards to warn traders of the presence of pirates, and by the friends on land of pirates lying in ambush off the coast.

NAVIGATION BY PIGEONS

In the dialogue termed the Kevaddha Sutta of Dighha[3] of the fifth century B.C. the Buddha states: 'Long ago ocean-going merchants were wont to plunge forth upon the sea on board a ship taking with them a shore-sighting bird. When the ship was out of sight they would set the shore-sighting bird free. And it would go to the east and to the south and to the west and to the north and to the inter-mediate points and rise aloft. If on the horizon it caught sight of land thither it would go, but if not it would come back to the ship again.' The story of Noah and the Mesopotamian *Epic of Gilgamish* show that this device must have been practised by Sumerian captains back in the third millennium B.C.[4]

It would be interesting to know whether Minoan merchant cap-tains ever employed this device, hardly necessary when they were sailing to the Cyclades, but not to be despised for longer voyages out of sight of land, since stars are not always visible, even on Mediter-ranean waters. Cosmas Indicopleustes records this practice in Ceylon as late as the sixth century A.D. but there is no mention of it in the Homeric poems. But what of the pigeon which Jason set loose to ascertain whether the Argo could pass through the clashing rocks?

1. *Odyssey* XIV 86, XVI 425, etc.

2. Thucydides I, 4; Cleidemus quoted by Plutarch (Thesrus, Chap. 19) even refers to police work executed by Jason.

3. Professor I. W. Rhys Davids, *Journal of Royal Asiatic Society*, 1899, p. 432; and compare W. H. Schoff, *The Periplus of the Erythraean Sea*, 1912, pp. 228, 229.

4. R. C. Thompson, *The Epic of Gilgamish*, 1928, 52, verses 145–55; Uta-Napishtim (the Sumerian Noah) released in succession a dove, a swallow, and a raven.

Was this a reminiscence of the bird that every good captain of a Minoan or Mycenaean ship would have taken with him on a long voyage?

ODYSSEUS'S SHIP

In the fifth book of the *Odyssey* we are given a brief but graphic description of the construction of a sea-going ship. The trees, poplar and fir, were felled with double axes, trimmed with an adze to the required shape, bored with a drill, and fastened together with pegs and what were termed *harmoniai*, a word used by Galen of the union of broken bones by the mere apposition of their surfaces, and therefore in Homer's passage presumably implying that the ship was carvel-built, not clinker-built. The other evidence agrees with this: indeed all ancient ships in the Mediterranean may have been carvel-built.

Representations of Odysseus's ship on classical vases often interpret it as a war galley, but this is obviously wrong. Homer states very explicitly that it was a broad cargo ship, and I suspect that the word *ikria* (decks), if it does not imply a fully decked ship like the one on the Mycenaean vase from Enkomi, at least implies a half-decked ship with fairly substantial decks fore and aft.

The hull was probably strengthened by the insertion of U-shaped transverse frames just below the gunwale, struts which would serve as thwarts for the rowers in long boats or small boats, or would carry the deck in the larger cargo boats; two such frames appear to be suggested on the Enkomi ship referred to on page 97.

TRADE WITH EGYPT AND PHOENICIAN COAST

Direct trade with Egypt seems to have been slight during the Early Minoan period. Egyptian influences are certainly discernible in the shapes of some of the stone vases and in the designs and occasionally in the shapes of Early Minoan seals, but many of these influences might have come indirectly from places where Egyptian culture was prominent, such as the ports of Syria and Palestine, and it should be remarked that after the appearance of Proto-Dynastic bowls in a sub-Neolithic context at Knosos, the earliest imports of Egyptian objects re the fragments of a faience bowl and the necklace of faience beads found at Mochlos in Tomb 6, of which the earliest interment dated from the Early Minoan II period. A few scarabs of the First Intermediary Period (Dynasties VII–X inclusive) found their way to Crete, and some Cretan ivory seals of the Early Minoan III period seem to have been influenced by Egyptian scarabs of that period, but most of the actual imports of Egyptian seals date from the Twelfth or Eighteenth Dynasties. Not till the Twelfth Dynasty do we find any hint of Cretan influences on Egypt, and even then the evidence is a little ambiguous.

M. Money-Coutts Seiradhaki has pointed out the analogies between the Cretan lids in steatite with the handle carved in the form of lying dogs and the lid of a vase in the Beirut Museum from Byblos with the handle in the form of a squatting bull.[1] The bull looks like a Sumerian animal, but the material, green schist, and the incised herring-bone decoration recall such east Cretan art as the *pyxis* from Maroneia. The Mochlos lid was found with an Early Minoan II burial and the other Cretan example was presumably of about that date. The Byblos vase was found by Montet below the Twelfth Dynasty temple II on that site in a foundation deposit dated about 2100 B.C. The exact date of this deposit is open to question but it was certainly contemporary with the Middle Kingdom and Schaeffer is inclined to date it slightly earlier than the deposits found later by M. Dunand. This correlation agrees well enough with the limits 2300–2100 B.C. which I have suggested for the Early Minoan II period.

If the Byblos vase could be reckoned as Cretan, it would be the earliest Minoan export that we know of to a foreign country, but it may well have been made in Byblos. One motive of Egyptian art which has sometimes been supposed to have been derived from, or at least influenced by, Minoan art is the spiral decoration which suddenly becomes popular under the Twelfth Dynasty, especially in the form of rapport designs[2] and quadruple spirals arranged in chequer

1. M. Money-Coutts, 'A Stone Bowl and Lid from Byblos', *Berytus*, 1936, p. 139.

2. Most English dictionaries do not define this phrase, which is employed by many archaeologists; I should define a rapport design as an all-over, interlocking, net-like pattern suggesting but not necessarily implying the influence of textiles.

fashion. Spiral decoration was characteristic of the Neolithic cultures of the Danube basin and of the Chalcolithic pottery of Thessaly and Thrace. Running spirals appear very early in the Bronze Age in the Cyclades and Crete may have derived its spiral decorations from those islands. It has been suggested that spiral ornaments were derived from a late Palaeolithic source or from Sumerian metal work. Egypt, however, had known simple spirals in the Pre-dynastic period and later, but was practically devoid of spiral decoration from the Fifth Dynasty period to the First Intermediate Period when we do find some scarabs with primitive spiral curls or tendrils. These, however, were comparatively scarce and gave no hint of the abundance of quadruple and interlocked c spirals which appeared under the Twelfth Dynasty and induced Matz to suggest an Aegean origin for them. The adopting of the spiral into quadruple squares or other rectangular patterns, including the meander, which is only a rectilinear version of the spiral, may have been carried out by Egyptian craftsmen familiar with rectilinear designs in textiles and matting.

The Egyptian meander patterns at least are unlikely to have been derived from north of the Balkans, but it is not impossible that Egyptian textiles might have penetrated to the Danube valley. It is a curious and perhaps not altogether insignificant fact that the spiral and meander designs, which were a thousand years later to be the symbols of the labyrinth of Minos on the classical coins of Knosos, became popular in Egypt and in Crete at the time when Amenemhat III constructed his great 'labyrinth' in the Fayoum and a Cretan prince constructed his 'labyrinth' at Knosos. I imagine indeed that the word 'labyrinth' would never have acquired its modern significance of maze but for the fact that Amenemhat's great funerary temple was more or less contemporary with the earliest palace at Knosos, and so invited comparisons between the two. The Egyptian temple was 'labyrinthine' in the modern sense but had nothing to do with the double axe, the *labrys* from which the Cretan palace derived its name; but long after the destruction of the latter building the folk-lore about the Minotaur and the maze-like building he lived in was confirmed and crystallized by the maze-like intricacies of the great temple in the Fayoum, which existed up to Roman times.

Another evidence of intercourse with Egypt is provided by the symbols obviously borrowed from the hieroglyphics of that country by the Cretans in their Hieroglyphic Script A. Here we must cut out from Sundwall's list such naturalistic representations as a man's leg or a scorpion or a ship, symbols which might arise independently in both countries, and confine examples of intercourse to such conventional designs as have a specially Egyptian character and meaning, the Ankh sign, the symbol of life, Ana, the palace sign, Byty, the bee-keeper sign, perhaps Ka, the raised hands sign for 'worker' or 'activity', and the 'adze' sign (adzes indeed might occur anywhere, but Egyptian and Minoan adzes had handles of a peculiar form). We cannot, however, quote any Cretan exports to Egypt in the Early Minoan III or Middle Minoan I periods.

MINOAN EXPORTS TO EGYPT, SYRIA, AND CYPRUS

Minoan vases were exported to various parts of the Levant. Tomb 6 A at Lapithos in Cyprus contained a Middle Minoan I A spouted jar associated with pottery of the types known as Early Cypriot II and III, and metal vases of the same Minoan period were found at Tod in Upper Egypt in chests inscribed with the name of Amenemhat II (1929–1895 B.C.). A Middle Minoan vase was found at Level II (2100–1900 B.C.) at Byblos in Syria. Beakers resembling Middle Minoan I B examples from various Cretan sites were found in Stratum II at Alisar and in Level IV A at Bogaz Koï in Asia Minor, Middle Minoan II A sherds were found in a later deposit at Byblos, and in the Middle Ugarit II period (1900–1750 B.C.) at Ras Shamra, and in Egypt at Haraga Middle Minoan II sherds were deposited at Lahun before 1700 B.C., perhaps about 1750. A Middle Minoan II B spouted vase was found at Abydos in a tomb belonging to the end of the Twelfth or beginning of the Thirteenth Dynasty.

The converse side of this picture is a Babylonian cylinder seal from Platanos of the type current in Hammurabi's reign (1792–1750 B.C., according to Dr Sidney Smith), and an amethyst scarab of late Twelfth or early Thirteenth Dynasty type from the lowest deposit of the Psychro Cave. Two other cylinders dating from the First Dynasty of Babylon are recorded from Crete, but these were not found in datable contexts. Perhaps it was at this time that the Cretans became acquainted with the use of papyrus and called it after Byblos, by the name from which was derived the modern Greek word for a book and the English word for the Bible.

Cretan traders also probably visited the city of Alalakh, capital of the little Syrian state of Mukishe, and its excavator, Sir Leonard Woolley, was at first inclined to stress Minoan influences on its architecture, frescoes, and pottery. After further excavations, however, it became evident that some of the frescoes, stone lamps, and pottery that had recalled Middle Minoan III to Late Minoan I A designs in Crete had been thrown away some time between 1350 and 1275 B.C. Indeed the most definitely Aegean pottery consisted of imported Mycenaean and Cypriot vases and was not Minoan at all, and the quasi-Minoan features in frescoes and on pottery of the so-called Nuzi ware remind us of Heurtley's description of Philistine vase motifs as 'patterns that had gone out of currency in their own country' and were perhaps due to a certain number of Minoan refugees calling or even settling there after 1450 B.C. when an Achaean dynasty was probably ruling at Knosos.

The food and raw materials exported from Minoan Crete to Egypt probably included oil, olives, wine, and perhaps dried grapes and almost certainly timber, especially cypress.

A curious export from Greek lands to Egypt was that of lichens used there for breadmaking, even to the present day when they may be purchased under the name of *sheba*. Greek lichens have been found in Middle Dynastic deposits at El Assassif, Thebes, and also elsewhere in Middle Kingdom tombs. Persson points out that the distance from the Peloponnese is not so very much greater than that from Crete, but I think that in the Middle Dynastic period the lichens would have come rather from Crete or the Dodecanese, though in the Late Dynastic period they were doubtless imported from the mainland.

EGYPT AND THE KEFTIU

The Late Minoan I A period (1580–1550 B.C.) was the time when Queen Hatshepshut ruled Egypt and developed peaceful trade with her neighbours. The tomb paintings of her chief architect Senmut depicted foreigners in Minoan costume bringing tribute to Egypt in the form of vases, fillers, and various gifts so accurately portrayed that we can confidently assign them to the Late Minoan I A period. Unfortunately so little of this painting survives that we do not know what name was assigned to these foreigners. Were they or were they not the same people mentioned in later tomb texts as coming from 'the shores of Keftiu'? (See Fig. 54.)

Even some of the supporters of the theory that Kaphtor meant Crete have suggested that the Aegean vessels brought to Egypt from the land of Keftiu were perhaps not Minoan but Late Helladic works from Mycenae or some other site on the mainland. The Late Minoan I A period (1550–1500 B.C.), parallel with the second half of the first Late Helladic period on the mainland of Greece, was the period when Minoan art exercised its strongest influence on that of the Peloponnese and southern Greece in general, so that it is often hard to say whether an individual vase was made on Crete or on the mainland. Large metal jugs with a decorative band level with, or just below the base of the handle were characteristic of the Middle Minoan III B to Late Minoan I A period at Knosos and were found in the Second Shaft Grave at Mycenae; and they were also represented on the offerings brought by Aegeans in the tomb paintings of Senmut (about 1510 B.C.) and of User-Amon.

A large palace amphora of the type found by Seager at Mochlos and by Evans in the north-east house at Knosos seems also to be represented in Senmut's tomb. The patterns below the top row of handles on this vase were interpreted by Evans as a second row of handles. Mr Alexiou's discovery of a fine Late Minoan II vase with plastic figure-of-eight shields, which also occurred on the silver 'siege rhyton' from Mycenae, suggests that these patterns should be interpreted as similar ornaments.

The so-called 'Vapheio cups' shown in the paintings of Senmut and User-Amon are Minoan rather than Helladic in that their shape is rather squat and they lack the raised horizontal rib which appears on so many of the Mycenaean examples. (See Fig. 54.)

The gold cups which gave their name to this shape from the *tholos* tomb at Vapheio near Sparta must, I think, be imports from Crete or works of a Cretan resident on the mainland, not Mycenaean work as suggested by Snijder and Miss Kantor. The rather squat shape and the free-field naturalism with no attempt at balanced groups are Minoan characteristics.

User-Amon was succeeded in the office of Grand Vizier by his nephew, Rekhmire, whose tomb was closed about 1450 B.C.; in this tomb the Foreigners are said to come from the land of Keftiu, the islands (or coasts) of the Green Sea, and the wording of the Egyptian would allow us to consider the words 'coasts of the Green Sea' as in apposition to 'Keftiu' and so explaining its meaning, but would also allow us to supply an 'and' between 'Keftiu' and 'the islands', differentiating one from the other. There is no radical difference, however, between the foreigners that would enable us to claim one group as coming from the land of Keftiu and another as coming from the islands. Wainwright emphasized that the foreigners of Rekhmire's tomb are less Minoan in their dress than those of Senmut and the vases they bring include Syrian or Anatolian as well as Minoan forms. Indeed he would regard all the Keftiuans labelled as such as coming from Cilicia. Supporters of the theory that Keftiu meant Crete regard the progressively less Minoan appearance of its inhabitants in later tombs as due to the careless copying of earlier paintings, but the appearance of Late Minoan I B vases in Rekhmire's tomb, whereas only Late Minoan I A forms occur in Senmut's painting, implies that the former is not a mere slavish copy of the latter and this conclusion is supported by the statement of N. de G. Davies that the foreigners represented in Tombs 71, 39, and 131 at Qurna (those of Menkheperrasenb, Puimre, and Amen-user respectively) seem to have been studied afresh in each instance.

Nothing can be inferred from the order of the places mentioned in Rekhmire's inscription, since the offerings of the 'Great Chief of Keftiu and the Isles (or Coasts) of the Green Sea' are sandwiched between the offerings of Punt and those of Nubia.

The linguistic evidence is hardly conclusive. Keftiu seems to be the same country that is called Kaphtor in the Hebrew and Kaptara in the cuneiform records, and it is quite certain that this country must be either an island or a coastal district. The Philistines are said to have come from Kaphtor, and we can no longer, as Macalister did, regard them simply as Minoan refugees. Their pottery is rather a local variety developed from Mycenaean pottery of the Late Minoan III c type. The Philistine invasion of Egypt, however, was much later than any references to Keftiu in the Egyptian records, and the Pelethim of the Hebrew records were accompanied by Cherethim who might have been Cretans.

The cuneiform references to Kaptara are not much more helpful. The French excavators of the palace at Mari on the Euphrates interpreted Kaptara to mean Crete.

The Keftiuans are depicted bearing bull's head rhyta like the steatite one found in the Little Palace at Knosos. We may even have one of these rhyta that were sent to Egypt still existing, namely the fine bull's head rhyton formerly owned, and published, by my friend Dr Charles Seltman. Its history is obscure, since it turned up in France without any proper information as to its source in the collection of a man who had acquired it from Egypt. I have handled it, and personally regard it as genuine, especially as the forgery of Minoan antiquities was not well developed at the time when it would appear to have been acquired by its former French owner, and experts have testified that the alkaline deposit on the less exposed surfaces would have taken many years to form.[1]

A few Minoan vases have also turned up in Egypt, the most celebrated being the fine jug in the Marseille Museum known as the 'Marseille Oenochoe', but our information about this and one or two other vases that I think were Minoan imports from Crete, rather than Helladic imports from Mycenae, depends on the statements of dealers from whom they were bought.

The only certain example of a Late Minoan I B vase in pottery derived from a proper excavation in Egypt is the baggy alabastron found in Grave 137 at Sedment dated to the reign of Thutmose III. Of the twelve vases illustrated by Miss Kantor on her Plate VII and labelled 'Late Bronze I–II Aegean', I am inclined to regard vases A, C, D, and L as Minoan and the rest as Helladic vases from Mycenae or some other site on the mainland.

Miss Kantor observes that many of the Keftiuan decorative motives seem to be Egyptian, and it would probably be a mistake to consider the repertory of these designs as a reliable reproduction of Keftiuan textile patterns; but these patterns do not occur on Egyptian kilts, nor are they arranged in the same way on any other Egyptian garment so far as I remember, and it may therefore at least be argued that they were intended to give the general effect of a Keftiuan kilt.

1. Information given me by Seltman himself; note that no published known prototype existed for a forgery of this type before 1914 and that before 1926 the vase was already in France.

I see no reason to suppose they were merely intended to fill 'gaping blanks', since the Egyptian had no *horror vacui* like the Indian artist, and was perfectly willing to leave a blank space when he thought it appropriate.

Miss Kantor's law of the 'diminishing accuracy of successive representations' may have more validity with regard to the later tombs, but I do not think it applies to Rekhmire's tomb, where the designs, as Vercoutter remarks, are characterized by their originality. Unfortunately the figures have been repainted and altered in this and in other ancient tombs. We should like to know whether the original paintings made any difference between the Keftiu and the Men of the Isles and their offerings. Why were the alterations made? Was it because the Aegeans had ceased to come to the Egyptian court, and if so when did that occur? Alexiou's alabaster vase (Fig. 50) suggests that direct relations between Egypt and the harbour town of Knosos lasted probably up to the middle of the fifteenth century B.C. We shall see that there are reasons for supposing that an Achaean dynasty may have ruled over Knosos in the Late Minoan II period from 1450 to 1400 B.C. approximately, and if this is so it would seem that the death of Rekhmire more or less coincided with a drastic reduction of direct communications between Crete and Egypt, but not necessarily their suspension. One argument which must be faced by the supporters of the theory that Keftiu is Cilicia is the absence of any reference to any name like Kaptara in the cuneiform records of the Assyrians and the Hittites, and to which they would presumably answer that it was known by another name to these nations. Eastern Cilicia was apparently part of the country known in the cuneiform records as Kissuwadna, but coastal Cilicia might have been termed Kaptara or some such name, though Gurney includes the coastal district also under the former name. Furumark quotes Kabderos, father-in-law of Mopsos, in support of the equation of Kaptara with Cilicia, but the Hittite bilingual text referring to Mopsos dates from the eighth century B.C. and does not mention Kabderos or Kaptara.

M. J. Vercoutter has recently answered the criticism that the kilts of Rekhmire's Keftiuans are un-Egyptian by claiming that the fringed division of the kilt is really central and not really different from that of the Cup-Bearer in the fresco at Knosos. Nevertheless this kilt does differ from the type with the codpiece illustrated in Crete by the steatite vases from Hagia Triada and by representations on engraved gems. The crux of the matter is whether we are to interpret this difference as a distinction between Minoan and Keftiuan kilts or as a change in Cretan fashions (conceivably introduced from Mycenae) in the second half of the fifteenth century B.C. This later type of kilt without codpiece is the form that appears at Knosos in the Late Minoan II 'Captain of the Blacks' fresco, and at Mycenae on the inlaid daggers and later on frescoes and gems.

CRETAN TRADE WITH THE CYCLADES

There is no evidence of trade between Crete and the Cyclades during the Neolithic period except the presence on Cretan Neolithic sites of knives made from what looks like Melian obsidian. In the first Early Minoan period there is ample evidence of connexions between Melos and Crete in the Pelos ware of the former and the Pyrgos fabric, but the impression I form from this is that Cycladic people were settling in Crete rather than Cretans in the Cyclades. The Pelos ware develops naturally into the Early Cycladic II pottery of Melos and other islands of the Cyclades, whereas the similar Pyrgos pottery of Crete comes to a dead stop and is replaced by pottery of completely different forms and decorations. Obviously the Minoan Cretans continued to import Melian obsidian, but I have a strong suspicion that it was coming in Cycladic, not in Minoan ships, in the Early Minoan I period.

With the development of the Middle Minoan culture and the building of the palaces early in the second millennium B.C. the position changed. The Cretans developed a merchant marine and probably a navy of their own, and they began to compete successfully with Phylakopi and other Cycladic cities, and perhaps it was because the Phylakopi merchants were being squeezed out of the Aegean Seas that they pushed into the western Mediterranean and left traces of their pioneering enterprise at Marseille and on the Balearic Isles, many centuries before the Phocaeans or even the Phoenicians had penetrated to those waters.

Before the fall of the first city of Phylakopi we already find local pottery imitating the light-on-dark wares of Early Minoan III and Middle Minoan I A type in Crete.

The second city of Phylakopi saw the importation of Minoan vases of Middle Minoan I B and Middle Minoan II A type and the imitation of them by local potters. On Kythnos there was a hoard of bronze tools of Middle Minoan types, including an axe-adze.

At the same time Phylakopi was also importing grey Minyan pottery from the Greek mainland, and if its sphere of influence was being curtailed by Minoan Crete there is still no evidence that it formed part of the Minoan empire; indeed it seems probable that Phylakopi may have owned some of the other Cyclades, since its traders dominated this area.

In the third Middle Minoan period Cretan influences became more marked at Phylakopi and it is not unlikely that Crete might even have dominated Melos and some of the other Cyclades. In the Temple Repositories at Knosos Evans found beaked jugs with curious Cycladic birds painted on them and suggested that 'these bird vases may have held some welcome offering to the priest-kings in the shape of Melian wine'. Cretan objects found in the second city of Phylakopi include bull's head rhyta. One quarter of the city was even turned into what was almost a Minoan residential quarter, with pillar crypts and splendid frescoes of Minoan type including one of flying fish in which the art of the Cretan fresco painter is seen at its best. Similar pillar crypts and frescoes occurred in the contemporary city on the island of Thera, and the islanders also made use of a linear script which looks like a variant of the Minoan Linear Script A.

Thucydides, in the first book of his history, tells us that 'Minos, the earliest of whom we hear, formed a navy and conquered what is now the Hellenic sea for the most part and the Cycladic islands, and ruled over them, becoming the first founder of many of them, driving out the Carians,[1] and establishing his own sons as rulers; and piracy, as was natural, he removed from the seas, so that more revenues might accrue to him.' Unfortunately, we are uncertain how far the tradition quoted by Thucydides refers to the Achaean King Minos mentioned by Homer and how far it reflects the glories of an earlier, pre-Hellenic Minos of the Middle Minoan period.

1. We do not know exactly why Thucydides believed there were Carians in the Cyclades, but it seems probable that by Carians he meant people akin to the Leleges, a subject population in classical Caria (see Chapter 3).

MINOAN AND MYCENAEAN TRADE WITH THE WEST

Trade with the West developed slowly, perhaps first up the Adriatic coasts, since copper daggers of a type known in the Early Minoan graves of the Mesara were found at Remedello near Brescia, at Monte Bradone near Volterra, and at Pangia in what was later to be known as Etruria; and before the end of the Early Minoan period Cretans were already importing the volcanic stone known as liparite from the Lipari islands as a substitute for, or an improvement on, Melian obsidian.

It is possible of course that some of this western trade may have been carried on not by Minoan Cretans but by Cycladic traders from Phylakopi on Melos.

Isolated vases of a kind made in Melos in the Middle Cycladic period have been found (without context) as far west as Marseille and the Balearic isles, and a stone axe of what seems to be probably Naxian emery at Calne in Wiltshire. The faience beads, however, of Levantine manufacture scattered over Europe, especially Britain, and dated by Piggott between 1550 and 1100 B.C. must be evidence of Mycenaean, not Minoan, trade with the West.

Recent excavations in the Lipari Isles uncovered some Vapheio cups of the Late Minoan I A period, which were at first hailed as Minoan imports, but these vases are not coated completely inside with glazed paint but have only a band of paint below the rim inside, and it would, therefore, appear that they must be not Cretan imports but Late Helladic I vases from Mycenae or some other mainland site.

Most of the Aegean imports to Sicily also seem to be Mycenaean. I know no certain example of a Minoan vase from that island, and though the bronze rapiers from Plemmyrion at Syracuse look like Minoan rapiers I would not like to assert that they could not have been brought on Mycenaean ships. There is, however, a very strong folklore tradition, recorded in its most complete form by Diodorus Siculus but also mentioned by Herodotus, concerning Minos's expedition to Sicily in pursuit of Daedalus, his murder there by the local King Kokalos, and his burial in a tomb of which the description by Diodorus reminds us of the temple tomb at Knosos.

We should, however, guard against the assumption that this proves that a Minoan expedition was sent to Sicily by a pre-Achaean king of Knosos, first because, as we shall see later, the Minos who is supposed to have made the expedition may have been an Achaean king of that city, and secondly because the Greeks confused the legends of a Bronze-Age architect named Daedalus with the Dedalic school of sculpture of the eighth and seventh centuries B.C.

Diodorus was using classical writers on Crete and supplementing their stories by the folklore of his native Sicily. Herodotus seems to have been using Samian sources and puts the siege of the city of Kamikos in Sicily by the Cretans, who were angered at Minos's death, in the third generation before the Trojan war, that is somewhere in the first half of the thirteenth century B.C. But what were the architectural remains attributed to this Daedalus which still existed in Diodorus's day? Pareti suggested that the Sicilian Minoa was not a Bronze Age foundation by Minoan Cretans or even Mycenaeans, but was connected with Selinus, itself a colony of Megara Hyblaea and so perhaps possessing legends originally derived from the Minoa near Megara on the Saronic Gulf (the mother city of Megara Hyblaea). This theory has been well criticized by Dunbabin, who emphasizes the resemblances between the Tomb of Minos as described by Diodorus and the Temple Tomb at Knosos which was buried and unknown to that writer.[1] Dunbabin therefore believes that the name Minoa, like other cities of that name in the Levant, does imply a connexion with Crete in prehistoric times.

Besides the rapiers of Plemmyrion we also find a form of spearhead that might have been imported from Minoan Crete in the form of a bronze spearhead with a long tapering blade, which is easier to parallel in the graves of Zafer Papoura than in Sicilian graves. Nevertheless no indisputably Minoan pottery has been found in Sicily, and rapiers of the Plemmyrion kind, though far more common in Crete, have also been found in the earlier shaft graves at Mycenae, so that even if the Sicilian examples were made in Crete, which is not certain, they may have arrived in Mycenaean ships.

The distribution areas in Sicily of these bronze weapons that can be derived from Aegean sources is almost confined to the neighbourhood of the three cities of Syracuse, Thapsus, and Acragas. These

1. 'Minos and Daidalos in Sicily', *Papers of the British School at Rome*, 1948, p. 8.

sites correspond to Thucydides's description, in the sixth book of his history, of the areas occupied by the Phoenicians. Now the Phoenicians did settle in Sicily in large numbers, but the settlements of which we have clear evidence were planted by Carthage and the western Phoenicians in the western part of Sicily, and it seems not unlikely that Thucydides was crediting to the Phoenicians the founding of trading settlements which had really been established by Mycenaean colonists in the fourteenth and thirteenth centuries B.C.

We may therefore agree with Dunbabin that the Sicilian legends of Daedalus confuse two periods, the first in the late Bronze Age when Minoan and Mycenaean adventurers came to Sicily, and the second when Rhodians and Cretans colonized Gela in 688 B.C. and their 'dedalic' sculpture was the dominant external influence. To the earlier period more probably belong the stones of the fortifications of Kamikos, the 'columbethra', the reservoirs of Daedalus, and the structures of the tomb of Minos and of the temple of Aphrodite at Eryx. The so-called *tholos* tombs of the Second Siculan period have sometimes been derived from Crete; but Levi denies this, and in fact their plan is more reminiscent of early rock cut tombs in Euboca than of anything in Crete. Occasionally we find Aegean types of skulls differing from the normal Siculan type (including two spheroid skulls from Pantalica and others from Castelluccio).

Minoan connexions with Malta and Pantelleria are harder to establish. The oriental features of the Maltese Neolithic culture and their rather general parallels in Cretan Neolithic or Early Minoan culture seem to depend rather on a common heritage from Syria or Anatolia than on a direct connexion with Minoan Crete. Perhaps the most striking individual parallel is that between the fine Cretan Neolithic squatting figurine in the Giamalakis collection and those of Neolithic sites such as Hal Saflieni in Malta. It suggests, as Hawkes remarked, that the original colonists of Malta must have arrived before the end of the Cretan Neolithic period in all probability, even though there is no suggestion that they came from Crete; J. D. Evans, however, dates the earlier Neolithic settlements in Malta late in the third millennium B.C.[1]

1. J. D. Evans, 'Prehistoric Culture Sequence in the Maltese Archipelago', *Proceedings of the Prehistoric Society*, 1953, p. 41.

LAND TRANSPORT IN CRETE

Crete has no rivers suitable for inland transport so that most materials must have been man-handled or carried on pack animals, because the mountainous character of the island left no possibility of the roads fanning out after the fashion of the desert tracks of Egypt, Syria, and Mesopotamia. There might be a choice of ways, but these ways were always narrow, and when it was a question of crossing a saddle from one valley to another there was, and still is, often no choice available. Human porters seem to have carried their loads on poles balanced on the shoulder, varying according to the weight of the burden from a short pole with two evenly balanced packages to a long pole carried by three or four men, a method employed in Egypt from the early dynasties onwards. I can recall no evidence for the use of hods or headbands to assist the porterage of loads on the back.

A clay model of Middle Minoan I date from Palaikastro (Fig. 17) illustrates the type of wagon used; it was doubtless drawn by oxen. The model presumably represents a wagon with solid wheels and no means of pivoting the front axle. This was not such a bar to progression as might be imagined, since Miss Seton Williams records seeing in Turkey in 1951 a wagon, with solid wheels revolving with the axle and with no pivot for the front axle, turning corners slowly but without undue difficulty; similar examples are illustrated by G. R. H. Wright and J. Carswell.[1]

Stockholm Museum has a copper model of a rather similar type of vehicle from north Syria, and though this particular example cannot be accurately dated we have evidence that wagons were in use in the Orontes valley in Syria about 2000 B.C., and the Cretans who were in close touch with ports such as Byblos probably imported the idea from that country.

Professor Childe suggested the following dates for the introduction of wheeled vehicles: in Mesopotamia 3000 + (B.C.); in the Indus Valley 2500 ±; on the Central Asian steppes 2500; in north Syria, on the Khabur and Upper Euphrates, 2200 ± 100; in the Orontes valley

1. V. Gordon Childe, 'The First Wagons and Carts', *Proceedings of the Prehistoric Society*, 1951, p. 177, and Wright and Carswell in *Man*, March 1956, Note 39.

Fig. 17a. Palaikastro model wagon

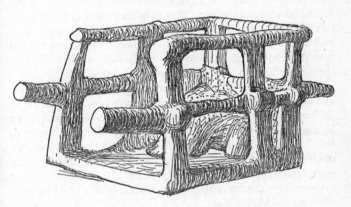

Fig. 17b. Litter from Dove Shrine, Knosos

2000 ± 100; in Crete and central Anatolia 1900 ± 100; and on the mainland of Greece 1550 ± 30.[1]

The use of the domestic ass as a pack animal may go back further in Crete, though I cannot recall any evidence for that animal on the island before Middle Minoan times or any representation of an animal

---

1. The people of Mycenae had horse-drawn chariots by this date and they may have had ox wagons as early as the Cretans.

with panniers before the Late Minoan III period.[1] Childe suggests that oxen may have been used for ploughing before they were employed for drawing carts, but I know of no Minoan evidence either for or against this suggestion.

WAR CHARIOTS

Spoked wheels appear at a very early date at Chagar Bazar, but the earliest appearance of the war chariot with spoked wheels in the Aegean would appear to be the example carved on the grave stele of the Mycenaean king buried in the Fifth Shaft Grave at Mycenae, dated about 1550 B.C. Since the earliest representation of a horse in Minoan art is on a Late Minoan II gem dated 1450–1400 showing a horse being transported on a galley, there is a distinct possibility that the war chariot and the horse were only introduced to Crete in the Late Minoan II period, perhaps by the Mycenaean dynasty which may have been ruling at Knosos at that time, though there is a seal from Avdhou in Crete showing two men in a chariot drawn by two *agrimia* attributed to the Late Minoan I period (Fig. 18).

The Minoan army certainly had no cavalry and probably no organized chariotry. The war chariot seems to have been an invention of the Sumerians, but their chariot, with its four solid wheels, and drawn by asses, must have been rather a slow, clumsy affair. The capture of Babylon by the Kassites, who had domesticated the horse, revolutionized the warfare of the Middle East. Before the middle of the second millennium B.C. a properly organized chariot arm was serving the purpose of cavalry in all the armies of the greater land powers of the Near and Middle East.

By the sixteenth century B.C. the war chariot had spread to the Greek mainland, not indeed the improved light chariot with a six-spoke wheel which we find illustrated on the later Hittite monuments and on Egyptian monuments of the Eighteenth Dynasty, but the rather slower four-spoke wheel type that appears on the earlier monuments of the Hittites, from whom the Mycenaean Greeks may

1. A figurine of Late Minoan III date from Phaistos shows a horse with two *pithoi* slung pannier-fashion, as is the practice today among the travelling potters of Thrapsanos. See D. Fimmer, *Die Kretisch-Mykenische Kultur*, 1924, p. 114, Fig. 102.

have adopted it.[1] The earliest representations of the Mycenaean chariot given on the sculptured *stelai* from the shaft graves are rather summary, and we must not therefore overstress the fact that there is only one horse and only one man in the chariot. Nevertheless it is quite possible that at Mycenae the oldest form of chariot had only one horse and that the charioteer also used the spear against his opponent.

Fig. 18. Goat chariot from Avdhou

The normal method, however, where the chariot had two horses and two men, one to drive and one to fight with spear or bow, is already illustrated by a gold ring from the Fourth Shaft Grave at Mycenae. The chariot with its four-spoke wheels and low box-like car perhaps made of basketwork is similar to those of the *stelai*, but is here drawn by two shaggy ponies.[2]

1. I do not imply that a six-spoke wheel must be faster than one with four spokes, but simply that the six-spoked form on the monument is much lighter and less clumsy than the four-spoked variety.

2. Not the fine Arabian breed illustrated on Late Minoan frescoes, vases, and gems, but something more like a modern Cretan pony; conceivably the so-called 'Celtic' variety of *Equus agilis*.

This form of war chariot was particularly favoured by the Indo-European speaking tribes and was probably a major cause of their widespread conquests and expansion. It is referred to in the *Rig Veda*, the earliest Sanscrit poems in India, in Homer's *Iliad*, and in other epic poems in Greece; it continued in use later in Cyprus, in Etruria, and among the Celts, and was still employed by the Britons when Caesar invaded Britain.

The yoke, which was appropriate for an ox-cart and which had been intended for a Sumerian war chariot, must have been rather an awkward device for a swift horse-drawn vehicle. Contenau even goes so far as to say that 'the capacity of the horse's effort is only equal to its resistance to strangulation', a superb epigram but perhaps exaggerating the difficulties. The yoke, I believe, was probably not taking the main stress of drawing the chariot, which would be taken by traces attached to the collar or breast-band, but was serving the same purpose as the shafts of a modern carriage in keeping the car in its proper position. The Homeric word *lepadna*, as Miss Lorimer observes, comprised both the collar or breast-band and the girth, which was set very far forward and attached to the collar at its top-ends just behind the base of the neck. The traces are not usually illustrated, but must surely have been attached to this dual *lepadna*, which continued to be popular throughout the classical period. This form of harness and yoke already appear clearly on the Avdhou gem (Fig. 18). The straps of the *lepadna*, which would have been of leather, broaden towards the bottom.

Some chariots of the Late Minoan II–III period illustrate another device that may have been intended to relieve the strain on the horses' necks, consisting of a long pole or thong stretching from the rim of the car to the tip of the chariot pole and attached by straps lower down to the pole.

In the Late Minoan II–III period the normal chariot was apparently what Evans termed the 'dual chariot', and is illustrated by the signs on the 'chariot tablets' of Linear Script B from Knosos, and by the fresco of the two princes in a chariot from Tiryns on the mainland. The curving projection at the back gives rather the impression of a rail, though in fact, as Miss Lorimer observes, it must be a solid affair. It may still, however, have been rounded off by a flat rail which, with the addition of the extended platform of the car, would have afforded greater facility for the warrior to mount the car while it was in motion; and this I suggest may have been the purpose of the projection at the back of the dual chariot. It would also probably allow the car to carry a third person if necessary.

It must be remarked that the horse on the ship of the Late Minoan II seal, and indeed all the horses depicted on Mycenaean frescoes or vases, is a fine animal with a small head, powerful fore and hind quarters, and small joints, recalling Shakespeare's splendid description in *Venus and Adonis*:

> Round-hoofed, short jointed, fetlocks shag and long,
> Broad breast, full eye, small head and nostril wide,
> High crest, short ears, straight legs and passing strong,
> Thin mane, thick tail, broad buttock, tender hide:
> Look what a horse should have he did not lack,
> Save a proud rider on so proud a back.

In a word, Mycenaean horses look as if they had good Arabian blood in them, and would be much superior in speed to what Ridgeway used to term 'those quarter-bred animals of the Parthenon frieze'.[1]

Did the Minoan Cretans know how to ride? The evidence from Cretan sealings would suggest that equitation was practised by goddesses rather than men,[2] since the earliest unmistakable picture of a mounted warrior in Crete is on a cremation urn from Mouliane often assigned to the tenth, but by Desborough to the ninth century B.C.[3]

Nevertheless Mycenaean Greeks both in the Peloponnese and in their colonies were riding horses in the thirteenth century B.C.[4] and the riding of asses had been known in Egypt in the days of the Middle Kingdom and of horses by the inhabitants of the Persian uplands apparently in the third millennium B.C.

The negative evidence from Crete is unreliable, and it seems probable that riding was practised in Crete certainly by the thirteenth century B.C. and perhaps considerably earlier, whether the art was learned from Mycenae or from Egypt, Palestine, or Syria.

1. A quotation from a lecture.

2. D. Levi, 'La Dea Micenea a Cavallo', *Studies Presented to D. M. Robinson*, 1951, p. 108.

3. V. Desborough, *Protogeometric Pottery* (1952), p. 269.

4. M. S. Hood, 'A Mycenaean Cavalryman', *Annual of the British School at Athens*, 1953, p. 84 ff., Figs. 47, 48; C. F. A. Schaeffer, *Ugaritica II*, 1949, p. 158, Fig. 61C.

The Minoans also employed open litters or carrying chairs. Our earliest surviving evidence for this form of transport consists of a model carrying-chair found in the Dove-Shrine deposit in the Temple of Minos (Fig. 17*b*).

The normal Minoan carrying-chair illustrated both by the Middle Minoan II model referred to and by a rather fragmentary fresco of Late Minoan I date from the Palace of Minos consisted of an open litter enclosed by a railing, attached to two carrying poles, and containing a chair for the occupant.

The Mycenaean Greeks, however, improved on this model by adding a vaulted cover[1] resembling on a smaller scale the hood of the covered wagon of the Scythian steppes, and illustrated by a clay model found in Stratum VI at Tepe Gawra (a settlement dating back to Early Dynastic[2] times on a mound now enclosed by the Assyrian walls of Khorsabad).

Pendlebury even goes so far as to say that 'the normal method of progression for the rich man was a palanquin', and he may be right, though the evidence is rather scanty for Minoan Crete.

It would be rash to assume that the Cretans ever had goat-carriages drawn by their own wild goats, despite the appearance of the chariot drawn by two *agrimia* on the Late Minoan I seal from Avdhou quoted above.

1. J. M. Cook, 'Pelino Omoioma Mykenaikou Phoreiou', *Kretika Chronika*, 1955, p. 152.
2. I refer, of course, only to the Sixth Settlement.

CHAPTER 5

Minoan Art

MINOAN art, the art of the Cretan Bronze Age, differs in spirit considerably not only from its contemporaries in the Near East, but also from its immediate predecessor, the art of Neolithic Crete.

Art for art's sake seems, I know not why, to have been a Neolithic invention and appears all over the world whenever the inhabitants reach that stage of culture, whereas late Palaeolithic art and its more recent offshoots, such as the cave paintings of eastern Spain or the relatively modern cave paintings of the Rhodesian caves, were grafted in magic. They were intended to serve the practical purpose of aiding the hunters, though doubtless the painter derived an artistic pleasure from his work.

Neolithic art on the other hand was non-representational and severely abstract in the main. If men, animals, birds, fishes, or flowers were represented at all they quickly became patterns. Features that originally had had a structural use on vases were also turned into patterns, which are termed by the archaeologist 'skeuomorphic' designs, because they had derived their *morphe* or shape from the *skeuos* or household article on which they had originally performed a practical function. Thus the stitched seams of a leather bottle, or the ribs or studs of a metal vessel may be painted as skeuomorphic patterns on pottery imitations of such vessels (Plate 1 and Fig. 3).

The 'art for art's sake' of the Neolithic potter may have been fostered by the settled agricultural life of those times, but whatever the cause was it is clear that Neolithic Cretans conformed to the general rule. The pottery of the earliest Bronze Age in Crete also continued to be adorned only with very simple patterns of a severely geometric kind such as painted vertical or diagonal lines, occasionally cross-hatched, incised dots, or semicircles – a poor and uninspired repertory, but completely devoid of any suggestions of magic.

It is evident that we cannot speak of an art common to the whole of Crete during the first Early Minoan period (2400–2300 B.C.) which was marked by the infiltration of small bands of settlers from various directions, each with its own particular style of pottery; indeed the complete fusion of these different elements of the population was scarcely complete before the beginning of the first Middle Minoan period (1950 B.C.).

Fig. 19. Minoan torsion designs

We can only surmise the origin of these bands of settlers from the artistic affinities of their arts, from those of Early Minoan II patterned ware and of Vasiliki pottery, with certain Anatolian wares; and from those of Pyrgos with those of the 'Pelos' variety in the Cyclades (Fig. 22).

The rectilinear patterns of Early Minoan III pottery were only a continuation or elaboration of those of the previous period – a zigzag line with triangles, a band of chevrons, a pattern like the triglyphs and metopes of a Doric frieze, and so on. More important than the rectilinear decoration was the introduction of curvilinear ornaments, which had scarcely ever appeared before except in the form of concentric semicircles on Early Minoan II pottery. Whole circles filled in with colour or with hatched segments or other hatched patterns also occur. Running spirals (a Cycladic pattern) appear sometimes joined by a curious leaflike scroll. This incipient interest in natural history is very slight and tentative at first, the most amusing

Fig. 20. Zakros sealings

example being a sherd on which the familiar opposed triangles or 'butterfly' pattern has been turned into a goat by adding a head with a pair of horns at the apex of one of the triangles. Perhaps this new naturalistic art may have started in the Mesara, since it is rare on the pottery but very evident on the ivory seals, which are common in the great round tombs of the Mesara. Here we find not only lively if somewhat primitive designs of men, animals, birds, scorpions, fishes, and even ships, but also meander patterns and quadruple spirals best paralleled in Egypt. A favourite animal on these seals is the lion, which still existed on the mainland of Greece and of course in Syria, but not, I think, in Crete.

SPIRAL DECORATION

The origin of spiral decoration in general does not concern us here and I think it had more than one origin; its derivation from gold or copper wire or from the spiral coils of shells or from textiles will all fit individual instances, but break down if interpreted as universal sources for spiral ornaments.

It is clear, at least, that a fashion in spirals spread over the Levant towards the end of the third millennium B.C. In Egypt the fashion is illustrated by small scrolls on scarabs of the First Intermediate Period, finally developing into four, or sometimes six, interconnected spirals outlining a roughly quadrilateral area. Similar quadruple spirals appear in Crete on the bases of seals of gold and of ivory from the Mesara, and on a stone *pyxis* from Tholos B at Platanos. The pattern is capable of developing into a spiral network of the kind fashionable in Egypt in the Eighteenth Dynasty, and in the Late Bronze Age in Crete, and on the mainland of Greece.

TORSION AS A DECORATIVE PRINCIPLE

The first real attempt to probe into the basic principles of Minoan art was made by Professor Friedrich Matz in his work on early Cretan seal stones, in which he distinguished two fundamental methods of decorating the surface of a vase, which we may translate as 'zone decoration' and 'surface decoration'. Furumark, in his works on Mycenaean pottery, prefers to employ the terms 'tectonic' and 'unity' decoration for the same two methods.

The peculiarity of Minoan surface decoration, first noted by Matz, was its partiality for 'torsion' or twisted motifs. The zone decoration in which horizontal bands of ornament play the leading part is indeed 'tectonic' in the sense that it emphasizes the structure of the vase, the greatest width, the mouth and neck, the handles, and the foot. The 'surface' or 'unity' decoration, on the other hand, treats the whole vase as a free field for a single design, or even several independent designs, without stressing any particular structural feature of the vase.

If the base of a cylindrical or round stamp seal has a frieze of animals on the circumference, or even two animals arranged in the *tête bêche* position (which is only the circular frieze reduced to its simplest form), the effect of a moving frieze can be obtained by turning the seal round, but this is not torsion. Torsion occurs when a motive which might be expected to run vertically or horizontally twists like the line of a corkscrew up and across the surface to be decorated. This can occur in purely rectilinear ornaments, but it is perhaps not surprising that it should have been particularly popular in areas where spirals were in vogue, such as the Aegean or the Danube basin. Indeed Matz in his book on Cretan seals was inclined to regard this as a European element in Minoan culture, but in his latest article on torsion he has emphasized the fact that, though torsion was certainly characteristic of large areas in Central and Eastern Europe, it was also characteristic of a wide area in the Levant including not only the Aegean, but also south-eastern Anatolia, which so strongly influenced Crete, the Cyclades, and the Greek mainland at the beginning of the Bronze Age.

Matz has contrasted the torsion style with the more widely distributed systems of the *Winkelband* or 'Zigzag Line' and the 'Meridian system', a vertical division which in one form or another occurs in most parts of the ancient world, and has come to the conclusion that the source of torsion as an aesthetic principle is to be sought not so much in Europe as in Anatolia.

Matz's account of the diffusion of torsion seems reasonable and is not incompatible with an idea of my own that the technique of decorating the surface while the vase was being turned on a mat may have contributed to its development. Indeed the technique of manufacture may have contributed something also to the zigzag band and meridian systems. Zigzag bands are common, if not inevitable, in basket work, so that the *Winkelband* might be considered as a skeuomorphic ornament derived from basketry even though the potters who developed this theme were probably quite unconscious of its origin.

Similarly meridian decoration might be derived from leather bottles with vertical seams, though it is only occasionally that we can assert such a derivation with confidence.[1]

Torsion decoration might arise naturally, I think, if a potter painted his vase while turning it on a mat or some such base. All hand-made vases, unless they are so big that the potter has to walk round them, must be turned round during the process of manufacture. When the potter's wheel was introduced the wheel would normally have been stopped before the decoration began (unless the ornament

1. For example on certain bowls and bottles of Bronze Age date in Cyprus.

was of a very simple, band-like character), and if any decoration was carried out while the wheel was still moving, this would be easy to detect. With vases turned on a mat, however, the turning would have been so slow and so easily controlled that decoration could

Fig. 21. Designs on Early Minoan I vases

easily have taken place while the vase was being turned, and this would have been apt to produce torsional effects, which later might be deliberately cultivated as an aesthetic principle. Other causes doubtless contributed to the torsional style, but I think it may be significant that the earliest motives of this nature seem to occur on hand-made or hand-turned pottery, and that they seem to be absent from Mesopotamia, Syria, and Egypt where the potter's wheel was introduced at very early dates. In the Aegean area itself torsion is particularly dominant in Crete and rarer in the Cyclades and on the mainland until it reappears under Cretan influence at the beginning of the Late Bronze Age.

MINOAN ART AND THE EIDETICS

Now it is true that we may claim the Minoan civilization as the first European civilization, as distinct from the semi-barbarous though often artistic cultures of the north, but this is no explanation of the uncanny qualities of Minoan art in the Middle and Late Minoan periods, qualities less obvious during the Early Minoan period. Minoan art is not only unlike its predecessors; it is also unlike all its successors, with the exception of arts directly influenced by it such as those of Mycenae and the Cyclades. G. A. Snijder offered an ingenious explanation of these peculiarities suggesting that they were character-istic of the artistic products of a group of people whom the psycho-logists term 'eidetics', and that these peculiarities were also to be noticed in the late Palaeolithic art of Spain and France and in related cultures of more recent times, such as the Eastern Spanish School or the Bushmen paintings of Rhodesia. This condition is very rare among European adults, and not very common among children, but is a well-attested phenomenon. Just as anybody who looks at the sun or a lighted lamp and then at a blank wall will see a little purple lamp or sun for a second or two, so an eidetic person will retain the vision of a whole picture or landscape if he transfers his gaze from it to a blank surface. This vision, which is not merely a mental picture, is termed an *eidos* and the people who are liable to such visions are termed 'eidetics'. This condition was first studied by the German scholar, E. R. Jaensch, who published his researches in 1933 in a work entitled *Die Eidetik*.

Children with eidetic vision are sometimes unable to distinguish clearly between their eidetic visions and what they see in the ordinary way. This condition is termed the phase of eidetic unity, and usually does not last long, but may persist longer with half-witted or slowly-developed children, and it is suggested by followers of Jaensch that it might be more prevalent and last longer with primitive peoples.

The Minoan ability to portray figures in rapid movement with a vividness hardly equalled before the invention of photography could be easily explained if the Minoans were eidetics, since the artist would then only have had to trace along the outline of his eidetic

Fig. 22. Designs on Early Minoan II vases

vision. This great facility is, however, accompanied by certain weaknesses. The eidetic artist is apt to concentrate on the outline and to disregard the internal bony structure which does not appear in his vision. The figures therefore sometimes tend to be slightly insubstantial, to float in air rather than to stand firmly on the ground.

Snijder's theory attracted me at first and has been supported to some extent by Pendlebury and Platon, but on a closer examination of it I doubt whether it is a satisfactory explanation of Minoan art in general.

Can the realism of Minoan frescoes be explained by assuming that the artist saw his subject as an eidetic vision? Minoan frescoes may perhaps seem fresh and natural compared to the splendid but more formal beauties of Egyptian wall-paintings, but they are not quasi-photographic representations like the bisons of Altamira in Spain. Indeed Minoan paintings abound in conventions, some obviously borrowed from Egypt, such as the procession motives, or the distinctions between the red flesh of the men and the white flesh of the women, but other conventions seem to be native Minoan. Most uneidetic of all the Cretan artist's conventions is his naturalization of the lotus flower. The photographically correct drawing of this plant on Egyptian paintings appeared too stiff to be true to the Minoan artist, who proceeded to gild the lily by painting his lotus if not 'as large as life' at least 'twice as natural'.

This idealistic tendency of the Cretan artist is well stressed by H. R. Hall in his comparison of the cat on the Hagia Triada fresco with those on Egyptian paintings of the Twelfth and Eighteenth Dynasties.

The Minoan borrowed his idea from Egypt, and his cat is in one sense a better cat than the Egyptian, in another a worse one. It gives the idea of the cat, its stealthiness and its cruelty, better than the Egyptian paintings which hardly give any such idea at all. But they are more accurate in detail; they are correct portraits of the animal taken from her in repose, and in the Eighteenth Dynasty example clumsily put into a scene meant to represent action, though all the actors with the possible exception of the butterflies, are as calm and peaceful in gesture as is the cat. Compare the Cretan cat, which is incorrectly drawn, but gives a masterly and true impression of the animal when hunting.

Hall proceeds then to contrast the purely Aegean conception of a swallow in flight on a sherd from Melos with the very dull copy of an Egyptian goose found on the same site at Phylakopi.

This difference between Minoan and Egyptian artistic practices may be observed also in the Late Bronze Age.

The octopods and dolphins of the first Late Minoan period are not correctly drawn in detail but are magnificently alive, whereas the Red Sea fish and crabs of Queen Hatshepshut's relief at Deir-el-Bahri are as accurate and lifeless as the diagrams of trilobites in a textbook of palaeontology.

Forsdyke stresses this same feature with reference to one of the gold cups from Vapheio: 'The trapped bull bellows in anger and its hind quarters are twisted the wrong way round. Such distortion is manifestly impossible, but the Minoan artist would not check at this exaggeration so long as it served to emphasize a mighty struggle and disposed a pair of legs nicely for his design.'

Surely the eidetic artist postulated by Snijder would have been more accurate and less idealistic in his draughtsmanship. The inaccuracies of eidetic art are of a different kind and consist of combining incongruous details which individually are photographically accurate.

Mrs Groenewegen-Frankfort speaks of 'the absolute mobility' and 'unhampered freedom' of Minoan figures whether human or animal and the artist's delight in moving patterns. . . . 'There is a sense of the organic even when organisms are not depicted. . . . This not only makes for a dynamic coherence of disparate motifs but gives each one of them a curious independence as if they were charged with life.'[1] She also points out how often the dominant movement in one direction is restrained by a counter-movement in a different direction such as animals in the flying gallop pose with the head turned backwards, or the falling man on the Harvester Vase from Hagia Triada.

Snijder also attempted to detect eidetic characteristics in Minoan sculpture, architecture, and even vocabulary. Minoan architecture is certainly rather queer and haphazard so that it has been rightly dubbed 'agglutinative' because rooms and wings of various shapes and sizes were added as the need arose, but I doubt if they are so very much more 'agglutinative' than the plan of the City of London, which from medieval times onwards has mainly expanded by cellular growth, nor do I see any great resemblance between a Minoan palace and a nomadic camp (to which Snijder compares it), since the latter

1. H. A. Groenewegen-Frankfort, *Arrest and Movement*, 1951, p. 191 f.

is usually laid out on a much simpler and more regular plan to meet the needs of defence against surprise attack.

It should be remarked that Snijder's best parallels between Minoan and eidetic art occur not in the Early Minoan period, as might be expected if they were primitive traits, but rather in the third Middle Minoan period, and that they might be more explicable if we supposed that a painter capable of seeing eidetic visions had played a leading role as a fresco painter and perhaps formed a school of his own, instead of trying to interpret all Minoan art in terms of eidetic visions.

MINOAN POLYCHROMY IN POTTERY AND FRESCOES

The naturalizing of geometric designs, which is barely noticeable in Early Minoan III and Middle Minoan I A pottery, becomes increasingly prominent in the Middle Minoan I B style. Purely geometric designs such as hatched triangles or spirals now not only alternate with branches, daisy chains, and triple flowers, but also intermarry with them, so that a design which starts as a hanging spiral may suddenly bloom into a cluster of berries. Among the new designs is a swastika (a very ancient motive in Mesopotamia but new to Crete). The commoner form of polychromy, especially on cups, is the alternate repetition of the same motif in white and orange on the usual black ground. The old principle of torsion is still active in the diagonal arrangement of many of the motifs, one of these torsion designs being the old Early Minoan III one, the scorpion parade, now arranged as two lobe-shaped leaves joined by a stem. Large round blobs are a favourite motif, either arranged as a frieze or forming the knots of a net pattern.

Another form of decoration, not very common in northern Crete but very popular in the Mesara, was the so-called barbotine type, consisting usually of thin strips of clay usually applied in the torsional style to jugs with beaked spouts and with no painted or only very simply painted ornaments. Another form in which the surface is worked up with a tool to form prickles like rose thorns is more characteristic of the Middle Minoan II period.

In eastern Crete pottery decorated in this Middle Minoan I B style not only began rather earlier than it did in the centre of the island (?1900 B.C. as against ?1870 B.C.) but also persisted right through the Middle Minoan II period, when the pottery that we know as Middle Minoan II A and B was in vogue at Knosos and Phaistos.

The colours employed on Middle Minoan I B vases included a modification of the old orange-yellow, a new red approximating to crimson in hue, and a brilliant white employed not only for separate ornaments but also to coat zones or panels of barbotine 'prickle' ornament between the areas adorned with polychrome ornaments (especially in the Mesara). The shapes favoured included 'fruit stands', bridge-spouted vases, beaked jugs, 'tea-cups', 'Vapheio cups',[1] and, in Knosos and along the north coast up to Gournia, chalices with strap handle and a crinkled rim obviously imitating a metallic type – one vase of this form in silver was actually found at Gournia in a grave.

These chalices are quite important from a chronological point of view since they are clearly related to, and probably contemporary with, some Hittite vases found in the fourth city at Boghaz Koi or in the city termed Alisar II in Cappadocia.

FIGURES IN THE ROUND

Very little plastic work of importance has survived from the first Middle Minoan period. The fashion of carving the handles of ivory seals in the form of an animal or a bird, so popular in the Early Minoan III period, had died out, and we have only one steatite figure, the one from the round tomb at Porti in the Mesara, that should probably be assigned to this period since the proportion and modelling of this figure show a marked advance on any of the earlier human figures.

The cheaper forms of Middle Minoan I figures, however, are well represented among the dedications at the various 'peak sanctuaries' in the form of figurine men or women, or animals, or parts of them. The earlier types of these are represented by those from the oval house at Chamaizi in eastern Crete consisting of standing male figures with the right hand raised to the chin and the left hand by the belt, to which is attached a short dagger, and of standing female

1. A truncated conical shape like that of the gold cups found at Vapheio.

figures with both hands raised to the chin, with a long, flaring skirt, and with a roll on the head that might be interpreted either as a 'Tam o'Shanter' form of cap, or as a method of hairdressing.

The later figurines from the peak sanctuaries are of the kind made familiar by the finds from Petsopha, the sanctuary above Palaikastro. Two fragments of a figure painted in the Middle Minoan II style were found in the Second City of Phylakopi on the Cycladic island of Melos.

Such figurines were obviously the cheap art of the period, but of the figures in gold, bronze, or ivory which must certainly have existed we have nothing surviving except the Porti figurine already mentioned.

We are therefore no more able to conjecture what the best work of Minoan modellers and carvers might have been at this time than we could have estimated the work of Pheidias if the Parthenon marbles had not survived and we had been dependent on reconstructing their probable forms from the cheap plaques and figurines in clay dedicated on the Athenian Acropolis.

In the Middle Minoan II b period (1830–1700 B.C.) we begin to encounter beautiful seals in hard stones engraved in a naturalistic style (cf. Fig. 34). This development is partly due to an increasing mastery over the materials by the artist, who was now using a tubular drill and a saw as well as a graver and so could cut hard stones such as agate, crystal, and emerald, and partly due to the fact that the invention of a linear script had provided an easy method of writing clay labels and so rendered the seal less important as a means of communicating a message.

Seals were now articles of luxury rather than business necessities and those who ordered them could command the services of good craftsmen. Indeed the best Middle Minoan II b seals were never surpassed in grace and finish. Prism seals with three or four sides still continue to be made, but the best engraving occurs on flattened cylinders, on lentoid or bean-shaped seals, on discoid seals with a design on both flat sides or with one side modelled to form a grip, or on signets (a form borrowed from the Hittites of Asia Minor). One design which recurs on several seals of the Middle Minoan II b and Middle Minoan III a periods was compared by Pendlebury to a Jacobean cherub, and by Evans to an Ishtar mask; I have myself wondered whether it was not a modification of the winged sun disk of Egypt turned into a grinning face by the irrepressible Minoan artist. I think that, whatever was the origin of this device, Marinatos is probably right in associating it with the faces on seals or clay sealings from Mochlos, Phaistos, and Zakros and with Greek archaic representations of Gorgon masks.

To the Middle Minoan II B period also belongs a unique amethyst scarab from the lower levels of the Psychro Cave, which by its material and modelling, should be Egyptian work of the Twelfth or at latest of the Thirteenth Dynasty but bears on its base a Minoan design consisting of two beaked jugs and some concentric circles arranged round a device usually interpreted as a rayed sun.[1]

The naturalism which was soon to blossom in the frescoes already appears on the seals in a developed form. A fine flattened cylinder in rock crystal shows a Cretan ibex bounding over its native rocks with a tree in the background, a perfect illustration of the scene so aptly described by Xan Fielding in his book *The Stronghold*:

> With no apparent means of propulsion (for its legs were invisible in motion) and with its shoulders flattened by perspective and half-concealed in dust, it came hurtling horizontally across the cliff – a disembodied head hanging on to the air by its horns.

This is certainly the finest verbal description of the pose which archaeologists term the 'flying gallop' and which the Minoan artist loved to portray (Fig. 34). Fielding's description perhaps explains why so many ancient representations of the ibex portray the head and horns too large for the body.

Of the ivory figures now in European or American museums and reported to have come from Crete it is better to follow Nilsson and not to quote them as illustrations of Minoan art, though the gold and ivory snake-goddess in Boston is usually reckoned as genuine and the Toronto figure known as 'Our Lady of the Sports', wearing the male dress for the bull ring like the ladies in the Toreador Fresco, bears a strong resemblance to the leaping figures from the Late Minoan I deposit.[2]

1. Pendlebury, *The Archaeology of Crete*, p. 119 and Fig. 19, No. 5.
2. Evans, *The Palace of Minos*, Vol. I, p. 337 and Vol. III, p. 305; but Marinatos, Mallowan, and Glotz consider the Boston statuette to be a forgery.

CHAPTER 6

The Early Minoan Period

THE Neolithic period in Crete did not end in a catastrophe; its culture developed into that of the Bronze Age under pressure from the infiltration of relatively small bands of immigrants from the south and east, where copper and bronze had long been in use. This early metal culture of Crete might be termed a Copper Age, but since the exact date when tin first became available to the Cretans is hard to define, it is best to follow Sir Arthur Evans, who christened the culture between the Neolithic and Iron Ages in Crete the Minoan culture, after Minos the legendary king of Knosos, and who divided the Minoan epoch into three periods: Early, Middle, and Late Minoan with three sub-divisions each.

Professor Doro Levi has recently put forward a heretical theory, based on the absence of Early Minoan pottery at Phaistos, that there was no Early Minoan period at all, properly speaking, and that the Middle Minoan period directly followed the Late Neolithic with the intervention of only some very short-lived transitional fabrics that might be described as Early Minoan.[1] It must be admitted that at Knosos also Early Minoan pottery is very scarce, and almost non-existent in the Palace of Minos where the walls of the earliest palace usually rest on or are embedded in the latest Neolithic deposits.

His theory, however, does not explain the existence of extensive Early Minoan material not only in the Mesara but also especially in east Crete where such material is sometimes stratified over Neolithic or under Middle Minoan I deposits. The absence of Early Minoan material on the palace sites at Knosos and at Phaistos may be explained by the cutting away of such deposits caused by the terracing required for the excavation of the great Middle Minoan I palaces.

The Early Minoan period, however, must have been much shorter

1. See articles in *Illustrated London News*, 19 January 1952, 2 December 1953, 30 September 1955.

than was supposed by Evans, whose absolute chronology was based on synchronisms with the contemporary culture of Egypt and Mesopotamia, and was dependent on the validity of what was then termed 'the shorter chronology' evolved by Dr Édouard Meyer, but which has now proved to be not short enough.

THE FIRST EARLY MINOAN PERIOD

Thus the Early Minoan I period which Evans was obliged to stretch from 3400 to 2800 B.C. is dated 2600 to 2400 by Matz, and I am inclined personally to date it 2500 to 2400 B.C.

The Early Minoan I culture is not a unity at all. I doubt if any of the more important Late Neolithic sites were abandoned. At Knosos and at Phaistos there is an absence of the new dark-on-light painted pottery found elsewhere, but this, I think, is merely because the local Neolithic pottery developed into Sub-Neolithic fabrics better baked, of finer material than that of the preceding period, and characterized by vertical burnishing, but obviously derived from the Late Neolithic types.

It is likely, too, that some of the pottery of Late Neolithic types, found by the Germans at Kumarospilio in the far west and by the Greeks at Hellenes Amariou, may belong to the Early Minoan I period. On such sites we may assume that the inhabitants were still of Cretan Neolithic stock.

The foreign influences that were already perceptible, however, in the Late Neolithic period, may now be observed to be infiltrating into the island by three main routes, from the Cyclades, from Anatolia, and from Syria.

Graves from the Early Minoan I period are scattered thinly throughout east and central Crete, at Zakros, Hagios Nikolaos, and Patema in the extreme east, at Sphoungaras on the Merabello coast, at Trapeza in Lasithi, at Miamou in the Mesara, and at Kanli Kastelli in central Crete.

Houses of the Early Minoan I period are scarce however, and it is clear that many people still lived in caves.[1] Of the thirty-three excavated sites recorded by Pendlebury sixteen were burials or bore traces of having been burials (twelve from caves or rock shelters),

1. Unless one believes with Levi that this period did not exist.

while only at Mochlos and at Hellenes Amariou were actual walls of stone houses recorded, though it is of interest to note that Komo, the port for ships departing for Egypt, and the little island harbour town of Mochlos on the gulf of Merabello were both founded in the Early Minoan I period.

No copper tools that can be dated as certainly Early Minoan I have yet been found, and it is not improbable that the Cretans of that period continued to use stone tools. Evans has also assigned to this period two or three stone figurines which appear to represent a transition between the Late Neolithic squatting type and a standing type, because of the abnormally wide flanks and very short legs. This characteristic, however, can hardly be quoted as evidence for an Early Minoan I date, since standing figurines were already made in Neolithic times. The use of stone instead of clay, however, may, as Pendlebury suggested, indicate an Early Minoan I date. One such figurine from central Crete is in alabaster, one from Knosos is in a marble-like stone, while a third from Gortyn is in breccia.

At Pyrgos near Nirou Khani, Xanthoudides excavated a large rock shelter which had been employed as an ossuary in Early Minoan I and later times. There was no stratification, but the Early Minoan I material, which could be identified on stylistic grounds, was abundant. Here the excavator found not only incised bottles and *pyxides* like those of Pelos, with vertically pierced suspension lugs,[1] but also beaked jugs of west Anatolian forms with simple rectilinear designs in a reddish brown lustrous paint and a grey smoked fabric with burnished decoration of which the most characteristic shape was a tall chalice, shaped like an hour glass, of a type sometimes called the Arkalochori chalices, from the site where they were first found by Hazzidakis. Evans derived these from the footed bowls of later Neolithic pottery, but now that we have more evidence from excavations in the Dodecanese and Asia Minor it appears that this ware is also in a sense Anatolian, being related to wares in the Dodecanese and Samos; but it is reasonable to assume that the people who made the incised bottles and *pyxides* characteristic of the Pyrgos cemetery near Nirou Khani, of Tholos A at Koumasa, and of the Kanli

1. A feature characteristic of the contemporary Early Cycladic vases in the Cyclades and distinguishing them from the succeeding Early Cycladic II vases with horizontally pierced lugs.

Kastelli (Fig. 23) cemetery must have come from the Cyclades where such pottery is characteristic of the very earliest deposits in Melos and Antiparos. The earliest and most primitive form of *tholos* tomb in Crete, at Krasi on the edge of the Pedhiadha district, also resembles Cycladic forms. The marble figurines found near Knosos, in the Mesara, and in eastern Crete are still clearer evidence of influence from those islands, though possibly at a later date.

Archaeologists have often been puzzled over the apparent absence of a Neolithic culture in the Cyclades, although tools which seemed to be made of Melian obsidian were discovered in early Neolithic deposits at Knosos. Saul Weinberg is probably right in explaining this by his assumption that the earliest Bronze Age culture of the Cyclades overlapped with Cretan Neolithic and with the Middle Neolithic culture of the mainland.[1]

The Early Minoan I and II pottery, characterized by jugs with high-beaked spouts and a buff surface adorned with simple linear designs in red or brown lustrous paint, found in east Crete, in the Mesara, and in the Kanli Kastelli cemetery, must have been introduced by immigrants from the south-west coast of Asia Minor.

Much of the Early Minoan I pottery from Knosos, Phaistos, and other sites, however, consists of burnished, sub-Neolithic wares but with a thinner fabric and baked much harder than the Neolithic pottery. In eastern Crete the transition to the Bronze Age was more marked, but even there we find little suspension *pyxides* in a grey sub-Neolithic fabric at Hagios Nikolaos near Palaikastro (including, however, a tall horned lid like a Trojan form) while Tomb 5 at Mochlos contained clay ladles of Neolithic type. At Knosos the sub-Neolithic vases included open bowls, handleless cups, ladles, and pedestalled bowls. A few burnished sherds, others with stripes of chalky white or crimson paint, and one or two fragments with dark-on-light designs may presumably be regarded as imports from other parts of Crete where those fabrics were more normal products.

1. See R. W. Ehrich; *Relative Chronologies in Old World Archaeology*, pp. 96 and 97; and S. Benton, 'Haghios Nikolaos near Astakos in Akarnania', *Annal of the British School at Athens*, 1947, p. 156.

THE SECOND EARLY MINOAN PERIOD

The second Early Minoan period was dated 2800–2400 B.C. by Evans, 2400–2200 B.C. by Matz, and I have myself suggested 2300–2100 B.C. as a not unlikely date, after taking into account the latest revisions in Egyptian and Babylonian chronology.

During this period the eastern peoples and the Mesara developed their Copper Age culture to a new height, though the north and west lagged behind them. Metal tools and weapons are relatively scarce but always of copper or with a very low proportion of tin, to which the Cretans probably had no direct access.

Fig. 23. Early Minoan II vases from Kanli Kastelli

Our knowledge of the pottery and of the burial customs of the Early Minoan II period has been considerably extended by the recent excavation by S. Alexiou of a burial deposit in a cave shelter at Korphi tou Vathia near Kanli Kastelli.

This deposit like others of its kind was devoid of any real stratification, not because it had apparently been robbed, but rather because of the funerary rites concerned. The question arises whether we are to interpret the Korphi tou Vathia shelter as a collection of primary burials or to treat it rather as an ossuary where burials of different dates were collected, and where it would therefore be impossible to separate individual burials and the grave goods dedicated with them. The cave shelter at least afforded a fine series of late Early Minoan I and Early Minoan II pottery comparable to that of Pyrgos. Here there were no gold jewellery or delicate vases of stone as at Mochlos, and we can therefore regard it as the grave furniture of the peasants. The confusion in the deposit might at first sight suggest that the burials had been robbed of their most expensive offerings, but the excavator is convinced that this was not the case (a conclusion supported by the fine preservation of the pottery) and he suggests that the evidence of fire and of burnt bones, human as well as animal, not only at Kanli Kastelli but at many other contemporary burial sites, such as Pyrgos, Sphoungaras, Gournia, and Kato Zakros, indicate that burnt sacrifices formed an essential part of the funeral ceremonies.

The pottery consists chiefly of two fabrics, a smoked grey ware and a ware with simple rectilinear designs in glaze paint on a buff surface. The shapes of the smoked ware include not only chalices of the Arkalochori type but also squat *pyxides*, *pyxides* with high necks intended for cylindrical lids like the Early Minoan I suspension vases from Miamou and Hagios Nikolaos, conical cups with one handle, two-handled beakers, and beaked jugs (all three west Anatolian shapes, reminding us of vases at Troy and elsewhere), ovoid jars, carinated jars with cylindrical necks (reminiscent of early Maltese shapes), cylindrical *pyxides*, conical jars with tripod feet (another west Anatolian form), and small ovoid jars with everted rims – a very comprehensive series suggesting foreign influences, especially from Anatolia. The ornaments of the vases with burnished designs that appear on Arkalochori chalices occur also on contemporary vases from the Dodecanese or Samos.

Another fabric from this site was a red ware stained in the firing, and so the forerunner of that later ware of the Early Minoan II B period known as Vasiliki ware, but having irregular, shallow grooves in the surface made by a comb. The vases in this technique were mostly beaked jugs of Anatolian forms recalling those of the painted ware found with them, and varying in form from a jug with a very high beaked spout, like that from the Hagios Onouphrios deposit, to a type where the mouth is almost horizontal with only a slight dip downwards towards the handle, like the jugs acquired by Ormerod in Pisidia, or ones found by Seager in stone at Mochlos, by Xanthoudides at Platanos, and by Bent in pottery from an Early Cycladic grave on Antiparos.

The dark-on-light painted ware of Kanli Kastelli was of the kind first identified by Evans when he assigned the jug from the Hagios

Onouphrios deposit near Phaistos to the latter part of the Early Minoan I period. Professor Banti has recently suggested that such vases belong rather to the beginning of the Middle Minoan I period, and it is true that the fabric seems to last into that period, but evidence that Evans and Pendlebury were probably right in their dating of the Hagios Onouphrios jug is afforded from Kanli Kastelli, where the shapes in this fabric included such jugs. Pendlebury's distinction between the Early Minoan I jugs with rounded bases and the Early Minoan II ones with flattened bases may not be absolutely reliable (the two forms may overlap) but it is not contradicted by Alexiou's evidence. Other shapes in this fabric included tankards not unlike Early Helladic forms on the mainland, but also paralleled in Asia Minor: squat little jugs on three short legs (a Trojan form); mugs like two-handled coffee-cups; other cups with handles set very low down; conical cups with two small lug handles; an *askos* with tubular spout; and a one-handled mug with four short legs.

The decoration consisted of vertical, horizontal, and cross-hatched lines occasionally employed in panels (Fig. 22). The maximum variety achieved consists merely of painting slanting lines on the spout, horizontal on the neck and vertical on the body of a beaked jug. This tendency to stress the structural features of the jug may have been introduced by the new settlers from their Anatolian home, since it soon dies out in Crete and is replaced by an all-over system of decoration which Matz calls 'surface decoration' and which Furumark prefers to call 'unity decoration'. Cycladic influences are naturally less noticeable at the inland site of Kastelli than they were at Pyrgos or even in the Mesara, but there was a cylindrical *pyxis* with incised decoration of Cycladic type and blades of what was presumably Melian obsidian.

Three copper daggers were found belonging to Mrs Maxwell-Hyslop's Type 16,[1] a local Minoan variety appearing first in the Early Minoan II period and developing parallel with a similar Egyptian one in the Early Minoan III period. One of these Kastelli examples had the blade formed of two thin plates welded together. One or two beads of yellow steatite were discovered in the same deposit.

1. Maxwell-Hyslop, 'Daggers and Swords in Western Asia', *Iraq*, 1946, pp. 18, 19; similar daggers have been discovered in Early Bronze Age deposits at Alisar in Anatolia, at Tarsus in Cilicia, and at Lapethos in Cyprus.

The absence from Kanli Kastelli of the mottled pottery known as Vasiliki ware confirms Pendlebury's view that the latter was an Eastern fabric typical of the Early Minoan II B period, appearing at Vasiliki before the end of Early Minoan II A, later exported to other parts of Crete, and imitated at Palaikastro, Trapeza, the Mesara, and elsewhere. By the end of the Early Minoan II period potters had begun to coat Vasiliki ware with a red slip which was mottled red

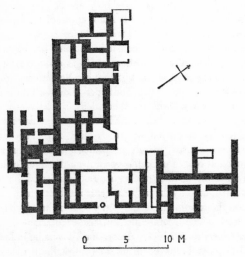

Fig. 24. Early Minoan II house at Vasiliki

and black. This mottling was at first presumably accidental and caused by baking the vases in an open fire, but later seems to have been deliberately cultivated to produce an ornamental effect.

The irregular surface of the walls at Vasiliki was covered with a red lime stucco which has a surface almost as hard as Roman cement. This cement, though convenient, was not an unmixed blessing since, like charity, it covered a multitude of sins, and encouraged a carelessness of structure to which the Minoan mason was only too prone; but it did provide an ideal surface for internal decoration, and was one of the reasons why such a brilliant school of fresco painters developed in the Cretan palaces of later times.

The so-called 'House on the Hill' at Vasiliki not only affords the clearest example of Early Minoan II B pottery stratified over Early Minoan II A ware, but is also by far the most luxurious building of that date so far excavated in Crete. It is, indeed, a small palace and the prototype in miniature of the splendid buildings later to be erected at Knosos, Phaistos, and Mallia. It is orientated with its corners towards the cardinal points of the compass, a practice normal in Mesopotamia and the Middle East generally, but abnormal in Egypt and in the Aegean, and it is possible that this architectural orientation is due to the people who introduced Vasiliki pottery, with its Anatolian forms. Unfortunately the site is badly denuded and all that remains is the lower parts of the south-west and south-east wings of the building. It is impossible to reconstruct the original plan, but it seems not unlikely that the various wings were grouped round an open court in the centre.

The remainder of the building consists of rectangular rooms of all shapes and sizes, sometimes united internally by long passages, and illustrating that typically Minoan labyrinthine, agglutinative architecture which was to culminate in the Palace of Minos.

Simpler houses of the old 'but-and-ben' type,[1] and amplifications of these with three or more rooms, must have been common, though actually we can illustrate their forms not so much from surviving houses as from ossuaries which preserved the plans of earlier houses. A fine series of such ossuaries dating from the Early Minoan III and Middle Minoan I periods was excavated at Palaikastro by Bosanquet, and we may suspect that features of pre-existing house plans are preserved in some of the subsidiary buildings attached to the great round tombs of the Mesara. Later in the Middle Minoan I period we find small cities of the dead, a complex of small rectangular houses arranged in streets like the great Islamic 'city of the dead' at Cairo. Such cemeteries of the Middle Minoan I period exist at Mallia on the north coast and at Apesokari in the Mesara.

Similarly at Mochlos, where the earliest burials belong to the Early Minoan II period, Tomb 2 reproduces the 'but-and-ben'

1. Two-roomed houses with an outer room opening into an inner room; see p. 51 and Figure 5.

type of house we have remarked at Magasa in the late Neolithic period. Later Tombs 4, 5, and 6 were united into one complex with 4 A in the centre looking curiously like a Mycenaean *megaron*.[1]

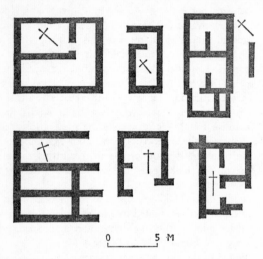

Fig. 25. Early Minoan II ossuaries at Palaikastro

Early Minoan Jewellery from East Crete

No jewellery has survived from the Early Minoan I period and for the two succeeding periods we depend mainly on the results of Seager's excavations at Mochlos.

Tomb I produced a small cylinder seal in silver with a large opening (sign of an early date), and some almost obliterated figures that looked more Mesopotamian than Minoan. It might perhaps have been imported from Syria, and oriental imports of this kind must have stimulated the production of ivory seals, of which only one or two were found at Mochlos, but many in the round tombs of the Mesara (see page 151). Alleged undisturbed deposits of Early Minoan II jewellery were discovered in Tombs 6 and 19 at Mochlos. In the former Seager found two long necklaces of crystal beads, and a

1. For the late Bronze Age type of house termed a *megaron* see p. 306.

still longer one of beads of stone, faience, and shell,[1] sprays of gold (olive?) leaves, a fine gold chain with seven leaf pendants, two pins with crocus flower heads, and fragments of gold armlets. The grave also contained a small silver cup. An ivory seal of the Mesara type (broken and riveted in Minoan times) bears a whorl and spiral design foreshadowing many designs popular in the Middle Minoan period, while another bears a design of two cynocephalous apes sitting back to back. A seal of the latter type was found on the town site of Mochlos in an Early Minoan III deposit, thus raising a suspicion that some of the gold jewellery from this tomb may really have dated from the Early Minoan III period, to which probably also belong the silver diadems found in Early Cycladic graves on Syros and Siphnos.

An animal mask in gold leaf, two drop pendants in silver (perhaps from ear-rings), a large disc in gold leaf, a short necklace of gold and crystal beads, two delicate chains with pendants in gold, and a miniature bronze lion also came from this tomb.

The jewellery from Tomb 19 (also dated Early Minoan II by Seager) included four gold hairpins with daisy heads (a type also found in the Chrysolakkos cemetery at Mallia), two head-bands, a gay but rather nondescript necklace of stones of different kinds, a heavy gold chain of double links, a fine chain with leaf pendants, three leaves from a spray, fragments of armlets, and three stars to be sewn on a garment, all in gold.

The jewellery from Tombs 2 and 4 would appear to be representative of the Early Minoan III period in the main. Connexions with the Cyclades are suggested by the gold diadems with punctured or impressed designs (four dogs on one and two human eyes on another) from Grave 2 and the chalcedony pigeon pendant from 4, recalling silver diadems with punctured designs from Syros and Siphnos and chalcedony pigeon pendants from the latter island, all found in graves of the Third Early Cycladic period (corresponding to Early Minoan III in Crete).

Smaller quantities of jewellery occur in other graves at Mochlos, notably in 12, 21, and 22 where, however, it is hard to distinguish between the Early Minoan burials and those of later date.

---

1. R. B. Seager, *Explorations in the Island of Mochlos*, Figs. 8–12; what I have termed faience he calls porcelain, but it is not porcelain in the English sense of that word.

The Mochlos jewellery also included flat, short tubular, flattened spherical, and pearshaped beads in rock crystal, carnelian, limestone, shell, and faience.

Gold ornaments securely dated to the third Early Minoan period are hard to find but we may probably include in this small category the gold ornaments found in the upper stratum of Tholos A at Platanos in the Mesara. The ornaments are abundant but less beautiful than those of Mochlos, and it appears that at this period the flourishing ports of the Merabello coast were setting the fashion for Crete, and that the Mesara, though prosperous enough, was more provincial and lagged behind the east in development.

Perhaps the best workmanship was displayed in a pendant shaped like a hollow cone suspended from a chain with very fine links in a very pale gold, that must certainly contain a proportion of silver, as did all the native alluvial gold of the Levant. (The term 'electrum' is only applied to such a natural alloy if it contains about thirty per cent of silver or nearly that proportion.)

The jewellery from Tholos A at Platanos also included two small heart-shaped ornaments of very thin gold leaf, one of them with a pretty border of repoussé dots. Twenty-two cylindrical beads of gold leaf were also found there, usually adorned with simple lines or grooves, often of the torsion type embossed or incised, and in two instances decorated with appliqué spirals of gold wire.

Seals and Miniature Carvings in Ivory

The second Early Minoan period saw the beginning of Minoan sculpture in ivory, and of figurines that no longer remind us of the Neolithic ones but of early Egyptian and Libyan types.

A number of Early Minoan figurines have been preserved in the round tombs of the Mesara and from the cave of Trapeza in Lasithi, but all except the most primitive examples from the 'larger tholos' at Hagia Triada belong to the Early Minoan III period, and some of the best carvings were in the form of figured handles to ivory stamp seals. This progress in modelling may have been partly stimulated by the importation from the Cyclades of the Early Cycladic figurines, of which considerable numbers would appear to have been imported into the Mesara and of which occasional examples have been found on other Cretan sites.

The ivory for the figures of Lasithi and the Mesara was probably imported from Syria rather than from Egypt, but the style of the carving is purely Minoan. Indeed some figures from Trapeza with that curious garment variously described as breeches or as a divided apron are reminiscent of certain Late Neolithic figurines from Crete rather than of anything from the Cyclades or from further east in the Levant.

During this period Crete was subjected to strong cultural influences from Anatolia and Syria, from where stamp seals of steatite and other materials were introduced, and Cretans perhaps imitated these and began for the first time to manufacture seals of their own from imported ivory and from native materials such as steatite.

Before the introduction of a written script the stamp of a well-known seal was the only guarantee that an article or package had belonged to or had been dispatched by a particular person or organization. The purpose of the seal was therefore mainly a practical one, but the necessity that the design should be easily recognizable fostered the growth of an art in gem cutting.

The principal forms current in the Middle East at an early date, the cylinder seal favoured in Mesopotamia, the stamp seal popular in Syria and the Levant in general, and the Egyptian scarab made in the form of the sacred beetle, were all of them bead seals which might be strung on a necklace or worn on the wrist like a wrist-watch. By the opening of the Early Minoan period these forms might be found anywhere in the Levant, though their popularity in individual countries remained as stated above. Another form of seal introduced into Crete in the Early Minoan III period was the signet, a form popular among the Hittites and other people of Anatolia. The Cretans might have copied any of these forms, and in later times did so, but their earliest attempts at making bead seals (if we except the rather doubtful examples assigned to the Early Minoan I period) were the Minoan modification of the cylinder seal.

Copper Working

Early Minoan copper work is represented by a few examples, well dated, from eastern Crete and by a much larger but less securely dated series from the round graves of the Mesara. Of the daggers, the most primitive type (also found in Early Minoan II graves at Mochlos) is flat and leaf-shaped with two rivet holes at the outer corners of the slightly concave base, and three of these were found in the Early Tholos A at Koumasa. A triangular type with strong midrib (perhaps to be dated Early Minoan III and represented by three silver examples, Nos. 212, 213, 214 from Tholos (at Koumasa) is of interest for its western connexions. Childe calls it a Minoan type and suggests that it inspired Chalcolithic examples at Remedello in Cisalpine Gaul and at Monte Bradoni in Etruria, but this form seems to be rather more common in Italy than in Crete.

More sophisticated and perhaps later in date is a dagger with a long slim blade, a strong midrib, and two or four rivet holes.

Copper tweezers with splayed tips have also been found in Early Minoan graves at Mochlos, at Koumasa in the Mesara, and at Kanli Kastelli in the Pedhiadha.

The Art of the Stone-cutter

Perhaps the finest artistic achievement of the Cretans in the second Early Minoan period is their astonishing skill displayed in the cutting of stone vases, and their artistic taste in exploiting the colour variations of breccia, conglomerate, or such stratified stones as calcite. They also made stone vases out of green, black, and grey steatite, limestone, schist, marble, and white calcite (all local stones) and more rarely of imported stones. Xanthoudides believed that the fragments of an obsidian rhyton from Tylisos were of Nubian rather than of Melian obsidian.[1]

These stone vases were first blocked out with a tubular drill and then finished by hard grinding with abrasives. Stone vases had been a feature of the Neolithic culture of Cyprus but the shapes there were quite different. This sudden blossoming of stone vases in Crete therefore requires some explanation and probably implies influences from Egypt; and we do occasionally encounter an Egyptian shape, though the more striking and exotic forms of the stone vases are of Anatolian origin, like those of the pottery vases.[2]

1. *Vaulted Tombs, etc.*, p. 105, discussing a core in a similar transparent obsidian from Tholos B at Platanos; this, however, was written before the Italian discovery that Giali near Cos also produced a transparent obsidian.

2. Sinclair Hood believes (perhaps rightly) that many of these vases belong to the Middle Minoan I period.

The Mesara Culture and its Tholoi

Local differences in the shapes of the stone vases from the Mesara, Lasithi, and Merabello suggest that there were several local schools of stone carvers during the Early Minoan II and III periods. Many of the stone vases from the Mesara had so small a cavity inside that they can hardly have been intended for any use except as dedications to the dead. These vases were so numerous that over three hundred were found in the walled Trench α in front of Tholos A at Platanos, but the Mesara vessels, unlike those of Mochlos, belonged mainly to the Early Minoan III and Middle Minoan I periods, and the materials employed were chiefly steatite or serpentine, much easier to cut than the hard breccias favoured by the Mochlos artists.

To the Early Minoan II period, however, we may perhaps assign the 'pepper-and-salt' trays from Tholos A and Trench α at Platanos, consisting of oblong blocks with two or more cups sunk in them, and compared by Xanthoudides to the so-called *kernoi* still used in the liturgy of the Orthodox Church.[1] These Early Minoan *kernoi*, if we may call them that, had holes for suspension and incised rectilinear decoration.

Oblong trays with two or three compartments had already occurred in pottery at Knosos as early as the Middle Neolithic period, sometimes with a flat base and sometimes furnished with four short legs, and it is therefore not impossible that a similar rite for the dedication of the first-fruits of the year may have persisted in Crete for some five thousand years. Similar vessels were also used in Predynastic Egypt, though, of course, not necessarily for the same purpose. The Platanos *kernoi* were all fashioned from a soft red ironstone. Six oval double *kernoi* were also found in the same cemetery. Most of the *kernoi* belonged, I imagine, to the Early Minoan II period, but the early character of some vases from Tholos A makes it possible that the type dates back to the Early Minoan I period.

The dark-on-light pottery forms include small beaked jugs, 'teapots', bowls with tubular spout and handle at right angles to the spout, miniature *hydriae*, two-handled bowls, cups with one or two handles, and bird-shaped *askoi* (in one instance with a ram's head)

1. S. Xanthoudides, 'Cretan Kernoi', *Annual of the British School at Athens*, 1960, pp. 9–15 and Fig. 2.

with a misleading superficial resemblance in form to Mycenaean vases of a thousand years later (Fig. 23). Some of these vases, however, belong to the Early Minoan III period and a few, especially the miniature *hydriae*, appear to have been Middle Minoan I A in date.

Most curious of all is a vase which I hesitate to describe as a votive pair of trousers, but do not know what else to call it. Xanthoudides's term for it is a cylindrical belly open at the top standing on two long tubular legs.

Village sites of this period have scarcely been examined in the Mesara, but Xanthoudides has noted the existence of one or two settlements, and remarked that probably many of the Early Minoan settlements remained undiscovered, because their ruins underlie the modern villages, the settlement corresponding to the round tomb of Marathokephalo below the village of Maroni, that of Dhrakones below Phournopharango, and that of the tombs of Christos, Koutsokera, Salami, and Hagia Eirene below Vasiliki, where Middle Minoan I sherds have been recorded.

The round tombs of the Mesara were communal graves and have sometimes been claimed as the ancestors of the beehive tombs of Mycenae, but they belong to a different category. The essential features of a Mycenaean *tholos* grave, as it is usually termed (though without classical authority of the phrase), are that it is cut in the slope of a hillside, and approached by a level or nearly level entrance passage – it is in fact a chamber tomb lined with stone masonry. The Mesara tombs, on the other hand, stand in the open plain, and most of them could never have been completely roofed with corbelled vaulting, especially with the relatively small stones employed in the existing walls. Only the smaller *tholos* at Hagia Triada and the one at Kalathiana might possibly have been roofed in this fashion. All the others must have been completed with a lighter form of roof in wood or mudbrick or something of that sort.[1] If there is any relationship between the *tholoi* of Mycenae and the round tombs of the Mesara it must have been a collateral one, since both might ultimately have been derived from the Neolithic round buildings of Khirokitia in

1. Compare Dr Johnson's account of the roofing of a Hebridean hut in *Samuel Johnson, Writer*, 1926, by S. C. Roberts, pp. 169, 170, and the account of a Macedonian hut (Pendlebury, loc. cit, p. 64, footnote 2).

Cyprus, though the positive evidence for such a descent has not yet been produced.

There exists, however, in the Cyclades a group of small primitive *tholoi* that might be claimed as intermediate between Khirokitia and Crete. These primitive *tholoi* are often free standing, but they are so small, and the stones employed in them relatively so large, that the task of covering them with a roughly corbelled vault presents no problem at all. In Crete such primitive *tholoi* are not uncommon in Lasithi, a backward district, at the very end of the Bronze Age, but that they also occur even in the Early Minoan I period probably under Cycladic influence is shown by the instance of such a tomb at

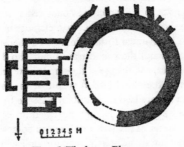

Fig. 26. Tholos A, Platanos

Krasi (in the Pedhiadha province politically, but geographically only just off the edge of the Lasithi plain), containing some silver ornaments, an ivory seal shaped like a human foot, two daggers, and some pins of bronze.

We may perhaps claim Tholos A at Koumasa, a tomb containing two Cycladic figurines and incised pottery of Early Cycladic I types (a *kernos* and *pyxides* with vertically pierced lugs), as only an improved and more elaborate form of the Cycladic primitive *tholos*.

The Mesara round tombs continued in existence till the end of the Middle Minoan I period, and in that period a small *tholos* tomb, rather primitive still but a little nearer the mainland type, was erected at Apesokari on the southern edge of the Mesara. In the late Bronze Age we shall find occasional examples of the mainland type of *tholos* tomb in Crete, but I should hesitate on the present evidence to derive either the mainland from the Cretan or the Cretan from the mainland. I should imagine rather that there were two originally independent but converging lines of development in Crete and on the mainland. If there was any direct influence from one to the other, Crete is more likely to have influenced the mainland before 1550, the mainland more likely to have influenced Crete after 1450.

The Early Minoan tombs of the Mesara have also been quoted, especially by Evans,[1] as evidences of Egyptian and Libyan influence on Crete. Sir Arthur cited as instances parallels from Hierakonpolis and Nagada for certain types of figurines in Crete, and the analogies between the forms of the round tombs of the Mesara with those of the *mapalia* or round huts which persisted in Libya up to Roman times. Professor Banti has thrown doubts on such influence from Pre-dynastic Egypt, but Pendlebury countered with the remark that it was really only the western or Libyan element in the Pre-dynastic culture that Evans claimed to have influenced the Mesara, citing not only the figurines and the round tombs, but also the type of dress, the side lock of hair, and the use of the simple bow armed with broad-tipped arrows of the chisel-bladed type that the French term *petits tranchets*. Libya is only two days' sail on a caique from the Mesara, a fact emphasized by Lt-Col. Hammond when he escaped in a caique to Tobruk at the end of the Battle of Crete in 1941.

It is not unnatural that eastern Crete, through which came most of the trade from the Dodecanese, Syria, Cyprus, Palestine, and Egypt, should have led the way in the Early Minoan period.

The prosperity of Pseira and Mochlos in the Early Minoan II period was considerable. Mochlos is now an island separated from the mainland of Crete by about a hundred and fifty metres of water, but we have to allow for the subsidence of the eastern half of Crete since Minoan times. In the Early Minoan II period Mochlos was probably united to Crete by a narrow spit of land affording a good harbour on either side according to the wind. The prevailing winds are N.N.W. to W.N.W., and it would therefore be the eastern harbour that would be most employed by Minoan merchants and fishermen.

It is more difficult to account for the prominence of Pseira, which was always an island, and, as Seager remarks, 'aside from the harbour the island could have offered little to attract settlers of any sort even in Minoan days'. He points out, however, 'the excellent harborage

1. *The Palace of Minos*, Vol. II, p. 37-9.

for small craft offered by the sheltered cove. . . . It is exposed solely to the east, and an easterly gale is a thing of rare occurrence in Cretan waters. . . . Even in the present day the port of the ancient Minoan town is constantly used in case of a sudden gale by the numerous sponge fishermen who work the Cretan waters on their way to and from the Libyan coast.' Indeed sponge-diving was probably a local industry at Pseira in Minoan times. Perhaps the purple fisheries were another, as they certainly were in Middle Minoan I times on the island of Leuke off the south coast of Crete. Pseira, however, is a barren island which can never have afforded sustenance for its population, who must have depended largely on trade and imported their food, other than fish, from the mainland.

THE THIRD EARLY MINOAN PERIOD

The third Early Minoan period (?2100–2000 B.C.) is a very short transitional period of which the most remarkable feature is the expansion of central Cretan sites, such as Knosos and Phaistos, at the expense of the east Cretan sites, which began to decline. Pendlebury's picture of this period for eastern Crete is rather grim: only a few new sites; at Vasiliki the great house on the hill is in ruins with the small huts of squatters built against its walls; no certain habitation of Early Minoan III date was known to him, though some of the Middle Minoan I houses at Pseira, Mochlos, Palaikastro, Hagia Triada, and Tylisos may well have been erected on earlier foundations, or even have been adaptations of earlier houses. At Knosos the only structure of importance assigned to the Early Minoan III period by Evans was the great *hypogaeum* near the south porch, but since there are no more Early Minoan III sherds than Neolithic ones from this excavation, Pendlebury is probably right in assigning it to the Middle Minoan I period to which most of its pottery belongs.

The paucity of habitations datable in the Early Minoan III period may be due to their continued occupation in the following period, as is indicated, perhaps, by the fact that it is much easier to point out Early Minoan III burials.[1]

In the Mesara, communal round tombs built in the Early Minoan II

1. At Galana Kharakia, near Viannos, Platon recently opened two communal tombs of the Early Minoan period with the remains of over 300 *pithos* burials.

period continue to have burials, and some of the great round tombs such as those of Porti, Christos, and Vorou were first erected in the Early Minoan III period. In eastern Crete burials of Early Minoan III period may be quoted from Palaikastro, from the ossuaries, and from the later tombs at Mochlos, and from rubbish dumps at Gournia. The mottled pottery and the dark-on-light ware still survive but the most characteristic pottery of the period has designs in matt white paint on a black or dark brown slip, triangles, segments of circles, and even running spirals. Partial hatching is common, and a segment of a circle may have the two corners hatched but not the centre. One two-handled mug has a St Andrew's Cross flanked by panels of vertical lines looking rather as if it had anticipated a motif of over a thousand years later.

The shapes include trough-spout tea-pots, beaked jugs, round, vertical, and conical cups with or without handles, and conical bowls. Among the straight-sided cups is the prototype of the Vapheio cup which was to become so popular in the Middle Minoan II and Late Minoan I periods.

Influence from Egypt and the Levant

The evidence from Pseira is confusing. Seager found plenty of Early Minoan III pottery and therefore inferred that this period was a long one, but he found it all in rock pockets under the houses of Late Minoan I date, and in some instances the Early Minoan III cups merged imperceptibly into those of the following period. Nevertheless, despite the shortness of the Early Minoan III period and the absence of houses datable to it, there are some important changes in Minoan art that appear to have taken place at that time. One of these was the replacement of pottery with dark-on-light patterns by vases with light-on-dark patterns, a phenomenon that seems to have taken place about the same time on the mainland of Greece. Pendlebury suggested that the Minoan Cretans disliked plain ware, and when they found that the 'mottling' of Vasiliki ware was too chancy an affair, they experimented after a very brief and unsatisfactory attempt to return to the incised and punctured patterns of Early Cycladic and Cretan Neolithic type, by covering the pots with red glaze, on which they painted simple designs in white paint.

The increasing importance of Knosos and the valleys round it was marked by some new building and perhaps by the founding of the town of Tylisos (which probably retains its Minoan name).

Foreign imports from Egypt began to come into the Mesara and the Cretan seals of this period have designs closely paralleled by those of the Egyptian seals and scarabs of the First Intermediate Period (Seventh to Tenth Dynasties).

Some of these Egyptian motifs, however, and even the ivory of which the seals were made, may have been introduced from Syria rather than directly from Egypt (since wild elephants were to be found in Syria at least as late as the fifteenth century B.C.). One saucer with a design of concentric circles in thick oily red paint discovered at Mochlos with Early Minoan III pottery was reckoned by Frankfort to be an import from Syria, and he quoted as other instances of Syrian influence the animal-shaped ivory seals found at Platanos and Kalathiana. Some ivory seals of this date have on them a parade of two, four, or more scorpions swimming round like goldfish in a bowl, and this motif develops before the end of the Early Minoan III period into the tennis racket motif of Middle Minoan I vases, a motif sometimes regarded as more Mycenaean than Minoan. The fact is that the origins of this motif, the scorpion parade and the single or double tennis racket developed from it, are purely Minoan motifs. It is only the late development of this motif, when the tennis rackets are attached to a central stem and treated as the leaves, that is Mycenaean more than Minoan. Strictly speaking this motif never resembles a tennis racket though it does rather resemble a lacrosse racket, but the Minoan examples always have the twist to one side, which preserves the twist of the scorpion's tail (Fig. 30). Other seals have a kind of swastika made up of four spirals, which became a very popular motif with many variations. Some seals have representations of the Minoan ships of the period, which we discussed in another chapter. Other seals have rectilinear meander patterns or spiral variations of them on the bases, motifs that became suddenly popular on Egyptian–Libyan seals of the Sixth Dynasty and continued on those of the First Intermediate Period (though isolated examples of spirals and meanders occurred later).

An ivory signet from Hagia Triada shows a cable design surrounding an Egyptian draught-board with three men (shaped like chess pawns) on top, while another Early Minoan III seal from Crete

Fig. 27. Designs on Early Minoan III vases

actually shows us a Cretan sitting on a high-backed chair playing draughts. There is nothing Egyptian about this seal except the draught-board, and the reverse, showing a seated figure with a two-handled vase, perhaps taking it from the oven, is purely Cretan.

The connexions between Egypt and Crete, however, should not be exaggerated, and Miss Kantor stresses certain fundamental differences, particularly the absence of the Cretan torsional or interlocked ornaments, as a basic element in Egyptian design.[1]

Quadruple spirals do appear on some Middle Kingdom scarabs, but as an all-over ceiling pattern they seem not to occur before the new Kingdom.

At Pyrgos on the north coast we find clay chests or *larnakes* with rounded corners and side handles for passing a rope through to carry them. In the Early Minoan III period and at Pachyammos on the gulf of Merabello there were not only Early Minoan *larnakes* of this type, but also burial jars like super-*pyxides* with lids into which the bodies must have been thrust with great difficulty, either by trussing tightly (as Evans suggests) or by breaking the bones.

Cycladic Influences

Early Cycladic idols in marble were imported into central Crete and imitated locally both in the Mesara and in the district round Knosos. Relations with the Cyclades are perhaps also indicated by the appearance of spirals (running spirals and a line of s spirals) on the painted pottery, and still more clearly by the appearance of small *pyxides* with incised spirals. As examples we may quote an Early Minoan III *pyxis* in stone (the variety not stated) with running spirals in relief from Tholos B at Platanos, and a fine schist *pyxis* with carinated profile, complete with lid and spirals in relief, from Maronia near Setea.[2]

Relations with the Cyclades of course had never been broken, but they are more apparent in the Early Minoan I and III periods than in Early Minoan II, when east Crete was being infiltrated by settlers from Asia Minor, and I think it would not be unfair to say that whenever the Cycladic influences are more important than those of Asia

1. It is true that torsion designs occur on one or two metal vases from the Tod treasure, but these, if not actual Minoan imports, at least display very strong Minoan influence. A. Vandier, À *propos d'un dépôt, etc.*, Syria, 1937.

2. H. Kantor, op. cit., Plate II, J and F.

Minor, then central Crete, from Knosos to Mallia on the north, is more important than the part of eastern Crete from Hagios Nikolaos to Palaikastro.

The little incised *pyxides* found in the Vat Room deposit at Knosos (earliest Middle Minoan I A), despite the resemblance of their patterns to certain Neolithic vases, should be reckoned rather as instances of Cycladic influence.[1]

In accordance with this transfer of power and influence from east to central Crete it may be noted that the quality of the stone vases at Mochlos shows a marked decline. The vases are smaller and usually of black steatite instead of the fine variegated breccias popular in the Early Minoan II period. The Lasithi plain, however, seems to have been prosperous, having direct contacts with the Mesara, perhaps through Lyttos and the Pedhiada, and so with trade connexions to Syria and Egypt.

Some of the seals were clearly influenced by Egyptian types either in forms (such as the scaraboid seals) or in decoration – for example a curious double sickle effect which Evans traced back to an Egyptian type with two reversed lions. The button seals, however, may well represent a Syrian tradition, and even when the designs are paralleled in Egypt the Cretan forms of the animal-shaped seals are sometimes nearer to the original Syrian prototype. In some of the ivory seals the handle was skilfully carved in the form of an animal – a sitting monkey (as at Trapeza in Lasithi or at Platanos in the Mesara) or an ox (Platanos).

One Platanos seal has a cynocephalus ape squatting in the ritual attitude familiar in Egyptian representations of that animal, but the incised design on the base consists of three lions contorted in a fashion which no Egyptian artist would have tolerated, but which came naturally to a Cretan artist trained in the 'torsion' school of art (see Chapter 5).

Cretan, too, is the habit of treating a cylinder seal as if it were a button seal, drilling the suspension holes through the short axis and executing the design that was to give the impression on the flat sides, thus making nonsense of the whole principle of a cylinder, which was intended to roll out the design.

1. Unless one follows Levi in practically eliminating the Early Minoan culture; on that supposition the patterns could well be survivals from the Neolithic repertoire.

CHAPTER 7

The Middle Minoan Period

THE URBAN REVOLUTION IN CRETE

It rarely happens that one historical period is neatly divided from its successor by a widespread catastrophe, and in the absence of such an event the line of demarcation chosen between two successive periods will often seem arbitrary. The late Sir Arthur Quiller-Couch used to refer to the mysterious cataclysm of A.D. 1485 which (to judge by the history books) suddenly plunged Britain from the Middle Ages into modern times. The line of demarcation between Early and Middle Minoan may seem almost equally arbitrary, but just as there is a real distinction between the England of Henry VI and that of Elizabeth I, so there is a real and significant difference between the simple village communities with their large communal tombs of the Early Minoan period and the rich sophisticated culture of Middle Minoan Crete, with its cities and palaces, its marine supremacy, and its expanding trade with Egypt, Syria, and Anatolia, and with the barbarian north.

Early in the second millennium B.C., Crete was the scene of an urban revolution which developed with startling rapidity, providing not only a model for similar but later events in Greece, but also a channel through which flowed the cultural products and influences of the older civilizations of Mesopotamia, Syria, Anatolia, and Egypt into the less developed lands of Europe.

The immediate causes are obscure and doubtless bound up with local politics. We can see dimly what happened but not why it happened, and we would give much to be able to read the letters of a Minoan Margaret Paston.

The north-east coast of Crete with its island ports, which had provided the main driving force during the Early Minoan period, now sank into relative obscurity and was eclipsed by the centre of the island, where large cities with splendid palaces appeared at Knosos and Mallia in the north and at Phaistos in the Mesara. We gain the impression that a large part of the island was united under a strong central government, at least a confederacy if not an empire, which not only exploited the rich agricultural plains of the Mesara, the Pedhiadha, Herakleion, Mallia, and the Mylopotamos valley but also carried on a thriving foreign trade with Egypt and the Near East.

TOWN PLANS IN MINOAN CRETE

Architectural planning develops to heights unprecedented in Crete, but it is still the planning of individual architects for particular buildings or at most a group of buildings. There is no town planning as it was understood in the contemporary cities of Egypt.

It is true that no Middle Minoan sites have been excavated completely, like the Late Minoan settlement of Gournia or the Sub-Minoan one on Karphi, but the British excavations at Palaikastro and those of the French at Mallia afford us some idea of the central and poorer quarters of a Middle Minoan city, while the villas of Tylisos and the houses in Gypsadhes illustrate the houses of the upper classes.

The governing principle underlying the lay-out of Minoan towns and villages is well illustrated by the 'House on the Hill' of the Early Minoan II period at Vasiliki (Fig. 24), though it can hardly be termed town-planning. The big man, whoever he was, grabbed the best site and built his palace or large house there, and his relatives and dependants built houses round it. There was therefore an accidental but quite noticeable tendency for towns and villages to be centrifugal, with streets radiating out from one central building and united laterally by roughly concentric streets. This is very noticeable in the Late Minoan town of Gournia.

Defensive considerations seem to have played no part at all in the lay-out of a Minoan settlement until very late on in the Bronze Age. There are no city walls like those of the Early Bronze Age settlements in the Cyclades. I think, therefore, that the tendency of the small houses to cluster round the big house of the village was not so much due to a desire for security against robbers, pirates, or foreign raiders, but was simply because the prehistoric Cretan, like his modern counterpart, was naturally sociable and gregarious.

There are relatively few isolated farms in Crete. A smallholder may have a hut that he occupies for special purposes at some season of the year, but his home is in a village if possible. The unsociable Englishman prefers to live near his work even if he has to walk miles to visit his neighbours, his pub, or his chapel. The sociable Greek prefers to live in a crowded village among his friends and relatives and near his church and his café, even though he may have to walk miles to till his fields or trim his vines, and I think the prehistoric Cretan was like him.

Huddling in a crowded village for company, however, is one thing, but deserting the fertile coastal valleys to live in bleak upland dales is quite another matter, and I think Lehmann makes a good point when he observes that in the periods when a strong central government, such as the Minoan power, or the Roman empire, or the Duchy of Venice, kept the sea free of pirates the coastal plains were well populated, but in the bad times when piracy was rife, such as the Early Iron Age or the Homeric period or the Hellenistic period or that of the Saracen raids, people tended to abandon the coastal villages for those in the uplands.

The Middle Minoan period, however, was very prosperous, and perhaps the fleet of Knosos was already controlling the central Aegean. The question how far 'Minos' of the classical legends was a 'Minoan' king in the sense of belonging to a non-Hellenic race is of course very debatable, and I think that Ridgeway was right in calling him an Achaean,[1] but Herodotus may also have been right in admitting the possibility of an Aegean sea power before that of Minos.

THE HYPOGAEUM AT KNOSOS

A vaulted *hypogaeum* or chamber cut in the soft rock, with a spiral staircase leading into it, was dated Early Minoan III by Evans, whose section restores a passage leading to the south, the whole forming an elaborate entrance system to a hypothetical predecessor of the Palace of Minos. But there is no evidence for this underground tunnel to the south, and I can see no point in the large vault if this was an entrance system. It resembles more an underground granary, since there is no sign of cement or plaster and the rock here is too sandy and

1. W. Ridgeway, 'Minos the Destroyer, etc.', *Proceedings of the British Academy*, 1909.

porous to be suitable for a cistern. Evans dated it to the third Early Minoan period, but Pendlebury pointed out that the Early Minoan III sherds found in it were not much more numerous than the Neolithic, and was inclined to assign it to the Middle Minoan I A period.

THE FIRST PALACE OF MINOS

Early in the Middle Minoan I A period the top of the Kephala mound was levelled for the construction of the first palace, and any Early Minoan structures that might have existed were swept away so that in the central court late Neolithic buildings directly underlie the

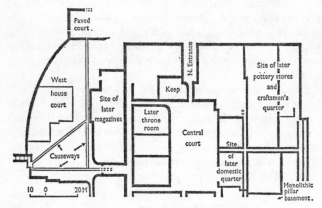

Fig. 28. Plan of earlier Palace of Minos

paving of the central court (a condition paralleled in several parts of the Palace of Phaistos).

The general plan, which in its main outlines continued to dominate the later buildings, consisted of a great, rectangular court surrounded by isolated blocks which Evans termed *insulae*.

The north entrance was flanked by two towerlike blocks. The western tower, which Evans termed the 'Great North Keep', was constructed of very massive blocks of limestone, with foundations sunk deep into the Neolithic earth, enclosing small, windowless cellars known as the 'dungeons'. Sir Arthur used to relate with glee how he had once shown a party of German tourists round his excavations when he had a workman employed at the bottom of one of the dungeons. The Germans had looked surprised and inquired why the man was down there. Sir Arthur had replied 'we had some trouble with that man, in fact he has been down there for several days', and he used to add that they had gone away much impressed with British discipline.

The rounded corners of this early keep were evidently a characteristic of the early *insulae*, since another such corner was preserved even in the latest reconstruction of the block containing the Late Minoan II throne room. Indeed repair and cleaning operations carried out by Dr Platon and myself in 1945 proved that the main scheme of the ceremonial rooms immediately west of the great court go back to the earliest days of the palace. The throne room as it stands belongs to the Late Minoan II period, but below the floor of the ante-room leading to it was an earlier floor of the type known as *mosaiko* – a sort of crazy pavement of irregular stones of different shapes and colours fitted together – that should not be later than the Middle Minoan III A period (1700–1600 B.C.). Immediately south of this the pillar shrine and the temple repositories behind it date from the Middle Minoan III B period (1600–1550 B.C.), but the east Pillar Crypt behind had an earlier floor covered with pure Middle Minoan I A material – sherds, broken lamps, and burnt bones of oxen, sheep, and pig – implying that the main plan of this area must go back to the earliest days of the first palace (Plate 7).

The west quarter of the earliest palace, however, projected farther into the west court than does the present façade, and there was originally direct access between the west and central courts. The domestic quarters on the east side of the great court consisted of a series of rooms built terrace fashion down the hill and served by what Evans called the east-west corridor, with a staircase at its west end giving access to the central court.

In the Middle Minoan I B period[1] (1900–1850 B.C.) some important building operations were conducted, of which perhaps most important was the construction of the great Stepped Portico, a splendid

1. It is dangerous to employ this phrase except at Knosos because the Middle Minoan I B pottery in east Crete and the Mesara may have started earlier.

covered approach to the south end of the palace from the terminus of the great south road that brought the produce from the Mesara ports and from Egypt. The Portico is so ruined that its reconstruction cannot be attempted in detail, but we can surely see how it made the right-angled turn to cross the Vlychia ravine, where the great south road split into three branches – one entering the Stepped Portico, one entering the west court by a long ramp, and a third continuing almost on the line of the modern motor road towards the harbour town of Knosos. To this period belongs also the setting back of the façade facing the west court, and it is not unlikely that there may have been some precursor of the later west porch giving indirect access to the central court at its south end.

MIDDLE MINOAN I CEMETERY AT KNOSOS

The Middle Minoan I A houses of the city have hardly been excavated, but Middle Minoan I A sherds are common everywhere. In 1935 under Sir Arthur Evans's auspices and guidance (and at his expense) I opened a rock shelter on Monasteriako Kephali, the acropolis hill west of the Minoan city. It proved to be a continuation of the rock shelter previously tapped by R. J. H. Jenkins, who found Middle Minoan III *pithos* graves there.[1] I also found remains of about three *pithos* graves of Middle Minoan III date and a considerable quantity of pottery of that period, but, underneath and separated from it by a sterile layer of fallen rock representing a collapsed roof, I found the remains of an ossuary of Middle Minoan I date with one complete skull, a number of crania, and plenty of bones. There was, however, no possibility of distinguishing between those of one skeleton and of another.

The most interesting individual find was a limestone head (published in *Journal of Hellenic Studies* Vol. LV and also by Pendlebury in his *The Archaeology of Crete*). It has a distinctly Sumerian appearance, and Frankfort compared it to Early Dynastic sculpture from Mesopotamia, that is sculpture of the middle of the third millennium. The head, however, was found in the Middle Minoan III deposit, and though its battered condition makes it quite likely that it may have

1. Unpublished; H. G. G. Payne, 'Archaeology in Greece', *Journal of Hellenic Studies*, 1934, does not mention them.

Fig. 29. Designs on Middle Minoan IA vases

een derived from the Middle Minoan I deposit, it certainly cannot
e dated earlier than about 1900 B.C. on the Cretan evidence and
might be later. It might of course have been an *antica* even then,
cquired in the course of a raid on the Syrian coast, but the stone
ooks not unlike a hardened variety of the local marl known as
ouskouvas.

The back view of this head looks very like those of the Palaikastro
oys. The latter, however, if not Egyptian work, were clearly influ-

Fig. 30. Designs on Middle Minoan IB vases

enced by it, whereas the Knosos head, though not Sumerian handy-
work, was influenced by oriental sculpture, perhaps from Syria
(Plate 14a).[1]

THE OVAL BUILDING AT CHAMAIZI

The Middle Minoan I A building excavated by S. Xanthoudides at
Chamaizi on the high ground separating the coastal plain north of
Tourloti from the Seteia valley is unique, the only oval building of
Minoan date. Some well-intentioned but misguided attempts have
been made to interpret this structure as an intermediate form between
circular and rectangular houses, an explanation which might possibly
suffice for some early houses on the mainland of Greece, but will
certainly not do for Chamaizi, since there are no round houses preceding it.

Mackenzie pointed out that the interior walls were all set at right
angles and explained it as an ordinary house with an open court in
the centre. He suggested the oval wall outside was simply dictated by
the space available on the crown of the hill (Fig. 31).

Platon, who interprets it as a variety of peak sanctuary, stresses the
evidence for cult worship indicated by an altar and an ash stratum, by
the presence of three large idols and the head of a fourth, and by the
fact that the so-called well would neither collect nor hold much water,
and would be far more suitable for a *bothros* or sacred rubbish pit. The
filler, the lamp, and the cylindrical vessel can all be paralleled at the
Koumasa shrine.[2] For the apsidal plan Platon cites the survival into
Protogeometric times of apsidal models of shrines in pottery, quoting an example in the Giamalakis collection (Fig. 68). The evidence
is rather inconclusive, but Platon may be right since the Chamaizi
building has no exact parallel in domestic architecture.

House A at Vasiliki also belongs to the Middle Minoan I period
and is a normal example of Minoan agglutinative planning. The individual rooms are rectangular and well constructed but have been
added when and where the occasion demanded, so that the overall
plan appears accidental. One might say that the house had grown over

1. Professor Mallowan states that the head is certainly not Sumerian but
probably an archaic work from north Syria.
2. Xanthoudides, *Vaulted Tombs of the Mesara*, p. 50 and Plate XXXIII.

the ground like an ivy plant. Most of these Middle Minoan I houses were destroyed by Middle Minoan III buildings, though at Chamaizi there was no reoccupation. Since Middle Minoan II pottery is

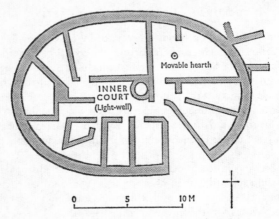

Fig. 31. Middle Minoan I house, Chamaizi

confined to so few sites it is not unnatural to attribute the destruction to the same catastrophe which caused great destruction at Knosos during that period.

THE SECOND MIDDLE MINOAN PERIOD

The second Middle Minoan period (1850–1750 B.C.) is hard to define in most parts of Crete where pottery of Middle Minoan I B and even of Middle Minoan I A type continued to be made, but at Knosos and at Phaistos the period[1] can be more accurately represented both by its pottery and by architectural reconstructions and improvements in the Palace of Minos.

The semi-independent *insulae* of the Middle Minoan I palace (Fig. 28) with the open passages between were now for the first time

1. At Phaistos, however, we must date the beginning of this period not later than 1900 B.C. (see pp. 191, 197).

linked up into a single structure. The west court was extended by destroying some early houses, levelling the whole area, and digging three great circular pits known locally as *koulouras*. Evans and Pendlebury interpret these as dug simply to receive the broken pottery from the palace rubbish dumps. It is evident, however, that the similar but smaller *koulouras* in the west court of the palace at Mallia were intended for use as cisterns or granaries, since they were lined with plaster and often have a central Neolithic pillar to support a wooden roof. The rubbish found in the Knosos *koulouras* is no evidence for their original purpose, since all granaries and cisterns, when they go out of use as such, degenerate into rubbish pits. More serious objections to identifying the Knosian *koulouras* as granaries or cisterns are that they have no plaster lining, no central pillar to carry a roof, and are very large and awkward to roof.

The level of the old north-west court was raised and a broad flight of steps led up from the south side to meet the paved causeway crossing the west court towards the west porch. The alterations to the ceremonial block of state rooms between the west and central courts are rather hard to detect, as they have been obscured by later improvements, but they apparently included the construction of the west magazines and the setting back of the façade facing the central court, and so might have contained in some form the pillar shrine facing the central court.

It is clear at least that the Vat Room and the two adjacent pillar crypts preserved the plan they had in the Middle Minoan I period.[1] The old North Keep had its dungeon basements filled in, and its remains now served only as a substructure for the west side of the new north entrance with its broad ramp running up to the central court.

West of the main north gate there was constructed a smaller and more private entrance, associated with a fine new lustral area, and with a passage that skirted the remains of the old North Keep and communicated with the north-west corner of the central court near the rounded corner of the *insula* that later contained the throne room.

1. Evans's excavations proved this for the Vat Room, and the material found by Platon and myself in 1945 below the Middle Minoan III paving proved the Middle Minoan I A date at the two pillar crypts (Plate 7).

Fig. 32. Designs on Middle Minoan II A vases

To the latter half of the Middle Minoan II period Evans assigned the earliest fresco with a human figure in it, that of the Saffron Gatherer, of which the fragments were found above a Middle Minoan II floor laid down over one of the 'dungeons' of the old North Keep. Snijder pointed out, however, that the stratification of the room would allow it to be assigned to a Middle Minoan III A or even Middle Minoan III B date, and in view of the advanced character of the fresco such a date is probably to be preferred.

In the north-east part of the palace some new rooms were built for the Royal Pottery Stores which contained some of the finest polychrome pottery (Middle Minoan I B and Middle Minoan II A) found on the site, and south of these a special magazine for the great knobbed *pithoi*, dated Middle Minoan II B.[1]

The most radical alteration to the palace, however, was the construction of a great new domestic quarter in a cutting of the hillside on the east side of the great central court, and although this quarter was again remodelled in the Middle Minoan III period, certain features still existing, such as the terrace walls of the cutting, the south wall in the light-well of the 'Queen's *megaron*', and the walls of the lower east-west corridor, date from the Middle Minoan II period, as does also the elaborate drainage system of this quarter.

Some idea of the general appearance of the Minoan town at this time may be gathered from the details of the town mosaic, of which fragments were found in a Middle Minoan II B stratum north of the domestic quarter.

THE THIRD MIDDLE MINOAN PERIOD

The Middle Minoan II period ended about 1700 B.C.[2] in a disaster perhaps caused, as Pendlebury remarks, by 'the first of that series of earthquakes which periodically laid the palace in ruins'. The damage was soon repaired but it is possible, however, that the Cretan marine never quite recovered its control of the Levantine seas, since, as Miss Kantor has noted, exports of Minoan pottery to Egypt and Syria

1. This date is confirmed by the similar but smaller examples found at Phaistos sealed by a floor of the later palace.

2. Conceivably the earthquake of 1730 B.C. recorded by Schaeffer, *Stratigraphie comparée*, etc., p. 6.

seem to stop after the Middle Minoan II period though they still continued to the Cyclades and the mainland of Greece.

There is no sign of internal decay, however, in Crete. At Knosos the third Middle Minoan period is that of the greatest building activity. In the palace of Minos the domestic quarter was remodelled and the east-west corridor, though still existing in a modified form, was replaced as the main line of communication in the domestic quarter by the Grand Staircase, a splendid structure rising from the Hall of the Colonnades (Plate 15) right up to at least two storeys above the level of the central court. The central space in the Hall of the Colonnades was unroofed and acted as a light-well for all the storeys of the staircase. These light-wells, so reminiscent of modern hotels or blocks of flats, are a typical feature of Minoan architecture, and were the natural solution of the problem of lighting a large number of small internal rooms.

At Knosos the light-wells are normally situated at one end of the room, but the architects of the palaces of Phaistos and Hagia Triada in the Mesara sometimes illuminated a long room on the ground floor by a light-well in the middle of the room.[1] The light-well at the bottom of the Grand Staircase, known as the Hall of the Colonnades, was bordered on the north by the lower east-west corridor which thus still preserved something of its old importance as a main line of communication in the domestic quarter.

A few steps along the corridor was a door opening into the west end of the Hall of the Double Axes, so called because the double axe recurred as a mason's mark on the stones of the light-well at its west end. This was the chief room, the throne room of the domestic quarter, and the impressions of a wooden throne with pillared canopy above may be seen in the mass of melted gypsum plaster adhering to the north wall of this hall.

Opposite the throne, in the Hall of the Double Axes, a short 'dog's leg' passage led into an elegant little room which has been christened the 'Queen's *megaron*', with light-wells on the east and south sides, a small lustral area or bathroom on the west side, and a passage leading to the Queen's private lavatory (Fig. 33).

1. These light-wells are distinguished by their fine ashlar masonry, whereas the interior wells (not subject to the damp) usually had rough surfaces with rubble masonry that would have been covered by painted plaster.

The lustral area or bathroom differs from the usual type in that its floor is not sunken, so that there are no steps leading down into it. Also it still contains a clay bath and, though the painted ornament of this shows that it was made long after the construction of the room, it may still reflect its original purpose. The convex fluting of the column has been restored from those of the columns in the lustral area at the Little Palace. The terminus of the south road, where it joined the Vlychia bridge, is now supported by a massive viaduct, perhaps the most imposing structure still visible at Knosos.

The entrance from the north-west was made much more impressive. The steps leading from the oblong court at the end of the Royal Road were preserved, but were flanked on the east by a platform forming a royal box where the King could receive or review deputations, and the east end of the court was blocked by another flight of steps, the whole forming a Theatral Area (Plate 8) analogous to the earlier example at Phaistos, on which it was presumably modelled. The eastern steps led up to a private entrance to the palace flanked by what Evans termed the north-west 'lustral area', leading past the old North Keep direct to the throne room. Presumably only important visitors or officials would have been allowed to enter this way, and such persons may have had first to purify themselves by some ceremony in the lustral area.[1]

Structural innovations of this period include the regular employment of light-wells to give light to inner rooms; the replacement of the *kalderim*, or cobbled floors characteristic of the Middle Minoan II rooms, by the type called *mosaiko*, consisting of irregular slabs of almond stone with the interstices filled with red or white plaster; the replacement of high-column bases in breccia by low ones in limestone; and a fondness for inserting *kaselles* or stone-lined cists in the floors of magazines. The south-west wing of the palace was disused and private residences encroached on it.

One of the most notable features at this period is the excellent sewage and drainage of the domestic quarter of the palace (Fig. 33*b*).

The Queen's lavatory with its traces of a wooden seat and arrangements for flushing, and the system of drains and sewers connected with it (Fig. 33*a*), are one of the most interesting refinements of the palace

1. If these 'lustral areas' had been only sunken bathrooms, one would have expected to find some drain for the surplus water.

The first floor of the domestic quarter clearly reproduced the plan of the ground floor, and we have sufficient evidence to infer the existence of an upper Hall of the Colonnades giving access to an upper hall of the Double Axes and beyond to an upper Queen's *megaron*. Further, the upper Hall of the Colonnades has a fresco consisting of representations of figure-of-eight shields of the regular Minoan type, representing a spiral frieze as hanging above, which

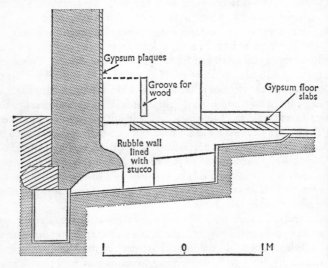

Fig. 33 a. Section of Queen's lavatory, Knosos

enabled Evans to put forward an ingenious and, I think, convincing deduction. The lower Hall of the Double Axes has a similar spiral frieze but without representations of shields, and Evans suggested that, since the most important room in the domestic quarter could hardly have been decorated merely with a narrow spiral frieze, we might infer that the actual shields were hung on the wall behind the throne, and he therefore caused replicas to be made and hung there.

The shield fresco was badly damaged but could be restored in detail from a Mycenaean reproduction of it on the mainland in the Palace of Tiryns.

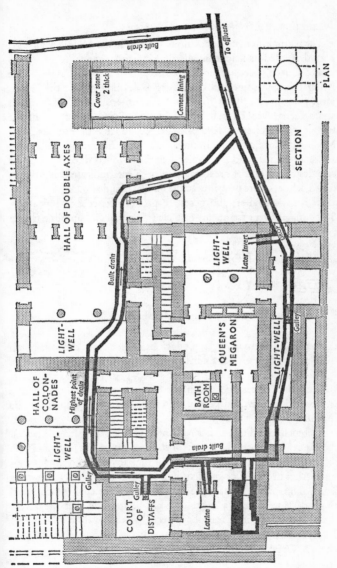

Fig. 33 b. Drainage of domestic quarter

Naturalism in Middle Minoan III Frescoes

The naturalism that became more marked in the Middle Minoan II period reached its height in Middle Minoan III times. A fine fresco in the Queen's *megaron* at Knosos depicted dolphins, at least one flying fish, and some fish resembling *melanouria* (which the French term *blades*). The flying fish was a favourite motif at this time. It appears engraved on seal stones, and modelled in faience in the temple repositories at Knosos. The second city of Phylakopi on Melos contained a splendid mural with flying fish, surely painted by a Cretan painter, and a few pieces of floral fresco discovered in the city destroyed by the great eruption on Thera indicate that Minoan fresco painters were probably active on that island also.

At Knosos painters also began to produce frescoes in low relief. Some magnificent fragments of a charging bull and an olive tree in

Fig. 34. Middle Minoan II B seals

this technique were uncovered which had fallen from the little porch overlooking the west side of the north entrance to the Palace of Minos.

The Middle Minoan III B period (1600–1550 B.C.) was characterized by the appearance at Knosos of some remarkable miniature frescoes with crowds of people represented in a very impressionistic manner (Plates 11 and 12).

A French expedition under M. André Parrot excavated at Mari on the Upper Euphrates the palace of its king Zimri-Lim (?1790–?1760 B.C.), a contemporary of Hammurabi of Babylon who finally captured Mari in 1760 B.C. (or according to some authorities a few years later). This palace contained some miniature frescoes which recall those of Knosos, and a suggestion has been made that they were influenced by Minoan frescoes, especially as the palace accounts of Mari record imports from Kaptara (usually regarded as Minoan Crete, though Wainwright and Furumark interpret it as Cilicia).

The Mari frescoes, however, appear to be over a hundred years earlier than the miniature frescoes of Knosos (which may well have been influenced by them rather than have influenced them), since if we exclude the doubtful instance of the Saffron Gatherer, which might possibly be Middle Minoan III A, there are no figured frescoes in Crete before the Middle Minoan III B period. To the Middle Minoan III period, however, we may certainly assign some fresco fragments from the lower east-west corridor at Knosos, consisting of a dado with imitation marbling (a curious anticipation of the earliest Pompeian style) with a labyrinthine pattern above it executed in dark brown on a yellow ground. It has been suggested also that Minoan frescoes were influenced by those of Level VII at Atchana (intermediate both geographically and chronologically between those of Mari and of Crete).

From the Loom-Weight Area in the Palace of Minos came some other fresco fragments of Middle Minoan III A date with two diagonals crossing at right angles, a design paralleled by a similar fresco in the great central court at Phaistos, and by a design on an engraved gem depicting a man seizing a bull by the horns.

The earliest miniature fresco is represented by some fragments found in a cist in the thirteenth magazine at Knosos (a cist which was filled in during the Middle Minoan III B period). It shows a columned building with horns of consecration on the roof, and with double axes stuck in the capitals of the columns, obviously a shrine of some sort, though not exactly corresponding to any other one I recall; it was presumably painted in the Middle Minoan III A period.

To the Middle Minoan III B period certainly belong the more famous miniature frescoes discovered in strata probably dating from before the great earthquake, fallen from an upper room in the old North Keep. The scene illustrated a typical Minoan pillar shrine, such as existed in the central court of the palace, flanked each side by a line of court ladies sitting and ostensibly watching a dance, but obviously more interested in their own conversation. The less distinguished spectators were indicated by sketching the outlines of the heads on a brownish-red background for the men and on a white ground for the women. A long tongue of white ground inserted into a red pattern makes it clear that there was no segregation of the sexes at the Minoan court (Plate 11).

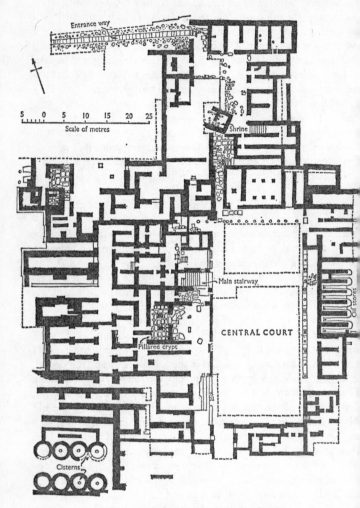

Fig. 35. Middle Minoan Palace, Mallia

Some of the spectators at this Cretan *fête champêtre* are shown standing in an olive orchard, and another fragment that may belong to the same scene shows an enthusiastic group of men waving spears, not, I think, in any hostile gesture, but rather, as Pendlebury remarks, 'like a cheering football crowd'.

From the great East Hall of the domestic quarter came some badly mutilated pieces of a magnificent fresco known as 'the Ladies in Blue', a conversation piece like the ladies in the miniature frescoes but on a heroic scale.

Frescoes with human figures, however, were almost confined to Knosos and its neighbourhood, the only other examples of Middle Minoan III date so far discovered being at Tylisos, where Hazzidakis found some fragments showing some court ladies walking from right to left, another with a design interpreted as a fan, and some small pieces of an interesting miniature fresco depicting a line of boxers like those on the steatite 'Boxer Vase' of Hagia Triada.

If it be true, as Professor Banti maintains, that Minoan painting, whether on frescoes or on vases (apart from the Knosian school), was not interested in human figures, this cannot be due to influence from the Greek mainland, which as yet had no frescoes, but might possibly be due to influence from Mari or Atchana.[1]

The Middle Minoan III period, however, also witnessed another development in frescoes that owes nothing to Mari, though it may have been influenced by Egyptian painted reliefs: namely the Minoan invention of frescoes in relief.

The Knosian Faience Industry

Even in the Early Minoan II period, faience beads had been imported into eastern Crete from Egypt, and perhaps Cretans had already learned the trick of making faience beads; but it was not till the beginning of the Middle Minoan period that we find attempts to decorate boxes with inlays of shell and faience. In the Vat Room deposit at Knosos, dating from the earliest period of the Palace of Minos, Evans found not only beads of blue and green faience but also fragments of shell and faience that had evidently been employed in an inlay as the ground work for quatrefoils of some other material.

The most remarkable inlay, however, of which we have any con-

1. L. Woolley, *A Forgotten Kingdom*, 1953, p. 76.

siderable remains consists of the fragments of the so-called Town Mosaic (Plate 6), discovered in a filling of Middle Minoan III A date near the Loom-Weight basement and themselves therefore apparently dating from the Middle Minoan II B period.

Numerous small plaques have survived illustrating the typical urban houses of the period with two or three storeys. Most of the roofs are flat, but one house has a penthouse roof to its third storey attic, and a slight outward slope on the roofs of the second floor rooms flanking the attic. Other plaques, presumably from the same mosaic, depict trees, animals, water, the prow of a ship, and some negroid figures. It has been suggested that the whole scene may have represented the siege of a town by the sea like that on the silver rhyton from Mycenae, but no actual incidents of battle have been identified.

This faience industry seems to have been confined to Knosos, and perhaps to the Palace of Minos itself, since fragments are so rarely found on other sites.[1] A lucky chance has preserved for us some important examples of this industry in the temple repositories of the palace. Two large cists sunk in the floor of a room at the back of the pillar shrine that faced the central court had been filled with a number of superfluous dedications which had evidently been removed from the shrine but had been too holy to give or throw away, and had been covered by a later floor. Among these objects was a Greek cross in grey and white marble.

The orthodox explanation of this cross is that it was not a religious symbol but might have formed a centre piece in some mosaic, though the mere fact that it was found in the temple repositories presumably indicates that it belonged to a dedication of some sort. The most striking of these offerings were two faience figurines, one of the Snake Goddess and another of a priestess or votaress (Plate 9). The goddess is a stately, rather early Victorian figure in a dress with a long spreading skirt and tight laced bodice leaving the breasts and lower arms bare. On her head is a high tiara around which coils a spotted snake whose tail intertwines with another snake which coils round her body and whose head appears at her girdle. A third snake coils over her shoulder and she holds its tail in her left hand.

1. The faience vases recently discovered at Mycenae are considered by the excavator to be probably of Syrian fabric, not Knosian or Mycenaean.

The priestess or votaress lacks the head part of the headdress, the left arm, two pieces of the hair, and parts of the skirt and apron. The flat cap with its raised medallions was found separately, and was probably crowned with a small figure of a spotted cat or leopardess which has a hole underneath corresponding to a hole in the cap.

There were also miniature models of votive robes in the same fabric adorned with designs of saffron flowers and girdles; small bowls with upright handles, and cockleshells or figure-of-eight shields moulded round the rim, and a small beaked jug with a band of running spirals in relief (copied from a metal prototype). The colours of these objects varied from white through pale green to emerald, through pale blue to turquoise, and from yellow to a chocolate brown; and the same naturalistic tendencies that appear in the contemporary frescoes and seal stones manifested themselves in the faience. Other fragments from the same deposit represented argonauts, cockleshells, and flying fish. Perhaps the finest of all the faience plaques, however, were two reliefs showing a cow suckling its calf, and another animal, usually (but I think wrongly) described as a goat, suckling its kid.

Minoan Gaming Boards

The debris from the western cist included globular, almond-shaped, and segmented beads, and pieces of inlay from a gaming board, of which we should be unable to form any conception but for the discovery of more numerous fragments of another gaming board in the so-called Corridor of the Draught Board. The latter (Plate 13) must have been a truly magnificent affair, measuring nearly a metre long and half a metre wide. The wooden base has perished, but a considerable part of the ivory framework and inlay has survived. The border had a line of faience daisies in relief with a central boss of rock crystal. The general design of the board consisted of four large rosette positions at one end, and ten smaller roundels at the other divided by parallel ribs of segmented bars.[1]

1. Gaming boards have also been found in Egypt, Cyprus, and Mesopotamia; see C. J. Gadd, *Iraq*, 1934, p. 45, and 1946, p. 66.

MALLIA

About twenty-two miles east of Herakleion along the north coast lie the ruins of another great Minoan city of which we do not know the name (though Marinatos has suggested that the ancient name may have been Tarmara)[1] and which we therefore call Mallia, after the large modern village which lies some two and a half miles west of it. The Greeks spell the name with one 'l', but most foreign authorities have followed the French excavators in spelling the name with two 'l's.

The ancient site was occupied in the Late Neolithic and throughout the Early Minoan period, but the remains from these periods were scanty. The inhabitants were perhaps backward, and continued to make pottery of Neolithic and Sub-Neolithic types during the Early Minoan I and II periods, and pottery of the Vasiliki style during the Early Minoan III period. The site was first tested by the discoverer Joseph Hazzidakis, but later the French School at Athens took over the site and excavations have taken place during a period of over thirty years under the successive directions of Renaudin, Chapouthier, Charbonneaux, Demargne, and others.

The position of this Minoan city is quite different from that of Knosos since the coastal plain is here much narrower, and Mallia was therefore itself a port.

The Palace of Mallia

The earlier palace, like the first Palace of Minos, dates from the Middle Minoan I period and is formed of a complex of rooms grouped round a central court, but seems never to have consisted of isolated blocks with open passages between like the early *insulae* at Knosos. The blocks into which the Palace of Mallia was divided should be considered rather as functional parts of a building planned as a unity from the first (Fig. 35), persisting, with some changes, into the Middle Minoan III period.

1. 'Some General Ideas on the Minoan Written Documents', *Minos*, 1951, p. 42.

Thus Block 1 consisted of the central block of the west façade, bisected by the great corridor which may have been open to the sky. The walls of this block were very thick and we may perhaps infer the existence here of a second storey. Two varieties of local stone were chiefly employed in the construction. The late Quaternary sandstone, quarried on the coast nearby, was easy to cut and was always used when good ashlar masonry was required. For inner walls, where strength was desirable but where a rough face could be covered with

Fig. 36. Designs on Middle Minoan III vases

a coat of plaster, the builders employed another local stone, much harder and less tractable, known locally as *sidheropetra* or 'ironstone', a very hard knobby limestone, half-way to a marble. In addition to these materials, interior walls of no great importance were sometimes built of mud bricks, now accidentally fired by the conflagration that destroyed the palace.

Block IV in the Mallia Palace seems to have been occupied by the palace artists and citizens, since it includes two workshops, one of an ivory carver and the other of a coppersmith. Block V was a 'keep', reminding us slightly of the early North Keep at Knosos but here constructed with huge blocks of 'ironstone', in the rough masonry often termed Cyclopean (because its most imposing example was the fortress walls of Tiryns, said to have been built by the Cyclopes).

Block VI contained some small but important rooms entered from and lighted by a loggia that was open to the central court. A small room entered from the north side of the loggia contained a hoard of ceremonial weapons, including the great bronze sword with its crystal hilt, a bronze dagger, and a battle-axe in brown schist sculptured in the form of a hunting leopard or cheetah straining at the leash. Chapouthier describes this block as 'shut in on itself' and suggests it may have been the palace centre for the 'Cult of the Hearth'.

The pottery here was still in the Middle Minoan I style, with the exception of one or two vases probably imported from Knosos, but the hieroglyphic inscriptions were of the developed type, some of the signs even betraying a tendency to develop into their counterparts in Linear Script A.

The absence of Middle Minoan II pottery at first induced Chapouthier to suggest that the hoard belonged to the Middle Minoan III period, but Evans protested that the hieroglyphic tablets found in a passage in the north-west part of the palace must be earlier, and his protest was justified by Chapouthier's later investigations in 1946 proving beyond all doubt that the hieroglyphic sealing hoard must have belonged to the earlier palace. Further Chapouthier himself stressed the relatively archaic form of the sword compared to the other swords found at Mallia. Evans had even dated the earlier Mallia sword to the transition from Early Minoan III to Middle Minoan I; Pendlebury dated it Middle Minoan I; and it cannot be later than the Middle Minoan II period to which we may, I suggest, assign the destruction of the first palace.

The battle-axe is a Cretan variant of the series of ceremonial battle-axes scattered all over Europe in the second millennium B.C. and often associated with the dispersion of the peoples speaking Indo-European languages.[1] The richest series of these axes is from south Russia, but perhaps the most famous and certainly the most splendid examples were the battle-axe of lapis lazuli and the three of a jade-like green-stone from Treasure L at Troy. The Royal Treasure at Alaca in Asia Minor has also provided us with a fine example, in silver and gold.

In the Aegean, however, such battle-axes are rare and exotic objects, and the only other example I recall from Crete is a fragment in stone in the Giamalakis collection in Herakleion.

The Mallia weapon, like the ones from the Trojan treasure, was obviously intended for ceremony, not for use in battle, since the thin blade of fragile schist would have split at the first blow, but it is an admirable example of Minoan art in the first phase of that naturalism that was to culminate, in the Middle Minoan III and Late Minoan I periods, in vase painting, in the palace frescoes, and in the miniature arts of the gem cutter, the ivory carver, and the modeller in faience.

The presence of documents in the developed form of the hiero-glyphic script indicate clearly that the site continued to be occupied during the Middle Minoan II period, but the pottery in use, as on most Cretan sites except Knosos and Phaistos, continued to be painted in the style that Evans termed Middle Minoan I B.

In general the Mallia Palace suffered less from the Middle Minoan II earthquake than that of Minos, and the reconstruction carried out at the beginning of the Middle Minoan III period was therefore far less sweeping than that at Knosos; but for that very reason it is often a delicate question whether a particular wall belongs to the earlier or the later palace, and most of the walls above the later floor levels seem to have been built in the Middle Minoan III period.

Perhaps the clearest distinction between the structures of the two palaces was shown in Block III where excavations by Chapouthier

---

1. R. W. Hutchinson, 'Battle Axes in the Aegean', *Proceedings of the Pre-historic Society*, 1950, p. 52f. and Plate IV, No. 2; V .G. Childe, *The Aryans*, 1926; H. Hencken, 'Indo-European Languages and Archaeology', *Memoirs of the American Anthropological Association*, 1955.

revealed under the Ante-room III 9 the remains of a fine stuccoed room with benches and two magnificent rapiers of Middle Minoan III date. The magazines of Block XI and the great east-west corridor in Block I certainly belonged to the scheme of the first palace. Gallet de Santerre even gives Middle Minoan III A as the *terminus ante quem* for the earlier sword.

Little enough can be said as yet about the earlier town though a house on the coast has yielded a series of Early Minoan I–II vases and one of the town cemeteries started in the Early Minoan III period.

The town site has not been excavated in full, but the French have probed and uncovered to give us some idea of the lay-out of the second city, which was built to replace the one destroyed in the Middle Minoan II period.

The Cemetery of Mallia at Chrysolakkos

The first ossuary at Chrysolakkos was evidently used by the poor folk. The pottery, with its rather clumsy Anatolian shapes, beaked jugs, and 'tea-pots', is typical Early Minoan III, like that of eastern Crete, and is adorned both in the 'dark-on-light' and in the 'light-on-dark' styles with the latter predominating. Where mottling occurs it seems to be not later than Early Minoan III times, and before the end of that period a second ossuary was in use which continued into the Middle Minoan I period. The building of the first palace was obviously accompanied by a rapid expansion of the town, and two islets off the coast (named respectively after Christ and St Barbara) were used for cemeteries. To the same period belongs the construction of the royal burial ground of Chrysolakkos, 'the Gold Hole', a name obviously derived from the plunder taken from it by tomb robbers of later times, and comparable to the term 'treasuries' which the classical Greeks applied to the beehive tombs of the mainland. One piece of jewellery, at least, escaped this looting – the glorious gold pendant in the form of two bees (or wasps?) sampling a berry, discovered in 1945 by P. Demargne (see p. 196 and Fig. 37).[1]

South of the cemeteries, by the sea, lay a considerable town of which we do not yet know the extent, but of which the ruins always

1. R. Higgins, 'The Aegina Treasure Reconsidered', *Bulletin of Institute of Classical Studies*, 1957, p. 27.

seem to have Middle Minoan III pottery on top and Middle Minoan I below. The islet of St Barbara also had some Middle Minoan I houses, including one that had belonged to a fisherman.

Adjoining the palace on the west was an important quarter with fine houses of the Middle Minoan III period and a well-paved street with a drain at the side, but here too the houses overlay a thick deposit of Middle Minoan I sherds with the smaller, flimsier foundations characteristic of that period on this site.

South of the palace lay Quarter E, with stuccoed halls and corridors that were evidently earlier than the latest phase of the palace, since in some instances they were overlaid by its western wing.

In general the houses of the later town were built better than the earlier, with more regular plans, though often on the same sites. A Minoan house agent, if such existed, would doubtless have described them as 'furnished with all modern conveniences', paved and stuccoed corridors, reception halls, bathrooms, store-rooms, light-wells, etc.

We may take as specimens of the more luxurious residences the fine villa (excavated 1946–8) in Quarter Z east of the palace, or the house with frescoes in Quarter E south of the palace. A recent report[1] outlines the probable extent of the city.

It was at one time supposed that the Minoan city had suffered its second destruction at an earlier date than Knosos because the latest pottery seems to be a rather late variety of Late Minoan I A but the discovery of at least one fine vase of Late Minoan I B marine style in House 2 and the certainty that Late Minoan II is a local Knosian style suggest that Mallia was also perhaps destroyed about 1400 B.C. by the same catastrophe.

There was some slight reoccupation of the town site in Late Minoan III times and some sherds of that period were even found in the palace, where I believe the diagonal building to be a reoccupation shrine corresponding to that of the Double Axes at Knosos; but the chief glories of Mallia belong to the Middle Minoan period.

Chrysolakkos, the chief cemetery of the Middle Minoan I period at Mallia, seems to have become less fashionable towards the end of the Middle Minoan period, if we may judge from the fact that the

1. P. Demargne and H. G. de Santerre, 'Mallia, Maisons', *Études crétoises*, 1954.

Middle Minoan III graves are much poorer than the earlier ones, and it seems probable that we have not yet discovered the richest cemetery of the later period.

GOURNIA PALACE

To the Middle Minoan III period may be assigned the construction of the small Palace of Gournia (Figs. 43 and 57) on the Merabello coast. It is hardly more than a large villa, but is obviously aping its betters, since it has a small theatral area recalling that of Knosos, but its ashlar façade with set-backs, and the alternation of round pillars and square piers in the portico facing the court, were obviously modelled on those of Mallia. We cannot say very much about the inner rooms, which were disorganized when the building was turned into workmen's flats in the Late Minoan I A period.

There was further building activity in the latter part of the Middle Minoan III period at the eastern sites, reconstructions of houses at Pseira and Mochlos, *pithos* burials at Pachyammos and Sphoungaras, and copper smelting at Chrysokamino. Copper slag has also been found on a Middle Minoan III B dump which I tested at Knosos, on Monasteriako Kephali, but I do not know from what mine the Knosians derived that ore.[1]

At Zakros in the far east a new village was planted at a site where one would have expected to find earlier habitations, since it has one of the best streams of fresh water in the whole island. Perhaps there had been earlier settlements washed out by floods like the one of 1901 so graphically described by Hogarth.[2]

THE PALACE AT PHAISTOS

At Phaistos in the Mesara, as at Knosos, the Early Minoan strata had been cut away when the site was levelled to build the earlier palace, so that it is often difficult, despite the long and careful investigation by a distinguished series of Italian archaeologists, to determine the form of the earlier buildings. The evidence for the sequence of the various structures has been well discussed and summarized by Professor Banti,

1. H. Payne, 'Archaeology in Greece', *Journal of the Historical Society*, 1935.
2. D. G. Hogarth, *A Wandering Scholar*, p. 161ff.

her deductions reviewed and criticized by Platon, and fresh evidence has been produced by Levi's recent excavations in the south-west corner of the site.

The pottery preceding the earliest structures of the palace was of the Middle Minoan I A type comparable with that of the Vat Room deposit at Knosos.

Pendlebury dated the building of the first palace to the Middle Minoan I B period, but Professor Banti objected that she found Middle Minoan I B, Middle Minoan II A and Middle Minoan II B, and Middle Minoan III A sherds in the same deposits, which might be explained either by supposing that certain types continued much later in the Mesara, or by supposing that there was some error in Evans's chronology. She dated the destruction of the first palace about 1600 B.C. and inferred from the synchronism of these various styles of pottery that it could not have lasted more than 150–200 years, perhaps not much over 50. Her minimum estimate seems low but her maximum might well be correct. In an admirably clear statement she stresses the difference between the vases found on the floors – presumably the pottery in use just before the destruction of the first palace – and the pottery of the debris above, which includes earlier types with more varied shapes, greater use of polychrome ornament, and frequent examples of barbotine ornament. This early Middle Minoan I A pottery is easily paralleled at Knosos and in the Kamares cave, but at Phaistos was not found on the floor anywhere except in the south-west House, which Pernier always considered to have been contemporary with the first palace, but destroyed at an earlier date. This evidence should not be ignored, but it hardly seems to justify the dating of the palace by this small unimportant room which might well have been cleared down to an earlier level in the later days of the first palace.

I should prefer, therefore, to date the first palace late in the Middle Minoan I B, or at latest early in the Middle Minoan II A period, and this dating is supported by the latest excavations of Doro Levi, revealing three stages of the first palace of which we hitherto only knew the latest. In the second of these phases, Rooms XXVII and XXVIII formed a single room with a central partition, and in this deposit Levi found a glorious series of Middle Minoan II A vases apparently unmixed with other styles. The most obvious remains of the first palace are in the west court, where the façade for the later palace was set back, and the lower levels of the rooms immediately behind the earlier west façade were covered by the paving of the west court, thus preserving for us the plan of these rooms of the earlier palace. The present 'theatral area', which reminds us so much of the one at Knosos, did not exist in early Middle Minoan times in that form, since the west entrance was only a narrow unimposing doorway. Yet it was in a sense more obviously theatral than that of Knosos, seeing that the steps at the north end of the west terrace lead to nothing but a perpendicular rock face, and can only, I think, have been intended for the use of spectators watching some spectacle (dance or parade or whatever it may have been) taking place in the outer west court. The space between the theatral steps and the western entrance to the palace was partly occupied by a three-roomed shrine, of which the central room rose higher than the side ones, like that depicted on the miniature frescoes of Middle Minoan III date at Knosos or like the gold model of a shrine of the dove goddess from Shaft Grave 3 at Mycenae.

Of the three small rooms behind this façade, number two contained the bench for the cult objects normal in Minoan shrines. Below this was the earliest shrine, consisting simply of a rectangular rock-cut trench with a circular cavity in the middle. The triple shrine presumably belongs to the third phase of Levi's earliest palace and will therefore date not earlier than Middle Minoan II, probably Middle Minoan II B (that is about 1800 B.C., with a few years' margin of error). In 1953 Levi also excavated another room east of the room uncovered in an earlier campaign. The character of these two rooms, with their gypsum paving and dadoes surmounted by fresco, and the fine quality of the Middle Minoan II A pottery made it evident that these are not merely early houses but clearly a wing of the earliest palace; one room contained a stuccoed bench bearing a number of fine vases, and another two stucco consoles. Here was found a sort of dice-box in terracotta, containing what appears to be a die in the form of a small ivory disk with the numbers indicated by inlaid silver dots, as well as two possible 'chess pawns', in the form of a small lion's head and an ox's hoof, in ivory.

It would appear that those rooms marked on the earlier plans of Phaistos as pre-palatial, in the south-east and north-west parts of the

Sherds of the Early Neolithic I period

I

Early Neolithic I vase from Knosos

Early Minoan III vases

a Middle Minoan IB vases

b Middle Minoan IIA vases

4

Middle Minoan I figurines from Petsopha

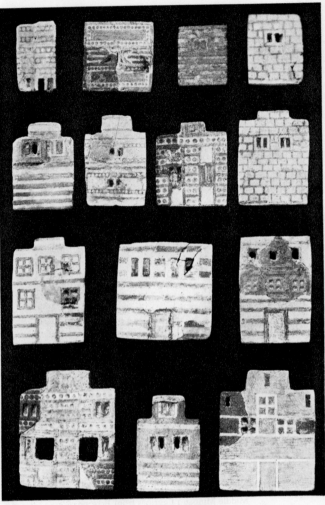

Town Mosaic in faience of Middle Minoan IIB period

East Pillar Crypt, Palace of Minos

Theatral Area, Palace of Minos

Snake Goddess group in faience from temple repositories, Knosos

b Temple Tomb, Knosos

a Great Viaduct, Knosos

Miniature fresco, Palace of Minos

11

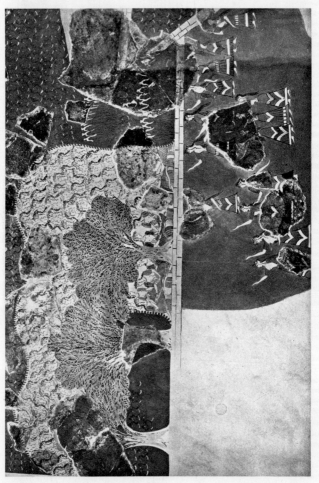

Miniature fresco, Palace of Minos

Royal gaming board

13

a Stone head from Monasteriako Kephali, Knosos

b The Phaistos Disk

Hall of the Colonnades, Knosos

Bronze statuette illustrating the Minoan bulljumping sport

a Bull Rhyton, Little Palace, Knosos

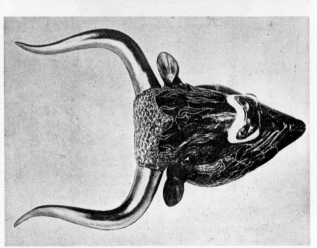

b Fresco of the Young Prince, Palace of Minos

Late Minoan I vase from Pachyammos

Late Minoan II polychrome vase from Isopata

Late Minoan III sarcophagus from Hagia Triada

Cult objects from Karphi Shrine

Geometric vases, Khaniale Tekke

Geometric clay house, Khaniale Tekke

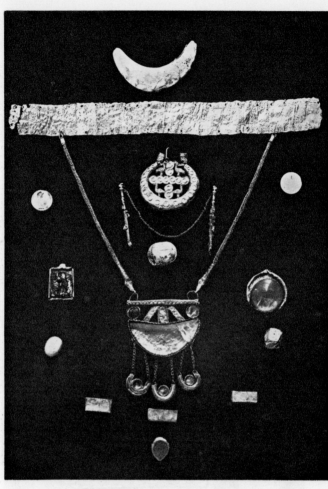

Jewellery from Khaniale Tekke Tholos

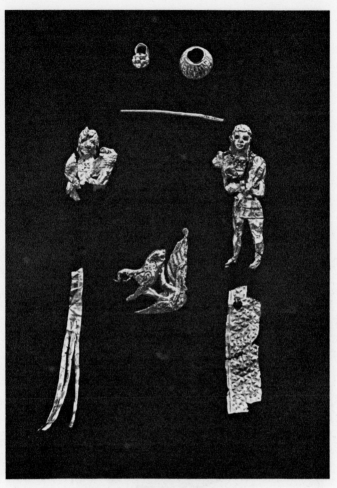

Jewellery from Khaniale Tekke Tholos

Polychrome vase from Khaniale Tekke Tholos

Hammered bronze figures from Dreros

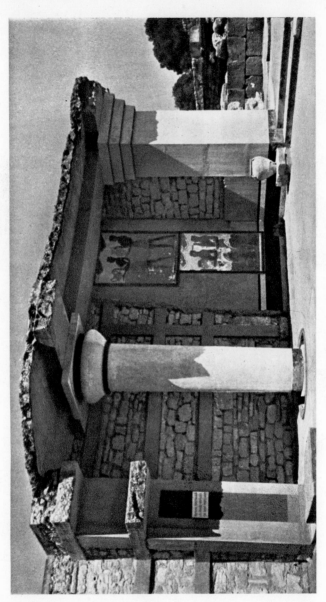

South Propyleum and Procession Fresco, Knosos

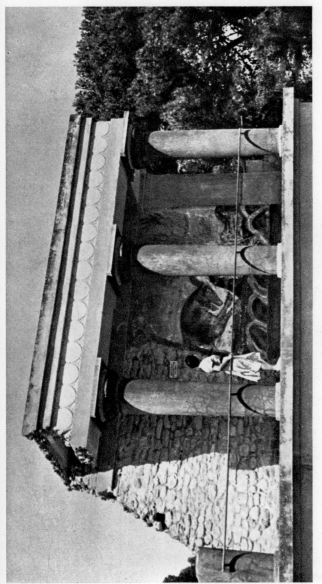

North entrance to the Palace of Minos

Central court, Palace of Phaistos; Mount Ida in the distance

Corridor opening off Great Court, Palace of Phaistos

Magazines, later Palace of Phaistos

site, should rather be regarded as belonging to these earlier phases of the first palace revealed by Levi's recent explorations.

If the earlier palace at Phaistos was destroyed by the earthquake of the Middle Minoan II B period which, we have suggested, may have been connected with the great Levantine disaster assigned by Schaeffer to 1730 B.C., the Cretans of the Mesara seem to have recovered from it quickly.

On the ruins of the early palace was constructed a still more magnificent building. The west façade was set back seven metres and the paving of the outer west court covered the ruins of the early shrine, which was replaced not by another shrine but by a grand staircase leading to an imposing propylaea or entrance hall giving access to the central court and to the upper floor in a curiously indirect manner. The central court may also be approached through the fine 'lustral area' or 'bathroom'.

It may be remembered that the 'western approaches' to the palaces of Knosos, Mallia, and Phaistos have this in common. If the entrance is a magnificent one it is very indirect; if it is direct it is very narrow. Security may have been the object aimed at in each instance; what was feared perhaps was not so much attack by foreigners as palace intrigues and local revolutions.

The new propylaea covered over some magazines of the first palace, but the central court and the magazines to the north of it were incorporated in the later palace.

The magazines immediately north of the entrance possessed storage jars, of which one contained a quantity of grape seeds (the earliest recorded from Crete). I have suggested 1900 B.C. (rather than Levi's 2000) as a likely date for the earliest palace, but even so it is clear that Middle Minoan II A ware was plentiful at Phaistos when the current pottery in east Crete was Middle Minoan I B and when developed Middle Minoan I A was still prevalent in north central Crete.

Other substructures of the earlier palaces were uncovered by Levi under the western part of the central court. All round the palace on the slopes of the hill were houses, which the Italians are only beginning to explore, but which show that the town of Phaistos passed through the same vicissitudes as the palace.

The Italians have suggested that the enlarged west court may have been used for the toreador sports, and spectators may have watched not only from the slopes but from the windows of the palace, and because of this, the staircase joining the west court to the little court in the north-west wing was preserved and incorporated in the later palace.

Immediately south of the great propylaea system was an important series of magazines opening off both sides of a broad corridor which at its east end opened out into a two-columned hall (perhaps, it is suggested, an administrative office for the palace treasures) with a broad portico facing the central court.

The southern and most of the eastern part of the palace has been destroyed by later buildings and denudation of the site.

The north side of the great court was united to the north quarter of the palace by a broad corridor, originally perhaps open to the sky. The doorway leading to the princely apartments to the north was closed by a double door flanked by two half columns and two niches adorned with frescoes. This corridor existed in the first palace, but the floor was raised in the second palace. The store-rooms each side of the corridor form two large rectangles, indicating the measurements of the halls on the first floor, for which they had formed the sub-structures. North of this lay the fine hall with its central light-well (a peculiarity of Phaistos and Hagia Triada anticipating the Tuscan *atria* of Pompeii); it seems to have served as an ante-room to the splendid hall with its two annexes, the Phaistos equivalent of the Knosos Hall of the Double Axes. From this hall a dog's-leg corridor led to some private apartments with bath and lavatory, corresponding somewhat to the Queen's suite at Knosos. It is to be remarked that there is very little in the way of fresco decoration. The best rooms at Phaistos relied on the fine quality of their masonry and on a very liberal use of gypsum for doors, dadoes, and floors.

Little can be said about the Minoan town of Phaistos, but the nature of the ground makes it obvious that most of it must have lain on the southern slopes and on the plain at their foot.

The later palace, like that at Knosos, was apparently largely destroyed by the great earthquake of Middle Minoan III, perhaps more so than that of Knosos since it was not rebuilt as a palace. There was some reoccupation in the palace, but the ruling prince evidently decided that it would be better to build a new palace, and the site he chose was the western end of the same ridge on which Phaistos stands, a very beautiful position but far less defensible, perhaps showing that the Minoan fleet was still controlling the seas round Crete. (But see p. 173.)

But though the new palace, of which we do not know the ancient name and which is therefore called Hagia Triada after the little medieval chapel there, was first constructed later in the Middle Minoan III B period, it is better to consider it in the main as a building of the following period.

MIDDLE MINOAN JEWELLERY

Parallels to the Mochlos head-bands were also found in the Mesara in the form of three broad bands, and many fragments of others, often with a decoration of repoussé dots round the edge and with holes for attaching them. Twenty-one small disks (10·8 cm. in diameter) of very thin gold leaf, each with two holes for attaching it perhaps to a garment, were found in the same deposit, together with a disk with carved surface and six attachment holes, two rings of gold sheeting (possibly from the rim of a vase), three almond-shaped beads and three round ones, three finger rings of thin wire, and six rivet heads of gold.

With the exception of the pendant and of a few beads from the lower stratum, the gold seems to be pure, implying that the native silver had been removed from it.[1]

Of the gold ornaments from the Mesara, especially those from Koumasa, the majority would appear to have belonged to the Middle Minoan I period, or possibly to the Middle Minoan II, since it is hard to differentiate between the remains of these two periods except at Knosos and Phaistos. The Mesara goldsmith no longer confined his attention to decorating his work with repoussé and incised designs, but had also developed the techniques of granulation and of cloisonné work with gold wire (from Tholos B at Koumasa) in the form of a sitting toad. The same tomb also produced some gold beads (one in the form of a lilac seed capsule), and two small pierced disks of gold, which are paralleled by those on the gold bee pendant from

1. The alluvial gold of the Near East regularly contained varying percentages of silver; compare A. Lucas, 'Silver in Ancient Times', *Journal of Egyptian Archaeology*, 1928, p. 40.

Mallia and on three pendants among the so-called 'Aegina treasure' in the British Museum. R. Higgins suggests that this treasure may have been part of the gold looted from the cemetery at Chrysolakkos and from which the latter derived its name of 'the gold hole' and which he assigns very plausibly to the seventeenth century B.C. (though some scholars had tried to assign it to as late as the eighth century B.C.). The most obvious Minoan piece is the gold cup with the quadruple spirals, but the 'Master of Animals' pendant must surely

Fig. 37. Gold bee pendant, Mallia

be either Minoan or Mycenaean, and the other pendants also have Minoan parallels in some detail or another.

Fortunately the finest of all Minoan jewels was actually found in Chrysolakkos during the French excavations there. This is the splendid gold pendant in the form of two bees (or wasps?) soldered together at the heads and the tips of the abdomens (Fig. 37). The legs of gold wire held a ball decorated with granulations, and the same technique was employed on the eyes and the bevels of the abdomen. From the tips of the wings and the point where the abdomens meet hang gold disks like those of the 'Aegina treasure' pendants.

MIDDLE MINOAN CHRONOLOGY

Levi's recent excavations prove that Middle Minoan II A pottery was already in use in the earliest palace at Phaistos, and the discovery of metal vases of that style at Tod in Upper Egypt in a deposit dated to the reign of Amenemhat II (1929–1895 B.C.) indicate that that style can hardly have started later than 1900 B.C.[1]

I therefore suggest the following amendment of the Middle Minoan Chronology which I put forward in 1954.

	Knosos Early Minoan III	Northern Villages Early Minoan III	Phaistos Early Minoan III	Mesara Villages Early Minoan III	East Crete Early Minoan III
2000					
1950	M.M.IA	M.M.IA	M.M.IA	M.M.IA	M.M.IA and M.M.IB
1900	M.M.IB M.M.IIA		M.M.IB and M.M.IIA		
1830	M.M.IIB		M.M.IIB		
1750*					
1600	M.M.IIIA	M.M.IIIA	M.M.IIIA	M.M.IIIA	M.M.IIIA
1570	Pre-Seismic M.M.IIIB	M.M.IIIB	M.M.IIIB	M.M.IIIB	M.M.IIIB
1550	Post-Seismic M.M.IIIB				
	L.M.IA	L.M.IA	L.M.IA	L.M.IA	L.M.IA

* Or 1730, if the Cretan earthquake is the same as Schaeffer's one.

THE GREAT EARTHQUAKE OF 1570(?) B.C.

At Knosos the Middle Minoan III palace was badly damaged by a great earthquake, but the clearest evidence of this catastrophe comes from an area just below the south-west corner of the central court. Here two small but well-built houses have been crushed by blocks hurled southwards from the adjacent palace walls. In this, as in most Cretan earthquakes, the shocks evidently came from the north, probably from the epicentre on or near the island of Thera. One of

1. R. W. Hutchinson, 'Minoan Chronology Reviewed', *Antiquity*, 1954, p. 155.

these houses Evans termed 'The House of the Fallen Blocks', from the great palace blocks which destroyed it and which still lie there. It appears to have been the abode of a stone cutter who made stone lamps. The other house Evans termed 'The House of the Sacrificed Oxen', since it contained two pairs of horns of bulls of the great *primigenius* type and the remains of painted tripod altars.

Evans aptly quoted a line of Homer to the effect that 'the Earth-shaker delighteth in bulls' and suggested that the Minoan king had decided that this area should not be rebuilt but remain sacred to the 'earth-shaker' and had sacrificed bulls there to Poseidon the god of earthquakes, or to whatever Minoan god was the equivalent of Poseidon.[1]

The palace was quickly restored and the ruins that we still see represent for the most part this reconstruction at the end of the Middle Minoan III B period, though the north-west portico and the north-western lustral area seem not to have been rebuilt, and the cists below the Middle Minoan III floors were filled in.

1. A. J. Evans, *Palace of Minos*, II, p. 296; Pendlebury op. cit., p. 155; evidence for the epicentre of the earthquake is provided by the cracks which start at ground level on the north and travel diagonally south and upwards, exactly like the cracks made by the earthquakes of 1926 and 1935.

CHAPTER 8

Minoan Religion

PRE-HELLENIC ELEMENTS IN CRETAN RELIGION

THE inhabitants of Crete during the classical period had, like those of the mainland of Greece, inherited many beliefs and religious practices from Bronze Age times, but they were well aware that this inheritance differed from that of the ordinary Greeks. The mainland had been occupied by a Greek-speaking population since early in the second millennium B.C. By the middle of the second millennium, probably, Greeks were already settling in Crete, but only in comparatively small numbers, and these Mycenaean Greeks had already adopted many Cretan cults and religious customs. Even on the mainland we find survivals from Minoan or at least pre-Hellenic religion, but in Crete these non-Hellenic elements were much stronger and tended to survive much longer.

Herodotus in a suggestive passage of the second book of his history remarks that Hera, Hestia, Themis, the Graces, and the Nereids were among the oldest deities of Greece.[1]

In Hera and Themis we seem to have a reflection of the great mother goddess of the Minoan Cretans, and in Hestia of the Household Goddess who, according to Euhemerus, had founded Knosos.[2] In the Graces and the Nereids we may perhaps have a reflection of those rather vague groups of two or three goddesses so often represented on Minoan and Mycenaean gems, but it is often difficult to distinguish what is genuinely Minoan in the legends about them. Let us therefore concentrate on a much less important figure, but one where the Minoan element seems to have been less diluted by later tradition. I refer to Akakallis, daughter of Minos. Her name is not

1. Herodotus II, Chap. 50.

2. See F. Jacoby, *Fragmente der Griechischen Historiker*, 1923, p. 63 (a passage from Lactantius quoting Ennius's Latin translation of Euhemerus's *Sacred History*).

Hellenic and the reduplication of the first syllable certainly occurs in some Minoan names. Further it was a name for the narcissus, and plant-names, as Marinatos has stressed, are often survivals from the pre-Hellenic vocabulary. The special characteristic of Akakallis was her aptitude for arranging that her sons (usually by the god Apollo) should be suckled by animals. Such stories occur elsewhere, the best known being that of Rhea Silvia and her twins Romulus and Remus, but few girls can have displayed such a facility in this practice as Akakallis. Thus her twin children Phylakis and Philander by Apollo were reared at Tarrha by a goat, her son Kydon at Kydonia was suckled by a bitch, and her son Milatos by a wolf. (I cannot name foster-parents for her other children, but I doubt if that resourceful maiden would have suckled any herself.)

The association with Minos, the pre-Hellenic name of the daughter, and the consistency of the stories suggest that these really are derived from pre-Hellenic folklore, and also strengthen our belief, supported on independent evidence, that many features of the cult and tradition surrounding Apollo were derived from some pre-Hellenic god.[1]

The most startling heterodoxy of the Cretans in classical times was that the Zeus they worshipped had been born as a baby in Crete, had grown to manhood, and had finally been buried there. The Greeks did not so much mind the story of Zeus's birth, which was accepted by Hesiod, but the legend of his death and burial was regarded as down-right blasphemy even by the Cretan Epimenides in his poem on Minos quoted by Saint Paul. The fragment preserved and brilliantly restored by Rendel Harris from a passage in a Syriac commentary has been translated as follows:

> The Cretans carved a tomb for Thee, O Holy and High,
> Liars, noxious beasts, evil bellies
> For thou didst not die, ever Thou livest and standest firm
> For in thee we live and move and have our being.

Well might orthodox Greeks be shocked at the Cretan picture of the lord of Olympus, but the question arises: why did the first Greek settlers identify their Sky-Father with a god who lived his complete

1. Perhaps the 'Master of the Animals'; see p. 207.

life and died like a man in Crete? The natural inference is that this god, whose name appears to have been Velchanos, was an important deity worshipped on the island by the Minoan Cretans.

It is therefore worth our while to examine briefly the main outlines of the story of Zeus's birth in Crete.

THE BIRTH OF ZEUS

The oldest extant version of the story of the birth of Zeus is the one presented by Hesiod in the *Theogony* written in the eighth century B.C., but the main outlines of the story go back well into the middle Bronze Age, since they appear in Hittite texts of the second millennium B.C., where we find the parts of the Greek gods, Ouranos, Kronos, and Zeus being enacted by Anu, Kumarbi, and the weather-God Teshub, deities of that element of the Hittite peoples that spoke the Hurrian language.[1]

Hesiod recounts how Kronos, the son of Heaven (Ouranos) and Earth (Gaia), mutilated his father at his mother's suggestion and became the supreme deity. Kronos, believing that he too would be destroyed by his son, used to swallow his children until Rhea his wife secreted her latest-born son Zeus and sent him to Lyktos where his grandmother, Gaia, received him and hid him in a dark cave on the wooded Aegean Mountain (the Goat's Mountain). Kronos was induced to swallow a stone wrapped in swaddling bands believing that he had swallowed his latest son also. The story is crude and primitive, and we might naturally have imagined it to be ancient, though I think few (before the discovery of the Hittite texts) would have suspected it to be an ancient Hurrian tale. The elaboration of this story and its association with Cretan place-names must be the work of Cretans, and the elaboration must have taken place in the Bronze Age, before the Dorian colonization of Crete, since it is not typical of Doric folklore elsewhere. Hesiod, of course, was a Boeotian, but he lays the scene in Crete. His 'Goat's Mountain' must almost certainly be the fine massif now called Dikte, and the cave would probably be that of Psychro. It should be remarked, however, that the name Dikte

1. Compare O. R. Gurney, *The Hittites* (Penguin Books, 1952), p. 190; note that Anu reigned for nine years in Heaven as Minos did for the same period on earth.

as applied to this mountain has only been revived by modern scholars and Hesiod himself never mentions Dikte. The Psychro cave, however, was surely one of the places where Zeus's birth was celebrated, and whatever cave Hesiod alludes to must have been situated not very far from the site of Lyktos, which is near the modern village of Xydhas.

The 'goat' of the 'Goat's Mountain' is usually identified by scholars with Amaltheia, the goat which was said to have nourished the infant Zeus. Now it is only writers of the Hellenistic period or later that refer to Amaltheia as a goat; earlier authors such as Pherekydes and Pindar call her a nymph. Nevertheless the motive of a divine child reared by an animal is a primitive one, as we have noted above with regard to the legends of Akakallis (p. 200), and classical authors very often humanized and softened down the more primitive elements in their traditional folklore. Some later author, perhaps Euhemerus, stated that Amaltheia was the daughter of the Cretan King Melisseus, who may himself be only the humanized version of the wild bees that brought honey to the infant god.

Strabo, the geographer, asserted that the birth cave of Zeus was on Mount Dikte, and Aratos confused the tradition further by saying that Zeus was reared 'in fragrant Dikton on Mount Ida'. Hellenistic traditions seem to have placed Mount Dikte east of the isthmus of Hierapetra, since Strabo, writing in the time of Augustus, denounced the absurdity of placing Dikte near Mount Ida, from which he said it was 1000 stades distant, whereas only 100 stades separated it from Cape Samonion in the far east. Bosanquet emphasized that during the classical period the cults of Dictaean Zeus were all situated in the east end of the island, and he suggested that the ruins at Palaikastro, where there was a temple dedicated to Dictaean Zeus, might represent the city of Diktaia, which Diodorus said had been founded by Zeus near his birthplace. The map of Crete drawn up in the fifteenth century A.D. by the Venetian Coronelli places Dikte near the site of the conical mountain termed Modhi and the town Dittea a little to the south-west.

Obviously we have rival stories from various districts all claiming that the birth cave of Zeus was situated on their territory. The Eteo-Cretan story represented by the traditions recorded by Strabo, Diodorus, and Coronelli and summed up by Bosanquet must have identified the birth cave with some as yet undiscovered cave near Modhi.[1]

Hesiod's story of the birth cave and the 'Goat's Mountain' must have been the canonical version in Lyktos and probably throughout the district we now term the Pedhiadha, though Marinatos has suggested that at an earlier date the cave of Zeus might have been identified with that of Arkalochori, which is nearer to Lyktos, and that the tradition might only have shifted to Psychro after the collapse of the roof of the Arkalochori cave.

A third tradition certainly associated Zeus's birth with the Idaean cave that underlies the main peak of Psiloriti and overlooks the plain of Nidha, 5000 feet above the sea. This was the cave most commonly accepted as the Birth Cave in Roman times, and dedications show that it was a sacred place before 1400 B.C. It was not, apparently, frequented in Middle Minoan times, when the Kamaras cave overlooking the Mesara may possibly have been a place where the local inhabitants celebrated the birth of Velchanos, the Minoan Zeus.

THE CURETES

Closely associated with the cult of the infant Zeus was that of the Curetes, attendants of the young Zeus.

A hymn dating in its present form from the third century A.D. but obviously derived from a much earlier prototype, invoking the young Zeus (here regarded not as an infant but as a young man) in the name of the Curetes, was discovered at Palaikastro in the country of the Eteo-Cretans on a site where there had been an earlier temple dedicated to Dictean Zeus.

According to Diodorus the nine Curetes were earth-born like the Titans, though others said they were children of the Idaean Dactyla. The Curetes were said to be 'the first to gather sheep into flocks, to domesticate the several other kinds of animals which men fatten, and to discover the making of honey. In the same manner they introduced the art of shooting with the bow and the ways of hunting animals,

---

1. R. C. Bosanquet, 'Dikte and the Temples of Dictaean Zeus', *Annual of the British School at Athens*, 1940, p. 60; the fame of Diktaia was remembered even by Ariosto, who calls it the richest of the hundred cities of Crete (*Orlando furioso*, Canto XX, verse 15).

and they showed mankind how to live and associate together in a common life, and they were the originators of concord and of a kind and orderly behaviour.'[1]

This rather sophisticated account hardly sounds like genuine folk-lore; I suspect it to be an account by Euhemerus or some such writer of the origins of the Neolithic civilization. Diodorus also records that the Curetes invented swords and helmets and the war-dance, but this is probably only an explanation of the ritual dance performed at festivals of the birth of Zeus. Later traditions refer to them as sons of Zeus, or confuse them with the Corybantes who had Rhodian associations and appear in inscriptions from Hierapytna, a city with very strong Rhodian connexions.

The legend of the dancing Curetes, however (when not confused with the Corybantes), seems to be purely Cretan.

This dance has been compared to the leaping dance performed at Rome by the Salii, the armed priests of Mars. The eastern districts of Crete, as remarked by Evans, the very districts where the Eteo-Cretans maintained themselves till a late date, are still famous for their *pedhiktos* or leaping dance.

THE DEATH OF THE CRETAN ZEUS

No legend has survived at all concerning the manner of the death of Zeus and presumably even the suspicion of it would have died out of the popular memory but for the celebration of rites by local inhabitants near the reputed site of his tomb. There is no literary reference to his death before the passage from Epimenides quoted by St Paul (but not mentioned by other Greek writers in any extant passage before Euhemerus and Callimachus).

Nilsson assumes that the Cretan Zeus was a vegetation god, born and dying each year like Osiris, but there is only one possible classical reference to the annual birth and none to the annual death, unless we are to assume that the annual spreading of carpets on the throne of Zeus in the Idaean Cave was a ceremony associated with the annual death.

Nevertheless, although these Cretan legends of Zeus seem to be saturated with pre-Hellenic myths, it is hard to identify any of them

1. Diodorus Siculus, Book v, Chap. 65.

in the representations on Minoan seal-stones. There are some seals showing a young male figure descending from Heaven who may well have been Velchanos, but there is no Bronze Age seal or other representation showing the birth of Zeus, or the Curetes dancing round him. On the contrary most Minoan gems suggest that goddesses were more important than gods to the Cretans of the Bronze Age and probably of the Neolithic period also.

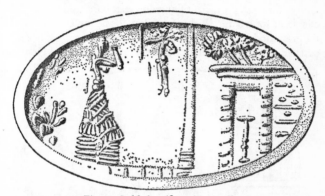

Fig. 38. Gold ring (from Knosos?)

The prominence of legends referring to the young Zeus in the Iron Age is perhaps almost an accident, due to the fact that this particular Minoan deity, who may possibly have been only a deified king, happened to have been identified with the main deity of the Greek settlers.

MINOAN DEMONS

Minoan demons, which were always depicted as performing some religious rite, such as pouring libations or bringing offerings to a goddess, are consistent in type and must be carefully distinguished from the more varied and fanciful monsters devised by Minoan artists when they were aiming merely at decoration and not at any religious symbolism. They walk upright and behave like human beings, but their limbs end in paws, not hands or feet, their heads resemble those of lions or horses or asses, and their backs are covered with loose skin ending in a point like a wasp's tail. Levi has classified them as lion demons, while Evans believes they were derived from an Egyptian design showing TA-URT, the hippopotamus goddess, carrying a croco-dile. Nilsson regards them as an invention of Minoan fantasy. Their origin remains obscure but their functions seem certain.

MINOAN GODDESSES

One of the most prominent figures on seals is the goddess sometimes compared to Artemis, 'Lady of the Beasts', and sometimes to Cybele, the great mother goddess of Asia Minor. There is some excuse for both parallels, but the tendency of many writers, helped by Hesychios's

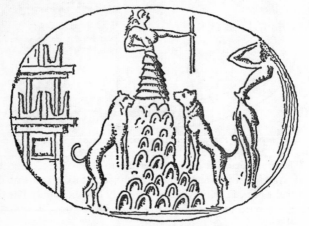

Fig. 39. Mountain Mother sealing

statement that Kybelis was a word for the double axe, has been to overstress the relationship of this deity to Anatolian religion and to the great mother goddess whom the Phrygians so appropriately addressed as 'MA'.

Nilsson has pointed out that the famous seal impressions showing the Minoan goddess standing on a mountain peak flanked by two guardian lions are relatively late; I would personally go further and regard them as Mycenaean sealings, although found at Knosos (Fig. 39). Earlier representations of the Minoan goddess depict her as a huntress like Britomartis or Artemis, rather than as the protectress 'Lady of the Beasts'.

Evans often seems to suggest that he regards most representations of goddesses on Minoan seals as personifications of the great mother goddess, but a fairer representation of his views is afforded by a quotation from a letter he wrote to Nilsson stating: 'I have always in mind the possibility that the goddess who appears in so many relations in Minoan scenes and impersonations may cover what was really regarded as separate deities with separate names equivalent to Artemis, Rhea, Athena, Aphrodite, etc. But as a provisional procedure it is convenient, in default of more definite knowledge, to treat the goddess as essentially the same great Nature Goddess under various aspects – celestial with the dove, chthonic with the snake, etc., etc.' We may recall how the Titan Prometheus in Aeschylus's play refers to 'my mother Themis and Earth, one shape with many names' (*Prometheus Vinctus*, lines 217 and 218).

THE LADY OF THE BEASTS AND THE MASTER OF THE ANIMALS

The huntress goddess figured on some Minoan seal-stones may have been called Britomartis, a name which, according to the late Latin

Fig. 40. Master of the Animals seal

author, Solinus, meant 'sweet virgin', a translation confirmed by an entry in Hesychios's Lexicon stating that '*britu*' was a Cretan word meaning 'sweet'. We need not, I think, be troubled by the fact that this goddess was worshipped as Britomartis in the east but as Dictynna in the west of the island. If Britomartis was an old Eteo-Cretan title (and it was certainly not Greek) we can understand its surviving longer in eastern Crete, where that language persisted till Roman times. In the west, however, where the country was flooded with Achaean colonists at an early date, it is natural that she might be hailed as 'The Lady of Dikte'. Worshippers had to enter her temple barefoot – possibly a Minoan custom.[1]

Parallel to the 'Lady of the Beasts' is her less prominent but well-attested male counterpart the 'Master of the Animals', a youthful figure usually depicted grasping two lions or other animals or birds by the throats. We do not know his Minoan name and it is difficult to attach a Greek name to him. The fact that the 'Lady of the Beasts' was called Artemis in archaic Greek times might suggest that we should call the 'Master of the Animals' Apollo, especially as the cult of that god was said to have been introduced from Crete to Delphi, but there is really no evidence to show that Apollo was represented as 'Master of the Animals' in archaic Greek art.[2]

THE SNAKE OR HOUSEHOLD GODDESS

Another deity very popular in Minoan times was the one known to archaeologists as the Snake Goddess, from the fact that one or more snakes are usually found coiling round the body or arms of the figures representing her (Plate 9). Her worship seems to be concentrated in small shrines in the palaces and the large houses, and she is therefore regarded by Nilsson as pre-eminently the domestic or household goddess. The snake had probably nothing to do with the snakes that appear in underworld cults in classical Greece. It was the house snake that was fed and revered as the genius, the guardian angel of the house, according to a very widespread superstition. The cult of the household snake has not entirely died out even now. In some parts of Greece peasants will sprinkle breadcrumbs round a hole in the floor regarded as the snake's door, or will pour milk into it. If the snake appears it will be hailed as 'master of the house' (*noikokýres*) or 'genius of the place' (*topákas*).[3] Similar practices are recorded from Albania, from all the Slav countries, from Lithuania, Italy, Sweden, and India (all countries characterized by their use of Indo-European languages). It is true that in classical Greece the cult of the house snake does seem sometimes to be confused, or at least associated,

1. It was certainly the normal practice among the Semites.

2. Mrs Chittenden prefers to correlate him with Hermes; see *Hesperia*, 1947, p. 187.

3. But I cannot quote any recent example from Crete.

with a cult of the dead, and we find the snake worshipped under titles such as Zeus Ktesios, Zeus Meilichios, or more commonly as the Agathos Daimon. This, however, was quite foreign to the Minoan and Mycenaean practice where the snake was not a deity but simply, in all probability, the emblem of a goddess.

A similar snake goddess seems to have been worshipped during the Bronze Age in Palestine where a *stele* was found at Tell Beit Mirsim in a deposit dated about 1600 B.C., carved with a representation of a goddess with her snake curling round her body.[1] This *stele* was practically contemporary with the faience figure of the Snake Goddess found in the temple repositories at Knosos. Unfortunately the goddess of Tell Beit Mirsim lacks both a head and a name.

The classical deity who embodied most of the spirit of the Minoan Snake Goddess was certainly Athena, not the fierce warrior goddess of Olympus as Homer represented her, but rather the maiden goddess as Pheidias saw her, the calm, benignant patron of the city, still faithful to her bird (the owl), her snake, and her pillar, all familiar elements in the cult of the Household Goddess, the Snake Goddess of Crete, by one tradition the birthplace of Athena.

Just as Athena was worshipped as Polias, the patron goddess of the city, so was her snake regarded as 'Oikouros', the household snake of the city and we can imagine the consternation of the Athenians when that snake refused its food on the occasion of the invasion by Xerxes and his Persians.[2] Nilsson has most aptly quoted a passage from Kipling's story, *The Letting in of the Jungle*: 'Who could fight against the Jungle or the Gods of the Jungle when the very village cobra had left his hole in the platform under the peepul.'[3] Sir John Forsdyke has recorded his memories of a more gallant house snake which refused to desert the Macedonian village of Kalenovo when the human inhabitants fled, and which therefore drew rations from the British unit which occupied it in the First World War. I spent a night there in 1924, but unfortunately cannot substantiate whether the snake was then still carrying out its duties.

1. W. F. Albright, *The Archaeology of Palestine* (Penguin Books, 1949), Fig. 20.
2. Herodotus, Book VIII, Chap. 41.
3. *The Second Jungle Book.*

EPIPHANIES IN THE FORMS OF BIRDS

The sacred bird was just as characteristic of the Minoan Household Goddess as it was of Athena Parthenos but it was usually a different bird in Crete. The birds associated with her in Middle Minoan deposits, such as the doves of a shrine from the Loom-Weight Basement, or from the temple repositories, or from Late Minoan shrines such as Gournia or Gaze, or Sub-Minoan shrines such as Karphi and Prinias, are often hard to identify, but when they have any characteristics at all they resemble doves rather than owls. Most of them can only be termed small birds. A bird on the double axes in the cult scene on the Hagia Triada sarcophagus is almost certainly a raven.

The miniature shrine from which the 'Dove Shrine Deposit' gained its name is particularly interesting, since it consists of a trilithon of three pillars with beam-end capitals, each surmounted by a 'dove'. It recalls somewhat the very interesting pillar-shrine of Roque-Perthuse in South France[1] (though without the human skulls and horse-head frieze of the latter). The Roque-Perthuse monument only dates from the fourth century B.C., but the Ligurians who probably erected it were a very old-established and conservative element of the population of those parts.

The epiphany of gods and goddesses in the form of birds must have been equally familiar in Mycenaean mythology. Even in classical times we have Zeus's eagle, Athena's owl, and Aphrodite's doves, but in Homer's poems such epiphanies are more numerous and varied. Athena and Apollo appropriately turn themselves into vultures to watch the battle between Hector and Ajax. Hypnos (sleep) approaches Zeus in the form of a kite. Athena on other occasions appears as a swallow or as a heron.

If then the chief gods and goddesses of the Minoan pantheon were worshipped by the Mycenaean Greeks, we should be able to identify many of them. Which, if any, of the Hellenic goddesses are we to identify with the Minoan goddess whom Evans regarded as the 'Nature Goddess' whose symbol appears to have been the double

1. Compare F. Bénoit, *L'Art primitif méditerranéen de la vallée du Rhône*, 1945, p. 14 and Plate 29.

axe and whose sacred birds appear to have been doves? The double axe might suggest that she was Cybele and the doves that she was Aphrodite. Indeed the naked Mycenaean goddess with the doves probably was Aphrodite, but our Cretan goddess of the double axe was respectably attired in full court dress.

It is at least arguable that 'the very holy one' of Crete may have been nearer to Athena than to Aphrodite, since at Corinth, a great centre of Mycenaean culture, we find the cult title 'Hellotis' (recalling the Cretan festival Hellotia dedicated to Ariadne) assigned to Athena.

ARIADNE

The first literary reference to the name Ariadne occurs in the *Iliad*, where Homer records that Daedalus prepared a fine dancing place for her in Crete.[1] Nilsson has suggested that in view of the importance of dancing in Minoan times, the said dancing place might have been prepared for the goddess Ariadne rather than for Minos's daughter, though the classical readers of the *Iliad* would certainly have interpreted the passage as referring to the princess Ariadne. Nilsson even suggested that the tales of the rapes of Ariadne, Helen, and Persephone all reflected the rape of a Minoan vegetation goddess.[2]

The name Ariadne is simply a Cretan epithet signifying 'very holy', and its modern equivalent would seem to be *Panagia*, 'The All Holy', the regular name in modern Greece for the Virgin Mary. This name, of course, is not confined to Crete, but it may not be devoid of significance that, whereas in many parts of Greece only women swear by the name of the Virgin, in Crete her name is regularly on the lips of the men also, as it might well be on an island where in Minoan times goddesses had been more important than gods,[3] and where the natives referred to their 'motherland' and not their 'fatherland'.

Some of the classical legends about Ariadne are concerned with her death. Sometimes it was said that she died in child-birth, as in the

1. *Iliad*, Book XVIII, I.
2. *The Mycenaean Origins of Greek Mythology*, 1932, p. 170.
3. Compare Charles Seltman's reference to 'the age-old potent wish to regard Nature as Feminine and Godhead as Female'. (*Women in Antiquity*, 1956, p. 166).

story current at Amathus in Cyprus, a legend perhaps alluded to in the eleventh book of the *Odyssey*, where it is stated that Artemis (who presided over births) slew her in Dia. Plutarch, on the other hand, tells how Ariadne hanged herself on a tree when she was deserted by Theseus on Naxos. This story, and another told by Pausanias to the effect that Helen had been hanged on a tree in Rhodes on the orders of Polemo, have been quoted to prove that both Ariadne and Helen were originally goddesses connected with the Minoan tree and pillar cults.

The Greeks themselves were puzzled over these inconsistent stories and some tried to distinguish between the goddess Ariadne wife of Dionysus, celebrated by a joyous festival, and Ariadne the daughter of Minos, for whom a mourning festival was celebrated. Nilsson, however, suggests that both festivals were probably in honour of the same deity, a goddess of the spring, since it is customary to celebrate the death of a vernal deity with mourning and the resurrection of the same deity the following spring with rejoicing.

Neustadt even goes so far as to compare the dance of Ariadne with modern customs associated with the first of May, and the story of Theseus diving into the depths of the sea to receive a wreath from Amphitrite with the custom of drenching the representative of the vegetation spirit in modern country festivals. This is rather a speculative suggestion, but probably there are ancient survivals in the celebrations of the first of May. For centuries before 'Labour Day' was invented the first of May was celebrated as Lady Day. Who was the original Lady to whom it was consecrated? Not, I think, the Virgin Mary and perhaps not even the 'very holy one' of Minoan Crete.

EUROPA

Another Cretan heroine who might perhaps once have been a goddess is Europa. The orthodox legend represented her as a Phoenician princess, the sister of Kadmos and of the elder Minos, and stated that she was carried off to Crete by Zeus, who appeared to her in the form of a bull. Coins of Phaistos and Gortyn of the fifth century B.C. show a woman usually identified with Europa sitting in what appears to be a willow tree, an identification supported by the occasional presence of a bull or bull's head. But why should she be sitting in a willow tree? Vürtheim has related the names of Europa and Velchanos to *rhops* and *helike*, two Greek words meaning willow, pointing out that the willow tree was sacred to Hera on Samos. This sort of speculation is rather hazardous, but there is perhaps a slightly better case for associating Europa with tree worship than Ariadne.

TREE AND PILLAR WORSHIP

A very distinctive feature of Minoan religion and of the Mycenaean cults derived from it was the worship and veneration paid to trees and pillars, stressed by Sir Arthur Evans in his monograph *The Mycenaean Tree and Pillar Cult*. Worship of trees and sacred boughs was widespread in Europe in ancient times, and the classical work in English on primitive religions by Sir James Frazer was termed *The Golden Bough*.

It was Evans, however, who pointed the moral of the connexion between trees and *baetyls* or sacred stones, which often continued to remain sacred even when their shrines had been taken over by the followers of an iconoclastic religion such as Mohammedanism. The most famous example of such a *baetyl* still revered in modern times is the black stone at Mecca, but another example is quoted by Evans from a Mohammedan shrine at Tekekioi near Skoplje, where the sacred pillar, venerated by Christians and Mohammedans alike, was regularly anointed with olive oil, just as Jacob used to anoint his stone at Bethel. The Tekekioi pillar, which is roughly square, reminds us of the square piers in Minoan pillar crypts, and the resemblance between them is strengthened by the sunken hearthstone behind it on which candles were lit every night, reminding us of the sunken stone trough that often accompanies or surrounds the piers of pillar crypts at Knosos. On the other side of the pillar at Tekekioi there was a stone base where the votary stood to pray, finishing his prayer by embracing the stone so that his fingers touched behind it. He then visited the Tekke, the grave of the saint, with water drawn from a neighbouring spring. Over the headstone of the grave grew a thorn bush hung with rags, dedicated by pilgrims to the shrine. In 1927 I saw a similar bush decorated with rags beside a stone with a natural hole through it near Lapsista in western Macedonia, a village then

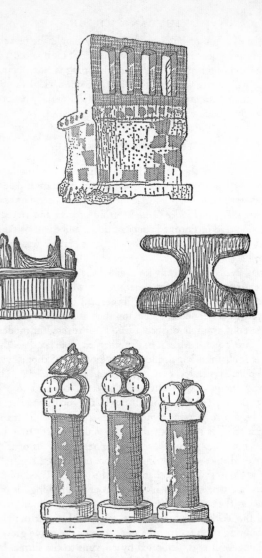

Fig. 41. Furniture of Dove Shrine

occupied by refugees from Anatolia, but before 1922 by the Greek-speaking Mohammedans known as Valláhadhes.

In both these modern instances we find the association of the *baetyl*, the sacred stone, with the sacred tree, stressed by Evans as typical of the Minoan–Mycenaean civilization. The classical cult of Athena Parthenos at Athens also shows the pillar associated with the sacred tree, the olive, and with the sacred bird, Athena's owl. The cult of Poseidon Erechtheus provides an instance of the sacred spring.[1]

We need not, indeed must not, assume that all pillars were necessarily sacred, and Nilsson points out that even the affixing of sacred symbols such as *bucrania*, or the tripod of Apollo, to a column or wall does not necessarily imply its sanctity. Clearly the pillars of pillar crypts served an obvious structural purpose in supporting the room above them, and we must not attach too much value to the fact that occasionally the double axe appears as a mason's mark on the stones of one or two of these pillars. Nevertheless I think Evans's term 'pillar crypts' is in the main justified, and their religious associations are supported by the remains of burnt offerings, pottery, lamps, and animal bones which Dr Platon and I found between the Middle Minoan I and the Middle Minoan III floors of the east Pillar Crypt of the Palace of Minos when we were carrying out repairs there in 1945.

A Mycenaean *crater* from Curium in Cyprus (No. C 391 in the British Museum) has a scene apparently showing two women adoring a pillar together with a chariot scene on one side, and on the other side what appear to be two pillar crypts, one above the other, with a couple of women adoring the pillar in each (Fig. 42).

SACRED SPRINGS

Sacred springs presided over by a goddess were characteristic of the Minoan religion and continued into classical times when the deities of the springs were worshipped as the Nereids, as Herodotus tells us; indeed traces of the cult have persisted into modern times since

1. Professor Mallowan's excavations at Chagar Bazar in Syria and at Arpachiyah produced various analogous features: goddess, figurines, birds, double-axe amulets, with the addition at Arpachiyah of *tholoi*, also in deposits of the Tell Khalaf period.

Neraïdes is still used in the sense of 'fairies'. There is a rock-cut spring-house just above the cemetery of Mavrospelaion dating from the Middle Minoan period, but it was rather bare when excavated; perhaps the best surviving example is the small shrine erected over the outflow of the spring at the caravanserai south of the Palace of Minos.

The gypsum Spring Chamber with its little niche for an image

Fig. 42. Women worshipping in pillar shrine

was constructed like the rest of the caravanserai in the transitional Middle Minoan III B–Late Minoan I A period but continued as a place of worship right to the end of the Late Minoan III period, long after the caravanserai had ceased to be used for its original purpose and was lying in ruins. The date when the Spring House ceased even to be visited as a shrine is indicated by the Protogeometric rubbish choking the basin.

DOMESTIC SHRINES IN PALACES AND HOUSES

The domestic shrines of the palaces and larger houses during the Middle Minoan period seem to comprise two main forms. The simpler type, intended to serve only the needs of the family, may be seen at Knosos in the House of the Priest and the House of the Chancel Screen, and consisted of a room with a kind of chancel screen, with pillars and a central passage between the ante-chapel and the sanctuary.

The other form of domestic shrine was obviously intended to satisfy the needs of public worship for other people outside the inhabitants of the palace, and consisted of two or three rooms to which probably only the priests were admitted screened from the public by a fine façade, and a triple porch of which the centre portion rose higher than the flanks, the roof of each porch being crowned by a pair of Horns of Consecration. Such was the shrine that faced the west side of the central court at Knosos, and its appearance may be gauged from the shrine represented in the miniature frescoes (Plate 11).

This form of palace shrine was adopted by the Mycenaean Greeks of the mainland and is illustrated by the small gold models of the Dove Shrines found in the third Shaft Grave at Mycenae. The earlier shrine of the Middle Minoan 11 palace at Phaistos seems also to have been of this type, so far as we can judge from the extant remains.

Another and simpler type of palace shrine, however, appears before the end of the fifteenth century in the palace at Hagia Triada. This consists of an oblong room entered through a small porch from one of the narrower ends and with a ledge for the images and cult objects at the innermost end of the long room. This was to become the regular form in the very latest Minoan period, and bears such a resemblance to the Mycenaean *megaron* and to the simplest form of Greek temple that one might suspect Mycenaean influence.

In Crete only the shrines of this type at Gournia and Hagia Triada can be dated as early as Late Minoan I and some scholars would prefer to assign even these to the Late Minoan III period. Other similar shrines either date very late in the Late Minoan III period (the Shrine of the Double Axes, the one at Prinias, and, I think, the one at Mallia also), or even in the Sub-Minoan period (Karphi).

On the mainland the Mycenaean building underneath the later Hall of the Mysteries at Eleusis was also of this type, though with some special features of its own.[1] There seems to be no obvious Minoan prototype for this kind of shrine, unless we are to take the rather different domestic shrine of the south-east house at Knosos as the prototype.

1. W. B. Dinsmore, *The Architecture of Ancient Greece*, 1950, p. 24, Fig. 10.

MINOAN SHRINES AND SANCTUARIES

The places where Minoan worship was carried out differed consider
ably from those of the Greeks in that there were properly speaking
no public temples, though they were not without places for public
worship. The holy places were peak sanctuaries, cave sanctuaries
spring houses, and domestic shrines. Certain funeral ceremonies were
also carried out near tombs in small adjacent chambers, which
seems to have been the practice in Early Minoan times with the
great tombs of the Mesara and perhaps even with the smaller tombs
of eastern Crete. The family tombs of Middle Minoan II–III and
Late Minoan times either possessed a *dromos* or entrance passage or
a small fore-court which could be used for the funeral rites. Spring
houses had a basin from which the worshippers drew the holy water
and a niche for images and lamps, if we may judge from the very
scanty evidence.

Cave sanctuaries seem to have had practically no structures at all
except a tenuous wall dividing the congregation from the priest
and the sanctuary; rough walls of this kind were found in the cave
sanctuaries of Eileithyia at Amnisos, and that of Zeus at Psychro.

PEAK SANCTUARIES

The Middle Minoan I period was marked by a new fashion in public
worship, in the form of the so-called 'peak sanctuaries', which remind
us of the 'high places' mentioned in the Book of Kings and inveighed
against by the prophets of Jehovah. The Cretan high places, however
seem to have been ultimately converted to Christianity, and it seems
likely that peaks now bearing chapels dedicated to the 'Lord Christ'
or to the 'Precious Cross' once bore shrines dedicated to the Cretan
Zeus. Iuktas certainly was sacred to the latter and was even regarded
as his burial place, though the church on its southern summit, originally monastic, is at present dedicated to the Virgin Mary.[1]

The Minoan sanctuary on the central peak, excavated by Evans,

1. An exception to the general practice according to which chapels erected
   mountains previously sacred to Zeus were on the mainland dedicated to
   Elias, but on Crete to the Lord Christ.

consisted of a broad hall (8 metres wide and 5 metres deep) approached through an outer room, and flanked by two narrow passages – a plan somewhat resembling that of the more or less contemporary temple of Tell Ai in Palestine.[1]

The sanctuary continued in use till the Late Minoan I period and some of the walls may date from that period, but the sanctuary probably preserved the same plan from Middle Minoan I times onward.

The inner room had a floor of white plaster, perhaps of later date, but the same feature also occurs in the Middle Minoan I shrine on the Prophet Elias peak above Mallia, where there was a sanctuary with a similar plan, but where the inner room had a plaster bench on three sides of the interior.

These peak sanctuaries were, of course, particularly subject to denudation by natural causes, and often the only signs of their former existence are the remains of votive offerings caught in crevices of the rocks, and sometimes evidence of sacrificial fires.

This group of sanctuaries has been reviewed recently in a good article in *Kretika Chronika* by Platon,[2] who lists the following examples: (*a*) Palaikastro, (*b*) and (*c*) Zakros, (*d*) Chamaizi and (*e*) Piskokephalo Seteias in eastern Crete and (*f*) the Prophet Elias of Mallia, (*g*) Endikti, (*h*) Karphi (both in Lasithi), (*i*) Iuktas near Knosos, (*j*) Koumasa and (*k*) Christou (both in the Mesara) in central Crete. No peak sanctuary has yet been reported from western Crete, but probably this is merely due to the fact that this area has even now been less thoroughly explored than the centre and the east of the island.

Some of the figurines from Piskokephalo described by Platon appear to be too developed in style for the Middle Minoan I period, and I should be inclined to date them Middle Minoan II or III.

One of the oddities of Piskokephalo is the series of very naturalistic representations of the rhinoceros beetle (*Oryctes nasicornis*), presumably regarded as a field pest which the worshippers hoped to render innocuous. Myres has quoted other examples of dedications of this sort. From the Iuktas sanctuary came clay models of weasels and from Palaikastro figurines of hedgehogs. The animals dedicated at

1. See M. V. Seton-Williams, *Iraq*, 1949, p. 81, Fig. 4.
2. 'To Ieron Maza', *Kretika Chronica*, 1951.

these sanctuaries, however, were not all pests, but more often domestic animals or even wild animals and birds. Platon enumerates sheep and goats, birds, pigs, dogs, hedgehogs, swallows, and ibex among the dedications. The figurines of oxen vary from twenty-five millimetres to perhaps half a metre in length, to judge from the size of a fragmentary head found at Piskokephalo.

Since Middle Minoan II pottery is practically confined to Knosos and Phaistos,[1] it is not surprising that we cannot quote examples from these sanctuaries except Iuktas, clearly datable between 1850 and 1700 B.C.; but it is likely that several of these sanctuaries continued to be frequented throughout much of the Middle Minoan period.

Marinatos was the first to stress the important clues towards determining the nature of the deities worshipped at the various sanctuaries afforded by the nature of the dedications. Thus the deity worshipped at Arkalochori was presumably a god or goddess of war, to judge by the quantity of swords and other weapons dedicated there.

The offerings at the Kamares Cave, on the other hand, were chiefly in the form of pottery. The cave which he excavated at Amnisos, however, is the only one where we can confidently name the goddess worshipped, namely Eileithyia, the patron goddess of childbirth. Here, as at Kamares, the offerings were mainly of pottery, and their paucity and poor quality suggests that Eileithyia may have been principally a goddess of the poor. We are reminded of Statius's fine description of the Altar of Pity in Athens.[2]

> Who asks is heard and night and day
> May go and seek the goddess' aid
> To ease her solitary complaints.
> Scant ritual, no sacrifice
> No incense flame ascends on high
> With tears alone her altar's wet.

Doubtless Eileithyia was also worshipped in villas and palaces but I think her cave at Amnisos was a shrine of the people.

The offerings from the peak sanctuaries, even from that of Iuktas, have given us a poor selection, but the sites were so exposed and the traces of sacrificial fires so evident that we cannot argue from the

1. The Kamares Cave is hardly an exception since it was a shrine obviously frequented by the inhabitants of Phaistos, from where it is clearly visible.
2. *Thebais* XII, 485–8.

absence of more valuable offerings which might have been burnt, looted by treasure hunters, or simply weathered away.

Sick persons also appear to have dedicated models of the limb or organ they wished to be healed. The concentration of these peak sanctuaries in eastern Crete might support the idea that the goddess worshipped was Britomartis. Platon, on the other hand, has suggested it was the great Earth Mother (interpreting Maza to mean Ma Ga, Mother Earth). There is, however, no conclusive evidence that the deities worshipped at the peak sanctuaries were inevitably goddesses, and it would not surprise me greatly if the deity worshipped had not sometimes been the 'Master of Animals' (especially if Mrs Chittenden's theory is correct that the Greek equivalent of this deity was Hermes and that his symbol was a pillar or a cairn of stones, for which the Greek word was *herma*).

MIDDLE MINOAN SHRINES OF THE HOUSEHOLD GODDESS

The palace shrines of the Household Goddess are less illuminating from one point of view, since, although they include objects of artistic value, these must represent only a small proportion, and that not necessarily a characteristic selection, of the objects originally dedicated in them. Thus both the Dove Shrine of the Middle Minoan II B period (Fig. 41) and the temple repositories of the Middle Minoan III B period were presumably concerned with the cult of the same goddess, but a comparison of the preserved dedications from them will show how little there is in common:

Dove Shrine	*Temple Repositories*
2 Pillar shrines	1 Figure of Snake Goddess
1 Altar with sacral horns	1 Figure of votaress
1 Hollow-sided altar	1 Cow suckling calf
1 Pair of sacral horns	1 Antelope suckling kid[1]
1 Beam-end capital	1 Fragment of votaress
1 Trilithon shrine with birds	2 Model robes
1 Carrying chair	Flying fish
	Painted shells
	1 Marble cross
	1 Stone table of offerings

1. Usually but wrongly described as a goat.

LATE MINOAN SHRINES OF THE
HOUSEHOLD GODDESS

A much more representative picture of the furniture of a shrine o the Household Goddess, but on a far poorer scale, is afforded by tha of the Civic Shrine at Gournia, of which the furniture seems chiefly if not entirely, to date from the Late Minoan III period. This include a clay figure of the Household Goddess, the head of a similar figure an arm with a snake twisted round it and tightening the grasp of hand holding a straight chisel-like object (certainly not a sword bu conceivably a torch), another hand with a snake coiling round it and the head of a snake formerly attached to something. There wer also three snake tubes with multiple heads and sacral horns in relie the fragment of a fourth, and a tripod altar of clay with the base o what was presumably a fifth tube attached to it. Other clay object from the shrine included two birds of different sizes and a sherd from a *pithos* with a double axe in relief (Fig. 43).

Two shrines were reconstructed from the ruins of the palaces a Knosos in the very latest Minoan period.[1] Of these the 'Fetish Shrine constructed in the ruined lustral area of the Little Palace had littl except a pair of Horns of Consecration, and the four strange stalag mitic formations, one vaguely resembling a woman and another child, which induced Evans to name it the 'Fetish Shrine'. The 'Shrine of the Double Axes' had no natural fetish stones but was bette equipped otherwise. It was constructed in one of the small rooms o Middle Minoan III date near the south-east corner of the great cour of the Palace of Minos. The room, though only 1½ metres square was divided into three parts by its different floor levels. A shallov ante-room opened into the main chamber which had a floor o stamped clay containing a number of vases, including a tall plain jar a tripod vase, a bowl with three upright handles, three other bowls and a stirrup vase decorated with a sprawling octopus in that specia variety of Late Minoan III C painting which Pendlebury termed 'the Middle-East Style'. The north end of the room was occupied by a narrow shelf containing the main objects of the cult, one bell-

1. The diagonal building at Mallia (Fig. 35) seems to be a third example but, if so, it had lost all its cult furniture.

shaped idol that must represent the Household Goddess, two other bell-shaped figurines, one with a bird on its head, a male votary holding a bird as an offering, a female votary with incised features, the features being filled with powdered gypsum in the Neolithic

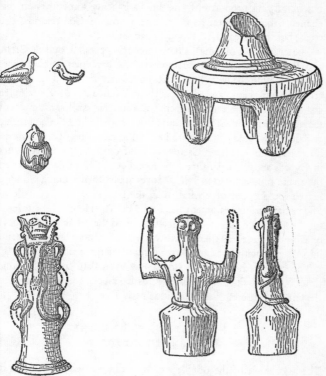

Fig. 43. Furniture of Gournia shrine

fashion, two pairs of Consecration Horns in stucco with clay cores, each with a socket in the centre presumably to hold the shaft of a double axe. A small double axe in steatite, from which the shrine derives its name, was found leaning up against one of the pairs of Horns, but was too small to have been erected over it. Sometimes indeed the space between the horns is occupied by a bough and occasionally the shaft of the double axe between the horns sprouts leaves.

It will be remarked that certain features recur in these household shrines: statuettes of the goddess, double axes, snakes, and birds, but in varying proportions, the emphasis being sometimes on one element, sometimes on another. The Horns of Consecration also recur, but these are universal on Minoan shrines.

The snake tubes of Gournia have interesting parallels outside Crete, and Evans collated a convincing series of examples of clay tubes connected with the household snake cult, some with modelled snakes crawling up them, and derived them from a type of drainpipe characteristic of the earlier palace at Knosos. The earliest examples of these snake tubes in Crete are those from the Middle Minoan I shrine at Koumasa. Some of the more interesting examples of snake tubes, however, come not from Crete at all but from Late Bronze Age sites in Cyprus and Philistia. One tube found at Kition in Cyprus shows the snake tube converted into a dove-cot, with the Dove Goddess herself looking out of a window in the fashion so characteristic of Phoenician shrines. Another tube, found in 'The House of Ashtoreth' on the Philistine site of Beth-Shan dated to the reign of Rameses II of Egypt (c. 1292–1225 B.C.),[1] shows two snakes crawling round and into the tube with two little doves perched on the handles.

The cult of the Snake Goddess may even date from Neolithic times in Crete, since figurines of birds have been found along with the female figurines of the Neolithic period.

THE DOUBLE AXE AND THE HOUSEHOLD GODDESS

The association of the double axe with the Household Goddess is puzzling but well attested. M. Mayer, as long ago as 1892, pointed out that the double axe was the traditional weapon of Zeus of Labraunda, a name obviously connected with Labyrinthos and with *labrys*, the Lydian word for a double axe, and we now know that Zeus of Labraunda was simply a Hellenized version of the old Hittite weather-god, Teshub. A. B. Cook and others have therefore argued that the double axe must be the symbol of the Thunder God, the Minoan

1. Possibly six years later for both dates.

Zeus (as the hammer was of Thor in the Scandinavian mythology). The suggestion seems very plausible at first sight, but the Minoan and Mycenaean evidence does not support it. The double axe is regularly the symbol of a goddess and in particular of the Household Goddess.[1]

It has been suggested that the double axe was simply the sacrificial weapon with which bulls were slaughtered for the sacrifices, and this is supported by the frequent appearance of double axes between the horns of bulls' heads represented on vases and gems. This seems better than the previous interpretation, but I am still puzzled why the sacrificial weapon should have been considered so appropriate for the Household Goddess. That the double axe was a sacred symbol is clear enough, and many of the existing examples such as the colossal bronze ones of Nirou Khani, the miniature gold ones of Arkalochori, and the small steatite one of the Shrine of the Double Axes would have been quite useless as tools or weapons (Fig. 46, 6).

We do, however, find a number of good, strong, work-a-day double axes in Middle and Late Minoan deposits on various sites, and very often associated with tools such as saws, double adzes, and chisels. I suspect, therefore, that the common double axe, when it was not a religious symbol, was the tool of a woodman or carpenter rather than a weapon, and possibly this might be a reason why it was considered appropriate for the Household Goddess. Professor Mallowan has suggested to me that the original idea of the root *peleku* was 'splitting', and this is supported by the modern Greek words *peléki* (cut stone) and *pelekízo* (to cut stone – used of a stone mason).

The Homeric *pelekus*, which was certainly a weapon and usually regarded as a double axe, derived its name from the Accadian word *pilaqqu*, which must surely have meant originally some other form of battle-axe, since double axes, though they occurred very early in Mesopotamia, were comparatively rare in that country.

ALTARS AND HORNS OF CONSECRATION

Various explanations, mostly very unconvincing, have been offered for the Horns of Consecration on Minoan altars and roofs of shrines.

[1]. Goddess figurines, birds, *tholoi*, *bucrania*, and double axes are also characteristic of the deposits of the Tell Khalaf period at Arpachiyah in Assyria. M. E. L. Mallowan, *The Excavations at Arpachiyah*, 1933, Figs. 45, 46, and 51.

They have been compared to symbols of mountains, regarded as fire-dogs, or connected with the lunate objects of Early Iron Age date from Central Europe and Italy. More often and more plausibly they are assumed to be derived from the horns of the sacred bull. Examples of the Jamdat Nasr period (3000 B.C.) have been found at Tell Brak in Syria, at Nuzu in Mesopotamia, and at Tepe Hisar in Persia, and examples of later date at Alisar and Kusura in Asia Minor.[1]

An abnormal, but I think probable, example of the Horns of Consecration was found at Mochlos in an Early Minoan I deposit. Normal examples of these horns occur on the miniature altar of the so-called Dove Shrine deposit of Middle Minoan II B date. From the Middle Minoan III period onwards such Horns of Consecration are normal on Minoan shrines and altars, or as bases for the shaft of a double axe, and they are equally common on Mycenaean shrines on the mainland – to judge by their representations in frescoes, vases, and gems. Gaerte also proposed to associate with them the small bell-shaped objects of clay of Middle Minoan I date which sometimes have two horns on top and have been classed as votive bells (Evans), votive robes (Hazzidakis), images of the goddess (Chapouthier), or ritual masks (Platon).[2]

A hieroglyphic sign resembling these curious objects occurs on some of the clay tablets from Mallia.

Minoan altars were nearly always very small, resembling incense altars or fire-altars rather than the temple altars of Greece or Rome, and no surviving Minoan altar could have been used for the sacrifice of any animal larger than a small kid. Nevertheless, representations of a trussed ox show that these animals were sacrificed, and one gem depicts an ox on a large table or altar with four low legs. Besides the altars we also have a large number of what are termed libation tables, or tables of offering, sometimes with a flat, sometimes with a low or high pedestal, but always with one or more round hollows in the upper surface. Occasionally, as on the triple-hollow table from the Dictaean Cave and on one or two from Palaikastro, they may bear short inscriptions in Linear Script A. The Middle Minoan sanctuary in the palace at Phaistos contained a rectangular clay tray em-

1. M. E. L. Mallowan, *Iraq*, 1947, Part 2, p. 184, with bibliography.

2. See p. 223 and compare N. Platon, 'Nouvelle Interprétation des idoles cloches du Minoen Moyen I' in *Mélanges Charles Picard*, 1949.

bedded in the floor with the usual central depression and with a flat rim adorned with incised spirals and figures of sheep (the latter confined to one long side and part of one short side of the tray, except for a solitary sheep at each corner). Eighteen sheep are represented, but I have no idea whether this number has any significance.

Mallia has one or two stones with a depression in the centre and a whole series of smaller depressions round the circumference of the stones. These are usually regarded as a special variety of tables of offering, though Evans suggested they were intended for some sort of game.

Tables of offering seem to appear when the *kernoi*, the multiple vases attached to a central support characteristic of Early Minoan and Early Cycladic tombs, disappear, so that it is not unlikely that they fulfilled a somewhat similar function, comparable, as Xanthoudides suggested, to that of the *kernoi* employed in the liturgy of the Orthodox Church and concerned with the offerings of first-fruits.

Triangular or leaf-shaped ladles of limestone occasionally bearing letters of Linear Script A incised on them would also seem to have been utensils in Minoan shrines. The best known example, and the one with the longest inscription, was that found at Troullos near Arkhanais.

Still more certainly associated with Minoan cults were the small tripod hearths, little round tables with broad lips and three short legs made of pottery or of plaster. Examples occurred in the Shrine of the Double Axes at Knosos, in the Gournia Shrine, and piles of five were found in the Little Palace at Nirou Khani. Examples have also been found on the mainland at Mycenae and Tiryns, and at Delos in the Cyclades. Most of the examples are Late Minoan, even Late Minoan III in date, but a possible prototype of Middle Minoan I date was found outside the round tomb at Porti in the Mesara, in the form of a round table with a slightly raised border but with no tripod legs. There is no very conclusive evidence that they were used as braziers, though a different form of brazier found in Late Minoan III tomb at Zapher Papoura (No. 32, P.T.K., Fig. 46) still held some charcoal, and the fixed hearth in the *megaron* at Mycenae was adorned with painted decoration reminiscent of that of the tripod altars of Middle Minoan III B date from the House of the Sacrificed Oxen at Knosos.

THE CULT OF THE DEAD

All peoples have some rites associated with the burial or disposal of the dead, but their views on the possibility and nature of any after-life vary extremely.

Nilsson has emphasized that the general conception of Hades in the poems of Homer as a gloomy place where the ghosts were but pale, twittering shadows[1] was contradicted by the picture of Elysium, where the more heroic spirits enjoyed a more enjoyable existence, and he suggests that the presence there of Minos's brother Rhadamanthos indicates the Cretan origin of this mythical paradise.[2]

Burial rites seem to have been very simple during the Cretan Neolithic period. The dead were not cremated but laid out in caves or rock shelters, and the funeral offerings now surviving consist only of pottery, though we must not exclude the probability that other more perishable materials such as food, clothes, and wooden implements were also offered. Similar burials in caves continued during the first Early Minoan period.

Built graves, cist graves, small rooms, and even structures like a house with two or three rooms appeared in the Early Minoan I period. Towards the end of the Early Minoan III period the grave goods became richer and included gold jewellery, beautifully cut stone vases, and engraved seal-stones; the use of *larnakes* or clay coffins appeared in the Early Minoan II period and later became common.

In eastern Crete the dead seem to have been buried separately and their bones later transferred to small family ossuaries resembling houses, with anything from one to six rooms, but resembling Neolithic rather than contemporary houses. 'The houses of the dead, in fact,' says Pendlebury, 'were the traditional houses of the living of a bygone era' (Fig. 25).

In the Mesara, however, the Early Minoan period is marked by the appearance of the so-called *tholos* tombs – large communal burial places, which Glotz regarded as tribal tombs and which certainly must have been designed to serve some larger community than a family, possibly a *génos* (clan), but hardly so large a unit as a tribe. Xanthoudides's report on the method of burial does indeed state that

1. As in the Eleventh Book of the *Odyssey*.
2. *Odyssey* IV, 560–9.

'some of them contained the bodies of many hundreds or even thousands of bodies',[1] but the individual reports of tombs hardly suggest the presence of so many burials. Xanthoudides records that although great fires had been lit in some of these tombs, he found no reliable evidence for cremation. 'In places the floor was burnt almost to terracotta, and stones were split by the heat. In the Porti *tholos* almost the whole of the thick burial stratum was blackened by the fire and smoke, and many of the skulls and bones were made quite black. Yet other scholars' examination of these remains has confirmed my view that there is no case of burning the body at burial. The fire came later, and the bones turned black from exposure to the heat and smoke at close quarters.'

What was the purpose of lighting these fires inside the *tholoi*? Frankly we do not know. It might have been to obtain light, or to fumigate the tomb from the flavour of death, or for a funeral sacrifice or feast. Yet no one of these suggested reasons would have necessitated so large a fire. Small huts of stone were often erected beside or against these round tombs, and these held vases of stone or clay of a later date than the tomb itself. A walled trench outside Tholos A at Platanos contained hundreds of small stone pots. Here we have clear evidence of a cult of the dead, implying, I think, a belief in an after-life, even though Xanthoudides may well be right in suggesting that they were vessels kept for the descendants to pour libations rather than for the actual use of the departed. Alexiou has given us a clear and interesting account of what he believes to have been the grave rites in the Early Minoan cemetery that he excavated near Kanli Kastelli, where the whole contents of the burials had been preserved by a later fall of rock. The confusion of skeletal material observed also at Pyrgos, Sphoungaras, and Kato Zakros might have been due to later disturbances, but this could not be true at Kanli Kastelli nor in the later ossuary of Middle Minoan I date which I excavated on Monasteriako Kephali, where a similar fall of rock had prevented later interference; these last two instances might indeed be explained by the transference of bones from primary burials else-where to their final resting place in the ossuary, but Alexiou remarks that the Zakros burials appeared to be primary interments. He

1. *The Vaulted Tombs of the Mesara*, p. 134; his use of 'cist' as a translation for *larnax* is rather misleading.

therefore considers that the clear traces of fire and the presence of animal bones, sometimes burnt but at Krasi unburnt, should be explained by supposing that funeral sacrifices were performed inside the tomb and that these caused much of the confusion of the skeletal material; and he would regard the traces of fire and animal bones recorded by Taramelli at Miamou as evidence of similar rites rather than as traces of a previous occupation of the cave shelter as a dwelling place.

The use of the round communal tombs continued in the Mesara till the end of the Middle Minoan I period or later, but the normal method of burying in the Middle Minoan period seems to have been to crush the bones into large *pithoi*, usually specially made and painted for this purpose, though sometimes ordinary domestic store-jars were utilized for the purpose.

The *pithos* was then inverted and either simply buried in the ash, as at Pachyammos and at Sphoungaras in eastern Crete; in a small walled enclosure, as in one instance at Porti; or in chamber tombs cut in the soft rock, as was the practice at Knosos in the Middle Minoan II and III periods. The evidence for Middle Minoan I burials at Knosos is rather scanty, but some burials at least were made in *larnakes* and the bones later transferred to cave shelters used as ossuaries. An unpublished but quite certain example of a cremation in a *pithos* of Middle Minoan III date was discovered by Sinclair Hood in his excavations at Knosos in 1955.

Burials in *larnakes* continued during the Middle Minoan period but the *pithos* burials which in some parts, particularly in eastern Crete, continued throughout the Late Minoan I period were common during the Middle Minoan period from 1800 to 1550 B.C.

In the Late Minoan period chamber tombs used as family graves were the normal practice throughout Crete, but they varied greatly in type from the Mycenaean kind with a long narrow *dromos* (an entrance passage cut horizontally into the slope of a hill) opening out into a round, oval, or square chamber cut out of the *kouskouras* (the local white marl) with a vaulted roof, to large, built chamber tombs cut in more level ground, with steeply sloping *dromoi* leading through a passage or outer chamber into a rectangular chamber, all except the outer *dromos* being lined with fine ashlar masonry. To the latter group may be assigned the Temple Tomb at Knosos and the Royal Tomb at Isopata.

Wooden coffins or biers were presumably sometimes employed, though the first certain remains of a coffin in this material were found in 1952 in a Late Minoan II chamber tomb at Katsaba excavated by Alexiou. Similar tombs continued to be dug throughout the Minoan period, but the Late Minoan III period was characterized by the extensive use of clay coffins or *larnakes* painted in the style of the period, sometimes in the form of rectangular chests on four short legs with a pitched roof, perhaps reproducing, I suggest, the dowry chest which up to modern times has been one of the most important articles of furniture in a Cretan home.

The burial rite was until a late period almost invariably inhumation. Apart from the Middle Minoan example quoted on the preceding page, the only clear evidence for Minoan cremation seems to be the graves excavated by H. van Effenterre in the cementery of Olous.[1]

THE MYCENAEAN RELIGION IN CRETE

Ventris's readings of the Linear Script B texts have provided us with a list of Mycenaean deities who were, if we accept his readings, worshipped in Crete in the Late Minoan II period, including Zeus, Hera, Demeter, Athena (with the title *potnia* = lady), Poseidon, and Dionysus. Enyalios appears (not Ares), as indeed one might expect, since scholars have always argued that the worship of the latter was imported from Thrace. It is strange to find Dionysus, who was also supposed to have been a later importation from Thrace, but his absence from Olympus only implies that his cult was not popular in Ionia before 700 B.C., not that it had not reached Crete or the mainland. Apollo appears only under his cult title Paian, I believe (but negative statements on the evidence from these texts are more dangerous even than positive ones!). Ventris also records priestesses of 'The Winds'.[2] We should not be surprised to find the winds as gods when we reflect that the cult of the Kassite god Buriash probably must have been established before 1200 B.C. in Attica, where, as Boreas, he became so acclimatized as to be reported in Athenian folklore as carrying off the maiden Oreithyia,[3] the daughter of Erechtheus and mother of Kalais and Zetes who sailed with Jason on the Argo.

1. *Études crétoises*, 1948, Chap. 2, 'La Nécropole d'Olonte'.
2. M. Ventris and J. Chadwick, *Documents in Mycenaean Greek*, p. 387.
3. The maiden's name has a good Mycenaean ring to it.

CHAPTER 9

The Social and Economic Life, Industries, and Agriculture

'ON the organization of the social group, the remains from pre-historic times leave the field free for the imagination and do not furnish us with any information. It is not impossible, however, to imagine the vague outlines of what might have been the evolution of the Aegean societies.' So said M. Glotz in 1921, and, though we know more than we did then, speculation and imagination still play an uncomfortably large role in any attempt to reconstruct Minoan society.

Already in the Neolithic period, however, we can perceive the development of village communities of peasant farmers, while at Knosos the community must have been several hundred strong at least, almost developing at the end of the Neolithic period into a small market town. We may imagine that the average lowlander tilled the soil, his own or another's, and that the highlanders would be mostly hunters or shepherds driving their flocks from the low-land to the highland pastures and down again according to the season.

It is much less difficult to reconstruct the economic life of the times than the social and political. Was there a king, an oligarchy, or a primitive democracy? Was there a tribal organization? Was the society patriarchal or matriarchal? Was Crete split into small city states or were there larger units?

It has been suggested that the large round tombs of the Mesara, which, according to their excavator Xanthoudides, had contained hundreds of successive burials, were tribal tombs and implied a vigorous tribal life extending from early in the Early Minoan period to the end of Middle Minoan I or II, and that the tendency to abandon these and construct smaller tombs coincided with a political change when the tribal units weakened and were merged in the dynasties of the priest-kings who built the palaces of Knosos, Phaistos, and Mallia.[1]

On the mainland, if we can trust the account given by Homer some centuries later than the events recorded in the *Iliad*, the tribal system was more broken down in Greece at the time of the Trojan war than it was in Scotland in A.D. 1745. The account in the *Iliad* was coloured by the conditions of Homer's own time, but in general his account of the 'Heroic Age' rings true. The late Professor Chadwick was the first to define clearly the social characteristics of an age of migrations and unrest, but the old Greek poet Hesiod had dimly apprehended these peculiarities when he inserted his 'Heroic Age' between his Ages of Bronze and Iron.

Heroic periods parallel to that of Greece had existed, as Chadwick pointed out, in various parts of the world and at various times, but were always marked by certain common features, including the establishment of new dynasties, often claiming descent from a god because the founder was not related to the previous royal family and often, like Sargon of Akkad, with no claim to power save through their own military prowess (though the latter's name actually means 'the true King'). Such heroic ages were those of the Aryan migration into India in the second millennium B.C., the Viking settlement of Iceland in the ninth century A.D., recorded by Ari Frodi, and the Maori settlement of New Zealand.

Race movements of this type are marked not only by epic poetry celebrating the heroes after the nation has settled in its new home, but also by a great break in the traditions of the families that played major parts in the migration. Very often these families, who could not trace their genealogies beyond the great event, claimed to have been descended from gods. Herodotus has recorded with admirable humour how the Egyptian priests in Thebes had shown him round their temples and had told him of a previous visit paid by the historian Hecataeus of Miletus. They told him how Hecataeus had boasted of his family, which 'went back to a god' in the sixteenth generation before, and of how they had shown him the statues of their priests, three hundred and forty-five successive generations of noblemen, the fathers

1. Halbherr estimated 200 burials for the larger *tholos* at Hagia Triada. The social unit served by such a tomb would presumably correspond not to a tribe but to something like a clan (the Greek *génos*).

succeeded by their sons, yet none of them had been gods or even demi-gods, nor had any god ruled in Egypt since Horus, the son of Osiris. And Herodotus states that the priests repeated this story to him 'though I told them no family history of mine'.[1]

Herodotus, of course, was poking fun at the insularity and snobbishness of Hecataeus, but an important historical conclusion may be drawn from the story. Sixteen generations before Hecataeus there was probably a major crisis in Greek history, a period of upheaval and migration, whereas Egypt had not suffered such a 'Heroic Age' since the days of the Hyksos kings.

Chadwick's principle that breaks in the genealogies, when the family 'went back to a god', as Herodotus says, implied a break in the folk memory and therefore a period of unrest was ingeniously applied by Myres to the traditional pedigrees of the heroic families of Greece. He found three major breaks in folk-tradition when families went back to a divine ancestor, and these were 1400, 1260, and 1100 B.C. The earliest of these, 1400, corresponds with the catastrophe that overwhelmed Minoan Crete, the latest corresponds to the Dorian invasion of the Peloponnese and the final extinction of the Mycenaean power. The 1260 crisis is less obvious at first sight. It was a couple of generations before the Trojan war, but, since dates from genealogies must not be taken too literally, it may be a reflection of the Phrygian infiltration of Asia Minor, the consequent collapse of the great Hittite Empire, and the establishment of the dynasty of Pelops in Greece.[2] Myres's 1400 agrees with 1410, the date given for the elder Minos on the Parian Marble Chronicle. Myres's three crises, however, are based on the pedigrees of Greek families and therefore do not help us much for the history of Minoan Crete before 1450, the approximate date of the first Mycenaean settlers in Crete.

The great migration of the Indo-European speaking group of peoples which had such an effect on India, Mesopotamia, Asia Minor, and eastern Europe seems scarcely to have affected Crete at all, which was then about to enjoy its most peaceful and prosperous years.

1. Herodotus, Book II, Chap. 143.
2. The final collapse of the Hittite Empire, of course, did not happen till after 1200 B.C., but Hittite weakness and Phrygian pressure must have begun two or three generations earlier – one Mita caused trouble to Arnuwandas IV.

PATRILINEAR AND MATRILINEAR SUCCESSION

Archaeology can tell us much about the economic conditions of Minoan times and something about the religion, but it is more difficult to imagine the social and political structure. How much of this survived the Achaean and Dorian settlements? What customs are so peculiarly Cretan that we can assume them to have survived in a changed form from Minoan times?

We have already discussed the religious survivals, which are certain and many, but did anything survive of the social and political structure? It is sometimes assumed that Minoan society was, if not matriarchal, at least matrilinear, but the evidence for this is slight and has been overstressed, especially by those scholars who connected Minoan culture with the Carians of Asia Minor, where matrilinear succession persisted into the fourth century B.C.[1]

The neighbouring country of Lycia affords the only certain example in the Aegean of a country where children were regularly named after their mothers, not their fathers. Herodotus regards this as unique though he describes their customs as partly Cretan, partly Carian, so that it is evident that if matrilinear succession ever existed in Crete it had died out before the time of Herodotus.[2]

Matrilinear succession would therefore seem to have been the rule at an early date for certain coastal districts of Asia Minor that received Cretan settlers during the Late Bronze Age, but this does not necessarily prove that such succession was normal in Minoan Crete. It should be noted, however, that by the laws of Gortyn the son of a free mother and a slave father was a free citizen, and Aristotle tells us that the older peoples in Crete continued to obey the laws of Minos.[3] The Achaean heroes of the *Iliad* and the *Odyssey* all traced their descent through their fathers, with the possible exceptions of the two Epeian heroes, Eurytus and Cteatus, who are dubbed 'Moliones' by Nestor after their mother Molione.

Nevertheless even if matrilinear succession had prevailed in Minoan

1. See W. Ridgeway, *The Early Age of Greece*, 1901–31, Vol. II, p. 76.

2. Herodotus VI, Chapter 37.

3. R. E. Willetts, *Aristocratic Society in Ancient Crete*, 1954, p. 34, and Aristotle, *Politics*, 1271 B.

Crete[1] the king must still have exercised great power not only as leader of the armed forces but also as viceroy of the gods, and in particular of the Cretan Zeus from whom he claimed descent, and was thus the chief executive officer in every department of the state, civil, military, and religious. Many centuries after the abolition of kings as civil magistrates or generals in the field, cities such as Athens and Rome continued to appoint kings as priests to perform those rites which only kings could perform, and Professor Thomson[2] has suggested that these would include the regulation of the calendar, and has reminded us that, of the early philosophers, Thales claimed to have been descended from the Theban royal clan of the Kadmeioi, and Herakleitos from Kodros, the last true king of Athens through the royal family of Ephesus.

THE EIGHT-YEAR CYCLE

Weniger has argued that the Olympian calendar was originally based on an eight-year cycle with two periods, as were perhaps also the Delphic festivals termed the Septerium, Herois, and Charita, and perhaps even the Pythian Games with their biennial cycle.[3]

Athenian folklore about Minos introduces the same period of eight years, and although these stories are post-Minoan and the prince they refer to was almost certainly an Achaean prince, yet they were old enough to be familiar to the author of the *Iliad*. According to the orthodox legend as told by Philochorus, the Athenians had to send seven youths and seven maidens as prey for the Minotaur every eight years (or every nine years as the Greeks would say), in payment for the death of Minos's son Androgeos. Every eight years Minos went up into the mountain to converse with his father Zeus (and this tradition was known also to Homer). This custom of Minos has been compared to the practice known in many parts of the world of putting the king to death after he had reigned a certain number of years. There is no clear evidence in Greece of kings being put to death at the

1. A very doubtful assumption.

2. G. Thomson, 'The Greek Calendar', *Journal of Hellenic Studies*, 1943, pp. 52–65.

3. L. Weniger, 'Das Hochfest des Zeus in Olympia', *Klio*, 1912; it should be remembered that the ancient Greeks counted inclusively, and therefore their nine-year cycle is what we should call an eight-year one.

end of a certain period, but there is evidence that their spiritual powers needed in some places to be renewed at the end of eight years by a fresh consecration of communion with the deity. At Sparta every eighth year the Ephors had to watch the sky on a clear moonless night for appropriate signs, and if they saw a meteor they decided that the king had sinned against the gods, and he was forthwith suspended from his duties until he had been reinstated by the oracle at Delphi or by the one at Olympia. This eight-year period represents a correlation of the lunar and solar years, being the shortest period when the longest day of the year can be made to coincide with a full moon.

Solon introduced this cycle to Athens when he intercalated three months to reconcile the current lunar year with the solar one, but the system was much older in Crete, and not long before Solon's reform the Athenians had summoned the Cretan seer Epimenides to purify the city after the murder in 621 of Cylon's conspirators.

VILLAGE ECONOMY

It is easier to reconstruct the life of a village than that of the court. The economy of a Neolithic village in Crete may to some extent be reconstructed from that of some of the poorer villages of today, after making allowances for differences in tools.

Most families would probably have had a piece of land from which they produced a little wheat or barley, some olives, almonds, or grapes perhaps. For vegetables they would probably have gathered what the modern Greek calls 'grasses', but it must be remembered that these included the wild varieties of lettuce, celery, asparagus, and carrots, which all grow wild in Crete and which have pre-Hellenic names, as have also the olive and the vine.

The village industries would include those of the potter, the carpenter, and the mason, though at a pinch most countrymen would have been able to construct a house for themselves. The place of the smith would have been taken by the man who chipped and ground stone tools.

Spinning and weaving, of course, would have been done in the house by the women of the family, a fashion that has not even yet entirely died out. There was no silk or cotton, but there was plenty of wool and probably flax, and the shape of certain clay sarcophagi of late Minoan date, obviously imitating wooden chests, suggest that the maiden of that day (and perhaps the Neolithic maiden also) treasured a family dowry chest in which she had stored the garments laid by for her wedding.

FOOD SUPPLIES

How far can we assert that the average Neolithic Cretan was a farmer, or was still a pastoralist or even a hunter? No direct evidence, I think, has yet been found of the production of grain in Neolithic times in Crete, though from the mainland we have evidence of wheat, barley, and millet being grown in the Neolithic period. It is very probable, however, that the Neolithic Cretans were growing some form of grain, since true millstones have been discovered in Late Neolithic contexts at Miamou in the Mesara and at Magasa in the east (the latter example being an upper millstone fitting into a hollow of the saddle quern below). Of course all prehistoric mills were of the saddle-quern, never of the rotary, type.

It is likely enough, however, that in the Early Neolithic period there may have been more shepherds and hunters than farmers.

Hunting and trapping must have played a larger role than in modern times, but perhaps less than one might expect. There is an odd suggestion that to the Minoan Cretans hunting was a sport rather than a trade. Seal-stones do indeed show men shooting at ibexes, boars, and bears, but the scenes showing men attacking lions, if not purely fictitious, must refer to lions kept specially for royal sports, as they certainly were at a later date in Assyria. Herdsmen and shepherds must have lived a life not very different from those of today, and we must imagine the shepherds driving their sheep up into the little enclosed mountain plains in the summer and down to the lowland pastures near the villages of the foothills in the winter.

A good account of the domestic animals is provided by K. F. Vickery in his excellent monograph *Food in Early Greece*. Even in Neolithic times the Cretan was hunting hares, rabbits, and stags (varieties not stated), as shown by evidence from Late Neolithic deposits at Miamou. Roe deer (? the *Anoglochis cretensis*) is reported from a Late Neolithic level at Phaistos.

From Early Minoan I deposits we hear of domestic sheep, goats, and swine, and for the first time of dogs (variety not stated)[1]; hares (*Lepus cretensis*) and hedgehogs (*Erinaceus nesiotes*) are also reported from this period.

At Tylisos the Middle Minoan levels produced a long-horned ox resembling *Bos primigenius*, *Bos brachyceros*, and a large variant of *Bos domesticus*; agrimi or Cretan ibex (*Capra aegagrus creticus*), domestic goats (*Capra hircus*), wild boars (*Sus scrofa ferus*), and domestic swine (*Sus domesticus indicus*).

Hunting and fishing must have contributed greatly to the family larder, and some of this work was probably carried out by professionals who devoted their whole life to hunting the abundant ibex,[2] wild boar, three kinds of deer, and perhaps wild oxen, as well as shooting the pigeon, partridge, pheasant, quail, and other birds, or trapping the skin animals such as martens, badgers, and wild cats, or fishing the offshore waters of the island; these, in the days before they had been spoiled by dynamiting, must have yielded in much greater supply than today all the modern varieties of fish, including tunny, red or grey mullet, sea bass, sea bream, lobster, braize, crab, sole, mackerel, parrot wrasse, sargue, sea perch, sprats, octopus, and cuttle fish. Of freshwater fish there would not be much except crabs and eels.

Shellfish were also eaten by Neolithic Cretans, and shells of mussels, sea-crab, lobster, limpet, oyster, and whelk were found in Neolithic deposits, as well as *Murex trunculus*, the last presumably exploited not as much as food but for its purple dye; both kinds of murex are indeed edible but *Murex brandaris* is said to be the better food, and I have found shells of both on a Middle Minoan III dump at Knosos.

The Late Minoan I levels at Tylisos added red deer (*Cervus elephas*), Swiss lake-dwelling sheep (*Ovis aries palustris*), horse (*Cavallus*), and the Cretan hunting hound (*Canis creticus*). Late Minoan III strata on the same site produced also remains of a domestic goat (*Capra hircus*) and a domestic ass (*Equus asinus*). Keller recorded thirty-two jaws of sheep or goat from Tylisos and seventeen of domestic swine.

---

1. But the dog's lower jaw from the Krasi tomb implies an animal of medium size.

2. At Tylisos *agrimi* bones abounded in all the levels.

The last-named were relatively more numerous, but cattle less numerous, than at the present day.[1]

The domestic fowl was not introduced into Crete in the Bronze Age, despite Glotz's suggestion to the contrary, but the Bronze Age Cretans may have possessed the *Chenalopex*, the small domestic goose of Egypt illustrated occasionally on Minoan seals.

We have evidence from Neolithic deposits of the existence at Knosos of short-horned cattle, swine, and goats, at Phaistos of short-horned cattle and of horned sheep of the Cypriote type, at Miamou of cattle, sheep, goats, hares, and rabbits, and at Magasa of sheep or goats.

A dog's head in pottery of Neolithic date at Knosos resembled that of a Saluki hound (like the dog buried about 3000 B.C. at Sakkara in the tomb of Queen Her-neit, and the dogs depicted on the Mycenaean fresco of a boar hunt at Tiryns in the Peloponnese).

Domestic animals were reared by Cretan farmers in the Neolithic period. Sheep and domestic goats are recorded from Late Neolithic sites, from Knosos and its harbour town, from Phaistos and Miamou in the Mesara, and from Magasa.

The sheep include not only *Ovis palustris* (the Swiss lake-dwelling variety) but also *Ovis orientalis* (the horned type still found in Cyprus). Pigs, apparently *Sus indicus*, are recorded from Phaistos, and from Knosos and its harbour town, and so are cattle, both the Cretan short-horns (*Bos creticus*) and a long-horned variety which is more of a puzzle. Cretan art of the Middle and Late Bronze Age is addicted to portraying toreador sports with a long-horned bull resembling the *Bos primigenius* of central and northern Europe. Hazzidakis found horns of bulls of this type both in Middle and in Late Minoan deposits at Tylisos; in some instances the horns had been cut, obviously to render them less dangerous (probably for the ring).

Keller considered that the short-horns might well have been introduced by sea, but that the great *Bos primigenius* would have been too difficult to transport in the relatively small ships available. Feige on the other hand considered that the Cretan long-horns were a local domestic breed (perhaps akin to the *Bos primigenius*).

No fishing tackle seems to have survived from Neolithic times,

1. J. Hazzidakis, *Tylissos à l'époque minoenne*, 1921, p. 76.

but we possess a two-pointed fishing spear of Early Minoan date from Hagios Onouphrios, and a lead sinker with a notch at each end, part of a large barbed fish-hook, and three complete barbed fish-hooks of bronze, measuring 9·5, 7·2, and 2·6 cm. in length respectively, from the Late Minoan I village of Gournia (Fig. 46, 1, 2, and 5). Fish-traps were also employed.[1]

AGRICULTURE

The basic tools for agriculture in the Near East are the pick, the mattock, and the zimbeli or two-handled basket, with the addition of the plough for grain crops. The spade is not a Levantine tool even today; it exists as an exotic foreigner used for special purposes, but the man who goes to plant vines or olives or vegetables will only use a pick to loosen the soil, and a mattock to scrape it into the basket with which he dumps it where required.

The plough, as illustrated by sign 27 of the Minoan Hieroglyphic Script, was probably entirely of wood, since no metal fittings seem yet to have been identified on Minoan sites (Fig. 44). Probably it was of the *autó-gyes* (all-in-one-piece) form recommended by Hesiod with beam and share made from one block, but with the stilt added separately. That the form shown in the Hieroglyphic Script is a fair representation of the Minoan form is indicated by the fact that a similar plough was used in Crete in Roman times and persists even today. Hesiod recommended that the

Fig. 44.
Minoan plough

share of a plough (if not *autógyes*) should be made of oak, the beam of holm oak, and the stilt of laurel or poplar (*Works and Days*, v, 435–6).

In the Neolithic period grain was probably cut by a wooden sickle with obsidian teeth, but in Late Minoan times a bronze sickle was used of the type described by Professor Childe as 'tangential' since the line of the handle forms a tangent to the curve of the blade.

---

1. An interesting example of uncertain date but possibly Early Minoan was found near the modern village of Mochlos in 1955 by the British School expedition conducted by Mr John Leatham; probably a number of the methods described in Oppian's *Halieutica* were also employed (*Halieutica*, III, pp. 72–91).

It was usually hafted by a tang fastened with one or two rivets, though miniature examples of Mycenaean date from a tomb at Enkomi in Cyprus had a socket for the handle. Such Minoan sickles were thus distinguished from the Egyptian ones where the blade was either bent forward towards the handle to form an angled sickle, or bent back to form a balanced sickle. Three of the Gournia sickles, however, belonged to Childe's 'looped' variety and must therefore have been either angled or balanced sickles.[1]

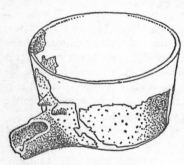

Fig. 45. Olive-oil separator

The cultivation of the olive was attributed by Greek tradition to the goddess Athena, and though Athenian patriotism might claim that this implied the olive was first cultivated in Attica, Cretans would certainly have claimed that this proved the olive was first cultivated in their island[2] and could appeal to the Peloponnesian legend which stated that the cultivation of that fruit had been introduced to Olympia by the Cretan Herakles.[3]

Middle Minoan deposits have yielded olive presses and olive separators. The oil was doubtless prepared in a manner still employed in the island. The fruit was first beaten off the tree with sticks and then winnowed from the leaves with a winnowing fork. The fruit was then drenched in hot water, crushed in a simple press, and placed in settling vats. When the oil had risen to the surface, the water was drawn off through a plugged spout at the bottom of the vat. Settling vats of this kind have been found at Mallia (from the Middle Minoan III period), and at Gournia and Vathypetro near Arkhanais (both of the Late Minoan I period).

1. V. G. Childe, 'The Balanced Sickle', *Aspects of Archaeology in Britain and Beyond*, 1951, p. 39 f.
2. For the tradition that Athena was born in Crete see p. 209.
3. The Idaean Dactyl of that name, not to be confused with his more famous namesake.

It seems not improbable that the drenching of the olives was carried out in great bronze cauldrons like the ones found at Tylisos (still notable for its fine olive orchards) unless indeed these were used for boiling the must, a normal process in the preparation of wine after the treading of the grapes.

Bees would certainly have been kept for honey. Sign 86 of the Hieroglyphic Script B is a bee, and perhaps a still better representation is the splendid gold pendant of Middle Minoan I date from the Chrysolakkos cemetery at Mallia (Fig. 37).[1] Perhaps the Minoan Cretans also made *petmez* out of their grapes. Whether they supplemented honey by planting carob bean trees is more uncertain. Sign 96 of the Hieroglyphic Script looks like a carob bean pod, but may simply be a copy of the corresponding Egyptian sign. The carob tree is native to the Mediterranean, but seems to be mainly associated with the southern shores of that sea. There are plenty of carob trees in Crete today in the parts from Mallia eastwards, which suggests that they have been introduced from Syria or Palestine,[2] and the European variants of the name from Spain to Greece are but thinly disguised varieties of the Semitic name.

Almond seeds have been found in Neolithic levels at Knosos, and in a Late Minoan I deposit at Hagia Triada, but there is no evidence to show whether the Cretans ever crushed them for oil; the wild almond trees are not uncommon in the neighbourhood of Knosos.

Date palms were not native to Crete, but they are represented in Middle Minoan art, and I have seen impressions of their leaves in the volcanic dust on Thera at a level which appeared to belong to the Early Bronze Age and was at least anterior to 1500 B.C.

Remains of figs have been found in a Late Minoan I deposit at Hagia Triada, and the so-called wild fig tree is not only common on the island but has a pre-Hellenic name. The quince (the Kydonian fruit) was supposed to be indigenous in the island. Pears, grapes, and olives, if not actually indigenous, must at least have been introduced at an early date and all occur in a wild form. Apples, too, were intro-

1. Unless these insects are wasps as suggested by one scholar. One of the Knosian tablets as translated by Ventris records a dedication of honey to the goddess Eileithyia.

2. But there are also large plantations of carob trees in the Rethymnon district.

duced, probably before the end of the Bronze Age, but I have never seen a crab-apple tree on the island. Other fruits such as cherries and plums had probably not yet been introduced to the island from Persia.

Wheat, lentils, and oil occur in Middle Minoan I deposits at Mallia, and their absence or scarcity from earlier deposits is probably accidental, since wheat is attested in Neolithic deposits at Olynthos in Macedonia.

Wine was certainly made from grapes from the Late Minoan I period onwards and perhaps much earlier.[1] Evans suggested that beer may have been made from Early Minoan times onwards, but Vickery has remarked that the 'tea-pot' vases of that period are rather small for beer. They would have been quite suitable, however, for *phaskó-milo* or other herbal teas of that kind.

In Egypt at least we know that wine was made from grapes in Early Dynastic times, and on the mainland of Greece the Middle Helladic people, who are not likely to have learned their wine-making from the north, also drank wine, so that we may assume that Cretans were making wine early in the Middle Minoan period and probably before that time.

The words for wine in Greek, Latin, and in the west Semitic dialects all seem to have been borrowed independently from a common source, probably some language current in the Mediterranean in prehistoric times and not improbably a language spoken in Minoan Crete. When we reach the Middle Minoan III period, evidence for garden vegetables becomes more abundant and from Knosos we have evidence of broad beans, 'Egyptian beans',[2] garden peas, lentils, as well as wheat and barley.

Crete abounds in edible herbs, and the pre-Hellenic names of mint, calamint, sesame, silphium, and wormwood suggest that these were all known to and used by the Minoan Cretans. Sesame alone bears an Akkadian name borrowed from Mesopotamia.

Kitchens seem not to have been very elaborate, and fixed hearths

1. The recent find of grape-seeds in a stone jar of the earliest period of the palace at Phaistos probably implies that grapes were dried as raisins then. D. Levi, *Illustrated London News*, 29 September 1956.

2. Evans does not state the name of the carbonized beans which his workmen recognized as a variety still imported from Egypt.

which were normal in Cretan Neolithic houses fade out in the Middle Minoan I period, from which we can quote only two examples at Mallia and none at all at Knosos.

There are no bread ovens like those of Troy and Thermi, though the Cretans may possibly have baked unleavened bread of the Arab type in the embers, and a strange clay oven found at Mallia in a house of the Late Minoan I period evidently represents an attempt to brighten the home life by some more exotic method of baking the food.

Most of the cooking, however, was carried out on portable braziers, which were common enough in Minoan houses and palaces.

EXPORTS AND TRADE

The large numbers of oil jars in the palaces of Knosos, Mallia, and Phaistos emphasize the interest taken by the royal princes in the olive trade. It is unlikely, I think, that the pressing of olives was a government monopoly, though it is possible that the export of oil and olives may have been mainly in royal hands, and it is extremely probable that a tithe or some similar agricultural tax was paid in olives and exported to Egypt either salted or in the form of oil.

Grain may also have been accepted as taxes, but there would have been no real surplus of this except the local surplus in the Mesara, and this would doubtless have been distributed to less fortunate parts of the island.

INDUSTRIES

The industrial life of Crete has changed far more than the agricultural, and this is not merely due to the mechanization of modern times. It is true that the island now can profit from all manner of industrial tools and methods unknown to ancient Crete, but most of such products are imported and the island is no longer the industrial centre it used to be in Minoan or even in Neolithic times.

The development of large cities such as Knosos, Phaistos, and Mallia created a demand for luxury industries which no longer exists in modern Crete and scarcely existed there during the classical period. Besides the ordinary craftsmen, such as the coppersmiths, masons, carpenters, potters, and the unskilled labour employed by them, and the food producers, such as the farmers, herdsmen, shepherds, hunters, and fishermen, or distributing agents, such as the merchants, boatmen, carters, and muleteers, we also find a number of purely luxury craftsmen, such as the gem cutter, the fresco painter, the ivory carver, the goldsmith and silversmith, the faience manufacturer, and the maker of stone vases, who handled not only soft stones but also much harder materials such as crystal and basalt. The close association of these luxury trades with the palaces of the kings and nobles is reflected in the stories of Daedalus and Minos, and is exemplified by the lapidary's workshop in the Royal domestic quarter of the Palace of Minos, by a workshop for casting bronze tools and implements and a supplementary one for making the stone moulds in the Mallia Palace, and by the great bronze founder's oven at Phaistos situated only a few yards from the central court of the palace.

A theocratic state, such as the Kingdom of Minos appears to have been, must have employed a large number of men and women as priests and priestesses, scribes, and acolytes or attendants of some sort or another in the service of the state cults of the Earth Mother, the Cretan Zeus, and other deities. It is impossible even to guess at the number, but the proportion of religious to secular officials must have been analogous to that in Egypt, and their power and influence no less than those of the Egyptian priests.

It is also difficult to assess how far the princely villas round the Palace of Minos were the residences of royal princes, hereditary nobles, high secular officials, priests, or a combination of any of these.

For a picture of an industrial centre occupied with the necessities rather than with the luxuries of life we must turn to Gournia, that pleasant little seaside town on the Gulf of Mirabello.

In the Middle Minoan III period there had been, indeed, a small palace or large villa on the crown of the hill, but by the Late Minoan I A period this had fallen into disrepair and been cut up into small tenements. From 1550 to 1450 or perhaps 1400 B.C. Gournia may be regarded as the Minoan equivalent of a small town in the potteries district of Staffordshire. No less than five of our scanty supply of Minoan potters' wheels were found in this little settlement.

One building had evidently belonged to a carpenter and produced a splendid saw, various chisels, an awl, a drill, and some other tools, while another had been a bronze foundry and contained moulds for casting double axes, chisels, etc.

METALLURGY

One of the more intriguing problems of Minoan industry is the sources from which the island derived its metals, since the native supplies were not rich. The scanty silver they possessed may have come from the Cyclades and the tin from Crisa (which would explain the early Cretan connexions with the Delphi district).[1] The Minoan upper classes seem to have possessed a fair quantity of gold, but they had no good local supply and must, I think, have imported Nubian gold through their trade with Egypt.[2] It has often been suggested that the copper ores of Crete were worked in Minoan times but the positive evidence for such working is slight.

At Sklavopoula on the west coast two small outcrops of malachite were tested in classical times possibly as early as the fifth century B.C. The quartz veins north and east of Kandanos have been worked more extensively, but apparently not before the time of the Roman occupation of the period, and other quartz veins were worked at Kambanou at a later date. The earliest mention of a Cretan goldmine is by Idrisi, the Arab writer of the twelfth century A.D., who refers to the existence of a goldmine at Rabdh el Djohn (the Arabic name for the Khania district).

The only copper ore deposits that we can confidently assert to have been exploited by Minoan miners are those of Chrysokamino.[3]

A copper axe was found in one of the Late Neolithic houses at Khosos but this was probably imported. Copper objects are still very

1. A. Lucas ('Silver in Ancient Times', *Journal of Egyptian Archaeology*, 1928, p. 319) notes that we have no evidence of silver being produced in Greece before the seventeenth century, but the relatively large proportion of silver objects in the early Cyclades graves suggests that the Siphnian mines may have been tapped before 2000 B.C. See O. Davies, *Journal of Hellenic Studies*, 1924, p. 89; C. F. C. Hawkes, *The Prehistoric Foundations*, 1940, p. 291.

2. The very name Nubia means El Dorado, the Land of Gold.

3. A. Mosso, *The Origins of Mediterranean Civilization*, p. 219; compare also the analyses quoted by T. Burton Brown in *Excavations in Azerbaijan*, 1948, pp. 192-7.

uncommon in the Early Minoan I period but quite common in the following period.

Minoan Weapons before 1700 B.C.

The earliest form of copper dagger from the round tombs of the Mesara is often miscalled triangular, but actually has a blade like a laurel leaf cut so that the top has a concave or more rarely two concave curves. Two rivet holes show how each blade was attached to its handle. The Early Minoan III deposits of the Mesara tombs contained more daggers of this type but associated with other blades that really do deserve to be called triangular, having a strongly marked midrib and a tang with one or two rivet holes for hafting, a form with

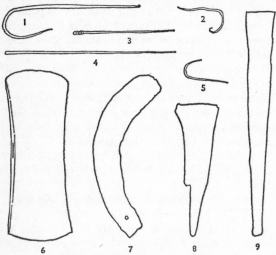

Fig. 46. Minoan bronzes, Palaikastro
(1, 2, and 5 fish-hooks, 3 and 4 needles, 6 double axe, 7 sickle,
8 axe-adze, 9 chisel)

widespread connexions, since examples of it occur in Copper Age contexts in Sardinia, in Sicily, and in Italy; three daggers of this form in silver were found in Tholos B at Koumasa.

The strange double-pointed blade from Hagios Onouphrios may probably be regarded not as a dagger but as a fish harpoon. The independence of the Cretan armourer at this period is emphasized by the absence of Early Minoan II shapes in Mrs Maxwell-Hyslop's typology for western Asia.[1] The third Early Minoan period was marked by improvements in the copper dagger, but there is still no evidence of actual bronze, doubtless because the Cretans at that time had no easy access to tin, which was then still scarce enough to be reckoned as a precious metal, as is shown by the torque of that material found in an Early Bronze Age deposit at Thermi on the island of Lesbos. The ordinary daggers resemble Mrs Maxwell-Hyslop's Type 16 and have a rounded base with three rivet holes. Some slim daggers with strong midrib and rounded base from the Mesara already foreshadow the rapiers of the Middle Minoan III–Late Minoan I period, though they themselves cannot be later than the Middle Minoan I period and may well begin in Early Minoan III times. These daggers are of bronze and terminate in a small tang for attachment to the handle, though Palaikastro has only the old tangless variety at this period and Mochlos only one dagger of the new type.

The Cretans had also evolved a long sword at least before the end of the Middle Minoan II period, though it was perhaps still rather a rarity since our only surviving example is the splendid ceremonial sword with its crystal pommel found in an intermediate deposit in the Palace at Mallia, and that would not have been a very suitable weapon for actual warfare. Possibly, however, we may assume the existence of work-a-day cut-and-thrust swords also. The stratification suggests that this sword is earlier than Middle Minoan III, and so does the absence of a tang, but a date after 1800 is not impossible.

Another rather broad dagger form with no marked midrib, but relying for strength on its thick blade, and with three rivet holes in its slightly curved base is usually dated Middle Minoan I-III. The best-known example is the one from Lasithi, incised with a design showing a man with a hunting spear awaiting the charge of a wild boar. This particular dagger probably dates from Middle Minoan III, and I doubt if any dagger of this form is earlier than Middle Minoan II because the shape does not occur among the daggers from the Mesara round tombs which are rich in daggers. This would imply that the depot of bronze implements from the oval house at Chamaizi was still occupied in the Middle Minoan II period; indeed this shape

1. *Iraq*, 1946, pp. 18, 19.

lasts from Middle Minoan II to the Late Minoan I period. This type of dagger does not occur in Mrs Maxwell-Hyslop's West Asiatic series but was imitated in Celtic circles as far west as Britain, where similar forms occur in the Early Bronze Age (?1800–1300 B.C.) associated with double axes in stone. The Lasithi dagger is asymmetrical and might even be interpreted as a halberd. Associated with daggers of this type in Middle Minoan III hoards we find work-a-day double axes, double adzes, axe-adzes, single shaft-hole axes, and fine-toothed saws, including one magnificent example over 1·6 m. long.

The bronze figurines of the Middle Minoan period may more properly be considered under the heading of fine arts rather than industry, and depended more on the skill of the modeller than of the bronze caster. The industrial art of the coppersmith is better displayed in the manufacture of bronze vases and cauldrons.

Minoan Weapons after 1700 B.C.

The defence of the island in Middle Minoan times was probably entrusted to the fleet, since not only do the cities and villages lack defensive walls but the tombs usually contain no weapons save girdle daggers, the side-arms that were part of every Minoan gentleman's normal attire. With the Middle Minoan III period, however, we find that long rapiers with pronounced midribs, rounded shoulders, and a short tang for insertion into the hilt became comparatively common, and a splendid series of those of Late Minoan I date were found by Hazzidakis in the cave at Arkalochori, a sanctuary doubtless sacred to some warlike deity, possibly the goddess who is seen striding along brandishing a long sword on a flat-cylinder of Late Minoan I A date from Knosos.

Another fine sword of this type was found in the Middle Minoan III burial in Tomb 2 and a shorter example in Tomb 20 at Mochlos. The latter tomb also contained three spearheads with split sockets formed by folding a flat plate round the shaft, and binding it with a cast ring at the lower end.

The double axes from Arkalochori, including miniature examples in gold and silver, were mostly of a kind that would be useless in warfare, and confirm Dr Marija Gimbutas's theory either that the double axe was a sacred emblem of the goddess, as suggested by Evans and as it obviously very often was, or that when it was cast in a practical form it was not intended as a weapon, but was a tool of a wood-man or a carpenter or even a butcher. It may have been also used to kill the sacred bull, but I suspect it was primarily a woodman's axe (Fig. 46, 6).[1]

The Arkalochori types of rapier and spear were quickly adopted on the mainland by the princes of the Shaft Grave dynasty at Mycenae.

Two splendid rapiers of this type with gold-plated hilts from the later palace at Mallia must be dated not later than Middle Minoan III A, but the same type of sword persisted both on Crete and on the mainland into the fourteenth century B.C.[2]

This style of rapier was improved by some swordsmiths in Knosos or Mycenae by converting the short handle tang (its great weakness) into a flat plate long enough to hold three or more rivet holes and flanged at the sides to grip the inlaid handle of wood or ivory. Further, the hand was protected by a horned guard over which the handle flanges were extended.

Swords of this type persisted into the fourteenth century both in Crete and on the mainland, and recently a representation of such a weapon has been identified incised on one of the stones of Stonehenge.[3]

Cut-and-thrust swords, except the great sword from Mallia, are not proved to have been used in Crete before the twelfth century B.C.[4]

BOWS AND SLINGS

Crete was renowned for its bowmen and slingers even in classical times and presumably they would have been still more prominent in prehistoric times before the development of body armour. No metal slingstones, like the leaden examples of classical times, have been discovered in purely Minoan strata, and we must assume that the Cretan slingers of the Bronze Age, like David, simply selected

1. 'Battle Axe or Cult Axe', *Man*, April 1953; I had suggested this view three years previously in my 'Battle-axes in the Aegean' (*Proceedings of the Prehistoric Society*, 1950, p. 58).

2. F. Chapouthier, 'Deux Épées d'apparat', *Études crétoises*, 1946; and for the date, H. G. de Santerre, *Kretika Chronika*, 1949, p. 377.

3. Compare R. J. C. Atkinson, *Proceedings of the Prehistoric Society*, 1952, p. 65, Plate 21, and O. G. S. Crawford, *Antiquity*, 1954, p. 25, Plate 1.

4. H. W. Catling, 'Bronze Cut-and-Thrust Swords in the Eastern Mediterranean', *Proceedings of the Prehistoric Society*, 1956, p. 102.

suitable pebbles from the beaches and river beds. Seager, indeed, at Pseira found three small rooms filled with beach pebbles which his workmen identified as slingstones. This 'primitive arsenal' perhaps belonged to the Middle Minoan period, since it was overlaid by a house of the Late Minoan I period. Clay sling bullets like those of Hassuna do not seem yet to have been identified.[1]

Archery was practised early in the Bronze Age, and from Early Minoan II to Middle Minoan I times the Cretans seem to have used a simple bow of Libyan type with chisel-pointed arrowheads, not of flint presumably, as in Egypt and Mesopotamia, but of obsidian.[2] (Evans, *Huxley Memorial Lecture*, 1925, p. 22.)

Pointed bronze arrowheads with a tang for hafting in a reed shaft appear before the end of the Middle Minoan period.

The 'composite' bow strengthened with keratin from *agrimi* horns appears to have been introduced into the island from the east not later than the Late Minoan I period but never superseded the simple bow which remained common in Crete.

In the Late Minoan II armoury deposit at Knosos Evans found two boxloads of bronze arrowheads associated with tablets in Linear Script B, some with the sign of an arrow, and others with that of an *agrimi* horn, an indispensable material for the manufacture of composite bows.[3] Since this deposit, however, dates from the period when we have inferred the existence of an Achaean dynasty at Knosos it might only be evidence of the employment of composite bows by the Mycenaean Greeks.

In general the composite bow seems to have been a northern weapon. The classical Greeks associated it with the Scythians and it persisted till modern times among the Turks, but the earliest example

1. V. G. Childe, 'The Significance of the Sling, etc.', *Studies Presented to D. M. Robinson*, I.

2. The seal illustrated by Evans may not be genuine, but the Mallia hieroglyphs also illustrate a bow and an arrow with chisel point, possibly however copied from an Egyptian hieroglyphic, Mallia sign 14 (Chapouthier, 'Écritures minoennes', *Études crétoises*, 1943, p. 65 and Fig. 25); but the chisel point is far more obvious on the Cretan hieroglyph than on the Egyptian, so that the evidence on the whole supports the existence in Crete of such arrowheads.

3. Compare H. L. Lorimer, *Homer and the Monuments*, 1950, p. 289, Fig. 37. The essential characteristic of the 'composite' (as distinct from the compound bow) is that it is bound with sinews on the outside of the curve and with keratin or true horn on the inside to increase its strength and flexibility.

of its use is by the Mesolithic inhabitants of Denmark. The Cretan and Mycenaean Greeks may have learned the use of this weapon from the Anatolian states of Hatti or Mitanni. Homer describes such a bow, but rather as if it was an exotic novelty, and the self-bow or the compound bow (of two pieces of wood) continued to be the normal form in Crete well into the classical period.

The flat bronze arrowheads of Mycenae, and the Cretan ones resembling them, are no improvement on arrowheads manufactured over a thousand years earlier in Persia. In the Late Minoan III period hollow-based arrowheads of Mycenaean type do appear in graves of Zapher Papoura and at Phaistos, while the Hunter's Grave in the former cemetery has some barbed arrowheads with a hollow-based tang that look like a compromise between the Minoan and Mycenaean forms.[1]

DEFENSIVE ARMOUR

The defensive armour of the Late Minoan period included a full length body shield with a figure-of-eight outline, probably implying a wooden frame covered with leather several folds deep. A semi-cylindrical shield with a curved top reminding us of Homer's description of the shield of Telamonian Ajax as 'like a tower' was fashionable on the Greek mainland but seems only to appear in Crete in the Late Minoan III period, presumably introduced by Mycenaean Greeks.

The small round parrying shield does not appear in the warfare of the Near East much before 1400 B.C. (though a different kind of parrying shield was known and used in Egypt at a much earlier date). By 1350 B.C. however, Ugarit smiths were making the slashing swords which this later type of shield was intended to parry, and the Hittites were using round shields of this form against the Egyptians at the battle of Kadesh in 1280 B.C.

There is no evidence that Minoan Cretans ever wore armoured corselets or greaves, except a large piece of bronze plating from a Phaistos tomb identified as part of a *mitra* or body-belt and fragments that might have belonged to another. From Mycenaean graves we can only quote one solitary instance of a metal greave from a tomb at Enkomi in Cyprus (despite the numerous references by Homer in

1. Evans, 'Prehistoric Tombs of Knossos', *Archaeologia*, 1905, Fig. 28.

the *Iliad* to 'the well-greaved Achaeans', which may refer to leather leggings like those shown on the warrior vase from Mycenae).[1]

The Cretans, however, had several forms of helmet during the Bronze Age. The simplest form seems to have consisted of a cap made from a single sheet of metal and is illustrated by a Middle Minoan III sealing from Zakros depicting a conical helmet with earguards, a long, narrow appendage presumably representing a chinstrap, and a short upright spike on the peak, probably for the attachment of a plume.

A second type of helmet is the built-up type best illustrated by a representation of it on a polychrome vase from the Tomb of the Double Axes at Isopata, showing a close-fitting cap consisting of horizontal bands (presumably of leather) with a knob on top, earguards, and an extension at the back to protect the neck. The best known variety of the built-up helmet, however, has the horizontal bands strengthened with horizontal rows of split tusks of the wild boar, arranged so that the curves of each row face in the opposite direction to those of the rows immediately above and below it. On the whole boars-tusk helmets seem more characteristic of the Greek mainland than of Minoan Crete. Plates for such helmets have been found on six grave sites in the Peloponnese, on three in Attica, and on one in Boeotia. At Menidhi and in one tomb at Mycenae sufficient were found to allow of the restoration of such a helmet. Representations of boars-tusk helmets appear on ivories from Sparta and Menidhi, on fragments of a faience vase from the third Shaft Grave, on the silver rhyton from the fourth Shaft Grave at Mycenae, and on a gem from the Vapheio tomb, showing a helmet adorned with two *agrimi* horns (or metal imitations of them). Against this series Crete can only set a few boars-tusk plates from a Late Minoan III tomb at Knosos, the design of a boars-tusk helmet on an ivory fragment from Knosos, and the representations of four helmets with *agrimi* horns on a Late Minoan I sealing from Hagia Triada, on a polychrome vase from Tomb 5 at Isopata, on a bronze double axe in the Giamalakis collection, and on a vase from Katsaba.[2] Repre-

---

1. Diodorus makes it plain that 'greaves' were not necessarily of metal, since Celtiberian greaves were made of hair (*The Library of History*, Book v, Chap. 33).

2. See A. Xenaki-Sakellariou, *Bulletin de Correspondance Héllenique*, 1953, pp. 46–58 and S. Alexiou, 'The Boars Tusk Helmet', *Antiquity*, 1954, p. 211.

sentations in fresco also occur at Mycenae (one of them on a tripod hearth) and perhaps at Tiryns. The bronze helmet with cheekpieces made from one piece of metal found by Persson at Dendra is without parallel on the mainland, and is compared by Miss Lorimer to some on the Boxer Rhyton from Hagia Triada, but it would be rash to claim this helmet as Minoan without further evidence. Fortunately one Minoan helmet in bronze has recently been found in the Warrior Graves at Knosos by Hood and de Jong. It is a conical helmet of thin bronze plate with cast knob for plume and cheekpieces (or earguards) riveted on (Fig. 47). It is the more important, not merely because it is our only surviving Minoan helmet, but also because this form of helmet seems to be the prototype of the group of so-called 'bell helmets' scattered across Hungary up into north Germany, and sometimes called the 'Beitsch' type from the site where an example (now in the British Museum) was found in a bog, associated with a dagger (or halberd) and a couple of ingot 'torcs' dated to about 1400 B.C.[1]

From Middle Minoan III times onwards Minoan warriors also carried spearheads with split sockets bound at the ends by rings of the same metal. The socket was cast flat and then

Fig. 47. Late Minoan II helmet, Ayios Ioannis

hammered round the shaft and fastened by a ring, a much simpler though less elegant and durable method than casting the whole spearhead, socket and all, in a bivalve mould.

In the Late Minoan II period, the type of weapons current at Knosos is well illustrated by three found in the Warrior Graves by Hood and de Jong at Ayios Ioannis. The swords were rapiers with horned or cruciform guards and flanged tangs to hold the inlaid handle of bone, wood, or other material, which was attached by rivets. Three of these spearheads still have split sockets fastened with a ring, but now completely cast in a mould except the ring which was

1. Compare H. Hencken, 'Beitsch and Knosos', *Proceedings of the Pre-historical Society*, 1952, p. 36.

added later (Fig. 48). One spearhead is a heavy type with a leaf-shaped blade and a tang, a type well known and distributed over the Aegean in the Middle Bronze Age, but in the Late Bronze Age rare, perhaps completely confined to Crete. Hood compares it to medieval boar spears. A second, a beautiful weapon with a long ogival blade, is also a rare type probably confined to Crete (where there is one example from Gournia and another in the Giamalakis collection). The two small spearheads with leaf-shaped blades probably belonged

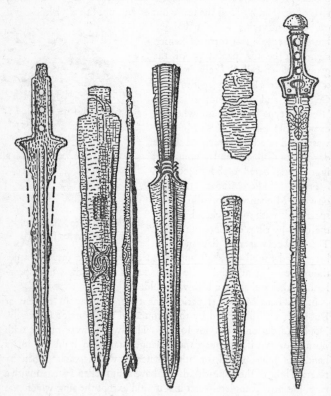

Fig. 48. Late Minoan II swords and spears, Ayios Ioannis

to javelins or throwing spears. The normal equipment of the warriors buried seems to have been a short sword with cruciform hilt, or alternatively a tangless dagger and a spear.

THE SOCIAL STRUCTURE

The architecture of the Minoan cities reveals something of the social structure. The Palace of Minos is surrounded by a number of minor palaces aping the amenities of the great one. Thus the Little Palace, the Royal Villa, the South House, and the South-East House all have lustral areas, the Royal Villa has a special throne room, and the South-East House a domestic shrine. Most of these houses were appendages of the Palace of Minos, and were presumably occupied by important officials, whether priestly or secular, some perhaps members of the royal family.

The Little Palace and the Unexplored Mansion to the west of it stand apart both literally and figuratively, and must surely have been the residences of persons important in their own right, such as the Crown Prince or the Queen Mother.

The palaces at Phaistos and Mallia had apparently no such minor palaces in their vicinity, and this fact might be used to argue that Knosos controlled the central part of the island, at least during the Middle Minoan III and Late Minoan I periods.

There are no visible traces in Crete of that primitive democracy which Jacobsen claims to have perceived among the city states of southern Mesopotamia at an early date,[1] but on the other hand there is no suggestion of a ghetto system or of rigid distinctions, and the little houses of the poor nestle up against the walls of the palaces and rich villas. We cannot even guess at the political rights of the various elements of the population (whether male or female), but there seems to have been much greater social freedom between the sexes than in most ancient societies. Women went unveiled in *décolleté* dresses and mixed freely with the men at the public festivals. They danced in public before the men and even took part in the dangerous toreador sport, dressing in the male costume for the purpose.

Minoan Crete would appear, therefore, to have been governed by

1. H. Frankfort, Mrs H. Frankfort, J. A. Wilson, and T. Jacobsen, *Before Philosophy* (Penguin Books, 1949), p. 141.

a paternal theocracy, not unlike that of Egypt, and to have consisted of states where the proletariat probably had few or no political rights and was heavily taxed, but otherwise not unduly oppressed, where there was probably a rather top-heavy upper class of princes, nobles, and priests, and a very small middle class, but no very rigid caste system. There must also, I think, have been a fair number of slaves, but not, surely, a majority of the population, since we have no examples of the large workmen's suburbs that we find in Egypt, nor of the *latifundia* of Imperial Rome, those large plantations founded on huge gangs of slave labour.

In the Late Minoan II period we are conscious of the difference between Knosos and its immediate surroundings including Tylisos and Amnisos, which appear to be Mycenaeanized and were very probably ruled by a Greek prince, and the other parts, which may have still had Minoan princes perhaps paying tribute to Knosos.

MYCENAEAN SOCIETY IN CRETE

Ventris's decipherment of the Linear Script B texts has offered to those who accept his transliterations the possibility of reconstructing the outlines of the social structure in Mycenaean Greece and in such parts of Crete as had Mycenaean settlers at a date some five hundred years before the poems of Homer were in all probability written. Professor L. R. Palmer has accepted this challenge and has defined the chief members of the Mycenaean society in the following terms:

(1) The *anax* or 'overlord' elected from a single royal family

(2) The *lawagetás* or war leader chosen for a war or campaign

(3) The *teléstai* or feudal barons who gave war service in return for land[1]

(4) The *hieréwes* or priests

(5) The *damiówergoi* or workers including both free peasants and artisans

(6) The *doúloi* or slaves

Palmer is able to quote parallels from other early societies speaking Indo-European languages, such as the Hittites, the Indo-Iranians, and the Germans; but the bards who are so prominent in Homeric and

1. Paralleled at Olympia in the Peloponnese in the sixth century B.C. (though presumably in a different sense) in the meeting between Elis and Heraea.

in early Celtic society are lacking, unless they are included among the priestly class.

Let us, however, compare his analysis with the picture of the archaic Dorian society in Crete as drawn in a recent book by R. F. Willetts,[1] who bases his conclusions mainly on a study of the laws of Gortyn as they existed between 700 and 400 B.C. The laws in question were drawn up in a Dorian city several hundred years after the close of the Bronze Age, but many features, such as the tribal organization depicted, must have survived from prehistoric times, and have not been exclusively Dorian. At Gortyn (and in most other Cretan cities of that period so far as we know) there was the *startagetás* in place of the army leader of the *lawagetás* type,[2] but no kings or barons. The city was governed by magistrates called *kósmoi*, assisted by others termed *títai*, by a council, and by an assembly. These discrepancies do not matter much and could be explained as a normal development from a Homeric kingdom to a city oligarchy. But these Dorian cities also had a tribal system consisting of *pýlai* (tribes), *phratríai* (septs), and *géne* (clans), which had existed in non-Dorian Athens before Solon reorganized its constitution and which must have been common in Mycenaean times (I omit features which seem to be exclusively Dorian). I shall not, therefore, feel quite happy about Professor Palmer's reconstruction of Mycenaean society until he finds some reference to this tribal system, which should have been far more active and obvious in the thirteenth century B.C. than it was in the days of Homer.

The differences between the art of Knosos and the rest of Crete between 1450 and 1400 B.C. may be assessed fairly, but the differences in the social and economic life are much harder to gauge, especially as the Mycenaean people of the Late Minoan I period had absorbed so much of Minoan culture and religion. Nilsson has remarked, 'I must emphasize again that the Mycenaean Greeks were a mixed people who to a great extent took over Minoan culture and religion.' This is surely true and underlines the difficulties of deciding what is Minoan and what is Hellenic. Some gods, objects, and practices we

1. *Aristocratic Society in Ancient Crete*, 1955.
2. The military leader of the clan gathering or *startos*, which is only another form for *stratos*, the normal Greek word. For an army, the *phratria* was the equivalent more or less of the Roman *curia*, and the Saxon hundred.

may identify confidently as definitely Minoan or definitely Hellenic, but there remain a large number of marginal instances which we cannot classify so confidently.

MUSIC AND DANCING

It is certain that music, associated with dancing, played a large part in the life of Minoan Crete, and that it was closely bound up with religious ceremonies and festivals, though we must not assume that there was no secular music. Even in modern Crete we find, quite apart from the official music of the Orthodox liturgy, certain tunes associated with particular occasions and festivals. Thus the carol singers sing one particular air on Christmas Eve and another in honour of St Basil on New Year's Eve, while a third traditional song is sung to the bride at weddings. The folk dances too, the *khaniotikós* of the west, the *pendozáleis* of the centre, and the *pedikhtós* of the east have each their own appropriate airs, less limited in number but still not very numerous.

Minoan Music

Classical folklore credited the Cretans with having introduced several forms of musical performance to the mainland. Thus the *nome*, the solo hymn to Apollo accompanied by the singer on the lyre, was said to have been first performed at Delphi by Chrysothemis the Cretan, the *paean*, or choral hymn to Apollo, was also derived from Crete, and the *hyporchema*, the choral song and dance executed at Delos, was termed Cretan by Simonides, its invention attributed to the Curetes, and its introduction to Thaletas of Gortyn, who introduced Cretan rhythms to Sparta.

It seems likely, then, that some of the old Minoan music was not entirely lost; but what was its character? Mosso records that from the lowest levels at Phaistos, that is from the Late Neolithic period, came a bone horn similar to some still used by peasants of the neighbourhood and two bone tubes of unequal length, which he suggested might have been part of a *syrinx* or 'Pan's pipe'.[1] One of the Minoan seals depicts a woman blowing a conch horn, but the music that can be achieved by this means is rather limited, and they were perhaps

1. But surely these might be a set of double pipes of unequal length, like the pair illustrated on the Hagia Triada sarcophagus.

employed for summoning the people to attend festivals or other gatherings. Galpin notes the wide distribution of such conch horns, but seems to be unaware of the Minoan examples.

Triangular harps of the kind which the Greeks termed *trigonon* were known in the Cyclades during the Early Bronze Age[1] and an instrument like the classical lyre with seven strings would appear to have been well known in Crete from Middle Minoan I times since it appears as a symbol in the Hieroglyphic Script.[2] Sometimes the symbol is shown with only four strings. This is perhaps only a convenient simplification, not necessarily an attempt to depict a tetrachord instrument, though it may be noted that the four strings of the primitive Kafir harp of Persia are tuned to a tetrachord.[3] One example of the Middle Minoan symbol shows an instrument with eight strings, presumably implying a heptatonic scale.

The Late Minoan III painted sarcophagus from Hagia Triada depicts a seven-stringed lyre of classical type with a tortoise-shell sounding board, perhaps tuned to a double tetrachord with the central note belonging to both tetrachords. The double pipe, which appears on this sarcophagus, had also been known in the Cyclades in the Early Bronze Age,[4] but we must remember that the sarcophagus belongs to the period when Mycenaean influences were very strong in Crete, and that the bronze figurine of Late Minoan I date in Leyden cannot be quoted as a piper since his hands are broken off at the crucial point. The Geometric *phorminx*, however, had only four or five strings, and this fact has been used to support the idea that the Greeks, like the Celts, had a pentatonic scale without semitones, but the evidence seems unconvincing.[5] Both seven-stringed lyre and double pipe seem to disappear after the Bronze Age, only to

---

1. It is a variety of the Mesopotamian upright harp termed a *zakkal*; compare F. W. Galpin, *The Music of the Sumerians*, Chap. 3.; H. F. Lutz, 'A Larsa Plaque'; and T. Alvad, 'The Kafir Harp' *Man*, 1954, No. 233.

2. Galpin, op. cit.; but the Minoan instrument is Egyptian rather than Sumerian in shape.

3. T. Alvad, op. cit.; the five strings of certain Greek lyres do not prove a pentatonic scale; thus Alvad speaking of a five-stringed harp from Kafiristan thinks it was probably tuned as a diatonic tetrachord. It seems less probable that the instrument should be tuned pentatonically.

4. U. Kochler, in *Athenische Mittelungen*, 1884, pp. 156–62.

5. R. P. Winnington Ingram, *Classical Quarterly*, 1956, p. 169.

be reintroduced in the seventh century B.C., but here again the negative evidence should not be pressed, and the four-stringed *phorminx* could possibly have been tuned to a tetrachord like the Kafir harp. The seven-note scale seems to have been indigenous to Western Asia and perhaps to have spread westwards with the Indo-European peoples, but it never crushed the pentatonic scale in the Celtic areas, while in China we even hear of an earlier heptatonic scale being changed to a pentatonic by royal decree.[1]

For percussion instruments the Minoan Cretans possessed cymbals and the Egyptian rattle called a *sistrum*, but I can quote no evidence for the existence of a drum.

Minoan Dancing

A widespread tradition credited the Cretans with the invention of dancing, a tradition ridiculous in itself but reflecting the great role played by dancing in Cretan life from Minoan times up to the present day.

Fig. 49. Late Minoan dancers, Palaikastro

It has been suggested that we may have illustrations of the classical Cretan dance termed the *hyporchema* in the group of dancers in bronze from Olympia and the pottery group of dancers with a lyre player in their centre of Late Minoan I date from Palaikastro (Fig. 49).

1. F. W. Galpin, op. cit., p. 139; S. Piggott, *Prehistoric India*, 1950, p. 270.

If this suggestion has any foundation in fact we may have a descendant of the *hyporchema* in the *pendozáleis*, the only modern folk-dance in Crete where the performers grasp each other's shoulders in the manner of the groups from Palaikastro and Olympia. The musician still stands in the centre, and his instrument is still called the *lyra*, though it looks more like a three-stringed lute than any ancient type of lyre illustrated in classical art.

We have no evidence as to whether the Minoan Cretans affected airs in five or seven time, such as occur in later Greek music. I suspect, however, that most village dances of Minoan or of classical Crete were in four time, which would suit the simpler metres based on trochees, iambics, dactyls, spondees, or anapaest rhythms, and that they no more resembled the complicated rhythms of the choral dances of Pindar and Bacchylides than English folk-dances resemble those of the Royal Ballet.

Modern Cretan folk dances may be divided into two groups, which nearly but not exactly coincide in their distribution with the eastern and western divisions of the Cretan dialect. From the Malevizi eastwards the local dances are the *maleviziotikos*, the *herakliotikos*, and the *pedhiktós*.

West of Malevizi and including the Ida range other local dances, such as the *pendozáleis* and the *khaniotikós*, are based on an entirely different principle, and I suspect that the *geranos* or 'crane dance', which Theseus was said to have seen the Cretan maidens dancing, and himself to have introduced to Delos, may have been a dance of this kind.

The twice-yearly migration of the cranes is a very noticeable event at Knosos, and the cranes really do perform a dance resembling a *khaniotikós*, graphically described by Miss Rawlings in her novel *The Yearling*:

> The Cranes were dancing a cotillon as surely as it was danced at Volusia. Two stood apart, erect and white, making a strange noise that was part cry and part singing. The rhythm was irregular like the dance. The other birds were in a circle. In the heart of the circle several moved counterclockwise.[1] The outer circle shuffled around and around. The group in the centre attained a slow frenzy.

1. The two musicians still operate in the course of a *khaniotikós*, but the dancers move clockwise.

In the eighteenth book of the *Iliad* Homer describes a dance 'such as Daedalus made for Ariadne in broad Knosos' with the youths and maidens hand in hand dancing in a circle (for that is what must be implied by the comparison to a potter's wheel) and then again dancing in two ranks facing each other.

There exists a curious parallel to Homer's Cretan dances in a place where I should least have expected it, at Chichicastenango in the Quiche district of Guatemala. The 'Bull Dance', as described by Aldous Huxley, is danced about Christmastime, though the people start preparations for it in the previous Lent. The story, which is told in verse, refers to a bailiff who entrusted the care of his master's bulls to some herdsmen, but Huxley did not follow the details of the plot. The dance had two figures like those described by Homer but in the opposite order. First, two lines of dancers alternately advance on each other and retreat. Huxley compares this movement to that of 'Here we come gathering nuts in May', and east Cretan dances would produce a similar effect if danced in two lines facing each other instead of in a circle.

In the second Guatemalan movement, compared by Huxley to the 'Grand Chain' of the Lancers, the two groups of dancers circle round the whole area in groups of two who circle round each other. Since Huxley informs us that practically all the local music and folklore of that district is of Spanish, not of Maya origin, I suppose this dance of the bulls should ultimately be derived from some old Spanish dance. Moreover, the *toritos* wear bull masks which must make them look very like Minotaurs. Is it conceivable that this was an old Mediterranean dance known to Homer and danced in Minoan Crete?[1] The evidence is far too slight to support such a theory, but scholars have sometimes tried to derive the toreador sports of Spain and southern France from that of Minoan Crete.

MINOAN SPORTS

The most popular sports in Minoan times seem to have been boxing and the bull ring. The representations of boxers (usually in pairs, but also shown in procession) in relief on steatite vases or in miniature

1. Was it perchance something like the *karpaia*, the 'cattle-lifting' dance of the Aenianians and Magnesians. Compare the account given by Athenaeus in *Deipnosopishtae*, I, 15.

frescoes indicate them with leather boxing gloves of the classical cestus type, so that we can assert that the traditions of Greek and Roman boxing go right back to the Bronze Age. Representations of boxers on Mycenaean and Geometric vases and the accounts of boxing in the Homeric poems suggest that this sport never died out.[1]

The sport of the bull ring was obviously the more exciting and more dangerous, and naturally was therefore represented more often in art. The bull was not pursued on horses and overthrown, as in the rodeo sports popular in Thessaly in classical times, nor was it apparently slain by an armed matador, as in the modern Spanish bull ring. The main object of the Minoan sport seems to have been to stand in front of a charging bull, catch him by the horns, and vault over on to his back (Plate 16). Girls as well as youths indulged in this practice, but for this purpose they wore male attire. We are reminded of the old Athenian folk tales about Theseus and Minos and of the seven youths and seven maidens who were sent from Athens to be the prey of the Minotaur. We also have representations of the netting of bulls (the most famous being those of the gold cups found at Vapheio near Sparta). There is no indication that this is part of the toreador sports, but Seltman has pointed out the parallel between this scene and the one described by Plato in his account of Atlantis which, he has suggested, might contain folk memories of Minoan Crete. The relevant passage from the dialogue called the *Critias* states how 'wild bulls were turned loose in the precinct of Poseidon. The ten kings, left all alone, prayed to the God to make them capture the beast which he desired, and then set forth, unarmed, with only staves and nets. The bull which they secured they dragged to the block of brass and cut the bull's throat over the block, according as the law commanded.'

The question whether Plato's Atlantis was Minoan Crete is, of course, highly speculative and debatable, but both the netting and the sacrifice of bulls occurred in Crete in the Bronze Age, and the latter, at least, must have been a religious ritual.

Even the bulljumping and the boxing have been considered to have been religious rituals, but this is not substantiated by evidence and pending further investigation it is better to regard them as usually-

1. The chronological gap between Hagia Triada and archaic Greece is bridged by occasional representations of boxers on Late Mycenaean and Geometric vases.

secular sports, though doubtless practised on days of religious festivals.

We have no evidence for any ball games like that played by Nausicaa and her maidens in the *Odyssey*.

For indoor games we have the evidence of dice and the royal gaming board, but no clear idea of the sedentary games in which the Cretans of that period indulged. Of the gaming boards found elsewhere in ancient Egypt, Cyprus, Elam, Assyria, and Sumer perhaps the closest parallels to the Minoan board are the splendid inlaid examples from the Royal Cemetery at Ur, but the number and arrangement of the holes are different, and I would hesitate to assume that the Sumerian game was played in the Palace of Minos.[1]

1. Compare C. L. Woolley, *Ur Excavations*, 1934, pp. 274–9, Plates 95–8; E. D. van Buren, in *Iraq*, 1937, pp. 11–16; C. J. Gadd, in *Iraq*, 1934, pp. 45–50.

CHAPTER 10

The Decline of Knosos and the Growth of the Power of Mycenae

THE Late Minoan period in Crete opens brilliantly with no obvious signs of the decay of Cretan power that was to set in later, despite the great loss of life and the extensive material damage that must have been caused by the great earthquake which rocked the island in the second quarter of the sixteenth century B.C.

At Knosos there had been widespread damage to the Palace of Minos, but this had already been repaired before the end of the Middle Minoan period, so that Evans was able on this site to classify his deposits as pre-seismic or post-seismic Middle Minoan III B according to whether they had preceded or succeeded the great earthquake.

The Late Minoan I A period (1550–1500 B.C.) was marked at Knosos by various reconstruction works, including the final form of the entrance systems on the west and south sides of the Palace of Minos. The Late Minoan I B period (1500–1450) was not marked by any major architectural work, and the succeeding period Late Minoan II (1450–1400) had no building in the palace except the reconstruction of the throne room block. There were, however, a number of minor repairs executed in the Palace of Minos, including a number of new frescoes, on which we remark a tendency to imitate in stucco the veining of marble dadoes, a curious anticipation of a trick characteristic of the earliest wall paintings at Pompeii in the so-called 'encrusted style'. The best-preserved fresco of the Late Minoan II period is that of the guardian griffins in the throne room (paralleled at a later date by a similar fresco at Pylos) with its interesting attempt at shading.

The trade balance with Egypt and the Levant had swung now from Knosos to Mycenae, but Egyptian vessels of value still reached Crete, as is proved by Alexiou's discovery of stone vases in a Late Minoan II tomb of the harbour town of Knosos. One of these was a fine

267

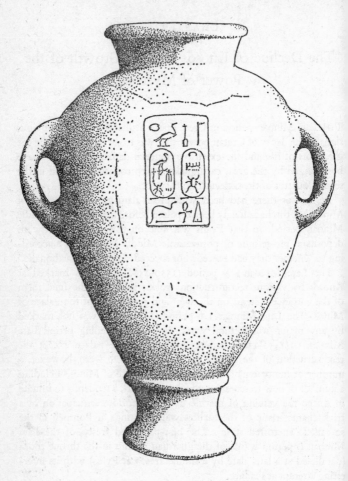

Fig. 50. Alabaster vase from Katsaba

'alabaster' jar (Fig. 50) bearing an incised inscription translated as 'the good god – Men-kheper-re – son of the sun – Thutmose perfect in transformation endowed with eternal life' and referring to the great Thutmose III.

The most striking and significant difference, however, between the late Minoan I B and the Late Minoan II A deposits at Knosos is the replacement in the latter of Linear Script A by Linear Script B in the palace records discussed in Chapter 3, which certainly implies that Knosos and perhaps much of central Crete was then under an Achaean dynasty, whether this was achieved by conquest, by a dynastic marriage, or by the *coup d'état* of a Mycenaean general serving over a Minoan army.

MYCENAEAN INFLUENCE ON CRETE

Even before Ventris's revelations of the mainland characteristics of Linear Script B, various scholars, such as Karo, Praschniker, and Snijder, had pointed out the presence in Late Minoan II art of features that seemed to imply influence from Mycenaean Greece, and K. Müller in particular had stressed some non-Minoan characteristics in the 'palace' amphorae from the *tholos* tomb at Kakovatos in Elis. Even when the motives were Minoan, the Mycenaean artist was apt to stylize them and turn floral elements into abstract patterns. Minoan artists, of course, had also stylized floral patterns from an early date, but the whole-hearted tectonic treatment of the palace amphorae at Knosos was different and might be due to Achaean influences.

Yet even a Greek occupation of Knosos in 1450 B.C. does not quite solve the problems of the Knosian frescoes. Human figures, formed patterns, linear borders, and frieze decoration had all appeared at Knosos, Amnisos, and other sites in the north of Crete during the Late Minoan I A period. It would not help our inquiry to push back the Greek occupation before 1550 because there were no frescoes on the mainland before 1400 B.C. The natural inference is that these features, like the relief frescoes, were a local growth of the Knosian school (perhaps influenced from abroad but certainly not from Mycenae).

THE TRANSITIONAL PERIOD AT KNOSOS

The only *kouloura* hitherto still open in the west court was now covered with paving, and the only earlier building still left standing near the palace on this side was the north-west Treasury. The west porch in its present form, with its reception room and porter's lodge, was constructed at this time, and the Corridor of the Procession widened, but the South Propylaeum, which gave access from the same corridor to the state apartments on the first floor, was narrowed.

The palace façade on the west side of the central court was advanced, and the court itself paved with limestone slabs (though only a small proportion of these still remain *in situ*). The shrine and the staircase between it and the throne room block were reconstructed. The north-west entrance with its lustral area had never been rebuilt after the Middle Minoan III earthquake, nor had the great stepped portico on the south side, but it is clear that the old Middle Minoan I bridgehead over the Vychia ravine was still in use, because it was during the transitional Middle Minoan III B–Late Minoan I A period that the charming little caravanserai was constructed for the accommodation of travellers from the Mesara and from the south in general, implying that the bridge was still in use though the Stepped Portico it had previously served was in ruins.

The reception rooms consisted of a small pavilion approached from the palace side by a short flight of steps with a single column in the position termed *in antis* – that is half-way between the *antae*, or corner-posts, of the sidewalls. This room was adorned with a frieze of red-legged partridges and hoopoes.

Adjoining the pavilion with the partridge fresco there was another small room with a footpath fed by a conduit from a spring on Gypsadhes Hill and with its overflow filling a drinking trough for the animals that had accompanied the travellers. A few yards to the west lies a little spring house lined with gypsum slabs, and with a small niche at the back, intended perhaps to hold a lamp or a figure of the guardian deity of the spring; and indeed this spring seems to have continued as a 'Holywell' long after the abandonment of the caravanserai and even of the palace.

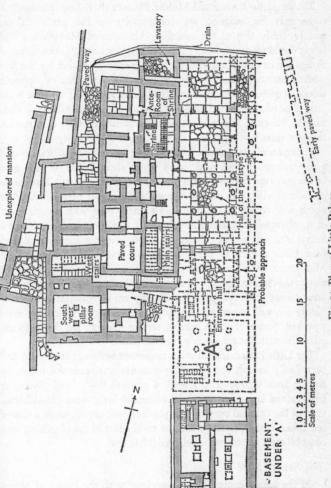

Unexplored mansion

Paved way

Lavatory

Drain

Early paved way

Ante-
Room
of Shrine

Ante-
Shrine

West
stairs

South
west
pillar
room

Paved
court

Main stairs

'Hall of the peristyle'

Entrance hall

"A"

Probable approach

N

"BASEMENT
UNDER 'A'

0 1 2 3 4 5   10   15   20
Scale of metres

Fig. 51. Plan of Little Palace

The Little Palace

To the same transitional Middle Minoan III B–Late Minoan I A stage may be assigned the construction of the Little Palace, and probably also of the so-called 'Unexplored Mansion', a still larger building immediately west of the former, but unexcavated except for its east façade. Both buildings are remarkable for the fine ashlar masonry of their exterior walls facing each other on opposite sides of a narrow but well-paved road running parallel with the main arterial north-south road, and both were built into the slope, so that, like the Palace of Minos, they had more storeys on their east than on the west sides.[1]

The main entrance to the Little Palace from the east passes through a fine columned propylaea, from which short flights of steps give access northwards into a peristyle court reminding us of a Hellenistic or Roman villa, though the eastern half of it has perished. Off the north-west corner of the court lies a small room with a stone drain in it, obviously a bathroom.[2] South of this there was originally a lustral area, restored as a shrine in the latest reoccupation period, and mud brick packed in between the wooden columns of the Late Minoan I A lustral area, thus preserving the impression in the burnt clay of the convex fluting of the now vanished pillars. From the south-west corner of the peristyle a noble gypsum staircase, of which two flights are still preserved, led to an upper storey which has now vanished. South of this a narrow service stairway led down to the pillar basements at the south end of the palace.

The Little Palace, like all other important buildings at Knosos, had been badly looted, but one of its treasures was preserved for us by having been thrown into a well, a glorious bull's head rhyton or filler carved in black steatite and originally fitted with gilded horns. One of the original eyes, with a pupil of rock crystal set in a rim of red jasper, is still preserved and the vivid effect of the bloodshot eyes of a bull must be seen to be believed (Plate 17a).

The South House

Of the houses more directly associated with the Palace of Minos

1. A very common practice in Crete both in Late Minoan and in modern times (as noted by Seager; see page 286).
2. The opening is too small for a sewer.

the most splendid was the South House rising to a height of at least four storeys on the southern slopes of the Kephala. It seems more dependent on the palace than the Little Palace or the Royal Villa and may, I imagine, have belonged to some important official. It is at least significant that the occupant of this house, constructed in the transitional Middle Minoan III B–Late Minoan I A period, was allowed to encroach on the line of the old Stepped Portico.

Another entrance perhaps existed at the south-east corner of the building, leading into the light-well of the main hall of the house (a miniature version of the Hall of the Double Axes in the Palace of Minos, but with a small lustral area opening off its north-west corner). West of this hall on the same floor there lay a pillar crypt of which the religious associations were clearly emphasized, since on one side of the central gypsum pier stood a conical base of the same material of the kind reserved for the sacred double axe, while on the other side stood a more enigmatic gypsum base with three round holes in it. Below the ground-floor rooms there were cellars. These were also constructed as pillar crypts, but there is no obvious sign that they were employed for any religious purpose, though they were well constructed with a lavish use of gypsum for walls and stairs. The door into one of these rooms could be locked from inside or from outside by inserting a bronze pin into the wooden bolt. The wooden bolt has perished, but the bronze pin was found still in position in its diagonal slot.

The House of the Frescoes

Such were the mansions of princes and nobles, but to realize the astonishing degree of luxury and refinement attained by people of more moderate means we have only to examine the House of the Frescoes, lying between the west court of the Palace of Minos and the Royal Road uniting the theatral area to the Little Palace.

A small projecting wing on the north side contained an entrance lobby and an office for a doorkeeper (like the French, the Minoan Cretans seem to have been rather addicted to employing *concierges*). The lobby gave access to two corridors on the east side, and on the west to a long narrow room opening into a large room where the fresco fragments were found neatly stacked in layers, apparently in preparation for a replacement which never took place. The quality of the frescoes is as good as that of any in the palace, and their combination of extreme naturalism in the treatment of the fauna against a highly stylized background of flora and rocks is typical of Late Minoan I A frescoes, and may be remarked also on the wall paintings of the caravanserai and of the villa at Amnisos. But, although the technique is Minoan, the subjects have an exotic, half-Egyptian flavour (compare the papyrus and the blue monkey).

Late Minoan Innovations at Knosos

The domestic quarter of the Palace of Minos, east of the central court, seems to have remained without any major reconstructions, presumably because it had been cut into the side of the Neolithic tell, and had therefore suffered less damage from the great earthquake. Even in these parts of the palace, however, a considerable amount of redecoration took place, especially in the form of new frescoes. Relief frescoes die out in this period, but include one magnificent specimen, the 'Priest-King' relief in the porch connecting the Corridor of the Procession with the central court, and a ceiling pattern of rosettes and spirals on a blue ground from the same area where the Miniature Frescoes of the previous period were found. It is probable, too, that the splendid fragment of relief fresco at Pseira showing two court ladies (originally restored as one court lady) may have belonged to this period.

To this period may belong the so-called 'medallion' *pithoi* of the Palace of Minos. Evans dated those Middle Minoan III but admitted that the examples in the domestic quarter continued in use right up to the time of the destruction of the palace in 1400 B.C. Pendlebury remarks that on grounds of style these *pithoi*, or at least the examples with moulded grass ornaments, should belong to the Late Minoan I A period, and his dating is supported by the fact that the medallion *pithos* in the room behind the central pillar shrine west of the central court rests on an earlier pavement and has the later pavement built round its base.

Amnisos

Another fine villa with frescoes was erected early in the Late Minoan I A period at Amnisos, traditionally the naval headquarters of King Minos. It should be noted that Minoan ideas of what constituted a suitable site for a harbour varied considerably from our own. They did not, of course, despise a natural, land-locked harbour like Soudha Bay, but they were less fussy and were quite content with a site that had a promontory jutting out, flanked on each side by a beach, so that boats could be beached on one side or the other according to the wind, and Platon has pointed out that most Minoan harbours possess such a promontory. Amnisos, however, hardly possesses even this convenience since the rock projects very little, and even that hardy sailor Odysseus commented on the poorness of its harbour. Why then should Minos have chosen it as his naval headquarters? The rocky eminence that lies between the modern aerodrome and the shallow bay of Amnisos may have cut some of the force of the prevailing north-west winds but only if they were more west than north, and Marinatos is probably justified in assuming that the coastline has sunk here since Minoan times (as it certainly has at Nirou Khani only a few miles farther east) and that a sandspit had probably connected the Kastro rock to the small island lying off shore, thus providing the necessary facilities for beaching ships. The 'Naval Officer in Charge' at Amnisos appears to have done himself well. His villa lies on the east side of the isolated hill known as Palaeochora, protected by it from the prevailing north-west winds, and consisted of a two-storey building with some very good ashlar masonry in the more important parts. At the north-west corner there was a typical Minoan hall, repeated in duplicate on the first floor, and served by two corridors and a flight of stone steps. The chief reception room was on the first floor, with two pillars in the centre and with fine floral frescoes adorning at least three of the four walls.

LATE MINOAN FRESCOES

The so-called House of the Frescoes between the Palace of Minos and the Royal Armoury contained the remains of fine murals neatly stacked as if they had been intended to be replaced on the walls after some reconstruction. One scene represents a gay picture of wild flowers and rocks with two blue monkeys. Some of the flora is definitely Cretan, including the earliest naturalistic representation of a yellow rose (*Rosa foetida*, or the Austrian briar), but the blue monkeys and the papyrus plant are exotic features probably copied from

Egyptian murals (though Platon has suggested that the scene represents a royal park rather than one taken from the wild life of Crete).

So-called rosettes occur much earlier in Mesopotamian and Egyptian art, but these might represent some other flower, and Meillet has argued that both 'rose' and 'lily' were old Aegean words, not necessarily of Minoan origin, but at least current in the Levant at a very early date.[1] Among the plants native to Crete on this and on the Amnisos frescoes were lilies, irises, vetches, and myrtle.

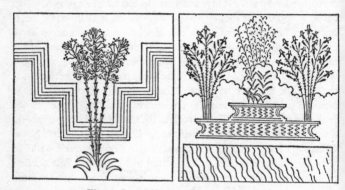

Fig. 52. Late Minoan I frescoes, Amnisos

Rather more formal than the Monkey Fresco, and perhaps to be assigned rather to the Late Minoan I A period, is the attractive frieze of red-legged partridges and hoopoes adorning the entrance hall of the Caravanserai. The fauna and flora of this painting were all native to Crete, and the multi-coloured balls that look like Easter eggs were probably intended to represent river pebbles of Cretan breccia.

To the same period (Late Minoan I A) belongs the room with garden scenes at Amnisos, a different scene for each of three walls in a room, depicting lilies on one wall, irises on another, and on the third other plants not growing wild as in the Monkey Fresco, but formally planted out in stone vases like the crocuses of the Saffron Gatherer.

From Hagia Triada in the Mesara comes what is, perhaps, the finest of all the Minoan naturalistic frescoes. The scene shows two cats stalking a pheasant and the hindquarters of a roebuck leaping over

1. A. Meillet, *Aperçu d'une histoire de la langue grecque*, 1930, p. 65.

rocks in what appears to be the natural scenery of a Cretan dell. There is certainly no suggestion of a park here, except the odd fact that the cats are not Cretan wild cats but domesticated Egyptian ones.

To the Late Minoan I A period may also be assigned two Knosian frescoes that were imitated much later on the mainland in the Mycenaean palace at Tiryns. Indeed the great mural painting from the Upper Hall of the Colonnades, representing a row of 'figure of eight' oxhide shields, could never have been restored but for the better preservation of a miniature copy of it at Tiryns.

The other fresco which provided a model for one at Tiryns was the Toreador painting which originally probably adorned the walls of some room or loggia above the so-called 'School Room'. The technique of this highly difficult and dangerous sport is clearly defined in this painting which shows a girl, dressed like a boy, standing in front of a charging bull which she grasps firmly by the horns, preparing to vault over the animal. A youth has just succeeded in vaulting over the animal while another girl stands ready to catch him when he alights. One might almost adopt the old army phrase and describe the scene as 'bull-vaulting by numbers'.

In this painting we may notice certain characteristics which mark the decline of the splendid naturalistic frescoes of the Middle Minoan III B–Late Minoan I phase and herald the grandiose but rather blatant art characteristic of the Late Minoan I B period at Knosos. Human figures, hitherto mainly confined to the miniature frescoes, become more prominent. The charging bull, though spirited enough, is greatly inferior to the splendid animal in the relief fresco of the North Porch. Another characteristic of this new type of fresco, which seems confined to Knosos, is the multiplication of subsidiary friezes (sometimes imitating coloured stones) of a quasi-architectural kind. These traits may also be seen in the later Mycenaean paintings of the mainland, but we must beware of attributing the Knosian examples to Greek or Mycenaean influence on Knosos, since on the latter site they appear about a hundred years earlier than they do on Mycenae or at Tiryns.[1]

Other frescoes of this period (1550–1500 B.C.) at Knosos include a

1. We may, however, infer that the Mycenaean art of Mycenae and Tiryns was influenced by the school of Knosos, not by those of Mallia or the Mesara.

gay little piece from the Queen's *megaron*, perhaps depicting a girl dancer whirling round in a quick dance with her curls flying out. It must be admitted, however, that the analogy of similar representations of hair flying upwards on seals seems usually confined to small figures of deities descending from heaven on their worshippers. I have never seen it suggested that this figure represents a goddess making her epiphany, but that is what the analogy from the gems and sarcophagi would suggest. Another fresco fragment from a small room opening off a continuation of the Corridor of the Procession shows part of a procession, with men carrying a palanquin on which a figure in white robes is seated on a camp-stool.

LATE MINOAN I A POTTERY

The pottery of the Late Minoan I A period (1550–1500 B.C.) was distinguished by its superior baking, and Pendlebury remarks on 'the clink' that is heard when a Late Minoan I A sherd is dropped on a hard surface'. In the far east of the island, at Zakros and Palaikastro, the transition to this style was gradual. We find there the same leaf and scroll patterns executed both in the light-on-dark and in the dark-on-light techniques, and not infrequently the same vase will have superimposed bands of ornament in alternative styles. One vase from Palaikastro, a pear-shaped jar with basket-like handle formed of the horns of an ibex of which the head projects in front, reminds us of the bull's head projecting from one of the vases depicted in Rekhmire's tomb.

Cups shaped like tea-cups were also quite common and adorned usually with sprays of leaves, and there were also a number of 'flowerpots', flaring conical or pear-shaped jars with a hole in the bottom of each. There were jugs of various shapes, some rather squat with bridged spouts, others taller and pear-shaped with plain or with beaked spouts. Rhyta, or fillers, were popular, varying from the old 'peg-top' form which had appeared in the Middle Minoan period, to an elegant ovoid variety, or a long conical type which appeared in Crete at the beginning of the Late Minoan I A period in steatite and was copied in clay, especially in eastern Crete and later on the mainland (where there is at least one example of the sixteenth century from Prosymna in the Argolis).

The conical rhyton was the most common form in the hands of the Keftiuans and the People of the Sea represented on the Egyptian tomb paintings. Some fragments of handsome rhyta of this shape in hard stones such as Spartan basalt were found at Mycenae (associated

Fig. 53. Late Minoan I A vase designs

with Late Helladic III pottery) and just such a filler was borne by the celebrated Cup-Bearer in the Late Minoan I B fresco at Knosos.

We also find some handsome ovoid jars with multiple handles, forerunners of the palace amphorae of the Palace of Minos in the Late Minoan II period (though the latter were made to suit Achaean tastes, perhaps even by Achaean potters). One of the finest was a splendid vase found at Pachyammos (Plate 18).

Baggy alabastra of a type common in Egypt during the Twelfth Dynasty were imported into Crete and imitated in pottery with wavy bands of paint imitating the veined calcite of their Egyptian prototypes. Most curious of all the Late Minoan I A vases were some polychrome libation vessels found at Isopata in the form of high, slim buckets with double looped handles and with the body of the vase treated like a fresco, since it was coated with a lime plaster before

Fig. 54. Minoans in Tomb of Senmut

the polychrome designs were applied (Plate 19). The most interesting and best preserved examples of these vases were those from Tomb 5 at Isopata, one with a design of a boars-tusk helmet of the type more familiar on the mainland but also known in Crete, the other with a design of a figure-of-eight shield. The more numerous examples from Hagia Triada only retained faint traces of their original decoration, but the painted sarcophagus from a tomb near that site (though later in date) illustrated the purpose of these vases. They were for libations in front of the sacred double axes at other Minoan shrines.

CARVED STEATITE VASES

From the Palace of Hagia Triada come one complete and two fragmentary vases in steatite with designs in low relief; fragments of similar vases have been found at Knosos, one representing a procession

f youths carrying bowls, another an archer disembarking from a
oat, and a third a building on a hill (perhaps a peak sanctuary, as
laton suggests). The complete vase from Hagia Triada is a conical
up with the design of a young prince (perhaps the 'Minos' of that
ay, as Forsdyke has suggested) giving orders to an officer of the
uard with his men behind him. One of the fragmentary vessels is a
onical rhyton with parallel zones of sporting scenes in low relief,
aree of boxing and one of the toreador
port.[1] The second fragment from Hagia Tri-
da, the shoulder of an egg-shaped rhyton,
epicts a harvest festival, a marching crowd
f peasants carrying what look like pitch-
orks, shouting, laughing, and singing, with
ae man giving the time by a *sistrum* (the
gyptian rattle) and led by a priest in a
uilted cloak.[2] The Harvesters' Vase is the
aost lively and vigorous relief that we
ossess until late in the classical period. To
ae same period I would assign the celebrated
old cups found in the *tholos* tomb at
apheio near Sparta, though the pottery
und with them belongs to the Late Helladic
t or Late Minoan I B period. The two cups
ave repoussé designs, one showing the net-
ng of wild bulls and the other the decoy-
g of them by a tame cow, and were both
bviously the work of the same artist. They
e supposed by most authorities to be im-
orts from Crete, I think rightly, first because
f the highly naturalistic style of the relief;
condly because the decoration is of the free field type with no at-
mpt to divide it into zones; and thirdly because this rather squat
rm of Vapheio cup is a typically Middle Minoan form and unlike
ae Helladic forms.

Fig .55.
Late Minoan I B vase

The Late Minoan I B period (1500–1450 B.C.) corresponds to the

1. Compare Hutchinson, *Town Planning Review*, October 1950, Fig. 10.
2. Illustrated everywhere, but compare especially F. Matz, *Kreta Mykene
ruja*, Plate 67.

first half of the Late Helladic II period on the mainland and is cha
acterized by pottery with designs of fishes, seaweed, etc. at Knosos a
Gournia, Palaikastro and Zakros, but it would be a mistake to assur
that it everywhere succeeded the floral and spiral designs of L
Minoan I A (Fig. 55). This marine style was never very common a
was probably a local style either of Knosos or of some eastern site, sin
we do not find it at Mallia, and only rare examples of it at Phaist
though the best fresco in this style is the fine floor with a mari
design under the Late Minoan III floor of the shrine at Hagia Triad

Collared rhytons in this style occur at Palaikastro and Zakros, a
a vase of this shape (which does not occur in the Late Minoan I
period) is shown along with Vapheio cups and conical rhyta bei
brought as tribute to Pharaoh by the islanders represented on t
tomb of User-Amon, vizier to Thutmose III in the earlier part
his reign.

The neck of a faience rhyton of this shape was even found at Ash
the capital of Assyria, and a complete example except for the mou
and neck at Mycenae. A few Late Minoan I B vases were export
to Egypt and of these we may quote the fine *oenochoe* (jug) in t
Marseille Museum acquired in Egypt, a tall alabastron with imitati
marbling from a tomb in Sedment, a bridge-spouted jug in Ne
York, purchased in Egypt in 1860, and a squat alabastron fro
Armant in the British Museum, acquired in 1890. The last is som
times reckoned as a Helladic vase on the ground that the shape is
mainland one, but the shape is more common in Crete than is oft
realized, and the decoration is very close in style to the jug in Ne
York (though not, I think, painted by the same man).

The majority of the Aegean vases found in Egypt at this tim
however, seem to have been imported from the mainland of Gree
and we may consider the fifteenth century B.C. as the period wh
Mycenaean traders began to supplant Cretans in the ports of Egy
and the Levant.

Finest of all the Late Minoan I B vases is the stirrup jar (so-call
because the false neck with a handle on each side bears a vague reser
blance to a stirrup) from Gournia, with a terrifying fiercely ali
octopus writhing all over the body of the vase.

Many of the floral motives of the Late Minoan I A vases continu
but usually in a modified or stylized form. Ivy leaves devel

wo or three stalks, the realistic palm tree of Middle Minoan III
imes develops into a kind of flower, in which form it became very
opular in the succeeding period on Late Minoan II and Late Hella-
ic II vases. Favourite neck ornaments were foliate bands, garlands of
endant crocus blooms, and a double band of reserved rosettes. A
avourite pattern on the lip, especially on the large vases, was the one
riginally described by Evans as 'the notched plume' but later re-
hristened by him 'the adder mark' because he considered it was
erived from the markings of an adder's skin. The marine ornaments,
vhich are particularly rich on the rhyta of eastern Crete, com-
rise octopods, whorl shells, nautilus, starfish, and a rock formation
ooking rather like coral (but certainly nothing of the sort).

LATE MINOAN FRESCOES AT KNOSOS

t Knosos, where Late Minoan I B pottery occurs but is not very
lentiful compared to that of Late Minoan I A, the main indications
f change are to be seen in the palace frescoes.

The most important fresco of this period is that adorning the walls
f the Corridor of the Procession, where a string of figures was shown
ringing offerings to the king in a manner recalling that of contem-
orary paintings on Egyptian tombs and temples. Only the lowest
arts of the figures are preserved, but they include both men and
omen, some of them doubtless bringing vases of metal or of stone,
ke the Cup-Bearer from the South Propylaeum, others carrying
usical instruments, culminating in the double row of figures in the
outh Propylaeum and the splendid figure of the Cup-Bearer himself
the only surviving example of the head and upper half of a figure
om the procession, though several legs and quite a number of feet
ave survived.

If the Cup-Bearer with his fine aquiline features, long curly hair,
ther light brown eyes, powerful shoulders, trim muscular limbs, and
ery slim waist is to be taken as representative, even in an idealized
rm, of Sergi's 'Mediterranean Man', we must admit that the type
an attractive one, and I think that in the main Sergi was right. It is
least beyond dispute that men with similar features and figures may
ill be found in Crete at the present day, especially in the mountain
stricts.

283

Late Minoan II frescoes tend to imitate in stucco the veining of marble plaques in dadoes, a curious anticipation of the Pompeian 'encrusted style'.

At Knosos the reconstruction of the throne room and the heraldic fresco of the Griffins may be credited to the Achaean dynasty and so may the 'Captain of the Blacks', showing a Minoan (or Mycenaean?) officer leading off some Nubian troops at a smart double, found near the earlier House of the Frescoes.[1] On style alone I should have assigned the 'Campstool Fresco' and 'La Parisienne' to this period though Evans and Pendlebury assign them both on stratigraphical grounds to the Late Minoan I B period. At Knosos no more relief frescoes were designed, but there was a considerable amount of painting in the flat, of which the most important was the mural from the throne room.

NIROU KHANI

In the bay immediately east from that of Amnisos lay a small Minoan port and a very interesting little palace associated with it. The Palace of Nirou Khani, as it is called,[2] was built at the beginning of the late Minoan I A period and was excavated by Xanthoudides and published in 1922. We gain the curious impression that the port and palace together formed the Headquarters for the Propagation of the Minoan Gospel to the infidels in other parts of the Levant, since the palace was stocked with cult objects, four large bronze double axes, forty tripod altars, and other ritual objects, stone lamps, vases, etc. far beyond the needs of a much larger palace and presumably intended for export (perhaps to the land of Keftiu). On the south side of the east court was found the remains of a large pair of Horns of Consecration and pieces of a fresco with sacral knots.

The palace is small but very well built and designed. The main hall, with its inlaid doors dividing into two parts like the Hall of the Double Axes at Knosos, opens on to the east court and forms the centre of the living quarter. The ground floor of the north side is

1. Pendlebury, op. cit., p. 200. The artists however were probably Cretans since no fresco of this date is known on the mainland.
2. By all archaeologists, though the local inhabitants often call it 'Koukini ti Khani'.

given over to domestic store-rooms with corn bins and *pithoi* for wine and oil. The south wing has most of the missionary stores, altars, lamps, etc. The whole building must have had at least one more storey since there are staircases in both the north and south wings.

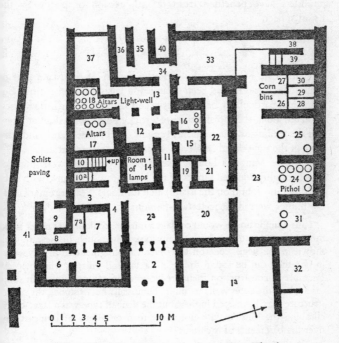

Fig. 56. Plan of Late Minoan I palace, Nirou Khani

The sinking of the coastline since Minoan times has resulted in the flooding of some of the port installations, but we can still see two rock cut basins, a long mole, and traces of some other buildings (warehouses, perhaps).

At Mallia the palace and the town both continued to be occupied, but their importance seems to have diminished greatly, and this area may now have been under the control of Knosos. Perhaps the gulfs of

Merabello and eastern Crete were also under the same control, but i
so they seem to have benefited by it, and the towns of these areas may
well have found the remote control exercised by Knosos less irksom
than the more direct control probably exercised by Mallia in th
Middle Minoan period. Ports such as Pseira and Mochlos woul
doubtless have benefited from the suppression of piracy by th
Knosian fleet.

PSEIRA

The first Late Minoan period was the heyday of the island port o
Pseira which had indeed been occupied in Early Minoan II times bu
flourished particularly between 1550 and 1450 B.C.[1] The little houses
clustered along the top and sides of a rocky point, with steps at inter
vals descending to the harbour, remind one of many an island har
bour of the type called '*skála*' (= staircase) at the present day.

The Late Minoan I houses, like those of Gournia, were built o
large, roughly-squared blocks of the local grey limestone, with slab
of schist (also found on the island) used for floors. Seager remarks tha
the houses were built in terrace-fashion.

Thus a single house would contain a number of floors yet never stand
more than two storeys high at any one point. Such houses are wel
shown in the siege scene on the silver vase fragment from Mycenae
in fact they can be found today in Cretan hill villages which closel
resemble in construction their predecessors of Minoan times. In som
cases where the outer walls are built of unusually heavy stones, the super
structure may have been higher, but the general type was a large hous
climbing the hillside with not more than one floor of living-room
over the basements of each tier.[2]

No palace was discovered here but there are some comfortable houses
such as those termed Houses A and B, both larger than anything a
Gournia except the small palace on that site.

One house overlay a more ancient building of which the thre
rooms were filled with beach pebbles, which the workmen identified

1. Or 1400 B.C.; see page 290.
2. R. B. Seager, 'Excavations at Pseira' *Anthropological Publications c
Pennsylvania University*, 1912, p. 13. This form of house is still very commor
in Crete, especially in the villages of the foothills.

as sling-stones. This earlier building, not exactly dated by the excavator but presumably belonging to the Middle Minoan rather than
the Late Minoan I period, may have served as a primitive arsenal.

One small but well-constructed house even possessed a fine relief
fresco, the only example found outside Knosos, and a sure indication
that the relationship between the capital and the island must have
been close and friendly. The existing fragments, which had fallen
from an upper storey, show that the subject illustrated was two ladies
or goddesses (originally thought to be only one) in richly embroi-
dered court dresses, reminiscent of the Middle Minoan III B 'Ladies
in Blue Fresco' at Knosos.[1]

GOURNIA

Our most complete picture, however, of the lives of the ordinary
citizens of the Late Minoan I A period is afforded by the ruins of the
little industrial town of Gournia on the Gulf of Merabello, and we
owe this picture to the splendid perseverance of Miss Harriet Boyd
(later Mrs Boyd Hawes), who uncovered practically the whole settlement, a feat never attempted previously and but rarely since. All
honour is due to her hard and unspectacular work on this site, without
which our account of Minoan culture would be a very one-sided and
misleading story of palaces and villas. The town of Gournia lies on a
small knoll a few hundred metres from the coast, and it seems to have
been scantily occupied ever since the first Early Minoan period (Fig.
57). The first serious building on the site, however, occurred late in
the third Middle Minoan period when a small palace or large villa
was erected on the crown of the hill in obvious imitation of the great
palaces of Knosos and Mallia. Like Knosos it boasted a theatral area
on a very small scale, but there was no gypsum here, so the masonry
of rubble with an ashlar facing of sandstone was rather modelled on
that of Mallia, with the same small setbacks of the façade and with
the same alternation of square piers and round pillars of the portico
facing its central court.

The internal arrangements of this small palace are rather obscure
and cannot be restored with any confidence, since the building would
appear to have been destroyed by the Middle Minoan III earth-

1. R. B. Seager, op. cit., Plate v; parts of two figures wrongly united as one.

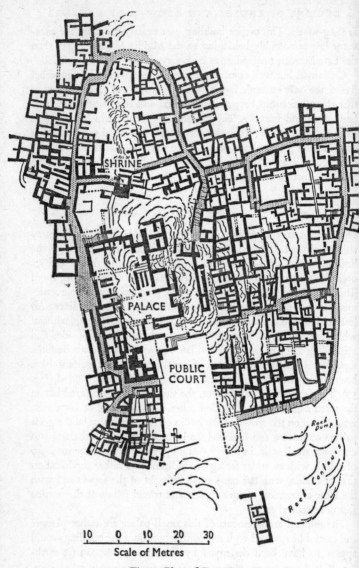

SHRINE

PALACE

PUBLIC
COURT

Rock
Dump

Rock Contours

10 0 10 20 30
Scale of Metres

Fig. 57. Plan of Gournia

quake, and had been turned into workmen's flats in the Late Minoan I A period (presumably by the independent actions of refugee squatters rather than by any order of the local Housing Committee). A regular industrial settlement grew up round this nucleus, with streets radiating out from the centre and with lateral communications provided by two curving streets of the German *Ringstrasse* type (Fig. 57).

The artisans' houses are small and tightly packed together, and the surviving rooms seem to be chiefly store-room basements. The living-rooms must have been mainly on the first floor, often reached by stairs rising straight from the street (a practice for which I could quote modern parallels in Crete). Gournia, of course, was only a little market town, what would now be termed a *komópolis*, with small local industries catering for the agricultural and fishing hamlets in the neighbourhood, but the evidence for them is very complete. We possess no less than five clay disks from the tops of potters' wheels, a carpenter's workshop with a number of bronze tools including a fine saw, a fragment of a cross-cut saw, double axes, large and small chisels, an auger, the point for a drill, a coppersmith's forge, and an oil factory for pressing olives. Just below the crown of the hill at the end of a small cul-de-sac leading out of the inner *Ringstrasse* lay the remains of a small civic shrine, the humble precursor of many a temple to Athena Polias, and the first of its kind to survive to our times, since earlier shrines had always been attached to a palace or a villa if they were in a town, though peak and cave sanctuaries of a public character had existed in the country. The furniture of the shrine still surviving seems to belong chiefly, if not entirely, to the Late Minoan III period, but it seems probable that there was a shrine on this spot in the Late Minoan I period.

HAGIA TRIADA

In the Mesara the damaged palace at Phaistos was reoccupied, but was replaced as the official residence of the reigning prince by a new and smaller palace erected at the west end of the same ridge, a site known to us as Hagia Triada.

This palace seems to have been built just after the great earthquake in what Evans termed the post-seismic Middle Minoan III B period and probably lasted till 1400 B.C.

Certain local peculiarities mark off the architecture of these Mesar͏ palaces from those of northern Crete, notably a partiality for gypsur͏ dadoes rather than for fresco decoration and a habit of locating ligh͏ wells in the middle of the longer halls rather than at one end.

Nevertheless Hagia Triada has produced two splendid frescoes i͏ the Late Minoan I naturalistic style (see p. 276), the more famous o͏ the two being the Cat Fresco described above. The other fresc͏ was a marine design with octopi and fishes adorning, not a wal͏ but the floor of the little shrine which used to be assigned to th͏ Late Minoan III period, to which its second floor level certainl͏ belongs, but which must, I think, have been first erected in the Lat͏ Minoan I period. The position of this shrine is very interesting sinc͏ it is accessible both from the palace and from the town and we seer͏ here to have the transition from the purely palatial shrines of Knoso͏ Phaistos, and Mallia to the civic shrine that we noticed at Gournia.

It was originally supposed that the absence of Late Minoan II pot͏ tery on this site implied that the palace had been abandoned befor͏ 1450 B.C. but now that we know that late Minoan II pottery in Cret͏ is practically confined to Knosos, it seems more natural to suppos͏ that the Hagia Triada palace was destroyed in 1400 B.C., though it ͏ clear that the town site was soon reoccupied.

The pottery is chiefly of the Late Minoan I A type, and the fev͏ examples of Late Minoan I B vases found in this area were probabl͏ imported from some other part of the island.

To the Late Minoan I A period I would attribute the constructio͏ of a beehive tomb excavated by Miss Vronwy Fisher, Mr V. Des͏ borough, and myself on the Kephala ridge about half-way betweer͏ the Zapher Papoura cemetery and that of Isopata (Fig. 58). The tom͏ had been badly looted in Minoan times and employed as an ossuar͏ in the Late Minoan III C period, but there were a few remains fron͏ the earlier burials, while the sherds found in or behind the walls wer͏ all Middle Minoan, except two sherds that were probably Lat͏ Minoan I A.

The tomb resembles in some respects Wace's first group of *tholoi* a͏ Mycenae, but the side-chambers in the fore-hall and the fact that th͏ tomb is not cut into a slope are Cretan features and recall the Roya͏ Tomb at Isopata, which seems to date from the end of the Lat͏ Minoan I A period.

THE SECOND LATE MINOAN PERIOD

The second Late Minoan period (1450–1400 B.C.) is a chronological division which, however, has no cultural significance except in the neighbourhood of Knosos, where it was characterized by the art that we term Late Minoan II. Elsewhere pottery of Late Minoan I B

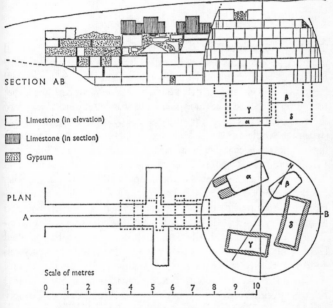

SECTION AB

☐ Limestone (in elevation)
▨ Limestone (in section)
▦ Gypsum

PLAN

A ———————— B

Scale of metres
0 1 2 3 4 5 6 7 8 9 10

Fig. 58. Tholos tomb on Kephala

style, or in some places of Late Minoan I A style, persists without much change, though occasionally some eastern site such as Palaikastro or Gournia may reveal the fact that the deposit belongs to the second half of the fifteenth century B.C. by the presence of a Late Minoan II vase imported from Knosos or by Late Minoan II motifs on a local vase.

At Knosos the only major construction in the Palace of Minos during the Late Minoan II period was the reconstruction of the throne room block, and even this was less radical than has been supposed, since the *mosaiko* pavement of Middle Minoan III A type recently revealed under the present floor of the ante-room indicates that the plan has been little altered since that date, and I suspect that some sort of throne room existed here even in the Middle Minoan I period (see p. 165). The Temple Tomb was repaired and re-used.

ROYAL TOMB AT ISOPATA

The Royal Tomb at Isopata consists of a large rectangular burial chamber (7·90 m. by 6·07 m.), walled by splendid ashlar masonry sometimes bearing masons' marks, approached through a fore-hall (6·75 m. by 1·58 m.) with two shallow side-chambers or niches roofed by corbelled vaults terminating in flat lintel blocks. Much of the corbelled vaulting of the fore-hall had also persisted up to 1941 (when the whole tomb was destroyed by General Ringel). The roofing of the main chamber is a more doubtful problem. Evans and Fyfe restored a keel vault rising nearly eight metres high which would have implied the existence of a burial mound. This is not impossible, but the analogy of some smaller tombs with similar plans and structure of the fourteenth century B.C., excavated by Schaeffer at Ras Shamra in Syria – a site in close commercial relationship with Crete – suggests the possibility that Isopata might have possessed a corbelled barrel vault.[1] Another parallel to the Ras Shamra tombs is the curious door or window in the back wall, apparently backed by virgin soil. I understand, however, that this communicated probably with the Minoan ground surface by a narrow shaft, through which possibly offerings or libations may have been poured. It would be not unnatural to suppose influences from Ras Shamra, where this form of tomb is more common, but the Isopata example seems to be about a hundred years earlier than any of its parallels at Ugarit. The long earth *dromos*, or entrance passage, cut in the earth resembles those of Mycenaean tombs, except that the Isopata tomb follows the Minoan practice of

1. C. F. A. Schaeffer, *Ugaritica*, 1939, p. 32 f. and Plates XVI and XVII; and 'Fouilles de Minet el Beida et de Ras Shamra', *Syria*, 1929, p. 29.

being sited on the crest, not on the slope, of the hill so that the *dromos* has to slope steeply down instead of running level into the slope as on the mainland.

The tomb had contained one or more royal burials of the second Late Minoan period, from which were preserved some fine vases in Egyptian alabaster and also painted vases of clay in the Late Minoan II style. The jewellery and richer objects that it must once have contained had been looted long ago, but one small stirrup cup in the

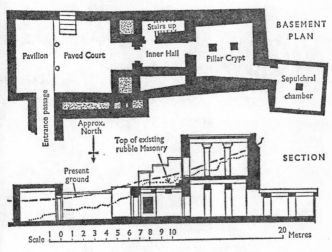

Fig. 59. Plan and section of Temple Tomb, Knosos

Middle-East style of the Late Minoan III period (see page 310) showed that the tomb continued to be used till the end of the Bronze Age. The Late Minoan II B period was illustrated by the latest burial in the Temple Tomb, which till recently constituted the only evidence for the smaller vases of this period. The Late Minoan II A period is now illuminated also by the Five Warrior Graves from the Hospital Site at Knosos and by a rich tomb at Katsaba, and the very latest period before the destruction of the palace (which I prefer to regard as still Late Minoan II B, though it corresponds to Furumark's Late Minoan

Fig. 60. Late Minoan II vase patterns

III A 1) is illustrated by Alexiou's tomb from Katsaba, with the alabaster vase of Thutmose III, and by another chamber tomb which I opened near the Temple Tomb.

LATE MINOAN SEALS

The seal-stones of the Late Minoan I A period begin to exhibit a slight decline from the best work of the Middle Minoan II B or Middle Minoan III periods, but there are still plenty of fine stones.

The commonest shape is the lentoid. The amygdaloid, or almond-shape, grows longer and acquires grooves on the back side. Flattened cylinders no longer occur, but there are some examples of true cylinders. A representative group of clay sealings of this period was found at Knosos in the south-west basement; the designs include one of a youth holding two mastiffs on leash, others of dogs with collar, and a curious scene showing a young Minotaur sitting on a camp-stool with an attendant pointing to a kneeling ram.

Late Minoan II seals are still finely cut, but characterized by increasing stylization.

Naturalistic motives had, of course, often been stylized by Minoan artists from a very early period, but the whole-hearted tectonic treatment practised on the 'Palace Style' vases and gems of that period was very different from anything in the Late Minoan I period, and might well be due to Mycenaean influences.

Jerzy Pilecki, in his discussion of heraldic devices in Mycenaean art, has also stressed this tectonic treatment practised by the Mycenaean artist in his engraving of seal stones.

He divided the antithetic groups of Mycenaean art in general, and of seal-stones in particular, into three types. The first of these was the triangular, pedimental, or architectural group which characterizes so many Mycenaean gems, and not a few found in Crete also; it has no obvious prototype in Aegean art before the Mycenaean period but is an old oriental type, possibly borrowed from the Hittites. The finest monumental example of this type in the Aegean is, of course, the famous relief over the lintel of the Lion Gate at Mycenae.

Pilecki's second type is the rectangular, or frieze type which, he suggests, might be considered as a repetition of monumental motifs derived from compositions over lintels, or excerpts adapted from interior friezes. The lintel suggestion is not convincing, but there are plenty of prototypes for Pilecki's second group both in Minoan and in Mycenaean friezes.

Pilecki's third group is the 'miniaturist', where the old Minoan miniature reacts on the Mycenaean heraldic type, sometimes bending and squeezing the design to fit the circular field of the gem, sometimes adding extra motifs either as significant emblems or as landscape features.

Pilecki then proposes a curious theory that the supporting figures of an antithetical group were not merely guardians, but representations of the deity with whom they had an ideological identity, and supports it by those strange designs where the bodies of two lions or other beasts unite in the centre in a single head or mask, and quotes the double-headed eagle of the Hittites as a similar example. Here it is hard to follow him, since his theory seems to depend on representations of very ambiguous meaning, though there may well sometimes have been a confusion of ideas between a deity and his or her sacred animal, especially when there was a possibility that the deity might appear in that form.

Pilecki, however, is probably right in stressing the civic significance of so many heraldic groups in Mesopotamia, and the double-headed eagle appeared as the city arms of Lagash long before the Hittites adopted it. It would not then be surprising if the Lion Gate group at Mycenae represented the civic arms of that city, or the family arms of its ruling family, as suggested by Persson.

Fig. 61. Sealing with warrior frieze

The engraved gems of the Late Minoan II period in Crete and of the Late Helladic II period on the mainland are marked by an increased use of the wheel and the bow-drill, and therefore, though spirited enough, rather more slap-dash in execution than the beautiful engravings of the Late Minoan I period. We witness the beginning of what Wason terms 'the drill style', which was to be spread far and wide in the Early Iron Age.[1]

Many of the seal-stones of the Late Minoan II period were still cut in the old free-field, naturalistic style, though some of these may have been cut in the Late Minoan I period. But others appear more Mycenaean than Minoan, with their tendency towards heraldic and pyramidal groups and their fondness for an exergual line, as if the design had been an excerpt from an architectural frieze. These

1. C. R. Wason, 'The Drill Style in Ancient Gems', *Liverpool Annals*, 1936, pp. 51–6.

Mycenaean characteristics are displayed to the full on the famous Mountain Mother sealings from Knosos, showing the goddess on her sacred mountain guarded by two lions, with her temple behind her and with a male votary saluting her in front (Fig. 39).[1]

What should be our test whether a gem is Minoan or Mycenaean? Hood refers to 'the element of torque or feeling for the round which is habitual in all Minoan engraving', but I think it is a pity to generalize and so weaken the force of Matz's torsion principle, which surely demands not only a feeling for the round but a definite twist, often a spiral twist. Where torsion occurs the work probably is Minoan, but Mycenaean works may and do have a feeling for the round. In addition to torsion, I would suggest that Minoan engravers disliked symmetrical, pyramidal, and heraldic devices, which appealed to the Mycenaean artist. Unfortunately many gems and some of the gold rings, such as the so-called Ring of Nestor, the Thisbe Treasure, and the so-called Ring of Minos, are seriously suspected of being forgeries. Hagen Biesantz has recently tried to answer Nilsson's complaint that 'there seem to be no indications of a technical kind which allow a sure decision' by formulating some rules for the detection of forged gems and rings claimed to be Minoan or Mycenaean work.

The forgeries, he suggests, will betray themselves by one or more of the following faults:

(1) the occurrence of antiquarian details not substantiated elsewhere (not damning by itself as Biesantz admits)

(2) representation of a subject belonging to another artistic circle

(3) the mixing of two different styles which are not part of a regular development

(4) the association of several examples on grounds of style by one hand, when one of these works is known to be a forgery

(5) the occurrence of more modern technique (in perspective for example) than was normal on seals of similar style

(6) appearance of the correct picture in the impression, whereas the Minoans and Mycenaeans produced the correct picture on the original so that the impressions from originals show such anomalies as left-handed swordsmen

(7) outraging of the unity of 'time and place' in the composition.

1. Mesopotamian influences are more evident in Mycenaean than in Minoan art, and the Mountain Mother may ultimately be derived from Ninharsag.

This scheme provides some useful tests, though I do not feel quite happy about Biesantz's seventh criterion. The Ring of Nestor, with its four unrelated or at least not closely connected scenes, certainly does look very odd and must be suspected on other grounds also. It is true also that Minoan and Mycenaean seal-stones in general do depict one isolated scene or incident, but there are gems, especially from Crete, which look rather like excerpts from a frieze and which very possibly reproduce motives from the frescoes of palaces and villas. I refer of course not to objects bought from dealers, like the cylinder from Hagia Pelagia, but to the certainly genuine examples found in excavations such as the gold ring from the Agora at Athens, or the seal impressions with marching warriors from Knosos (Fig. 61).

On the whole Biezant's criteria are useful and save us from rejecting all gems and rings not found in archaeological excavations – a counsel of despair which would deprive us of most of our material so far as gems and rings are concerned. Of the seals from Warrior Grave 3 at Ayios Ioannis, the fine lentoid seal 21 and the prism lentoid 22 seem to be good native Minoan work, but No. 20 might be Mycenaean, and the cylinder 23 might be Syro-Phoenician work from somewhere like Ugarit or Byblos.[1]

The cylindrical bead seal from the Royal Tomb at Isopata and the two lentoids from the Tomb of the Mace-Bearer are typical Minoan work, and I think the same is true of the fine gold ring found there because of its asymmetrical arrangement, a question of some importance since so few gold rings have been found in Crete in archaeological excavations and doubts have been raised concerning the genuine character of those bought from peasants or dealers. The Isopata ring shows four women indulging in an orgiastic dance in a field of lilies, and the goddess herself has deigned to visit her worshippers in the form of a small figure descending from the sky with her locks flying upwards, as do the locks of all Minoan deities making their epiphanies from the heavens.

Seals found in tombs, of course, are quite often earlier than the other objects associated with them. Thus the lentoid carnelian from the Late Minoan III A Tomb 99 at Zapher Papoura cannot itself be much later than the Late Minoan I B period, and the splendid gem

1. M. S. F. Hood and P. De Jong, *Annual of the British School at Athens*, 1952, p. 275 and Fig. 16.

found by Bosanquet in a very late *tholos* tomb at Praisos cannot be later than the Late Minoan I A period.

It seems likely that the other Minoan cities continued during the second Late Minoan period to subsist in a comfortable but provincial obscurity, deprived of any external power they may once have possessed, and rapidly losing even their commercial power to Mycenae and Pylos and the new Achaean colony at Knosos.

If we exclude the abnormal site of Knosos, it is easier to find examples of Late Minoan II vases in the far east at Palaikastro and at Zakros than at sites farther west, and there is more evidence of building and prosperity, yet there is no evidence there of an Achaean settlement. Perhaps the Eteo-Cretans from Seteia eastwards were 'Quislings', glad possibly to escape from the heavy hand of Minoan Mallia, and therefore perhaps not unwilling to establish friendly relations with the new Achaean power at Knosos. There is not much evidence on this point, but there is at least a faint suggestion that the east end of the island was relatively prosperous and on friendly terms with Knosos.

CHAPTER II

The Decadence of Minoan Crete: The Mycenaean Empire

MINOAN power terminated in a sudden and widespread but rather mysterious disaster. At Knosos Evans found abundant evidences of the destruction of the Palace of Minos by fire, and of its systematic looting, but very few human bones. If its inhabitants were not carried off wholesale into captivity, they must have had time to escape. Moreover the Minoan culture did not vanish overnight like the Minoan empire. After an interval refugees of the same race and religion apparently, and indeed with the same culture but on a much lower standard, began to squat and even build shrines in the ruins of the palaces and villas of the princes and nobles. It is possible that the upper classes were nearly wiped out by the great disaster, but it is clear that a large number of the common people must have survived.

A lucky chance enabled Evans to date this disaster with considerable accuracy. Painted pottery of the type found in the reoccupation period at Knosos was found in Egypt in the city of Akhetaten at Tell-el-Amarna founded by the heretic Pharaoh Akh-en-aten and abandoned after his death. Such pottery must therefore be dated between 1375 and 1350 B.C., and even though we now know that this pottery is a Mycenaean not Late Minoan fabric, this does not affect the chronology, since the same Mycenaean pottery is found at Knosos in strata immediately on top of the debris from the great fire.

But what was the cause of this catastrophe, which was not confined to Knosos but seems to have been experienced all over the island? The same destruction (followed, accompanied, or preceded by looting) seems to have affected Phaistos and Hagia Triada in the Mesara, Tylisos, Amnisos, Nirou Khani, Mallia, Pseira, Gournia, and Mochlos in the north, and in the east, though perhaps to a lesser degree, Palaikastro and Zakros.

What was the cause of so widespread a disaster? Was it caused by foreign invasion, by internal revolutions, or by natural causes such as earthquakes and floods (which curiously often cause fires as well)? It is clear that Mycenae benefited by the collapse of Crete, but this does not prove that the mainland Greeks were the primary cause of it.

Sir Arthur Evans, after considering the possibility that the great Cretan catastrophe at the end of the Late Minoan II period might have been caused by an invasion from the mainland, had rejected this idea in favour of the theory that the disaster was due to a terrible earthquake or series of quakes, and to the floods and fires that so often follow in their train. The most celebrated flood legend in Greece, that of the Thessalian Deucalion (not to be confused with the Cretan hero of that name), was traditionally supposed to have taken place about 1330 B.C. There were flood stories also on some other islands, such as Rhodes and Samothrace. If we could follow the suggestion made by Frost, and supported by Marinatos and Seltman, that Plato's story of Atlantis, that civilized island overwhelmed by a marine flood, was a garbled account of the destruction of Minoan Crete preserved in Egyptian records, then indeed we might have a folk memory of the catastrophe of 1400 B.C., but this interpretation at present lacks confirmatory evidence.[1]

Marinatos has supported the theory of the destruction of the Minoan empire by natural causes, but in a new form. He would associate the abandonment of Amnisos, and of other sites on or near the north coast of Crete after the Late Minoan I period, with the great eruption that blew up a large part of the Cycladic island of Thera and submerged a large area, leaving three islands, Thera, Therasia, and Aspronisi, as the only portions of what had been known as *Kalliste*, the 'fairest' of the Cycladic Isles. A large part of the present Thera is now buried in volcanic ash and pumice to a depth of thirty metres, and one of the strangest sights I have ever seen is the fields of flourishing vines and tomato plants growing out of lumps of pumice stone with apparently no other soil to support them.

Theophanes, the Byzantine historian, in describing the much smaller eruption on the same island in A.D. 726, tells how the pumice reached the shores of Asia Minor and Macedonia, and to this day it

---

1. K. T. Frost, 'The Critics and Minoan Crete', *Journal of Hellenic Studies*, 1939, p. 189; S. Marinatos, 'Perí toú thrýlou tis Atlantidos', *Kretika Chronika*, 1950, p. 195; C. Seltman, 'Life in Ancient Crete', *History Today*, 1952, p. 332.

is easy to pick up small lumps of pumice anywhere along the north coast of Crete.

Marinatos, arguing from the size of the prehistoric crater (eighty-three square kilometres in extent and six hundred metres deep), maintains that the great eruption which he assigns to about 1500 B.C. must have exceeded that of Krakatoa in A.D. 1883, and must therefore have been accompanied by an even greater series of tidal waves and earthquakes affecting all the neighbouring islands, including Crete. I should prefer to have dated this eruption of Thera about 1400 B.C. (though there may of course have been two serious outbreaks of the volcano) since the absence of Late Minoan II pottery except at Knosos can now be explained on other grounds. Otherwise I favour the theory of Marinatos, who points out that the Krakatoa eruption, with its much smaller crater of only 22·8 kilometres, caused tidal waves twenty-seven metres high, devastated the coasts of Java and Sumatra, and was responsible for the loss of 36,000 lives. Now Thera is only one hundred kilometres north of Crete, but at one point the sea reaches a depth of over 1800 metres, so that the tidal waves of the Cycladic earthquake should have been considerably higher and more frequent than those of Krakatoa.

A Cycladic settlement on Thera, with pottery imitating Late Minoan I types, was overwhelmed and buried in the debris from this earthquake, and it is not unnatural to suppose that the island and coastal settlements on the north of Crete, such as the harbour town of Knosos, Amnisos, Nirou Khani, Mallia, and Gournia were destroyed at the same time or shortly afterwards by the tidal waves and earthquakes.

Marinatos had supposed that Knosos had escaped serious destruction by reason of its greater height and distance from the sea, but I think the palace may have been destroyed by earthquake and fire at that time, even though it may have escaped the tidal waves.

The absence of the Late Minoan II culture (1450–1400 B.C.) from sites other than Knosos, except for an occasional import, can now be better explained by the presence of an Achaean dynasty at Knosos, rather than by assuming that Knosos persisted later than the other Cretan cities. The late Sir William Ridgeway always maintained stoutly that the Minos of the legend of Theseus and the Minotaur must have been an Achaean king, and his theory, till recently rather unpopular, has now been magnificently vindicated by Ventris's reading of the Linear Script B tablets as documents in 'Achaean' Greek, using the term Achaean not in the limited sense in which it was applied in classical times but in the wider sense in which it is used by Homer in the *Iliad*.

Among other causes which may have contributed to the abandonment of Cretan sites was the failure of Minos's naval expedition to Sicily. This story was already known to Herodotus, probably from his Samian sources, who would be familiar with the west Cretan version of the legend as told in Kydonia. Kleidemos again knew of it in the fourth century, but his attempt to conflate it with the tradition that Daedalus was born in Athens makes his story unconvincing.[1] Diodorus Siculus, who completed his history in the reign of Augustus, gives a coherent and reasonable account, which would appear to be derived partly from fifth-century sources like Herodotus, partly from Cretan historians of the Hellenistic period, and partly from the folklore of his native island of Sicily. How strong those Sicilian traditions were in the second decade of the fifth century B.C. is proved by the action of Theron, the tyrant of Akragas, who discovered what he claimed to be the bones of Minos, and sent them back to Crete to be reburied there. Herodotus, in the seventh book of his history, gives an account of this western expedition of Minos in pursuit of his runaway engineer, Daedalus, but does not mention the name of the Sicilian king, Kokalos. Herodotus, presumably drawing on his Samian–Cretan sources, gives some interesting details, such as the five years' unsuccessful siege of the city of Kamikos by the Cretans after the death of Minos, and the very interesting local detail that all the peoples of Crete had taken part in this expedition except the citizens of Polichne and Praisos. The most interesting item provided by Diodorus, obviously derived from the Sicilian legends, is his description of Minos's burial place as 'a tomb of two storeys, in the part which was underground they placed the bones, and in that which lay open to gaze they made a shrine of Aphrodite', a description which reminded Evans of the form of the Temple Tomb at Knosos, a royal tomb that the classical Cretans never saw, since it was buried

---

1. For the confusion between a legendary artist named Daedalus of Bronze Age date and the alleged founder of the Dedalic School of sculpture see p. 340; and for Samians in Crete see p. 350.

for some three thousand years. The resemblance between the tomb and Diodorus's description may be a coincidence, but it is easier to explain it by supposing there had been a genuine tradition of such a tomb underlying the Sicilian folklore.

The fire that destroyed Minoan halls would have had less effect if the central pillars had not been of wood, and this accounts for the good preservation of most of the pillar crypts with central piers of ashlar stonework. The account of Samson's destruction of the Philistine palace at Gaza becomes less fantastic and more credible if we imagine him as pulling together two central Mycenaean wooden columns probably affected by dry rot.[1]

Ruined adobe houses tend to retain their walls. The material – clay – unlike stones, is not worth the trouble of carting away to be used elsewhere for other constructions. If the inhabitant of a destroyed adobe house should return and desire to build another on the same spot he simply levels the walls and builds his new house at a slightly higher level. This is the explanation why mounds consisting of the accumulation of prehistoric villages of mudbrick houses are so much higher as a rule than sites of the classical and historic periods, where building materials were re-used and the levels of the new buildings did not differ much from that of their predecessors. I think, therefore, that the great disaster approximately dated 1400 B.C. may probably have been due to natural causes, such as earthquakes followed by fires and in the coastal cities tidal waves, without excluding the possibility that it may have been aggravated by human actions, such as raids and revolutions following the collapse of the Sicilian expedition. In the nineteenth century A.D., when Ireland was struggling for Home Rule, it used to be stated that 'England's misfortune was Ireland's opportunity', and we may perhaps claim that in the fifteenth and fourteenth centuries B.C. Knosos's misfortune was Mycenae's opportunity.

During the fourteenth century B.C. Achaean settlers seem to have colonized most of the more fertile parts of the island, and enslaved many of the native population. The more virile elements of the

1. Professor Mallowan, however, points out that the Mesopotamian records reveal many evidences of such destruction; probably palaces and temples were easier to fire than cottages, because there would be more timber and more air space.

native Cretans fled to the hills and founded new villages, such as Axos in the Mylopotamos district, Prinias on the watershed between the northern plains and the Mesara, Karphi in Lasithi, and Vrokastro and Effendi Kavousi in the Merabello district.

EFFECTS ON MINOAN TRADE

Even in the sixteenth century, trade with the western Mediterranean seems to have been in Mycenaean rather than in Cretan hands, while in the fifteenth century Mycenae managed also to capture most of the trade with Egypt, Cyprus, and the Levant in general.

In Crete, however, the Minoan culture persisted in a weakened and decadent form. There are few imports of Egyptian alabaster vases, little jewellery or engraved gems in comparison with the previous period, and no painted frescoes, with the one curious and abnormal exception, the painted sarcophagus of Hagia Triada. Fresco painters and all the best gem cutters seem to have emigrated to the mainland, where there were richer patrons and a better market for their work. The pottery immediately succeeding the catastrophe in Crete, which in Furumark's classification is Late Minoan III A 2, I would term simply Late Minoan III A, preferring to regard the short-lived style which he terms Late Minoan III A 1 as simply the last pottery of the Late Minoan II B period. This is merely a matter of convenience, so that we may keep Evans's correlation of the great disaster with the end of the second Late Minoan period. The contemporary Late Helladic III A 1 style of the mainland is a well-balanced if rather dull style, with ornaments, derived mainly from the Late Helladic I repertoire, usually confined to the shoulder and with only horizontal girding bands decorating the belly and foot of the vase.

REVIVAL OF MINOAN SHRINES

Of the larger settlements in the lowlands perhaps the only examples we can quote as surviving without great change through the fourteenth century are Palaikastro and Zakros in the far east. There was more continuity, however, in the religious than in the civic life of the Minoan towns, and shrines of the reoccupation period can be quoted from most of the great Minoan centres. At Knosos two small rooms in the south-east part of the ruined Palace of Minos were reconstructed and converted into a shrine of the Household Goddess, dubbed by Evans the Shrine of the Double Axes. Here were preserved all the essential features of a Minoan shrine, but in the cheapest form. (See p. 222.) We gain the impression on the whole that the reoccupation of the lowlands of Crete by Minoan refugees was rather a gradual process, and that the first movement came from the priests. The worship at the old shrines revived before the civil life did, but by the thirteenth century B.C. civil life was also beginning to recover. At Mallia the structure that the French excavators cautiously describe as 'the diagonal building' (Fig. 25) should also, I think, be regarded as a shrine of the reoccupation period, though no sacred utensil or vases from it seem to have survived. These small shrines recall the simplest form of the '*megaron* house' and look forward to the simplest form of the classical temples, the so-called *templum in antis*, which is simply a long narrow room entered through a porch with two columns between the *antae*, or side-posts, though the Late Minoan examples usually have either only one column or else none at all between the *antae*. But if the architectural form of these shrines has been affected by northern models, the ledge at the back and the figurines and other furniture, when preserved, remain solidly Minoan to remind us that the deity and the ritual are Cretan.

The furniture of these Late Minoan III shrines is a travesty of those that had existed in the Minoan palaces.[1] The figurines of the goddesses are of pottery, or occasionally of bronze, but not of ivory or faience, though small faience beads of ladies or goddesses in flounced skirts are found. There are few stone vases, except at Palaikastro which seems to have escaped the worst of the disaster; pedestal lamps in stone still occur there, but the pedestals are shorter than formerly and have a moulded band half-way up. Steatite bowls of the 'bird's nest' and 'blossom' type still continue at Palaikastro, but many, perhaps most, of these may probably have been family heirlooms made in Middle Minoan times and still in use. Occasionally stone vases are found on other sites also.

1. See Plate 21 and Fig. 43. The date of the town shrine at Gournia might be Late Minoan III or Late Minoan I, but its furniture is unquestionably Late Minoan III.

In general the Eteo-Cretan country east of Seteia seems to have escaped from the worst effects of the floods, and earthquakes, and so to have been better able to hold out against Achaean colonists. Thus Zakros has one of the best-constructed and most comfortable houses of the period.

POTTERY OF THE REOCCUPATION PERIOD

The Late Minoan III A pottery of this reoccupation period starts with stirrup jars, deep bowls, cups, jugs, and *larnakes* adorned with degenerate versions of Late Minoan II 'Palace Style' motifs, and combines them in a loose, rather tasteless fashion developing into a 'close style' in which the main object of the painter seems to be a *horror vacui*, a terror of leaving any part of the vase undecorated (Fig. 62), in great contrast to the rather industrialized, but very competent, decoration of the contemporary Late Helladic III A vases introduced by the Achaean colonists, who usually confined their main ornaments to the neck and shoulder, and only painted well-spaced girding bands on the body and foot of the vase.

Mainland influences are discernible, however, also in the Late Minoan III pottery, especially in the increasing popularity of certain shapes such as the squat alabastron, the 'pilgrim bottle', the *kylix* (a champagne cup), and the small pear-shaped amphora with three handles, all forms occurring in Crete at an earlier date, but hitherto much more popular on the mainland.

During this period we may observe the gradual adoption of the Minoan–Mycenaean style based on the Late Minoan II of Knosos by other Cretan areas which had been wont to use and manufacture pottery of Late Minoan I A and Late Minoan I B types during the second half of the fifteenth century. Furumark has discerned two main groups in this Late Minoan III A pottery, one basing its decoration on the old 'free-field unity' system native to Minoan Crete, and the other on the banded-zone system introduced by the Achaean immigrants. At first the whole vase was covered by horizontal zones of ornament with no special regard to the tectonic divisions of the vase, but this was soon replaced by a more balanced system whereby the main decoration was confined to the broadest part of the vase, where the handles and spouts were placed. Later still this tectonic arrangement was further emphasized by subdivisions into vertical panels, or by breaking up the intervals between the handles and spouts into triangular quadrants. The vertical panel division is particularly characteristic of many of the larger vases of the Late Minoan III A style. Western Crete, where the Minoan population, though well distributed, had always been relatively sparse, naturally succumbed more easily to the Achaean infiltration. The first extensive Mycenaean settlement in the west of which we have archaeological evidence would appear to be that at Atsipadhais, where the tombs are filled with Late Helladic III A and B pottery and contain a number of Mycenaean 'dollies', the little clay figurines so typical of Late Helladic III B sites on the mainland and easily distinguishable from Cretan figurines.

Another cemetery of chamber tombs in the west, outside Khania, contained both Late Minoan III A and Late Helladic III A vases, and the same mixture occurred in the Zapher Papoura cemetery excavated by Evans near Knosos. Typical Late Minoan III A pottery was also found in chamber tombs at Kalyvia in the Mesara, in *larnax* burials at Gournia, Hierapetra, Seteia and other sites in eastern Crete, and in the 'Bathroom' in block C at Palaikastro.

The Late Minoan III A *kylices* differ from their mainland contemporaries in having hollow pedestals.[1] The 'Vapheio cup' has died out and been replaced by 'tea-cups' and by small cups with straight sides and a handle perched on the flaring rim. Bridge-spouted saucers with a handle at one side, or opposite the spout, or without any handle at all, are quite common.

The circular *pyxis* reappears as a Cretan vase-shape, and for the first time we encounter domed covers for lamps as in Rhodes.

In the luxury arts of the Late Minoan III A period it is often hard to distinguish between Minoan and Mycenaean work, but the best patrons were the Achaean princes and the best Cretan workman had probably emigrated to the mainland. Frescoes appear on various sites on the mainland, but no frescoes have survived in Crete except the unique and very interesting painting adorning a sarcophagus in a Late Minoan III chamber tomb at Hagia Triada (Plate 20). No other

---

1. Two-handled goblets with characteristic decoration and fabric are found in Late Helladic II deposits on the mainland and occasionally at Knosos, but not elsewhere in Crete.

sarcophagus is decorated in this fashion, but we are entering on a period when pottery ones with designs painted on the clay were to become normal, and Nilsson has suggested that this was the grave of a Mycenaean chief and that the local Minoan painter employed to decorate the sarcophagus had used the technique and the motifs which he would have employed to decorate a Minoan shrine.

A few engraved gems have been found associated with Late Minoan III A pottery (for example Tomb 99 at Zapher Papoura), but most seals assigned to this period are dated purely on grounds of style. They include some haematite cylinder seals with a mixture of Minoan and oriental subjects, reflecting influences from Syria or Cyprus. A tomb at Aptsa, dated 1400–1350, contained a prism seal that looks about 500 years older than the objects associated with it.[1]

The Late Minoan III B style of pottery[2] (1300–1200 B.C.) is rather more uniform than its predecessor. The absorption by the Achaean power of those areas of Crete where the Late Minoan I style had reigned resulted in the development of a pottery style in which were mingled late Mycenaean elements along with motifs derived from the older traditions of the Late Minoan I A and Late Minoan I B styles and others derived from the Knosian Palace Style of the Late Minoan II period. The general effect is rather dull, and neither the ornaments nor the paint are the equal of the contemporary Mycenaean pottery imported from the Peloponnese.

GEMS

Gem engraving still continued, as is illustrated by the remains from the lapidary's workshop at Knosos. The shapes are normally lentoid, the material steatite, and the designs include not only such old favourites as the cow suckling its calf and the lion springing on a bull, but also representations of dogs attacking goats, sheep, or oxen. A seal from Arkhanes illustrates the motif of a well-known Mycenae dagger, namely the hunting cat attacking wild duck.

A certain amount of jewellery also occurs in Late Minoan III B

1. S. Xanthoudides, 'Ek Kretes', *Ephemeris Archaiologiki*, 1904, p. 1 and Fig. 4.
2. Furumark calls this Late Minoan III B 1 and his Late Minoan III B 2 corresponds to my Late Minoan III C.

chambers. Thus Tomb 7 at Zapher Papoura had a gold-plated bronze ring with the design of a sphinx, and a necklace of beads with the double argonaut design, which appears also on beads from a tomb near Phaistos. Further jewellery was found in Tombs 66 and 99 at Zapher Papoura, in Tombs 3 and 6 at Isopata, and in the Mavrospilaion cemetery.

THE MIDDLE-EAST STYLE

By 1200 B.C., or perhaps a little earlier, we are conscious of a new form of pottery decoration, a last dying flicker of the old Minoan spirit, in what Pendlebury terms the 'Middle-East Style'. It certainly was absent from western Crete, which seems to have been almost completely Hellenized and where the best pottery is all Mycenaean, but the new style was current in central Crete, both at Knosos and in the Mesara, and was exported in some quantities to Rhodes, while isolated examples have been found at Kalymnos, in Attica, Asine and Delphi and even as far west as Scoglio del Tonno near Taranto.

Not many vases of this style from Crete have been published, and the examples from Karphi were often so affected by weathering that it was impossible to illustrate their designs, but the published examples from Crete include a small stirrup jar from the Royal Tomb at Isopata, a tankard from the Psychro Cave,[2] and some sherds from Hagia Triada.[3]

The characteristics of this style as defined by Pendlebury are 'the use of thick solid elements in the decoration, usually fringed and combined with a forest of fine lines and closely hatched subordinate figures. The

Fig. 62. Late Minoan III C vase ('Middle-East style')

1. W. Taylour, *Mycenaean Pottery in Italy*, 1958, pp. 108, 131 considers most of these to be Rhodian, as some may well be, but not, I think, all of them.

2. D. G. Hogarth, 'The Dictaean Cave', *Annual of the British School at Athens*, 1900, p. 103.

3. M. Borda, *Arte Creteo-Miceneo del Museo Pigorini di Roma*, 1946, Plates XXXVII, XXXVIII.

octopus motive is a favourite one and though clearly distinguishable it has become divorced from all reality and is treated as a pure pattern.' The most imposing vases adorned in this style are some large stirrup jars from Rhodes, and it is of course quite possible that these were local Rhodian imitations. The Cretan origin of the style, however, may be inferred from the fact that vases in this style from other districts are always stirrup jars, and only in Crete do we find different shapes, such as deep bowls and bridge-spouted tankards, in this same style. Elsewhere, both in the west and in the east, we find simply a gradual decay of the Late Minoan III and Late Helladic III styles.

A SYRO-PHOENICIAN CULT IN CRETE

The trade routes with Egypt and the East, however, were still open, and the Achaean merchants were quite ready to exploit them.

To the Late Minoan III period in general belongs a series of metal statuettes representing the Syrian god Reshef, usually in bronze but occasionally in some other material such as silver. They have been found in various parts of the Levant and must have been made, neither in Crete nor in the Peloponnese, but in some Phoenician or Syrian factory.

Recently an example of such a bronze figure with round shield and sickle-bladed sword, of the type which the Egyptians called a *khepesh* (and which some archaeologists wrongly dub a *harpe*) was found by the French excavators at Delos. H. G. de Santerre and J. Tréheux, in publishing this figurine, give a list of similar statuettes, which they do not claim to be complete, but which seems much fuller than any other.

Fig. 63. Reshef figure from Sybrita

This list of de Santerre and Tréheux emphasizes the overwhelming evidence in favour of a Phoenician or south Syrian factory for these works, but they were popular imports into Greece and Crete in the Late Minoan III period, as may be seen by the following supplement to this list of thirty-eight figurines:

39, 40	bronze statuettes in Athens from Mycenae and Tiryns
41	figurine from Sybrita, Crete, in the Ashmolean Museum, Oxford
42	silver figurine in the Ashmolean from Nezero in Thessaly
43	bronze figurine from Thermon
44	bronze figurine found at Schernen in east Prussia
45, 46	two statuettes found at Olympia
47, 48	four geometric statuettes from Delphi
49	the 'Karapanos' statuette from Dodona

His title in the Karatepe inscription, 'Reshef of the Birds', suggests a comparison with the Minoan 'Master of the Animals' and with figures such as the gold figurine from 'the Aegina treasure'.

This deity was the young 'Baal' of Phoenicia and could be hailed as Teshub, Hadad, Mot, or Seth according to the nationality of his worshippers. It is possible of course that the Mycenaeans and the Cretans of Late Minoan times may have equated him with Apollo, or the Minoan 'Master of the Animals'.

THE FOLK-MIGRATIONS OF THE
TWELFTH CENTURY B.C.

The twilight of the Minoan and Mycenaean cultures is illuminated by some references to the peoples of the Aegean in the contemporary records of the Hittites and the Egyptians. In the third year of the reign of Mursil, Great King of the Hatti (about 1331 B.C.), the official records refer to a country called Ahhiyawa, associated with the name of a city called Millawanda. Many scholars believe that the country in question was an Achaean state, either in the Peloponnese or in one of the Aegean islands such as Cyprus, and that Millawanda was Miletus, which claimed to be a colony of Milatos in Crete. Some years later, perhaps still in the reign of Mursil II or perhaps in that of his successor Muwatallis (1306–1282 B.C.), often referred to as

Mutallu, a letter was written by the Great King of Hatti concerning Tawagalawas, son of Antarawas, a vassal of the King of Ahhiyawa, based on Millawanda. This letter has received rather more publicity than it deserved because the Swiss scholar Forrer identified these princes with Eteokles, son of Andreus, legendary kings of Orchomenos. Most scholars, however, now reject both this identification and also Forrer's attempt to identify a certain Attarissyas, King of Ahhiyawa and a contemporary of the Hittite king Tudhalias IV (1250–1220 B.C.), with Atreus, the father of Agamemnon. The dates fit, but neither the form of the words nor the places associated with these names seem suitable. G. L. Huxley compared Attarissyas to Teiresias, and Sayce even preferred to identify Attarissyas with Perseus. Tudhalias may be the same name as the Greek Tantalus, but it does not follow that we can identify the father of Pelops with any particular Tudhalias, or Achilles's opponent Telephus with any particular Hittite prince named Telepinush.

The one inference that we can draw from these Hittite records with some degree of probability is the existence, somewhere in the Levant, of an important Achaean power during the thirteenth century B.C., and this is confirmed by the archaeological evidence. How many such states there were is more debatable, but that of Mycenae was certainly the most important, and those of Pylos, Orchomenos, and Thebes also of considerable standing.

The Hittite empire collapsed about 1190 B.C. and we therefore hear no more about Achaeans in the records from Boghaz Koi. Here, however, the Egyptian records help us with some references to the extraordinary ferment that was brewing in the international affairs of the Near East at this time, a ferment that began with the destruction of Hatti and the racial movement of the Phrygians from Macedonia into Asia Minor, and culminated in the attacks of the sea raids and the land raids on Egypt. Priam's campaign against the Amazons on the Sangarius River and Agamemnon's capture of Troy are all part of the same story, but so many pieces of the jig-saw puzzle are missing that we cannot form a coherent picture of the whole. The first invasion of the northerners broke against the shores of Egypt even before the collapse of Hatti when, in 1221 B.C., the Egyptian Pharaoh had to repel a Libyan fleet that attacked the Delta supported by a motley group of allies whose names suggested that

they came from Asia Minor. The only national contingent we ca
identify with absolute certainty is that of the Lycians, though th
Tursha are perhaps to be identified with the Tyrsenoi, the Asiati
nation which colonized Etruria.[1] The Shakalsha have been identifie
with the people of Sagalassos and the Shardana with Sardians c
Sardinians. In favour of the last-named identification is the fact tha
the Shardana wore helmets with two horns and carried very lon
swords and small round shields like the figures found in the Nuragh
cemeteries of Sardinia (though the Nuraghic culture is not suppose
to begin before 1000 B.C.) Some of the Shardana, whoever the
were, remained in Egypt and were incorporated as mercenaries i
the Egyptian army.[2] Some of the raiders used cut-and-thrust sword
with narrow tang of a type that became popular in Europe.[3]

The most interesting to us, however, of the Libyan allies are th
Akwasha, who are identified by most historians with the Achaean
and the people of Ahhiyawa in the earlier Hittite records. The ver
same year (1221) Meneptah had had to contend with revolts i
Palestine in the cities of Gaza and Askalon, later celebrated as strong
holds of the Philistines. Indeed the Philistines may have already bee

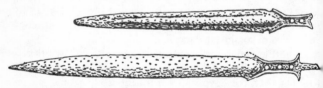

Fig. 64. Swords from Mouliana

infiltrating into this coastland since, under the name Pulasati, the
appear as one nation among the motley horde of northerners tha
overran Syria and Palestine and attacked Egypt from the north-ea
in 1190 B.C.[4] Of the previous raiders from the west only the Shakalsh

1. But when and how many? For the theory that the Etruscan nation gre
up in Italy, see M. Pallottino, *The Etruscans* (Penguin Books, 1955), Chapter
2. See also R. Dussaud, *La Lydie et ses voisins*, 1930, p. 37.
3. C. F. A. Schaeffer, 'A Bronze Sword from Ugarit', *Antiquity*, 1955,
226.
4. For J. L. Myres's suggestion that Pulusati = Pelasgians, see *Who We
The Greeks?*, 1930, p. 143.

appear again, and the Akwasha are not mentioned. Of the new names the identifications for Thekel and Weshesh are very uncertain, but fresh evidence has appeared in support of the theory that the people termed Denyen in the Egyptian records were those that Homer calls Danaoi, a term he used as a rather loose equivalent of Achaeans. The recent decipherment of a Phoenician text at Karatepe in Cilicia suggests that these Denyen were the inhabitants of the plain of Adana, a district which still recalls their name and which was traditionally colonized by Mopsos of Argos, shortly after the fall of Troy.[1] The same people also appear as Danuna in the Assyrian records. The curious stories of Danaus and his brother Aegyptus, to which we owe the Greek and modern European names for Egypt (which its inhabitants have always termed Musri), must go back to the traditions of the land raid of the northern peoples on Egypt. The old Bronze Age powers of the Aegean had disappeared or were in a state of collapse. Hatti, Knosos, Troy, and even Mycenae became heaps of ruins, but the successors of these powers had lived long enough in contact with the Bronze Age civilization of these cities to have absorbed much of their culture, and the new states that emerged from the ruins, Phrygia, the late Hittite states such as Carchemish, and the small city states that arose in Greece, though simpler than their predecessors, preserved much of their cultural heritage.

Wace and Albright, for different reasons, would date the transition from the Sub-Mycenaean to the Protogeometric Period not later than 1000 B.C. Desborough's 970 B.C. depended on the date formerly assigned to stratum IV at Tall Abu Hawam in Palestine, now dated fifty years earlier by Van Beek (see Wace and Albright in *The Aegean and the Near East*, edited by S. Weinberg, pp. 134 and 163 respectively). The period between the Dorian invasion and Homer remains very obscure. Whatever we may think of the validity of Ventris's system, there seems little doubt that Greek was spoken in Crete in 1500 B.C. and that the percentage of Greek speakers rapidly increased. Why then was the native script abandoned, and was there a period of complete illiteracy at the end of the Bronze Age before the introduction of the Phoenician alphabet which, with the addition of a few letters,

1. R. D. Barnett, J. Leveen, and C. Moss, 'A Phoenician Inscription from Eastern Cilicia', *Iraq*, 1948, p. 56; see also G. L. Huxley. 'Mycenaean Decline and the Homeric Catalogue of Ships', *University of London Bulletin*, 1956, p. 19.

was to become the official Greek alphabet and the ancestor of all th
modern alphabets of Europe? The date and the method of this trans
mission is still a matter of dispute, but a recent survey of the evidenc
by Margot Falkine has suggested a date between 900 and 863 fo
the transmission, which she thinks may have come via Rhodes.
Signorina Guarducci, however, has suggested that Crete may rathe
have been the medium. By 750 B.C. the modified Phoenician scrip
was in use in Athens, Thebes, Corinth, Thera, and Melos as well a
Crete and Rhodes.

It would appear that the *Iliad* and the *Odyssey* must have bee
composed during the eighth century. 'Homer, then,' says Sir Mauric
Bowra, 'stands at a point where an ancient poetical tradition ha
just been touched by the new art of writing and to this we may ow
some of his subtlety and aptness. But it is to the purely oral art behin
this that we must turn when we wish to examine his relation witl
the past.'[2] This statement needs to be qualified. The art of writin,
was not 'new' in the eighth century B.C., but, even if it had no
died out, it seems that the number of writers must have diminishe
and that oral transmission played an important role in epic poetry

'Heroic poetry', Finley remarks, 'is always oral poetry; it is com
posed orally, often by bards who are illiterate, and it is recited in
chant to a listening audience. Formally it is at once distinguishabl
by the constant repetition of phrases, lines, and whole groups of lines.

The procedure of the composition of an epic lay by an illiterat
poet who dictates it to a literate scribe is illustrated by the Creta
poem *The Song of Daskaloyannis*, composed in A.D. 1796 by a
illiterate cheesemaker and taken down in writing by a literat
shepherd.[3]

1. M. Falkine, *Frühgeschichte und Sprachwissenschaft*, 1948.
2. *Homer and his Forerunners*, 1955, p. 14.
3. See V. Laourdas, *Tó Tragoudhi toú Dhaskaloyánni*, I, 991–8.

CHAPTER 12

The Dorian Colonization, Oriental Influences, and the Growth of the City States

THE DORIAN INFILTRATION INTO CRETE

THE classical traditions concerning the entry into the Peloponnese of the people who spoke a Dorian dialect associated this event with 'the return of the Herakleidai', Herakles's three sons, Temenos, Aristodemos, and Kresphontes, who founded kingdoms, presumably with Dorian support, in Argos, Sparta, and Messenia respectively; and one generation later a certain Tektamos, son of Doros, with a mixed band of Dorians, Achaeans, and Pelasgians was stated to have founded the first Dorian dynasty in Crete.

These traditions must not be taken too seriously, since they have certainly been corrupted, sometimes unintentionally, and sometimes deliberately doctored by later genealogists seeking to bolster up the claims of Hellenistic kings to heroic pedigrees.

Herodotus, however, writing in the fifth century B.C., gives another less detailed account of the Dorian infiltration, which may not be far from the truth in its general outlines. 'In the time of King Deukalion[1] the Dorians lived in Phthiotis, in the time of Doros the son of Hellen they occupied the land under Ossa and Olympus which was called Histiaiotis. From Histiaiotis they were expelled by Kadmeians and dwelt in Pindos, being called Macedonians. Thence they moved to Dryopis (the later Doris) and from Dryopis they came to the Peloponnese and were called Dorians.'[2] Herodotus at least offers us an intelligible and not incredible account of a north Greek tribal group not so much 'moving down the spine of Pindus' (in Wade Gery's phrase), but rather across the mountain

1. Traditionally the late fourteenth century B.C. Thucydides, I, 12; Herodotus, I, 56.

2. See N. G. L. Hammond, 'Epirus and the Dorian Invasion', *Annual of the British School at Athens*, 1932, pp. 131–79.

317

masses shutting in the west sides of Thessaly and the Spercheius district, raiding the fertile lowlands of Boeotia, being repelled by the princely cities of Orchomenos and Thebes, and finally settling on the north side of the Gulf of Corinth in the district later known as Doris.[1]

Moreover Herodotus's account can be reconciled with the legends of the Herakleidai. The first Dorian settlements on the Peloponnese may well have been started by exiled Achaean princes trying to regain lost kingdoms or to usurp those of other princes. We might also be inclined to trust the tradition that the first Dorian settlement in Crete was planted one generation after the foundation of the three Dorian kingdoms in the Peloponnese, but for two awkward passages in Homer suggesting the possibility of early Dorian settlements in Crete and in the Dodecanese before 'the return of the Herakleidai'. The significance of these passages, which admit of more than one interpretation, must now be briefly considered.[2]

The first of these consists of some famous lines from the *Odyssey* Book XIX, 175 ff.) describing Crete and its inhabitants. 'In it are countless people and ninety cities. One tongue is mingled with another. In it are Achaeans, and great-hearted Eteo-Cretans, and Kydonians, and Dorians, in their three tribes, and divine Pelasgians.'

These lines might seem appropriate to the time when Homer wrote (? the eighth century B.C.), but look strange as a description of Crete before the Trojan war. Does Homer's description refer to Crete of the ninth and eighth centuries B.C., or were there really Dorians in Crete in 1200 B.C. or earlier? Strabo, in citing the passage from the *Odyssey*, also quotes a note on it by the historian Staphylos,[3] who stated that the Dorians were in the east, the Eteo-Cretans with their city of Praisos in the south, while the remainder (the Achaeans and Pelasgians), who were the strongest, held the plains. Now in classical times, and perhaps even in Homer's day, the Dorians controlled

1. For the passes traversed see N. G. L. Hammond, 'Epirus and the Dorian Invasion', op. cit., Fig. 7.

2. According to Ventris's and Chadwick's readings of the Mycenaean texts we must allow for the possibility of early settlers coming by sea from the Adriatic side, as Hammond also stresses (loc. cit.) on archaeological and topographical grounds.

3. Staphylos's date is rather uncertain; he has been dated as late as 300 B.C. and must at least be later than the foundation of Naucratis, but he was presumably quoting an earlier tradition.

the Mesara and most of the coastal plains except that of Kydonia. If, therefore, there was ever a time like that described by Staphylos, when the Achaeans and Pelasgians held the rich plains and when the Dorians were confined to the extreme east beyond Seteia and Praisos, such a state of affairs could only have existed at the beginning of the Iron Age before the Argive colonization of Knosos, when we might suppose the existence of small Doric communities in the east, planted probably by colonists from the Dodecanese. Such settlements, however, must have been relatively small and unimportant compared with the Dorian colonies planted later by Argives and Lakonians in the plains of Rethymnon, Herakleion, the Pedhiadha, and the Mesara districts. Even when the Dorians did arrive in Crete they adopted for the most part the local place names, and there are practically none that we can call certainly Doric in origin. Hierapytna, which embodies a north Greek word for rock, might possibly be a Dorian name, but places like Gortyn and Arcadia presumably owe their Peloponnesian names to Achaean settlers.[1] Even such an aggressively Dorian city as Lyttos bears a pre-Hellenic name meaning 'upland'.[2] River names we expect to include a large number of pre-Dorian and even pre-Hellenic names, just as the river names in England and France tend to be Celtic. It is surprising, however, that such an overwhelming proportion of the city names should be pre-Hellenic and it suggests that the classical population of Crete must have been characterized by a large percentage of Minoan blood. On a map of Hellenistic sites in Crete, I noted twenty-one that had modern Greek names (of which the ancient equivalents were unknown), eighteen that seemed to have pre-Hellenic names, three ancient Greek names, and two of Venetian origin. Many of the cities famous in classical times bear names that must date back to the Bronze Age if not earlier, cities such as Kydonia, Phalasarna, and Sybrita in the far west, Rethymnon and Lappa in the middle west, Knosos, Tylisos, Rhaukos, Phaistos, Pyranthos, etc., in the centre, Lyttos in the middle east, and Eteia and Praisos in the far east. During the very gradual process of the Hellenization of Crete, large numbers of the native

1. It has been suggested that Gortyn is a Pelasgian name.
2. The description by Polybius (Book IV, Chaps 53–5) of Lyttos as 'the most ancient city of Crete' might possibly imply that it was the earliest Dorian colony; the statement is certainly untrue in any other sense.

population were absorbed into the new states as slaves and dependants, but the more independent elements of the population retired to the hills, and we find settlements of Geometric dates, but still Sub-Minoan in character, occupying hilltop villages at Kavousi and Vrokastro in the east, at Karphi, a key site commanding the road from the coastal plain at Mallia to the upland plain of Lastithi, at Prinias, another key site commanding the most direct route between the north coastal plain and that of the Mesara, and another at Axos commanding another north-south road.

SUB-MINOAN CITIES OF REFUGE

Karphi

The village of Karphi ('the Nail') lies on the saddle just below the jutting peak from which the modern name is derived and which forms a landmark for sailors from Cape Stavros eastwards almost as far as Milatos. 'The Nail' itself was perhaps already a peak sanctuary in the Middle Minoan period, when it must have attracted worshippers from villages in the plain of Lastithi or in the valleys immediately to the north of it, but the pottery from that village site is chiefly in a late version of Pendlebury's 'Middle-East Style'.[1]

The foundation of the Sub-Minoan village on the saddle of this mountain is evidence of a gallant attempt by refugees of Minoan race, whose fathers had known better conditions, to construct something that might recall a small market town comparable to Gournia, but on a site that was exposed to bitter weather in winter and that had obviously been chosen for reasons of defence rather than of comfort. Nevertheless Karphi, like Gournia, also possessed its civic shrine, consisting of a large room entered from the east side, and two smaller rooms on the west side. Towards the north side of the large room there still stand the remains of a large altar, but, if a north wall to this room ever existed, it must have fallen down the precipice on to which the shrine abuts. The cult statues and objects in clay (Plate 21) are particularly interesting, and illustrate how the Minoan cult of the Household Goddess persisted in its native form long after the collapse of the political power of the Minoan state. One of the Karphi

1. M. Seiradhakis suggests that the patterns were influenced by Mycenaean textiles.

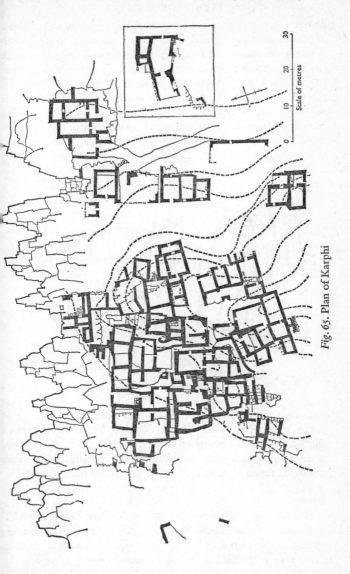

Fig. 65. Plan of Karphi

Scale of metres

0 10 20 30

figurines was taller than the others and had birds instead of Horns of Consecration on her diadem, so perhaps we ought to regard her as the goddess and the two smaller figurines as only attendants (whether human or semi-divine), like the clay votaress in the Shrine of the Double Axes, the faience votaresses of the Snake Goddess in the temple repositories, or the two maidens who stood on each side of the Bronze Apollo of Dreros. (See p. 344 and Plate 27.) The cult objects from this shrine also include a charioteer group, a curious tripod altar with three looped legs and three bulls' heads attached, and a tetragonal clay altar.[1] The period of occupation perhaps lasted from 1050 to 950 B.C.

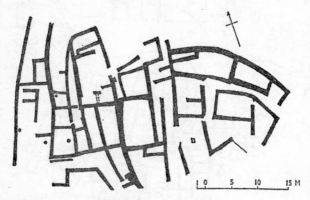

Fig. 66. Houses at Vrokastro

The path leading up from the plain of Lasithi to the village of Karphi served as a primitive 'Appian Way', or Street of Tombs, with small *tholos* tombs opening on to it. The chambers of these tombs were normally rectangular, but were covered by rude, circular vaults resting on rough squinches.

Vrokastro

A similar city of refuge was built at Vrokastro on a lofty hill overlooking the Merabello coast, an easily defensible site, but less uncomfortable than Karphi. The house-plans still ambled about in

1. M. P. Nilsson, *The Minoan-Mycenaean Religion*, 1950, Fig. 81.

the 'agglutinative' manner of Minoan towns, and the streets still had drains along one side, but the long *megaron*-like rooms may reflect Achaean influences. It is still very hard, however, to define where one house ends and another begins. Pendlebury suggested that the existing remains may have belonged to three houses, two of them entered from the south, and a third running east and west with no means of entrance visible.

Kavousi

At Vronda (or 'Thunder Hill') Kavousi, a peak sanctuary had existed in Middle Minoan days, as at Karphi, and the name of this site, coupled with that of Effendi Kavousi, the name of the great

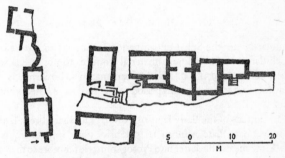

Fig. 67. Houses at Kavousi

mountain overlooking this area and conspicuous along the whole stretch of the Merabello coast, suggests that the deity of the peak sanctuary at Vronda was in all probability the Cretan Zeus, Velchanos.

Here also, on 'Thunder Hill', Minoan refugees gathered in the latest Minoan period and built a small city of refuge, of which Miss Boyd excavated the scanty remains, a forecourt and one or two other rooms. The rooms were constructed with shale slabs set in clay mortar, and were of better masonry than those of Vrokastro, where there was only dry stone walling, and not very good specimens of the method at that.

S. Alexiou has recently excavated a very interesting shrine of a goddess (very probably Eileithyia), on a site near Kavousi, called Pachlitzani Agriadha, founded apparently at the very end of the Late

Minoan III period but frequented by worshippers as late as the sixth century B.C. The little oblong building, with its ledge for the sacred objects, resembles the Late Minoan III household shrines as founded at Knosos, Mallia, Hagia Triada, and Gournia, but the figurines (all feminine) dedicated there include Sub-Minoan, Dedalic, and archaic examples, and one Dedalic plaque represents a naked goddess of the Qadesh type popular in Syria in the Late Bronze Age but rarely, if ever, represented in Minoan art.[1] A large cylindrical clay base with a cable pattern may have belonged to the cult statue of the shrine, possibly (Alexiou suggests) a figure like the one in the Ashmolean Museum said to have come from western Crete, and also paralleled by some cylindrical figurines from Praisos.

THE SUB-MINOAN PERIOD

Furumark dates the Sub-Minoan period from 1075 to 1025 B.C., but Brock dates the Sub-Minoan material from his tombs at Knosos between 1020 and 970 B.C. Sub-Minoan material, however, is rather plentiful in Crete, so that this period might well have lasted a hundred years.[2]

The pottery of the Early Iron Age displays no sharp break from the latest Minoan; Late Minoan III C fabrics glide imperceptibly into Sub-Minoan, and the latter into Protogeometric far more so than on the mainland, where the break between the Sub-Mycenaean and Protogeometric pottery is more defined, especially in Attica, where the repulse of the Dorian invaders who had overrun the Megaris and threatened Athens (a repulse traditionally associated with the self-sacrifice of the last King Kodros) allowed the development of a new Protogeometric style, which strongly affected many of its neighbours.

In Crete, however, the Sub-Minoan pottery was conservative, and the introduction of new shapes and ornaments correspondingly gradual. The Sub-Minoan pottery is perhaps best illustrated by the east

1. The so-called 'Ring of Minos' had a naked goddess, of course (Evans, *Palace of Minos*, IV, p. 957), but was that ring genuine? See Biesantz, op. cit. The naked females on a Middle Minoan vase from Mallia are genuine, but are they divine? See P. Demargne, *Explorations des Nécropoles*, 1945, Plate XXXVII, No. 1.

2. For evidence in favour of the earlier date see W. P. Albright in *The Aegean and the Near East*, 1956, p. 163.

Cretan tombs at Erganos, Vrokastro, and Milatos.[1] The pottery shapes included *larnakes*, *cratera* of a type very popular in Cyprus, stirrup jars, *kylikes* of champagne glass form (a shape that had died out elsewhere), cups with open trough spouts, small beaked jugs, and vase stands. The decoration includes degraded forms of the Minoan octopus.

THE EARLY PROTOGEOMETRIC PERIOD

The next fifty years (970–920 B.C.?) was marked by the appearance in the Knosian tombs of the Early Protogeometric pottery produced by the reaction on the Sub-Minoan pottery of Protogeometric pottery of an advanced character imported from Athens.[2] Thus Tomb 2 at Knosos comes early in the Knosian series,[3] but contained an Athenian *lekythos* of a form characteristic of the Later Protogeometric at Athens, while most of the ground was left in the natural colour of the clay, a trick inherited from the local Sub-Minoan tradition in the island. Some neck-handled and some belly-handled amphorae were probably actually imported from Athens, and certain ornaments such as cross-hatched and chequered panels on lozenges.

Nevertheless the Cretan tradition was so strong that the Early Protogeometric of Knosos, and still more that of Vrokastro, might almost be classed as a variety of Sub-Minoan. Cremation associated with iron weapons was now the rule, but inhumations still happened occasionally, and cremation was not unknown even in the Sub-Minoan period. The later burial in the Mouliana tomb may indeed have belonged to the Geometric period, as argued by Xanthoudides, and the Tylisos example is also open to question; but there can be no doubt at all about the Sub-Minoan date of the cremations in *pithoi* uncovered by van Effenterre at Olous.[4]

The instances of cremation at Vrokastro are on a different footing, because that site was a Sub-Minoan city of refuge occupied by people of Minoan race but probably lasting throughout the Protogeometric and into the earliest Geometric period.

---

1. Of these cemeteries Erganos is the earliest, since the published vases are Late Minoan III C in style.
2. (or 1020–970 B.C.?) V. Desborough, op. cit., pp. 247–9.
3. Brock, op cit., even calls it Sub-Minoan.
4. H. van Effenterre, 'La Nécropole d'Olonte', *Études crétoises*, 1948.

The Early Protogeometric pottery is well illustrated by tombs from Ayios Ioannis, Fortetsa, and the district round Knosos in general – chamber tombs like the Late Minoan types but usually with shorter *dromoi* or no *dromos* at all. Cremations were normal but inhumation also occurred. Many Sub-Minoan vase-shapes continued, such as the globular stirrup jar, the *amphoriskos*, the 'feeding bottle', the *crater*, and the three varieties of *pyxis*, but the 'bird vase' developed three legs, and the stirrup jars and deep bowls conical bases. The old Minoan and Mycenaean form of *crater* was replaced by a high, bell-shaped variety and neck-handled and belly-handled amphorae appear (following their Attic prototypes fairly closely).

Most vases had plain girding bands separating the shoulders from the belly and the belly from the foot. The main painted ornaments comprised simple linear patterns such as concentric circles on the shoulders of the amphorae, hatched triangles on those of the stirrup jars or small jugs, and wavy lines on those of the *amphoriskoi*.

At Vrokastro the Protogeometric period is best represented by the contents of Chamber Tomb 1. Here, however (as might be expected in this Eteo-Cretan district), the influence of the Attic Protogeometric style is much weaker than at Knosos.

Only one vase, a neck-handled amphora, seems to be derived from an Attic vase form; the remainder are variations of Sub-Minoan or Sub-Mycenaean forms. The bronze tripod stand from Chamber Tomb 1 is of Cypriote type parallel to one from Tomb 11 at Fortetsa.

The Early Protogeometric period is well illustrated by Tomb 6 at Fortetsa and Tomb 1 at Ayios Ioannis. The latter, opened in 1939 and published 1960, contained the only recorded inhumation of this period, as well as at least one cremation in a cinerary jar with lid. Associated with the inhumation were a bronze belt and two iron spearheads. The other vases in this grave were five neck amphorae, one *amphoriskos*, four simple craters and one with pedestal base, four *oenochoae*, one jar, one *pyxis*, one stirrup cup, twenty-eight deep bowls, and nine or possibly ten cups. Three bronze rings and three clay beads might have belonged either to the inhumation (which was a man) or to the cremation.

Tomb 6 at Fortetsa contained two imported vases, a footed bowl certainly imported from Attica, and an *oenochoe*, probably from the same source from which the Protogeometric style seems to have expanded into other parts of Greece. The native tradition was represented by a splendid *crater* with panel designs consisting of two affronted goats like those of the Mouliana *crater* on one side, and of ships on the other.

The Middle Protogeometric period (920–870 B.C.) is illustrated by Tombs 3, 4, and 5 in the Fortetsa cemetery and by some cremations in the Khaniale Tekke tombs; Sub-Minoan shapes such as bell *cratera* and stirrup cups still persist. The necked *pithos* was also a common form. The ovoid cremation *pithoi*, rather clumsy in shape, had double-arc handles, sometimes alternating with a pair of vertical ones, and a very broad shoulder of geometric ornament. In this period there would appear to have been increased contacts with Cyprus, and Cyprian imports include a bronze tripod stand on which stood a bronze cauldron and two iron spears of Cypriote type, from Tomb 11. A few Cypriote vases appear and a large number (especially the duck-shaped *askoi*) appear to reflect Cypriote prototypes.

Tha Late Protogeometric period (870–850 B.C.) was short and ill-defined, but is perhaps best illustrated by Tomb 50 at Fortetsa. It is marked by the appearance of a new vase shape, the *hydria*, perhaps imported from the Cyclades, though it is derived from a Mycenaean prototype, and by the fact that the false spout of the stirrup cups is no longer closed but open.

THE TRANSITION TO THE GEOMETRIC CULTURE

The transitional 'Protogeometric B period' (850–800 B.C.) was contemporary with the reigns of Shalmaneser III and Shamshi Adad V in Assyria, and of Mesa, King of Moab, and with Athaliah's massacre of the prophets in Judah.

The 'Protogeometric B' pottery is marked by some new vase shapes and decorative motifs, but the fabric and technique remain the same, and many of the older vase forms continue, such as the bell *crater*, necked *pithos*, *kálathos*, bird vase, and straight-sided *pyxis*. To this period belongs a group in the Giamalakis collection including a unique clay shrine (Fig. 68). A shape new to Crete was the stemmed *crater*, which seems to have been imported from Early Geometric circles outside the island, probably from the Cyclades.[1] The new

1. R. W. Hutchinson and J. Boardman, 'The Khaniali Tekke Tombs', *Journal of the British School at Athens*, 1954, Plate xxv, No. 19.

decorative motifs include standing concentric semicircles, well known in Crete in the Early Minoan I period, but in this instance reminiscent of the Protogeometric pottery of Thessaly, the Northern Sporades, and Attica. With the pottery of the short Early Geometric period (820–800 B.C.) Cretan art resumes the even tenor of its way with the intrusive, oriental elements now fully absorbed and digested into the local style. A typical shape is a neck-handled amphora with rope handles from lip to shoulder (the shoulder often decorated with a horizontal s) and with a pear-shaped body adorned only with a few horizontal girding bands. To this period belongs the pottery from the 'Bone Enclosures' at Vrokastro with belly-handled amphorae, one of them equipped with a lid of the 'votive shield' type,[1] vases which Miss Hall called 'covered bowls' but which in Attica would have been termed *pyxides*, small jugs of the *lekythos*, or oil flask, type varying in size and shape but often recalling contemporary vases in Cyprus, and the solid (earlier) form of *kálathos*, a shape resembling a waste-paper basket and indeed obviously derived from a basket prototype. The open-work

Fig. 68. Protogeometric B shrine

form of *kálathos*, which reveals its origin still more clearly, also appears in this period.

The rather scanty jewellery from these tombs at Vrokastro included two pendants and some globular beads of rock crystal, small disc beads in faience, and Egyptian beads in blue glass.

The weapons included slashing iron swords with double-curved hilt and projecting tang for the pommel, spearheads with sockets folded in the old Minoan fashion but in iron, and knives with curved blades. To the same period may be attributed the contents of the *tholos* tomb at Rusty Ridge, near Kavousi, and the material acquired by Evans from Plai tou Kastrou.

1. Hutchinson and Boardman, op. cit., Plate XXIII.

THE MATURE GEOMETRIC CULTURE

The Mature Geometric period (800–770 B.C.) corresponds roughly with the reigns of Adad-nirari III in Assyria and of Joash in Israel. Egypt at this time was weak, and suffering from the oppression of various war-lords. First the Libyans set up a dynasty of kings, of whom the best-known was Sheshonk, and these were followed by an Ethiopian dynasty founded by Piankhi, who captured Memphis in 775 B.C.

To this period belong many vases from the Knosian Chamber Tombs, and probably also Miss Benton's Class 2 group of cast tripod

Fig. 69. Gold band from Khaniale Tekke

cauldrons.[1] We may also attribute to it the gold head-band (Figure 69) from the Khaniale Tekke treasure, which is clearly related to the embossed bands from Athens dated by Kunze 'very early in the eighth century', a dating confirmed by the recent discovery of an

1. S. Benton, 'The Evolution of the Tripod-Lebes', *Annual of the British School at Athens*, 1935.

embossed gold band inside a Late Geometric vase near Koropi in Attica.[1]

The pottery of the Mature Geometric period (800–770 B.C.) includes ovoid *pithoi*, often with conical lids with knob handles, and with four handles alternatively vertical and raking, dividing the main shoulder zone into panels of geometric ornaments, meanders, zigzag bands, etc. The lower part of the vase was simply adorned with broad bands of dark paint alternating with groups of thin girding lines, and sometimes the broad bands carried a line of concentric circles in matt white paint. Other common shapes were *hydriae*, slim amphorae, and a variety of small jugs from globular to spindle shapes, usually paralleled by contemporary shapes in Cyprus or in Corinth.

To the Geometric period in general I would assign the gradual desertion of the Sub-Minoan cities of refuge if (like Karphi and Vrokastro) they were too high and uncomfortable, or their gradual conversion into Greek city states if (like Lato, Prinias, and Axos) they were on more comfortable and accessible sites. Lato is the best illustration of the latter group since Prinias is too denuded, while at Axos the earlier buildings have been destroyed or covered by later ones.

Lato

By the eighth century, in all probability, Lato had not only established control over the little plain of Lakonia and the important east and north-west coast road, but had also probably planted a colony at Lato pros Kamara[2] (the present Ayios Nikolaos) which possessed a natural landlocked harbour.

The city of Lato proper, erected mainly on the saddle of a twin-peaked hill, certainly straddles the period from the Sub-Minoan to archaic Greek times, but the individual buildings are very hard to date accurately. This is the more unfortunate because the so-called

1. J. Cook, 'A Geometric Amphora and a Gold Band', *Journal of the British School at Athens*, 1951, p. 45; and, generally, W. Reichel, *Griechisches Goldrelief*, 1942; P. Jacobsthal, however, in *Greek Pins*, p. 18, dates my band from Khaniale Tekke to late eighth century.

2. Literally 'Lato towards the arch', presumably referring to a well-known bridge, since it is not likely that any vaulted building existed old enough to give a name to the port at so early a date.

agora, or 'market place', of Lato (Fig. 70) shows the town centre of a Greek city in its simplest and most primitive form. If you look forwards, its *prytaneion*, or 'presidency', may be regarded as the prototype of a French *hôtel-de-ville*, or of an English town hall, or, if you prefer to look backwards, as the descendant of a Minoan palace

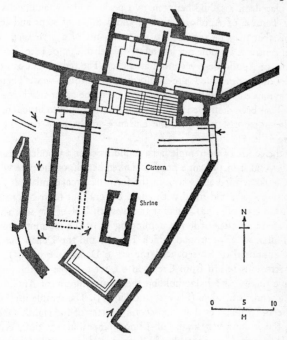

Fig. 70. Town centre, Lato

approached through its 'theatral area'. Immediately facing the steps of the last-named was a trapezoidal piazza with a cistern in the centre, and beyond that a small civic temple behind which was an *exhedra*, or shelter, open to the piazza along one of its long sides and perhaps serving, I suggest, as a dining-hall for the town councillors, like the *tholos*, the round shelter, at Athens. The municipal architect of Lato deserves to be complimented, first on his economic utilization of the very small space available, and secondly, on his ingenuity in using two towers of the inner town wall to provide an imposing entrance (almost in the manner of a Hittite *bit hilani*) for his *prytaneion*.

Dreros

A slightly similar civic centre exists at Dreros, near Neapolis, also placed on a saddle between two peaks, and containing a very early Temple of Apollo, a cistern, and a flight of steps and some rooms that may be regarded as the remnants of a *prytaneion*. The town centre as a whole is a less interesting than that of Lato, but the temple of Apollo deserves more attention. The temple consists of a single room orientated almost north-east to south-west. There is no obvious entrance; there might have been one at the north corner, which has been destroyed by a modern lime kiln, but so little remains of the north-east wall that the entrance might have been in the centre of it (Fig. 73).

In the centre of the temple lies a round base for a wooden column, and beyond it in the same line is a sunken hearth, of the type which the Greeks termed an *eschára*, in the form of a rectangular pit lined with stone slabs and filled with ashes. Beyond but more to one side lay a table of offerings. Against the western half of the south-west wall stood an altar of horns, reminding us of the far more famous horn altar at Delos around which Theseus and the Delian maidens were supposed to have danced the crane Dance (see p. 263) after his victorious return from Crete. In the west corner of the Dreros temple there was a ledge holding the bronze figures of Apollo and two attendant maidens (Plate 27 and Fig. 73). The temple itself does not seem to be older than the second quarter of the eighth century B.C., but it has a very odd, Sub-Minoan appearance with its central column, central hearth, table of offerings, and ledge at the inner end for the sacred images.

Prinias

A somewhat similar city existed on a hill overlooking and commanding what is at present the main north-south road linking Herakleion to the Mesara. The ancient name of this site is not known but it is now termed Prinias from the village immediately south of it. The ancient town was situated on a natural acropolis first occupied in Late Minoan III times, when it obviously formed a city of refuge, like Karphi or Vrokastro, for Minoan refugees forced up into the hills by the Greek invaders, but unlike those sites was not abandoned in the archaic Greek period.

The Italian Mission under Pernier excavated two temples here, of which the earlier and more important dated from about the middle of the seventh century B.C. It may be considered as a variety of the so-called *templum in antis*,[1] but, as at Dreros, there are several features that remind us not so much of an archaic Greek temple as of the little shrines of the Late Minoan III period, especially the ones at Hagia Triada and at Mallia. There was only one square pier between the *antae* of the porch (instead of the two columns normal in a *templum in antis*), and there were also apparently two wooden columns in line with this, in the middle of the *cella*, resting on low stone bases of the Minoan–Mycenaean type to support the cross-beams for a flat roof, and a central hearth between them. The central post of the entrance from the porch to the *cella* (which had an internal width of 5·94 m. against a length of only 9·75 m.) supported a stone transom with female figures carved in low relief on the soffit, and with an animal frieze on the front of the transom. Above the transom at each end were two seated female figures which helped to carry the true lintel. Fragments have also survived of low reliefs showing a procession of mounted spearmen, probably set up, not like an Ionic frieze between the architrave and the cornice, but as a parapet *sima* like the terracotta example with a procession of chariots from the temple of Dictaean Zeus at Palaikastro.[2]

THE LATE GEOMETRIC CULTURE

The Late Geometric period (770–735 B.C. according to Brock's dating) is chiefly represented by the contents of family chamber tombs excavated by the British School at Athens in the neighbourhood of Knosos and by some of the finds from Levi's excavations at Arkadhes.

The burials were normally cremations in ovoid *pithoi* with recti-

1. The term for the simplest form of Greek temple, entered by a porch with two columns between the *antae* or side-posts.
2. R. C. Bosanquet, 'Dicte and the Temples of Dictaean Zeus', *Annual of the British School at Athens*, 1943, p. 60, Plate 17.

linear geometric decoration in zones, and usually with conical lid adorned in the same manner. The smaller vases sometimes include small flasks decorated with concentric circles, either imported from Cyprus or more commonly emulations of such vases by the Cretan potters. Other imported vases include Late Geometric vases from Attica and the Cyclades, Protocorinthian *skyphoi*, and occasionally examples of *bucchero* looking rather like Lesbian *bucchero*. Almost identical limits are set by Miss Benton for her third class of cast bronze cauldrons with hollow rectangular or double T-shaped sections for their legs and with light flat handles (775–725 B.C.). This is the period that witnessed the reign of Jeroboam II in Israel and almost coincides with the reigns of Assurdan III, Assurnirari II and Tiglath Pileser III in Assyria, and with the Bubastite dynasty's rule in Egypt.

To the second half of the eighth century B.C., perhaps, may be assigned an interesting series of small terracotta plaques found at Vavelloi, near Praisos, in the Eteo-Cretan country. These depict warriors like those of the bronze tripods, and, though they are inferior artistically, they may be used to supplement our idea of the art of this period because they are on a larger scale and preserve in Mrs Dohan's words, 'the salient features of geometric art, a long neck devoid of modelling, a rope-like arm, a long sharp chin, an eye in the middle of the cheek, and a prominent crested helmet'. She proceeds to compare these figures with the bronze ship and figure from a tripod stand which is one of the dedications in the Idaean cave, and should belong to the end of the eighth century B.C.

THE CRETAN ORIENTALIZING CULTURE

The period from 735 to 680 B.C. is termed by Brock the early Orientalizing period. Tiglath Pileser III of Assyria (745–727 B.C.) had overrun Urartu and Syria and had carried off into captivity the two tribes of Israel and part of another one that lived east of the Jordan. Shalmaneser V (727–722 B.C.) had overrun another part of Palestine, though the actual capture of Samaria and the enslavement of its population was carried out after his death by his successor

---

1. S. Benton, 'The Evolution of the Tripod Lebes', *Annual of the British School at Athens*, 1935, p. 113.

Sargon II (722–705 B.C.). Sargon also captured Carchemish, the capital of the last surviving Neo-Hittite state of any importance, and Payne pointed out that, whereas the lions on Protocorinthian vases of the eighth century resemble those of Late Hittite sculpture, those on Corinthian vases of the seventh century resemble Assyrian forms. But culture is more spread by refugees than by conquering generals, and Sargon's conquests of Urartu and Damascus are reflected in the appearance of great bronze cauldrons with bull or griffin head handles of Vannic type, not only in Greece, but as far west as Etruria,[1] and of ivories of Syro-Phoenician type in the same countries.[2]

The early Orientalizing pottery of the graves round Knosos reflects these events, not by Assyrian vase shapes, but by the appearance of decorative motifs of oriental origin on native vase shapes. Some new shapes appear but they are borrowed from Cyprus or the Greek mainland not from Assyria, but the gay polychrome patterns including large cable patterns, the oriental tree of life, lotus garlands, and other stylized designs painted in the crusted technique in fugitive matt colours do remind us of the painted bricks of Assyria as found at Assur, and to a lesser degree at Nineveh. This polychrome work is confined to the neighbourhood of Knosos in Crete, though a few vases in a similar technique have been found near Athens. A favourite shape in this Knosian fabric was a *pithos* with cylindrical neck, ovoid body, and high inverted conical feet, derived, I suspect, from a shape popular in the Cyclades in the Early Bronze Age, revived in east Crete in the Middle Minoan III to Late Minoan I period, and again in the Cyclades and in Euboea in the Geometric styles of these districts. The lotus and bud garland, which recalls those of contemporary Rhodian vases, could have been borrowed from Assyria, since it appears sculptured in low relief on the floor slabs of Ashurbanipal's palace at Nineveh; but it appears in Assyria in this form only after Esarhaddon's conquest of Egypt, whereas it was an old Egyptian pattern, well known also in Syria, and had appeared among the ivories of Ahab's palace at Samaria.

1. K. R. Maxwell-Hyslop, 'Urartian Bronzes in Etruscan Tombs', *Iraq*, 1956, p. 150; P. Amandry, 'Chaudrons à Protomés de taureau en Orient et en Grèce', *The Aegean and the Near East, Studies presented to Hetty Goldman*, pp. 239–61.

2. R. D. Barnett, 'Early Greek and Oriental Ivories', *Journal of Hellenic Studies*, 1948.

The Dedications in the Idaean Cave

The mixture of oriental ideas was also reflected in a fine series of bronze shields with embossed and incised designs found by F. Halbherr and P. Orsi during their excavation of the Idaean Cave. More recently this material has been splendidly published by E. Kunze, who spread the dates of the shields over a hundred and fifty years, from the end of the ninth to the first half of the seventh century, and divided them into four groups without any very clear development from one to the other, though he noted the stylistic parallels between individual pieces and individual works of art outside Crete, such as the parallel between the earliest shields and the gold head-bands from the Dipylon cemetery at Athens. His dates have been criticized as too early by F. Matz and also by Miss Sylvia Benton, who has submitted a classification employing Kunze's numbers for the shields and relying for her chronology on synchronisms with the well-dated series of Protocorinthian and Corinthian vases.[1]

One Idaean shield belonged to the '*Herzsprung*' series (that derive their name from the type-site of the same name in North Germany). The characteristic of a '*Herzsprung*' shield is that its ornament of concentric bands of decoration is broken by indentations in the inner bands, sometimes even extending into the central boss of the shield. These indentations may be U-shaped or V-shaped in Western Europe, but only the latter kind have been found in Greece. Shields of this form were widely distributed in Europe during the eighth and seventh centuries B.C., and examples have been found in Ireland, Spain, Germany, Bohemia, Italy, and in the Aegean in the Idaean Cave, at Delphi, at the Samian Heraeum, and at Idalion in Cyprus. At least three of the Greek examples were found at Panhellenic sanctuaries, and the examples from other parts of Europe may well be related to the trade routes by which the Baltic amber was distributed. Cretan graves of this period do sometimes contain amber beads or jewels with amber inlay, though the amber in them seems to be less abundant than that of many Mycenaean graves in the Peloponnese. The Idaean shields, and the fragments of similar shields from Palaikastro, were not only decorated in an exotic manner, but seem too flimsy and too magnificent for ordinary warfare. They look like

1. S. Benton, 'The Date of the Cretan Shields', *Annual of the British School at Athens*, 1939, p. 52, and E. Kunze, *Kretische Bronzereliefs*, p. 1.

ceremonial shields, and, since the legendary Curetes were associated with both sanctuaries, it has been suggested that these shields were employed in a ritual dance or play celebrating the birth of the Cretan Zeus.

Oriental parallels are noted in an admirable article by H. Hencken who has remarked that the net-like treatment of the lion's mane on some Cretan shields, compared by Miss Benton to those of Early Corinthian lions, already occurred on the manes of Assyrian ivory lions apparently dating 'from the reign of Assur-nasir-pal II (884–859 B.C.)'[1] and that banded wigs like those of the sphinx on Shield 59 (one of Kunze's later group and dated about 650 by Miss Benton) are best paralleled by finds at Delphi in a hoard that can hardly be later than 700 B.C. Hencken also points out that the 'Hunt Shield' (of Kunze's earlier group and dated about 650 B.C. by Miss Benton) has oriental parallels in the ninth century rather than later (such as sculptures of Assur-nasir-pal II, Hittite reliefs from the Citadel Gate at Senjirli, and ivories from Ahab's palace at Samaria) though one feature in the design, the vulture on the back of the lion, recalls Assyrian examples of the eighth century (a relief from the reign of Tiglath-Pileser III (745–727 B.C.) and a bronze bowl from Nimrud from a palace restored by Sargon II (722–705 B.C.), with a Phoenician inscription on a doorway recording that the wing of the palace in which it was found contained plunder acquired during his campaign against Pisiris, King of Carchemish.

The round shields with concentric bands of ornament were only more splendid variations of the current war-shield which had replaced the indented shield typical of the Dipylon period, and of which we may see representations on the Hunt Shield from the Idaean Cave and on the bronze bands found in a tomb near Knosos, depicting a battle scene between bowmen in a chariot and foot soldiers.

The oriental influences discernible among the offerings in the Idaean Cave were not, however, confined to the bronzes (which were mainly a local Cretan product, despite their differences in style), but were also indicated by actual ivories imported from the Orient, including two single figures of naked goddesses of the Qadesh or

---

1. Here, however, Hencken was misled by Barnett's previous dating since later evidence suggests that most of the ivories were not earlier than Sargon II (714–700); compare R. D. Barnett, *The Nimrud Ivories*, pp. 133–5.

Astarte type native to Syria and Phoenicia, and a fragment of a group consisting originally of two figures back to back, supported by a column capital with a collar of leaves recalling the so-called Aeolic capital (of which the immediate prototypes were to be found in Syria and Palestine).[1]

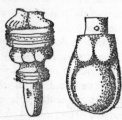

Fig. 71. Ivories from Idaean Cave

Nor were these ivory fragments the only imports from Syria and Phoenicia from the Idaean Cave. Two complete bronze bowls from that site and a fragmentary one from the Acropolis at Athens clearly resemble some of the bowls found in the north-west palace at Nimrud,[2] and appear to have been products of a Phoenician or south Syrian School of art very strongly influenced by Egyptian work, as is shown by the recurrence of such Egyptian works as the winged solar disk and the *uraeus* headdress of the sphinxes. Two other fragments of bowls from the Idaean Cave resembled an example from Idalion in Cyprus, and we may assume that some of these oriental influences were entering Crete by way of Cyprus and the Dodecanese.

The 'bronze gong' from the Idaean Cave, showing a god, attended by two wingless demons, wearing a curly Assyrian beard and brandishing two lions, may probably, as suggested by Herzfeld, have been imported from the neighbourhood of Lake Van.[3]

It appears, therefore, that the earliest bronzes from the Idaean Cave should be dated nearer to Miss Benton's 685 than to Kunze's 800, and perhaps ± 725 B.C. might be suggested as a possible date.[4] To

1. The oldest is an early tenth century example from Megiddo v; cf. W. F. Albright, *The Archaeology of Palestine*, 1949, p. 126.

2. Kunze, op. cit., p. 159, following H. Layard, *Nineveh and its Remains*, 1858, Plate 57.

3. See V. R. Maxwell-Hyslop, 'Urartian Bronzes in Etruscan Tombs', *Iraq*, 1956, p. 159; any Urartian bronzes should be dated not much before, and not much later than, 714 B.C., when Sargon II sacked Musasir the Urartian capital and when Urartian refugees must have been common all over the Levant.

4. This of course refers to the bronzes originally found, not to any found by Marinatos recently in his Mycenaean deposit.

Syro-Phoenician influence may be attributed some fragmentary figures in gold leaf which I found in the lower burnt stratum in the *dromos* of the destroyed *tholos* tomb containing the seventh-century treasure at Khaniale Tekke. The figures are in double gold leaf, which had presumably once covered a core of some less durable material such as wood.

The most complete figure is that of a man clad in a short tunic belted at the waist and carrying a ram on his shoulders. The upper half of a man or a woman (?) carrying a ram or lamb was found near, but this had been more damaged by the funeral fire. There were some other gold fragments in the same deposit that might have belonged to a larger figure. The oriental influence is very strong here, but I am convinced they are Cretan imitations of Phoenician work, not imports. They seem at least to be completely outside the currents of Dorian art, and may be products of that ill-defined school termed Eteo-Cretan by Langlotz and Matz, and more tentatively by Demargne.[1]

In the plastic arts, represented by sculpture, modelling, and carving in stone, clay, bronze, gold, and ivory, the Cretan school played a very important part in the eighth and early seventh centuries B.C., and its works are often characterized by the style which archaeologists have termed 'Dedalic', a word that is useful but rather ambiguous unless it is very carefully defined and employed. Greek folklore was hopelessly confused over the legendary craftsman Daedalus, who was said to have worked for King Minos before the days of the Trojan war, and a much later artist, the traditional founder of the Daedalid School, the man who, in the words of Diodorus, had been 'the first to give them [i.e. statues] open eyes and parted legs and outstretched arms, for before his time artists made statues with closed eyes and hands, hanging down and cleaving to the sides'.[2] Now if such an artist did really exist, and if Diodorus is not merely employing a legendary name to typify the work of a school, that artist must have lived in the eighth and not the fourteenth century B.C.

It is clear at least that when we encounter the word *Daedalidae*,

---

1. R. W. Hutchinson and J. Boardman, 'The Khaniale Tekke Tombs', *Annual of the British School at Athens*, 1954. P. Jacobstal, *Greek Pins*, p. 20, considers the more damaged figure to be a man, and that both are carrying calves; he considers that they come from the same workshop as the Idaean pendant.

2. *The Library of History*, Book IV, Chap. 76.

or 'sons of Daedalus', it has nothing to do with the legendary artist of the Bronze Age, but simply refers to this archaic school of Cretan artists, just as the term *Asclepiadae* does not mean the actual sons of Asclepius but simply the Coan school of doctors, and *Homeridae* not the sons of Homer but the school of epic bards and reciters. Archaeologists, however, have come to employ the term 'Dedalic' of the sculptural style characteristic of, though not confined to, Doric-speaking cities in the eighth and early seventh centuries B.C., and though 'Dedalic' in this sense does not coincide with the sense in which Pausanias might have understood it, it is nevertheless probable that most of the works, particularly the wooden statues which he

Fig. 72. Cretan imitation of Egyptian scarab,
Khaniale Tekke

attributed to *Daedalidae* and to sculptors such as Dipoinis and Skylles, reputed as pupils or even sons of Daedalus, would be reckoned as 'Dedalic' in the modern sense also.

No major sculptures have survived in Crete from the Protogeometric and Geometric periods, and if such works ever existed they would have been made of wood. It is not likely that any great works of art have perished, since the bronze and clay figurines surviving from those periods, as illustrated by finds from the Psychro Cave, are chiefly but the degenerate offspring of the latest Minoan types, naturalistic in intention but feeble in execution.

The rise of the Proto-Dedalic style in Crete practically coincides with the reign of Esarhaddon in Assyria (681–669 B.C.), and with the

estruction of the Phrygian power of Midas by the Cimmerians.
Egypt Psamtek had founded a new native dynasty in 661 and had
alisted Greek mercenaries in his service. This renewed contact be-
ween Greece and Egypt was reflected in a new influx into Crete of
gyptian scarabs and beads of faience, which appear at Knosos and
lsewhere in tombs of the Late Orientalizing period (680–635 B.C.)
nd in some of the decorative motives that appear on the polychrome
ithoi at Knosos. We also find imitations of scarabs with quasi-
gyptian designs, though whether any of these were made in Crete
r whether they were all imported from Cyprus or Syria is more open
o question. More important was the Egyptian influence on the rising
chool of sculpture. In Crete and other Doric-speaking districts,
gyptian influence is most obvious in the treatment of the hair which,
n Dedalic statues, is often treated like a heavy Egyptian wig, and
n the walking pose with the left foot forward. Egyptian influence
vas short-lived and is chiefly noticeable during the reign of Psamtek
661–609 B.C.), but it occurred at a very important period, when
Greek sculpture was at a very impressionable stage of its development.

THE PROTO-DEDALIC STYLE IN SCULPTURE AND MODELLING

The forerunners of the new Doric style which we know by the name
of 'Dedalic' are a small group of figurines appearing between 685
and 680 B.C. and lasting till 670 B.C. The style of this group has been
termed by Jenkins Proto-Dedalic, and it already illustrates the dominant characteristics of the Dedalic style.

The head is regarded from a frontal point of view, almost as a
mask, and has no proper profile view. Instead of the weak, round
faces of the sub-Geometric heads, with their retiring foreheads,
pointed retroussé noses, and a general lack of proportion between
the features and the face, we now have a long, narrow, V-shaped
face with a low but not retreating forehead, features roughly modelled but not out of proportion to the face, and a very pointed chin.
The hair is generally treated like a perruque, suggesting Egyptian
influence, but there are also examples of long braided locks.

Jenkins notes that the Cretan examples have a broader face and a
more individual treatment of the eye, with strongly marked brows

and two incised lines for the upper lids, distinguishing them from Proto-Dedalic heads from other parts of Greece. The new Dedalic style affected not only figurines of clay or bronze and jewellery, but also had a notable effect on a very ancient craft – the making of *pithoi* or large stone jars with moulded ornaments, a craft going back through the Minoan age into the Cretan Neolithic period. The *pithoi* of the Bronze Age or of the early Iron Age had for the most part been content with simple skeuomorphic patterns, such as imitations in relief of the rope slings with which such jars were moved.

The Dedalic artist (not only in Crete, but also in Boeotia, in the Peloponnese, and in the Cyclades) added friezes on the necks or shoulders of the *pithoi* with figures in relief – horses, warriors, sphinxes, lions, or chariots.[1]

Some of the Cretan relief *pithoi* are hard to date accurately but perhaps the one most likely to be contemporary with the Proto-Dedalic figures is a small group with figured decoration (modelled freehand and not in moulds); a fragment in this technique from the Psychro cave, depicting a leaping goat, is now in Oxford.

THE EARLY DEDALIC STYLE

The second, or early, Dedalic period (670–655 B.C.) was marked by the fact that the pointed chin was now rounded off; the face, though still long and narrow, was no longer V-shaped, but U-shaped.

Crete, or at least Dorian Crete as distinct from the Eteo-Cretan cities, seems to lag somewhat behind the other Dorian districts in artistic ability. There are plenty of Early Dedalic heads in the Herakleion Museum, and some in European or American museums from sites such as Vavelloi, but the quality of the work is very indifferent and sometimes individual features remind us of Sub-Geometric types.

The head is regularly too large for its body and the waist is about half-way down the figure (this applies not only to Cretan figures but also to Proto-Dedalic and Early Dedalic figurines in general). The hair is usually in a perruque. Both the figurines and the figures on the relief *pithoi* were cast in moulds.

1. Obviously cheap substitutes for bronze *pithoi*, such as the splendid example recently found at Vix in France.

One statuette in stone from Malles in eastern Crete seems to belong to this period. What remains of the head shows the long oval face and perruque hair, and the thin arms hanging from the shoulders may be paralleled by seated clay figures of Protocorinthian fabric. The Dedalic style reached its peak in the Middle Dedalic period (655–630 B.C.), which Jenkins divides into three stylistic phases.

THE MIDDLE DEDALIC STYLE, FIRST PHASE

In the first phase, though the faces of the heads are still oval with rounded chins, the increased breadth of the foreheads gives the general impression of a V-shaped countenance rather than the U-shape of Early Dedalic heads. The modelling is much better than before.

There is no Cretan free-standing statue of this period to set beside the Nikandra statue from Delos, but some stone reliefs and a number of clay statuettes illustrate the current fashion.

The most striking sculptures in stone are the procession of the horsemen and the goddesses from the soffit of the transom from Temple A at Prinias[1] (the two goddesses sitting above the transom are later, and must be due to a reconstruction of about 600 B.C.). To the same period should belong the middle of a relief of a running figure found at Knosos in the spring of A.D. 1936 in a mixed deposit, quite out of any sensible context, but obviously derived from a seventh-century work. The broken pottery heads of the period include an interesting example found at Knosos in the later strata above the Little Palace.

The finest bronze of this period (if it really is Cretan, as I think it is) is a bronze head from Olympia in the Karlsruhe collection – a very strong individual work, with its trapezoidal face, thin-lipped, faintly smiling mouth, and up-curving brows, but with the low flat cranium that is so characteristic of seventh-century heads in Crete; it is also one of the earliest, if not the earliest, example in Greece of hollow casting in bronze.

1. S. C. Casson, *The Technique of Early Greek Sculpture*, 1933, p. 66 and Fig. 22.

THE MIDDLE DEDALIC STYLE, SECOND PHASE

The second phase of the Middle Dedalic style (650–640 B.C.) is termed by Jenkins that of 'the Auxerre group', because its best and most characteristic work is the charming female statuette found at Auxerre in central France, now in the Louvre, and illustrated in almost every general book on Greek sculpture. The flat boardlike figure, with features and details cut out in the soft limestone by a knife, suggests the influence of woodcarving. Some archaic funeral monuments in the form of *stelai* from Prinias display an even simpler technique, since here all details are simply incised in the soft stone, giving an impression of low relief. These *stelai* are of some importance, since they are the earliest figured tombstones in Greece since Mycenaean times. The only complete *stele* surviving depicts a woman dressed in the Doric *peplos*, with a spindle in her hand, standing on a low base (suggesting that the dead woman is receiving the ritual of a consecrated heroine). The fragmentary *stelai* from the same district show either similar figures of women or else warriors dressed as heavy-armed hoplites, with large round shields and two spears. Sometimes the dead hero is approached by a much smaller figure, obviously representing a living member of his or her family. The clay figurines include a very interesting series excavated by the French at Anavlochos, a head from the Little Palace at Knosos, and another from Arkadhes.

Some moulds for clay plaques found in the Peloponnese at the Argive Heraeum and Perachora may have been Cretan work of this period.

To this period also may be assigned the splendid group of *sphyrélata* (or hammered) bronzes found in the little temple of Apollo at Dreros described on page 332 and regarded by Matz as Eteo-Cretan rather than Doric works of art.[1] There were indeed Eteo-Cretans at Dreros, as we know from a fragmentary inscription in their language found on that site, but Demargne is surely justified in claiming that these figures are closely related to the Middle Dedalic art of this period.

In the early seventh century, and indeed probably up to 650 B.C.,

1. Compare H. Megaw, 'Archaeology in Greece 1935–6,' *Journal of Hellenic Studies*, 1936, p. 152 and Fig. 11.

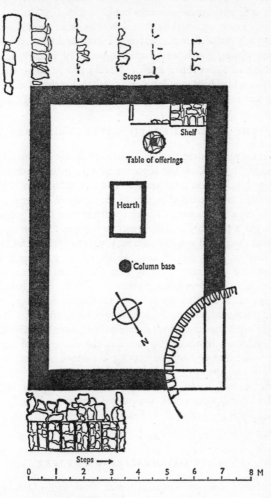

Steps →

Shelf

Table of offerings

Hearth

Column base

N

Steps →

0 1 2 3 4 5 6 7 8 M

Fig. 73. Temple of Apollo, Dreros

the *cire perdue* method of casting bronze was not practised in Gre
lands and, while small statuettes could be cast solid, large statuet
or statues were executed by the *sphyrélaton*, or hammered, techni
whereby a wooden statue was first carved and then covered w
bronze plating which was riveted together, or in later times fix
with a hard solder (Plate 27). Gold could also be employed for t
plates instead of bronze and was used for the colossal gold statue of Ze
dedicated at Olympia by Periander, the famous tyrant of Corinth.

THE MIDDLE DEDALIC STYLE, THIRD PHASE

The third phase of the Middle Dedalic Sculpture (640–630 B.C.) w
christened by Jenkins 'the Mycenae group', from the fine Deda
metope block found at Mycenae.[1] The faces on heads of this peri
are shorter and squarer than that of the 'Lady of Auxerre', and t
cheeks are almost parallel. A fine bronze statuette of a youth four
at Delphi is probably a Cretan work of this period. Among the cl
heads of this period was one with very carefully painted facial detai
modelled on a clay pilgrim flask which, up to 1939, was in Berlin
The painted vases contemporary with these Dedalic heads are tho
of Brock's Late Orientalizing period, which he dates between 6
and 630 B.C. In the chamber tombs of the Knosos district polychron
ovoid *pithoi* continue. At Arkadhes the polychrome *pithoi* of Knos
did not occur, but there were occasional and more tentative attemp
at polychromy reminding us rather of the colouring of east Gre
vases rather than of Assyrian painting, combined occasionally with
motif or vase shape.

One curious motif, consisting of pot-hook spirals ending
panthers' heads, occurs both on a painted *pyxis* from Arkadhes and
a relief *pithos* from Kastelli Pedhiadhos, suggesting that their wor
shops were closely related (if not identical).

LATE ORIENTALIZING POTTERY

The painted vases contemporary with these Proto-Dedalic, Ear
Dedalic, and Late Dedalic heads is that of Brock's Late Orientalizin

1. A. J. B. Wace, *Mycenae*, 1949, Plate 107; Jenkins, loc. cit., Plate VI, No.
2. Jenkins, op. cit., Plate VI, No. 6.

eriod, which he dates between 680 and 630 B.C. In the chamber tombs
t Knosos the polychrome ovoid *pithoi* continue, and the smaller vases
with decorations simply on the dark varnish, consisting of a fusion
f geometric and oriental ornaments, is also paralleled on other sites
though polychrome vases are still confined to the district of Knosos).

Vases were also imported and imitated from Cyprus, Corinth, the
Cyclades, and Athens. At Arkadhes, in the Pedhiadha, Levi excavated
n interesting series of tombs of this period.[1] The vases here tended
o be more rustic and provincial than those of Knosos, though
Demargne's verdict that 'some of the products are often barbarous'
eems unduly severe. I should prefer personally to say that the Arkadhes vases were the products of a very lively and original peasant
rt, often quite prolific in ideas and fancies, less sophisticated than
hose of Knosos but also more original.

The more common shapes include ovoid *pithoi*, *hydriae*, tall *pyxides*,
ugs of various Cypriote shapes, and cups. A tankard from tomb R is
n odd combination of a Sub-Minoan or Sub-Mycenaean shape,
with an orientalizing decoration consisting of a large cable band.
Some jugs have the plastic head of a horse or ass issuing from the
houlder. One vase in Oxford is shaped like two owls back to back
influenced by the owl-shaped vases in the white-shaved ware of
Cyprus). Some jugs were influenced by examples from Rhodes or
ome other east Greek site.

Relief Pithoi

The Early and Late Orientalizing periods were marked by a fine
eries of *pithoi* with decoration in relief. Making store-jars with rope-
work or medallions in relief was an old Minoan fashion which perhaps
never entirely died out, but the relief *pithoi* of the eighth to sixth
enturies B.C. were characterized by oriental motifs such as sphinxes,
ffronted lions, and cable patterns on the main zones of ornament
n the neck and shoulders. Sometimes horses appear instead of lions,
nd a fine *pithos* from Prinias shows the *Pótnia Therón*, or Lady of the
Beasts, flanked by two horses, though, as Dunbabin remarks, 'the
ttitude and proportions of these suggest that they might have begun

1. D. Levi, 'Excavations at Arkadhes', *Liverpool Annals*, 1905; one vase
learly imitates an Urartian bronze cauldron; compare R. D. Barnett, *The
Aegean and the Near East*, Plate XX, No. 2.

life as lions, and the long muscular raised forelegs look like lion's legs'

Thrapsanos, in the Pedhiadha, is the chief manufacturing centre for such large jars in modern times, and I suspect that the archaic centre was not very far from that village. Of the sites that have produced archaic relief *pithoi* or fragments of them, Afrati, Gonies Astritsi, and Kastelli Pedhiadhos are all in the Pedhiadha area, while Knosos, Arkhanes, Prinias, Phaistos, and Embaros have easy access to it. A more eastern centre may have supplied Dreros, Anavlochos Praisos, and Lithinais, but Plati could equally well have imported from the Pedhiadha. Dunbabin, however, has plausibly argued that the potters of the archaic *pithoi* may have worked in their own village and travelled to work in other parts of the island in the summer, like the modern potters of Thrapsanos and Margaritais.

ENGRAVED SEAL-STONES

To the combined Minoan-Mycenaean traditions of the Eteo-Cretan and of the descendants of Mycenaean colonists we may perhaps attribute the persistence in Crete of the art of gem engraving. The art of writing may have died, or become very rare, before the end of the Bronze Age.[1] There was apparently no survival of the Bronze Age scripts such as occurred on Cyprus. The rare Eteo-Cretan inscriptions surviving from the classical period were all cut in Greek characters Yet this very decay of literacy on the island may have helped to preserve the art of gem-cutting since seals always have an enhanced importance in an illiterate or semi-literate community. Unfortunately the Cretan seal-stones of the period between 1050 and 700 B.C. have not been adequately studied or published. In the nineteenth century A.D. most seals of this period, if not betraying obvious signs of connexion with Cyprus, Etruria, Phoenicia, Egypt, or Mesopotamia, were loosely grouped together as 'Melian' or 'Island' gems, very unsatisfactory titles, though many seals did indeed come from the islands and some even actually from Melos. These seals were regularly cut in soft stones, usually steatite. Many were poorly executed, but the best examples are of some merit and often remind us of

---

1. Compare M. Bowra, *Homer and his Forerunners* (Andrew Lang Lecture 1955): 'There is no evidence that the Mycenaean script continued anywhere in Greece after *c.* 1200.'

Minoan or Mycenaean gems, either by the technique of their cutting with wheel and drill, or by the reproduction of old Aegean motifs, such as the *agrimi*, or the lion seizing a bull, or by the '*tête bêche*' arrangement of foreparts of animals. Wason has shown how the use of the drill in cutting such stones migrated from the Aegean to Mesopotamia and back again. Knowledge of the drill did not die out, but the degrees in which drill, saw, or graver were used varied with the fashions of individual schools. Sometimes Aegean and Hellenic elements are so blended that a seal is hard to date. Thus an engraved gem with two walking mules and a line of vertical chevrons was classified by Forsdyke as Late Minoan III B, but as Geometric by Casson, and the chevrons might belong to either period; Evans, however, assigned it to the Hellenic period, and I think correctly so, since the treatment of the mules resembles that on black-figured vases rather than that on Mycenaean *cratera*.

POST-DEDALIC ART

The last twenty years of the seventh century and the first twenty years of the sixth century B.C. were marked by sculptures, figurines, and relief *pithoi* transitional between the Dedalic art and the fully developed archaic style of the sixth century, and this transitional group has been christened Post-Dedalic. To this group we may plausibly assign the two seated goddesses perched above the transom of the door of Temple A at Prinias. These figures have been called 'Dedalic', but they are clearly later than the cavalry relief of the figures sculptured on the transom of the same temple, and more developed in style than the Auxerre goddess or the statue from Eleutherna; presumably the seated goddesses were executed in a later restoration of the temple.

To the same Post-Dedalic group belongs also a bronze figure of a *kriophóros*, or a man carrying a ram, dated 650 by Kunze and Neugebauer, but by Demargne more reasonably dated to 600 B.C., and till 1939 in the Museum in Berlin. The general conception of a *kriophóros*, however, had not altered so very much since the Late Minoan period.

We cannot say very much about the pottery of the Post-Dedalic period in Crete because the rich cemeteries of the Knosos–Fortetsa area, which had provided such abundant material for the period between 950 and 630 B.C., quickly peter out. Was there another severe earthquake, or did Knosos suffer from a political disaster, or is the deficiency merely due to the fact that we have not yet discovered the cemeteries of the period after 630 B.C.? In other parts of the island the absence of cemeteries may be only apparent, but the immediate neighbourhood of Knosos has been so thoroughly tested by excavations and trial pits that it seems strange that so few tombs of the sixth and fifth centuries have been discovered. The district was not altogether deserted; sculptures, inscriptions, vases, and coins of this period do turn up, but no Greek buildings of any importance have been uncovered, though Roman buildings abound. A certain number of Attic black-figured and red-figured vases were imported, but the local potters seem to have produced nothing but domestic ware. The population must, I think, have declined in number, and a curious twilight descended on Crete which, in the classical period, seems to have acted mainly as a recruiting ground for bowmen and slingers for the richer cities of the mainland. The best Cretan artists emigrated, the sculptors Dipoinis and Skyllis to the Peloponnese, and the architects Chersiphron and Metagenes from Knosos to Ionia.

THE CRETAN TWILIGHT

A story in Book III of Herodotus's history provides a 'news flash' from Crete in the sixth century B.C. We hear how some Samian adventurers, who had failed to overthrow their local tyrant Polykrates, had seized the island of Siphnos and, when they had been evicted from that, had sailed to western Crete, expelled the Zakynthians who were occupying the site of Kydonia, and refounded that place as a Samian city. The Samians enjoyed their ill-gotten gains for five years, during which time they had founded a temple, later to become famous, in honour of the Minoan goddess Diktynna, but in the sixth year they were defeated by the Aeginetans, who captured the city and enslaved all its inhabitants, Samians and Cretans alike.

This is an isolated story, and an incomplete one too, but if these events were at all typical of what was happening in other parts of the island, we can perhaps understand the paucity of Cretan buildings and works of art attributable to the sixth and fifth centuries B.C.

Praisos, indeed, kept the Eteo-Cretan flag flying for a while and, in the time of which the historian Staphylos wrote, still controlled ports on both the north and the south sides of the island[1] and probably also the district round Eleia (Palaikastro) in the far east. But she gradually lost these outlying possessions to her Dorian enemies at Hierapytna and Itanos, and was finally completely destroyed by them about 144 B.C.

To the Eteo-Cretan twilight of the early sixth century we may perhaps attribute such works as the terracotta chariot *sima* from the Temple of Dictaean Zeus at Palaikastro and the curious fragment of a plate from Praisos with a splendid black-figure group of Herakles or some such hero grappling with a sea monster, or possibly Peleus wooing Thetis, on one side and a very dull horseman (surely by another painter) on the other.

Later still, probably about 560 B.C., is the fine clay head and shoulders of a clay statue from Praisos of a young god, perhaps Apollo, perhaps the young Cretan Velchanos, the latest surviving work of any importance from the Eteo-Cretan school of modelling, and here we may end our account of the prehistory of the island, for Dorian Crete in the classical period was a very different place, less cultured and less comfortable, a motherland of warriors, and sometimes of pirates, rather than of artists and architects.

1. Staphylos's own date has been set rather doubtfully about 300 B.C. I should prefer to date Staphylos much earlier, but since he was born at Naucratis he can hardly be earlier than the sixth century B.C.

BIBLIOGRAPHY

BIBLIOGRAPHY

GENERAL

These references will not always be repeated after the individual chapters but most of them are relevant to all the chapters.

Åberg, N., *Die Bronzezeitliche und Früheisenzeitliche Chronologie*, III and IV, 1933.

Baikie, J. M., *Sea-Kings of Crete*, 1921.

Bossert, H. T., *The Art of Ancient Crete*, 1937.

Burrows, R. M., *Excavations in Crete*, 1908.

Childe, V. G., *The Dawn of European Archaeology*, 5th ed., 1950.

Cottrell, L., *The Bull of Minos*, 1956.

Demargne, P., *La Crète dédalique*, 1947.

Dussaud, R., *Les Civilisations préhelléniques dans le bassin de la Mer Égée*. 2nd ed., 1914.

Eliadi, M. N., *Crete Past and Present*, 1933.

Evans, A. J., *The Palace of Minos*, Vol. I, 1921–Vol. V, 1935.
    Scripta Minoa, I, 1909.

Evans, A. J., and Myres, J. L., *Scripta Minoa*, II, 1952.

Fimmen, D., and Reisinger, *Die Kretisch-Mykenische Kunst* (chiefly written by Fimmen in 1915), 1926.

Glotz, G., *La Civilisation minoenne*, 1921.

Hall, H. R., *Ancient History of the Near East*, 11th ed., 1942.
    The Civilization of Greece in the Bronze Age, 1928.

Hutchinson, R. W., 'Minoan Chronology Reviewed', *Antiquity*, 1954, p. 155.

Kantor, H. J., 'The Aegean and the Orient in the Second Millennium B.C.', *American Journal of Archaeology*, 1947.

Mackenzie, D., 'Cretan Palaces', *Annual of the British School at Athens*, 1904–8.

Matz, F., *Die Frühkretischen Siegel*, 1928.

Montelius, O., *La Grèce préclassique*, 1928.

Pendlebury, J. D. S., *The Archaeology of Crete*, 1939 (easily the best general account of the Minoan culture).

Schaeffer, C. F. A., *Stratigraphie comparée et chronologie de l'Asie orientale*, 1947.

Snijder, G. A., *Die Kretische Kunst*, 1936.

CHAPTER I: THE ISLAND OF CRETE

Allbaugh, L. G., *Crete (A Case Study of an Undeveloped Area)*, 1953.

Bate, Dorothea, *Geological Magazine*, May 1905, p. 196.

BIBLIOGRAPHY

Chalikiopoulos, L., *Die Halbinsel Sitia*, 1903.

Elliadi, M. N., *Crete, Past and Present*, 1933.

Lehmann, H., *Geographische Zeitung*, 1939, p. 212.

Marinatos, S., 'The Volcanic Destruction of Minoan Crete', *Antiquit* December 1939.

Pashley, R., *Travels in Crete*, 1837.

Pauly-Wissowa-Kroll, *Realenzyklopädie der klassischen Altertumswissenscha* article on Crete, 1922.

Pendlebury, J. D. S., *The Archaeology of Crete*, 1939 (especially for surfa topography routes and distribution of sites).

Sharpe, R. F., *European Animals: Their Geological History and Geographi Distribution*, 1890.

Rawlin, V., *Description physique de l'île de Crète*, 1869.

Renz, C., 'Progress of the Geological Exploration', *A.J.S.*, 1947, p. 175.

Schaeffer, C. F. A., *Stratigraphie comparée et chronologie de l'Asie occidentale*, 194

Spratt, T. A. B., *Travels and Researches in Crete*, 1865.

Thomson, J. O., *History of Ancient Geography*, 1948.

Tournefort, J. P. de, *Voyage au Levant*, 1717.

Trevor Battye, A., *Camping in Crete*, 1913.

Vickery, K. F., 'Food in Early Greece', *Illinois Studies in the Social Scienc* Vol. xx, No. 3, 1952 (an invaluable monograph).

For further works on the island, see also the bibliography given by X Fielding in *The Stronghold* (1953), a most readable account of the Sphak district.

CHAPTER 2: THE STONE AGE

Evans, A. J., *The Palace of Minos*, I, 1921, p. 1–32.

Franchet, L., 'Rapport sur une mission', *Nouvelles archives des missions scie tifiques*, 1911.

Furness, A., 'The Neolithic Pottery of Knosos', *Annual of the British School Athens*, 1953.

Hutchinson, R. W., 'Cretan Neolithic Figurines', *Ipek*, 1938, p. 50.

Matz, F. (ed.), *Forschungen auf Kreta*, 1942, article by U. Jantzen.

Muller, V., *Frühe Plastik*, 1929, p. 1–6.

Pendlebury, J. D. S., *The Archaeology of Crete*, 1939, Chap. II.

Pernier, L., *Il Palazzo di Festos*, I, 1932, pp. 67, 105.

Schachermeyr, F., *Die Ältesten Kulturen Griechenlands*, 1955.

Weinberg, S., 'Neolithic Figurines and Aegean Inter-relations', *Americ Journal of Archaeology*, 1951, p. 121.

    'The Relative Chronology of the Aegean', *Relative Chronologies in O World Archaeology* (ed. R. W. Ehrich), 1954.

CHAPTER 3: THE CRETAN PEOPLES, LANGUAGES, AND SCRIPTS

Physical Characteristics of the Cretans

Angell, J. L., 'A Racial Analysis of the Ancient Greeks', *American Journal of Physical Anthropology*, 1944, pp. 329–76.

Buxton, L. H. D., 'The Inhabitants of the Eastern Mediterranean', *Biometrika*, 1913, p. 92.

Duckworth, W. L. H., 'Human Remains at Hagios Nikolaos', *Annual of the British School at Athens*, 1903.

'Ossuaries at Roussolakkos', *British Association Reports*, 1903, 1910, 1912.

Evans, A. J., 'The Prehistoric Tombs of Knossos', *Archaeologia*, 1905.

'The Tomb of the Double Axes', *Archaeologia*, 1911.

Hammond, N. G. L., 'Epirus and the Dorian Invasion', *Annual of the British School at Athens*, 1933, p. 131.

Hawes, C. H., 'Some Dorian Descendants', *Annual of the British School at Athens*, 1903, 1910.

Hawes, C. H., and Duckworth, W. L. H., *Proceedings of the British Academy*, 1908, 1909, 1910, 1912.

Koumaris, J., 'Notes anthropologiques sur quelques crânes', *Revue anthropologique*, 1934, p. 245.

Luschan, F. von, 'Beiträge zur Anthropologie von Kreta', *Zeitschrift für Ethnologie*, 1913, pp. 320–52.

Senyurek, M., 'A Short Review, etc.', Appendix I, *Early Anatolia*, by Seton Lloyd, 1956.

Sergi, A., *The Mediterranean Race*, 1901.

Xanthoudides, S., *Vaulted Tombs of the Mesara*, 1924.

Languages and Scripts

Beattie, A. J., 'Mr Ventris's Decipherment of the Minoan Linear B Script', *Journal of Hellenic Studies*, 1956, p. 1.

Bennett, E. L., *A Minoan Linear B Index*, 1952.

'Fractional Quantities in Minoan Book-keeping', *American Journal of Archaeology*, 1950.

The Pylos Tablets, 1951 and 1955.

'The Mycenae Tablets', reprinted from *The Proceedings of the American Philosophical Society*, 1953.

Blegen, C., 'An inscribed tablet from Pylos', *Ephemeris Archaiologiki*, 1955.

Bosanquet, R. C., 'Inscriptions from Praesos', *Annual of the British School at Athens*, 1910, p. 258.

Caratelli, Pugliese G., 'Le Iscrizione Preellenici di Hagia Triada in Creta e della Grecia Peninsolaria', *Annuario*, 1945.

BIBLIOGRAPHY

Chadwick, J., 'Greek Records in the Minoan Script', *Antiquity*, 195
    The Decipherment of Linear B, 1958 (Penguin Books, 1961).

Chapouthier, F., *Les Écritures minoennes au palais de Mallia*, 1930.

Conway, R. J., 'The Pre-Hellenic Inscriptions of Praesos', *Annual of the British
    School at Athens*, 1902, p. 125.

Cowley, A. E., 'A Note on Minoan Writing', *Essays in Aegean Archaeology*
    1927.

Daniel, J. F., 'Prolegomena to the Cypro-Minoan Script', *American Journal*
    Archaeology, 1945.

Dow, S., 'Minoan Writing', *American Journal of Archaeology*, 1954.

Evans, A. J., *Cretan Pictographs and Pre-Phoenician Script*, 1895 (originall
    published in *Journal of Hellenic Studies*).

Evans, A. J., and Myres, J. L., *Scripta Minoa*, I–III, 1921.

Georgiev, V., *État actuel des inscriptions créto-mycéniennes*, 1954.
    Lexique des inscriptions créto-mycéniennes, 1955. (Both in Russian but wit
    French summaries.)

Gordon, C. H., 'Notes on Minoan Linear A', *Antiquity*, September 1957,
    124.

Hencken, H., *Indo-European Languages and Archaeology*, 1955.

Kober, A. J., 'The Minoan Scripts: Fact and Theory', *American Journal*
    Archaeology, 1948.

Kretschmer, P. K., 'Die Ältesten Sprachschichten auf Kreta', *Glotta*, 1931.

Mann, S. E., 'Mycenaean and Indo-European', *Man*, February 1956.
    'Documents in Mycenaean Greek', *Man*, November 1957.

Meriggi, P., *Glossario miceneo* (in Italian), 1957.
    'Relations entre le Minoen B, le Minoen A', *Études myceniennes*, 1956.

Minos: A journal published by the University of Salamanca devoted to th
    study of Aegean Scripts with articles in English, French, German, an
    Spanish, 1951– .

Nuño, B. Gaya, *Lexicon Creticum* (in Spanish), 1953.

Palmer, L. R., *Achaeans and Indo-Europeans* (Andrew Lang lecture), 1955.

Pernier, L., 'Il disco di Festos', *Ausonia*, 1909.

Peruzzi, E., 'Bibliography of Linear A Script', *Minos*, 1957, p. 99.

Platon, N., Reviews in *Kretika Chronika* (in modern Greek), 1954.

Sundwall, J., 'Die Kretische Linearschrift', Jahrbuch des archeologische
    Instituts, xxx.
    'Der Ursprung des Kretischen Schrift', *Acta Academiae Abo*, 1920.

Treweek, A. P., 'Chain Reaction or House of Cards', *Institute of Classic
    Studies Bulletin*, 1957, p. 10.

Ventris, M., 'A Note on Decipherment Methods', *Antiquity*, 1953.

Ventris, M., and Chadwick, J., *Documents in Mycenaean Greek*, 1956.
    'Evidence for Greek Dialect', *Journal of Hellenic Studies*, 1953.

Webster, T. B. L., 'Mycenaean Records, a Review', *Antiquity*, 1957.

CHAPTER 4: THE MINOAN MARINE, TRADE, AND COMMUNICATIONS

Barnett, R. D., 'Early Shipping in the Near East', *Antiquity*, 1958.

Casson, L., 'Fore and Aft Sails in the Ancient World', *Mariners' Mirror*, February 1956.

Childe, V. G., 'The First Waggons and Carts', *Proceedings of the Prehistoric Society*, 1951, p. 177.

Clark, G. D., 'Horses and Battle-axes', *Antiquity*, 1941, p. 56.

Clowes, G. S. L., *Sailing Ships*, Part I, reprinted 1951.

Cook, J. M., 'Pelino Omoioma Mykenaikon Phoreion', *Kretika Chronika* (in modern Greek), 1955, p. 152.

Evans, A. J., 'The Early Nilotic Libyan and Egyptian Relations with Minoan Crete', *Journal of the Royal Anthropological Institute*, 1927.

Faulkner, R. O., 'Egyptian Seagoing Ships', *Journal of Egyptian Archaeology*, 1941.

Furumark, A., 'The Settlement at Ialysus and Early Aegean History', *Opuscula Archaeologica*, 1950.

Hood, M. S. F., 'A Mycenaean Cavalryman', *Annual of the British School at Athens*, 1953, p 89, Figs. 47, 48.

Hyde, W. W., *Ancient Greek Mariners*, 1947 (with good bibliography).

Kantor, H., 'The Aegean and the Orient in the Second Millennium B.C.', *American Journal of Archaeology*, 1947, pp. 1–68.

Kirk, G., 'Ships on Geometric Vases', *Annual of the British School at Athens*, 1949, p. 23.

Lorimer, H. L., *Homer and the Monuments*, 1950, pp. 307–28.

Marinatos, S., 'La Marine créto-mycénienne' *Bull. Corr. Hell.*, 1933, p. 170 f. (still the best general account of this subject).

Ormerod, H. A., *Piracy in the Ancient World*, 1924.

Pendlebury, J. D. S., 'Egypt and the Aegean', *Studies Presented to David Moore Robinson*, Vol. I, 1951, p. 184.

Piggott, S., *Prehistoric India*, 1950, pp. 273–82.

Ridgeway, W., *The Origin and Influence of the Thoroughbred Horse*, 1905.

Rose, J. Holland, *The Mediterranean in the Ancient World*, 1924.

Starr, C. G., 'The Myth of the Minoan Thalassocracy', *Historia*, 1955, pp. 282–91.

Taylour, W., *Mycenaean Pottery in Italy*, 1958.

Vercoutter, J., *Essai sur les relations entre Égyptiens et Préhellènes*, 1954.

Wainwright, G. A., 'Asiatic Keftiu', *American Journal of Archaeology*, 1952, p. 196.

CHAPTER 5: MINOAN ART

Alexiou, S., 'Protominoikai Taphai', *Kretika Chronika*, 1951, p. 275.

'Nea Stoicheia dhia ten Ysteran Aigaiaken Chronologian', *Kretika Chronika*, 1952, as summarized in *Antiquity*, 1953, p. 183.

'The Boar's Tusk Helmet', *Antiquity*, 1954, p. 214.

Banti, L., *Il Palazzo minoico di Festos*, Vol. II, 1951.

'Il Sentimento della natura nell'arte minoica e micenea', *Essays dedicated to A. Keramopoullos*, 1953.

'Myth in Pre-Classical Art', *American Journal of Archaeology*, October 1954.

Bosanquet, R. C., and others, *Unpublished objects from Palaikastro*, 1923.

Bossert, H. T., *The Art of Ancient Crete*, 1937.

Chapouthier, F., and others, 'Fouilles de Mallia', *Études crétoises*, 1922.

Childe, V. G., *The Dawn of European Civilization*, 5th ed., 1950.

Childe, V. G., and others, *Essays in Aegean Archaeology Presented to Sir Arthur Evans*, 1927.

Dawkins, R. M., and Laistner, M. L. W., 'The Excavation at the Kamares Cave in Crete', *Annual of the British School at Athens*, 1913, p. 1.

Dunbabin, T. J., 'Antiquities of Amari', *Annual of the British School at Athens*, 1947, p. 184.

Evans, A. J., *The Palace of Minos*, 1921.

'The Prehistoric Tombs of Knossos', *Archaeologia*, 1901.

'The Tomb of the Double Axes, etc', *Archaeologia*, 1907.

Fimmen, D., *Die Kretisch-Mykenische Kultur*, 1924.

Forsdyke, E. J., *Minoan Art* (Hertz Lecture to the British Academy), 1929.

Frankfort, H., *Studies in Early Pottery of the Near East*, Part II, 1927.

Hall, E. H., 'Excavations in Eastern Crete, Sphoungaras', *University of Pennsylvania Anthrop. Pub.*, 1910.

The Decorative Art of Crete in the Bronze Age, 1907.

Hawes, C. H., *Crete, The Forerunner of Greece*, 1909.

Hawes, H. Boyd, and others, *Gournia, Vasiliki, and other Prehistoric Sites*, 1908.

Hazzidakis, J., *Tylissos à l'époque minoenne*, 1921.

Les Villas minoennes de Tylissos, 1934.

Hutchinson, R. W., 'Prehistoric Town Planning in Crete', *The Town Planning Review*, October 1950.

'Minoan Chronology Reviewed', *Antiquity*, 1953.

Heaton, N., 'On the Nature and Method, etc.', *Tiryns*, 1912, p. 211.

Hutchinson, R. W., Eccles, E., and Benton, S., 'Unpublished Objects at Palaikastro and Praesos', *Annual of the British School at Athens*, 1940.

Kantor, H., *The Aegean and the Orient in the Second Millennium B.C.*, 1947.

Karo, G., *Die Schachtgräber von Mykenae*, 1930–3.

Levi, D., Reports in *Illustrated London News*, 19 January 1954, 12 December 1953, 29 September and 6 October 1956.

Maraghiannis, G., and Karo, G., *Antiquités crétoises*, 1908–15.

Marinatos, S., 'Protominoikos Taphos . . . Krasi', *Archaiologikon Deltion*, 1932, p. 102.

Crete and Mycenae, 1960

Matz, F., *Die Frühkretische Siegel*, 1928.

'Torsion', *Abhandlungen der Akademie der Wissenschaften und der Literatur, Mainz*, 1951.

Pendlebury, J. D. S., *The Archaeology of Crete*, 1939.

Guide to the Palace of Minos, 2nd ed., 1954.

BIBLIOGRAPHY

Pendlebury, J. D. S., and others, 'Excavations in Lasithi', *Annual of the British School at Athens*, 1906.

    'Guide to the Stratigraphic Museum', *Annual of the British School at Athens*, 1931.

Pernier, L., and Banti, L., *Il Palazzo di Festos*, 1935–51.

Seager, R. B., 'Vasiliki', *Transactions of Pennsylvania University*, 1907, p. 218.

    'Excavations in the Island of Pseira', *Anthrop. Publications Pennsylvania University*, 1910.

    Explorations in the Island of Mochlos, 1912.

Snijder, G. A., *Kretische Kunst*, 1936.

Taramelli, A., 'Ricerche archeologiche cretesi', *Mon. Ant.*,1899, pp. 289–446.

Vandier, J., 'À propos d'un dépôt de provenance asiatique trouvé à Tod', *Syria*, 1937, p. 174.

Wace, A. J. B., *A Cretan Statuette in the Fitzwilliam Museum*, 1927.

Xanthoudides, S., *Vaulted Tombs of the Mesara*, 1924.

Xenaki-Sakellariou, A., 'La Représentation du casque en dents de sanglier', *Bulletin de Correspondence Hellénique*, 1953, p. 46.

CHAPTER 6: THE EARLY MINOAN PERIOD

Aberg, N., *Bronzezeitliche und Früheisenzeitliche Chronologie*, IV, 1933.

Alexiou, S., 'Protominoikai Taphai para to Kanli Kastelli, Herakleion', *Kretika Chronika*, 1951, p. 275.

Bosanquet, R. C., *Unpublished Objects from Palaikastro*, 1923.

Ehrich, R. W., and others, *Relative Chronologies in Old World Archeology*, 1954.

Evans, A. J., *The Palace of Minos* (especially Vol. I), 1921.

Frankfort, H., *Studies in Early Pottery*, Part II, 1927.

Furness, A., 'Some Early Pottery of Samos, etc.', *Proceedings of the Prehistoric Society*, 1957, p. 173.

Hall, E. H., *Excavations in Eastern Crete, Sphoungaras*, 1910.

Hawes, H. Boyd, *Gournia*, 1908.

Hazzidakis, J., 'An Early Minoan Cave at Arkalokhori,' *Annual of the British School at Athens*, 1913, p. 35.

Hutchinson, R. W., 'Minoan Chronology Reviewed' (with bibliographical references), *Antiquity*, 1954, p. 155.

Marinatos, S., 'Protominoikos Tholotos Taphos para to Khorion Krasi Pedhiadhos', *Archaiologikon Deltion*, 1932, p. 112.

Matz, F., *Frühkretische Siegel*, 1928.

    'Die Agais', *Handbuch der Archaeologie*, 1950, p. 227.

    'Torsion', *Abhandlungen der Akademie der Wissenschaften und der Literatur*, 1951, p. 9.

Mellaart, J., 'Preliminary Report ... Southern Turkey', *Anatolian Studies*, 1954, p. 75.

Pendlebury, J. D. S., *The Archaeology of Crete* (Chap. II B), 1939.

Pernier, L., and Banti, L., *Il Palazzo di Festos*, I, 1935; II, 1951.

Schachermeyr, F., 'Vorbericht über eine Expedition nach Ostkreta', *Archae-ologischer Anzeiger*, 1938, p. 465.

Seager, R. B., *Excavations on the Island of Pseira*, 1912.
  Explorations in the Island of Mochlos, 1912.
  'The Cemetery of Pachyammos', *Anthro. Pub.*, 1916.
  'Vasiliki', *Trans. Pennsylvania University*, 1907, p. 218; 1912, p. 118.

Xanthoudides, S., *Vaulted Tombs of the Mesara*, 1924.

CHAPTER 7: THE MIDDLE MINOAN PERIOD

Aberg, N., *Bronzezeitliche und Früheisenzeitliche Chronologie*, IV, 1933

Banti, L., 'Cronologia e Ceramica del Palazzo Minoico di Festos', *Annuario*, 1940.

Bosanquet, R. C., *Unpublished Objects From Palaikastro*, 1923.

Bossert, H., *The Art of Ancient Crete*, 1937.

Chapouthier, F., 'Fouilles de Mallia', *Études crétoises*, 1922.

Demargne, P., 'Crète et Orient au temps d'Hammourabi', *Revue Archéologique*, 1936.

Dussaud, R., 'Rapports entre la Crète ancienne et la Babylonie', *Iraq*, 1939, p. 53.

Evans, A. J., *The Palace of Minos* (especially Vol. I), 1921.

Forsdyke, E. J., *Minoan Art*, 1929.

Hall, E. H., *The Decorative Art of Crete in the Bronze Age*, 1907.

Hutchinson, R. W., 'Prehistoric Town Planning in Crete', *Town Planning Review*, October 1950.

Kantor, H. J., *The Aegean and The Orient in the Second Millennium B.C.*, 1947.

Levi, D., Reports in *Illustrated London News*, 19 January 1952, 12 December 1953, 30 September and 6 October 1955.

Mackenzie, D., 'Cretan Palaces', *Annual of the British School at Athens*, 1904–8.

Pendlebury, J. D. S., *Aegyptiaca*, 1932.
  The Archaeology of Crete, 1939.

Pernier, L., *Il Palazzo di Festos*, I, 1935.

Pernier, L., and Banti, L., *Il Palazzo di Festos*, II, 1951.

Petrie, F., *Buttons and Design Scarabs*, 1925.

Platon, N., 'To Ieron Maza', *Kretika Chronika*, 1951 (a comprehensive survey in modern Greek on the peak sanctuaries).

Sakellariou, A. Xenaki, 'Minoikes Sphagidhes, etc.', *Kretika Chronika*, 1949.

Santerre, H. G. de, 'Mallia, Aperçu historique', *Kretika Chronika*, 1949.

Seltman, C., 'A Minoan Bull's Head', *Studies Presented to D. M. Robinson*, 1951.

Smith, S., 'Middle Minoan I–II and Babylonian Chronology', *American Journal of Archaeology*, 1945, p. 1.

Vandier, J., 'À propos d'un dépôt de provenance asiatique trouvé à Tod', *Syria*, 1937, p. 174.

CHAPTER 8: MINOAN RELIGION

Banti, L., 'Culti di Haghia Triada', *Annuario*, 1941-3, p. 9.
    'Myth in Preclassical Art', *American Journal of Archaeology*, 1942, p. 307.
Chittenden, J., 'The Master of Animals', *Hesperia*, 1947, p. 187.
Cook, A. B., *Zeus*, 1914-40.
Demargne, P., 'Culte funéraire, etc.', *Bulletin de Correspondence Hellénique*, 1932, p. 76.
Deonna, W. J., 'Tables antiques d'offrandes, etc.', *Bulletin de Correspondence Hellénique*, 1934, p. 1.
Evans, A. J., *The Palace of Minos*, 1921-36.
    'Mycenaean Tree and Pillar Cult', *Journal of Hellenic Studies*, 1901.
    The Earlier Religion of Greece in the Light of Cretan Discoveries (Frazer Lecture), 1931.
Frazer, J. G., *The Golden Bough* (abridged version), 1929.
Hesiod, *The Theogony*.
Mylonas, G. E., 'The Cult of the Dead in Helladic Times', *Studies presented to D. M. Robinson*, 1951.
Nilsson, M., *The Minoan Mycenaean Religion*, 1950 (the best general introduction on the subject).
Persson, A. W., *The Religion of Greece in Prehistoric Times* (Sather Lecture), 1942.
Picard, C., *Les Religions préhelléniques*, 1948 (with a very good bibliography and synthesis of the various authorities).
Platon, N., 'To Ieron Maza, etc.', *Kretika Chronika*, 1951, p. 96.
    'Nouvelle interprétation des idoles cloches, etc.', *Mélanges Charles Picard*, 1949, p. 833.
    'Ta Minoika Oikiaka Iera', *Kretika Chronika*, 1954, p. 428.
Rose, H. J., *Primitive Religion in Greece*, 1925.
Taramelli, A., 'The Prehistoric Grotto at Miamu', *American Journal of Archaeology*, 1897, p. 297.
Ventris, M., and Chadwick, J., *Documents in Mycenaean Greek*, 1956.
Xanthoudides, S., 'Cretan Kernoi', *Annual of the British School at Athens*, 1912.
    The Vaulted Tombs of the Mesara, 1924.

CHAPTER 9: THE SOCIAL AND ECONOMIC LIFE

Alexiou, S., 'The Boar's Tusk Helmet', *Antiquity*, 1954, p. 211.
Alvad, T., 'The Kafir Harp', *Man*, 1954.
Armstrong, E. A., 'The Crane Dance in East and West', *Antiquity*, 1943, p. 71.
Chadwick, H. M., *The Heroic Age*, 1912.
Curwen, E. C., 'The Significance of the Pentatonic Scale in Scottish Song', *Antiquity*, 1940.

BIBLIOGRAPHY

Demargne, P., *La Crète dédalique*, 1947.

Evans, A. J., *The Palace of Minos*, 1921–36.

Forbes, R. J., *Metallurgy in Antiquity*, 1950.

Galpin, F. W., *The Music of the Sumerians*, 1932.

Glotz, G., *La Civilisation égéenne*, 1923.

Gordon, D. H., 'Swords, Rapiers and Horseriders', *Antiquity*, 1953, p. 66.

Hawes, H. Boyd, *Gournia*, 1908.

Hazzidakis, J., *Tylissos à l'époque minoenne*, 1921.

Hencken, H., 'Beitsch and Knossos', *Proceedings of the Prehistoric Society*, 1952, p. 96.

Lorimer, H. L., *Homer and the Monuments*, 1950.

Marinatos, S., 'Le Temple géométrique de Dréros', *Bulletin de Correspondence Hellénique*, 1936.

Myres, J. L., *Who were the Greeks?*, 1930.
   'Minoan Dress', *Man*, 1950, p. 1.

Nilsson, M. P., *Homer and Mycenae*, 1935.
   'Primitive Time Reckoning', *Acts–Soc. Litt. Human. Lund*, 1921.

Pendlebury, J. D. S., *The Archaeology of Crete*, 1939.

Ridgeway, W. G., *The Early Age of Greece* I, 1901; II, 1931.

Ridington, W. R., *The Minoan-Mycenaean Background of Greek Athletics*, 1935.

Swindler, M. H., *Cretan Elements in the Cult and Ritual of Apollo*, 1913.

Thomson, G., 'The Greek Calendar', *Journal of Hellenic Studies*, 1943, p. 52.
   'From Religion to Philosophy', *Journal of Hellenic Studies*, 1953, p. 77.

Vickery, K. F., 'Food in Early Greece', *Illinois Studies in the Social Sciences*, 1936, No. 3 (an excellent account).

Wace, A. J. B., *A Cretan Statuette in the Fitzwilliam Museum*, 1927.

Winnington Ingram, R. P., 'The Pentatonic Tuning of the Greek Lyre', *Classical Quarterly*, 1956.

Xanthoudides, S., *The Vaulted Tombs of the Mesara*, 1924.

CHAPTER 10: THE DECLINE OF KNOSOS

Alexiou, S., 'The Boar's Tusk Helmet', *Antiquity*, 1954, p. 183.

Biesantz, H., *Kretisch-Mykenische Siegelbilder*, 1954.

Blegen, C., *Prosymna, The Helladic Settlement Preceding the Argive Heraeum*, 1937.

Burn, A. R., *Minoans, Philistines and Greeks*, 1930.

Childe, V. G., 'The Final Bronze Age in the Near East', *Proceedings of the Prehistoric Society*, 1948.

Clarke, J. G. D., 'Horses and Battle-Axes', *Antiquity*, 1941, p. 50.

Demargne, P. and de Santerre, H. G., 'Fouilles exécutées à Mallia, 1921–48', *Études crétoises*, 1953.

Evans, A. J., *The Palace of Minos*, 1921–36.
   'The Prehistoric Tombs of Knosos', *Archaeologia*, 1905.
   'The Tomb of the Double-Axes', *Archaeologia*, 1913.

Furumark, A., *The Mycenaean Pottery, Analysis and Classification*, 1941.
The Chronology of Mycenaean Pottery, 1941.
'The Settlement at Ialysos and Aegean History', *Opuscula Archaeologia*, 1950.
Hall, E. H., *The Decorative Art of Crete in the Bronze Age*, 1907.
Hazzidakis, J., *Tylissos a l'époque minoenne*, 1921.
Hawes, H. Boyd, *Excavations at Gournia*, 1908.
Hood, M. S. F., 'A Mycenaean Cavalryman' (with a useful bibliography on horses and chariots), *Annual of the British School at Athens*, 1948, p. 84.
Hood, M. S. F., and Jong, P. de, 'Late Minoan Warrior Tombs', *Annual of the British School at Athens*, 1952, p. 49.
Hutchinson, R. W., 'Prehistoric Town Planning in Crete', *Town Planning Review*, 1950, p. 261.
Kantor, H., *The Aegean and Orient in the Second Millennium B.C.*, 1947 (particularly valuable on the relations with Egypt).
Karo, G., *Die Schachtgräber von Mykenae*, 1930-3 (the final and comprehensive account of the Royal Shaft Graves opened by Schliemann and Stamatakis).
Muller, K., 'Die Funde aus den Kuppelgräbern von Kakovatos', *Athenische Mitteilungen*, 1909, pp. 269-305.
Pilecki, J., 'La disposition héraldique dans la civilization minoenne', (in Polish with French summary), *Swiatowit*, 1937, p. 15.
Rodenwaldt, G., *Der Fries des Megarons von Mykenai*, 1926.
'Die Fresken des Palastes', *Tiryns*, 1912.
Santerre, H. G. de, and Treheux, G., 'Dépôt égéen et géométrique de l'Artémision à Délos', *Bulletin de Correspondence Hellénique*, 1948, p. 148.
Seager, R. B., *The Cemetery of Pachyammos*, 1916.
Stubbings, F. H., *Mycenaean Pottery from the Levant*, 1951.
Wace, A. J. B., *Mycenae, An Archaeological History and Guide*, 1949.
'Chamber Tombs at Mycenae', *Archaeologia*, 1932.
'The Date of the Treasury of Atreus', *Antiquity*, 1940, p. 233.
Weinberg, S., and others, *The Aegean and the Near East (Studies Presented to Hetty Goldman)*, 1956.

CHAPTER II: THE DECADENCE OF MINOAN CRETE: THE MYCENAEAN EMPIRE

Alexiou, S., 'Nea Stoicheia', *Kretika Chronika*, 1952 (English summary in *Antiquity*, 1954, p. 183).
'The Boar's Tusk Helmet', *Antiquity*, 1954, p. 211.
Allen, T. W., *The Homeric Catalogue of Ships*, 1921.
Barnett, R. D., 'A Phoenician Inscription from Eastern Cilicia', *Iraq*, 1948, p. 56.
The Nimrud Ivories, 1957.
Blegen, C., *Prosymna*, 1937.

Borda, M., *Arte Creteo-Miceneo del Museo Pigorini di Roma*, 1946.

Bosanquet, R. C., Dawkins, R. M., and others, 'Excavations at Palaikastro', *Annual of the British School at Athens*, 1901–5.

Burn, A. R., *Minoans, Philistines and Greeks*, 1930.

Burton Brown, T., *The Coming of Iron to Greece*, 1954.

Catling, H. W., 'Bronze cut-and-thrust swords in the East Mediterranean', *Proceedings of the Prehistoric Society*, 1956.

Childe, V. G., 'The Final Bronze Age in the Near East', *Proceedings of the Prehistoric Society*, 1948.

Evans, A. J., *The Palace of Minos* (especially II and IV), 1921–36.

'The Prehistoric Tombs of Knosos', *Archaeologia*, 1905.

'The Shaft Graves and Beehive Tombs', *Archaeologia*, 1929.

'The Tomb of the Double Axes', *Archaeologia*, 1906.

Finley, M. I., *The World of Odysseus*, 1956.

Forsdyke, E. J., *Greece Before Homer*, 1956.

British Museum Catalogue of Vases (Vol. I, part I), 1925.

Furumark, A., *The Mycenaean Pottery*, 1941.

The Chronology of Mycenaean Pottery, 1941.

Hawes, H. Boyd, *Gournia*, 1908.

Heurtley, W. A., 'The Relationship between Philistine and Mycenaean Pottery', *Palestine Quarterly*, 1936.

Huxley, G. L., 'Mycenaean Decline and the Homeric Catalogue of Ships', *London University Bulletin*, 1956.

Kantor, H., *The Aegean and the Orient in the Second Millennium B.C.*, 1947.

Lorimer, H. L., *Homer and the Monuments*, 1950.

Loud, G., *The Megiddo Ivories*, 1932.

Marinatos, S., 'The Volcanic Destruction of Minoan Crete', *Antiquity*, 1939.

Mylonas, G. E., *Ancient Mycenae*, 1957.

Myres, J. L., *Who were the Greeks?*, 1930.

Santerre, H. G. de, 'Mallia, Aperçu historique', *Kretika Chronika*, 1949.

Seltman, C., 'A Minoan Bull's Head', *Studies Presented to D. M. Robinson*, 1951.

Smith, S., 'Middle Minoan I–II and Babylonian Chronology', *American Journal of Archaeology*, 1945, p. 1.

Wace, A. J. B., *Mycenae*, 1949.

Weinberg, S., and others, *The Aegean and the Near East*, 1956.

CHAPTER 12: THE DORIAN COLONIZATION, ORIENTAL INFLUENCES, AND THE GROWTH OF THE CITY STATES

Amandry, P., 'Chaudrons à Protomés de taureau, etc.', *The Aegean and the Near East*, 1956, p. 239.

Barnett, R. D., 'Early Greek and Oriental Ivories', *Journal of Hellenic Studies*, 1948.

The Nimrud Ivories, 1957.

BIBLIOGRAPHY

Benton, S., 'The Date of the Cretan Shields', *Annual of the British School at Athens*, 1939, p. 52.

'The Dating of Helmets and Corselets in Early Greece', *Annual of the British School at Athens*, 1940, p. 75.

'Bronzes from Palaikastro and Praisos', *Annual of the British School at Athens*, 1940, p. 49.

Brock, J. K., *Fortetsa*, 1956 (the first comprehensive survey of Cretan pottery of the Early Iron Age).

Burn, A. R., *Minoans, Philistines and Greeks*, 1930.

The Age of Hesiod, 1936.

Conway, R. S., 'The Prehistoric Inscriptions of Praesos', *Annual of the British School at Athens*, 1902, p. 125.

Crowfoot, J. W., and G. M., *Early Ivories from Samaria*, 1935.

Demargne, P., *La Crète dédalique*, 1947 (the best general survey of this period).

Desborough, V., *Protogeometric Pottery*, 1952.

Dohan, E. H., 'Archaic Cretan Terracottas in America', *Metropolitan Museum Studies*, 1931, p. 127.

Dunbabin, T. J., Review of *La Crète dédalique*, *Gnomon*, 1947, No. 132, p. 19.

'Cretan Relief *Pithoi* in Giamalakis Collection', *Annual of the British School at Athens*, 1952.

The Western Greeks, 1944.

Effenterre, H. van, 'Reports on Excavations in Eastern Crete', *Bulletin de Correspondence Hellénique*, 1933, p. 293; 1938, p. 694.

Ferté, E. C. de la, *Les Bijoux antiques*, 1956.

Gray, D. H. P., 'Metal Working in Homer', *Journal of Hellenic Studies*, 1954.

Guarducci, M., *Inscriptiones Creticae*, 4 vols., 1935–50. (With commentaries in Latin, a regional survey of all classical inscriptions from Crete.)

Halbherr, F., 'Three Cretan Necropoleis', *American Journal of Archaeology*, 1901.

Hammond, N. G. L., 'Epirus and the Dorian Invasion', *Annual of the British School at Athens*, 1932, pp. 131–79.

Hartley, M., 'Early Greek Vases from Crete', *Annual of the British School at Athens*, 1930, p. 75.

Hencken, H. C., 'Herzsprung Shields and Greek Trade', *American Journal of Archaeology*, 1950, p. 205.

Hogarth, D. G., 'The Dictaean Cave', *Annual of the British School at Athens*, 1900, p. 70.

Hutchinson, R. W., etc., 'Unpublished Objects from Palaikastro and Praisos', *Annual of the British School at Athens*, 1940, p. 38.

Hutchinson, R. W., and Boardman, J., 'The Khaniale Tekke Tombs', *Journal of the British School at Athens*, 1954.

Jacobsthal, P., *Greek Pins and their Connexions with Europe and Asia*, 1956.

Jenkins, R. J. H., *Dedalica*, 1936.

Kirsten, E., *Das dorische Kreta*, 1942.

Kunze, E., *Kretische Bronzereliefs*, 1931.

Lamb, W., *Greek and Roman Bronzes*, 1929.

BIBLIOGRAPHY

Levi, D., 'Early Hellenic Pottery of Crete', *Hesperia*, 1945.
    'Excavations at Arkades', *Liverpool Annals*, 1925.
    'I Bronzi di Axos', *Annuario*, 1933, p. 33.

Lorimer, H. L., *Homer and the Monuments*, 1950 (especially Chapter v).

Mallowan, M. E. L., 'The Excavations at Nimrud (Kalhu) 1953', *Iraq*, 1954, Part I, p. 59.

Marinatos, S., 'Report on Dreros Temple', *Bulletin de Correspondence Hellénique*, 1936, p. 219.

Maxwell-Hyslop, K. R., 'Urartian Bronzes, etc.', *Iraq*, 1956, p. 150.
    'Notes on some Distinctive Types of Bronzes etc.' *Proceedings of the Prehistoric Society*, 1956, p. 102.

Ormerod, H. A., *Piracy in the Ancient World*, 1924.

Payne, H. G. G., 'Early Greek Vases from Knosos', *Annual of the British School at Athens*, 1929, p. 229.

Pendlebury, J. D. S., *The Archaeology of Crete*, 1939.

Pernier, L., 'New Elements for the Study of the Archaic Temple of Prinias', *American Journal of Archaeology*, 1939.

Svoronos, J., *Numismatique de la Crète ancienne*, 1890.

Wason, C. R., 'The Drill Style on Ancient Gems', *Liverpool Annals*, 1936, p. 51.

Weinberg, S. S., and others, *The Aegean and the Near East*, 1956.

Willetts, R. F., *Aristocratic Society in Ancient Crete*, 1954.

Williamson, G. C., *The Book of Amber*, 1932.

INDEX

INDEX

*Some other Pelican books
are described on the
following pages*

THE DEAD SEA SCROLLS IN ENGLISH

G. Vermes

A 551

Many books have been written about the Dead Sea Scrolls since their discovery in 1947, but until now the ordinary reader has had little opportunity to get to know the texts themselves, and so to make any personal judgement of their value or relevance. In this volume a clear, faithful translation of the non-biblical scrolls from the Qumran caves is accompanied by brief introductory comment on each, and by a general description of the beliefs, customs, organization, and history of the Community they derive from. The teaching of this sect of Jewish schismatics sheds the light of comparison and contrast on to that of their contemporaries, the Christian dissenters, and also on to the mother faith of both – Palestinian Judaism. This book reveals the Dead Sea Scrolls as fascinating documents that give us new insight into the history and philosophy of religion.

ARCHAIC EGYPT

W. B. Emery

A 462

Between 1936 and 1956 archaeological discoveries at Sakkara, the necropolis of ancient Memphis, have produced evidence which has caused historians to revise many of their previous conceptions of Egyptian civilization of the first two dynasties (3200-2780 B.C.). The origins of the Egypt of the Pharaohs still remain obscure, but the new material uncovered by the pick of the excavator shows that the people of the Nile Valley at that remote period enjoyed a far higher degree of culture than has hitherto been recognized. Architecture and the arts had reached a degree of excellence which in some ways was hardly surpassed when the full flower of Pharaonic civilization was in bloom.

The aim of this book is to put before the reader a general survey of what we now know, through these recent discoveries, of the cultural achievements of the great people who lived on the banks of the Nile nearly five thousand years ago. While in no sense a textbook this absorbing study will make an equal appeal to the student and to the layman.

PREHISTORIC INDIA

Stuart Piggott

A 205

This book was the first to review the archaeology of prehistoric India in relation to that of Western Asia as a whole. Although the great cities of Harappa and Mohenjo-daro are well known, the peasant communities of the Indian Bronze Age in Sind and Baluchistan have received little attention since the time of their first discovery thirty years ago. Work in Iraq and Persia has thrown much light on Indian problems, and the contacts and relationships between these regions are described.

The story of Indian origins is discussed from the remotely ancient Palaeolithic period onwards, though the body of the book deals with the Bronze Age of western and northern India between about 3000 and 1500 B.C. which has produced most of the available archaeological material.

The book has been limited to the period before 1000 B.C., which allows for an examination of the archaeological and linguistic evidence for the Indo-European conquest of India under the Aryans. An attempt to assess the material culture of the writers of the *Rigveda* forms the concluding chapter.

THE ARCHAEOLOGY OF PALESTINE

W. F. Albright

A 199

This book is written for the reader who wants an up-to-date, authoritative, and clearly written account of the subject. The author has been engaged in active excavation and research in this field since 1920, and he has utilized his command of it to write a survey which emphasizes the most important and most interesting phases of Palestinian archaeology. Besides summarizing the results of the archaeological work of the past twenty years, during which the subject has been revolutionized, he brings the reader up to date with references to the very latest finds. Here for the first time the latest discoveries in Sinai and the sensational finding of the Jerusalem Scroll of Isaiah are set in their proper historical perspective.

The book contains chapters which explain how the archaeologist carries on his excavations, how the subject developed from a treasure hunt into a science, how civilization unfolded from the Stone Age to the height of the Roman Empire. There is a chapter on the races and languages, scripts and literatures of ancient Palestine, as well as a chapter on the everyday life of the people. Two chapters summarize the bearing of these researches on the Old and New Testaments, including previously unpublished material. A final chapter on 'Ancient Palestine in World History' places the book in the full current of the philosophy of history, showing how profoundly archaeological research is influencing historical and religious thought.

ARCHAEOLOGY IN THE U.S.S.R.

A. L. Mongait

The Soviet Union is a country of many different languages and peoples. So a book dealing with its archaeology must range from Stone Age Russia to the Greek colonies on the Black Sea – from the Slavs of what is now European Russia to the desert forts of Central Asia, held by Arab, Turkic, and other rulers.

This book is also fascinating for two other reasons. In the first place Soviet archaeology is almost unknown in the West, and the reader will discover that Russian achievements here fully match those in better known fields such as space travel.

Secondly Dr Mongait is a Communist, and this will be a chance for many people to see the Marxist interpretation of history applied to archaeology. There are many illustrations in the book.

THE AZTECS OF MEXICO

George C. Vaillant

A 200

Dr George Vaillant was that rara avis, a great specialist who could make his speciality as interesting to the layman as it was to himself. For many years curator of Mexican archaeology at the American Museum of Natural History, and acknowledged an outstanding authority on the early civilizations of Mexico and Central America, in this book he wrote what is still the most important account of the birth and death of one of the world's great civilizations.

In the eleventh century the Aztecs arrived in Mexico from the north. Even today their speech is much like that spoken by the Indians of Oregon and Montana. In less than a hundred years, rising on the ruins of the older Mexican cultures, they developed an extraordinary indigenous civilization. Here is the strange story of the rise, and of the even swifter fall under the impact of Cortes and his followers. Dr Vaillant vividly re-creates the Aztec way of life. In one fascinating chapter he takes his reader to the great Aztec city, Tenochtitlan, now Mexico City, in the days of the height of the Aztec power, and wanders with him through the town. We learn not only the history of the Aztecs and how their society was organized, but how the children went to school, modes of dress, and many interesting aspects of an ancient daily life.

'One does not know which to admire most, the care with which the details are assembled or the imagination which has constructed cultural and political history out of them. No reader of *The Conquest of Mexico* should miss this book' – *Time and Tide*

THE ANCIENT CIVILIZATIONS OF PERU

J. Alden Mason

A 395

Our detailed knowledge of the people of pre-Columbian Peru has grown enormously since 1940. Many expeditions have made excavations and published their reports. Regions archaeologically unknown hitherto have yielded their secrets, and far more is known of all of them. Especially is this true of the cultures that preceded the Inca whom Pizarro found and conquered in one of the great adventures of history. Four thousand years before his day, radiocarbon analyses now permit us to state with confidence, simple fishermen-hunters on the coast were beginning the long climb towards the extraordinary blend of communism and monarchy that was the Inca empire. Our concepts of the latter and of its history also have been altered somewhat by recent studies. This book presents a summary of our present knowledge and point of view regarding the development and nature of these past civilizations and their fascinating and diversified country, with 64 pages of plates.

PRIMITIVE GOVERNMENT

Lucy Mair

A 542

We take so much for granted the familiar forms of government – parliament, cabinet, ministries, law courts, and local authorities – that we are apt to forget which features constitute the essential elements of rule. These become clearer when we study how government has evolved to suit the needs of family, tribe, nation, and even empire.

Dr Mair has carried out field work on various widely differing systems which, in spite of the imposition of colonial rule, still in part obtain in East Africa. In these primitive societies it would appear that concepts of law and government were already understood and developed. In fact Dr Mair contends, contrary to some previous opinions, that no known society exists without them, even though their forms may be rudimentary.

Some such systems are quite outside the experience of western readers. For instance an apparent anarchy may prove, on examination, to be in reality a well-ordered kind of government. In one society political responsibility is diffused throughout the whole; in another men have built up a kingdom which could be compared with those of medieval Europe.

In this survey of the way in which government is conducted without modern technical equipment Dr Mair throws new light on its historical evolution.

For a complete list of books available please write to Penguin Books whose address can be found on the back of the title page